NAKED
CAME I

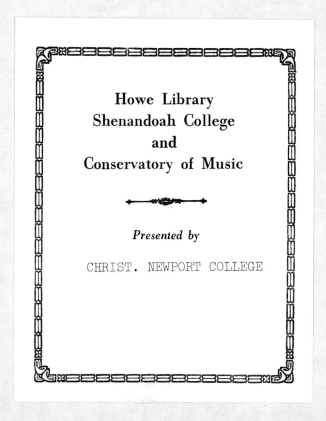

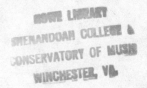
NAKED CAME I

A NOVEL
OF RODIN
BY DAVID
WEISS

William Morrow and Company/New York

For my wife:

Stymean Karlen

Naked came I into the world,
And naked must I go out.

Don Quixote, by Cervantes

The endpapers are drawings of Rodin sculptures by Lydia Fruhauf

TOP ROW: *St. John the Baptist/The Man with the Broken Nose/
Victor Hugo/Burgher of Calais*

MIDDLE ROW: *The Kiss/Adam/Eve/Eternal Spring*

BOTTOM ROW: *The Age of Bronze/Mignon (Rose)/
Thought (Camille)/Balzac*

CONTENTS

PART ONE
ONE
THE
FAMILY

CHAPTER 1

The father of the infant was a French peasant from Normandy.

Jean Baptiste Rodin had not expected to be the father of a son at the age of thirty-eight; he had two daughters, Clotilde and Marie, but they did not really count, and he was overjoyed. He had come to Paris because he had wanted to own land and had known that as a peasant he would never own land. But a son was the next best thing. A son would provide for his old age, carry on his name. Rodin meant red in Normandy, and all his family had red hair.

Papa paused, however, in the Mairie of the arrondissement. It was necessary to make a declaration to register his son, but neither he nor his wife, Marie, a thirty-four-year-old peasant from Lorraine, could write, and he turned to his wife's sister, Aunt Thérèse, and asked her to fill out the form. Aunt Thérèse could write; housekeeper, model, and occasional mistress of the painter Drolling, she had learned from Drolling.

Papa said, "We will call him François Auguste."

Aunt Thérèse wrote, "François Auguste Rodin, born November 12, 1840, at 3 rue de l'Arbalète, the twelfth arrondissement of Paris."

Papa said, "I will put away a louis to celebrate and to say Mass."

"He looks like a healthy one," said Aunt Thérèse.

"All Rodins are healthy," Papa said vigorously. Aunt Thérèse, for all her wit and charm, floated around in a never-never land, but he was practical. His thick, heavy features, like a block of rugged stone, took on the air of a troubled man. He pushed his stubby, square-fisted hand through his luxuriant dark red hair, his pride and joy, and still disturbed, scratched his Louis Philippe chin whiskers. He was a supporter of the monarchy, of the Bourbons, but how could he guarantee that all would turn out well for his son? This was the Paris of the *petite bourgeoisie*, he thought: they were becoming more important each day, and he was a peasant, his wife was a peasant, their ancestors had been peasants, although he had risen to be a not quite minor police official, a police messenger.

And the quarter in which they lived! *Mon dieu*, it was hardly better than a slum, and it was infested with prostitutes—they lived next door, all around them. But he could not afford anything better than this medieval labyrinth of twisting, narrow alleys and streets. The rue de l'Arbalète was stony and steep, and the cobblestones were as rough and jagged as mountain rocks. It was one of the ugliest, poorest quarters of Paris, yet he consoled himself with the thought that they were within walking distance of the Sorbonne and Notre Dame, that the district was dominated by the gray cupolas of the Panthéon and by many fine old churches, like St. Séverin, Ste. Geneviève, and Val de Grâce. Family piety would make up for the neighborhood, he hoped. Then as Papa thought of the house in which they lived his heart sank. There was no sidewalk in front of the house, which was yellow and gray, and a mixture of cracked stone, crumbling plaster, imitation Gothic turrets, and a yellow stucco roof. They rented one floor, the fifth, the top, the cheapest. They had to climb one hundred and one steep, winding, cracked steps to reach it. It had been a wonder his wife had survived her pregnancy; this one must be a strong one.

Aunt Thérèse said, "I like the name Auguste. I'm glad I named my first-born that."

How pitiful, thought Papa. He liked Aunt Thérèse, everyone did, she was pretty, cheerful, spirited, but what would become of her three illegitimate boys? Worse, when he scolded her, she was not ashamed. It was just that she had avoided the formality of getting married; she had a large heart—and a different father for each of her three sons.

At least he would give his son a name.

Aunt Thérèse gave Papa Rodin a kiss of congratulations, and he prayed that François Auguste would grow up to be pious, strong, and a minor police official—only the *bourgeois* were major police officials, and they could read and write. Then Papa was struck with an astounding idea. If Thérèse could learn to write, why couldn't his son? Mama would say he was out of his mind, but the failure to know how to write was why he was still a police messenger at only eight hundred francs a year. He would put the boy in school before he sent him out to work. François Auguste would get a good education and avoid the influence of the prostitutes next door.

Papa said with bravado, "I am not a republican, but it is good for a son to read and write."

II

When Auguste was five—the *François* had never been used—and preparing to enter the Jesuit school nearby, Aunt Thérèse gave him drawing crayons as a present which she had borrowed from Drolling without asking.

The Rodins lived near the rue St. Jacques now, on a cleaner street, and the child hoped that someday they would live on a wide one. The house was better, too, and they had the first floor. This afternoon he was alone with Aunt Thérèse, who had promised to watch him. Red-haired, stocky, shy, nearsighted, he was fascinated by the black crayons. When he pushed down on them, they made such distinct lines—he could really see them! Then he paused, he was making the kitchen table dirty.

Aunt Thérèse smiled encouragingly, said, "Use the floor."

Auguste nodded. He wanted to draw her—Aunt Thérèse had delicate features where Mama's were hardy—but he knew Papa should come first: Papa came first in everything. He squatted on the uneven stone floor of the kitchen, which was also dining room and living room, and sketched an outline of Papa. He liked the feel of the stone though it was too hard for the black crayon, which crumbled as he drew. But the outline had been distinct even at a distance. He noticed the brown wrapping paper which Mama had gotten when she bought potatoes for their dinner. Mama had put the wrapping paper aside to light the fire in the oven, but it did not crumble the crayon.

He perched cross-legged at the kitchen table, forgetting the dinner to be served, frowning, preoccupied; the crayon made a thick line, like Papa's lips. A scowl, that was right, but should he? Auguste altered the width of the line to make it clearer but so as to not alter it beyond recognition. He gave the body Papa's dumpy trousers, rumpled coat, thick belt. Then he was ashamed. Papa would be angry.

Aunt Thérèse said, "That's nice. I'll try to get you colors next time."

Auguste said nothing. Papa would be very angry.

The next week, when Mama bought cabbage and potatoes, he took the paper which they had been wrapped in and drew on it. The fish was wrapped more heavily, in newspapers, and he copied pictures from the newspapers. The greatest delight was when Mama bought butter, cheese, and eggs. Not only were they a delicacy for Sunday and their picnics, they were wrapped in white paper and the white was wonderful to draw on—everything was so clear that even with his weak eyes he could see all the details.

He drew people he knew: Papa, excited and flushed; Mama, patient and subdued; Aunt Thérèse, gay and smiling; his sister Marie, sweet and pleasing; his half sister Clotilde, pretty and perfect-featured. He could not halt. He hoped school would be as adventurous. He drew only when he was alone. He was still afraid Papa would not like it.

He heard Mama grumbling, "Auguste, what has happened to the wrapping paper? You didn't throw it out? We've nothing to light the fire."

He shook his head no, afraid his lips would stick together if he lied.

The next few days Auguste took only an occasional piece of wrapping paper and drew on both sides, but drawing excited him so he could not think of anything else. Then Mama hid the wrapping paper. Wood and charcoal cost sous but the wrapping paper came with the groceries. Auguste was afraid to use the floor, they would discover his secret.

Today the kitchen was lonely and barren until he sat in Mama's rocker and rocked with great zest, as she did. Then as the magic of his beloved twilight filled the room, he sat like stone on the edge of the chair. The changing and darkening light in the sky was a miracle, but he also loved the contrast of the darkness in the kitchen, and that, too, was changing and darkening. Everything was changing and darkening, and he was fascinated by the motion this suggested. Suddenly he started rocking again, only to halt, remembering Mama's words: "Papa, why does he sit in the dark?"

Mama puzzled him. Didn't she know? Couldn't she feel the great thing going on around her at twilight?

Mama's shopping basket hit the door as hard and loud as a rock, and Auguste's skin felt it was crinkling up like crepe paper.

Mama asked, "*Mon cher,* why do you sit in the dark?"

He grinned, unable to explain.

She quickly lit the oil lamp. Auguste wanted to cover his eyes, but she was scraping off the white cheese from the pure white wrapping paper. Busy with the other groceries, cabbage, potatoes, turnips, peppers, she did not see the paper fall off the table. It lay spread out on the floor and it was more than Auguste could resist. As Mama turned her back to prepare the supper, he grabbed a dark saucer, a flowered cup, and flung himself on the floor, over the white wrapping paper.

With the stubby crayon in one hand and the plate held fast over the paper with the other, Auguste drew the outline of the plate on the paper. He held the cup down and drew it the same way. He pressed his left hand down on the paper, opening wide his fingers, and outlined his hand. For a moment he didn't know whether to draw the lines up to his elbow or to stop below it. Some kind of judgment had to be formed and it was—he ended the line just below the wrist. He stared at the lines in his hand and began to fill in the hand on the paper in the same way. Another noise like a rock hit the door and there stood Papa.

"Auguste, get up from the floor!" Papa picked up the wrapping paper, crumpled it, and threw it toward the fire in the kitchen stove.

"Yes, Papa." He couldn't take his eyes off the paper, which had missed the fire, falling by the stove.

"What are you doing, playing with a cup and saucer? You're not a girl."

Auguste wanted to explain, but how could he? He looked at the crayon in his hand and smiled. Papa took off his dark blue jacket and pulled off his heavy shoes and gave a tired sigh.

Auguste grabbed one of the boots, unrumpled the wrapping paper, placed the boot on the paper, and bending down, started to draw the outline of the boot. Papa, tired, hungry, eating at once, didn't notice. Auguste returned to the floor, and when he saw that one of the table legs did not quite touch the floor, he shoved the drawing paper under the leg and with his crayon drew its outline on the paper.

This disturbed Papa. The bowl with the potato soup shook. Papa almost missed his mouth with his spoon, and splashed some of the food onto his chin whiskers. He regarded Auguste with annoyance and disgust while his son continued to draw. Now Auguste was staring at the potato in Papa's bowl and drawing it. Papa pushed the potato aside and covered it so that Auguste would stop sketching it, but Auguste started to draw the small plate that covered the potato.

Papa's voice rose. "Give me that paper." His red hair was streaked with gray now, and there were many new work lines on his face.

Auguste had never disobeyed Papa openly before, but he shook his head no.

"Mama, get me the strap."

Auguste wavered. His fist about the paper unclenched.

"Put it in the fire." Papa had the strap now, thick and heavy. Mama looked unhappy, but she never argued with Papa.

Auguste felt like the fire itself.

"*Mon dieu*, do I have to tell you twice!"

He had no alternative. Papa reached for the paper and he acquiesced. He thrust the drawings into the fire, feeling stricken.

"And the crayon. Quickly!"

"Please, Papa?"

"Now!" *Mon dieu*, was his son possessed of the devil?

The boy's clutch about the crayons was so tight his fingerprints could be seen, but the crayons went into the fire also.

"Auguste, go to bed!"

"Without supper?" Mama was upset. She hurried to Papa's side, implored, "Jean, he will get sick."

"Next thing we know, there will be crayons in the soup. Put him to bed. And don't give him a bowl when I'm not looking."

Mama cried, "He's too thin as it is. I'll say another Mass for him."

"No!" shouted Papa, his voice hoarse. He ignored her to concentrate on the pale, frightened boy. "You will not waste any more wrapping paper." Papa, mystified by Auguste's need to draw—it was too strange, coming from his own flesh and blood—became very authoritative to hide his confusion. "If I find any drawings around the house, I will spank you to an inch of your life. I must put you in school as soon as possible, before you become an idiot."

"No more drawing?" whispered Auguste.

"None." Papa was absolute. "You will go to school as soon as possible."

Auguste recoiled. He went to bed with a stomach-ache. Mama gave him a bowl of soup after Papa went out, but he couldn't eat or sleep.

When Papa wasn't home, the child took pieces of charcoal intended for the stove—just two or three, so that no one would miss them—and sketched on the walls of the narrow, dingy alley outside, although he didn't like the light, and he hoped it would be better in school.

III

The small elementary Jesuit school was within walking distance, and Auguste hurried toward it at first with eager strides. Val de Grâce was on the rue Val de Grâce, in an ancient building that once had been a military hospital, but it was also on the corner of the boulevard St. Michel and close to the more respectable St. Germain Quarter.

Auguste was in a high state of excitement, but he was taken aback by the gray, forbidding façade, the sternness of the middle-aged priest-teachers, who were testy, harsh, and absolute. They made him feel full of sin. There were no questions to be asked, only ones to be answered.

Val de Grâce was attached to a seminary, and religious instruction was the heart of its curriculum. Auguste had great difficulty memorizing the catechism. It also gave instruction in arithmetic, which Auguste did not understand; in Latin, which he loathed; in reading, writing, and penmanship, which in his case deteriorated into an ugly scrawl, made worse by his inability to spell even the simplest words; in geography and history, which he liked but did poorly in because of his nearsightedness; and in grammar, which in his mind was chaos. It was a poor man's school, despising leisure and any other such nonsense, determined to turn out boys who would work hard, be content with their place, and be deeply devout.

Art was taboo. When Auguste drew in his geography class, sketching a map of the Holy Roman Empire, it was torn up. When he did it again, a ruler descended harshly on his fingers. They hurt so much he could not hold a pencil for a week. Yet he had to draw; it had become the only thing that mattered. The next time Auguste was caught, he was whipped. But for all his shyness he was stubborn. Drawing had become his world. His teachers became inhumanly stiff faces whom he sketched with an unholy joy. He did caricatures of them, drawing secretly, making sure he would not be caught.

The only other thing that excited Auguste was the revolution of 1848. In the rioting, King Louis Philippe was deposed, and suddenly, unexpectedly, and pleasantly there was no school. At first Auguste was delighted. But the revolution stopped being a picnic, even for the boy, when freedom and a republic became the burning questions and the workers of Paris took up arms against the existing provisional government.

The arrondissement in which the Rodins lived became the center of the fighting. Rebels erected barricades on the boulevard St. Michel, near the school. Discharged workers, guns and spikes in hand, shouted, "La liberté ou la mort!" The "Marseillaise" was sung everywhere—by both sides.

Papa stopped working, Mama did not even shop, no one in the family was allowed out of the house—it was as if they were besieged. They had to exist on one potato a day through four days of bloody, savage fighting that exploded within their hearing.

Baudelaire fought behind the barricades for the republic; Balzac wanted to fight, but his insatiable curiosity drove him to explore the deserted palace and the workers' bloody quarters, seeing everything under the magnifying glass of his own mind. Hugo felt himself a god, and expected to become one of the leaders, perhaps *the* leader, believing himself the ideal mixture of imperial and republican, and gave his readers and listeners what they wanted—the glory of patriotism. Hugo was deeply disappointed when they chose Louis Napoleon as President instead. A most unfortunate choice, Hugo thought, puny, ailing, starved, imprisoned until recently, an outlaw a year ago, alone then except for his mistress, valet, and dog; but when he signed his speeches and proclamations *Louis Napoleon Bonaparte*, the magic name wiped out everything else.

Even Papa, whose royalist convictions had been shaken by the slaughter of the workers, was relieved when Louis Napoleon was elected President of France at the end of the year. He told his family it was good for France.

When school resumed, lessons were even more boring. Auguste thought, What was a world of dead kings when live ones were to be conquered? His eyes grew worse. He was so nearsighted now that he could not read properly, but no one knew enough to remedy this— and when he drew everything became large. He had become, without question, the worst pupil in Val de Grâce.

The Rodins were living on the rue St. Jacques now, a wide street not far from the boulevard St. Michel, the boulevard of the Left Bank painters. There was a statue outside their house that was supposed to be Cupid. Papa was offended by it—he thought a statue of the Virgin would be far more appropriate; Auguste was irritated that it was blistered and disfigured, but when he tried to clean it Papa scolded, "Are you going to be a gipsy? Have no future?"

The boy started to sketch the Cupid on lesson paper from the school, and Papa ripped it out of his hands and cried, "Auguste, you are impossible! We have a nice house now. You could have a nice house when you grow up. I moved close to the University Quarter to help you. But you do so badly in school, I don't know what to do with you."

It was a cry of despair, but Auguste felt despair, too. The new rooms were better, there were two windows in each room, glass in each window, and clean curtains and heavy iron gratings over the windows. But people still threw refuse into the street, and then washed it down to avoid the plague. There was always a damp chill in the house and street, and even here there was an odor for which he had only one name: the odor of poverty. To Auguste it was dreary, destitute, and miserable. But Papa was proud; Papa made twelve hundred francs a year now.

The next few weeks Auguste tried to be obedient, but his drawings were an escape from this world, a sanctuary, a feeling free. Aunt Thérèse gave him an old paintbox, and he colored everything in sight, especially the picture magazines Papa adored. Once again when he was supposed to be studying he drew and sketched and painted. He envied the taller boys, for he was short, stocky, with wide shoulders—a true peasant's build, Papa said—and he made his figures large.

He began to stay away from school, and one day this was reported to Papa. When Auguste came home the next afternoon, apparently from school—he had gone to look more closely at Notre Dame, he liked the pinnacles, the light, far-reaching buttresses, and the great west front with its towers, as if everything had been measured with a view to grandeur—and sought to explain this to Papa, Papa wasn't listening.

Papa said, "Voilà! I have an idiot for a son! He does not even know this is a day for school. He cannot even add and subtract." Without another word he thrashed Auguste with his heavy belt.

Auguste trembled violently, but refused to cry.

Mama stood there whimpering to herself, and Papa, exhausted afterward, collapsed into a chair, groaning, "You are sinful."

Mama was disappointed because Auguste showed no aptitude for religious instruction—she was pleased that Marie was very good, Clotilde, ah Mon dieu, that was another matter, all that Clotilde showed interest in was boys, but Auguste, even after four years at Val de Grâce, hadn't been able to memorize the catechism. She was beginning to doubt he would ever be prepared for his first Communion. And suddenly she said as Auguste stood there shaking but still not crying, "Auguste, you don't love me."

"Mama . . ." He couldn't speak. Of course he loved her. But he could not say it. Not now. He would draw her. When he felt better. When the tears stopped welling up inside. A light had gone out abruptly, as though a black, terrible wall of separation had risen between him and Papa.

Papa had not finished. Papa had recovered his strength. It was not his fault, he thought, it was the school that was to blame. He decided to send this numskull to his brother Alexander's school, at Beauvais.

IV

Uncle Alexander was competent, practical, and strict, and he set out with Norman vigor to educate his nephew. Auguste's prominent nose, his high, broad forehead, his firm mouth, his large head, suggested what his uncle called sensitiveness. Only one thing bothered Uncle Alexander—the boy's eyes, though bright, were small.

It looked quite hopeful, Uncle Alexander assured Papa. He was sure the Jesuits had failed, not Auguste.

Uncle Alexander resolutely concentrated on his favorite Latin and arithmetic—his students had to have orderly, disciplined minds—and Auguste was attentive, gained weight, and developed a width of chest and shoulders that made him very strong. His pale skin grew ruddy and his health flourished in the country air. But he learned nothing. His uncle, striving energetically to teach him, felt as if he were trying to penetrate marble.

After four years Uncle Alexander was forced to admit it was no use, the Jesuits were right. "The boy is virtually illiterate: he can read, but that is all. He knows no Latin, he cannot even say the conjugations, his spelling is horrible, like nothing I have ever seen, and his composition"—Uncle Alexander waved an excited, despairing hand—"it is incredible."

Auguste had tried to tell his uncle that he could not see the board properly, that his eyes hurt, but his uncle had not listened. And his passion for drawing had grown. Then everything became large, distinct. If he could only live in a republic of lines, lines brought things to life.

Uncle Alexander felt utterly defeated. He was glad to get rid of this block of marble, to return Auguste to Papa. He informed Papa, "Nothing will ever penetrate his thick skull. He is uneducable. The sooner you put him out to work, the better. I doubt he can even make a living."

CHAPTER 2

To Papa this was a grave nuisance: earning a living was the major fact of his life, and he feared that his brother was right, that the boy was good for nothing. Yet Auguste was fourteen; he had to learn a trade, the family's resources were still scanty, and it was essential that he provide for his own needs.

Papa greeted Auguste with the announcement that he had to go to work.

It was a lovely June Sunday, ideal for a picnic such as Auguste had enjoyed so much before he had gone to what had become a prison at Beauvais, but they were having dinner at home today. It was Papa's wish, and everyone was there except Clotilde.

"The question is," said Papa, "What kind of work?"

"I want to draw," said Auguste.

Papa went to whip him, then paused; it was not fitting on a Sunday. Mama sat sewing, to keep calm, and wished they were going on a picnic. And Auguste stood there like stone, unchanging, and Papa had to have something malleable to vent his wrath upon. Then he became angry with Clotilde for being absent from dinner, particularly without his permission: dinner was the core of his family life, the one time he felt *en famille*. He shouted at Mama, "Where's Clotilde? She's never home. And this is the best home we have had."

Mama said, "I don't know where she is."

"You should know! She's always out!" he exclaimed, feeling so put upon. "A daughter who is never home, a son who wants to be an artist. Pile up nonsense on nonsense. I move into the University Quarter the moment I can, we are close to the Sorbonne, the most learned part of Paris, and my son is a fool, a redheaded fool. Artist—I have no money for such nonsense. At least if you could spell, I could get you in the Prefecture of Police as a clerk, but now . . . ?" He shrugged vehemently, hopelessly.

Auguste thought, Yes, this is the nicest place we have lived in. They were higher up on the rue St. Jacques, the Sorbonne within sight, but even if he hadn't been a bad student he couldn't have gone, Papa didn't have the money or position for it. Auguste stared at Papa, sitting at the head of the oblong dinner table—at Papa regarding him as a spoiled child.

Papa was proud that in these quarters Auguste had a room for himself, and so had Marie and Clotilde, but Auguste had to earn his. In the daytime his room was the kitchen, while his sisters had the dining room and his parents the living room.

As Papa went over the different trades his son could apprentice himself in, Auguste—full of emotion—he had missed his family very much in Beauvais, even Papa—tried to absorb them all with his senses. Papa still had his broad shoulders, strong chest, muscular arms, heavy, square-fisted hands, the joints of his fingers covered with tufts of red hair. His face was furrowed with premature wrinkles. His voice was heavy, boisterous when happy, rough when angry.

Mama was blonde, with gray eyes and plain, flat features. She was deeply religious, with a perpetual expression of sadness, as if she knew life was essentially difficult and sinful. And Auguste noticed that she wore the same dress he had seen on her when he had departed for Beauvais years ago, redyed so many times the fabric was tattered.

Marie was too slender, too frail, thought Auguste, her reddish-blonde hair and pale face having the look of a medieval statuette, and her sweet expression was often one of resignation, like her mother's. But when she was happy and animated, as she was usually with him, she was pretty. Then her small oval face and blue eyes glowed and her appearance lit up despite the severe way she dressed. At the moment, he noticed, in a simple black dress with a trim high white collar—almost like a nun.

It was Clotilde who was the beauty. Clotilde, Papa's daughter by his first wife, now dead, was different from anyone else in the family. She was very vivacious, with a dark complexion, green eyes, and black hair.

He liked both Marie and Clotilde even though they happened to be his sisters.

They sat down as Mama brought in dinner with Marie's help.

Papa began to grumble again about Clotilde's absence. Then he saw Auguste sitting motionless, not eating, not speaking, looking dead. Papa flared. "Have you no shame over your poor marks?"

"I don't want to be a police official."

"Idiot, it takes brains to work for the Prefecture!"

"I know I could be an artist."

"Do you think a louis is a trifle? Work for it, find out. I paid five for this oilcloth." Greasy though it was, they had put it down for Sunday dinner.

"I should go to art school," Auguste said almost as if he were talking to himself.

Papa said sarcastically, "To the Beaux Arts, no doubt, Monsieur Rodin?"

"No, Papa, it is too soon. I need training."

"Of course. There is no telling where you will end up."

"At the Beaux Arts, after I get the proper training."

"I have one son," Papa lamented, "and he turns out to be an idiot."

Marie gazed at her serious-looking brother: his beardless, still childish face, his wide forehead, his square features, his long, fine nose, his determined mouth. He thought he appeared weak because of his gentle voice, his shortness, but this was deceptive, she reflected; he had a very stubborn will. She said, it was the first thing she had said all day, "Papa, maybe he should go to art school."

"No," said Papa. "There is character in his well-developed arms and his long nose, but next he will consider himself a gentleman and want to wear a frock coat and top hat."

"Perhaps he would become good enough for the Beaux Arts," said Marie.

Papa's ruddy face puffed out as he grew angry and sarcastic. "And, monsieur, what happens if you fail the Beaux Arts?"

"I won't fail," said Auguste with the assurance of the fourteen-year-old who faces a universe made for him to conquer.

"You can't even spell," said illiterate Papa. "Alexander says you are the worst speller he has ever had."

Auguste replied, "Mistakes in spelling are like the mistakes other people make in drawing. Papa, I don't find fault with *your* drawing."

"Idiot!" Papa raised a hand to chastise Auguste, but Mama pushed the meat in front of him, an infrequent luxury, and he couldn't resist the smell. Teeth in a mouthful of veal, he declared, "There are several thousand artists in Paris alone, but do they eat decent meals like this?"

"Paris is a painter's city," said Auguste. "That's why they live here. And we are close to the Beaux Arts."

"I said no Beaux Arts!"

"I couldn't get in, anyhow."

"Why not?" Suddenly Papa was offended.

"I am not ready. Not yet." He dipped his hands into the cold water, washing them very carefully. They were becoming important.

At this moment Clotilde entered. "Oh, not for dinner," she said. "I am being taken to dinner."

"On Sunday?" Papa was outraged. "You are only nineteen. Where are you going? Who is the young man?" His pride was greatly hurt.

Auguste thought Clotilde especially attractive today with her tall, lithe figure, her soft, warm flesh, her intimate manner.

She was wearing a hat with ostrich feathers.

"À *la mode*," Papa sneered.

She retorted that he was a skinflint.

Papa rushed on, "You're too dressed up to be honest—what splendid carriage brought you home? Is it waiting for you on the corner of the boulevard St. Germain?" Clotilde had become a lovely, dark-haired young woman and much too pretty for a daughter of his. It made him very uncomfortable. She did not want to become a seamstress, or even a milliner. She never wore simple morning dresses any more. And now she was insolent, refusing to answer his demand to know where she had been. He stated, "If this keeps up, I will have only one daughter." He put on his coarse chestnut-brown coat. "Now, don't keep Mama waiting. Eat your dinner."

"Papa, I told you I am being taken to dinner."

"You are mad."

"The carriage is waiting."

"And you are a Josephine to a Napoleon?"

"Papa, I came home to get a wrap."

"Who is the man?"

"Oh, my poor Papa, he has to know everything."

"You come of an honest marriage. You are beautiful enough, you might marry without a dowry."

Clotilde sneered, "Is this a family confessional?"

"You are insulting!" Papa glared at her, waiting for her to apologize and take her place at the Sunday dinner table.

Clotilde did not want to continue the quarrel, but she could not apologize. She had gone too far, she knew, but if she retreated now she would never have any freedom. And Gaston was waiting. Gaston was a great opportunity, wealthy enough to support her, frantically infatuated. Just a few minutes ago he had said to her that beauty such as hers was made in heaven and must be framed in gold. Yet even as she could not give in, she did not want to push Papa too hard. There had been other promises, most of them unkept. She wavered, not sure what to do.

Papa had no wish for a showdown, either, but he was afraid that if he displayed weakness now the rest of the family would take advantage of it, especially Auguste. And Clotilde would give in, he assured himself, she always had. Papa said, "Sit down, and we will consider the punishment later."

"What about my friend?" asked Clotilde.

"Invite the young man in," said Papa. "We always have food for one more mouth, and we can become acquainted."

But that was impossible, thought Clotilde. Gaston came from a good family, one of the richest in Rouen; if he set foot in here he would never want to see her again. As it was, it had been difficult to get him to promise to wait for her on the nearby boulevard St. Germain. "I'm sorry, Papa," she said, "but we've already made arrangements for dinner elsewhere." In this instant of defiance she felt quite beautiful.

"Because we're not good enough to meet him," said Papa.

"I didn't say that," said Clotilde.

"You don't have to. It is as obvious as those ostrich feathers you are wearing."

"He likes them."

"I don't." Papa reached out to pull them off, and she evaded his grasp. There was a minute of silence. The others sat like statues. And suddenly it was unbearable for Papa. As Clotilde went to fetch her wrap, he declared, "If you go now, do not come back."

"This is an order?"

"Yes," replied Papa, growing firmer as Clotilde stopped, apparently impressed. "You must obey."

"And if I don't?"

"I think you had better take all your things with you."

"But why?"

"You will end up in the woman's prison of St. Lazare."

Clotide looked stunned. Papa was ominously angry, and she was afraid.

"Mademoiselle, the woman's prison at St. Lazare has a thousand little ghastly barred windows. It is filled with prostitutes who are diseased, mentally ill. I know, I have delivered messages to the Prefecture there. And I don't want any daughter of mine to end there."

The look of horror turned to hatred in Clotilde's eyes. "You couldn't do that to your own daughter!"

"You wouldn't be my daughter then."

Mama said, "Jean, she is young, willful, but you can forgive that."

"After she has insulted me?"

"Oh, Jean, because she disagrees?"

"She disobeys. All the time. All my children disobey now," he said, aggrieved, determined to halt this, to set an example, to show his son his power before things got completely out of hand. "Even gentle Marie."

"Jean, you can't throw her out."

Papa controlled himself with an effort. How dare Mama defend her? Clotilde was not her child! And everybody was opposing him now! He could not back down—he had gone too far.

"If you love her," said Mama, "you will forgive her."

Papa did not answer. He was like stone.

Clotilde had not moved, but now she went to get her wrap.

Papa said, "Don't come back."

Mama renewed her plea to Papa to be charitable, and Marie joined in, then Auguste, but the more they opposed him the more he was driven to assert his authority. Clotilde picked up her wrap and ran across the room toward the door. Mama stood at the stove, stunned. Clotilde paused at the door, and in this instant both she and Papa hoped the other would give in, but neither could. She grew pale, and then was gone. Marie and Auguste hurried after her, and saw her vanish into a carriage at the corner.

Papa muttered, "She's no better than a prostitute—see!"

Mama cried, "Jean, how could you? You know she has no money to support herself!"

Papa banged on the table and said he wanted no more talk.

Auguste was shocked: Papa had called Clotilde a prostitute. It made him remember his first and only sexual experience. She had been the prostitute on the corner. She had looked about nineteen. Clotilde was nineteen. He had taken a big chance of disease with her. And it had happened so quickly, so suddenly, he had not had time to enjoy it. But he kept recalling the prostitute's heavy thighs, her naked body, her thick waist, her huge breasts; he could remember every detail of her body but nothing about her face. He should have sketched her, but she would have laughed at him. Real artists did naked women, and he had no francs for models. He had no francs for anything, he realized suddenly; the prostitute had given her body to him for free, amused and curious about his youth, considering it a triumph somehow to be his first.

Did Clotilde give her body for free? Then Auguste was shocked at himself for thinking such things about his sister.

He did not return to the table to finish his dinner, but stood at the door, where he had rushed after Clotilde, and Papa growled, "Now here, don't be a fool. Eat!"

"I'm not hungry."

"Then stand still."

"I'm standing still."

"Sit down. *Mon dieu!*"

Auguste knew it would be far better to obey, but he couldn't. He could hear his own breathing. Would Papa throw him out, too? Where would he go? The prostitute? Impossible. But he had to draw.

Papa glared at his son, who stood as stubborn as a rock. It was bad enough about Clotilde, but he couldn't lose a son, his only son, it would be too humiliating. Yet they were still like two stones when Marie offered a compromise. She said softly, "I know of a free school. The Petite École."

"What about room and board?" asked Papa.

"I can take care of it," said Marie. "Selling religious medals."

"Well, well, well." Papa was surprised. This was revolt from an unexpected quarter.

Marie, feeling that Papa was weakening, said, "The Petite École tries to develop draftsmen rather than artists, poor boys who can get into a drawing industry."

Papa demanded, "How do you know?"

Marie blushed. "I met a young man, Barnouvin, who studies there."

"Why haven't you invited him here?"

"Oh . . ." She made a vague gesture. "I just talked to him once or twice."

"Do you like him?"

"Papa, he's a painter."

"Don't distract me."

"But you said you don't like artists."

"Invite him. Let me judge."

"I don't know him that well."

But Marie had lost her usual resignation, her ascetic quality, thought Auguste. Even in her austere black dress she looked animated and pretty. He wondered how well she really knew Barnouvin.

Marie said hurriedly, "If Auguste graduates from the Petite École, he might get work in a goldsmith's shop on the rue Dauphine or become an engraver on the rue Auvergne or a cabinetmaker anywhere in Paris. He will be learning a trade, Papa."

Papa growled, "He couldn't graduate from anything."

Mama said, "Poor Auguste, he is trembling like a leaf. *Mon chat*, does it mean that much to you?"

Auguste nodded.

"That's not enough," Papa said icily.

"How much is his board, Papa?" asked Marie.

"I'm not a moneylender," said Papa.

"Ten francs a week?"

Papa did not answer.

"Twelve francs?"

"I said I am not a moneylender, a monster. Give what you can."

"I will give you what you need."

"Need?" Papa shrugged. "There is always need." Generosity was an extravagance he could not afford. He would have left Paris long ago if he could have done better in Normandy.

"Then he can go to the Petite École?" asked Marie.

"How do you know he will be admitted?"

"He will be admitted," Marie said positively.

Auguste thought that never had anyone looked as beautiful as Marie. He ran to her side and kissed her on the cheek, then embraced Mama, who gave him one of her rare smiles. He wanted to kiss Papa, too, or at least take his hand. Instead he found himself mumbling, "*Merci*, Papa," for Papa was grumbling, "One daughter a whore and one a saint, and a son who is a jackass." Papa felt like Job.

CHAPTER 3

A few days later Auguste was taken to the Petite École by Barnouvin. Barnouvin was doing this for Marie, whom he seemed eager to impress.

Barnouvin was a tall, lean, fair seventeen, high-colored, high-spirited, and opinionated, and delighted to display his superior knowledge and sophistication to this lad. He considered himself a superb talent, the logical successor to Delacroix, in his second year at the Petite École, which he was using only as an entry into the Beaux Arts.

Auguste envied the faint down that covered Barnouvin's chin, the start of a Vandyke, his charming eyes, his fine features, his humorous and flexible mouth—Barnouvin talked readily, while he had to grope for words. Barnouvin already dressed in the fashion of the day: tail coat, trousers with flaps, a soft hat, a pipe, and his hair long and curling over his open collar, in the fashion of the Latin Quarter.

The Petite École was on the rue de l'École de Médecine, in the quarter whose center was the École de Médecine, the Sorbonne, the École de Droit, the École des Beaux Arts, and the Observatoire. "They are the heart of French learning," Barnouvin said proudly, and pointed them out as they walked with quick, impatient strides over the wide, crowded boulevard St. Michel and then along the narrow and picturesque rue Racine.

Barnouvin, as he liked to be called, was a babble of information. He told the wide-eyed, attentive Auguste, "The Petite École was founded in 1765 by Madame de Pompadour's pet artist, Jean Jacques

Bachelier, as a school of the decorative arts; not of the fine arts, like the Beaux Arts. We're called the *Petite* to separate us from the *Grande*—the Beaux. But officially we have a fancy title." Barnouvin mouthed it as if it were an empire. "You are going to attend the École Impériale spéciale du Dessin et des Mathématiques."

Auguste did not laugh, as he expected.

"*Mon ami*," exclaimed Barnouvin, "you're not much of a talker!"

"Not much." What was there to say?

"Lecoq is, when he wants to be." He didn't tell Auguste who Lecoq was, but clearly Lecoq was a person of Napoleonic importance. "What trade are you studying? The Petite École turns out draftsmen rather than artists. In fact, Beaux Arts students say we are pupils with little talent who can't make the Beaux Arts. But they won't keep me out. What drawing industry do you want to get into?"

"I want to be a painter."

"Have you ever used oil?"

"No."

"I have. I'm an advanced pupil." Barnouvin said that as if he had already half conquered the Salon. "Have you worked with water color?"

"Yes and no."

"Yes and no! What kind of an answer is that? No doubt you are going to amuse yourself?"

Auguste shook his head no so intently that Barnouvin was startled. He said, "You are decided for the Beaux Arts?"

"I will try. After I prepare at the Petite École."

"Everybody tries. Next you will want to be Michelangelo."

"I have never seen his work."

"You know who he is?"

"A little. Not enough. I was always being taught Latin."

"And now you want to be an artist?"

Auguste shrugged. "If God wills. And I work hard enough."

Barnouvin stared at him as if he were a stranger, but they were at the Petite École and it was time to enter.

The school was in a striking seventeenth-century building. There were grounds in front, and they entered through a large iron gate set in a triumphal arch. Over the entrance of the building itself was the Latin inscription *Utilitas—Firmitas*. Barnouvin translated as Auguste looked bewildered. "Practicality—Solidity. Apparently your Latin didn't do you much good. Grand, isn't it?"

Auguste nodded, and stared at the statues of Hercules and Minerva set on each side of the entrance, two Ionic columns beside each statue. There was a contradiction here, he thought: despite these Greek touches the front was ornamental in a highly decorative baroque. The building itself was circular, and he didn't like the dome; he thought it oversized, in bad taste, more suitable for a church than an art school.

Barnouvin led him into the main hall, formerly a large salon which had been converted into a studio. The ceiling was high, the windows were long and large; the best light was on the north side. The walls were decorated with numerous drawings in charcoal, white, red, and black crayon, and with some paintings, mostly copies. At the rear, commanding the entire studio, was an elevated platform with a wide drawing desk and a man standing behind it. Facing the desk were a model-throne, a few stools, and about forty firmly built straight-backed chairs, with easels in front of the chairs and many drawings.

The students were young, anywhere from fourteen to eighteen, Auguste noticed with relief—he would not be too much out of place. There was no chaff, there were no jokes. He sensed that this was a serious business, not for the irresponsible or the idle; this was to make a living, to avoid the garret, the morgue, the Seine, the road, the paternal shop.

His heart beat rapidly as Barnouvin introduced him to the man on the elevated platform, Horace Lecoq de Boisbaudran.

"*Maître*, this is Auguste Rodin, who wants to enter the Petite École."

Lecoq looked intently at him. The teacher was dark, middle-aged, with a face full of shadows, thought Auguste, yet when he showed interest, as now, his brown eyes were full and bright—as if each new student was a new opportunity, a new challenge, a new birth, or perhaps, as his expression grew saturnine, a disappointment. It was an interesting face, Auguste told himself, long and lean, and marked by high, prominent cheekbones, a fine forehead, and penetrating eyes. Auguste felt himself transfixed by these eyes as Lecoq asked, "You want instruction in the fine arts?"

"Yes." How did Lecoq know? Barnouvin had told him that the Petit École concentrated on training artisans.

"Have you studied before?"

"No."

"What makes you think you can be an artist?"

"I have been drawing since five."

"On canvas?" Lecoq looked cynical.

"On wrapping paper."

Lecoq looked confused, and Barnouvin, who had heard the story from Marie, hurried to explain.

"Oh," said Lecoq, "another poor one."

Auguste nodded.

"Why didn't you come sooner?"

"I was in school, studying Latin and arithmetic."

"Wasting your time?"

Auguste gave him a glance of relief.

"Have you any work with you?"

"Won't I be admitted?"

Lecoq, distracted by a student, didn't answer, and Barnouvin whispered, "Fool, of course you will. There is no examination or tuition. He wants to know where to place you."

Lecoq's attention returned to Auguste, who stood there frightened yet fascinated, and he said sharply, "There are two types of students they wish on me. One type is a clerk, who wants to make straight lines, although there are no straight lines in nature, who wants to draw according to rule, although there are no rules in life. They usually end up in the Beaux Arts, imitating the classics. Their throats should have been slit at birth. But I have to teach them in this republic of art. Then there are the second type, who are rare, and where they come from you never know, who, à la Rembrandt, try to use their eyes, try to see their own way. Most artists see through their family, their teachers, their masters, the society in which they exist. But the second type, à la Rembrandt, learn to ignore these things and to see through their own eyes."

Auguste was in despair. He saw so little, so badly. He would never get into the Beaux Arts, or make the Salon, the only place one sold, let alone satisfy the Petite École, which had become in this moment Lecoq.

"But you expect art to radiate goodness and charity," said Lecoq.

"What should I do? I have no training in composition," said Auguste.

"So you will find your own level," Lecoq said indifferently. "You will learn to be an ornament maker, a clerk of straight lines."

Lecoq was about to ignore him when Auguste cried out, "My papa says I'm an idiot to come here. But I have to. I cannot say why, but I have to. And I can draw. I know I can."

Lecoq smiled: at least the boy could get angry. "Go ahead," he said.

Auguste turned to Barnouvin for advice and Barnouvin shrugged with such a mixture of insouciance and superiority that Auguste couldn't resist. He sat in an empty chair and picked up black crayon. Though everything felt awkwardly unfamiliar, as Barnouvin's face grew under his fingers he forgot his confusion. He could think of nothing now but the drawing, and when Lecoq halted him suddenly, he said unhappily, "I haven't finished."

"It's sufficient." Lecoq examined the drawing, then glanced at Barnouvin and said, "Your friend is not altogether flattering."

Barnouvin stared at the mouth, which was charming yet a little sly, and declared, "It is degraded. A scrawl. I do not look like this."

Lecoq said, "It is the way he sees you."

Barnouvin said, "A joke, a bad joke."

"I'm sorry," Auguste said quietly. "I didn't mean to do a caricature."

Barnouvin made a gesture of magnanimous forgiveness, and Lecoq said, "It is not a caricature. What did you say your name was, boy?"

"Rodin. Auguste Rodin."

"Next time you sketch such an elegant young man, Rodin, use a pen for the thin lines. Now there are too many smudges."

"I have never used a pen. I could not afford it."

"You will. You will get on, little by little, even without a sou. C'est bien."

"Merci, maître."

"But you will go into the morning class for beginners."

"I thought—" Auguste halted, unable to finish; it wasn't fitting what he was going to say.

"You thought, mon ami, that you are of the second type, à la

Rembrandt. That's yet to be proved. But you will have time. Now we are doing nothing but learning to draw. That is what everybody lacks today. You, too, Barnouvin," Lecoq added as he saw Barnouvin frowning.

Barnouvin said, "I work hard."

"All my students work hard," Lecoq said firmly. "It is the least we can do."

II

On Auguste's first day at school he was determined to work his fingers to the bone, yet a little apprehensive. Class began at eight in the morning and went on until noon, and he was one of forty. Lecoq informed him that before he joined the others in copying drawings by Boucher he must show that he could draw from memory. It was a ritual for all beginners who desired to be fine artists. The teacher told him, "This is training in a manner of seeing," then ignored him, but Auguste felt that this was another test, more to try his fiber than his skill.

He sat before a sheet of blank white paper and detested its blankness. He felt in a vacuum. He had white, red, and black crayons that Barnouvin had given him, but nothing else. He did not know where to start. This was worse than yesterday. No one was interested.

Barnouvin was copying a red chalk drawing by Boucher, traditional at the Petite École, for Boucher, who embodied the French rococo taste of the eighteenth century, was a hero here, having been the tutor of Pompadour. Barnouvin, seeing the pale, motionless boy, whispered, "Just do something as natural as breathing. Seeing is just as natural."

But there was nothing to see, thought Auguste. He wondered if Lecoq knew as much as Barnouvin thought the teacher did. What was seeing? It would be much simpler to copy. He looked over at Barnouvin, but his friend shook his head.

Lecoq stood behind him, said, "Draw something you know."

"A face?"

"If you wish."

"My father?"

"That's up to you." Lecoq placed a pen by his side, soft and hard pencils, charcoal, and said, "Every artist has to find the tools that are best for him. You choose your own." He smiled and walked away.

Auguste faced the blank white paper with a new determination. He tried the pen but it was unfamiliar, and found himself back with his own black crayon and charcoal, materials he knew. He made the head first, then drew in the features, making them protrude until they looked almost like sculpture—a man homely but sturdy. Then Auguste thought of Papa as he had been when he had agreed reluctantly to the Petite École, and Papa's lips became narrow with distaste, the jaw grew heavy, the neck thick.

Lecoq had returned. "Your father?" he asked, surprised by what he saw.

"Yes." He had an appalling fear the drawing would be torn up. It was coarse and Papa looked ugly—but it was Papa, he'd swear to that.

Lecoq was aware of the boy's anxiety, but he couldn't resist, the boy was so serious. "Monsieur Rodin, you are immoral."

"But that's the way he looks," Auguste cried desperately.

"Monsieur Rodin, you mean that is the way you see him."

"They are my eyes," Auguste stated decisively, stubborn suddenly.

"So ugly?"

Auguste winced, but had to motion yes.

Lecoq shook his head in wonderment.

"I'm sorry, maître, that you don't like it, but—"

"But," prodded the teacher, "you're not sorry you did it that way?"

There was no choice. Auguste wanted to lie, but he could not.

"You are not sorry?" repeated Lecoq.

Auguste picked up his black crayon, certain he was being dismissed despite the Petite École being free.

Lecoq said, "I'm glad you are not moral. Morality has ruined more young painters than anything I know."

"You like the drawing?" Auguste was surprised.

"I like that you didn't lie and didn't flatter. A drawing doesn't have to be pretty, it does have to be alive."

III

Auguste spent the next few weeks learning as much as he could about drawing from Lecoq. Barnouvin declared that Lecoq was the best teacher outside of the Beaux Arts, perhaps the best teacher in Paris in spite of Lecoq's violent and often expressed dislike of the Academy. Lecoq was proud of his dislike, and let his students know it. He enjoyed stating, "I know most of you come here only as preparation for the Beaux Arts, for its dry lectures, uninspired courses, the Prix de Rome, the Salon, honorable mention or medals, purchases from the state, and finally government commissions and election to the Academy itself. But there is no more imagination there, or vitality. Everything has to be sweet and decorous."

It did not alter Barnouvin's or Auguste's determination to get into the Beaux Arts, but Auguste agreed with Barnouvin now—Lecoq was a remarkable man, indeed.

Lecoq kept repeating, "Only three or four of you will ever amount to anything," but Lecoq made each student feel he was one of the three or four.

Auguste knew he should not trust this. He couldn't believe what was happening to him, even now, even after several months of Lecoq. Paying attention, which had been the hardest thing in the world, had become easy; he no longer felt fidgety; he felt that if he didn't pay attention he would miss something vital.

Lecoq stressed the use of visual memory; he insisted that they soak themselves in what they saw so that they would be able to reproduce it completely from memory. But he also taught technique, how to use pen and pencil as well as chalk and crayon and charcoal, to use material soft and medium and hard, to smudge in contours with the fingers, to use various colors. His favorites were what he called "à deux crayons, red and black crayon," and "à trois crayons, red, black, and white crayon."

He said, "Drawing is inseparable from painting. The line defines the concept, the form, the tone, the texture. There is the suave line, the lyrical line, the witty line, the decorative line like Boucher's. The great decorators, Boucher and Fragonard, drew incessantly; they made drawing an independent art form—in red or black chalk, in pencil, pen, and wash. As for character, Rembrandt and Michelangelo, ah, *mon dieu!* But you will discover that for yourselves."

Auguste was so held by Lecoq's enthusiasm he was afraid to interrupt, it might halt the flow, and the others felt the same way, for there were rarely any interruptions. In such moments Auguste was full of excitement.

Lecoq was saying now, "Drawing consists not only of what is set down, but of what is not. The pen moves and the artist is forever committed."

It was Auguste's first exposure to such strong feelings, and he wondered how any of them could become only artisans after Lecoq's fire.

When Lecoq said, "Above all, we must respect the dignity and integrity of the human body," Auguste sought to draw a human figure. He didn't know whether to make it male or female, draped or undraped. He found himself sketching a torso first, without sex, then legs, still without sex, then arms, a head—but now he was stuck. A head could not be neutral, neither could the body. He saw Lecoq loom up behind him. He expected the teacher to say, "Desist."

Instead Lecoq said, "Go ahead."

Auguste said, "I don't know enough about anatomy."

"You know the human body, don't you? Your own body? You've examined your own body?"

Auguste blushed. No, he hadn't, except in a casual and general way, but this was not something he could discuss.

"An artist who doesn't use himself as a model is blind."

Auguste started to sharpen his pencils, but Lecoq was persistent.

"No one sees the same way. I see blue, you may see green. I see trees, you may see bodies. Do it as you see it."

"But I can't do it from memory. I don't know how!" To admit more was to admit an innocence of which somehow it was to be ashamed.

"You are an innocent. To you they are all unrelated parts. You actually should be a draftsman, a clerk in a republic of straight lines."

"I don't want to be a draftsman. I won't!" Auguste stood up with such violence that he upset his drawing board, ruining the drawing. It hurt, but he hurt more from what Lecoq had suggested—he had trusted Lecoq.

Lecoq looked weary, anxious to be rid of this emotion which had become a nuisance; but when he saw the tears in the boy's eyes—and the boy could draw, that was evident—he said slowly, "You may come to the evening life class and draw from a model. But come early. It is very crowded."

IV

Lecoq was right. The evening class was crowded: it was the night for the female nude model. There were twice as many students as in the day classes, and they were freer, noisier, and older. Auguste had just turned fifteen and he felt self-conscious; most of these students were eighteen and nineteen, and some of them were in their early twenties, artists who toiled as artisans during the day and could study only at night.

The students formed a thick circle around the model immediately, and began sketching her, and Auguste found himself in the rear, at first able only to see her back. He had come late, delayed by arguing Papa into allowing him to go to the Petite École at night.

He was very nervous. The studio was chilly, it was December, and he was shivering. But he knew it was not the cold. He was not sure he could look at the naked model in the presence of others.

Barnouvin, sitting next to him, whispered triumphantly, "At the Beaux Arts they use only male models and copy the female form from oil paintings of classic nymphs, but Lecoq is advanced, an *homme précieux*."

Auguste nodded, ashamed to do otherwise, but Papa would be shocked, Mama would utter more Ave Marias, and Marie—it would be impossible to tell what his quiet sister would think.

Yet everyone seemed so impersonal. Lecoq presented the model as he might a cadavar in a dissecting room, discussing her figure as if it were an anatomy lesson, enumerating her parts methodically: the torso, the arm, the hand, the head, the lower limbs, the foot, the pelvis. And the model was the biggest disenchantment of all.

"A chambermaid from across the street," Barnouvin told him, annoyed. "Lecoq wanted a fleshy one."

Fleshy she was, Auguste agreed, trying to appear as grown-up as Barnouvin. Even so, he felt his heart palpitate as he got his first close look at her, although it was only from the rear. This was different from the prostitute on the corner.

Lecoq said in a dry voice, "This is a typical female body."

Auguste edged closer.

"It is up to you to infuse her with your own vision."

Auguste still hadn't drawn a line.

"Start with the hip and thigh. It will show the direction of her body."

Auguste did, then paused. All the nudes he had seen had been in paintings that illustrated a heroic event of antiquity. They were romantic, picturesque, idealized, but this model was nothing but a middle-aged working woman, not even a pretty *demimondaine*, who at least would have been inviting. Nonetheless, he was attracted by the insinuating profile of her back. He searched for a rhythmic line to convey motion, and tried a line that suggested an arched body, forward and upward.

Then the model pivoted so that all the students could view her from every angle—Lecoq did not believe a model should stand still interminably, but should move freely, to encourage the creation of motion and reality, and Auguste was shocked. From the front she was even heavier, far heavier than he had expected. Her breasts, growing flabby, were long and sagging; her stomach bulged like a lumpy mound; her hips were thick, wide, grossly muscular. The biggest disillusionment of all was her skin. Instead of being marble white, as he had imagined from the paintings of Ingres, a kind of white splendor, it was spotted with innumerable freckles.

He felt as if he were looking without seeing. As he stared at her, intently now, he felt also an embarrassing naïveté that he longed to conceal. He told himself that to study the figure correctly he should steep himself in solitude, and that was impossible here. She stood now with her hands over her pubic patch in an attitude that was supposed to suggest purity, but it was disturbing, drawing more attention to the black coarse hair. There was no beauty in her stolid body. He grew melancholy. Her figure was a stupid slander of the female body as he had imagined it.

He sought to copy her as carefully as he could, and Lecoq said, "Too obvious. Correct, and lifeless."

"I'm not finished."

"Time! Time! Time! That's only part of it!"

"Is it my lines, *maître?*"

"Short brushstrokes, long brushstrokes, they don't matter, as long as you have sensitiveness in your eyes. Your eyes must act as intermediary between you and the subject."

"I'm drawing what I see."

"What you feel. You feel well, but you do not see enough, *mon ami.*" He liked this boy, but who was to say who would succeed and who would not? When he had been at the Beaux Arts, they had said that Horace Lecoq de Boisbaudran was going to be another David, or Ingres, when he wanted merely to be the first and only de Boisbaudran. Now he rarely painted, *now* they said he was a born teacher, meaning that he was no longer expected to paint. "Let your drawing flow, Rodin—formal arrangements are not important. Use your eyes. There is an art to seeing; to see well is the most difficult thing of all, it requires genius."

Auguste yearned to tell Lecoq that his eyes hurt, that when he was far away from the model her outline blurred, but even while he was listening more aggressive pupils had pushed between him and the model. He was in the rear again, he could hardly see her at all. And he had not finished. He had not yet drawn her neck, shoulders, and arms. And he never would, he was afraid suddenly, for Lecoq strode over to the model, ordered her to rest, and she sat down with a heavy wool cloak over her pudgy shoulders to keep warm.

During this intermission Barnouvin introduced Auguste to a small group of fellow students. Henri Fantin-Latour, four years older than Auguste, was the talker of the group, with red hair like Auguste's, a mustache, and a young beard, and very much the model of the young artist. There was also Alphonse Legros, swarthy, short, intense, and quiet; and Jules Dalou, a student of sculpture, with a narrow, taut face, outspoken and energetic. But it was Edgar Degas, who was not even sketching, sitting there only as an observer, who was the one they listened to, who at twenty-two was knowing beyond dispute. Degas was slender, with a very long, thin face, full lips, and the most mocking, questioning eyes Auguste had ever seen.

Barnouvin said, "Such a heavy model—she turns my stomach."

"It's a waste," said Fantin-Latour. "The model is surrounded by a circle of idiots. We should paint from memory and at the Louvre. The Louvre is the best school of all."

Barnouvin said to Auguste, "Fantin never does a line without keeping the masters in mind."

"It is better than working here," said Fantin-Latour. "We expect a nymph and get a working woman. Even Delacroix and David have better taste than that."

"Ah," said Barnouvin, "Fantin is a scholar."

Degas suddenly said mockingly, "You are both arguing about the wrong thing. Draw lines, draw lines, from memory, from nature, from wherever they are. But theory, that's for the *canaille*."

"Lines?" Fantin said just as mockingly. "Our friend Degas hears this from Ingres and immediately he is the disciple."

"I am no one's disciple," growled Degas. "But I am not an idiot, either."

"And I'm an idiot?" demanded Fantin.

For an instant Auguste thought they were coming to blows, there seemed such bitter animosity between them; then Degas shrugged as if to say he couldn't be responsible for Fantin's idiocy and Fantin began arguing with Legros.

Auguste, after his initial shock, realized they adored arguing; without argument and disagreement they were bored—it was the one thing they had in common. And rebellion, rebellion against anything in the established art world, except Lecoq. In this there was a genuine *esprit de corps*, for when it came to the moment of contact they side-stepped. They called one another by their last names, as if in doing this they already recognized each one's individuality even if no one else did. He envied their free-and-easy conversation. They were bragging now about the girls they had had, should have had, and would have. Barnouvin went into detail, and they agreed this model was a bore. As Degas said, "*Canaille!*" Everyone the frail, long-featured Degas didn't like, which was almost the entire human race, was "*canaille*."

Dalou chimed in, "Even naked she's not worth a *nuit d'amour*." He insisted he had several girls who were "*ravishing*."

At the end of the intermission it was decided that after the next female nude class they would all go to a brothel.

Auguste sought to concentrate on the model, but they had distracted him. Dalou was sketching methodically, earnestly; Legros kept bringing his pencil to his lips to wet it, and never stopped working; Fantin-Latour examined her as if she were a classic in the Louvre; Barnouvin drew with a slight, wry smile on his lips; even Degas, the observer, was intent. It was all quite puzzling. Had they actually meant what they said? Or were they showing off, especially for his benefit?

Lecoq was saying, still dryly, "Don't martyrize the model."

Auguste came back to his own drawing, but again he was in the rear. By the time he got close enough once more to see her clearly, it was too late to complete the drawing, the class was over.

Lecoq saw his disappointment and said, "Finish it at home, from memory."

At home the following evening when he should have gone to bed, Auguste sat at the kitchen table, seeking to finish the drawing. How large, how very large, she seemed in memory. He kept thinking of Barnouvin's friends, a band of lunatics, but they had been fun and he had been part of them, at least while he had listened. He kept remembering the pictures of the *amours* of Eros and Psyche and he could hear Lecoq warning, "Don't use your pencil like an iron bar."

"Don't you hear me? *Mon dieu*, where are your ears?" It was Papa, standing behind him, staring incredulously at the not quite finished sketch. "What is that?"

"A figure, Papa."

"A female figure?"

"It's for the school."

"Naked?"

Auguste shrugged and tried to explain that this was the way one learned to draw, but Papa wasn't listening.

"*Mon dieu*, that I should have such a son!" he roared. "Eggs and bread have gone up to one franc ten sous, and you draw naked women!" Mama was down in her nightgown, aroused by Papa's voice, and so was Marie. Papa was in a quandary: this was not something to discuss in front of them. He grumbled, "He's wasting your money, Marie." He tried to take the offensive drawing from Auguste, but the boy slipped it inside his shirt and backed away.

Marie said, "Auguste, may I see the drawing?"

Auguste, blushing, said, "It's not finished. The figure is a little heavy."

"I'm not a child."

He could see the swell of Marie's breasts, always hidden by her austere clothes, under her thinner nightdress. She had a far better figure than the model. Yet she was his sister.

Marie said quietly, "You want to be an artist, don't you?"

Her directness startled him. Papa was scowling, Mama was whispering Ave Marias under her breath, but Marie looked completely composed. "Yes," he said. "A painter if I can get paints."

Papa shouted, "I have no money for such nonsense!"

"Of course," said Auguste.

"Of course," cried Papa. "Is that all you can say?"

Auguste shrugged with a gesture of resignation. He knew there was no money for such a luxury. Aunt Thérèse had said she would try to borrow paints from Drolling, but so far she had failed—Drolling hid his paints. Yet Marie had diverted them from the nude. If they would only go to bed now, perhaps he could finish it. If Marie weren't his sister, but no—it was wrong, she was too slight, too young, to be the model.

Mama said, "It's late. We should all go to bed. *Bonsoir, mon chat.*"

Auguste put out his oil lamp, then waited a few minutes until he heard Papa snoring, lit a candle, and returned to the drawing. It was difficult to see what he was doing, the candle kept flickering and wax spilled on the much smudged paper, but gradually he finished the neck and shoulders. He was just starting to do the arms when he heard a "shush" and Marie stood at his side.

He started to protest, and she smiled and whispered, "Ah, a 'Venus de Milo,'" pointing to the armless figure, and Auguste, who had felt caught in the act, didn't try to stop her from examining the drawing now.

She scanned it carefully, then said, "It looks real. Who is she?"

"A model from the evening class. A chambermaid, actually."

"Without any clothes?" Her voice took on a faint quiver.

"Nude. All artists have to learn the human figure."

"Is Barnouvin in your class?"

"Yes. He sat next to me tonight."

"Does he like it?"

"All the students do. When they get used to it. Marie, it is no longer the fashion to do Madonnas."

"How much do you need for paint?"

"Five francs. For a box with all the primary colors. Marie, do you like Barnouvin?"

A hesitant smile passed over her face. "Do you think he likes me?"

"He is in love with art. We all are," Auguste said with a new, sudden pride.

"No doubt."

He wondered if Marie was making fun of him.

"I'm glad you didn't give the model a straight back. Nobody has that kind of back, actually. I like her back."

"It was all that I really saw," he said intensely.

"Don't be ashamed."

"But it is not finished."

"Agreed. And don't fight, not with Barnouvin."

"We're friends. He introduced me to a group of students who are real artists already."

Marie smiled as if they shared a secret, and when he returned to the drawing she handed him a five-franc piece for paint and said he must go to bed, it was past midnight, Papa would be furious if he was found up at such an hour. Auguste nodded, she gave him a quick good-night kiss, and he was working intensely as she departed, drawing as if there would never be another opportunity.

V

The following week, after the next life class with the female model, Barnouvin drew the others close to him and declared that he knew the best *maison d'amour* in Paris, especially for the money.

Tonight, Auguste thought, Barnouvin had dressed to look particularly dashing. His light curly hair was unusually long under his broad-brimmed hat, and he wore gray trousers with a green-striped velvet jacket, tight boots, and a rolling collar.

Barnouvin said, "Petite École models, they don't know anything," as if he had tried them.

"What about Lecoq?" asked Auguste.

"What about him?" Barnouvin looked belligerent.

"Won't he mind?" asked Auguste.

"This is the real thing, Rodin. And Lecoq, our illustrious *maître*, would prefer that we have experience. It sharpens our pencils." No one laughed, but Barnouvin, enjoying his witticism, went on to tell how he had three mistresses: the one he was thinking of leaving, the one he adored at the instant, and the third he was courting with an eye to the future. Tonight was practice, merely practice.

Auguste didn't believe him, but the others were nodding, although Dalou growled that Barnouvin better have finer taste than he had had last time. Dalou said, "They were pigs, fat, ugly, dull," and Fantin-Latour added, "Dalou is right. We're not blind. We want young ones, not battle-scarred veterans."

As they prepared to depart, Auguste said desperately, "I haven't finished my drawing." He hadn't. He held it up to show the half-done arms; he had gotten down only to the elbows.

Barnouvin said, "You're the kind who never finishes. A perfectionist, who can't let his work go, who is afraid to let it go. Come, the girls will make you forget this model. And you're young enough to make love and draw at the same time." When Auguste still hesitated, he asked with surprise, "Is it that you've never known a girl?"

Auguste whispered after a long silence, "I knew one. When I was fourteen."

Fantin-Latour said, "Ah, a prodigy."

"It's just—" Auguste paused, not knowing how to explain it.

"No money," said Fantin-Latour.

"Not enough." It was one way out, thought Auguste. He felt the five-franc piece in his pocket and knew it must go for paint.

Barnouvin laughed. "Such a fidelity to truth, I almost believe it. Rodin, you can't escape *amour* by refusing to look at it."

"He's too young," said Fantin-Latour, feeling superior at nineteen.

"No, I'm not," Auguste blurted out, unable to accept that. "Barnouvin, how much?"

"Five francs if she likes you. Ten if she doesn't."

Dalou said, "I can assure you, if it's that cheap it's not worth it."

Barnouvin said, "I didn't say they were superb. I said they were the best for the money."

Thereupon they so insulted each other that it became impossible for either of them to withdraw, and the others had to follow them. It would have meant virtual ostracism if they did not, and so Auguste found himself trailing the others, afraid yet eager. He sensed there was reluctance in Degas, who was the oldest at twenty-two; not scruples, but a distaste for this kind of contact, and this made him feel a little less guilty. And he liked being part of the group; it was the first time in his life that had happened.

The *maison d'amour*, as Barnouvin insisted on calling it, as if that would make it more alluring, was on the rue Mouffetard, not far from where Auguste had been born. It was in the slum quarter, one of the shabbiest brothel districts in Paris. No one spoke as they plodded up the dirty cobblestone streets. The air reeked with the heavy stench of poverty. They passed an old man in rags, herding pigs. Most of the houses were unpainted, ugly, and squeezed in by other houses.

Auguste sensed that Degas wanted to turn back, and Fantin-Latour and the quiet Legros as well. Even Dalou and Barnouvin looked shaken. But they were committed. Then Barnouvin brightened: they were before the *maison d'amour* itself. It had gilded railings on a shabby balcony, and cheerful flower boxes, as if someone had to keep fresh the remembrance of a green and growing world.

Madame Clara, a large, blowsy, elderly woman, a type Auguste had seen on the streets many times in his childhood, sat them in the parlor. She asked Barnouvin suspiciously, "Cash or credit?"

"Cash," he said proudly.

She shouted upstairs, "Cash, *chéries*; it's Monsieur Barnouvin."

Auguste sat on the worn, faded *banquette* in the dingy parlor that had been converted into a red plush salon. He could hear the girls stirring upstairs. He avoided the eyes of the others, but noticed that several of them were self-conscious also, particularly Fantin-Latour and Degas. Suddenly Degas said this was a pigsty, and departed abruptly. There were cracked gilt mirrors on the wall; drab red plush was everywhere, and a thin carpet underfoot, with many worn spots.

Barnouvin asked Madame Clara, "The girls, do they have *savoir-*

faire? We have a newcomer, a young one, a peasant, but maybe he's a young bull."

Auguste blushed fiercely as he realized they were discussing him. He wanted to flee, but the girls were down. What a fraud this is! he thought. Most of them will never see twenty-five again. Six females paraded before them on pink mules, naked under their flimsy negligees except for their hip-high black stockings. Most of them avoided him, he was such an obvious *enfant*, but one girl, younger than any of the others—Auguste judged her to be no more than nineteen or twenty—sat down beside him, draped her long, black-clad legs over his, leaned close so that her breasts pressed against his chest, and whispered, "I like young ones—they can overdo."

Her breasts were still firm yet yielding, her legs were soft yet muscular; Barnouvin was right, she was different from the model, from the one prostitute he had known. Barnouvin ordered a cognac, and so did Dalou, but when she asked Auguste he shook his head, afraid to trust his voice, afraid it would change in mid-air.

She introduced herself as Georgette, and whispered, "Do you want to go upstairs, *mon chéri?*"

She pressed so close to him it was impossible to resist her. He nodded, and Georgette led him up a winding, shabby-carpeted stairway that took them to her room. He didn't notice what had happened to the others. Despite his distaste for the surroundings, he wanted her as he had never wanted anyone before except in his adolescent dreams.

Her room was a smaller, dingier version of the salon below, with a bed.

He saw wallpaper with pink cherubs in the style of Louis XIV, although obviously they had been done recently, yellow shutters, a *banquette*. And suddenly, even as he craved her, he couldn't move.

She asked, "Do you have ten francs?"

"No. Sorry." He turned to depart.

"Eight?"

"Five."

She pursed her lips as if in doubt, then said, "You want to be amused?"

"Why not?" What else was there to say.

"Am I pretty?"

"Yes." She *was* pretty, he thought, with beautiful eyes, good features not yet etched with age and wear, and a figure that was vivid under her negligee.

"You don't talk much."

He put the five-franc piece down. It was the only one he owned. It would have bought enough paint for a week.

Georgette chattered volubly while she undressed, and repeatedly called him *mon chéri*. He didn't believe it, but as she slipped out of her negligee, then stood up, naked except for her black stockings, he couldn't believe anything else. He saw her pink-nippled breasts, not yet worn, the roundness of her neck, the curve of her buttocks. And then she undressed him as if it were her pleasure, indolently, then quickly, never at the same tempo from one moment to the next. Her fingers trailed expertly over his loins, as she whispered, "Ten francs is the standard price, *mon chéri*, but for you . . ." And he forgot everything but the wild pleasure that went through him as they came together.

Afterward he told her he had never known anyone like her, that she was "*magnifique!*" remembering one of Barnouvin's favorite words.

Georgette was vain about her ability, and suddenly it was vital to her to explain herself; she said her trouble was not greed or laziness but too much "*amour*," she could not resist "*amour*," it had brought her to Paris from Lorraine in search of it.

Auguste thought of Clotilde—Marie had kept in touch with Clotilde, who was living with a government official on the boulevard Port Royal—and he wondered if she would end up in St. Lazare, the dreaded women's prison, as Papa had warned. Or here?

But once again it was Georgette who had to be appeased. He felt the arching of her back, the pressure of her breasts against his chest, the moistness of her lips, the clawing of her nails on his flesh; and he responded, first because he should, then because he had to, and finally because he couldn't halt and it had to last.

As before, it was too quick, he thought, although Georgette said, breathing hard, "You will be a good one when you grow up."

"Would you pose for me?" He knew this was wrong—Lecoq would be furious, Papa horrified, and he had no studio—but she had the best body he had ever seen, lithe and wild and fluid.

"Pose?" Suddenly she looked unpleasant.

"I'm a student," he explained. "An art student."

She laughed as if that was a formula she had heard before and despised.

Outraged, he dressed hurriedly. He knew the request had been a blunder, but he had his sketchbook with him. He always had it with him now, it had become a kind of diary, and she had such an interesting body, especially in motion, although he knew that whatever he drew would be a sentimentality.

He was at the door when she said, "*Adieu, mon chéri.*"

Then she smiled and he realized he had pleased her, too. He said, smiling back, "*Au revoir.*" As he departed, not waiting for the others, he thought it was strange but in some ways he had been more comfortable with her than he had been with his fellow students. At least she wasn't competitive. And he no longer felt rejected. Now that it was over, he felt vital. Tonight, at least, he was a man.

CHAPTER 4

School settled into a pattern the next few months: mornings were spent at the Petite École; afternoons Auguste and the others were encouraged to visit the Louvre, to study and copy the drawings and engravings of Michelangelo and Rembrandt, to become acquainted with the other masters; and two evenings a week were devoted to drawing from life with a nude model.

Auguste was fascinated by the Louvre—a new universe flowered before his hungry eyes. Fantin-Latour said, "The Louvre is the greatest art school of all," and the blossoming Auguste agreed, for he was seeing for the first time original Leonardos, Titians, Raphaels, Rubenses, Rembrandts, and Michelangelos, and he was delighted that he could choose his own masters. The vast gallery of the Louvre was filled with paintings he liked. Auguste didn't know where to start. He was attracted by Delacroix's "Dante and Virgil," Leonardo's "Madonna of the Rocks," Raphael's "La Belle Jardinière," but it was Michelangelo and Rembrandt who were his men. Suddenly tears filled his eyes, he had an overwhelming wish to see better.

He stood before their drawings and etchings and resolved to remember these as long as he lived. He thought Michelangelo's work vigorous, muscular, and powerful, Rembrandt's rude, jarring, and full of human feeling. He noticed also that Michelangelo's designs were vivid, with rapid lines, that the Florentine often used exaggeration and deliberate distortion, while Rembrandt created his own reality, without drapes, ornaments, or intricate embellishments, but with known faces, known love, using pen, pencil, and crayon to strike with all his might. Auguste yearned to fondle their work, but this was impossible, no one did such things, still the longing remained.

Many days he copied or drew from memory, it didn't seem to matter which any more, for he drew equally well either way now. He continued to carry his sketchbook with him everywhere, and he did hundreds of drawings.

He also fell in love with water color and oils in this first real experience with them. Wherever he gazed in the Louvre, his blood raced through his body. He had not known there was such splendor. Everything about the Louvre—the galleries, the students and artists studying, observing, and copying, the constant conversation about art—stimulated him to draw and paint. He had an enormous eagerness to learn and to discover more and more.

Day by day his drawings grew better. Auguste knew he would never know enough about the human body, but he found himself devoting most of his energy to torsos and heads. Here he preferred the male body; he felt it showed to better advantage than the female, it was stronger, there were so many more muscles in the back, shoulders, and torso. And every hand was different, expressive, lending itself to gesture and animation.

Auguste tried to pretend it didn't matter that he wasn't painting, but when Lecoq paused before him one spring morning and asked, "Why haven't you come to painting class? You are about ready for it, Rodin," he felt a new rush of energy.

He hadn't gone back with the others to the *maison d'amour*, although there had been many moments when he had craved Georgette, for there had not been any more five-franc pieces.

"Are you afraid?"

Auguste grew red.

"Oh, you have no paint."

Auguste said hurriedly, "You told us to draw with all our might, that one can never know too much about it."

"True, true, but you should start to work seriously with water color and oils. Unless you want to remain just an etcher."

"No, I—" Auguste paused.

"You can't afford paint. Too bad."

"How are my drawings?"

"A little too Rembrandtish, and they smell of the Louvre."

"But you sent me there."

"I sent you to the Louvre to use your eyes and hands, and to be independent enough to depend only upon yourself."

"What should I do?" cried Auguste from the heart.

"Do? You have no paint. We are a free school and Napoleon the Third cannot afford to supply everyone with paint. You will end up an artisan, an ornament maker. Too bad. You draw well."

"I can sketch Michelangelo's figures from memory."

"I know," sighed Lecoq. "I see it in your work. Try to get paint, and I will put you in the painting class and we will see what you can do."

The next day Auguste was moved into this class, to work with pastels, water colors, oils, copying the model or doing an invention of his own—there was complete freedom of method and experimentation—but he could not afford it. He told Aunt Thérèse about this advancement, and she said she would get paint from Drolling no matter what, even if she had to steal it. Several days later she handed him a slightly used box of paints.

The colors were beautiful, he thought. In a festive mood he experimented with different colors on the palette, sucking in his breath with pleasure, feeling *magnifique!* and full of *savoir-faire!* He had also measured himself this morning and he had reached five feet four, a two-inch gain in the last year—perhaps he should do a portrait of himself, many painters did. He went to look for an empty canvas. He found none that were usable, but finally there was one that could be scraped. He returned with this battered canvas and felt struck dumb. His paints were gone. Legros, who worked nearby, said he hadn't seen them; Barnouvin said to stop bothering him—he knew Barnouvin had not taken them, however, Barnouvin had an allowance and could afford paint. He looked on his chair, behind his easel, but there was no trace of the precious box of paints. Someone had stolen them. He sat there blinking back his tears. Suddenly the studio was desolate.

Auguste sat there all that night without drawing a line.

Aunt Thérèse was sympathetic, but said that Drolling had discovered the theft of the paint and now everything was under strict lock and key.

The next few painting classes Auguste was able to work occasionally, when he found a tube of paint discarded by a more prosperous student. Only it was rarely a color he needed: the best colors were always squeezed to the last drop, or other students got to the discarded tubes ahead of him. It became hopeless. Finally he just sat, unable to quit, but unable to work. He tried to sketch, but it was senseless to go on, Papa was right, he was a poor boy who never could be anything but a workman—a cabinetmaker, perhaps, or an ornament worker. There was no alternative. He wiped the tears from his eyes. He could not draw, there was no purpose to it now. He dried his eyes and decided to tear up his drawings. He had them between his hands when Lecoq halted him.

Lecoq insisted on seeing them.

"Why?"

"Don't ask why, idiot!" He had never seen Lecoq so irritated. "I'm the one to decide what's to be done with your drawings!" Lecoq stared at them, not really seeing them, thought Auguste, and said, "I'll keep them."

"Why?"

"Is that all you can say—why?"

Auguste stood up. "I don't have to stay here."

"No, *mon ami*, you don't. You don't have to do anything. You don't even have to draw, paint, eat, sleep. But you can't sit here all night and do nothing."

"I can go."

"And give up art?"

"I cannot afford paint or canvas."

"I know." Lecoq saw the boy standing there, bereaved, ready to ruin his life for the lack of a few sous, but no, it was more than that, it was a matter of very hard-to-earn francs, the common ailment of the student and the artist, so common no one cared about it. But this boy was one of his best pupils; he had a great susceptibility to emotion and a great need to be free, with luck he could become an *homme précieux*—but if not he was not the first, nor would he be the last. Yet this boy had improved so much it would be a waste to let him go now, and he had an enormous eagerness to learn. Lecoq said suddenly, abruptly, "I'll think of something, Rodin. But you cannot just sit here. Go to the modeling room. At least it will keep you occupied."

"Maître, I don't know anything about sculpture."

"You can learn. You learn very well when you are interested."

"I'm tired." He meant sick at heart, defeated.

"And don't you think I am!" Lecoq shouted. "Do you think you are the first promising student I have lost for a few francs? Teach you what I know, get you to where you can draw a decent line, where you can see for yourself! Go, I can't keep you here!"

Auguste, shaken by Lecoq's emotion, didn't know what to do.

"But Michelangelo was a great sculptor, too. It will not hurt you to learn. And it will help your figure drawing while we find a way to keep you in the painting class. Come on, I will go with you."

Auguste went hesitantly to the sculpture room. He stared at the wet clay, the heavy loads of plaster, terra cotta, and marble, the ladders, the stands, more tools than he could count. Most of it was a world new to him.

Lecoq said, "You are a strong lad, with fine fingers. At least if you don't succeed as an artist you will make a good molder or caster someday."

Lecoq was gone then, as if he had already expressed too much emotion.

There were only a few students in the sculpture room, but suddenly Auguste was glad that Lecoq had brought him. He felt drawn to the stone by a force outside himself. There were completed statues, and copies of famous works, and they were so beautiful and potent he wanted to caress them. He felt the clay under his strong fingers and he was full of new sensations. He wanted to shout, "I love this!" but he was afraid it would sound sentimental. Yet there was no need to feel handicapped here because he had to strain to see pictures on account of his nearsightedness. Now that was an advantage, for he didn't have to see but feel—the closer he was to the clay the better.

Day after day he found excuses to work in the statuary room. He lost track of time, he forgot about paints and canvases. It seemed to him that this work, unlike the drawing and painting, passed not through his mind but through his body. In spite of the hardness and coldness of the stone, there was a soft, enticing warmth to it. He no longer dreamed of the pretty prostitute who beckoned to him from a window near his home, of the enticing Georgette, of the dream girl who resembled Marie; he had a new love, he dreamed of the "Venus de Milo." When no one looked, he fondled her. He was full of a new, unbreakable desire—to hold the stone, carve it, shape it.

When Lecoq became aware of his absence and found him in the sculpture room and said he would have paint for him, that he should return to the drawing and painting classes, Auguste said, "I can't. I have to work here."

"Agreed. But sculptors have to know how to draw, too."

Auguste stood fixed to the floor.

"You want to be a sculptor, Rodin?"

Auguste nodded—as emphatically as he could.

"Sculpture is a very poor business. It needs enormous influence. Actually the only buyers these days are the government and the museums. It is an art without openings. Now there are no great lords, no great fortunes, no great patrons, as there were for Michelangelo. And the materials themselves are even costlier."

"Perhaps," said Auguste, "but I must work here." He stared at the copies of the "Venus," the "Victory of Samothrace," the "David." "I must work with stone. It is wonderful for the human figure."

"I see."

"May I stay here, *maître?* I will not quit this time. Please?"

"Do you think I am a man without a heart?"

"I will even apprentice myself to a foundry to learn casting."

"That's not necessary, not yet. Stay here, and in the life classes. More than ever, you will have to learn to draw."

Auguste wanted to thank Lecoq, but how? Never had he felt so much gratitude, wonderment, and beauty.

There was a moment of silence, and then Lecoq said, "Let us not get involved in thanks. Whatever is said will spoil it. Work, that will be enough. How many drawings have you made so far, Rodin?"

"Five or six hundred, I think. I have not counted them."

"You will do far more if you become a sculptor. Far more, *mon ami.*"

"Will you still teach me?"

"In some things. Now go, tell your papa, before it becomes too difficult."

Auguste walked through a night that was wet and cold. There were many puddles of water from the rain and the cobblestones were slippery. About a year had passed since Papa had given permission for the Petite École, but Auguste felt changed now, older, newer, and different. There was a tempest within him—Papa would call it a plague, but Papa should not be surprised, not any more.

The family was up, and the oil lamp made a sad blot of light in the center of the kitchen-dining room. It was chilly, although there was a fire in the stove; it was a stone house, and Papa said you never could heat stone properly. Stone was unfeeling, Papa said.

Auguste blurted out, "Excuse me, Papa, forgive me, please, but I'm going to be a sculptor."

"A sculptor!" Papa shrugged despairingly, looked heavenward, and declared, "You're not an idiot. You're insane!"

"I have the hands for it, Lecoq says."

"Lecoq says," shouted Papa. "You have the arms for a workingman. Pity, pity, such strong arms, to be a sculptor? What a waste!"

"I'm sorry, but I have to."

"Sorry? Do you get a wage?"

"No."

"How long will it take? A year? Five?"

"Five. At least. If I make progress."

"And if you don't?"

"Nothing is guaranteed, Papa. No work, no wages. Just free instruction, as before."

Marie volunteered, "He will have a trade."

"As a stonecutter?" Papa smiled skeptically. "He will make no more than I do," he said with a wave of his hand. "I do not give my permission."

Auguste braced himself to be thrown out, but Papa was more practical.

"You stay only if you pay."

Marie said, "I will pay, as before."

"Of course. You are a fool, like him. You have eyes only for that painter, Barnouvin, but does he have eyes for you?"

Marie's face burned, and as Mama said an Ave Maria for her

daughter's happiness Auguste said, "Barnouvin is one of the most promising students in the school."

"Thank you," Papa said sharply. "You know everything now. But you don't know how to make a living. You will die even poorer than I am. Make sure when you work with stone you learn how to be a stonecutter, so at least you won't starve." He trudged into his room, taking Mama with him.

Marie waited until they were out of hearing, then asked, "Is Barnouvin so good?"

"He is an outstanding student. But he likes many girls." He didn't want to say it, but she should know, it would be better later.

"I saw him Sunday, at church. He said he would draw me one of these days."

"You will make a lovely model."

"Are you sure about sculpture?"

"I know every stick and stone in the modeling room."

Marie's delicate face grew animated, and Auguste started to sketch her. She wore an austere black dress, which he realized she wore also because it hid dirt, cleaned easily, and did not show wear. He covered her figure with a more attractive dress. He sketched quickly. In a few minutes he had a complete drawing. He was pleased with the deep-set, feeling eyes. When he finished he handed it to her and said, "See if Barnouvin can do better."

Marie took it gently and said, "I like it, as I'm sure I will like Barnouvin's."

Auguste wasn't listening; he had taken the sketch back to make her more womanly. He announced, "When I get my own studio, I will do your portrait in bronze. You will see how much more expressive you will be then."

He could not fall asleep. Long after midnight he sat on his ancient bed, sketching the foundation for the head of Marie he intended to sculpt the first chance he got.

CHAPTER 5

The chance did not come quickly. Auguste decided he must get into the Beaux Arts as soon as possible, in addition to studying with Lecoq, and he put off anything that might interfere—even the portrait bust of Marie.

Lecoq said this stress on the Beaux Arts was idiocy, that he would be lost there; Barnouvin said he would never make it; Degas deprecated it and applied and was accepted; Fantin-Latour was taken in after failing the first time and was dissatisfied immediately; Dalou and Legros strove furiously to get in, and finally, using influence, were admitted; and Auguste threw himself into an orgy of work.

The next few years Auguste, preparing for his entrance into the Beaux Arts, toiled a back-breaking schedule. He was out of bed before the sun rose, readying his work for the eighteen-hour day ahead. With the dawn he hurried to Lecoq's studio. Lecoq, pleased with his passion, encouraged him to work on various figures for an hour and helped him plan this schedule. Another hour was spent sketching from memory. From nine to twelve he modeled sculpture at the Petite École. Promptly at noon he rushed over the Seine at the Pont des Arts to the Louvre, where he studied the drawings of Michelangelo and the sculpture with a voracious appetite. Two days a week he visited the Bibliothèque Impériale to study the drawings of Poussin, Lorrain, Watteau, Boucher, and Fragonard.

He never paused to eat. He nibbled his bread and chocolate as he rushed about Paris; he hardly ever walked, he traveled from class to class in a kind of dogtrot. There was just a sou for food, but he pretended not to mind, although he minded very much. Always hungry, often tired, he could not stop this feverish pace. He knew if he halted he would lose the comradeship of the masterpieces, their inspiration, the impatience to work—and all that would be left would be his wretchedness.

At closing time he had to be ordered out of the Louvre and the library by the guards. Still nibbling bread and chocolate, he rushed about Paris; only occasionally, when Marie slipped him an extra sou, was he able to afford a bowl of onion or lentil soup. There was never enough time. His next class, one which Lecoq stressed, was a drawing course in design at the Gobelin weaving center from five to eight; it was far away from the Louvre and the Bibliothèque Impériale, and he had to go on foot. After eight he went to his favorite classes: two nights a week working from the nude with Lecoq, and three nights a week studying with the animal sculptor, Barye, to whom he had been recommended by Lecoq.

With Auguste adamant in his resolve to study sculpture, Lecoq emphasized anatomy. He told Auguste, "Michelangelo was a great anatomist. Listen to Barye. He is the best anatomist of any sculptor today."

II

Barye himself was a study in anatomy, a frail, aging knot of creaking bones and aching muscles. Famous for his animals, especially his lions, Barye had to teach to support himself, and he hated it. Yet if he had to teach, he had to teach what was right; so although he was anxious, tired, and distracted when he came to class, he stressed that "anatomy is the backbone of sculpture."

No discussion among the students was more energetic than the continuous quarrels over the value to a sculptor, a good, practical sculptor who hoped to sell, of knowing anatomy. Auguste was for it when they studied at Barye's favorite studio, the Jardin des Plantes, and observed the grace of the lions; he adored their free, fluid movements. But he was not so sure he should focus on anatomy when a class was held in a hospital, where the greenish-yellow leg of a corpse was passed about to be studied. He almost fainted, for hours he was sick at the stomach. He could not quit, however; Lecoq would not allow it.

Lecoq insisted that Auguste must work as the teacher could no longer, as Lecoq should have, when the teacher had been Auguste's age.

Auguste was so grateful to Lecoq for his interest he could not disagree with him. Gradually as most of the studying with Barye concentrated at the Jardin des Plantes, he became fascinated by the animal models. There was no free material, and Auguste had no money to buy clay, plaster, or terra cotta, but he could draw, and he loved to draw animals, for they were generally in motion and their movements were spontaneous.

Unlike most of his fellow students, he preferred his models to move. Then he could see his models in the round. He was discovering that for himself at least, sculpture, unlike painting, had to be seen from every possible view. It was the most striking aspect of Barye's sculpture.

As Auguste absorbed this, he absorbed a new regard for observation, for nature, and for anatomy. But he refused to go to the hospital again to view the dissection of a corpse, though Barye said it was essential and Lecoq told him that most of the great Renaissance artists had done extensive studies of cadavers. Auguste loved the body when it was alive. To him it was the world's noblest creation, and this love grew long after he had forgotten the names of the muscles and he was a practicing sculptor.

III

Auguste also fell in love with Paris. His idol was still Lecoq, but the teacher did not share his worship of the city. Lecoq was acid on the subject of Paris. He thought Paris evoked excessive praise, especially from artists. Her beauty was a sentimentality, he declared. Paris was not really attractive, and it was no good pretending that she was. And when Auguste looked wretched because of what he said, he grew vehement.

Lecoq could see the towers of Notre Dame from his studio, on the quai Voltaire, but he did not think them as wonderful as Auguste did. When Auguste excused his lateness one spring morning as a need to sketch the cathedral, Lecoq stated, "Gothic architecture is impressive, but no one creates churches like that any more. And Notre Dame is not Paris. Paris is a dirty, labyrinthine city of dingy streets surrounding a few square miles of beauty. It is scraped plaster, *petite bourgeoisie*, shopkeepers, government clerks, keepers of cheap, dubious *pensions*. It is for those who have a genius for intrigue, compromise, who are masters at living on appearances. It is for success, and so few have success."

Auguste listened, not wanting to argue, yet he did not agree. But he found this endearing, for suddenly Lecoq was human. He continued to admire Lecoq, but with less idolatry now. For the first time he began to see the possibility that if he knew Lecoq better he might even like him.

Nothing could discourage his absorption with Paris. In the winter it was dark and cold when he went to class, often wet and foggy. In warmer weather, when everyone's window was open to let in fresh air, more frequently bad air was let out and the heavy cobblestones were difficult to walk on. But he loved the quais along the Seine, the open spaces of the Tuileries. These days, even as he walked, Paris, a medieval city of narrow streets and crowded tenements, was being transformed by Haussmann, with new streets, new gardens, new bridges. Auguste was proud of the new rue de Rivoli, the completion of the Louvre, and when the small houses that pushed in on Notre Dame were cleared away even Lecoq could not find fault. This Paris was becoming a city of wide spaces and far horizons. He had no wish to migrate anywhere. He felt that the new Paris was being created for the pleasure of the artist, for the worship of the eye.

He longed to tell Papa about the beautiful, fast-growing chestnut trees on the new boulevards, but Papa, although still not a republican, now grumbled constantly about the Second Empire of Louis Napoleon, who had proclaimed, "The empire is peace." Papa said, "Instead there has been one military adventure after another." Papa was angry with the Emperor, for there had been no raises in the Prefecture of Police for several years.

Auguste also liked the Madeleine, recently completed, and that it had been built in the Greek fashion rather than the Gothic or baroque. He was in a Greek period now, loving everything classical. The year before it had been the Gothic, with Notre Dame the pinnacle. But there were times he felt like a bird hopping about Paris, eating a worm here and there but always hungry. Often he felt in a race he would never win, which would never end. Then his constant loneliness was intensified and it took all of his considerable will power to keep going.

At such times his sketchbook was his only relief. He carried it with him always, everywhere. It became a diary as he filled it with thousands of drawings. He was forever coming home with his hands black from ink, crayon, and charcoal, and Mama was always washing them. He tried to draw as Lecoq advised, with spontaneity and verve, but also with painstaking care.

By the time he was seventeen he knew most of Paris as well as he knew his own hand. He did not dare think of girls—this was a demand that was too diverting, and he had no free time. Saturday nights he sketched from memory, for the figures he wanted to model for himself. Sunday he sought to rest, but that was impossible: the more he studied the more his emotion demanded that he model, but the more he studied the less energy he had. Yet on Sundays, when no one was about, he began to work on clay at home. He hid the clay in his closet, covering it with an old coat. Even Mama would complain about its presence.

At the end of the first year of this arduous schedule Auguste decided that he was not ready for the Beaux Arts; at the end of the second year he was afraid; at the end of the third year he felt he might be almost ready.

IV

Lecoq regarded him sadly when he asked Lecoq to recommend him for the entrance examination to the Beaux Arts, but Lecoq said, "Prepare a head for the committee and I will see what I can do."

"Will you recommend me?"

"No."

Auguste looked stricken.

"That would keep you out. My name is anathema there. You will have to find one more acceptable, but do the head—a name will occur to me."

Auguste hurried home, but Marie could not pose for him, she was busy on Sundays, their one free day. She went to church every Sunday; she saw Barnouvin there. For the first time he could remember, she refused to heed his pleas. She could not give up these Sundays, no matter how he implored. Finally, however, seeing Auguste's distress, Marie suggested, "Ask Papa to pose. Whatever he pretends, he will be pleased."

Auguste was not so certain, but the first Sunday Papa was in a good humor, several weeks later, he asked Papa to pose for him. It was a rainy Sunday and Papa sat in the kitchen, very bored: there was nothing to do, no place to go, it was too miserable outside. He could not eat again; he had eaten twice already and it was not yet noon, and it was too early to take a nap. But he looked startled and affronted when Auguste added, "Lecoq says if I do a head he'll find someone to recommend me for the Beaux Arts. But I need a model, Papa."

"Model?" echoed Papa. "Oh no. What kind of a fool do you take me for?"

"We could do it at home. Start today."

"I have no time."

"Time?" repeated Auguste. He broke off suddenly.

Auguste stood there despondent, his face pale and weary, and Papa felt sad. He didn't want to hurt his son, his only son, but who had started this bonfire in him? *Mon dieu*, the boy had become a whirling dervish, the way he ran around Paris. He could see that these eighteen-hour days were wearing the youngster to the bone. It had become a great worry. Auguste had become so thin and tired-looking. And in winter there was not enough money for a warm coat, for solid shoes, yet the boy insisted on trudging all over Paris, day and night, in rain and fog, ice and snow, to study, study, study, seldom getting home before midnight, seldom eating a decent meal. And even then—like a moth caught in a kerosene lamp, self-consuming—as Auguste ate he was preparing work for tomorrow, always tomorrow, changing, starting, but never satisfied, never finished. Papa shivered suddenly. How could he refuse Auguste now? He didn't have a heart of stone and he was not an unnatural father, and Auguste looked as if he had waited a lifetime for this opportunity. Yet he could not just say yes! Auguste must remember that he still did not approve, a workingman was a workingman and common sense taught that you must not overreach yourself. If there was only someone to blame! Papa wavered, but as he saw Auguste sit down, all energy and hope out of him, he said, "Will you get in?"

"Lecoq thinks I might."

"Might? Is no one ever sure?"

Auguste shrugged.

"And how will I know you will do it right?"

"I've copied heads by Houdon, in the Louvre."

"Houdon? Who is Houdon?"

"He was the best portrait sculptor of France. He did Franklin, Mirabeau, Voltaire."

"Voltaire—an atheist?"

"Papa, he was a great sculptor."

"No wonder it is such an unreliable world," mumbled Papa.

"It will be my first original head," said Auguste.

"Well, if you can do it in one sitting."

"One sitting?" That was impossible; he needed a whole sitting just to sketch the head. But Auguste said he would try, otherwise Papa would not sit at all.

V

The following Sunday, Papa wore his brightest blue jersey to bring out the blue in his eyes. Papa was deeply disappointed when Auguste did not even have any clay but spent the entire afternoon sketching in Papa's head on Ingres paper with black and red chalk.

Papa said he would not sit again, but the following Sunday, when Auguste promised to start the head itself, he allowed himself to be coaxed into posing. Despite his apparent annoyance, he was flattered. He sat upright and still, like the statues of Napoleon Bonaparte, which he liked, until Auguste said, "You're unnatural, Papa. I can't do you this way."

Papa marveled at the dexterity and swiftness with which his son rolled balls of clay on the table and rapidly modeled a figure. Auguste's hands were so alive, gathering the clay in his large palms and kneading it with his fingers; it was as if he performed a magic trick. But he was not an idiot; he wanted to appear impressive.

For a few minutes it looked as if there would be no modeling. The more Auguste sought to relax his father, the stiffer he became. Finally, just as all seemed lost, Auguste ordered his father to sit perfectly still.

Papa was shocked—how dare his child talk to him this way! But Auguste was so commanding in spite of his youth that Papa became immobile.

Then abruptly Auguste stuck Papa's lit pipe in his mouth. Papa loved his pipe. Suddenly Papa relaxed, puffing on his pipe, and his features were natural.

Auguste worked swiftly now, and Papa was sure the head would be done in a few hours. Instead, just as Auguste seemed to have finished the nose and lips, he stopped and said, "They're wrong. They're too aristocratic."

Papa was offended: he rather preferred the way he appeared in the bust now.

Auguste, however, ignoring Papa's protests, quickly wiped off the nose and lips so that he could get a fresh start the following Sunday.

Papa knew he should not sit any more: this would go on forever, and Auguste grew domineering at the modeling stand; yet it was interesting to see what his son thought of him, and it made him proud to think of all those at the Beaux Arts who would see his head—he, a lowly police official!

A month passed before Auguste thought the head might be ready. But now Papa wasn't certain. He told Auguste, "Tell the truth, don't flatter me." He stared at the bust again, said, "But I don't look like that." He liked the long, straight nose and firm chin, but the head was too round.

"You fidget too much, Papa."

"And you make me too old."

"A little," agreed Auguste.

"It is not my face," Papa stated, gathering assurance as Auguste seemed to lose his.

Auguste began to model again.

"Remember, do not make me older than I am."

Auguste stepped back from the bust, almost as if paralyzed.

Papa asked, growing afraid, "Is there anything wrong, Auguste?"

"The mouth is too heavy."

"You want some encouragement."

"No, Papa, no!"

"You're afraid it's going to be a failure. We ought to quit right now, before it gets worse." Papa started to rise reluctantly.

"Papa," he almost shouted, "some of my life is here." Instead he cried, "Please, keep still. Please!"

"Don't worry," said Papa. "It won't fetch a hundred francs." But Papa sat down, pleased and relieved.

"Papa, I've almost finished."

"Finished? Without my chin whiskers?" His fine, vigorous, masculine Louis Philippe chin whiskers, what an outrage! This head was perfectly smooth-shaven. "You're a sculptor. You should know better."

"I'm doing it in the style of the antique, the classic Greek and Roman sculpture. It is the style of the Beaux Arts."

"Nevertheless, it is not the way I look. No one will recognize me."

"It is the way I see you." Auguste's lips tightened.

"You're a child," said Papa.

"I'm the sculptor," said Auguste.

When the boy did not move, Papa went to alter the bust. But such a flash of pain shot across Auguste's face he paused. Moreover, he couldn't change it, he would make it worse. And suddenly Auguste placed himself in front of the bust to prevent Papa from touching it. Papa's hand rose instinctively to strike his son. The boy went pale, but he did not cringe and he did not move. Papa's hand dropped; he felt baffled. But he had to say, to save face, "You have to change it."

"I can't, Papa, I can't!" It was a cry from the heart, for understanding.

"You think it is finished?"

"No! Of course not! I'm never finished!" He said that with an anguish verging on despair, as if already this inability to be finally satisfied was a torture beyond enduring. "But it's the best I can do —now!"

Papa stood a minute more, feeling he should give in but not knowing how.

Auguste said, "Papa, I have to do it my way. I'm not sure that it is right, but as Lecoq says, I have to do my work the way I see it."

"Lecoq, Lecoq?" *Mon dieu*, at least that was a way out. "Let's see what he thinks about it. He is an expert, they tell me."

"Who tells you?"

"Oh, I have friends. And not all of them are in the Prefecture of Police. Invite Lecoq—if he is so fond of you, he will come here."

Auguste did not believe Lecoq would come to his home, but he could not admit it, not to Papa. He said, "*Merci*, Papa. I will when I have a reason."

"You have the reason. My head." Now that Papa was getting used to it, he rather liked the bust. "Or are you ashamed to have your fine teacher meet your father?"

"Lecoq is a very busy man."

"But not too busy to recommend you to the Beaux Arts."

"He is getting someone else to do that when I finish this head."

Papa grew positive. "The head is finished. Invite both of them."

"I don't even know who the other artist will be."

"They will come—if they think you have a future."

VI

Lecoq came. In addition, so did Hippolyte Maindron and Barnouvin.

Maindron, a friend of Lecoq's and Delacroix's, was a renowned sculptor. His work stood outside the Panthéon and in the Luxembourg Gardens: he was a Beaux Arts graduate, a member of the Salon, and his approval would assure Auguste's taking the entrance examination. Barnouvin was Marie's guest.

The family made it a festive occasion. Papa was proud, Marie was tremulous, Auguste was apprehensive, and Mama was joyful. Mama thought the head of Papa too ugly to please anyone, but she was delighted that Barnouvin had accepted Marie's invitation, although the excuse was that this Sunday dinner was an unveiling of Auguste's first original work and Barnouvin wanted to be present to congratulate him. Dearest to Mama's heart was the hope of seeing Marie married, and though she would have preferred a beau who was not an artist Marie was so happy, she was happy, too.

Mama borrowed linen and good dishes from Aunt Thérèse, who borrowed them from Drolling without asking—Drolling was in Aix, painting—and Aunt Thérèse cooked and served the dinner.

The bust had a place of honor in the living room, but Auguste insisted on keeping it covered with a wet cloth, saying it should be seen only at the proper time. He hoped that this would create more interest in the bust; instead everyone seemed to take him at his word and ignored the head.

Hippolyte Maindron arrived with Lecoq, and was seated at the head of the table, as the guest of honor, with Lecoq and Barnouvin on either side of him, so that he would have artists with whom to converse. Maindron was a sparrow of a man who loved making mammoth, monumental figures, with thin, spindly legs, a beak of a nose, sharp-pointed features, and a constant cough and complaints. His hair was long, his mustache was curled; he wore a beautiful green velvet jacket, which matched his eyes, and dark, tightly fitted trousers, which accentuated his thinness.

Lecoq wore blue cloth, a white cravat, and a light waistcoat, which quickly got stained. But it was Barnouvin's outfit that caught everyone's eye. Barnouvin wore a jacket of black velvet, a cambric shirt, wide gray trousers, and red leather boots. Auguste saw Mama wince at the fine clothes, as if Barnouvin were a Chevalier and already out of Marie's reach.

Yet Marie, although dressed simply, had skillfully framed her delicate oval features with a white lace collar, and her deep blue dress heightened the color in her cheeks. Marie was almost pretty, thought Auguste, animated and attractive, listening to every word as if it were a pearl of wisdom, particularly when Barnouvin spoke.

Marie sat next to Barnouvin, Auguste was across from her, and Papa sat at the other end of the table, while Mama—although a place was set for her—insisted on helping Aunt Thérèse. Mama was more comfortable that way; there would be no danger of saying the wrong thing.

Papa wore a jacket of cornflower blue, and his chin whiskers were carefully trimmed. He listened as he had not listened for years, although much of what was being discussed was foreign to him. He was proud of the Voltaire easy chairs he had borrowed for his guests, the pastel copies of Boucher and the small Italian landscapes on the wall—also borrowed—which would show that he approved of art. But he was worried about the cost; this dinner would take a week's pay, and Barnouvin had such a big appetite and strong republican views.

Yet Barnouvin was fond of his son: Barnouvin was always teasing him, saying now, "Auguste is so earnest he draws as if he has to become an officer of the Legion of Honor."

Papa complimented Barnouvin on his handsome Vandyke, his fine gray trousers, and Marie wished Papa weren't such a nuisance—Papa's good manners, if anything, were worse than his bad. But Papa was proud that the dining room burst with hospitality even as he shuddered at the expense—Maindron's appetite was as astonishing as Barnouvin's. Papa wondered if the real reason for the sculptor's coming was the prospect of a free meal.

It was quite a performance by Maindron. The more the sculptor was offered, the more he ate. His hunger seemed limitless. And the more he ate, the more he talked, but not about Auguste, his work, or the Beaux Arts.

As Maindron held forth about the difficulties of being a sculptor, Auguste developed a splitting headache. Maindron told Lecoq, "Sculptors starve to death. Horace, you are lucky you teach. I wish I taught instead of depending on patrons, and the State, which is always changing."

Lecoq replied, "It's curious. I don't think of myself as a teacher at all. I'm interested in my pupils, the good ones, but not as my children. I do the best I can with them—and that is all. It is a necessity, but I rarely believe in teaching."

"And I rarely believe in sculpture," said Maindron.

Barnouvin asked, *"Mon cher maître,* what do you believe in?"

Maindron said, "That is a good question." But he did not answer it, saying instead to Lecoq, "Horace, you are still better off, being a painter."

"Oh yes, yes, even if I were a Rembrandt," Lecoq said sarcastically.

"He was too outspoken. He was a fool," declared Maindron.

"Of course," said Lecoq. "All artists are fools."

There was a deep silence. Then Auguste, his headache growing worse, certain now that Lecoq and Maindron had come only to mock him, blurted out, "Am I crazy to want to sculpt? Is it such a wild idea?"

Lecoq said, "Just because you put your life and ego into stone doesn't mean anything will come out of it."

Maindron chimed in, "Sculpture is the most expensive way to make a living. You cannot model a sky, a haystack, like Millet. You need people for models, you need to pay them. I cannot think of any other art into which you put so much and get so little."

Mama asked, "Are you married, Maître Maindron?"

Maindron said, "I take care of my mother." For the first time his voice softened.

Lecoq said, "She is very old. And very sweet."

"And patient," said Maindron, "On warm days she sits in our garden, which is full of our hopes—statues that I have spent years on, that I have been unable to sell. The clay and plaster and marble alone of these statues come to thousands of francs, and I will never see that money. But it is better for her to sit in the garden than in my damp, chilly studio among the many piles of clay, plaster, casts, and tools. The studio is like a cemetery. I make believe I am a sculptor, as I make believe it is a virtue to have debts, but it is no virtue to be a sculptor."

Auguste was numb. Papa must be full of I told you so. And did they think he was utterly without ability?

Barnouvin said, "Maître, you are one of our most honored sculptors."

Maindron replied, "So are Carpeaux and Barye, and they have to teach to support themselves."

"So I am crazy," said Auguste. "But it is what I do best."

Maindron smiled indulgently.

"What I care about!" cried Auguste. "The only thing I care about!"

Maindron said, "Many men do not marry the girl they fall in love with."

As Auguste looked desolate, Lecoq spoke up. "If you want a safe life, become a clerk, a clerk of straight lines. But if you have to be an artist, it must not be because of the enthusiasm of youth, because it seems exciting, because it is a first love affair, but because you must. One does not become an artist because it is easy, but because there is nothing else."

"Yes," sighed Maindron. He stood up. "Where is the head?"

Auguste pulled off the wet cloth. It was Papa! He could see it in Marie's eyes, and Aunt Thérèse was smiling, already celebrating it.

Maindron and Lecoq were expressionless. Their contemplation was mechanical, thought Auguste.

Maindron asked, "Your father?"

"Yes."

"You left off his whiskers."

"They didn't fit."

"Fit what?" Maindron's voice was as cold as his face.

"The antique," said Auguste.

"Is the function of the sculptor to copy?"

"I'm a student."

"But this is supposed to be your father, isn't it?"

"Yes."

"Then you shouldn't have copied. Anything. Except your father."

"It looks like him otherwise, doesn't it, maître?"

Maindron was silent.

"Will I get into the Beaux Arts?" There was no more time to lose.

Maindron glanced at Lecoq, then Barnouvin. Their expression remained blank. He said, "You've worked in the style of Houdon. This has some of the shrewdness he gave his head of Rousseau." He looked at Papa. "It is not altogether inappropriate."

"I will get in?" asked Auguste, his first smile of the day appearing.

"I have the best academic training," said Maindron. "Faugh!"

Barnouvin said, "Mon cher maître, I hope to get into the Beaux Arts."

Lecoq said, "Certainly. All my students try to get in. But some realize I am right. Degas has dropped out, and Fantin-Latour, and Dalou and Legros still study with me although they are students there now, too."

Auguste wavered. He desperately wished to please Lecoq, but even more desperately he had to please himself. He said, "I would like to apply. Forgive me, maître, but I must."

There was another long, painful silence. Auguste could sense Papa straining to talk, yet somehow managing to restrain himself. His own throat felt so tight he could hardly breathe.

Maindron walked around the head and said, "You have shaped it with perspective. It has depth. And you haven't made the usual mistake of the academic sculptor, treating it like a picture, with a right side and a wrong side. But the Beaux Arts?" He shook his head disparagingly.

Auguste said, "They say it is the finest art school in Europe."

"Of course, of the eighteenth century," said Lecoq, "and full of *amour-propre*."

Auguste asked, "Maître Maindron, will you recommend me?"

Maindron said, "Why do students have to ask such difficult questions? If I recommend you, you will assume you have talent, when you need so much more. I am not an emperor, to evaluate your fate."

"You are objective."

"Fair, not objective. Who will pay for it if you get in?"

Marie wavered, and suddenly Papa said, "If you think it is worth while, I will."

Maindron laughed. "I cannot make a grandiose speech, monsieur, about your son's ability. Or promise him any success. But if he has stamina, like a Hercules, it will give him a good formal education."

"Then you will recommend me?" cried Auguste.

Maindron glanced at Lecoq, who hesitated, then nodded. Maindron said, "Apply for admission, and I will sign the application. And make sure you spell your name correctly. I have seen applicants rejected for less."

Auguste, full of thanks, tried to explain to Lecoq that he still adored his teaching, but Lecoq cut him short. Lecoq said, "You can continue to study with me—if you want."

"Indeed, yes, *maître*, very much."

"Then make use of it. Work harder."

"And you will help, Papa?"

Papa said indignantly, "Have I ever broken my word?" But *mon dieu*, what had he let himself in for with these fine gentlemen? He hadn't known that artists could be such gentlemen—yet if Marie got married it might be worth it. Barnouvin, in spite of his elegant clothes and manners, appeared genuinely attracted to her. Barnouvin was taking Marie for a carriage ride in the Bois de Boulogne, and Lecoq was pleasant to Barnouvin, which meant that Lecoq thought the young man had a future.

Mama beamed after the departing couple and blessed them with several Ave Marias, and Aunt Thérèse thanked Maindron and Lecoq for their graciousness, for being such charming guests of honor. Maindron answered, "It was our pleasure," and Lecoq, leaving with him, took his first close look at the bust and said, "It is too antique, but at least it has vigor."

CHAPTER 6

Auguste hurried to his examination for the Beaux Arts with confidence, but it was dissipated quickly. The test for the sculpture applicants was held in an enormous cold amphitheater which was circled
with Roman statues that were similar and lifeless. In the center was
a middle-aged male model, and the applicants were placed around
him in a formal, stiff semicircle.

Auguste was not allowed to submit the bust of Papa—it was against
the rules of the Beaux Arts to present original work—but had to
work from the official model with the other applicants. This initial
disappointment struck him as a bad omen. He was depressed by the
large number of applicants; it took away his feeling of individuality.
Then there was not enough time. They had two hours a day for six
days to complete the entire figure. That was not even enough time to
finish the head, he thought. He felt trapped. The examination was a
speed contest.

By the end of the second day he was still sketching the figure, feeling his way, groping, experimenting, when most of the applicants
had half finished. The statues circling the amphitheater were smooth,
with a glossy finish, and the applicants' work took on the same
smooth gloss.

But that was wrong, thought Auguste: the model's muscles sagged;
to make them smooth was to falsify. There was nothing beautiful
about the model, yet each applicant seemed determined to make his
figure outdo the others in beauty.

Then Auguste longed to touch the flesh. Because of the alphabetical arrangement he was in the rear. He could hardly see the figure, but if he could use his sense of touch it should not fail him. Yet when he made such an attempt, a cry of horror went up from the students. The examiners warned him that one more infringement of the rules and he would be barred for good. Thus while he continued to try to work at his own tempo, he found himself drawn into rushing, into having to finish with the others—it became more vital than anything else.

On the last day of the examination he was still finishing his statue, though almost all the others were done, when the examiner, a distinguished member of the faculty of the Beaux Arts, approached him. The elderly man, tottering as he walked, was enveloped in a long black frock coat like a pallbearer, his silver spectacles low on his nose because of his myopia. The examiner stared at Auguste—not the statue—with judicial severity. As Auguste continued to work feverishly—the two hours were gone but the forehead needed touching up—the examiner said, "Permit me."

Auguste stepped aside, almost hopeful, and the examiner wrote in a large clear hand, "Rejected."

Everything in Auguste cried out against this verdict. This was the best figure he had ever done, with depth, solidity, perspective, and movement, but as he protested he was shut up with a wave of the examiner's hand. He could apply the following year, and that was the only comfort he received. He noticed irritably that the examiner's hands were soft, flabby, with long, carefully cultivated fingernails— how could anyone sculpt with such weak hands? It made him very sad. Sculpture itself was demeaned by the flaccidity of the examiner.

Barnouvin was at Auguste's side, delighted with himself, swaggering and grinning and announcing, "I did my figure in the style of Boucher. It was beautiful. I was so virtuous. They loved it."

"You were accepted?"

"Naturally. *Mon ami*, I will fill the Beaux Arts with my paintings."

"Marie will be pleased."

Barnouvin didn't answer.

Had Barnouvin heard him? Barnouvin was waving to several friends who had been accepted also.

II

The next year Auguste modeled his figure like everyone else. He imitated the Roman figures that circled the amphitheater. He was careful to finish on time. He gave his statue a shiny polish. He thought it was an excellent replica: accurate to the cubic centimeter. And the examiner smiled as he saw it and wrote, "Rejected."

Auguste was stunned, but no one gave him a reason he could accept for this rejection. Some said it was the angle of his figure, others that he had failed to find the eighteenth-century style favored by the school, several that he had had bad luck, but none of these reasons satisfied him. Lecoq refused to discuss the issue, and Papa declared it was better not to be admitted quickly, easily, Auguste would appreciate it more when he did get in.

III

The third year Auguste shut out everything but the figure. During all the intervening months he planned how to sculpt; he did his drawings ahead of time, from memory. As he expected, the model was male, middle-aged, and unattractive, and he got a quick start.

By the end of the second day he was on the figure. He did the body in the classic Greek style—the Greeks had carved bodies whose beauty had never been excelled—and the Beaux Arts admired the Greeks. The modeling was still too quick, he thought; there was no opportunity to be unhurried, reflective, to find the model's inner meaning, but his feeling was favorable. When the figure was completed, he was satisfied that it was the best he had ever done. He was almost pleased with it. He saw other applicants staring at the statue jealously. That was the best sign of all. He felt he had won the acceptance for which he yearned.

The examiner, the oldest and feeblest he had had so far, seemed to have difficulty making out the figure. His eyes were glazed, he could barely find the report to write on, and the pencil fluttered as he wrote, "Rejected."

"Again?" cried Auguste. He knew it was heresy to question an examiner's decision but this was absurd. "Why?"

The examiner added to the examination form, writing by the name *Auguste Rodin*, "Impossible. No ability whatsoever. He has no conception of appropriateness. Any further examinations are a waste. Forty-first."

There were only forty-four applicants in the hall. Dumfounded, Auguste asked, "When do I take the next test?" How could they have listed him forty-first in ability? Was he so mediocre?

"There will be no more tests. You are rejected for good."

A chilled Auguste asked, "You mean my technique is wrong?"

"There is no technique. You have imitated the Greeks. Badly."

Auguste had to clutch his figure to keep his feet. He was exhausted; his eyes were red and watery—he could barely see his figure himself now; he throbbed with the ache of injury. He could not understand why this had happened. He felt lost, that his life as a sculptor was ended forever. He was an idiot. He should never have studied sculpture.

IV

Fantin-Latour greeted him at the exit of the Beaux Arts. Fantin could tell from Auguste's desolate expression what had happened. He said, "It is not bad luck, though you will think so for a time."

"Of course it is bad luck," cried Auguste. "Art in France and the Beaux Arts go together."

"Not always. Both Degas and I have just been rejected by the Salon, so what good was the Beaux Arts to us?"

"Neither of you finished the courses. And anyway, Degas is off in Italy." How he envied Degas and his income! Italy seemed a million miles away, utterly out of reach, forever and forever.

"Just the same, we are considered Beaux Arts painters. But that didn't get us into the Salon."

Auguste stared at Fantin-Latour, quite attractive with his light red beard, bushy hair, strong nose, and asked, "Were you waiting for me?"

Fantin-Latour shrugged noncommittally.

"To console me? Why?"

"You are desolate now, and you shouldn't be—you are a natural."

"But you were certain I was going to fail."

"You didn't have the right recommendation. I knew that from the start."

"Maindron? He's very well known. He's a member of the Salon."

"And you are Lecoq's favorite pupil. They would never let you in. That would mean a kind of approval of Lecoq, which they never could concede."

Auguste was aghast. He cried out, "Why didn't you tell me?"

"What good would it have done? Would you have left Lecoq?"

"How could I!"

Fantin-Latour accompanied Auguste as the latter turned down the quai along the Seine and asked, "What are you going to do now?"

Sick at heart, Auguste said, "Quit sculpture."

"And admit that the Beaux Arts was right?"

"What else can I do? I have to earn a living. Without a Beaux Arts degree I will not get any commissions."

"Talk to Lecoq first. He may be able to suggest work where you can still model. Promise?"

"Why does it matter to you?"

"I felt the same way when I was rejected by the Salon. But now I know it was stupid to regard it as a matter of life and death. Oh, it is important, but I find it harder to do work I don't feel than to be rejected. Not that it is easy to be turned down, but the other is worse. Promise me you will listen to Lecoq?"

"Our illustrious *maître*," Auguste said sarcastically.

"Our *cher maître*," Fantin-Latour said with surprising sincerity. "What little I've learned, I've learned from him—and in the Louvre."

Auguste promised, but it was difficult to keep. He went directly to Lecoq, but he wondered if Lecoq really had the right point of view. Rejected by the Beaux Arts, he felt like an unrequited lover, yet the teacher refused to regard it as an unmitigated tragedy.

Lecoq was accustomed to the exaggerated melancholy rhetoric of the disappointed student and long ago had come to the conclusion that situations tended to master men rather than men situations. It would be better for this young man to learn all the facts of an artist's life. He said to Auguste, "It was the best thing that could have happened to you. The Beaux Arts has become a classical school of wolf-sucking Romuluses, Hectors and Andromaches in many parting embraces, so sedate it turns one's stomach. It is breeding a race of pygmies, full of humbug and dullness." He saw Auguste's attention wandering and he declared, "Do you think Michelangelo needed a Beaux Arts?"

"I'm not a Michelangelo."

"You're a sculptor. A very promising one."

"They marked me forty-first. Forty-first out of forty-four. How could I be that bad?" He held his head as if he would never recover from that.

"So you are going to drown." Ah, this was becoming dangerous, growing emotionally involved in a student. So many years he had kept out of such involvements. "But perhaps I was wrong to encourage you."

"Could you recommend me for work?"

"I might."

"I would be grateful, maître."

"But not for what you have learned here?"

Auguste gulped, but he could only murmur, "I admire you, maître, I—"

"Admire? Either you are an artist or you are not, and everything else is of no consequence."

Auguste flinched.

"I didn't ask you to study with me. I never ask anyone. This is, I must remind you, a free school, free to come to and free to leave."

Auguste started for the door, pausing only when Lecoq shouted, "And now you blame me for your rejection by the Beaux Arts because your name has been associated with mine." Lecoq laughed harshly. "I am one of those teachers known as the outer seven—anyone we favor the Beaux Arts automatically bans."

Auguste halted, replied strongly, "Pupils of yours have been admitted, Dalou, Legros, Degas, Fantin, Barnouvin—"

"Many, many," Lecoq interrupted caustically. "But they were not my protégés, or they had sufficient influence to overcome the infamy of being associated with me. Good luck, Rodin, and good-by."

"I don't want to stop studying with you."

"You have learned as much as you can from me. But," he said with a magnanimous gesture, "I will recommend you for suitable work if it comes up."

"Merci, maître."

"A man does what he must."

"Yes," said Auguste, feeling a kinship in this. "I've been wanting to do the head over, but—"

"If you stop being a sculptor, you can't."

"Still, I think now, I would do it better."

"Even as the forty-first sculptor at the Beaux Arts?"

But Lecoq was smiling, and Auguste smiled back.

"Do it over, Rodin; it will be better for you."

Auguste, more thoughtful than ever, went home by way of the rue de Vaugirard, through the Luxembourg Gardens, where students, grisettes, and elderly gentlemen with pigtails from a different age wandered, staring at the statues, for this was really a large outdoor gallery where the graduates of the Beaux Arts displayed their work. He observed Maindron's "La Velléda," and thought that no artist today could be considered a great artist unless he did a large work, like this statue, one with the proper heroic attitude and classicism. But in his present, new mood he decided this was a sham sublimity; at this moment he wanted to see something barbaric, outrageous, upsetting.

At home Papa said, "You must go to work. I gave you the chance you wanted, but if the Beaux Arts won't accept you, you will never make a living as a sculptor. Even Aunt Thérèse and Marie admit this."

"I'll get work as soon as I finish your head."

"My head? You finished that three years ago."

"No, I never finished it."

"I will not pose. It is idiocy."

"I'll do it from the first head."

"Copy? That is no way to work! Maindron said you cannot copy!"

"But you won't pose."

"Le bon dieu, you are difficult! What good will a new head do? They didn't even look at the old one. And it was me. Me."

"Papa, I have to do a new head, even if it doesn't make sense to you." His last piece of sculpture, he thought sorrowfully, before he went to work and stopped being a sculptor for good. "You can pose or not, as you wish!"

After more arguing a compromise was reached. Papa agreed to pose for a head if Auguste went to work the instant it was finished. Auguste said yes, and immediately destroyed the old bust so that Papa would not change his mind and so that he would not be influenced by previous considerations. And as he molded the clay in his hand he felt a little better.

Papa was a crusty subject and lamented that he was being punished for his sins, but he posed promptly, faithfully, and attentively. He was delighted with the bust when it was completed. He did not admit that, it would suggest he had been wrong; he did say it would be more appropriate in bronze. Then it would last longer and give him a more becoming strength.

"Bronze is impossible," said Auguste. "There is no money for bronze." Yet he was pleased. Papa was right. This bust deserved bronze.

"Maybe somebody would buy it," said Papa.

"No one will buy it," Auguste said decisively. "I've no reputation, no standing, no patrons."

"I don't really want anyone to buy it," said Papa. "I'll keep it myself." As he saw Auguste smile he grumbled, "Someone has to take care of it. You are so impractical, it will crack in no time."

Lecoq, in the meantime, had recommended Auguste to a decorator, Monsieur Cruchet, and Auguste went to work for five francs a day. It was miserly pay, but the decorator left him alone and for this he was grateful. Most of his work was ornamenting sculpture, and he realized the wisdom of Lecoq's recommendation. If it was not sculpture, it was almost the next best thing.

Auguste continued to take an occasional class with Lecoq and Barye —to keep his hands active—but he felt in exile. He doubted he would ever become a full-time sculptor. Yet he found it impossible to stay away from modeling. When he did not put in a couple of hours of hard work with clay for himself, he felt guilty, worthless, stupid. He got into the habit of working in his room after his regular jobs, usually late into the night.

He still felt Papa's head was the last he would ever do.

CHAPTER 7

One evening Auguste came upon Marie crying bitterly. It was several months after his final rejection by the Beaux Arts, late at night; their parents were asleep, and she had thought no one could hear her and she could no longer restrain herself. Auguste took her into his arms instinctively, and she sobbed, "Barnouvin is marrying someone else."

"You're sure?" He couldn't believe her: Barnouvin had been seeing her almost every Sunday for the past two years.

"He told me. I have no *dot*, and she has twenty thousand francs, I hear. It will be enough to support him for years. A tall, strong girl with a mighty bosom, muscular legs, a model's waist, and twenty thousand francs."

Auguste sought to console her, but she wouldn't be consoled. She was certain it was the end of her life. He suggested, "I'll talk to him," and she was terrified.

"No, no," she whispered. "He would never forgive that."

"But if you have lost him already?"

"I haven't lost him. It's the *dot*."

"Maybe he loves her." Maybe it was better for Marie to believe this and learn to accept it.

"He loves me. He told me."

"Did you—" Auguste paused; it was too difficult to ask his own sister.

"Refuse him?" she murmured. "Sixty-six times, it seems. But if he had proposed . . . He was considering it, I'm sure, Auguste, but he can't stand staying poor."

"It is difficult," said Auguste.

"I will become a nun," she said with sudden decisiveness.

"Marie!" The thought of losing her, even partially, was almost too much to endure.

"What about yourself?" she asked. "Is there anyone you like?"

He couldn't fall in love; he was too poor, but he said, "I'm too busy."

"Mama will like my becoming a nun. She will feel she has given a daughter to God. And it will make up for Clotilde."

"Is it what you want?"

"I can't have what I want!" she sobbed. "There is no other place to go."

"You may be right, Marie," he said with humility. "It is not easy to be rejected by somebody or something you love and still go on, pretending you are not hurt."

Marie did not answer. She was on her knees, praying with all the vehemence of her devout nature. There was a mist before her eyes and her mouth quivered, but now her voice was firm. The confusion was gone from her mind and she felt almost at peace. Perhaps it was for the best, as Auguste had suggested, perhaps in her heart she had always been wed to God.

II

A month later Marie began her novitiate in the convent of Ste. Euthyme.

Marie seemed calm when it came time to say good-by to her family, but Auguste felt her tremble in his farewell embrace. What was to be done about it? At home she cried all the time; she had grown thin and worn.

"Yes, yes, I will be careful," she told a worried Mama.

Mama was not happy about Marie's decision; she thought Marie was not strong enough for the trials ahead. Mama, who in the last few weeks had gone completely gray with the evil news about Barnouvin, tried to appear composed, however, and said, "You will make a good nun. You have been taught to know right from wrong." But Mama looked exhausted.

Papa was deeply upset. He was certain his daughter had not been violated, yet somehow it was as if something worse had happened. One did not enter the Church as a hiding place if her heart was pure, and that was what Marie was doing. Yet he had to help her in any way he could. As they parted, Papa pushed a small silver cross into her hand, although he had no intention of applauding her decision.

Marie resolutely focused on becoming a good nun. She was clean, orderly, obedient, determined to sacrifice herself to God, but she could not forget Barnouvin. She grew pale, lost weight, and became weak and ailing.

Two years passed in this fashion while Auguste, unable to sculpt —as if sculpture had betrayed him as he felt Barnouvin had betrayed Marie—struggled to earn a living as a maker of ornaments. But he could not work at all when Marie came home, critically ill with peritonitis.

Auguste was by her side constantly, trying to give her his strength, his will, but she had no will or strength. All the wish to live had gone out of her. Much of the time her mind wandered, and she imagined herself strolling through the Bois de Boulogne with Barnouvin, or playing at a picnic with Auguste and Clotilde—and then Auguste stroked her cheek tenderly and Mama prayed continuously and Papa could not believe what was happening, Rodins lived to a ripe old age.

Then on an evening Auguste was never to forget, Marie came back to the present with a superhuman effort. They were sitting about her bed, and Auguste sensed she was trying to find strength to say something.

It was remarkable, she thought. She was not that important to bring such concern to all their faces; Auguste would be the one to make things great and artistic. They must forgive her for being so weak and tired, she couldn't lift her arms, and her legs felt as if they had lead attached to them. And there had been no settlement with God. For two years she had tried, she had done the best she could, but she could not stop feeling miserable.

She struggled to reach out to ask their forgiveness, and felt Auguste's hand in hers. She could not see it, but she knew it was his, it was so strong and flexible from his work, a sculptor's hand, however much he doubted. She tried to whisper this to him, but he was such a long way from her; he couldn't hear her, yet he seemed to understand.

For a moment Auguste felt Marie's hand quiver in his, then abruptly, without warning, her fingers tightened around his—roughly, not like her—and were rigid. He stood for a minute transfixed, not realizing what had happened, not able to. Then he knew. He dropped to his knees, his face on hers, to breathe life into her, but it was too late. Papa stood stunned, unbelieving, Mama collapsed with a dull moan, and Auguste wept with an anguish he had never known before.

III

Auguste had developed a manual dexterity that could cope with any plastic difficulty, but he could not cope with Marie's death. She had been his emotional twin, friend and solace and confidante, always faithful and fair, the one person he could always depend on. All other emotions gave way before his grief. He could not face his work, his sculpture. Somehow sculpture seemed responsible for her death —he was sure that if he hadn't been determined to be a sculptor she wouldn't have met Barnouvin and she would still be alive. It didn't matter to his troubled mind that Marie had met Barnouvin before he had, that she had introduced him to Barnouvin—the theme that ran through him was: "I'm responsible, I'm guilty, I must atone."

He decided to take her place in the Church. He did not consult anyone: not his family, not Aunt Thérèse, not Fantin or any of his artist friends, not Lecoq—although this gave him much guilt. He was certain Lecoq would be furious with this decision, at the best consider it desertion and at the worst an act of treachery, but he could not face Lecoq to explain. It would be too difficult. Lecoq would make him change his mind. It would be an unpleasant scene. In any case, he rationalized, he was not a sculptor and he had not been since he had been rejected by the Beaux Arts.

One rainy winter day Auguste began his novitiate as Brother Augustin in the monastery of the Fathers of the Holy Sacrament. It was on the rue St. Jacques, near his home, which was a comfort, although he was determined to remain in the holy order and find peace. If everything went properly, and he was certain it would, he would become a monk after two years as a novice. He had not told anyone except his family, and they had been too shaken by Marie's death to question his decision.

Mama had aged terribly since Marie's death. She wore only black now; she had shriveled in size; this sacrifice struck her as inevitable and fitting. Papa, who felt like an old creaking gate now, thought Auguste was stubborn like stone, the most stubborn son in Paris; he respected the Church as he respected anything that was strong, but it was no place for happiness. Yet it was no use arguing with this new humility of Auguste's.

Auguste thought he didn't want happiness, but consolation. Whatever the doctor's verdict, Marie had died of "virgin's melancholy."

The head of the order of the Holy Sacrament was Father Eymard, a dignified elderly priest with a reputation as a scholar, whose translations of Dante and Petrarch had been highly praised. His wide cheekbones and thoughtful eyes and firm chin had a Roman severity, but when he smiled a light seemed to glow about him. He greeted Auguste quietly and said, "I hope God will forgive me the sin of vanity if you find your true vocation here."

"I will try, mon père, I will do my best," said Auguste, shifting a little uncomfortably in his heavy brown cassock.

"You were a sculptor, Brother Augustin, were you not?"

"A student, mon père, that was all."

"And you have finished with art?"

"It does not matter. Not any more."

Father Eymard's brown eyes widened. "Do not be so humble, my son, that it becomes a sin. If one is blessed by God with an ability for art, it is not to be held lightly. One can serve beauty and God. Fra Filippo and Fra Bartolommeo served both with honor and distinction."

Auguste nodded obediently, thinking, I will never care about sculpture again.

"There is no hurry, Brother Augustin. You will find your vocation or not, as it pleases God. However, one should not enter our order as an escape, but as a fulfillment."

"I will try."

"Do not be sad. You have been given the ability to choose."

In the days that followed, Brother Augustin sought to submit to the discipline of the order. As the newest of the novices he did the humblest chores, sat in the lowest place, existed in a shadowed anonymity. He struggled to be free of vanity, ambition, pride, the sins of the flesh: to be one with God. He sought to find consolation in silence and contemplation, in austerity and obedience, in solitude and prayer. He could endure the days, which were full of prayers, chores, studies, meditations; it was the long, sleepless nights that were difficult to bear.

Night after night he tossed on his straw pallet. It was not the physical discomfort that troubled him—he had borne as much at home, and worse; it was the flame of sculpture which kept flickering within him that was painful to endure. He did not wish to be presumptuous, but if he could only make a head of Marie from memory the pain of missing her might be less. And he missed female companionship with a heartache he had not expected. At home there had been Marie and Aunt Thérèse and Mama to support him, to comfort him, whatever happened elsewhere, but even to contemplate this as Brother Augustin was wrong. This would destroy all his monastic aims, he thought. Yet sleep still was very difficult.

In the chapel he prayed for guidance, for forgetfulness, but when he did not visualize the head of Marie that should be done, his mind was full of objects his imagination was persuading him to model: a Jesus on the Cross, a Magdalen with the face of Clotilde, St. John in the wilderness, a St. Peter like Michelangelo's "Moses"; there were so many subjects, and they struggled in his mind like a great hungry mass against extinction.

He grew somber, gloomy, and hopeless even as he performed all the duties assigned him. Father Eymard watched him anxiously as his mood became worse and one day asked him, "Do you know Dante?"

"A little." Auguste was surprised by the question.

"Brother Augustin, we are not the enemy of art. And Dante was not an enemy of the Church. He detested its sins, as did St. Francis, but his *Divine Comedy* is that of a devout man. I have a new edition of the *Divine Comedy* with etchings by an artist, Gustave Doré, which are the most unusual I have ever seen. Would you care to look at them?"

He could not pretend. He admitted, "It will be a great pleasure."

He was amazed by the bite, the severity, the bitterness of Doré's etchings. They had a stunning power that was almost incredible. He sat in the monastery library wishing he could draw with Doré—here was a sovereign lord of creation hammering down doors with his anger.

Then he was afraid to draw, certain he had lost the ability. Yet if he could . . . Father Eymard, judging his mood, handed him paper and pen.

Auguste, drawing his own conception of the *Divine Comedy*, gentler and more sensuous than Gustave Doré's, was not unhappy for the first time in a long while. It was the first sketching he had done since Marie's death. He felt some energy return. He didn't mind the seclusion now. If anything, it was preferable, for he could work at a more sustained pace.

Father Eymard glanced at his drawing and said, "Good, good, you do not abuse your time."

Auguste thought that if he was allowed to draw, to model, he could eat frugally, care nothing for possessions, and manage to accept the vow of chastity despite occasional flares of passion.

He slept a little better now. The dark was not such an enemy any longer: he was visualizing many subjects to draw.

After he finished the *Divine Comedy*, Father Eymard assigned him work in the garden. By now Father Eymard was keenly aware of his need to work with his hands, and there were many things to be repaired in the tool shed.

Auguste told himself this was the will of God, and tried to be content.

One day, however, a few weeks after this assignment, when he came upon some wood outside the shed he found himself creating a figure out of it. He had almost finished when Father Eymard came upon him. He was certain he would be severely punished.

Father Eymard said quietly, "The wood is weak these days, Brother Augustin. Would you like some clay?"

Auguste blushed, and stammered, "Yes." Then he felt guilty.

Father Eymard didn't seem to notice. He said, "You may use the shed."

"Thank you. Thank you very much."

"It must be hard, Brother Augustin, not to work at your art."

"Oh no, *mon père!*" He prayed that God forgive him for such a falsehood.

"We are not an academy of art," sighed Father Eymard. "But such fine skill as you display is a virtue."

"Would you pose for me, *mon père?*" he implored, kneeling at Father Eymard's feet.

"It drives you hard, doesn't it?"

"Yes, yes."

"What a pity! We must not go against nature. Rise, my son; you will not be able to model me from that position."

The next few weeks Father Eymard could pose only infrequently, but when the Father was absent Auguste worked from memory. He drew with charcoal on rough paper, then did a statuette to serve as the model for the final figure. He tried not to imitate the antique, as he felt now he had done in part with the bust of Papa, or to beautify, but to interpret, to capture the essence of Father Eymard's features and nature.

When the head was finished, Father Eymard examined it carefully, then said slowly, "At least I haven't been vulgarly idealized."

Auguste folded his hands as he had been taught in the monastery, but he could feel them convulse with a kind of anguish.

"Brother Augustin, you do have skillful hands."

"Did I do it wrong, *mon père?*"

"Brother Augustin, I am supposed to judge morals, not art."

"I hoped you would like it."

"Of course." Father Eymard walked around the bust, studying it from all sides. "Do I really look like that?"

"I thought so."

Father Eymard put his hand gently on the bust and said, "You are a sculptor and I am not. I accept your judgment. It is a fine head." His tone grew lighter. "It shows me sufficiently homely to keep me from being vain, yet charged with enough emotion to make me human. Very human." He repeated that as if he wanted to remember it.

"Thank you, *mon père*."

"Thank you, Brother Augustin." He stood a moment in silence, as if seeking guidance from above, then said, "Perhaps you should be differently nourished. We are too monastic here to encourage your talents, and this is no longer an age for Madonnas."

Auguste felt as if he were turned to stone. This was another rejection, no matter how Father Eymard worded it.

Father Eymard said gently, "Not all men are suited to the contemplative life. It is not a sin. Perhaps the monastic life is not for you."

There was a long silence.

At last Father Eymard said, "I think you should accept this and return to the world, to sculpture. Otherwise I think you will wither here."

"In the service of God!" exclaimed Auguste.

"God's service takes many forms," said Father Eymard. "To force yourself to stay here will not work. It will only make you hostile and bitter. You will come to feel that your arms are cut off."

"Nothing seems real out there," Auguste declared, indicating the outside world with a flourish of his hand.

"What about sculpture?"

"Sculpture is not to be trusted."

"That is a mood. It will pass. Life has to be an up-and-down affair, but essentially it is positive, not negative. For you sculpture is the positive, just as for me the monastery is."

"It is very hard to be a sculptor."

"Is it easier to be Brother Augustin?"

"I chose it. I made a vow. A promise to God."

"Whether you are a believer or not is for God to judge, not man. The monastery is not a prison. The door is open to leave as well as to enter. And you may very well serve God better in the world. Don't be sad. It would be a greater waste if you stayed here."

"You consider me hopeless."

"Misdirected, not hopeless. I do believe you are capable of sacrifice, renunciation, self-denial—for sculpture, but not for God."

"Then why did I come here?"

"Because you were looking for a consolation you hadn't found in the outside world. But that isn't what you need, but faith and hope."

Father Eymard turned to the head and added, "May I have a copy of the bust when you put it in bronze?"

"Bronze?"

"I would like it to last, even in this temporal world. If that is not presumptuous?"

Suddenly Auguste felt powerless to resist. This plaster bust would be so much better in bronze—Father Eymard was right. He smiled and said, "*Merci, mon père.*"

"What for?" Father Eymard looked astonished.

"For posing. You were a very good model."

"I hope so. God bless you, Auguste Rodin." Father Eymard covered the bust so that it would be properly preserved.

IV

A few days later Auguste left the order of the Holy Sacrament. He had been in the monastery almost a year, it was January 1863, and he was going on twenty-three, and he had no desire to go home. He wanted to see his parents and Aunt Thérèse, but he could not live with them any more. So instead of going home first, he went to the Petite École.

As Auguste hoped, Lecoq was there teaching, but he was shocked by the teacher's harshness. Lecoq did not bother to say hello. He asked brusquely, "What do you want?"

Auguste was not certain what he wanted. To find his childhood here? To thank Lecoq, apologize, explain? His childhood was gone, and to apologize was too difficult. And the students were so young: had he been so young when he entered?

Lecoq said, "What did you expect to find?"

Auguste did not know. But Lecoq had been his guiding light. He tried to say that, and Lecoq cut him short.

"So you thanked me by going into a monastery."

"But I've left."

"Thanks very much. How grateful should I be?"

"I'm sorry, *maître*. I thought you would be glad." Auguste turned away.

"I'm glad when any of my pupils do good work. Have you done any good work lately?"

Auguste moved toward Lecoq, then halted, the teacher regarded him so angrily. Yet he had to ask, "Could I work here?"

"No!"

Auguste grew pale and whispered, "I didn't mean to offend you."

"You didn't offend me. You are no longer a student, you have no place here."

"I have no place anywhere. I won't be able to work at home, I can't afford a studio."

"Don't make it too tragic or nobody will care." But when Lecoq saw Auguste close his eyes to keep from crying, he added slowly and quietly, "I was sorry to hear about your sister. It must have been a great loss."

"It was."

Lecoq strode to his desk, which still dominated the large classroom, pulled from his drawer a dozen drawings, and handed them to Auguste. Auguste was astonished to see that they were his own drawings, done many years ago, when he had first come to Lecoq. They seemed so crude now, but Lecoq pointed to them and said, "I have a few more, but this should be enough of a lesson."

"Lesson? What kind of a lesson?"

"Whenever you grow desperate, look at these, and then you will realize how far you've come."

"Not far enough."

"Auguste Rodin, you will never grow up," Lecoq said with sudden and familiar exasperation. "You're young, you have your strength, physical and mental. But you won't appreciate that until you don't have it any more."

"Could I work with you? Privately? I'll work any way you wish."

Lecoq wanted to explode, but he could not quarrel with Auguste's humility. He had felt so strongly about Auguste that it had become a problem, although he had never admitted this to anyone, not even to himself. And now Auguste was asking for help he could no longer give. He stared at Auguste carefully. Auguste was more muscular, especially in the shoulders and the chest. His face had become heavier and manlier. Yet, thought Lecoq, there was still something boyish about Auguste; this pupil still had a potential so few of his students had ever shown. But to achieve it would be a long and arduous battle.

Auguste said, "I must work at sculpture. If I have learned nothing else, I have learned that."

"Then there is nothing else I can teach you."

"But, *maître*—"

"I was an artist, too, once. My studio was my life. My friends are welcome there."

Auguste stood blinking tearfully at Lecoq.

"The key is under the mat—if I am not home." When he saw Auguste still looking dazed, he explained, "I am sixty," as if it were the end of his life. "I have stopped exhibiting. If I haven't been recognized by now, I never will."

"Everybody recognizes you, *maître*."

"As a teacher. But at least my studio will be put to use."

"How can I thank you?"

Lecoq stared at him as if Auguste had suggested something ugly. "Work, work, work," he cried, "until you think your hands are going to drop off."

Auguste walked slowly out of the Petite École, past the statues of Hercules and Minerva, the Latin inscription over the entrance. He had read that only the first time he had entered, but now he repeated thoughtfully, " '*Utilitas—Firmitas*. Practicality—Solidity,' " as Barnouvin had translated. His Latin, as always, was shoddy. But this time he did not grow furious at the thought of Barnouvin. Father Eymard was right: time did take care of some things. But he was leaving part of his life here. He took a firmer grip on the drawings Lecoq had given him. They were like toys now, dearly beloved toys.

That evening, when Auguste visited his parents and told them of his departure from the monastery, he informed them also that he had rented a room for himself.

Auguste sensed that his parents were upset by this move, but he could not remain at home any longer. There were too many painful memories of Marie, he had an overpowering need to strike out for himself. . . . There were many reasons.

After Auguste left, Papa shut all the windows in the house. The north wind was blowing hard, the fire had ebbed in the kitchen, it was chilly suddenly in the house. Papa and Mama felt very lonely. It was not easy to understand. Now all their children were gone.

PART
TWO
THE
ARTISTS

CHAPTER 8

It was the Café Guerbois that became Auguste's home the next few months. His room on the rue Hermel was a bleak, tiny shell, his work as an ornament maker was drab and there was nothing to discuss with his fellow workers, and using Lecoq's studio and studying with Barye several nights a week, though it seemed essential, made him feel still like a student.

But he felt like an artist at the Café Guerbois. It was located on the grande rue des Batignolles, and within walking distance of his room and most of the studios of his friends. It was a run-down working-class district, not far from Montmartre, and many artists were beginning to live there. It was cheap, picturesque, rural, for the most part a suburb, and the artists were left alone. After the solitary year in the monastery Auguste had a strong need for talk, companionship, and the cheerfulness of the Parisian café.

The Café Guerbois was very Parisian. It had a clean, protected sidewalk for warm weather and a pleasantly spacious interior for the bad, cold days. The gaslight was bright, the artists sat in one corner and the workingmen in the other, and the huge stove in the center of the room heated both sides equally well. The *apéritifs* were cheap, the portions of food were generous, and the magnanimity of the owner extended elsewhere, too: a customer could sit all night even if he didn't order anything, and could say whatever he thought. The owner believed that nothing was ever really overthrown by talking, even art schools and certainly not the Emperor, even a pseudo one like Napoleon III, and these artists, particularly the talkers, attracted other artists, and some of them had money and spent it.

The owner knew he had only to glance at these artists to know they would never amount to anything. Fantin-Latour, the most talkative one, dressed neatly, but he had to take just one look at him to know this painter was impractical. And this Edgar Degas would seduce no one, not even an art dealer, with his insulting arrogant ways—he should have stayed in the law. It was true that Monsieur Manet always paid for himself and had an attractive manner, but he also was too easily offended. Then the youngest of the lot, Auguste Renoir, was the very opposite of Monsieur Manet, who at least was a gentleman. This Renoir talked no better than a common laborer and seemed interested just in keeping alive. The serious ones, Alphonse Legros and Jules Dalou, with their attitude that the future of French art rested on their shoulders, were really too ridiculous. And now this newcomer, Rodin, sat like a rock most of the time, as if he could afford to be independent, when none of them—fools! *mon dieu!*—could afford such an attitude. But business was business, the owner reminded himself, and *he* was not a fool. As long as they left a few francs, they could sit all night; the corner would be empty otherwise.

Tuesday and Thursday were their favorite evenings, especially after they had done a hard day's work. Auguste became a faithful customer after his long hours as an ornament maker, although thrifty from necessity, he rarely spent anything. He liked the glow of the gaslight, the smell of tobacco smoke, the round marble tables, the sausages, wine, and *croissants*. He also appreciated that the café was the cheapest in the neighborhood, and the warmest—he could never get warm in his room—and that he could be conspicuous or inconspicuous, whichever he preferred. Most of all he craved the company of the artists who frequented the place, all of them about his age and struggling and striving like himself.

On this chilly winter evening Paris was dark with a wet snow that had become gray rather than white. It made Auguste late, for walking was difficult. By the time he reached the café, it was crowded and Degas had to be squeezed against Fantin-Latour to make room for him.

Degas' long face grew longer and he seemed to shrink within his velvet coat as if all physical contact was obnoxious to him. Out of sheer annoyance he snapped, "Rodin, there is really no place here."

Fantin, seeing Auguste's distress, said, "It's not his fault he's late. He has to help his family."

"And you must hold forth eloquently about it," said Degas. "Charming." His look of distaste grew more obvious.

"If you're uncomfortable—" said Auguste, starting to rise.

"Don't you dare," said Fantin, pushing Rodin back into the chair. "Degas is in a bad humor. He has been rejected by the Salon, too."

"That is not true," flared Degas. "I did not even submit."

"You know very well you wanted to," said Fantin. "But you didn't because you were afraid you would be rejected. It's the same thing."

Degas looked disdainful, but did not reply.

Legros asked skeptically, "Rodin, do you really help your parents?"

Auguste said, "Yes."

Legros looked horrified. Legros, a Burgundian born near Dijon, was glad he was away from his family, it removed any attachment to them. He had sold already, but unquestionably Rodin never would, tied to his family. Legros asked, "How can you do your own work?"

Auguste said, "I can't most of the time." But he could not stop helping at home, however much he resented the burden, for Papa had retired on half pay, Mama was ailing, and they needed his support.

"No wonder you entered a monastery," said Legros. "I would have, too, if I had such a burden."

"Why did you enter?" asked the intense, passionate Dalou.

Auguste said slowly, reluctantly, "I was alone. In a crisis."

"And you thought you were finished as a sculptor," Fantin said sympathetically. "And the Church seemed a solution."

"It wasn't," Auguste said with a sudden burst of emotion. "I learned the litany, I tried to be full of brotherly love, but it was impossible. I wanted only to model. Anybody who tried to stop me, I hated. It wasn't rational, but I had no grace in me. The other novices were bloodless creatures to me because they were not interested in modeling. They were impure, not me. So it became a trap instead of a fulfillment."

Renoir said, "I can understand that. Anyone who tries to stop me from painting, I hate. I think I'd hate God if He tried to halt me."

Auguste was surprised. Renoir was usually cheerful and gay. He said, "I didn't hate God, I didn't reject Him, He rejected me. Afterward I realized that He did not want me as His priest."

Renoir asked, "Were you angry when you discovered this?"

Auguste said, "Surprised, not angry. It was as if I had realized that God was a great sculptor, a magnificent sculptor, and the universe was His model and Michelangelo His prophet. And that I must work out of this feeling, out of love, not hate."

"Hear! Hear!" said Degas. "How fine to have such noble sentiments, and how vital to have infinitely more."

"Go to church, be good to your family, work hard," itemized Dalou. "I hate to admit it, but Degas is right, it is a waste. Women, well, that is more profitable. What about them, Rodin? We never see you with any."

A week after his departure from the monastery Auguste had returned to the brothel that had been his first real experience, driven with an enormous craving for a woman, a fleshy woman, but the *maison d'amour* was gone. Driven even more by this craving, he had found other brothels, the rue Mouffetard, which went back to Roman times, was crowded with the hierarchy of whoredom. On this street and in the neighborhood were *brasserie* tarts, unemployed whores, free-lance prostitutes, prodigal harlots, a constant pairing, appropriate for almost any taste, of all prices and grades. But Auguste's sense of privacy, always strong, had grown, and he preferred not to discuss such matters.

Dalou prodded, "*Mon ami*, don't you believe in *nuit d'amour?*"

Auguste shrugged noncommittally.

Dalou said, "Sad, sad, sad." To Dalou, the only other sculptor in the group, this was tragic: loving women was the major fact of his life, next to his craving for official position. "You will never amount to anything."

Auguste thought, Who could tell? Perhaps genius was like an iceberg, most of it under water. As Dalou described the different women he had known the past few months, Auguste stared at his new acquaintances, Édouard Manet and Auguste Renoir, and sought to realize their deepest emotions.

They were as different as two men could be. Manet was the oldest of the group at thirty-one, Renoir the youngest at twenty-two. Everyone in Paris who knew anything about painting said Manet was full of brilliance, could paint in any style, David, Ingres, Delacroix, Courbet; but no one took Renoir seriously—Renoir was just a student. Manet was like a royal peach, ready to ripen any day now, with exceptional gifts, attractive, elegant, cultivated, well-to-do, generous, a *boulevardier*, who had done fine work already; desolate, however, because it had not been recognized by the Salon, yet with much to live for, but often melancholy.

But the thin, slightly built, fair-haired Renoir, humble in appearance, with the look of constant impoverishment, one of five children of a poor tailor, without any of the advantages of Degas and Manet, whose growing up had been a bouncing from one distasteful job to another, was always cheerful as long as he had a paintbrush in his hand. He could paint with mud if he had to; he was stubborn about only one thing—his need to paint.

Auguste felt at home with Renoir, who had much the same background and rarely tried to persuade anybody about anything. The others, however, ah! Auguste smiled to himself.

Fantin was loudest, saying, "Seven rejections. Excellent. Excellent." He went over the list of those who had been refused by the Salon, "Legros, Dalou, Manet, Degas, Barnouvin, Renoir, and myself." He gloated with satisfaction. "That will show what I've been telling everyone, that the Salon is dedicated to prettiness and fraud."

"Nonetheless," said Manet, "the Salon has the prestige. I would still exhibit in the Salon if they would have me."

Renoir chimed in, "So would I," and Dalou and Legros agreed, while Degas looked indifferent and Auguste was impassive.

"Just the same," said Fantin, "they are not exhibiting any of us."

"That's not unusual," said Manet. "I've been rejected before."

"But you shouldn't—you, of all people," said Fantin. "You are the most advanced of all of us."

"Oddly enough," said Manet, "you may be right. What do you propose?"

Fantin declared, "I do not believe that to be received or not received by the Salon is essential. But it *is* vital that we be exhibited, that our work be seen."

Degas said, "Create our own Académie de Peinture?"

"No," said Fantin, "but at least have something to say about which of our paintings are to be exhibited."

"Impossible," said Degas. "We can't depend on artists to choose. Nobody likes anybody else."

Fantin asked, "Don't you want the public to see your work?"

Degas said, "I'm not sure. Nothing about painting should be left to chance. And this kind of an exhibition would be only chance."

Fantin turned to the silent Auguste. "What about you, Rodin? Do you want to be exposed to the public view?"

"Yes," said Auguste, "when I have something ready."

"Ready"—Renoir shrugged—"I always have something ready." He sat at the round marble table, improvising on an old newspaper as they argued.

Auguste said, "And when I have something ready, I want it to be something I care about."

"*Mon dieu!*" cried Degas. "He expects to be satisfied. He is out of his mind!"

"No, I am almost never satisfied," Auguste said, "but there is no point in showing your own work unless you care about it."

"As far as the public is concerned," said Degas, "the only good artist is a dead artist."

Fantin asked, "You mean we should crawl back into our attics?"

Degas said, "Well, you are the student who knows the most about the Louvre. It is not altogether a handicap."

Fantin flushed, but seeing the others listening intently, he stated emphatically, "We must make our own exhibition."

"Ourselves?" Degas was shocked. He looked as if he had been asked to perform the labors of Hercules.

"Not directly," said Fantin, really speaking to the others now. "But if we scream loud enough the echo could reach Napoleon himself."

Degas sneered, "That *nouveau royal*, that *nouveau riche*."

Fantin shouted, "I have no intention of defending him, but he is our only hope."

"Our only hope," repeated Degas. "Our *homme précieux*, he has made our Empire ideal. It is an empire inspired by revolution, a dictatorship approved by the vote of the people, a republican monarchy, the Emperor says, which could as easily be a monarchical republic, except it is neither. It is an empire dedicated to *la cause napoléonienne*, and one of these days we will be asked to die for it. But will he die for us?"

They all smiled cynically: in this, at least, they all agreed.

But Fantin refused to be put down. He jumped to his feet and declared, "All the more reason we should appeal to Napoleon. He needs us."

Degas said, "That's not reason, that's emotion."

"*Nom de dieu*," cried Fantin, "it's better than being intellectual, than giving up before we begin." He gathered strength as the others waited for him to continue. "I have a plan. The vital thing is to get people to look at our work. And if we shout violently enough, through our friends, public figures we know, newspapers, we will make the Salon ashamed. They will have to give us our own exhibition." Fantin grew wild with excitement, infatuated with his idea. He gave such a superb performance that the idea assumed great importance. The thought of giving an exhibition apart from the academic setting of the Salon intrigued all of them, even Degas. Fantin added, "All we need is stamina. We will go on and on until they are filled with fatigue. We will stir them out of their apathy. Apathy is our enemy. We will make Paris aware. They will see our work after all."

II

To everyone's surprise, not only was their commotion heeded and taken seriously, but in April, Napoleon III proclaimed officially "Numerous protests have reached the Emperor concerning the works of art rejected by the jury of the Salon. His Majesty, wishing to let the public judge as to the legitimacy of these protests, has decided that the rejected works of art will be exhibited in another part of the Palais de l'Industrie. The exhibition will open in May."

The Salon des Refusés, as it came to be known throughout Paris, struck Fantin as the answer to his plan although many were regarding it as a joke, and he persuaded Manet, Legros, Dalou, and Barnouvin to exhibit with him. Degas refused at the last moment; Renoir, to his sorrow, had nothing ready, having suddenly changed his style.

Auguste, when he heard that the Salon des Refusés was official, decided to do a head—it would be quickest, simplest—and exhibit it. He still did not have his own studio, he had no money for material, he could not afford a model, and he had only a few weeks in which to complete his entry. But the thought of doing a head for a public exhibition, even an eccentric, undignified one such as the Salon des Refusés, filled him with the breath of life and gave him so much energy he had to plunge on.

Auguste searched for a handsome, distinguished gentleman to model, someone of the stature of Father Eymard, in the hope of impressing fashionable Paris, and found himself with only one subject available, and that a difficult one. Bibi was a derelict who loitered about Lecoq's studio for a crust of bread and who slept in the court below when it did not rain. But Bibi was always about, and he agreed to sit in return for a bowl of soup and occasional wine. Auguste did not want to sculpt this ruined peasant, but he was the only model he could find, and afford.

At first Bibi, with his flattened, broken nose which spread over much of his face, his sodden eyes, his dirty gray beard, his features mutilated by poverty, misery, and age, struck Auguste as hideous and it was hard for him to get started. Gradually, however, after Auguste had thrown away dozens of sketches, several came alive—he had seen many Bibis on the streets where he had grown up. And once he had the clay in his hands there was no stopping. As the head took shape, he grew haunted by Bibi; it was as if Bibi had been delivered to him by a force within himself.

There was power in the derelict's large head, he thought, and the face was a *dossier* of a man's fate. The broken nose, in particular, fascinated him. To get it just right he pressed down on it, ignoring Bibi's cry of pain. Never in his life had he felt such a broken nose. Had Michelangelo felt this way when his own nose was smashed? How had that disaster affected the great Florentine?

He labored night after night, avoiding all other activity. While he worked, nothing else existed. He swam in clay. It felt warm and noble in his hands, but the head remained a cold and silent lump.

A week before the submission of the entries to the Salon des Refusés he felt more dissatisfied than when he had begun. He could not show the head to anyone; he could hardly look at it himself.

Then the night he needed Bibi the most, the derelict vanished. No one in the neighborhood knew where Bibi was, and he could not do the head from memory, it would become sentimental and false.

Yet Auguste tried, although he was certain he was on the wrong track.

Several nights later, when Bibi, hopelessly drunk, staggered into the studio for more wine, Auguste knew that his doubts were right. There was a lawless look on Bibi and he had none of that in the head. He destroyed everything but the chin, which was almost right. He sat Bibi in a corner against the wall, propped up by an easel, but Bibi kept slumping to the floor. He handed Bibi wine which he had slipped into a small bottle at the café for such a moment. Bibi gulped it down, revived, and sat up with new life.

This might last only a few minutes, however, and Auguste went to work hurriedly. He pressed down upon the bridge of Bibi's nose as with a fist. Bibi, sopping over with wine, felt no pain and sat motionless. Auguste could almost taste the blood and bone and broken flesh. "The cartilage must be soft yet firm," he whispered to himself. It would be weeks, probably months, before he could capture the tension of the skin, the curve of the nose, the protrusion of the eyelids—how much there was to learn about the human face! He had to possess an anatomical brain. He took a deep breath, returned to work, then had to halt—Bibi had collapsed again, this time for the evening.

When the entries closed for the Salon des Refusés, Auguste was still doing the head over and had not submitted Bibi. He desperately wondered whether the head was worth completing, and although he knew he should not show it to anyone in its unfinished state he asked Lecoq to look at it.

Lecoq had respected the first law of sculpture: never look at unfinished work. Not once had he peeked under the wet cloth that covered the head between sittings. He was curious, but he was also surprised by this request, it was not like Rodin to waste his time. Lecoq said, "It's not ready."

"I know, I know! But should I continue?"

"You'll probably not sell it. He's very ugly."

"That's the way he looks."

"That's the way you see him. *Mon dieu*, he is ugly."

Auguste, sick at heart, was about to shatter the head into a thousand pieces when Lecoq halted him.

"Wait a moment!"

"Why?"

"I want to look at it again." Lecoq examined the head thoughtfully and said, "You've certainly gotten away from the Academy heads."

"What about the Salon?"

"You'll have trouble with the Salon, as you did with the Beaux Arts. Does that have to matter?"

Auguste was uncomfortable.

"There is too much love in the world, anyway, fake love." Lecoq felt the features, fascinated by their reality. "Finish it if you can."

"You don't think I can?"

"I don't know," said Lecoq. "It is quite a difficult subject."

Auguste studied the head. The nose was effective, but not decisive. That was the trouble. His mind was full of noses, but he was not yet committed.

"You didn't want my criticism," said Lecoq, "you wanted my approval."

Auguste said, "I'm unsure."

"Naturally. You're the kind of sculptor who will always be unsure, because you're never satisfied. You want to be, but something in you won't let you. Did it occur to you that this nose should be boneless?"

"Boneless?" This could be true. "I'll try it that way."

"Of course you will. You will try every way until you find the right way for you." Lecoq smiled. "Then it will become your way."

Auguste returned to the bust with new energy, which he realized now he had needed most of all. He was resigned to the fact that he would miss the Salon des Refusés.

III

According to a French proverb, "Only where the Beaux Arts is, is there art." Thus the Salon des Refusés was sneered at by the public from the start.

At the opening Auguste stood in the gallery devoted to the Refusés from the official Salon, and as he heard the roars of derisive laughter he thought it a catastrophe. He wanted to flee, although it was not his work, then he couldn't. Degas had him by the arm, saying, "Lucky us, that we didn't exhibit," and was steering him toward the painting that was evoking the most scorn. He wondered on which side Degas stood.

It was a picture by Manet called "Le Déjeuner sur l'Herbe"—a painting of a picnic with two well-dressed artists sitting on the ground beside a nude woman—that was creating the uproar. There was also another woman in the painting, in the rear, dressed, but apparently about to bathe; however, it was the proximity of the nude woman to the two clothed men that was evoking the derision and shock and cries of "Scandalous!"

Auguste thought it improbable that two such elegant gentlemen would sit on the grass with a naked woman, even such an attractive one, but Manet had painted a lovely nude, real and vibrant, and certainly not indecent, as many of the outraged viewers were declaring.

Degas was offended that the painting was hung so badly. "It's too high, the light is poor, it's surrounded by the wrong pictures. A deliberate act of revenge by the Salon judges. A janitor could have done better."

"I like the nude," said Auguste. "It is quite remarkable in a way."

"I would have made her more pink," said Degas. "But why is everybody so shocked? Giorgione did this combination of nude and dressed gentlemen three hundred and fifty years ago and it was considered a masterpiece."

Auguste said, "I prefer Manet's. His nude is direct, individual."

"Oh, Manet can paint," said Degas. "The trouble is, he is so skillful he hasn't settled on a style yet."

"Too much black, perhaps, à la Courbet," said Auguste, having a sudden need to show that he could be critical also, yet remain accurate. "But it is a fine composition, with excellent design. And I do like the nude."

Degas said, "Wait until you start making nudes. You'll end by making them more elegant. Classical Venus in the style of Cabanel. But I won't."

"I won't either," said Auguste. He saw Barnouvin approaching. Barnouvin looked well in his fancy waistcoat, peg-topped trousers, and canary-colored gloves, as if he had to compete with the paintings.

Auguste bowed formally, and Barnouvin tried to explain about Marie, "I was dreadfully distressed to hear about her fatal illness. I was very fond of—"

Auguste cut him short. "Do you like the picture?"

Barnouvin said, "No one can get through the exhibition without hearing about it. It's too bad. There are far better pictures here."

Degas said, "Yours?"

"What do you expect me to say—yours?"

Degas was amused. "Barnouvin, you are as vain as an art collector."

Barnouvin flared. "At least I wasn't afraid to exhibit."

Degas nodded. "Granted. It would be impossible to compete with your work, it is so sweet, clever, charming, and nauseating."

For a moment Auguste thought the two men would come to blows, or at least arrange a duel, for both were too aristocratic in manner to soil their hands. Then Barnouvin laughed harshly and said, "You're the expert, Degas. You copy Ingres with a fidelity worthy of a far better cause."

But Degas had turned his back on Barnouvin. Fantin-Latour was approaching with a flushed, irate Manet and a grinning Renoir. Renoir was enjoying the commotion, but Manet's fists were clenched. The crowd had melted away from the painting as if it sensed it was *his* work.

Fantin said to Manet in the hope of soothing him, "Degas likes it, and Rodin. Don't you?" he asked when they hesitated to answer.

Manet said bitterly, "They like my being reviled."

"Nonsense," said Fantin, "Courbet is reviled, and so is Delacroix, but that doesn't stop them."

Degas said, "There are a few things I do not care for in the picture, but you have accomplished some fine effects. The use of the nude in contrast to the dark background gives her a lovely luminous white."

Auguste said, "And she is real. Vividly real."

"Satisfied?" said Fantin, feeling a little better.

"No!" Manet shouted. "You were wrong, Fantin, to get me to exhibit here. I am ruined."

"Discussed, not ruined," said Fantin.

"Will they hang me next year, or after that?"

"You are incredible," said Degas. "You expect to go your own way, yet be accepted. It is not possible. The public is a great beast, *canaille*."

"And smells of the Salon," said Fantin, "which has its own stench."

"It is still the home of French art," cried Manet, "and without it, we are lost."

Degas asked, "Will you paint their way next year?"

Manet shrugged: why did he have to be tortured so? He simply wanted to be accepted, the Salon was *his* world—he was a man born and bred on the boulevards, at home in that world, unlike most of his contemporaries. But something kept happening to him. Inside his shell there was a secret self that kept forcing him to find his own vocabulary. It was not a matter of sincerity—he despised sincerity, for it made artists confuse morality with quality, but he no longer could be just charming or entertaining. It was as if two personalities were at war within him. It was even worse when he did not paint what he saw and felt.

Degas said, "Perhaps you shouldn't exhibit next year."

"No!" Manet cried. None of them were of any help. "I will exhibit next year, and any year I have a picture I care about."

"Then don't be ashamed," said Degas with surprising fervor. "If fame belongs to you, you will not be able to escape it," he added as if for him that was something to evade. "But we are not the tribunal, in any case. I like your painting. Sometimes I say to our friends when you are not around, 'What talent Manet has!' But that doesn't matter. El Greco did not think Michelangelo could paint. Your idol, Velázquez, was contemptuous of Raphael, yet you give Raphael the greatest compliment, you imitate him. So how can we judge? We are too close, too involved. Too lacking in faith, perhaps." Degas sighed. "Too anxious for a perfection we will never find. But if ever you get tired of this picture, I will be glad to hang it. Though," he added, unable to resist a touch of malice, "I should retouch it."

The others were quiet, arrested by Degas' awareness of what they were all thinking. Suddenly the gallery of the Institute was oppressive to Auguste: he prayed there would come a day when he would not have to depend on the Institute, or its child, the Salon, or anybody or any place, to have his work shown. Degas was right: how could someone else judge when most of creation was an act of faith? There was so much mediocrity and conventionality all around Manet's picture, while it caught the attention immediately with its clear tones, its luminous light, its superb design. They couldn't take that away from Manet, and yet his friend was so unhappy.

They stood there another minute, and then Manet said, "Perhaps you are right, Degas, but it is difficult to endure this abuse."

Fantin said cheerfully, "Soon this abuse will change to praise. With paintings like yours, we will destroy the Salon."

"I don't want to destroy the Salon!" shouted Manet. "I want to be exhibited where the most people will see me!"

"You're right," said Renoir, who had been silent up to now. "I wouldn't worry about being indecent, but how we can sell." Renoir, who rarely envied anyone, envied Degas and Manet, who did not have to wait for a buyer to be sure of their next meal. "Look about us! You can't expect a buyer to look at five hundred pictures. It is better to show in the Salon."

Manet asked, surprised, "There are that many pictures here?"

Degas said, "There are many bad pictures in Paris, *mon ami*," adding, "and some dreadful sculptors, too," with a sly glance at Rodin.

Auguste said with sudden resolution, "Renoir is right. We have to exhibit in the Salon whether we like it or not."

"And I am right," said Degas, "that it must not really matter."

"You are right," said Auguste, "and wrong. I wouldn't mix paint or clay for another person. No one will mix mine." Auguste's jaw grew firm. "We talk and talk, and some of it makes sense, but work makes more sense."

"Bravo!" cried Degas. "We have a laborer in our midst."

Auguste said, "And you sound as if you'd had dysentery last night."

Even Manet smiled at that: Degas' dyspepsia was a standing joke.

Auguste added, "One thing I've learned. Our work is our life, and we must make our order upon the world even if the world doesn't know we are here."

"Just the same," Manet cried with anguish, "there is so much commotion, they are likely to close this exhibition at once!"

But the others were telling themselves the Salon des Refusés wasn't too bad. They had to affirm this to give themselves the resolution to go on.

Degas went off with Manet, Fantin with Barnouvin, and Auguste with Renoir. It was an inevitable coupling, for each of them paired off with what they could afford.

Auguste and Renoir strolled along the Champs Élysées to the Arc de Triomphe. Between them they could afford only the cheapest bottle of wine, but neither, at this moment, could return to his impoverished room. They needed to have a citadel today, to feel at home with the real Napoleon, the conqueror, for they wanted to conquer Paris, too.

IV

His Majesty, the Emperor Napoleon III, did not close the exhibit, as the friends of the Café Guerbois had feared; but when he visited the Salon des Refusés and declared that the artistic level of the work was scandalous, vulgar, indecent, blasphemous, his denunciation aimed chiefly at Manet's picture, most of the artists involved declared that they would never again submit outside of the Salon. Napoleon III, who had a genius for changing his mind, was still proud that he had been magnanimous, but it was better to be decisive, and to denounce these artists was a fine way to be so. Thus he sanctified the Salon, certain he would be regarded as a great and impersonal ruler, only to be criticized for having allowed the Salon des Refusés in the first place. It made His Majesty very pessimistic about human nature. He wondered if it was really useful to encourage art.

V

Although Auguste was busier than he had thought he could ever be the next few months, working as an ornament maker, doing odd jobs as a cabinetmaker to support himself, to help his family, and to pay for his clay and occasional wine for Bibi, he modeled in a fury whenever he had the opportunity. It was always at night, when he was very tired, and this added to his difficulties.

Sculpture such as he was attempting now required great physical effort, and he felt he should practice it every day—if he didn't, his skill and technique and strength would vanish—yet such a schedule was impossible. Bibi was more irresponsible than ever, rarely about when he needed him. Many nights, trying to work from memory, he grew sleepy, his fatigue became irresistible, he lay down to relax a moment and fell asleep for the night, fully clothed, like a dead man. In the morning he was full of energy, eager to work, but he had to hurry off to his job, which he hated.

During these periods of rest, however, his constant thinking and feeling about Bibi impregnated him with a new spirit. The thought that this head must in some way personify Michelangelo permeated Auguste now. He studied pictures of Michelangelo when the Florentine was old. Bibi's skull was larger, which amused him, but the expression was the same: there was the imprint of misery, of age, and toil on both faces. And as this conception developed, he began to feel he knew Michelangelo; he read several biographies of the Florentine, including Vasari's, and returned to the sculpture in the Louvre and the Luxembourg Gardens. But there was nothing in Gothic sculpture to help him and he could not use the sharp ridge of the Romans nor the smoothly modeled plane of the Greeks. He had to disregard most of what he had learned in the studio, museum, cathedral, and library. This was the kind of face he had not seen anywhere in sculpture.

The nose was the axis on which this face had to be constructed. A mutilated face that had its own crucifixion. Features ravaged by striving. The forehead bent in, the beard bristly, the nose a ruin.

Then he felt he had it, and this eliminated everything else. He took the weekend off, although it could mean dismissal. He forced Bibi to pose four hours in a row, incredible for Bibi; he worked forty-eight hours without stopping. And now it was over. "The Man with the Broken Nose" had as much as he could give it.

He felt empty, despondent; the eyes were bleak, the mouth did not speak.

No one would bid for it, he thought, but he had to submit this head to the Salon. A year had passed since he had started Bibi. It had taken too long, he told himself. He needed a better model. One he could depend upon all the time. He carved his signature at the base of the head, his first signature: A. *Rodin*.

CHAPTER 9

"The Man with the Broken Nose" was rejected by the Salon of 1864 as being grotesque. Auguste was deeply disappointed; this was the first head that had pleased him, and he decided not to do any more heads.

He was carving the ornaments of the Gobelins Theater, on the avenue des Gobelins, focusing on the caryatids and foliage of the façade, hoping they would not look just ornamental and decorative, although the orders of the architect—who was determined to outdo Bernini—stressed curlicues and frills, when he saw a handsome young woman approaching.

It was a lovely spring morning, when Paris was at its best, and he stopped suddenly to stare at her. Unlike most Frenchwomen, who were sallow-skinned and short, she was tall and rosy-cheeked and looked freshly scrubbed. He liked the simplicity yet determination with which she moved. He knew she was a working girl because of her dark blue dress and bonnet, but she walked with distinction. He was certain there was nothing of the servant in her. Her carriage was amazing, and she carried her head with such an erect and statuesque pride he had to model it.

"Mademoiselle," he said as she passed him, "may I?" He hesitated, not sure how to express his wish.

She paused, not intending to answer, but caught by his intensity, it seemed beyond the usual flirtatious proposal.

He said hurriedly, "Mademoiselle, what a fine walk you have!"

This was different, she thought, she was proud of her walk. She said with dignity, "I come from Lorraine, from Joan of Arc's province." Then suddenly she was the peasant girl, asking suspiciously, "Why are you interested in my walk?"

"I'm an artist." He pointed to the figures he was ornamenting. He hoped she understood that they were not his design. "Can't you see?"

"An artist? You don't look like an artist." He wore a workingman's blue blouse and baggy trousers and looked like a laborer.

"I'm a sculptor."

"Oh!" She stared at him as if he were something strange indeed, as if she had never seen a sculptor before. "That's a queer life, isn't it?"

"Sometimes. What do you do?"

"I'm a seamstress. But I'm going to be a milliner on the rue Richelieu someday. I'm very good with a needle."

He sighed. "C'est magnifique."

"What? Being able to sew well?"

He was thinking of her figure. Despite the clothes that covered her from her fingertips to the end of her toes, she was built like a Venus, a buxom peasant Venus. And such pointed breasts! Were they natural? he wondered.

She decided that he was trying to make a fool out of her, and she started to walk away. Suddenly he moved after her, blocking her way. In this burst of energy he was impressive, she thought, with his thick chest and broad shoulders, a bull of a young man, although he was hardly any taller than she was. And she liked his strong aquiline features, the high cheekbones, the searching blue-gray eyes, his heavy reddish-brown hair down to the neck, his long vital nose, the almost harsh jaw. He reminded her of a cliff she had desired to climb as a child but had been afraid to try. Yet he was very much the man, she thought guiltily, and hoped she would be forgiven what she was desiring. She asked, "What do you want?"

"Mademoiselle, would you pose for me?"

"Pose? How?"

"As you are. I want to do your head." He was certain suddenly that she was a virgin. How could he tell her that he could not pay her? "Then we can have coffee and *croissants*, or wine if you prefer."

"Where?"

"My studio, on the quai Voltaire." She looked properly impressed, as he had hoped, and he added, "Just your head. You have a fine head." He verified his first impression, standing face to face. She had a fine long nose, wide regular cheekbones, a firm resolute chin and jaw, large brown eyes that shone as she spoke, and hair that was thick, yet silky and dark, which she wore in a long braid. He could imagine her running through the fields, wading joyously in a country stream. "Do you like the quai Voltaire?"

"It is a nice neighborhood."

"I can meet you after work. We can have dinner before, if you like."

Ordinarily she would have walked away then. She was a good country girl, in Paris only a few months, but he was more interesting than any other man she had met, yet he did not put on airs like most Parisians and there was a shyness in him that was reassuring.

He asked, "What time should I call for you?"

"No! No!" She would lose her job. "Meet me here."

"At seven?"

"At eight." *Mon dieu*, she needed an hour to run to her room, on the nearby rue Jeanne d'Arc, to prepare for the evening.

"What do they call you?"

"I was baptized Marie Rose Beuret, but they call me Rose."

"I prefer Rose," he said decisively. "I'm Auguste Rodin. I will be waiting for you."

II

Auguste was prompt, and when Rose did not appear at eight he was sure she would not come. But when she did, a half hour late, he took her straight to the studio. Rose longed to eat first, she was famished, and Auguste had not said a word about how well she looked; there was an urgency in him that made him impatient and domineering. He took her forcefully by the arm and led her to the studio on the quai Voltaire with a vigor she could not resist.

The studio was in the front of a fine old stone building, and Rose

could see the Seine and Notre Dame from the windows. She had no
chance to admire them; he lit the stove and gas lamp at once and
ordered her to sit.

Rose was surprised by the disorder and concerned about the dirt.
The only place that was orderly and clean was where he worked.
There was just one piece of sculpture in the large studio, the head
of an old, very ugly derelict in the corner, so ugly it made her shiver;
everything else was easels, paints, stands, palettes, brushes, pictures,
and other painting equipment. She was upset by the lack of sculpture. Suddenly she felt deceived. She rose abruptly to depart, crying,
"This isn't your studio!"

"I use it. It is the same thing." He pushed her back into the chair.

"I can't stay. You've lied."

"No, I haven't. Lecoq allows me to use this whenever I want."

"Who is Lecoq?"

"A painter, but he doesn't paint any more."

"Why?"

Would she never stop squirming! "He teaches. He says to sell is
too hard."

"Is he well known?"

"Yes, yes! Look, will you please keep still?"

"Then why do you continue? You say he is well known, yet he
cannot sell."

"You are a very poor model." He glared at her with sudden disgust.

"I'm hungry."

"Fine. It will give your expression more feeling. And you will
enjoy your dinner more afterward." He had to make sure first that
she would be a good model. When, however, Rose continued to
fidget, he offered her wine and soggy bread left over from Bibi, which
he kept for emergencies.

Rose hesitated over the wine and turned up her nose at the bread.
But he encouraged her to talk about picnics her family had taken,
and he pretended to listen attentively as he sketched her over and
over, and gradually she relaxed. The talk of food, the memories of
growing up, his seeming to share them—every so often he broke in
with a few words about the picnics his family had enjoyed—made her
feel more at home. She took on a simple gravity that reminded him
of Marie.

Suddenly Auguste was stricken with guilt. He had been too harsh. He sought to make her comfortable, placing a cushion behind her back. He told her that she was very pretty, that she did remind him of Joan of Arc.

From then on the modeling went better. Rose was no longer afraid, and her posing improved. And finally he took her out to eat. It was quite late, and he ordered very little, and she did also, wanting to please him, although she was very hungry. Then Auguste looked confused, as if he wished she had ordered more, yet was grateful that she had been considerate of his sparse purse.

III

The next few weeks she posed for him regularly. There was no flirtation. They did not seem in tune except when she posed. But Auguste was pleased with the way she was developing a discipline and character.

Thus he had a moment of terror when she said one night that she had finished. He felt trapped. What was he going to do about this girl? It was true that he had just lost his temper with her, when she had stirred at the wrong time, but she should understand, she should be more responsible—he was on the verge of getting her mouth. Yet now she made him feel like a bully. But if he was going to model her accurately, there was no time for politeness. If she would only sit down! When she sat properly, everything came together!

He felt desperate as she started for the door. She was a trouble-maker and he ought to let her go, but somehow the alternative was worse, and he mumbled, "I'm sorry." She paused, but she did not return to the modeling stand until he added hurriedly, "Of course I am, *ma petite amie.*"

Rose knew he meant that only as a sop, but she was pleased, though still bewildered. It was strange, he took such pains with her head and virtually none with her. And no matter how she praised the head, he retorted, "It is not good enough."

One evening she could no longer endure being treated so coldly and she stated, "Auguste, you must take one day off. You said you love picnics. Why can't we make a picnic this Sunday, and if it is warm, go swimming?"

He regarded her as if she were insane and said, "I cannot swim."

"Why not?" In the country everyone could swim.

"Do poor people know how to do anything?" he said somberly.

"I still want to take a day off this Sunday," she said. He had to treat her as a woman, at least once, or she could no longer endure this.

"We will go," he stated, "when I finish."

"You will never finish."

"It will be over soon."

"Never, never," she moaned, and started to weep.

"Don't you realize that when I finish you'll look like a queen?"

"No, I won't," Rose said between her tears. "I'm a seamstress and I'll always look like a seamstress."

"Rosette, look at the head. It is almost finished."

She straightened up, it was the first real endearment Auguste had used. He ran his fingertips over her eyes—his powerful fingers, drying her tears with a tenderness she had not known he was capable of.

"You do like me, Auguste?"

"Yes, yes, I do." All at once he longed to kiss her. But he was puzzled by his feelings toward her. He was certain he did not love her, yet there was a pain and a loneliness in him when she was away that surprised him. He could feel Rose waiting for him to caress her. She had such a fine body, as fine a body as he had ever seen, it was apparent even under the proper clothes she always wore, but if he went any further she would possess him. She would be unable to keep sex independent of love.

"Auguste, will you take me out Sunday?"

"Yes." He decided that he must stop seeing her as soon as he finished the head.

IV

Auguste took Rose to the Luxembourg Gardens the following Sunday. She was pleased, although she would have preferred Fontainebleau or Versailles, where she had never been, but he insisted on the Luxembourg Gardens. He said he had to show her the statuary there, that it was the best outdoor statuary in Paris; he also had to be near the studio, in case he wanted to work later. But for Rose it was enough to have Auguste close and treating her as a woman, not a model.

She tried very hard to be gay. It was a lovely June Sunday, with the kind of clear blue sky that Auguste called a painter's sky. The mild sun encouraged leisurely strolling. She liked the air of Luxembourg, it was peaceful and relaxed. She admired the stately elms, the sturdy chestnut trees, the cultivated gardens laden with flowers. And the couples sitting on the benches arm in arm, the tender wistfulness of those who were alone, the many mothers and nursemaids and children made her so aware of love.

He refused to sit and revel in this enchantment. He insisted on showing her every piece of statuary in the spacious gardens, and it seemed to her there were thousands: Neptunes, Dianas, Queens of France, poets, artists, statesmen. He was captivated by the fountains of the Médicis, and they bored her; she had never heard of Marie de Médicis, for whom the Luxembourg had been built.

So much *bric-à-brac*, she thought, but to complain would be folly.

Gradually her gaiety evaporated. She felt caught in a snare. He was speaking about the Parthenon, someday he must visit it, and she did not know what he was talking about. As they stood before a profusion of lilies, Rose asked in desperation, to return the conversation to a subject she could understand, "Are your parents alive? You never talk about them."

"What is there to talk about?"

"Don't you like them? I like mine." Rose, just turned twenty-one, missed her parents very much, indeed at this moment wished she were back with them in her native Lorraine, where she would not feel so lost.

"Like?" Auguste shrugged. He pointed to a statue of Venus nearby. "Isn't she beautiful?"

Rose felt something seething within him, ready to surge forth, as he absorbed the naked statue with his senses. Yet if she said she was upset by the brazenness of the body he would be offended. All at once she wished she were on the rue de Rivoli or the Champs Élysées, where everybody was properly dressed and she would not have to feel apologetic about her ignorance.

He asked angrily, "You don't like the statuary?"

The sun was in flood and drenched her with its warmth and she felt chilled. She ventured, "Does your father like it?"

He laughed harshly. "Papa likes when I make francs."

"Isn't he proud of your being a sculptor?"

"Proud? He thinks he is the best friend I have. He says I will never make a franc as a sculptor."

"What about your mother?"

"Mama? She lives behind a black veil now. She prefers the plaster virgins." He kicked the pebbles underfoot irritably.

"You see them, don't you?"

"Oh yes, I drop in on them about once a week. They live nearby." She longed to ask why he hadn't taken her to meet them, but didn't dare.

"Papa is having trouble with his eyes—we have a tendency to weak eyes in the family—and he's had to retire on half pay. Now that he has nothing to do, he has become a critic. He says things are going badly in France, one military adventure after another with Napoleon the Third, but then things are going badly everywhere, he says cheerfully. 'Look at Russia,' he tells me, 'revolutionary threats, fools, freeing the serfs, and the United States torn in half with civil war.' Papa says, 'They're fools, too, like the Russians, to think they can end slavery.' But Papa assures me that I'm young, I'll survive it."

"Does he really dislike your work?"

"Papa?" Auguste laughed. "He has a great ignorance of art."

We both have, she thought fearfully, and changed the subject. She suggested, "As a Parisian you must have known many women."

"Many!"

"Cocottes?"

He said sarcastically, "I've had hundreds of loves, mistresses, ma amie."

"Hundreds?"

"More," he said with a flourish of his hand. "Every statue I've started, every statue I've admired, was a mistress."

"Oh!" She laughed almost hysterically with relief.

He stared at her with an intent expression, then suddenly swept her broad-brimmed flowered hat off her head. "You mustn't hide your face."

"Do you like it?" she said even as she disliked herself for having to ask.

"You have good features, an excellent complexion."

She took his hand, and he almost let her hold it. Then as if this were a kind of capitulation, he walked out of her reach.

She was just about to walk away in her embarrassment when he said, "Now you are expressive because you are upset. Why can't you be so expressive when you pose?"

"You are impossible!" she cried.

"Rosette! Eve was a statue until God breathed life into her."

She had been raised as a religious daughter, a devout Catholic, but as she saw the grave sensuality of Auguste's expression—he was regarding her now as if her physical beauty were an act of divine will—she became confused.

"Rosette, no wonder I've been unable to finish your head. You've never shown me your real expression before. Come, we are near the studio. If we hurry, we can get there before dark, while the light is still good. I must get you with the sun on your face." He took her by the arm, firmly yet gently, as if now he must not harm her, she had become precious, and led her swiftly to the studio.

A marvelous animation had come to Auguste. There was still sun in the studio and he sat her in it, although this was contrary to his usual practice. She was a perfect Mignon. And what a virginal skin! It took the light so well! She must be a wonderful nude. Even in her clothes it was evident that her breasts were full and so were her buttocks, a body made to serve. He modeled playfully and quickly; his fingers moved briskly and of their own accord. To have finally caught her this way—he felt like a Napoleon who had achieved a *coup d'état*. And she sat so well, quietly yet alive, as if she realized the virtue of the moment. It was commendable. It gave her such a fine look. She was full of ignorance, but she was a fine model; she made him feel in flood tide with the plenitude and power of life.

Rose wondered if modeling was his only form of sensuality, yet even now he gave her an extraordinary sense of health and well-being. She tried to respond, and felt her desire for him growing.

When he finished capturing the expression that had fascinated him, time had been forgotten. There were shadows in the studio, the sun was gone, he could barely see her, but he had her lifelike now. He was closer to the spirit of a Mignon. He leaned over to kiss her, to thank her, and then he realized the neck was unfinished.

It was her foul taste, he thought irately, having to wear clothes that covered every inch of her body, even on this warm day. He didn't kiss her.

Instead he ripped open her dark blue blouse. She hurried to button it and he halted her. She had such a fine bosom if she would only show it. And now the neck was better. Then he saw her staring at his muscular arms, bare to the elbow, his own chest—he had loosened his shirt to feel free and cool. Her skin was pink with rushing blood. It was wonderful. The neck was better, not quite done, but better. He reached out to unbutton her to the waist, to get her precisely, and suddenly they came together, she desiring him even more than he wanted her.

Part of him remained detached, and he realized that she was an innocent, struggling toward him yet not knowing quite what to do. His bad luck, he thought, a virgin. But he had suspected as much; it was his own fault. And bad luck, *mon dieu!* he had all the bad luck, but they were committed.

Then even as she gave awkwardly, she was so passionate her blunders were forgotten. And he had been right about her breasts and buttocks—they were full, firm, splendid, quite splendid.

Afterward Rose was stricken with shame. At the moment of culmination she had been in ecstasy, but now she was full of guilt. She knelt on the floor, praying to God for forgiveness. She was grateful it was dark and he hadn't seen her naked body—she hadn't let him turn on the gaslight, he mustn't see her naked body, no man ever had, though his powerful hands had embraced all of her. Then she remembered this was not even his studio.

She stated this and he replied, "Lecoq never comes at night."

"Even so, I cannot return here now."

"Well, you can't go to my room. It is too small, poor."

"I won't come here."

"But we must finish the head."

All at once she felt like a fool. He did not love her, he only wanted to model her. He was an artist and artists were insane. Rose dressed hurriedly, refusing his help. Several buttons had been ripped off her blouse but it did not matter, she would manage somehow. She was on the verge of tears, but she would not give him the satisfaction. She refused to let him walk her home, to make an appointment for another sitting or for dinner. The instant she was dressed, she fled.

CHAPTER 10

Auguste told himself he did not care, but as he sought to work on Rose's head the next few evenings from memory—his moment of satisfaction with the bust had evaporated long ago—he minded very much. He went to the Café Guerbois in the hope of feeling better, it was his first visit in weeks, and only Fantin and Renoir were there. They were discussing the Salon, as usual. Fantin asked, "Voilà, where have you been?"

"Working. Modeling."

"Always working," said Renoir. "No one works harder than I do, but I take some time out to eat and drink."

"I've been very busy."

"A girl?" Renoir smiled knowingly.

Auguste denied that strongly. Rose, even for Renoir who had grown up in lower-class poverty, would be a fish out of water. A whore was a whore, but you expected more from a nice girl like Rose.

Renoir said, "You must have been jilted, you are so edgy."

"The head I'm doing, it's not finished."

Fantin asked, "Are you doing the head for the Salon?"

"Naturally. Where else can I exhibit?" growled Auguste, prepared to quarrel with Fantin, who was always denouncing the Salon.

"Rodin's right," said Renoir. "It is the stream we have to swim in."

Fantin said, "You are accepted by the Salon and everything is forgotten."

"Who wants to be political?" Renoir asked wearily.

Fantin said, "You destroyed the picture that was accepted."

"Afterward," said Renoir. "I didn't like it then. I realized it was academic, unnatural, too dark. I wanted to be accepted by the Salon, so I painted in the style of the Beaux Arts. But I was living in the past and I didn't like that."

Auguste said somberly, "I don't like anything I'm doing these days."

Renoir laughed. "It's a girl. I never work well when I'm unhappy."

Auguste said, "It shouldn't matter, being happy, unhappy."

"But it does," said Renoir. "It always does for people like us."

"And not for me?" said Fantin.

"You're different," said Renoir. "You, Degas, Manet, still have some of the *ancien régime* in you."

Fantin said indignantly, "Why, I'm the one who is most against the Salon!"

"That's why," said Renoir. "You have to *prove* you are against them."

Auguste sighed. "Do you feel so bad when things go wrong?"

"Worse," said Renoir. "What you need is a girl who makes no demands. Then you'll feel better, your work will improve, you might even make the Salon."

Auguste, grateful to Renoir for this advice, left soon afterward for a *maison d'amour* on the boulevard des Batignolles, a very good one, which had been recommended to him by Dalou. But when he reached the fashionable brothel he turned away. How could Rose have been so impudent? When she walked up the boulevards, how fine, how statuesque she looked!

The next day Auguste waited for Rose where he had first met her. It was quitting time; she always went home this way. His trousers and blouse were painstakingly clean. His long hair was neatly barbered. He felt anxious in a way he had never felt before.

Quitting time passed, and she did not appear. Perhaps she was so angry with him that she really had to avoid him. Just as he was sure of this, morose, pessimistic, certain she would not appear, he saw her approaching.

Then she saw him. She hesitated as if to turn away, but when he hurried toward her she ran toward him. They met halfway in the street, almost hit by a carriage going by, but unheeding. He took her outstretched hands, his pleasure obvious. But he could not take her to Lecoq's studio or to his own room. He tried to explain, stumbling, feeling clumsy, and she said, "Why don't you get your own studio?"

"I can't afford it."

"I'm alone," she said. "I could help."

"It's impossible."

"And if—when you sell my bust, you can pay me back."

"No, no." It wasn't the money or even pride, but if they lived together there would be responsibilities, it would be dangerous.

Rose seemed to read his mind. "I'll stay only until you finish the head, and you will be able to work on it as much as you like." She prayed to the Virgin to forgive her this lie, but she loved him very much. "I'll leave the moment the head is done. If you want."

"You wouldn't have to leave," he said, thinking he would like to do a full-length figure of her before their affair ended. "Not until we feel like it."

"Yes, Auguste. And if it doesn't work out, you would still have your own studio and the head."

He wondered if she was actually so guileless.

"You should have a studio. Then you really will be a sculptor."

"How do you know?" he asked suspiciously.

"Haven't you been telling me that this is what all sculptors need?"

She was right. And he could break off whenever he wanted. He was the man, and she was entering this situation of her own free will. Yet still he hesitated, wondering what it would really cost.

"I have a hundred and twenty francs saved. I haven't had to spend any money since we met," she said when she saw the look of surprise on his face. This was a small fortune in his present circumstances. "Here!" She pulled a bound handkerchief from her bosom and handed it to him. "A hundred and twenty. Count them."

Auguste was shaken. No one had offered him this much money for anything; on her skimpy pay she must have gone without many meals to save this.

Rose thrust it into his trembling hand. "It fits, see!" she cried. "It's a good omen. You'll be able to get a fine studio."

"On a hundred and twenty francs? It will be a stable." But then she looked so hurt, he hurried to add, "It is very nice of you to offer."

"It will be even nicer if you accept."

Auguste knew he should still refuse, but to have his own place to work—what a luxury! Then he would do good work, his own work, and once she got over her virginity many things would improve, even her posing. He said, "Remember, this is just a loan."

"Just a loan," she repeated with a cheerful smile as her heart sank.

Auguste started to walk away, absorbed in the thought of having his own studio, of finding it at once. Rose didn't say a word, stricken, standing as if paralyzed, and suddenly he saw this. He stopped abruptly, aware that he had been preoccupied, absent-minded, and said, "*Merci*, Rose."

"It is my pleasure." She could not keep the hurt out of her voice.

"You are upset."

"No, I'm not." That would spoil everything. "Why should I be?"

"Have you had dinner?" He was too excited to be hungry, but she must be.

"No."

"Come. We'll eat. Oh, not with this," he said, putting her handkerchief with the francs in his pocket. "I've saved several francs for us. We'll celebrate. With sausages and wine." Auguste, for the first time, linked his arm in her arm and escorted Rose to an inexpensive but good restaurant.

II

Auguste did not consult Rose about a studio. He went to his friends for advice when he found an old stable on the rue Le Brun, near where he and Rose worked. It was between the avenue des Gobelins and the boulevard St. Marcel, also close to where he had been born and had grown up.

Auguste stood at the entrance of the ex-stable, his mind already made up, though he knew all its disadvantages, while Fantin, Degas, Renoir, Dalou, and a new friend, the husky, good-looking, broad-faced Claude Monet, surveyed the premises. He expected them to be critical, but they might also make useful suggestions.

Degas studied the ancient roof with its many holes, the mildewed walls, the cracked windows, the doors that did not fit, the floor that was part earth and part cement, the interior, drafty and bone-chilling, yet spacious and light, and said, "It has size, if you don't get pneumonia."

Fantin said, "Don't be catty. It is dangerous, Degas. Rodin, you'll get your death of cold. Your fingers will freeze in no time."

Auguste said, "I'll put a stove in. To the ceiling."

"You'll need several stoves," Fantin replied. "And even then, it will be very cold. Do you really think you should take it?"

"I wish I had my own studio," Monet said.

Fantin said, "But you are always saying we must paint in the open air."

Monet said, "I stress that because we have become prisoners of our studios. We sacrifice color and light when we paint inside. Color —all colors vary and change and are transformed by the quality and intensity of light. But some work should be done in the studio."

Degas said, "Monet, it is time you learned that. Even our best landscapists, Millet, Diaz, Corot, don't really work in the open air. Whatever notes or sketches they make outdoors, they always complete their landscapes in their *ateliers*." Degas turned to Rodin as if that settled Monet. "Rodin, do you really think you can work here?"

"I have to. I've already moved in."

Degas asked angrily, "Then why did you ask us for advice?"

"You can keep me from being cheated."

"Whatever you are paying, you are being cheated."

Monet said, "It has no conveniences, but he will be able to work."

Degas cried out, "With mittens on his hands, smoke in his throat, and icy feet. This is no better than a cemetery plot. He is mad."

"It is not that bad," said Monet. "It has a high ceiling and good light."

"But the air," said Renoir. "It is so ugly, how can you believe in it?"

Monet said, "One does not have to fall in love with what he sees. The vital thing is to paint truthfully what we see, as *we see* it."

Renoir retorted, "*Mon dieu*, if what I painted didn't please me, I wouldn't do it. I can't bring myself to do a subject unless I'm happy with it."

"In either case," said Degas, "do you expect Rodin to dig up clay and hand it over as alabaster?"

"He will have his own studio," Monet said stubbornly.

"Of course," said Degas. "Then it doesn't matter if he fails."

Monet declared, "He still won't have to depend on anyone else." Monet was bitter because so far, no matter how he sought to regulate his life, he had been unable to afford his own studio. Rodin was lucky. The trouble with Degas was Degas thought he was an artist even when he was not painting.

Auguste said, "And I don't have to wait for a miracle to get a place to work. And I have a room next door. That is convenient."

Dalou promptly investigated and reported, "And a double iron bed. And a small place to cook. Who is she?"

"It is my studio," Auguste replied strongly.

"Certainly," said Dalou. "But who is she? A *Provençale?*"

Auguste did not answer.

Dalou asked, "Don't you want to share her with others?"

Renoir said, "Maybe it is none of your business."

Dalou ignored him. "You should see the room. No furniture except this old iron double bed, a chest of drawers, and no chairs except two stiff-backed ones. Nothing comfortable, nothing pleasant. What are you, Rodin, an ascetic? It is enough to discourage the most passionate *amour.*"

Auguste said curtly, "I don't like soft furniture, particularly chairs one can lounge in. It discourages work."

Dalou prodded. "But suppose the girl was La Dame aux Camélias?"

"No," said Auguste. "I don't like the play. It is sentimental slop."

"Yes," said Renoir. "Quite stupid. Dumas is, indeed, a man of genius to make us believe it. Rodin, are you still working for the octopus?"

Auguste nodded.

"*Mon dieu!*" shouted Dalou. "You are secretive!"

Auguste shouted back, "What is there to talk about?"

Dalou said, "Your work."

"Being a decorator!" Auguste burst out. "Everything pretty, refined!"

"And nauseating," said Degas.

"Precisely," said Auguste. "I do nothing I believe in, nothing I care about. I do work in alabaster, and that is the trouble. I am tired of prettiness, of bodies that are impossibly slender, elegant, obvious. I can understand why Michelangelo preferred the male body. At least it is more difficult to make pretty, refined, elegant. But I must do things in quantity, and with polish. I have become the inheritor of the worst of the school of Fontainebleau. Everything must be *petite*, yet rounded. No individuality, no variety, no imagination, no heat. I have to be decorative, ornamental. I must be so polite, so civilized, there is no fire in any of it. The nudes are fit only for eunuchs."

Renoir smiled sadly and said, "I know what you mean. *Mon ami*, I've had the same education. When I was fourteen I was painting cups and saucers by the dozens *à la Boucher*. At sixteen, when I graduated, I was ordered to paint porcelain *à la Chardin*. Then I became a painter of fans in the style of Madame Pompadour. By the time I was twenty I was regarded as a great success, I could do window shades with decorative figures from anybody: Poussin, Boucher, Fragonard. I was superb. They were the most beautiful window shades you ever saw. When I quit, having saved enough to study at the Beaux Arts, my boss was stunned. He said I was an idiot, that he was beginning to sell those window shades to some of the best boudoirs in Paris. He said if I learned to paint on canvas I would be ruined, a failure, I would lose all my skill with window shades. But I had to quit, to learn how to do nudes I like. Although I'll never learn at the Beaux Arts."

Auguste added, calmer now, "That's why I need this studio, no matter what the disadvantages."

Degas laughed cynically. "Besides, who cares what we do? And does it matter what we do?"

Fantin said, "It does matter. Manet is showing a new picture soon, 'Olympia.' I've seen it in his studio. It is a new thing in nudes."

Degas said, "Without legs as well as arms?"

"With a body we can all recognize. Even you, Degas. A wonderful nude."

Degas regarded him caustically. "You like everybody."

"I do not," insisted Fantin. "I don't like Bouguereau, Couture, Gérôme, Cabanel, Chassériau."

"You are still too generous to be a good artist," said Degas.

"And sometimes I don't like Degas," said Fantin.

"That hardly makes you a connoisseur," said Degas. "Sometimes I don't like Degas either."

Auguste led them out of the stable. He was tired of all the disputing, and he had found out what he wanted to know. They had forced him to clarify his own thoughts: this studio was better than no studio, whatever the discouragements. And he didn't want them to meet Rose, who was due soon.

Monet told Auguste, "Although I grew up in Le Havre, I was born near here," and Auguste grew interested and replied, "So was I."

They compared notes, and were pleased when they discovered not only that they had been born within a short distance of each other, they had been born only two days apart. They were amused to learn that their fathers had gone to the same Mairie of the same arrondissement on the same day to make the declaration of their births. Auguste and Claude Monet forgot everything else as they went off to see if the Town Hall was still standing.

III

Lecoq was displeased when Auguste told him of the new studio. He stared at the unfinished female head Auguste was carrying out and said, "It's a poor reason."

"Don't you like the bust?"

"It's not the head. It's the girl."

Auguste looked blank.

Lecoq said, "I know all about Mademoiselle. It's no secret. Is anything a secret from a concierge?"

"Then why didn't you say something?"

"What was there to say? Would that have stopped you?"

Auguste felt the blood rushing to his head as he saw Lecoq's obvious disapproval. Lecoq was right.

"It's not your moving out I object to," said Lecoq, although that was not completely true—he minded very much, but he must not admit that. "It's the way you are moving. Once you become obligated to Mademoiselle, the damage could be irreparable."

"I'll make my own decisions," Auguste insisted.

"Your mind will, but what about your sense of responsibility, your conscience? Oh, you can shrug them off now, but you are different from most artists. True, nothing comes ahead of your sculpture, but you do feel your obligations."

"Maître, I need a girl."

"A girl, not an obligation. She's wrong for you."

"I'm not marrying her."

"That doesn't lessen the obligation for one like you."

"She is a good model."

"And a good cook, housekeeper, and perhaps even a good mistress. But now you owe her something, and as time goes by the interest is compounded. Eventually your primitive instincts toward her, satisfied, will be buried, but she will be there, and no matter how much you desire a change you will remember how she helped you. Then you will discover that gratitude can be more demanding than anything else."

"I'm grateful to you."

"Yes." Lecoq looked severe. "It's dangerous." He had been playing a paternal role and Auguste, out of gratitude, had acquiesced. "But you owe me nothing, Rodin, nothing!"

"I owe you a great deal. But I—" Auguste stuttered to a halt.

"It comes hard, doesn't it?" snapped Lecoq. "It will be even harder when you want to leave her."

"Suppose I don't want to leave her."

"You will. Have you introduced her to your friends? Family? Me?"

"You're offended."

"No—except when you don't tell the truth, as now."

"She's a peasant."

"And your family?"

"I also like privacy."

"Splendid." When Auguste did not move, Lecoq cried out, "Go, go. I've served my purpose."

"I hoped you would be my friend."

"Well, what do you want?"

"You're so angry."

"The time to worry is when I'm not angry."

"I would like to keep in touch, *maître*."

"I'm not moving. The key to the door will be where it always was."

IV

Auguste took Rose to the stable studio the next day. She was appalled by the dirt and draftiness and disorder, and for a moment she felt her love was a curse. Auguste did not ask her whether she liked it, but assumed it was satisfactory. He showed her where he would work, where she would pose, and she could not object. The mere sight of Auguste, the way he moved, the strength of his voice, were sufficient to make her surrender to him.

She moved in with a small trunk she had brought from Lorraine. She arranged the bedroom primly, but she was certain the concierge knew they were not married. It lessened the joy of being with Auguste. He stood at the window, filled with the pride of proprietorship, and she felt so tired, so weak, so lacerated by his principles. The plaster that cemented them seemed about to dissolve; she felt on the verge of collapsing. But the thought of breaking off was even worse. When he said, "We will improve the studio," she forced a smile and replied, "Yes, we will make it a home."

He looked at her suspiciously, but as she made a place for him to work he gave her a thank-you kiss. The ugly stable suddenly shone with a bright light, and she resolved to make everything shine, whatever the effort.

V

And still Auguste's work went on at a merciless pace: making ornaments for the façades of buildings, gardens, fountains; doing small decorative figures for household use that were six-, eight-, ten-inch copies of Cellini and Clodion, Donatello and Michelangelo, polished, shiny, pretty, and without the character of the originals. He also did Gothic carving and ornamented cabinets to earn extra francs. His hands grew stronger, more fluid; his plastic skill was such that now he could ornament anything. But discontent gnawed at him and he became nervous, edgy. The more he worked on other people's work, the more he craved to do his own, and that was becoming more difficult instead of less.

Housekeeping was Rose's god. She lived to make the new quarters a home. She cooked and cleaned and made sure his tools were where he could lay his hands on them instantly—he was always losing them without her—and kept the cloths wet on the unfinished clay models. She discovered that he liked cabbage soup with pieces of pork and fish, and she tried to have it as often as possible, for it was also cheap. She was determined to make him happy. She smiled even when she did not feel gay, and sang when he wasn't working; when he sculpted, all noise was forbidden. She was pleased when he was pleased.

He resented her being happy, it made him feel he ought to be also, and he wasn't. He was still dissatisfied with her head. She was a poor, stupid model, he decided. Nothing seemed worth doing.

In this disgusted mood Auguste was brooding about the studio one Sunday. He had risen with the sun, unable to sleep, and he was angry that Rose had not stirred—didn't she care how he felt? That he was hungry? He knew he was being unreasonable, but he liked being unreasonable, as he felt the world was to him, and finally, unable to contain himself any longer, he burst into the bedroom.

Rose was emerging from her nightgown, and as she saw him instinctively she covered herself with virgin modesty. Even their moments of love she had insisted must be in the dark, for she was still unable to let him see her naked—and here it was broad daylight!

Furious, Auguste ripped her hands away from her breasts. Then suddenly he paused. He had been about to throw her out, she was no good, but now he knew what was wrong with the bust. It should be done with her hair down, as she was now, natural. He grabbed her by the arm and pulled her to the model stand. She looked bewildered, began to cry—had he gone crazy? it was immodest to see her this way, with her hair down.

"Stand still!" he shouted when she went to retreat.

"All my life—" she whimpered.

"You'll stay here and keep your hair down or get out!"

Rose looked terrified, thinking she should flee home for salvation, she felt very sorry for herself, but Auguste was working as he hadn't worked for weeks. She grew quiet, fascinated by the new aspect of the head.

Auguste was determined to make "Mignon" perfect at once.

Rose sat all day without food, rest, change, variation. Just as she was thinking that being a dutiful wife was too much, he halted with the first genuine smile she had seen in a long time.

He said, "Rosette, I have it. 'Mignon' is done."

She did not believe him. She sat there as one paralyzed.

"Don't you believe me?" He was indignant.

"I believe you." But still she sat as if turned to stone.

"Oh"—he glared at her—"you don't like the head. You never did."

"Auguste, I never said I didn't like her, except for the eyes. But it doesn't matter. I like to pose for you." What she meant was that as long as she posed he would not have any other models.

"How about dinner? Is there any food here?"

"Cabbage soup. Fish. A little Cointreau I've been saving for a celebration. Auguste, I do like the head. Why don't you put it in bronze?"

"Bronze casting is costly. And marble is even more expensive."

"Is that why you don't work in marble?"

"No one works directly in bronze or marble any more. Any mechanic can cast clay and plaster into bronze and marble, but it takes an artist to conceive and create the work. With clay I can do much with touch—alter, modify, add—but with marble, once I cut away I am forever committed. But if ever I have my work cast in marble, I'll supervise it, I'll touch it up, it will be my creation."

"I hope 'Mignon' is in marble someday," she said with sudden longing.

"She would be better in bronze. Marble would make her too pretty."

"You don't think I'm pretty?"

"No model is truly pretty to an artist," he declared, "unless she is worth doing in the nude."

VI

This refusal to pose in the nude was Rose's last refuge of innocence, but when he would not make love to her unless she did she could not hold out. She tried, but when a week passed with him lying coldly beside her it was as if she were suffering from a mortal deficiency. Finally she gave in.

Several Sundays after the completion of "Mignon," she was out of bed before him. She lit the stove, put the breakfast on, then sat. She wore her coat, but nothing else—without the coat she would have frozen. And when he entered the studio, looking for her—he was hungry—she stood up and let the coat fall at her feet. Naked, she was very white, standing as if in a trance, her eyes closed, on the verge of fainting.

She felt his touch, she was certain he was going to bring her to debauchery. Instead he said, "Straighten up. No, no, not stiff. You can move about. I prefer that you move, the body is more natural when it moves, and that will keep you warm."

Rose had to open her eyes then. A look of approval was spreading over his face as he saw that her figure was as splendid as he had thought.

"Pleased?" she whispered, finding it difficult not to cover her pubic patch and breasts with her hands.

"Hm . . ." Her breasts were full and firm, her buttocks perfect, and most important, her belly—which was often wrong even in young women—was just right, with just the slightest swelling. He felt like tying a blue ribbon around it to keep it exactly as it was. What a curve her belly had! He was astonished. But he shouldn't have been, he thought, in their coming together his touch, almost always infallible, his most treasured sense, had told him that she was beautifully formed. He said, "You have nothing to be ashamed of."

"But I've never done this before."

"I don't mean morally," he said sharply. "I mean your figure. You never really know a nude is good until she takes off all her clothes."

"I've taken care of myself."

"Yes, Rosette, and fortunately nature has taken even better care of you."

Auguste was sketching her while he spoke, as one might take notes, not seeking to capture her precisely but to suggest the figure to follow. Then he went at the clay, building the figure like an anatomist with a cadaver, sectioning, cutting, stripping, adding until he had established the body in its layers and functions. He worked tirelessly, assuming that rest was unworthy. She did not complain, sensing that the impression she made here was of vital importance.

Afterward he came to her with a new passion that awakened in her an intensity of emotion she had not known she possessed.

Work and love became their pattern the next few weeks, but there were moments when Rose was ashamed. Several times, not telling Auguste, she went to Mass to pray for forgiveness but she could not go to Confession.

As the figure, which he called "Bacchante," developed, his humor improved. Auguste still had not said he loved her, words she craved with all her heart, but he was eager to be with her.

The instant he had a free hour he insisted on having her pose.

CHAPTER 11

On a beautiful June day, when Rose was thinking that the weather was sublime, they must skip one Sunday of work and picnic, she thought she could be pregnant. One moment she was afraid to believe it, the next she wanted it to be true with an enormous yearning. Then when she went to a doctor to confirm her suspicions—without telling Auguste—and the doctor said she was pregnant, she was confused.

At the instant of certainty she longed to cry out with pure elation, "What a beautiful feeling!" but what would Auguste say? Her dread of his reaction stifled her happiness and pride. Yet as the doctor assured her that she was in perfect health and should give birth to a fine child, probably in January, she was filled with an immense longing for the child, whatever the consequences. This would be her triumph, if nothing else. Ever since Rose could remember, she had desired to be a mother. Then she was overwhelmed with bewilderment, and dreadfully lonely. She yearned so much to discuss this with another woman, but whom? Her own family was off in distant Lorraine; she still did not know Auguste's family, one night a week he went to visit them, without her; she had no friends, he hadn't introduced her to anyone, although she knew he went occasionally to the Café Guerbois to visit with his artist friends.

And however Rose's mind twisted, it came back to one overriding consideration: how would Auguste feel? Sometimes she thought he would feel triumphant; then she was certain he would be furious, he would throw her out or order her to get rid of the child and she couldn't. She toyed with the idea of going back to Lorraine, but that was impossible; she could not leave Auguste, not of her own accord, that was asking too much. Finally she decided to hide her pregnancy, although she knew this would be difficult. Auguste had not yet finished the "Bacchante," and when he modeled her he had the habit of caressing her contours to capture the right curves.

Rose got into the habit of posing with her belly held in, though she was afraid it would hurt the child within her and many times she had severe pain afterward. Then he scolded her for being too flat, saying, "The ideal Venus should be rounded. You mustn't pose. I've told you many times to be natural."

As the weeks passed, the pregnancy became more difficult to conceal. She could feel with her own hands the increase in the swelling —and his hands were so much more sensitive than hers.

What saved her for the moment was Auguste's absorption in his nude. He was determined to finish it for the Salon of 1866, for though "Mignon" had been rejected by the Salon of 1865, Manet's "Olympia," a nude, had become the discussion piece of the Salon of 1865. "Olympia" had created another scandal because Manet had dared to make his nude utterly realistic, not an idealized, mythological Venus. But despite the furor, or perhaps because of it, even Degas liked "Olympia," Renoir had been influenced to do nudes of his own, and Fantin felt triumphant—as if this vindicated both his praise of Manet and their opposition to the sterile standards of the Salon. Only Manet was unhappy, having no desire for the martyrdom descending upon him because he wished just to paint what he saw.

Auguste agreed with Manet. He had no desire for martyrdom, either, but what good were eyes if you painted or sculpted as others saw?

He sought to explain this one Sunday to Rose after having spent the previous evening at the Café Guerbois with Manet, Degas, Renoir, Fantin, and Dalou, but she only looked confused and disturbed. What was the matter with her these days? he wondered. She was so preoccupied! At least when he was absent-minded it was because of his work. But he must be patient with her, he told himself, she was ignorant and naïve in many ways. He tried again. "Rose, if this statue succeeds, I'll have a Venus to rival the 'Venus de' Medci.' "

" 'Venus de' Medici'?"

He could tell by the look in her eyes she didn't know what he was talking about. He said, growing irritated, "Don't you know anything about art?"

"I know who Michelangelo was, and Rembrandt," she said timidly, "and Fra Angelico. I saw copies of his pictures in church."

"Do you like their work?"

"I like Fra Angelico."

"And Michelangelo and Rembrandt? What about them?"

"Well, I don't know enough to say."

He pressed her, to justify breaking off, disgusted with her suddenly. "What about Delacroix?"

"Who is Delacroix?"

There was no communication here, he thought bitterly, but it was his own fault, he had known this from the start.

When she saw his anger, she said softly, "You mustn't ask me these questions. I'm not an educated woman." She could neither read nor write except to sign her name, but she loved him very much —indeed, more now that she carried his child. "If I sewed at home, would it disturb you?"

"What has that to do with the 'Venus de' Medici'?" he asked suspiciously.

Rose couldn't tell him that one of these days she would be unable to go to the shop. She said, "I could sew while you are modeling. Make more francs."

Auguste glared at her as if she were really an idiot. Imagine trying to capture the concept of a Venus with a needle in her hand! Suddenly he could not work. He sat down in a fury, staring at her.

"Forgive me, Auguste, for being such a poor model today, but I'm tired."

"I'm glad you are intelligent enough to explain that."

"Do I have to know about Michelangelo and Rembrandt and this other man, Delacroix?"

"No." He didn't want to admit this, but it was the truth. "Many models, most in fact, don't know anything about art. But you don't like being considered just a model."

"I'm not. I'm in love with you. Is that wrong?"

He shrugged.

"Are you in love with me?"

"Love is for people who adore Dumas. I prefer Balzac, and Baudelaire."

He was unfair, she thought, mentioning people she could not discuss. Suddenly she was ill with nausea. She had to run into the other room, and when he did not follow she was relieved although also hurt.

Auguste assumed that Rose was merely trying to attract his sympathy; he was certain that physically she was as sound as a horse.

He was sitting in the studio, wondering what to do about her, when she returned a few minutes later. She was pale but composed, and she said, "I can pose some more if you like."

"No, no," he started to say, then he paused. Now he knew what was wrong with the "Bacchante"—he had the belly wrong. "Wait a moment. Stand."

Rose stood, trying to control her trembling.

Auguste felt her stomach, then the "Bacchante." His frown grew. Her stomach was so developed. No wonder he could not get the "Bacchante" right. He stared at her and she burst out crying, and then he knew.

"It's true," she whispered.

"Are you sure?"

"Yes," she sobbed. "I went to a doctor."

"When is the child due?"

"January, probably, the doctor said."

"Six months. That's a long way off."

"Yes. You're glad, aren't you, Auguste?"

"Glad?" he shouted. "Did I ask for a child? Should I thank you? As it is, we can barely support ourselves." He was tempted to throw her out, but it was too difficult—she looked so helpless, wan, and it was his child, he was certain he was the only man she had known. But what to do? He didn't need any children, he didn't want any, not yet, it was a terrible struggle as it was for the two of them.

She asked hesitantly, "Could you tell your mother?"

"No. If I told anyone it would be my aunt Thérèse."

"Then you do want the child, *chéri*? After all?"

How could he tell her that he didn't work so hard out of choice? How much it hurt that he could not afford a comfortable bed? That he yearned to have a satisfactory home and studio, a luxury he had never known? And never would, he was certain now. But it was useless to complain. In this world it was all or nothing. It was one of the ancient and holy truths of this world. He had come from nothing, he would stay nothing. How could he want one more commitment? But she wouldn't understand. No one understood another's burdens and pain.

He said, "I'll talk to my aunt Thérèse. She'll know what to do."

II

Aunt Thérèse knew very well. She had had three children without being married. She had lost her prettiness, her hair had turned gray, her trim figure had shrunk, but she was still energetic and free in her thinking, and used to this kind of emergency. She said he must have the child and she wanted to meet Rose.

Aunt Thérèse and Rose got along at once. They talked woman talk that neither had ever talked to Auguste: what would be needed for the baby—Rose thought it would be a girl, girls ran in her family, but Aunt Thérèse was certain it would be a boy, she had three boys; what Rose should eat and wear; and some confidential things that they wouldn't let him hear.

He felt shut out, annoyed, but relieved by the way Aunt Thérèse managed everything. Aunt Thérèse made Rose's pregnancy sound so matter-of-fact his anxiety lessened. Yet he was still not at all sure he wanted the infant.

Walking Aunt Thérèse home afterward, he expressed these doubts.

His aunt paused on the boulevard St. Michel, where she had taken him strolling when he was a child, and replied, "Marriage is not a fixed, predictable thing. You never can tell how it will turn out."

"You never married, Aunt Thérèse."

"It was not my choice."

"You've managed."

"Not easily." She sighed. "It would have been better for my boys if they had had a father. I don't want you to make the same mistake."

"It would be a bigger mistake if I married her."

"I don't think so. She has good character."

"By becoming pregnant?"

"And you were not part of it, Auguste?"

He shrugged, as if to say that was the woman's problem.

"Besides, the way you are living, it is like being married."

"I am not married!" he said positively.

"You are living together. It is much the same thing."

"No, it is not. I can leave her whenever I want."

"Under these circumstances?"

"Other men do."

"You are not other men. You are Auguste Rodin."

"I'm nothing," he said bitterly, "and when the child is born I'll be less."

"You are a sculptor," Aunt Thérèse said proudly.

"An ornamentalist," he corrected. "No one is a sculptor part time."

"Rose will help you."

"But she has none of my interests."

"Rose worships you. She will do anything to please you."

"So would a servant."

"A servant wouldn't love you. You would be foolish to throw this away, the most precious thing a woman can give you. It's not a matter of morality, but of common sense."

"But, Aunt Thérèse, I don't love her, at least not as she loves me."

"Love is never equal, Auguste. You should have learned that by now."

"I know, but I won't be able to work with a baby around."

"I could take care of the infant. My boys are grown-up. I would love to have a child again in the house."

"That's no solution."

"Then Mama could, and it would bring her back to the real world."

"No, no, don't tell Mama or Papa. Not yet."

"Auguste, she is a good girl."

He was silent.

"And you are an accessory to the fact."

"Perhaps. Promise you won't tell the family, or anyone else."

"Are you ashamed?"

"That's not the point. Promise, Aunt Thérèse. Unless you don't want me to keep the child."

She knew he could be as stubborn as rock, and so she muffled her disagreements and doubts. "I promise, if you will let me see Rose during her confinement."

It was agreed, each knowing the other would keep his word.

III

Aunt Thérèse came to stay with Auguste and Rose at the time of birth, and he slept in the studio, close to his beloved unfinished "Bacchante," while Aunt Thérèse remained near Rose. He rented an extra stove for Rose and Aunt Thérèse which went to the ceiling, and though the bedroom was still drafty and chilly Rose was pleased by his consideration and tranquil with Aunt Thérèse in attendance.

A boy was born in a lying-in hospital, Maternité, on January 18, 1866.

Now Rose was sure Auguste would say he loved her. Instead he stood by her hospital bed and stared at the squalling infant, wondering whether this being with the puckered-up face—grotesque, wizened—belonged to him. And did it have to be so noisy?

Rose cried out in sudden despair, "Aren't you going to kiss me?"

He saw Aunt Thérèse frowning, and although he was proud that he made up his own mind he cared for Aunt Thérèse. He bent over and kissed Rose and said, "I'm glad it is a boy, *ma chatte*."

"Yes," she said. "We'll name him after you."

IV

At the Mairie of the arrondissement several days later Auguste registered the birth of his son as "Auguste Eugène Beuret."

Aunt Thérèse, who had accompanied him, was shocked. She was proud that she was a free thinker but this was cruel; her three sons had suffered from being forced to take their mother's name. She pulled Auguste aside and asked angrily, "Aren't you going to legitimatize him?"

"No."

"Not even give him your name?"

"He has Auguste. It is enough."

"Rose will be very unhappy."

"It's her child. Beuret will do."

"Auguste, you still resent her!"

"Did the fathers of your children give them their name?"

"They were wrong. And I never forgave them."

Auguste was silent.

"*Mon dieu!*" cried Aunt Thérèse. "Have you no feeling for Rose?"

"Sentimentality is a tyranny."

"But she does love you. She is the mother of your child."

"My little housewife, *oui*."

"Don't you love her at all?"

"You sound like Rose. One doesn't get love by asking. It is either there or not, and no one can do anything about it."

"You know you are the first."

"If I didn't know, she has let me know."

"What have you got against her? Is it because she doesn't know anything about art?"

"Oh, I could educate her. She could learn, but then she wouldn't be—"

"Such a good housekeeper," finished Aunt Thérèse. "That was the way the painter Drolling treated me. That was his excuse to avoid responsibility."

Auguste said curtly, "He was wrong."

"But you are not?"

"Rose can't even read or write."

"Could your father?" She smiled. "You know, I signed the declaration for him when you were born."

"Then sign it for Rose," he said. "But don't tell me how to live." He strode back to the desk to confirm the name, Auguste Eugène Beuret, and then with a strange look of satisfaction escorted her back to Rose, who was still in the hospital, saying, "I'll give her a present. I'll cast 'Mignon' in bronze. Then she can have it for good."

V

Rose was not interested in owning "Mignon." She was deeply hurt by his refusal to give their son the name of Rodin. He refused to discuss the matter, however, saying it was closed with a finality she could not question.

The situation was menacingly difficult. The decision of Auguste, relentless as it was, drove her to near despair. Rose told herself that he was thinking only of himself, yet she had neither the skill nor the strength to resist him or to escape him. And she did not blame him, but his sculpture. He was her first love, her only love. With all of her passionate nature she was sure she would never care for anyone else, and she could not admit that this was a mistake. He must love her, she decided, even if he couldn't say the words. But between Auguste, who was the hard stone, and the infant, who was the soft, she felt trapped in a grinding millstone. When she dared protest, he took on the chill of marble.

He returned to the modeling of the "Bacchante" when Rose was able to pose again, but it went badly. The figure, his first full-length nude, must not be "pretty"; its justification must not be simply beauty; it had to be real, not artificial. This was the most difficult work he had attempted, and the baby was driving him mad. *Petit* Auguste cried constantly, startling him out of the most intense concentration. There was no plan to the crying, it occurred at all hours. And when Rose posed she was distracted, a slave to the baby's caprices. He believed the "Bacchante" would be superb, if he ever finished it, but he never would with the baby around. The squalling drove him frantic. It was as if the infant were conspiring against his work. His black moods became frequent.

After weeks of torture he made a speech to Rose. They must give *petit* Auguste to his family until the infant outgrew the crying.

Rose disagreed. She broke into tears. Then the infant joined in.

Auguste had spoken kindly, if firmly, but now he became angry. It was a conspiracy. The baby was screaming loud enough to awaken the Emperor. He said abruptly, "You are involved in a sentimental indulgence. You can see him every week, and when he is older you can have him back."

She was sobbing so hard the mattress shook.

His resentment increased. Tears were the last thing he could endure. He said, becoming colder and colder, "I have so much work ahead, and it is getting impossible with the constant crying."

Rose wondered how he could expect her to surrender *petit* Auguste.

He didn't say. He got out of bed, strode out of the house, and did not return that night.

She was so grateful when he returned for breakfast the next morning that she agreed to leave their baby with his parents for the time being. She was physically sick at the idea, certain she was the unhappiest of mothers, yet the crying disposed of, he was more amiable. He made love to her that evening for the first time in weeks.

And she was pleased at the thought of meeting his family, although also afraid. Family was the core of her existence; she had missed that more than anything else since she had come to live with Auguste. She prayed that they would be merciful about her unmarried condition and understand that it was not her choice.

She asked him, "Do you think they will take offense?"

He said, "I don't know. But I think they will want the child."

"And we will have little Auguste back when he is older?"

"When he doesn't interfere. Now let's not waste any more time. As it is, seeing the family Sunday, I'm giving up the one free day I have for sculpture."

CHAPTER 12

Aunt Thérèse arranged for Auguste to visit his parents the following Sunday. She did not tell them about Rose or the baby, but said he had news for them, a surprise, something quite important, to lessen the shock.

Auguste was affectionate, walking over from the studio. The arrondissement was full of memories of growing up, and in retrospect they became pleasant ghosts. He showed Rose where he had gone to school at Val de Grâce and told her, "I was an idiot, *ma chatte*. It was near the Sorbonne, but as far as my teachers were concerned it was a million miles away. But we lived right between the Luxembourg and the Jardin des Plantes and within walking distance of both, and of course, in the middle of the Latin Quarter. Oh, Papa was sure my love affair with sculpture would come to a bad end. He would have lived elsewhere if he could have afforded it, but I loved the variety of buildings. The stone was alive, St. Étienne du Mont and the Panthéon and St. Séverin, and naturally, Notre Dame. I think I might have wanted to be an architect, if I had known what an architect was, but nobody in my family knew about such things, except Aunt Thèrése a little, and she was too busy struggling to bring up her children to talk about such things. We were too poor to have leisure."

Rose nodded, determined to be interested, though she knew neither of them could ever compete with the gentlemen of the Faubourg St. Germain, and she was apprehensive.

It was noon when they knocked on the door of his parents' small stone house on the rue St. Jacques. The baby was in a perambulator lent by Aunt Thérèse, and she opened the door. Papa and Mama stood behind her, trying to hide their curiosity but finding that impossible. It was as they had suspected: Auguste had a woman and a child!

Papa looked grim and foreboding, while Mama was vague and indecisive.

Rose bowed respectfully to them, and Auguste introduced her simply. "This is Rose, and our child, Auguste."

Papa and Mama stood on the stoop, saying nothing about coming in, and Aunt Thérèse explained hurriedly, "Petit Auguste is six weeks old. Isn't he healthy-looking? Your first grandchild, Jean!"

Then Papa, very solemnly, bestowed a glance upon the baby in the carriage, and Mama followed his example.

Rose, sensing dismay and criticism behind their politeness and yet a fear of offending Auguste lest he stay away for good, said timidly, "He is the image of Auguste, isn't he?"

"No, no, no," said Papa. "He looks like you, Madame ——?"

"Mademoiselle Rose," said Auguste.

In the embarrassed silence that followed, Rose was sure Auguste had done the wrong thing. But she stated with some pride, "He does have Auguste's mouth and eyes."

"Nonsense," said Papa. "Auguste has lighter eyes."

Auguste, annoyed at Papa's righteousness and Mama's timidity, came to Rose's defense. "The baby looks like both of us."

Aunt Thérèse said, "Of course he does. Jean, it is obvious."

Papa grumbled, "I might have been consulted sooner."

Auguste said, "You are being consulted now. But if it makes you unhappy, we can leave right now."

"Oh no!" cried Mama. "The child does look like both of you. Doesn't he, Jean? And a little bit like you, too, Jean?"

"Me, too?" Papa was surprised.

Rose ventured, "We would like to think so, Monsieur Rodin. It would make us very proud." She smiled gently and with a mother's caution lifted little Auguste from his carriage and handed him to Papa.

Papa stared at the infant squirming in his arms and saw that the diaper had slipped down and the baby's bottom was bare. "*Mon dieu!*" he exclaimed. "He'll catch cold."

Rose went to readjust the diaper, but Mama was ahead of her, saying, "I used to do this very well."

Rose said softly, apologetically, "Monsieur Rodin, I hope you will forgive me for being impulsive—if *petit* Auguste is too much of a burden . . . ?"

She went to take the baby back, but Papa halted her. "Burden! He is my grandson, isn't he?"

Rose, pathetically charming in her simple brown dress, nodded with a faint smile and said, "Yes, if you don't mind."

"*Mon dieu!*" declared Papa. "You mustn't be so distressed. Mind? I can tell by his hair. All Rodins have red hair. And he has our nose."

"Do you like him, monsieur?" asked Rose.

"He is as light as a feather," Papa said. He knew he should be stern—to have a child without marriage was a sin and destroyed the man's initiative—but the child's helplessness was appealing. He felt himself melting, although his arms ached from the weight of the baby. Papa smiled at little Auguste, seeking to coax a smile from the baby.

Mama said, gaining courage from Papa's approval, "Of course we like him. I always told Auguste and Marie if they ever had any children of their own they must bring them to us, whatever the circumstances."

Yes, thought Papa, however the flesh of his flesh had betrayed his bringing up. This infant was all that was left to him of the future he had vigorously created. How could he reject *petit* Auguste when it would mean rejecting his own blood? Retired, going blind, aging fast, he had no other future. He had been unable to admit it, but he had lived in terror of Auguste's being childless, of his branch of the Rodins dying out. *Petit* Auguste was a rescue. And this girl was a good girl, not one with fancy airs and a false elegance who would look down on them. They could meet as equals; she was at home in their world. Papa said, "He is going to be a big, fine boy. I can tell by the way he is gripping my arm that he is a Rodin."

Rose agreed, and when she went to take the infant back Papa

shook his head and said, "Thank you, but I used to carry Auguste, too."

"I know," said Rose. "He told me, and that he got his strength from you."

"Yes, yes," said Papa, "Rodins have always been very strong. But come in. The baby will catch cold out here. Mama, is dinner ready?"

"Almost," said Mama. "I made extra portions today. I thought there would be more than just Auguste." She took Rose by the hand and led her inside, and the others followed.

Where, Auguste wondered, had Rose acquired these manners? Rose was at home with his parents in a way she had never been with him. Did love put her at such a disadvantage? Or was it that she did not have to apologize for her lack of education with them?

Rose noticed that the house was furnished plainly but was very clean. Mama put a pretty brooch in her shawl as she served. Papa did not want to let go of the baby, saying, "See, *petit* Auguste doesn't want me to," as the baby seemed to hang on to him with an instinctive clutch, but he could not eat and he was hungry—eating had become his chief pleasure, and Mama had gone to special pains today. Rose put *petit* Auguste back in the perambulator while Mama proudly served three sous' worth of butter and ten of wine and a two-franc roast, the first in months.

It was one of Mama's best meals, Auguste thought happily, and Rose discussed cooking with Mama and the bringing up of children with Papa as if each were an authority and these were the most vital subjects on earth. Auguste was just beginning to feel relaxed—Rose and Mama had discovered they both came from Lorraine and were regarding this as a new bond—when Rose grew quiet, odd, strained.

Papa asked, "Is anything wrong?"

"No," Rose insisted, but she glanced at Auguste in anxious scrutiny.

Auguste nodded and said, "Papa, you are right. About the baby."

Papa was astonished: Auguste had never conceded he was right about anything.

"The baby has caught several colds. Our studio is badly heated, and until I move, which will take a few months, the child will be poorly raised."

Papa, sitting at the head of the table as of old, with Rose next to him, said, "Auguste, what an idiot you are!"

Auguste smiled, this was like old times.

"Why don't you say it? You want us to take care of the child for a while."

"Would you?" asked Auguste, apparently surprised.

"Do you want us to?" asked Mama.

"He does," said Papa. "He is not a lunatic. Rose, what about you?"

"Monsieur Rodin, I would—"

"Papa," he corrected her.

"Monsieur Papa," she said, "we would be greatly honored but—"

"You would prefer to keep this treasure for yourself," said Papa. "I do not blame you. You are a good mother. And we need good mothers. They say fewer children are born in France than in any of our neighbors, and that our birth rate is still dropping. We are growing afraid of big families, suspicious of the future. Yet the Emperor squanders them in one adventure after another. The Crimea, Austria, and now Italy. But we must not have *petit* Auguste growing up to think it is a misfortune to be a Frenchman. We can always have a piece of meat for him, and a pot of soup. I may not have a taste for museums, like my son, but I am not so provincial I cannot understand young love."

Rose's eyes filled with tears, and suddenly she threw her arms around Papa and kissed him.

Papa blinked to hide his own rush of emotion and said, "See, I am not such an ogre after all."

"You will be good to little Auguste, Monsieur Papa," Rose pleaded. "Oh, I know you will."

"I will sit with him when he eats, punish him when he doesn't," said Papa. "Put him to bed with Mama, be careful about his clothes, and take him to church when he is old enough."

Rose whispered her thanks.

Papa said, "And we will expect you every week."

Rose said, "If Auguste lets me."

"What do you mean, if he lets you?" Papa was righteously indignant.

"Sunday he works on his sculpture," said Rose, giving Auguste a frightened glance.

Auguste, pleased with the way things were going, beamed even when Papa said, "He can take Sunday off. Even God worked only six days."

Auguste said, "We can come in the evening, and Rose can come more often, when she isn't posing." Papa didn't object, as Auguste expected, and Auguste thought of another dinner, years ago, when Clotilde had spoken her mind about love. But he was a man. To a man many things were permitted and excused. And Rose was a girl his family could understand. Virtuous in her devotion to him; economical with a peasant frugality; devout when he allowed her to be; and faithful, always so faithful.

Then, several hours later, when it was time to depart, Rose burst into tears at the thought of leaving little Auguste.

"There, there," said Papa, consoling her, this time his arms around her. "We'll take good care of the baby."

"Forgive me for being weak," Rose sobbed. "But I'm going to miss him so."

"I'll bring him over," said Aunt Thérèse, "when Auguste isn't modeling."

"So will I," said Mama. Mama's face lit up in a way Auguste hadn't seen since the death of Marie. Mama could tell that Rose was a good girl, motherhood was natural to her; perhaps they would marry one of these days; Auguste needed someone like Rose to look after him.

Papa brought out more Cointreau, a taste he shared with Auguste; Auguste slipped some francs into Mama's hand when no one was looking; Aunt Thérèse joined in a country lullaby with Rose to soothe the infant, who had begun to bawl at all the commotion. Rose smiled genuinely now. If she had lost a son temporarily, she had gained a family. How eagerly she wished they could stay here until it was time to go to bed! But Auguste had work to do; she could tell by his sudden impatience, his complaining about the lack of light on these short winter days.

Papa insisted on walking them to the boulevard de Port Royal, and suddenly, at the moment to say good-by, kissed Rose, flushing as he did, and then Mama did, not to be outdone—Aunt Thérèse had been left with *petit* Auguste.

II

That evening Auguste did not model as late as he usually did. He was content to redo the contours of the "Bacchante," and then he halted and said that Rose should learn about good writers like Balzac and Baudelaire. He read her poems from *The Flowers of Evil*—he had discovered Baudelaire with an enthusiasm that stirred him deeply —and Rose grew drowsy and looked ill.

She found the poet's sensuality sickening and brutal. She felt as if Baudelaire were ravishing her. Auguste was speaking about the poet's "great tragic sense," and she covered her nakedness with her coat. And she was bored. When she yawned, no longer able to control herself—Auguste had been reading to her for an hour—he stopped abruptly, swore. Then he caught hold of himself. She was regarding him with an innocent appeal. Her soft body stretched toward him.

She was impossible to educate, he thought, but tonight he had no bitterness. He said with unexpected tenderness, "Rosette, my parents liked you."

She replied with as unexpected candor, "They like children."

Rose was remarkable, he thought; she would suffer for him no matter what he asked. He went to her with a new passion. But a contradiction surged within him. She disliked Baudelaire, yet when he embraced her she came to him with a tempest of senuality, without any regard but to possess him.

Afterward he told himself that it was ridiculous to educate her, it would spoil her rich caresses, her heaving breasts, her wanton love. She lay beside him voluptuously, and he noticed the more ardently he treated her the more sensual she became. She was a natural *volupté*, as long as she believed he loved her. But when he mentioned Baudelaire, that someday he would do sculpture based on this poet, she burst out, "He's wicked!"

When finally they halted their love-making, they were exhausted.

Auguste fell asleep, and she lay beside him, watching him breathe, thinking that though he had cheapened her, shattered her pride by refusing to marry her, to legitimatize their son, tonight he had healed her pride, made her feel straight and womanly again. Whatever he said or did not say, and she knew he would do as he liked whether she protested or not, he had come to her with love. It was her recognition and her redemption. And he was correct about the "Bacchante." She would pose in such a way that it would have to be a magnificent statue. He turned toward her, half asleep, and murmured, "Rosette, what a fine belly," as if she were one of the statuettes he adored.

Auguste had placed only one restriction upon her during all their love-making: she must make sure there would be no more children. And when dismay had shown on her face, he declared, "Rose, if you ever get pregnant again, I'll throw you into the Seine!"

CHAPTER 13

In their new surge of emotion "Bacchante," the queen in the studio and a prospective Venus, was reborn. And Rose, a good wife in bed, became a servant in the studio and a model in the evenings and on Sundays.

Auguste, feeling practical, competent, vigorous, went to work with a new zest to model Rose into the image of a wild, carefree, lusty goddess. He destroyed the old figure. He decided Rose must be *the* Bacchante.

She objected to this, saying timidly that *such* nudity would be coarse, one ought not show one's self in public naked, and he said he was disgusted with doing caryatids, he hoped he would never model another draped female as long as he lived—the glory of women was their bodies.

He pulled her coat, her one refuge, off her. She stood on the model's stand naked, trembling, still unable to hide her embarrassment and shame, and he gently caressed her hips and buttocks to capture her curves in their precise contours. She quivered, helpless under his touch. Then as he ran his hand along her waist to get her exactly right, his touch made her mad with desire for him. She leaned toward him with a passionate yearning and he exclaimed, "Fine! Fine! You have just the motion she needs!"

She paused as if paralyzed, rigid suddenly. He took her hips with both his hands and pushed them forward, and she felt she could no longer endure it. She was afraid for her soul. He had his hands

around her and she knew he could have anything of her, anything!
And in her naked hunger she felt dreadfully exposed. It was so
ruthless it was terrifying. And so was her love, she thought with a
mixture of pain and exultation.

"More emotion!" he cried.

Didn't he know how she felt?

He was shaping her posture again with his hands and saying, "It
isn't the loss of her virginity I'm interested in, it's the loss of her
innocence."

"Auguste, do I always have to be posing?"

"Always."

"And our love?"

"Work is love."

"Only work?"

"Rose, you've lost the posture I gave you." He felt desolate. She
was hopeless. She had sagged in at the hips, when a bacchante
should be gay, carefree, abandoned.

"You don't love me," she said, and hate came into her eyes.

"Not when you're so stupid you can't remember a simple position.
I'll get another model."

"No!" She put her arms out to him. "Say you love me."

"Good. Hold it. That's almost right." Auguste worked swiftly and
surely now, sketching her over and over, saying as he did, "The
beauty of a naked woman is the beauty of God. A bacchante must always be in ecstasy, full of animal impulses, possessed by a passion beyond her control. I've studied bacchantes on Greek reliefs and those
of Titian, and they are never decorous or decorative, but buoyant,
with an ecstasy of movement, of yearning, of imminent delight."

His eyes had such a beautiful glow, admiring her yearning, she
could not resist him. He made her feel like a goddess.

During the next few sittings the "Bacchante" shot up into
womanhood, over six feet tall, greater than life size, the height giving a sense of strength. He was unhappy about the armature, which
was weak, of inferior metal, but it was all that he could afford—and
he felt his work had the mastery he needed. He throbbed with satisfaction. Sculpture meant mastery: mastery of the body, mastery of
the model, mastery of the mind and heart and imagination.

He felt released when he finished the "Bacchante." The statue was grand and beautiful and permanent, he thought, and he embraced Rose with sudden joy. He said, "She should make the Salon."

Rose asked, "Can we visit *petit* Auguste now?" They hadn't seen the baby for several weeks, he had been so preoccupied with his modeling.

"Later, later," he said, struck with a new idea. "Get back on the stand."

"I thought you said the 'Bacchante' was finished." She was disheartened enough to scream.

"We'll see the baby next week. Put your arms out again, as if you were holding the infant. I'm going to do something you will really like."

Rose, feeling imprisoned, wondered whether she would ever have a genuine hold on him. The "Bacchante" towered over her, and she had a tremendous desire to smash it. But that was not possible. That would shatter everything.

II

Auguste, gratified although not completely satisfied with the finished "Bacchante," felt so light of hand and heart he worked the rest of the day. He knew Rose was disappointed at being unable to see the baby, but he was certain she would be pleased with the result.

She missed the infant increasingly as the posing went on for several weeks, but when she realized what Auguste was striving for she modeled willingly. He was doing a miniature foot-high figure of her with an infant in her arms.

The completed clay group gave her great happiness. Auguste was touched by her emotion. He had it cast in bronze, though he wondered if this was foolish, it took the last sou he had saved, and then handed the bronze to Rose as a reward for posing for the "Bacchante."

Rose, irretrievably snared by her love, pressed the mother and child close to her heart. Then regarding them as a wedding present, she stood them on her bureau as a token of Auguste's love. She was still embarrassed by her exposure to the world as the "Bacchante," but she knew she would treasure this gift all her life.

III

A few days later Auguste received his first commission. Dr. Harneau was a middle-aged Parisian who had been just appointed to the École de Médecine as a teacher, and he needed a bust for their foyer.

Auguste was surprised that the doctor had come to him, but he had been recommended by Fantin-Latour. The doctor wanted to look distinguished, for a hundred francs. This was a penurious fee, Auguste knew, but it was the first money he had been offered for his own work and he agreed without argument. He told the doctor it would take a dozen sittings, though that meant no profit, and the doctor was shocked. Dr. Harneau said, "That's too long. We mustn't waste time. Have you noticed that I resemble Napoleon the First, the conqueror?"

Dr. Harneau was as short as the conqueror, but Auguste saw no other resemblance. He nodded, however, thinking perhaps the same spirit was there.

A sudden cold wave hit Paris the Sunday the doctor came to sit. Icicles dripped outside the studio window, and the stove steamed with a bad odor. The doctor hesitated to put his silk top hat down upon the extra chair, though in spite of the obvious poverty the studio was spotlessly clean. He wondered if he should have allotted more to his bust out of his savings; this sculptor, Rodin, was obviously a mediocre one, living so poorly. The sculptor was commanding, however. The doctor sat down, and he was impressed by the way Rodin worked at a white heat. He was disappointed when no features appeared at the first sitting.

By the fourth sitting Dr. Harneau was very impatient. There were a nose and a forehead, but they were not his, they were not fashionable; he wanted to look like a cavalier and the sculptor was making him a *petit bourgeois*. Suddenly Dr. Harneau was sure this bust would ruin him. He said, "You are making me fat."

"You have jowls," Auguste said, trying to be polite.

"Not stout ones. Don't you have any ingenuity?"

Puzzled, Auguste consulted the half-finished bust again. It was accurate: Dr. Harneau was round-faced and plump.

Dr. Harneau, angry at the sculptor's stupidity, shouted that it must be altered; moreover, he was uncomfortable in the studio—the studio and the bust were both too full of suffering.

Auguste, standing there bare-armed although it was bitterly cold outside and only a little less cold inside, studied Dr. Harneau thoroughly, but he could not lie or flatter him. Not for all the salvation in the world. Yet he tried to be tactful. He persuaded the doctor to give him one more hour to complete a facsimile of the head.

"But only one," the doctor repeated. "I'm a busy man, Rodin."

Auguste worked feverishly, thinking the doctor had a small head and a fat face and wanted a large head and a thin face. Like Victor Hugo's now, the doctor said, disenchanted with the Empire, with the disaster in Mexico.

The facsimile was finished at the end of a nerve-racking hour for Auguste. Dr. Harneau, knowing he had the advantage now, looked at it contemptuously and stated, "It is still too coarse. God forbid, but it looks as if it has been done with a meat cleaver. The head is too flat, too tiny."

"Monsieur Doctor, a large head does not fit your short body."

"I did not ask for an anatomy lesson, Rodin."

"Monsieur, I simply mean I want to get beneath the surface impression."

"No, it is a horror." The nose, whose prominence had always irritated him, gleamed conspicuously; this murderer made his heavy face even homelier. He got to his feet, declaring, "It will not do. No one would respect me at the École." He grabbed his top hat and rushed out before Auguste could ask for the fee.

Auguste told Fantin-Latour about this and his friend said, "*Mon ami*, you should have fooled him and made him handsome. What harm would you have done?"

"Would you have done it?"

"For a hundred francs? You poor boy."

"Well, would you, Fantin?"

"Why do you think I do still lifes?"

IV

To remedy this disaster Fantin-Latour sent Auguste a young lady soon afterward with the advice "Be paid in advance." Auguste tried, but the closest he could come to asking for his sculptor's fee was to mention the cost of materials. The pretty young mademoiselle, Renée Dubois, replied that he must keep the head inexpensive, modest, simple, something for seventy-five francs, preferably in one sitting and at the most two, and would he please make sure his studio was warm? She got chilled very easily, even in April.

The materials took all of Auguste's money, and the day of the first sitting he had no fuel for the fire. Desperate, he sent Rose out to find whatever she could for fuel.

Scavenging, Rose returned with two pairs of broken old leather work shoes she had found in the garbage, beyond repair. She threw them into the stove to rekindle the dying fire; but just as Mademoiselle Dubois was seated comfortably, praising the warmth, the stench from the burnt shoe leather became overwhelming. When Rose threw water on the stove, the smell became worse and the sitter cried, "I don't feel well," and fainted.

They had to throw cold water on her to revive her, and that gave her a chill. By the time Auguste finished with the pharmacy, to bring Mademoiselle Dubois to a condition fit to depart, he owed the pharmacy ten francs. And she threatened to sue him for damage to her health.

It was too great a risk, he decided, using this studio for commissions. After obtaining a victoria for Renée Dubois he came home hating the studio. He announced to Rose that he was going to find a better studio if it killed him.

V

Several weeks later Auguste found a more usable studio, on the boulevard du Montparnasse, near the rue de Vaugirard and not far from their present quarters. "It will cost only twenty francs more," he told Rose, quite pleased. "A jewel, compared to the stable." There was only one problem: he had no money with which to move.

But through Papa he borrowed a cart, without a horse—he could not afford a horse. It would hold most of his belongings and sculpture, but not all, and he spoke to Fantin-Latour about this difficulty.

Fantin had an immediate remedy. He said, "We will all help you move. Renoir and Dalou and Monet and Legros and Degas."

"Degas and Dalou? They wouldn't soil their hands," said Auguste.

"Yes, they will. At least Degas might. It will give him a chance to criticize. And he likes you, Auguste, even when he sounds superior."

Auguste remained skeptical, but the morning of the moving they all appeared, sauntering in one by one, united only in their curiosity about Auguste, he was so secretive about his private life and his work.

They were surprised to find his studio empty except for a few statues and personal belongings—they had heard rumors about a mademoiselle living with him, not a tart but a country girl. But Auguste had sent Rose over to his parents with her personal things, saying that she would strain herself if she helped with the moving. Actually it had been because he felt it was none of their business and he didn't want their jeers and jokes.

He was gratified by their coming, whatever their mood: Fantin, the leader, with his carefully cultivated Vandyke and strong nose; Renoir and his fair mustache; Dalou with his gaunt, triangular features; the proud, challenging head of Legros, attractive to sculpt; Monet's square bearded face dominated by his fine sturdy white teeth; and Degas, inevitably trailing the others, pretending always to be just the observer, his long nose and large eyes still the dominant features of a face framed by a precisely trimmed Vandyke and mustache, and lined as sharply as the work of his favorite *maître*, Ingres.

Auguste had done several more small figures in the past few weeks and the others paused to examine his sculpture before they loaded him.

Fantin said, "You've done a lot of work, Rodin. Far more than you've talked about."

Auguste said, "What's the good of talking about it? That doesn't make it any better."

Fantin laughed. "You're as secretive as our friend from Aix, Paul Cézanne. And almost as stubborn. The moment anybody disagrees with Cézanne, he runs away."

"Not always," said Renoir. "Cézanne has asked for another Refusés."

"Because he was turned down by the Salon," said Fantin. "But none of you will support him now, having been accepted by the Salon."

Auguste said, "I haven't been accepted."

Degas said sarcastically, "Our famous and grandiose Salon de Peinture et Sculpture des Artistes Français. As I have always said, we have put too much stress on it. Most artists are hung because their teachers are members of the Academy and vote for them. Or they are even more dishonest, bartering with their colleagues, saying, 'I will vote for your student if you vote for mine.' Every year it is done many times. How can we take this seriously, this *peinture et sculpture léchée?*"

Fantin said, coming upon the "Bacchante," "I wager Rodin is taking the Salon seriously. This is your work, isn't it, Rodin?"

"Yes," said Auguste.

"Huge," said Fantin. "An entry for the Salon?"

"Probably," said Auguste.

Dalou said, examining the "Bacchante" closely, "You don't expect to sell this, do you, Rodin? What is she?"

"A Madonna," suggested Fantin. "Or a Diana?"

"Oh no," said Dalou, "she's too—"

"Lusty, wild," Renoir said. "Those sharply pointed breasts, the muscles bulging in her thighs, the convulsed hips. They're outspoken."

"Take care," said Dalou. "She will attack you."

Auguste wanted to retire into a corner, but he said, "She's a bacchante."

"A bacchante?" Dalou looked skeptical.

"An aphrodisiac bacchante," said Renoir. "Full of high spirits. I don't care what anyone says. She has *joie de vivre.*"

Dalou said, "She is pornographic."

Renoir said, "Don't get excited. You don't have to sleep with her."

Dalou said, "It's not that. But she is too big, too wild."

Auguste, angry, retorted, "I'm sick of idiotic Venuses *à la Boucher,* Dianas *à la Houdon.* Houdon did good portraits, but his Dianas are lifeless. And why must a nude always be just beautiful? Why can't I make my bacchante voluptuous if I want to, not just a stupid, vacuous face and body?"

Dalou said, "You'll never make the Salon with such an entry."

Auguste said, "Precious Salon. I wish we could sell somewhere else."

Renoir felt the "Bacchante" and added, "When a painting or statue makes you long to fondle her, then you know you've put together a nude."

Dalou exclaimed, "But what about taste?"

Renoir smiled and replied, "*Mon dieu*, you are concerned with unimportant things, Dalou. Are your eyes blurred? Can't you feel?" He pointed vehemently to the "Bacchante" and stated, "Any man who has such a touch for buttocks and breasts is a rising man. But you see everything upside down."

Dalou said, "I see what it is my business to see. I prefer my work to have more *savoir-faire*."

Renoir was disgusted. "Why, a statue isn't worth anything unless you want to caress it. Especially a nude. But you prefer to model courtly reminiscences of the *ancien régime*. You are determined to be a great success, doing portrait busts of fashionable women and respectable nudes, as Degas said, '*sculpture léchée*.' So one day you will be able to wear a silk hat and a fur-lined overcoat, carry a cane and yellow gloves, and treat all of us who are less successful with indulgent but contemptuous *bonhomie*."

Dalou declared proudly, "My work has been accepted by the Salon."

"Yes," said Renoir. "Your self-admiration is inexhaustible."

Dalou grew pale. For an instant Auguste thought Dalou was going to attack Renoir. Instead he turned to Monet, said, "If you are really a close friend of Monsieur Renoir, as you say, you would do him a great favor and stop him from painting. You can see that he hasn't a chance of success."

Monet shrugged. "Everybody who wants to create is mad." He picked up the head of "Mignon." "I like this. A strong, pretty peasant face."

Dalou, determined to show he could be generous also, examined the "Mignon" and said, "Now, this is better. This has a sense of life. Rodin, why do you waste time on huge works that nobody wants when you could be doing simple charming heads? Where did you find this model? At a public hall? The flower market? On the sidewalk? In a *maison d'amour?*"

Auguste said, "It doesn't matter."

Dalou said, "She doesn't look like a professional model. Your *amour?*"

Auguste was silent.

Dalou said, "She's pretty. Not a skinny-faced laundress or a beady-eyed *midinette*. It's a handsome face. Your sister?"

"My sister is dead."

"Didn't you have a half sister? You mentioned her once."

"It is not a relative."

"Don't keep her for yourself. She's very pretty."

Fantin interrupted, "Stop prying, Dalou. And it won't do you any good to be envious. It is a fine face."

"Yes," said Renoir. "May I carry her?"

Auguste nodded.

They began to pack Auguste's belongings on the cart, and Dalou and Fantin came upon "The Man with the Broken Nose." Dalou disliked it immediately, Fantin admired it, and Degas was amused.

Degas said, "I don't know whether you have an eye for beauty, Rodin, but you do have a genius for ugliness. It's grotesque."

Auguste said, "That's what the Salon said. They rejected it."

Degas shrugged. "Naturally. It's not orthodox."

Fantin felt "The Man with the Broken Nose," marveling at the rough texture, particularly of the nose, and asked, "May I carry this?"

Auguste hesitated.

Fantin said, "Don't you trust me? Do you want Dalou to carry him?"

Auguste said curtly, "I trust you. Not Dalou."

They had almost finished packing when they came upon the bust of Father Eymard. Auguste, encouraged by Fantin's and Renoir's interest, explained that he had done this head while he was in the monastery.

"It is precocious," said Fantin. "Why don't you exhibit it?"

"Where? The Salon turned down 'The Man with the Broken Nose,' and it is better."

"They're not ready for it yet," said Fantin.

Auguste added dryly, "Most people aren't. Father Eymard told me that he liked his head, but when he died last year his family had no use for it and gave it back to me."

Auguste was loaded now, the "Bacchante" carefully packed in the cart. As he draped her with wet cloths, Renoir stared at her and stated, "Look at the perfection of her pelvis, her fine bosom. She doesn't have a classic profile, but she certainly suggests a generous nature. And what a *derrière!* Everybody can understand that!"

Renoir's enthusiasm was so genuine and contagious they all laughed, even Dalou and Degas.

Everyone carried something as they left with many *après vous.* They were animated by a rare *esprit de corps,* united in this, if nothing else, the one formula they had to heed. Renoir held "Mignon" affectionately; Fantin walked carefully with "The Man with the Broken Nose" in his arms; Dalou carried Auguste's tools; Legros took the looking glass, which would have broken in the cart jolting over the rough, uneven cobblestones; Degas bore the lightest object, the bronze mother and child; the sturdy Monet helped Auguste with the cart.

It was a benign May morning, and a picnic mood pervaded. Much of the route as they traveled along the boulevard du Montparnasse was uphill, and it was as if they were emerging from darkness into light, from waiting into doing.

Paris rattled by, fiacres, victorias, landaus, cabriolets, livery coaches, horse-drawn buses. Then the neighborhood became worse and they passed peasants carrying chickens, holding them as lovingly as they held the sculpture; old men in faded blue denim; unpainted houses with slanting slate mansard roofs; houses squeezed in by other houses.

They reached the top of a hill, and Auguste could see the cluster of churches on his right, with Notre Dame in the distance, looking, as always, dramatic and beautiful. He felt as if he were turning his back on the past.

It was wonderful to be moving on this beautiful spring day, in the warm sun, with everything in blossom. Auguste felt young and happy again. There were splashes of bright sunlight on the cobblestones.

Then suddenly the cart stuck on a broken cobblestone. The "Bacchante" tilted dangerously. Auguste shuddered. He felt very tired all at once, alternately pushing and pulling the cart, although Monet was strong and helpful and occasionally the others lent a hand. In a moment of panic he thought he should have hired a horse, somehow.

Fantin took command and pushed the cart free. The "Bacchante" shifted back into place and Auguste sighed with relief. It was his one vital work, whatever the others felt.

Auguste put his shoulders to the moving with renewed energy as they approached the new studio, feeling like Atlas carrying the world on his back. The cart was loaded to the breaking point, but they were almost there. Another five minutes and the difficult part of the moving would be over.

He relaxed as they drew up before the studio. And suddenly Paris, which could be the most beautiful of cities, became the ugliest. The wheel of the cart cracked on a jagged cobblestone, and weakened by weight and overusage, crumpled into a splinter of spokes, and the cart careened out of Auguste's exhausted hands and crashed into a lamppost. The "Bacchante" toppled onto the cobblestones and smashed into many fragments.

Auguste stood, stricken with horror. Her skull had been crushed by a blow of the cobblestones. He thought she had been born for life and pride, but now it was as if everything had been given to be taken away.

Fantin went to pick up the pieces, but it was useless.

Dalou fingered the bent armature and announced, "It was the fault of the shoddy armature. It is hardly better than tin."

But it was more than that, Auguste thought bitterly, he could not count on anything, not even luck; he had been betrayed by his ambition.

Degas said, "What a shame! Rodin, it is a great misfortune!"

The others agreed as they unloaded him. It was no longer a picnic, but a funeral. The unpacking went swiftly. No one had the courage to touch the shattered "Bacchante," and Auguste couldn't. Auguste was without hope. They were telling him how sorry they were as they said their *bon jours* and *au revoirs*, and he replied with a melancholy smile.

People strolled by on the boulevard du Montparnasse in the mild midday sun, some avoiding the bits of clay, several kicking them; then a child began to play a game with the remains of the head. And he could say nothing. How small he was in the vast scheme of things! How unimportant! He had been a fool to think he could be an artist, a master sculptor.

The concierge came out on the sidewalk and asked, "Monsieur Rodin, does this garbage belong to you?" The concierge was annoyed by all this debris. Artists were so untidy.

"No," said Auguste. "Not any more."

The concierge looked bewildered, but the sculptor didn't explain. "Should I sweep it up?"

"Do whatever you want." Auguste felt so tired, so close to surrender, it terrified him.

PART THREE
THE
TRAVELS

CHAPTER 14

Now Auguste floundered into respectability. With the death of the "Bacchante," he resolved to devote all of his energy to earning a living.

He went to Lecoq, who had become head of the Petite École. He was not certain what kind of work to obtain, but he was certain Lecoq would know.

Lecoq did not know. The teacher knew what Auguste could not do. Lecoq said, "You cannot teach, you do not have the temperament for it. You cannot be a stonemason, it would ruin your technique forever. And you shouldn't be a *praticien*, dedicating yourself to *mise au point*; any workman with strong hands can be a hewer of stone and marble, and it will rub you the wrong way, you have no taste for doing other people's work."

"I have no taste for my own."

"How have you been earning a living?"

"As a *maître ornemaniste*. I am becoming a *maître* of detail, and I could dump it all into the Seine."

"Ah, *mon ami*, now you are full of renunciation."

"*Maître*, that's not correct."

"What is, Rodin? That you thought sculpture would be a *voyage romantique et pittoresque*? And you are disillusioned because it isn't. I never gave you the impression it would be."

"If you can't recommend me, who can?"

Rodin looked so tragic, Lecoq had to smile. Rodin seemed determined to suffer, and perhaps he should, thought Lecoq, perhaps he needed more discipline. But even as the teacher thought this, he realized that was a rationalization. Lecoq was tired, however, and out of patience, disturbed by his own problems, disliking his duties as an administrator, which left him with very little time to teach. He felt trapped by his new authority and increased income, yet he did not want to give up any of it. He decided to give Rodin the facts and let him make up his own mind. This was no longer the boy standing before him, but very much the man, except when asking for help.

Auguste stated, "I must make a better living. If I am going to work hard, I want to be paid properly for it."

Lecoq said, "I can recommend you to Carrier-Belleuse. He is one of our most famous and successful sculptors."

"I've heard of him. Wasn't he one of your pupils, *maître*?"

"Yes, but he doesn't mention that today. He has become fashionable. His portrait busts of Napoleon the Third, Delacroix, Renan, George Sand, others, have made him enormously popular. He has far more work than he can do himself. He employs assistants, although he doesn't consider them that."

"What does he consider them?"

"Employees. Menials. But he does pay better than anybody else."

"Am I good enough?"

"*Mon dieu*, you are in a bad state!"

"Will he hire me?"

"If I recommend you. Belleuse says I've wasted myself teaching, but that my pupils do learn the fundamentals. I've recommended many artists to him."

"Many?" Auguste looked uncertain.

"They come and they go. He is strict, and many sculptors cannot endure being an executant and not the artist of record. *Mon ami*, this is a serious step you are taking."

"Recommend me, *maître*? Please!"

Lecoq cautioned, "True, you will be sculpting, but you will learn very little, get no credit, do the very things I taught you to despise."

"Will you recommend me? As you say, he pays well."

"Better, not well." Lecoq sighed. "I hope you survive. You have such a solid foundation in sculpture, it would be a shame to see it crumble now." He had felt like a lighthouse for this young man, warning him against the hidden reefs and shoals and rocks, but perhaps this role had been presumptuous. He said, "I will speak to him. But don't feel crucified afterward."

II

Soon afterward Auguste went to work for Carrier-Belleuse. He felt it was a stroke of good fortune in spite of Lecoq. He told himself Lecoq had been too pessimistic, it was Lecoq's nature. Auguste was quite hopeful that this venture into the world of commercial sculpture would be rewarding.

He assured Rose, "I should be at home there, Carrier-Belleuse is a clever sculptor," and she agreed, knowing he needed this kind of encourgement.

Carrier-Belleuse was a handsome middle-aged man with a florid complexion, round, full features, and long wavy hair carefully set back from his high forehead. An eloquent face, thought Auguste, his flowing cravat and wide collar completing the impressive picture of an eighteenth-century artist-gentleman.

Carrier-Belleuse greeted him affably, a huge jeweled chain glistening against his stout stomach—Auguste had come recommended as a hard worker—and that was the last conversation they had. Carrier-Belleuse had no time to waste on employees. His portrait bust of Napoleon III had made him the most popular sculptor of the Second Empire. He no longer had time to sculpt; he spent all his time obtaining orders, and he had more orders than he could fulfill. *Objets d'art* from his studios decorated many fashionable salons. He was determined to carve a permanent niche in a rigid Parisian society which permitted only two classes in his opinion, the successful rich and the poor. He could not stand what he called "the stench of poverty." His memories of his own childhood poverty were still vivid, and he had sworn to take advantage of the one thing that could change this: money. And his regard for his own work was matched only by his regard for himself.

Auguste was assigned to Carrier-Belleuse's foreman, and from then on all he saw of the sculptor was the back of his head and heels. There was a printed edict in the studio: the *maître* must not be approached first. Everything, work, conversation, orders, *bonjours*, and *bonsoirs* were initiated by the *maître*.

Auguste could not even select the work he did. The sketches and designs were done by Carrier-Belleuse, then handed to the foreman, who placed them in front of Auguste, who constructed the finished clay models in the style of Carrier-Belleuse. Auguste, like all the other employees, was regarded as a copyist, an executant. When Auguste's clay models were cast in bronze and marble, Carrier-Belleuse signed them and sold them immediately.

"He's right," Auguste said sadly to Rose. "My name won't bring a sou."

"It will someday," Rose reassured him, though she wasn't at all sure.

"I wonder. Hardly one out of a hundred sculptors makes a living out of his work."

Auguste, because of the delicacy and skill he had acquired as a *maître ornemaniste*, was assigned to model miniature nudes, foot-high female and male figures for boudoir, drawing room, and staircase. He grew grim, for this constant preoccupation with the nude re-awakened his love for the abundance of the large figure, and this was forbidden by Carrier-Belleuse.

For Carrier-Belleuse the nude was a convenient vehicle for technical display, for mannered, formal prettiness, and to make money. His nudes were tremendously popular, for no one could take offense, not even the Emperor, since they were without sex.

The harder Auguste worked, the more difficult it became. He hated these nudes. He was back in the worst of the school of Fontainebleau. The male nudes had to be handsome and elegant—in the classic tradition, Carrier-Belleuse assured his devoted clientele, and utterly without strength. The female nudes were even more difficult for Auguste to do: they had to be *petite* pretty nudes in the style of Watteau, softly rounded in the fashionable shape of an hourglass, sugar-sweet.

"Fit *not even* for eunuchs," Auguste growled to himself. Not only had he sold his hands to Carrier-Belleuse, he had given him his brain.

He could not complain to Lecoq. Instead Auguste sought to give his nudes individuality, and the foreman destroyed them and he had to model the figures over, working overtime without pay.

When one desperate day, many nudes further on and months after he had started work with Carrier-Belleuse, he forgot himself and gave a male nude a vibrant, supple vitality, he was regarded as if he had committed murder. The foreman called Carrier-Belleuse, who was horrified by the muscles that had been placed on this male figure. He said harshly, "Rodin, you fancy yourself a Michelangelo, but you are a fool. Any more musculature like this and you are finished. It is monstrous. You are mad."

Auguste, who had felt he had looked upon the face of God while he had modeled the "Bacchante," now felt dull-witted and useless. He was doing the same kind of ornamental work he had done before, only on a more elaborate scale. But he conformed now. Although he knew he was underpaid—he received a very small portion of the substantial sum Carrier-Belleuse obtained for what was *his work*, actually —he was earning more money than he had ever earned before. He could not return to poverty, not willingly.

III

Auguste moved to Montmartre, within walking distance of Carrier-Belleuse's studios. He breakfasted with Rose, then went off to work. No longer did he visit his friends at the Café Guerbois or seek them out elsewhere, or give his evenings and Sundays to his own sculpture, except for an occasional, rare exercise. He was so tired and discouraged when he came home he seldom modeled, and then only small things.

"Trifles," he told Rose. Life had become routine and monotonous.

Rose was willing to pose whenever he wanted, but the suggestion made him raw. She was hurt by his disinterest. She was afraid he no longer needed her. She said, "Why don't you try another 'Bacchante'?" and he regarded her as if she were idiotic.

He felt very old; he was twenty-seven, he reminded himself; he would never have a chance to do his own work. And when Rose said they should take *petit* Auguste back, he shouted "No!" He gave no reason, but she knew better than to question him. All he had to do, he thought, was look at *petit* Auguste and know the child was the price he had paid for the "Bacchante," and now that was gone.

Sundays they visited the family and *petit* Auguste, and in good weather they went for walks in the Bois de Boulogne and on the Grand Boulevards. Auguste stayed away from the Louvre and the Luxembourg; they reminded him painfully that he was not even a *jeune maître*.

He was affectionate to Rose, as if he required something into which to pour his emotion. He tried to be friendly and gentle to the child. *Petit* Auguste resembled his mother more and more as the child learned to walk, yet the boy had Auguste's mouth and red hair. But the child cried easily, having discovered this was the way to get around Grand-père, who was as doting with his grandson as he had been severe with his son. And Auguste hated crying or any uncontrolled outbursts of emotion. So the child had to be very quiet when Auguste was present, which made everybody uncomfortable.

Occasionally Auguste bumped into Renoir, who was living nearby in the Batignolles Quarter, and heard that his friends were still struggling to be fine arts artists, to overcome the influence of the Salon, and he thought himself well out of it.

He continued to avoid the others, but one Sunday, while strolling with Rose on the boulevard de Clichy, he encountered Degas.

It was too late to retreat, and then Degas, with a courtly bow and a lifting of his Sunday silk top hat, said to Rose, "*Bonjour*, madame."

Auguste didn't introduce them, replying, "You look well, Degas."

"It is an illusion," said Degas. "But it pleases some to believe it."

"Are you ill, monsieur?" asked Rose.

"Not critically, madame," said Degas. "It is our Emperor who sickens me. He is so stupid, he is making everybody a republican, God help us!"

Auguste said, "He won't involve us in another war, however."

Degas said, "I would like to agree, but he is careless, our Emperor who tries to please everybody." Then noticing Auguste's uneasiness, although this young woman with him, while clearly not a lady, was handsome-looking and attached to him, Degas said, "Madame, it was nice to meet you," and strolled on.

Rose asked, "Who is he, Auguste?"

"Edgar Degas," Auguste said. "A friend, a painter."

"He's dressed so well," marveled Rose.

"He has his own income," Auguste said bitterly.

"You are envious, *mon chéri*."

"No, I'm not!" he declared, but he was, very much.

"Do you like Monsieur Degas' work?"

"Rose, that's not important."

"But do you?"

"He's honest. He paints what he sees, no matter what anyone else says."

"Does he like your work?"

"What does that matter?"

"He was so polite," she said wistfully.

"Oh, he has fine manners when he wants to. But you are lucky. He can be very cruel if he doesn't like you."

"He wasn't cruel to me."

"You are not important enough."

IV

After three years with Carrier-Belleuse, Auguste had grown heavier and broader in his chest and shoulders and arms. The constant modeling, one statue after another in a ceaseless procession, had made his hands tremendously strong and facile. He could do the figures with his eyes shut. He was somber, but it was becoming and he looked well, which he resented—he felt like a failure. He was certain that soon there would be no more time to become a sculptor. He saw only gloom ahead. He was going on thirty.

Then in 1870, Napoleon III stumbled into war with Germany. The Emperor, who was still flirting with imperial ambitions, who wanted to dominate Europe without the risk, found himself enticed into a military adventure more perilous than he had wished, in a war he didn't want, that he doubted he could win, leading an army he didn't believe in, with the growing realization that he was not a Napoleon in the field.

Almost everyone Auguste knew in Paris was positive that enlightened France would defeat barbaric Prussia. There were hardly any doubters. The country was pleased and relieved that Prussia would be put in its place.

Auguste, not having enough money to buy himself out of the

Army, was drafted into the *garde nationale*. He had not wanted to fight: he didn't hate the Germans. Once in the Army, however, he burst with patriotism for *la belle France*. Everyone was singing the "Marseillaise" and shouting, "*Vive l'armée française!*" Auguste had visions of marching triumphantly on Berlin, but he was assigned to a reserve corps that was kept in reserve.

He was appointed a corporal because he could read and write. He achieved two distinctions the bitterly cold winter of 1870–71—while Rose supported the entire family by earning a franc an hour sewing shirts for the soldiers—he had to wear wooden shoes because his feet froze and he was so solemn, so afraid his precious fingers would freeze, too, he became known as "the Solemn Corporal" and "the Corporal with the Wooden Shoes."

Meanwhile Napoleon III learned that his doubts were right. The war was won by Germany in six weeks when he was forced to capitulate at Sedan, though it was months before Paris fell and almost a year before the armistice was signed.

Occasionally Auguste's regiment was moved, but never into action. Their commander was more concerned with keeping his *garde nationale* unit intact to put down any disorders in Paris than with fighting the Germans.

Auguste, between his freezing feet and the threat to his precious hands, found himself in graver danger from the cold and the insufficient clothing furnished by the Second Empire than from the Germans. Then the cold aggravated his already weak eyesight. He came to hate the weather more than the Germans. The moment the armistice was signed, after the surrender of Paris to the Germans, the Corporal with the Wooden Shoes was invalided out of the *garde nationale* because his vision had grown so poor he could not distinguish targets just a few yards away. And this could be catastrophic. The commander, who was preparing to intervene in the civil war he expected to break out any day, wanted only soldiers who could distinguish a republican from a royalist.

Auguste came back to a starving Paris, still suffering from the bitter siege by the Germans. A war which had started pacifically had ended in hatred. The Prussians had bombarded Paris, forced the city to its knees by starving it, and the Parisians cried, "Foul!" considering this precisely the kind of degradation a provincial country like Germany would impose. And when Germany took Alsace-Lorraine as spoils of war, it was as if every Frenchman had been mutilated. It made Auguste, like most of his compatriots, far more hostile to Germany than he ever had been during the fighting. The peace terms became an open carbuncle on the body politic.

Now Auguste wanted to fight the best way he knew how, with his sculpture, but there was too much to do at home. Mama was quite ill from smallpox and starvation, Papa's eyesight had failed to a point where he could barely get around, Aunt Thérèse was away, seeking to get one of her sons freed from a German prisoner-of-war camp at Sedan, and the whole burden of the family had fallen upon Rose.

She told a shaken Auguste, "It is a miracle any of us are alive." But she was proud that she had scavenged enough food to keep the family going. "Cats, dogs, rats, roots, grass, were a blessing, and nobody asked if they were spoiled. When I got a miserable piece of horse meat, I was very lucky. It was horrible."

"And my statues?" He was sure they were all destroyed.

"Untouched. I wouldn't let anyone come near them."

He couldn't believe her. "Nothing cracked? Nothing crumbled?"

"Nothing. I kept them covered. I went to them every morning and night. I tended them just as you taught me, *chéri*."

Still skeptical, he examined the sculpture and saw that she had told the truth. There had been the cloths that had been constantly wet and changed, to keep the clay figures from crumbling. There had been the spraying of the clay, but not too much, or the clay would soften. There had been the constant dusting of the few bronzes. And the studio itself had been kept immaculate. He had done Rosette a grave injustice, he thought, doubting her. With sudden emotion he placed his hands on her shoulders and drew her close, searching for a way to express his gratitude. He kissed her tenderly. But he could not compliment her. He was not a flattering man.

Then Mama, in her sickbed, was ready to see him. Tears came to Auguste's eyes as he embraced Mama: she looked dreadful, just skin and bones—she had aged years in the last few months. And Papa, blinking back his own tears, had grown old, too. He looked helpless and tired.

Yet when Rose brought *petit* Auguste to the sickroom, Grand-père and Grand'mère did look better, as if the child was the one person of importance they had to please.

The next few days Auguste walked through much of Paris, looking for work. There was none anywhere, but one icy afternoon he encountered Fantin, who had been in Paris during the siege by the Germans.

Standing on the rue Bonaparte, near St. Sulpice, which had been hit by a German shell, Fantin was bursting with news about their friends. He told an interested Auguste, "It's strange, and mixed up. Manet, an ardent republican, enlisted in the artillery of the *garde nationale*, and Degas, an ardent anti-republican, enlisted in the infantry of the *garde nationale*, and because of his weak right eye was transferred to the same artillery. So with their opposite views they ended in the same place. And Renoir, who, as you know, is the most peaceful man you could find, was so aroused by the war he enlisted, too, determined to fight, and found himself in the *cuirassiers*, training horses, which he knows nothing about—he doesn't even paint them—and I hear never got to fire a single shot."

"What about the others?"

"Legros had settled in London just before the war, to teach, and Monet fled there to evade serving, Cézanne went back to Aix for the same reason, I was told, and Dalou paid his way out of serving."

"And yourself?"

"I was rejected. On account of my health. They said my lungs weren't strong enough."

Auguste thought Fantin looked quite well, but he didn't say anything.

Fantin hurried on. "The siege was horrible. For a while it looked as if the Germans were going to destroy Paris. I didn't think any of us would survive. What are you going to do, Rodin? You're not going back to Carrier-Belleuse, are you? I hear that he moved to neutral Belgium, providentially, at the start of the war."

Auguste shrugged. His hands had become so rough and frostbitten in the *garde nationale* he wondered if he would ever be able to sculpt again. Yet he longed so to model his defiance of the Germans.

Fantin asked, "How was the *garde nationale?*"

"Cold. Very cold. I still have the remnants of a chill in my system."

V

A week later Carrier-Belleuse offered Auguste work in Brussels. He wanted to refuse, he detested the work and Carrier-Belleuse, but he was penniless, there was still very little food in Paris and he was another mouth to feed, and no matter where he looked there was no work. Feeling he had no alternative, he accepted the job.

Everyone in the family was upset by this decision, even Papa, who was genuinely glad and relieved to have Auguste home.

The morning Auguste was to depart, Papa suddenly kissed him on both cheeks, praised his stubble of a new beard, and said, his voice trembling, almost cracking, "*Mon petit enfant*, you won't stay long in Brussels. Will you?"

"No," said Auguste. "Just a few months, Papa."

Rose started to cry, but when she saw Auguste frown she controlled herself. She said, "You will write, *chéri?*"

"I will write," he said, "to all of you."

"If you write to Rose, that will be enough," said Papa. "And Aunt Thérèse will read it to us."

"Don't worry," said Auguste. "I will take care of myself."

Mama said, gathering a little strength in her bed, beside which they stood to bid him farewell, "All we can do is wait."

Auguste stared at Mama with foreboding. He had a feeling that if he left her now, he would never see her again, she was so wan and gutted of energy. But he could not turn back; money was needed more than ever.

Rose picked up five-year-old *petit* Auguste and said, "Kiss your papa, *chéri*."

Petit Auguste did so dutifully, but his father's lips felt like a stone.

Auguste, feeling the child recoil, swung him in his arms gently, and the child grinned and everybody started to laugh, even Mama. And suddenly *grand* Auguste and *petit* Auguste embraced spontaneously, for the first time in their lives, and Rose whispered, "Be careful, *mon chéri*. Please."

Auguste said, "I will. I'll be back soon. The minute I've saved some money."

Papa said, "Every Parisian returns to Paris."

Auguste asked, "Even those born in Normandy?"

"*Mon dieu!* Even those born in Lorraine!" exclaimed Papa with a sly glance at Rose. "If our St. Joan were alive today, we would never have lost Lorraine to the Prussians. The *canaille*."

Mama reached out her hand with a rare display of demonstrativeness and murmured, "Don't use yourself too hard, *mon chat*, and don't despair. You have a long life ahead of you. Jean's family is strong."

"And so is yours," Auguste blurted out.

Mama smiled wearily and put her hand to his face, to his start of a beard.

Auguste held her hand to his lips for a long moment.

Then Rose said, "We'll count the days until you return."

"Yes," said Auguste. "But now I must go." At the door, leaning against the cold stone wall of the house, he felt a hideous chill sweep through him. Into his imagination came a picture of Dante's Inferno: what more would they have to endure before he saw them again? Then with a vigorous shake of his head he sought to free himself of such fears. He turned to Rose with a flash of authority he had not shown since he had done the "Bacchante" and told her, "You did so well, watching my statues during the siege, I'm appointing you guardian of my studio." Feeling he had recovered his self-control, pretending not to see their tears, he waved *au revoir*—he didn't trust his own voice—and strode off in the direction of the Gare St. Lazare and Belgium. He went swiftly so that he couldn't turn back. He thought of the group he must model of this departure, and it made the leaving a little easier. It might even give him extra money to send home.

CHAPTER 15

Auguste went to work at once for Carrier-Belleuse, but he had no money to send home. The *maître* shrewdly and deliberately paid him just enough to subsist on; Brussels was as indifferent to his talent as Paris, although he did a few new pieces; what he earned was barely sufficient to provide him with modest meals and a simple room. He lived on the rue du Pont Neuf, in the heart of Brussels, near where he worked. He didn't like Brussels, finding it a pale, poorer, smaller imitation of Paris. It made him lonelier than ever for Paris, though Paris was much worse off these days.

In March 1871 civil war exploded in France as the Communards—large groups of craftsmen, workers, clerks, artisans, shopkeepers—seized control of Paris, driven to it by the *debâcle* at the hands of Germany, the horrible starvation that had followed, and the desire to repeat the triumphant days of 1793. Bloody street fighting raged between them and the Versailles army, the forces of the right.

Day by day the news that reached Brussels became more terrifying. Auguste heard that the famine was even worse than during the siege by the Germans, that all contact had been cut off between Paris and the rest of the world. He wrote frantic letters to Rose, and was terrified when there were no answers, and the news from Paris, mostly rumor, worsened—and he heard that Paris had been ravaged and gutted, that twenty thousand Communards had been slaughtered by the victors, the Versailles army, many of them on the hill of Montmartre, close to where his family had gone to live. It was said that Montmartre had become a vast grave.

When he did not hear from the family for several more weeks, he was certain they had been massacred by the conquerors. He wanted to rush back to Paris, but no one was being allowed into the city, for street fighting was still going on. Auguste sought to absorb himself in his work, but he was full of anguish.

Carrier-Belleuse, considering Auguste experienced and efficient now, promoted him and allowed him to model from his own sketches and designs. They had to remain in the style of Carrier-Belleuse, but everything else was original with Auguste. These nudes took on some of Auguste's vitality, though they retained Carrier-Belleuse's polish and elegance. When the clay models were finished, they were signed by Carrier-Belleuse and then delivered to the caster, Monsieur Picquant, who cast them in bronze and paid Carrier-Belleuse's price. With the *maître's* signature their value doubled automatically.

Another week passed. The half dozen other executants, mostly Belgian, envied Auguste's independence—they still had to follow the *maître's* sketches and designs—but he felt guilty. Here he was working away on trash, he thought, when all of his real work must have been destroyed in the civil war. And although he was relieved when he heard from Rose, by way of a smuggled letter written by Aunt Thérèse, when Rose didn't mention his sculpture he was more certain than ever that it had been wrecked. Rose wrote:

Everyone is alive, and most of the fighting has ended, but there is hardly any food, no money, they are still burying the corpses—in the fields now, there is no more room in the cemeteries, and we are still waiting for word from you. Why haven't you written, *chéri?*

Auguste could not eat supper that evening. He was absolutely certain now that all his work had been demolished. He wrote Rose a frenzied letter, pleading for news of his beloved statues.

An answer came a week later. Rose wrote through Aunt Thérèse:

It was so wonderful to hear from you. All the fighting has ended, except for the execution of the rebels—many were killed against the walls of our street, but the starvation is worse. There are no cats and dogs left to eat, they were gobbled up during the siege by the Germans, and now we are down to roots. But if one has a few francs, an occasional egg and slice of bread can be obtained from those who smuggle it into Paris from the country.

Your statues are safe, I spend many hours in the studio, I wish I was filled out as much as they are, but today I think we could devour them if they would nourish us.

Forgive me, *chéri*, for complaining, I know it makes you unhappy, but Aunt Thérèse says you should know the truth. Mama is failing, we think now from a lack of food. If you have any francs, *chéri*, they would help.

Sleepless, and racked with despair, Auguste sought to ease his despondency by working in the studio. He worked all night, and he didn't even use a candle, not wanting to be seen there after midnight—he could model these nudes with his eyes closed. He finished the female figure, a miniature of Rose from memory, by dawn, before any of the others arrived. He had to admit that he had captured the best of Carrier-Belleuse: the nude was delicate, *petite*, graceful. And vital, he reflected with a wry, tired smile, with a touch of Rodin. Here was a nude to breed a man.

Then suddenly he knew what he had to do. He found a hammer and chisel and with steady hands—there must be no slip, although inside he trembled—he cut across the base of the statue: *Carrier-Belleuse*. In this instant he was grateful for the hundreds of nudes he had done for his employer. If he was a forger, he thought, in a sense so was Carrier-Belleuse. And his name was worthless, but Carrier-Belleuse's was not.

Auguste hid this nude, and that evening he went to the caster, Monsieur Picquant, with a deep sense of urgency.

Monsieur Picquant's foundry was located near the Bourse, in the center of Brussels. It was a flourishing business, thanks to Carrier-Belleuse, and the fat, nearsighted, elderly caster, who had an infallible touch, regarded Auguste suspiciously. It was not like the shrewd, calculating Carrier-Belleuse to entrust the payment of money to anyone else. But this somber, heavy-set Rodin was his chief executant.

Picquant asked, "This is a Carrier-Belleuse original?"

"Feel it," said Auguste a little apprehensively—had he involved himself too much in Rose?

Picquant caressed the female nude with practiced hands, then stared at Auguste and asked, "You are sure, Rodin, you are to collect the fee?"

"Yes," mumbled Auguste, very uncomfortable, but gathering courage as he remembered his family starving in Paris. "Monsieur Carrier-Belleuse had to take a trip to Antwerp, and he asked me to conclude the transaction."

"Hm," said Picquant. "It is a fine piece."

"You like it?" asked Auguste, excitement creeping into his voice.

"Yes, yes. Why?"

Auguste shrugged.

"Is it one of your copies, Rodin?"

"What do you mean, my copies?" Auguste asked in a burst of anger.

"Aren't you the executant?"

Suddenly Auguste felt empty, despondent. "Yes. May I have the fee?"

Picquant hesitated, but when the executant didn't move he slowly counted out fifty francs. Still the executant hadn't budged. He asked angrily, "What are you waiting for now?"

"Belleuse gets seventy-five for this kind of figure, monsieur."

"Are you sure this is *his* design?"

"Of course. Can't you tell?"

Picquant felt the miniature again and said, "The breasts and buttocks are a little firmer, larger than usual." He added with a knowing leer, "I guess our *maître* must have had a good *amour* before he designed this, and let himself go. It does have his signature."

"He will be angry when I hand him only fifty francs."

The caster counted out another twenty-five francs, more slowly.

Auguste said, "*Merci*, monsieur." This was the most money he had ever received for one day's work.

The caster insisted on Rodin's signature in receipt of payment.

II

Auguste returned to the studios after he mailed fifty francs to Rose. He tried to do several nudes, to forget what he had done and to make it up to his employer, but he could think of nothing but the signature and the seventy-five francs.

A week later there was a long letter from Rose, written again by Aunt Thérèse, thanking him for the fifty francs, saying that it had saved them from starving. They had been able to buy some eggs and rabbits smuggled in from the country and had made it into a nourishing *ragoût,* and Mama had liked it so much they could all kiss him. Mama was a little better, and if he could send a few more francs it would be wonderful, Mama might pull through.

He was trying to decide how to present another nude to the caster when he was called into Carrier-Belleuse's office. Monsieur Picquant was there, and the piece to which he had put his employer's name.

Carrier-Belleuse, furious, accused Auguste of forgery.

Auguste stood, waiting for the words that would end his artistic life.

"Rodin, I could have you arrested."

"What about the wages you owe me? I did three pieces this week."

"What will you do with the money in jail?"

"I did the work."

"And Monsieur Picquant will testify that you forged my name. Yes?"

"Yes." The caster nodded.

"You're fired."

"For signing my own work?"

"My work. Your work wouldn't bring five francs."

Auguste made no attempt to answer.

Carrier-Belleuse said, "You did it because you envy my popularity."

"I did it because I was tired of doing trash. It was my piece, really."

"You're an anarchist!" cried Carrier-Belleuse. "Stealing another man's property. Maybe you do belong in jail."

He waited for Auguste to abase himself, but Auguste couldn't.

Carrier-Belleuse hesitated. Then deciding that jail might create a scandal and reveal that others did the work he signed, he said, "At any event, you have exhausted my patience. I will expect you off the premises immediately or I will call the police."

III

When Auguste reached his room, he counted his money—seventeen francs. There was another letter from Rose, pleading for money. Mama was worse again, and he didn't have enough money to leave Brussels. He walked feverishly about Brussels the next couple of days, trying to eat on a franc a day while trying to decide what to do. The political news from Paris was better; all the fighting was over and it was reported that food was entering the city. Then when the walking increased his appetite, which he could not afford, he sat in his room, brooding, full of self-torture, crying out to himself, "What has happened to me? I began infatuated with sculpture and now it will not have me. What has been my mistake? Have I sinned? Whom did I hurt?"

He heard his door open. It must be the concierge, demanding the rent he owed, but he couldn't surrender his last eight francs. He was surprised to see Joseph van Rasbourg, a fellow executant with Carrier-Belleuse.

Van Rasbourg was a heavy, stocky, blond Dutchman, a native of Amsterdam and a little older than Auguste. He had heard about the dismissal. He thought it was a stroke of good fortune. While Auguste listened incredulously, Van Rasbourg explained, "You are a fine workman, Rodin, and I have good contacts. I have been thinking of leaving Carrier-Belleuse for some time, but I need someone to help me."

"An assistant?" Auguste asked bitterly, thinking he could be gotten cheap, so cheap.

"A partner, *mon ami.*"

"Why me? I have no capital, no friends."

"You have the strongest, quickest, best hands in the studio. I can get orders if I can fill them. But I need someone in the studio."

"While you do the selling?"

"We can both do the selling, Rodin. I'll sign all the work sold in Belgium, and you will sign all the orders for France."

"And how much will I be paid?"

"Equally. We'll be partners."

Auguste was stunned. He grew suspicious. He said, "But as I told you, I have no money to put in, I—"

Joseph van Rasbourg said strongly, "I want the best work done in my studio. And you are the best. You are a highly professional sculptor, commercial and quick. You have great facility, Rodin. You demonstrated it at Carrier-Belleuse's studios every day."

"You know why I was fired?"

Van Rasbourg laughed. "We've been told, to make sure no one else did it. But who forged whom?"

"I appreciate your feeling, but I would need money right away."

"Most of my savings have gone to the rental of a studio, but I can advance you enough for room and board."

"But not enough to take me back to Paris?"

Van Rasbourg grew intense and serious. "Gently, gently; this is no way to start. We can sign a contract so no one will have to worry about being cheated. It will be to your advantage. I may not be as good an artist as you are, but I am a better businessman. How much do you need?"

"It's not for me, it's for my family in Paris."

Van Rasbourg handed Auguste fifty francs, said, "I wish it could be more, Rodin, but I really have put most of my money into a studio."

Auguste had to blink to hold back his tears. He murmured, "How can I thank you?"

"Work. After all, there are many degrees of work, as there are of thanks. And maybe you are gambling, too. Is it yes, Rodin?"

Several days later Auguste strode into the office of Van Rasbourg's lawyer and signed a contract on the terms they had discussed.

CHAPTER 16

He was like a man who had been almost betrayed by his art and had been close to death, only to be redeemed by it at the last moment. He felt he had traveled a long, long way. Life was to be modeled, he thought, life was to be created. He sketched and designed and sculpted like a man freed from prison. There were many orders, and although the demands were conventional the thrust and lunge and life of his figures were his own.

Van Rasbourg was as good as his word. They were partners, with their earnings split evenly. Van Rasbourg was scrupulous in business matters.

There was one irritant. They had agreed that Van Rasbourg sign all the work done for Belgium, Rodin all orders for France, and no commissions came from France but Van Rasbourg was popular in Belgium. And since Auguste was more prolific than Van Rasbourg and spent all his time in the studio, hating the work of selling while his partner was clever at it, soon there were more figures by Auguste without his signature. He thought, in moments of bitterness, that the homes and buildings of Belgium were swelling with figures signed by Van Rasbourg out of Rodin. But at least this unsigned work was supporting him, although it was not improving his reputation.

Paris had returned to peace, though the wounds of the civil war remained, and correspondence was regular between Auguste and Rose now.

Mama was still very sick, Rose wrote him through Aunt Thérèse, but everything else had improved. She told Auguste how she had obtained work when he lost his job, earning two francs a day sewing more army shirts at home in the evening. During the day she had stood many hours in line to get rations for *petit* Auguste, the family, and herself, bread that was half sawdust, stew that was mainly roots. But now Aunt Thérèse was living with them and taking care of Papa, Mama, and the child while she was making five francs a day as a needlewoman at the Gobelins tapestry center.

He replied by sending Rose whatever money he could salvage from the business and his carefully watched expenses. He missed her very much, as he told her by letter; he missed his studio even more. Van Rasbourg was a decent man, but as fatigue accumulated with increased orders Auguste came to think that his real ability had been taken from him—he was no longer a sculptor but an artisan, head of a business, destined never to do the work he loved.

It made Auguste desire Rose and his studio more. He wrote her how much he missed her, enclosed sixty francs, and ordered her never to take her eye off his statues.

Rose obeyed him completely. She continued to tend his work with patience, diligence, and love. She was an expert by now.

Then at the end of 1871, Mama died. Auguste walked numbly through Brussels, went to the cathedral, but that was no consolation. He felt desolate. If he could have sent more money, he told himself, she would still be alive. Suddenly his loneliness was unbearable. He missed Rose beyond enduring.

He wrote Rose, ordering her to join him—Aunt Thérèse could take care of *petit* Auguste and Papa, and he would send money for their support. He was not sure Rose would come, in spite of the command.

When she arrived in Brussels on a clear, cold February day in 1872, he was very pleased. But he was unable to show his pleasure, to acknowledge his need of her. He met her at the railroad station with his usual reserve, and for an instant he thought they would begin with a quarrel. Rose wore black, since she was in mourning for Mama, and he was shocked to hear that there had been so little money at the time of Mama's death that Mama had been buried in an unmarked grave.

"What about the money I sent you?" he demanded.

"Papa was sick, too. Aunt Thérèse thought it was better to spend it on the living, *chéri*."

"An unmarked grave?" He couldn't get over that. He was horrified. "You couldn't do any better than that?"

"We did the best we could."

"If I had only known!"

"You couldn't have done anything, *chéri*." He glowered, but she had to go on. "So many people have died in Paris since you left, with the civil war, famine, plague, that even the rich were buried two and three in a grave. And as you know, most of those killed in the civil war were the poor."

"I know," he said curtly.

"Has it been hard here, Auguste?"

"Hard?" He picked up her baggage and led her out of the railroad station. "To be a sculptor is always hard. Did you have my work packed properly for shipping?"

"Yes. It should be here any day."

"Come. You must be hungry."

"I am, but not for food." Suddenly forgetting herself, she threw her arms around him, crying, "You are glad to see me, *mon chéri*?"

"I've got to get back to work. It's not fair to Van Rasbourg."

She looked confused, started to turn away. "Don't you want me here?"

He was very annoyed. "I sent you fare. What more do you want?"

II

But when his statues arrived undamaged—she had packed them precisely as he had ordered—he took her to the finest dinner he could afford, and that evening came to her with a gravity that had its own charm. It was their first night of love in a year and one of their most satisfying. Rose's pent-up feelings poured forth, and Auguste responded with a new emotion.

She whispered, overwhelmed with love, "I adore your beard, Auguste, it makes you look so strong, honorable."

He smiled. He had wondered when she would react to this surprise. He was proud of the long beard he had grown the past few weeks. It made him feel more mature; perhaps it had been a happy choice after all.

"Today," she murmured, "is the happiest day of my life."

He held her close.

"I worried so when we were apart."

"So did I, Rosette." She had taken many risks for his work, and he was grateful. In this she was a part of him and there was communication.

III

Auguste, however, wrote to Degas when he wanted the stimulation of ideas:

I was a *collaborateur* of Carrier-Belleuse, but it was never acknowledged by him, although I acquired his flair.

Now I am a *collaborateur* of Van Rasbourg: he signs our pieces for Belgium, I sign them for France. But we sell only in Belgium these days, even after all these months, so homes are filling with Rodins signed by Van Rasbourg, but perhaps it is just as well. They do not please me, but they do keep my hands active for the day I can return to Paris and concentrate on work I care about.

He was pleased when Degas replied promptly, more promptly than he expected, writing:

I would not hurry back to Paris. It is true that the Second Empire has departed now and we have the Third Republic, but it is difficult to say which is worse. The Second Empire was the strong gesture of a weak man, now the Third Republic is the weak gesture of a strong man.

And the *Bibliothèque Impériale* is now the *Bibliothèque Nationale*, but nothing has really changed. Where we were corrupt at the top, now we are corrupt at the bottom. We had a democratic emperor, now we have an empire of democracy, and it is hard to say which was worse.

But I am enjoying the opera, there is a great stir over this German, Wagner; it is supposed to be a sign of culture to favor a native of our enemy, but as far as I am concerned I cannot share this devotion. For myself, I continue to prefer Mozart.

Auguste wondered why Degas hadn't written anything about their mutual friends. Yet one could not prod the painter, it was the surest way to silence him. Then he heard that Degas had gone to America in the fall of 1872 to visit relatives in New York and New Orleans.

When Auguste wrote him again, it was the summer of 1873 and Degas was back in Paris. He said:

I hope you enjoyed your voyage to America. As for me, I am finding the art of Belgium much inferior to our own. The fine work is chiefly in Holland, which I hope to visit someday, but at the moment I am finding the cathedrals about all that is nourishing.

I have wondered, however, about our friends. I hear that there are the usual difficulties, that the art critics are still full of jaundice and the Salon is still misplacing those they don't like, in the *dépotoir*, but I have been thinking about submission to the Salon.

Finally I am beginning to do my own work again, and one of these days I may sustain something that will grip the attention. I am still not at my best, I still give too much energy to my *collaborateur*, although it is not his fault but the nature of the situation, and this city is not stimulating. Brussels is a Gothic hodgepodge, with a few fine buildings, but it lacks the variety of Paris, and much of the stonework is atrocious.

Give my regards to Renoir, Monet, and Fantin if you see them. I think I have finally gotten over the loss of my "Bacchante."

I, too, would like to travel, but New Orleans and New York, where you went, are as far away as the moon for me. The best I can do is the hope of visiting Italy in a year or two. I would very much like to see the "David" and the "Moses" before I become a Methuselah.

It was the end of 1873 when Degas replied. In the meantime Auguste's desire to visit Italy had increased, but he had been unable to save the money necessary for the trip; he was certain the business could not spare him; he still felt in exile, unable to find his own kind of people. He was growing old and detached, he thought. None of the work he projected seemed important. He had submitted "The Man with the Broken Nose" to the Brussels Salon of 1872 on the advice and enthusiasm of Van Rasbourg, and although it had been accepted—his first Salon acceptance—it had not aroused any attention at all. He decided he should do large pieces, but what? A feeling of sadness pervaded him, and he felt that was hardly the mood in which to model an attention-getting figure. Yet he was startled by Degas' pessimism, although he was pleased by the length and detail of his friend's letter. Degas wrote:

Thanks for your good wishes, *mon ami*. We wonder whether Brussels suits you and whether you are able to do any of your own work.

America was fascinating but exhausting, and I would not want to live there. The country is immense, and you travel for days and go only halfway. I saw many new things; New York is enormous, too, and so much activity. I think Americans are a people possessed with more energy than they know what to do with, and while they consider it a great virtue it tires me. They are never still, and New Orleans is a curious and strange mixture of America and *vive la France*. And made me yearn more for Paris. . . .

Most of us have been exhibited now, Manet, Fantin, Renoir, Monet, Pissarro, Sisley, myself, and only Cézanne remains rejected, always rejected, but it is a great foolishness. We are still dissatisfied, and Cézanne is always dissatisfied. For a man who doesn't like company, Cézanne tries very hard to be noticed, and laments loudly when he is not. Rejected four, five times, he refuses to resign himself. But of course he is dedicated to irritating the jury rather than pleasing it, so what else can he expect?

But I do not expect to win. When the Salon accepts us, we are hung as poorly as possible, too high, too dark, packed in with the wrong pictures, stuck in a corner, and the sculptors are even worse off, most of them are flat against the wall and made to look one-dimensional. I do not care, really, but Fantin says we must win in the Salon and Manet supports him.

Fools! The Salon are like women, the Salon want to be courted but they are not really capable of giving love.

I do not have to listen to critics saying, "*C'est magnifique*," a "*debâcle*," about the same item. All they know, it is a picture, it is not a picture. Beyond that they are guided by prejudice, bad taste, the current fashion, and they regard us as a novelty, soon to pass. We are still, at the best, a *succès de curiosité*, and at the worst considered *fou*. As I said, I do not care.

But now the argument is whether to continue to pursue the Salon, to fight for another Salon des Refusés or exhibit through a dealer. I am unhappy with all of them, and sometimes think it would be better if we didn't have to exhibit our work at all.

In the studio one has time for reflection. No one hurries me. If I have doubt, and I have doubt often, one can change.

Monet and Pissarro and Sisley think I am old-fashioned, however, they are devoted now to painting out of doors, a view I and Manet do not share. Did Ingres and Rembrandt do so? Or even Corot, their idol? But if I question this, they say I am caustic, and when I don't share their adoration of nature I am misanthropic.

The truth is, the best work is being done by Manet. Oh, not his "Le Bon Bock," which has brought him his first great success in the Salon, it is Dutch ale *à la Frans Hals*, but his newer work. What skill he has. If he would only decide on a style.

The others, well, Fantin is still imitating the masterpieces and is in a prison of photographic exactness, he has spent too much time in the Louvre, though he resents it when I say so. Renoir has fallen in love with a rainbow, the flesh, and Monet's painting has taken on a mistlike quality and he is obsessed with sunlight.

And as you may have heard, Dalou and Courbet supported the Commune. Dalou was put in charge of the Louvre, imagine that—we would never get in—and Courbet was appointed head of all the Fine Arts and abolished the Academy, the Beaux Arts, the Salon, and now Dalou has fled to London and is teaching with Legros, and Courbet is in jail and would have been abolished if not for influential friends.

There is some of Courbet I like, but his republicanism—faugh! It is like a pestilence, and even Manet is infected.

For myself, my eyes grow worse, my right eye was damaged in the war and I find it impossible to stand the brightness of the sun. I know it is a permanent injury, and I am oppressed with a feeling that I will go blind, but the doctors tell me that can be avoided if I am careful. Careful, I am no Beethoven, to paint while blind! As if I can shut my eyes now and paint only what is past, what I remember. I fear I have only a short time left. I am going on forty, and when you think of what Raphael accomplished, and that he was dead by forty, it makes one shudder. It isn't fair, but then what is?

So when Fantin talks about being an artist because it is noble and high-minded, it sickens me. We are artists, if we are, because we can't be anything else. All else is nonsense.

But then I am surrounded with nonsense. I hadn't intended to go on at such length, but I am encircled by writers these days. Hugo is back after his exile, holding forth in all his heroism and vanity, and it is fine to be a genius, but it is even finer to have taste. . . .

And what about yourself? You say Van Rasbourg is supposed to sell you in France, but has failed. Perhaps you have tried too hard to please. Are you still modeling for the lower classes at fifty francs a head, or has the Protestant culture corrupted you further?

Perhaps that is what is wrong with Van Rasbourg. But then if you don't look out for yourself, no one else will.

The next day Auguste could not start on a new figure. There was much in Degas' letter with which he didn't agree, but it made him deeply dissatisfied. He was homesick for Paris; he craved a change, almost any change; Degas' freedom of movement and activity made him feel stifled. But where could a man go without money or time?

Van Rasbourg came upon Auguste sitting motionless by his model stand and was surprised. His partner was always working. He asked, "What is wrong? A headache?" Auguste sat with his head in his hands.

"A big headache, Joseph."

His colleague squinted at him, puzzled, and asked, "Are you sick?"

"Sick of what I'm doing."

With a wry smile Van Rasbourg shrugged and said, "Who likes this business?" He took in the high-ceilinged studio with a look almost of disgust: the half-finished clay statuettes, many of them reminiscent of Carrier-Belleuse; Roman-style portrait busts that were finished except for the metallic luster of bronze; a pair of ornamental cherubs for the façade of a church. "I accept it. But I don't like it."

"At least you have some recognition to show for all the effort."

"Ah, so that is the headache." Van Rasbourg smoothed down his graying yellow hair. He had waited fifteen years for this opportunity, it would be unfortunate if it ended just as they were on the verge of flourishing, however much the work *was* devoid of spirit and content.

Auguste grumbled, "At one moment I am almost a sculptor, at the next almost a businessman. But never am I really either."

"Your standing has been advanced."

"Perhaps as a businessman. But no one knows Rodin the sculptor. Whatever we sell, it is signed Van Rasbourg, Van Rasbourg, Van Rasbourg."

"Yes, yes, yes," Van Rasbourg said quickly. "But it is not my fault that France does not order."

"At the rate I am going, I will vanish as an artist. I must get some recognition."

"It's not that bad," Van Rasbourg said firmly. "The average wage for a workday is five francs, and you were making only ten, twenty a day with Belleuse, but now you make as much as three, four hundred francs a week, and you could become prosperous if we expand and you save."

"No!" Auguste stood up with sudden decision. "I cannot go on this way!"

Van Rasbourg considered himself a fair man, kindly and modest. He thought Rodin was acting in an arbitrary and capricious manner, and turning everything upside down. He must not give in. Yet there was a far greater demand for Rodin's work than his own—Rodin's figures had a vitality and individuality he could not capture. But there was also a responsibility to the business. Aloud he said, "You need a vacation."

"That's not what I need." But a seed had been planted and Auguste grew attentive. He knew that even his own name on this work would not get him out of this vise, but a large, important, vital work might; otherwise he was battering his head against a stone wall. There was no such thing as instantaneous recognition, whatever the legends said, but life was becoming swollen with unoriginal pieces. He was always tired, nervous, displeased with what he was doing these days.

Van Rasbourg, sensing the crack he had made in the dike, suggested, "Why don't you take a real vacation? Visit Amsterdam. Look at Rembrandt."

"I can't," said Auguste. "I can't afford it."

"We have enough work in stock. If we run low, I can hire someone."

"From Carrier-Belleuse?"

"If you like. We can certainly pay more than he does."

"To copy, to be an executant, as we were, unrecognized, exploited?"

"He will get paid for what he does. To be an executant is not dishonorable. If he can sell any of the work he does, he can sign it."

"Oh, you are generous indeed. Just as you were when you calculated that you would sell far more in Belgium than in France."

"It's not my fault, Auguste, that France is backward."

Auguste stared sternly at Van Rasbourg, sure that deep down his partner was being contemptuous, but Van Rasbourg looked earnest and sincere.

Van Rasbourg urged, "You are very tired. You do need a rest. For my sake, *mon ami*, before it leads us into a quarrel we cannot repair, go to Amsterdam. You like Rembrandt now, you will love him when you see his work in the Rijksmuseum. His best work is there. Take a week. We will manage. Whatever is done while you are away will be shared."

Auguste, although convinced, hesitated. He still couldn't afford it.

"Next year you can go to Italy. We will raise our prices."

"Won't it ruin our business?"

"I doubt it. Auguste, how old are you?"

"Thirty-three." The last few days, since the letter from Degas, he had felt a hundred.

Van Rasbourg reached into his pocket and handed him a hundred francs. "A going-away present. For traveling." He waved aside Auguste's thanks; Auguste would work twice as hard out of gratitude when he returned.

That night, alone with Rose, Auguste told her that he would visit Holland for a few days without her. "On business," he said when she looked bewildered, and when she asked, "What will I do while you are gone?" he replied, "Take care of my studio. When I return, I will be working there more, and less in the shop."

With difficulty she kept from crying. Chilled, tense, shaking inwardly with unhappiness, she tried to warm herself by clasping him close. But he did not respond. He was thinking of what to visit first.

He left the next morning without telling her the exact day he would return. "In about a week," was all he would say. She blinked back her tears, feeling dreadfully put upon. After he strode out the door, she knelt by their bed and prayed to the Virgin for forgiveness: it was not her fault that they had not married, for then this surely would not have happened.

He went down the street swiftly, before he lost his courage and ran back to apologize for his abruptness. She would be an encumbrance if he took her. At the end of the street he turned in the hope of seeing her standing in the doorway so he could wave *au revoir*. When he didn't see her in the doorway, he was annoyed, although he had told her that she mustn't—it would be sentimental, and he disliked sentimentality. His jaw stiffened. He decided he was right not to have softened. He hurried on to enjoy Amsterdam.

CHAPTER 17

The moment Auguste arrived in Amsterdam he went to the Rijksmuseum. He paced slowly through the galleries filled with the finest collection of Rembrandts he had ever seen, and for the most part he was the only visitor. He paused often to stare at the accumulation of work, thinking how fitting it would have been to have all of Rembrandt's work here, instead of its being scattered all over the world. It left Auguste dissatisfied even as he was grateful for what he had seen in the Louvre.

He was irritated also by the badly lighted, stuffy museum. He was very much aware that many of the paintings showed the erosions of time. Cracks in the canvases were poorly hidden by thick layers of varnish; this was particularly noticeable in the *pièce de résistance* of the Rijksmuseum, "The Night Watch." Colors had faded and had a muddy quality. The framing was old-fashioned. Even some of the draftsmanship, usually admirable, was spotty and careless.

He remembered that Renoir and Degas did not always share his regard for Rembrandt. Renoir thought the Dutchman too melancholy and Degas thought him not melancholy enough. He remembered Renoir declaring, "There is hardly a pretty woman in any of his pictures, and his palette is so full of dirty colors, so much black, and I don't care for his brushwork." He recalled Degas standing at his elbow, saying, "You're not objective, Rodin, it is a commonplace to say Rembrandt is a great painter. Oh, I admit Rembrandt could draw when he put his mind to it, but I like Ingres better, his lines are far clearer. You should appreciate that. They're like sculpture."

True, perhaps, thought Auguste, yet Rembrandt's faults only strengthened his preference for him: of all the painters, he was his favorite. There was no sentimentality in Rembrandt, whatever Degas stated, and he was not infected with Protestant righteousness, as Degas claimed. His blacks were more than a color, they were a dimension, a depth, a delivering of the soul.

It became a dialogue in Auguste between his intuitive feeling for Rembrandt and the cynicism of his friends which urged him to love reluctantly. He felt not so much influenced as moved. Whatever they said, whatever the flaws, he was drawn back to these paintings as though they held his own life.

Day after day he visited the Rijksmuseum. There were other museums to see, but they could come later. He did not speak to anyone. He just stood, staring, absorbing, voyaging. It was not a world of breath-taking beauty, he reflected, often ugliness dominated. He was not infatuated with "The Night Watch," which was reputed to be one of the most famous paintings in the world, and had an entire room to itself. He thought it too large, too ornate, some of the composition awkward.

It was the faces that pulled Auguste back. He told himself that in these faces the painter revealed that a great darkness had settled upon his world. A ruined man, Rembrandt, had made an undying world with his hands and imagination and vision, even as everything was dying around him, within him, even as this world was humiliating him, declaring him a bankrupt, a failure, a beggar. Yet Rembrandt had continued to paint, not to avenge himself, not even to express himself finally, but because there had been nothing else.

Auguste, drawn more and more into this world with an intense sense of participation, thought the painter had not evaded the issue. Rembrandt, saturated with man's tragic struggle with fate, had depicted this struggle as he had seen and experienced it. The great issue between the spirit and the flesh had been joined. Amsterdam had come to regard Rembrandt as a wastrel, but eventually he had not cared.

Had not cared! These words hammered in Auguste's brain. He had no wish to imitate or idealize. Whatever he had read had stressed

Rembrandt's flaws, his carelessness, his extravagances—how Auguste hated extravagance!—his occasional bursts of vanity, his excesses. But here before him, thought Auguste, was an endless search for truth.

Without sentimentality Rembrandt had exposed painfully and laboriously the frailties, the decay of life, and the inevitability of death and dissolution—the dissolution often before the death. And finally the painter had come to care only for the inner self of his subjects, had concentrated on faces, faces that emerged out of darkness with, often, just a glimmer of light. These faces reflected the continuous struggle between light and darkness. Everything else was secondary.

Auguste did many sketches now. For the first time in years he had an overwhelming desire to plunge into new work. Once again his hand felt free and fluid as he spread his drawings over many notebooks. He was glad he had come alone. He was bursting with ideas, his own ideas, having nothing to do with Rembrandt, he told himself. He was a modern man, a nineteenth-century man. It was better to be solitary, to absorb for oneself, without the usual distractions, to turn Rembrandt's light and darkness on the unexplored places of his own mind. Whether Rembrandt painted a young Jesus or an elderly Jew, a robust Magdalen or a stout burgher, a humble serving-woman or his beloved Saskia, he painted a human being.

Such expressiveness gave Auguste a longing to sculpt a head, a Venus, an Adam, a poet, anything and everything that had the bracing vigor of stone. I was right to search for an inner life in my work, he thought, whether it was Bibi or Father Eymard or Dr. Harneau or Papa or Rosette, and I must never be diverted from this pursuit.

In the days that followed, Auguste eventually tore himself away from his investigation of Rembrandt and saw Rubens and Hals and Vermeer and Brueghel. He studied and enjoyed their painting, especially Rubens, whose work gave him the effect of sculpture, but there came a day he knew he had to depart.

Two weeks had passed, and Van Rasbourg and Rosette must be worried.

He still felt the attraction of Rembrandt, but it was not difficult to leave Amsterdam itself. He didn't care for the city, it was chilly, gray, misty this late winter, and dominated by the canals. The canals made him uncomfortable—he was a land animal—and the architecture was solid, plain, often bare and uncompromising in its severity.

He went to the Wester Kerk, the seventeenth-century Dutch Reformed Church where Rembrandt was buried, and was disappointed. The church, instead of being light and airy, was heavy and dark and smelled too much of ducats. He decided that Amsterdam was even more *petit bourgeois* than Brussels.

And on his last morning in Amsterdam as a farewell he visited Rembrandt's house on the Jodenbreestraat, where Rembrandt had painted much of his treasured work. It made Auguste sad, for the ancient dwelling gave him no sense of what had been created there. He noticed that it was in the old Jewish quarter, which had supplied Rembrandt with many of his subjects. He moved on, fascinated by this quarter, and a square farther along came upon the house where Baruch Spinoza had been born.

All the way back to Brussels his mind kept churning. Rembrandt, with his use of light and shadow, had created depths hitherto unseen. And Auguste was grateful to Van Rasbourg: without the hundred francs he would never have been able to stay two weeks. He arrived in Brussels believing he had penetrated a new world.

II

Van Rasbourg did not criticize Auguste's prolonged absence. The Dutchman was annoyed about the second week, but as he had expected, his partner worked harder now.

Rose greeted him tenderly, as if Auguste had been away for just a day, and Auguste, refreshed and stimulated, treated her with a new gentleness.

He said, "Yes, *ma chatte*, Amsterdam helped," and said nothing more.

His feeling as a sculptor had intensified; he realized for the first time that his talent was an energy that was increasing now in force. During the next few weeks he began to work hard in his studio, doing heads mostly, modeling a number at the same time.

The visit to Amsterdam had also given Auguste the courage to establish a new routine. Every time he grew restless, he took several days off to visit the museums and cathedrals of Belgium and Holland. This made Van Rasbourg unhappy, but he could not quarrel with it—the vacations had been his own idea. And whenever Auguste left, he made sure he had completed more work than they could cast; Auguste was no longer querulous about not having his own name on their work, it was as if he were waiting for the special figure that would satisfy him. So Van Rasbourg hid his growing discontent and was silent.

Rose, having no clue as to Auguste's departures or destinations, had to wait patiently for his return and occupy herself with tending his studio. He wandered through Bruges and Haarlem and Antwerp and The Hague, drawing, sketching, modeling in his mind, observing with a constant flow of feeling. Several times he returned to the Rijksmuseum, and wherever he journeyed he searched out whatever Rembrandts were available.

And then for several weeks he would be content to stay at home and work. Then he was aggressive and amorous with Rose. But still the concept of the major figure he longed to sculpt eluded him.

This more and more made the call of Italy and Michelangelo irresistible—it was inevitable, he told Van Rasbourg when he informed his partner of the need to go there.

"To see more masterpieces?" asked Van Rasbourg, a touch of sarcasm creeping into his usually soft voice. "How much more can you absorb?"

For an instant Auguste thought of quitting. Then he realized that Van Rasbourg's question was insignificant. His partner was not qualified to judge.

"Can't you wait? We have so many orders."

"No. If I don't go now, I may never go."

Van Rasbourg looked uncomfortable, but thought how wise he had been to get ahead with their work.

"Joseph, you know I've been planning to visit Italy for a long time, and the winter is ideal."

"When you say Italy, you say it as if it were heaven."

"I'm stirred by Michelangelo. I want to see his 'Moses' and 'David.' He makes me very angry with myself, he makes me feel I have done nothing."

Van Rasbourg warned, "You may never be the same."

Auguste said with sudden force, "Joseph, I will need an advance."

Van Rasbourg grumbled, "If you would do church sculpture, we could afford it. Your sacred work is beautiful. But you discourage such commissions."

Auguste said shrewdly, "Maybe Michelangelo will change my mind."

Or make him even more dissatisfied with their partnership, thought Van Rasbourg. But he knew there was no altering Auguste; when Auguste made up his mind, an earthquake wouldn't change him. "How much do you need?"

"Eight hundred francs."

"Eight hundred!"

"Is it too much? I think I can do it on seven hundred, *mon ami*, but I want something in reserve."

Van Rasbourg knew he would have required at least a thousand francs, but he complained, "Eight hundred? You will bankrupt us, Auguste."

Auguste waited for his partner to decide. He thought their success or failure depended on Van Rasbourg. He would not abandon his partner, but from now on he was concentrating on his own work.

At the last moment Van Rasbourg agreed to nine hundred francs, to show that his heart was in the right place. Auguste was pleased, and still determined to spend no more than seven hundred.

CHAPTER 18

The desire to see more gave him no rest. The instant Auguste had the money for Italy in his hand, he prepared to depart. Then just before he was to leave, he told Rose.

She was stricken by the news. Before, he had left for a day or two, or for several weeks at the most, but Italy was far away, he would be gone for months. "How will I manage, *chéri?*" she asked.

"That is easy," he answered. "You will stay home, in the studio, and watch my work, wet the cloths, the clay, so I can go to work when I return." He put on his light coat for the warmer weather he anticipated in Italy, and his blue blouse, which served many purposes and made him look more like a workman than ever. He had his map of Italy: Milan, Turin, Genoa, Pisa, and then the high spots, Florence and Rome. His plan was determined. As a tourist he would be an anatomist. He knew just where he wanted to go.

"When will you be back?"

"Soon."

"In a few days?"

"In a few weeks."

Rose looked around at the walls, splashed with clay and plaster, the dirt on the floor, the ugly cast-iron stove, the casts of heads, the few small figures of terra cotta, and grumbled, "I don't have enough money to pay the grocer, and as for the Cointreau you want, impossible! And now you are going off to Italy. Where did you get the money?"

He didn't answer.

"You run around all day, looking at museums and cathedrals, and leave me without a sou. How do you know that by the time you return I won't be out on the street with everything we own?"

"Don't you have any money?" he asked, surprised. He had given her some several weeks ago.

"A few francs. Not enough. Or should I beg from Van Rasbourg?"

"No!" He was emphatic suddenly. "Here." He handed her fifty francs, although it reduced considerably his margin of safety.

Rose accepted the money with a mumbled *"Merci,"* resolved to save at least half. She was resentful that he was not including her on the trip to Italy. He thinks I will be ridiculous, she told herself. She started to cry.

For an instant he almost exploded in a fury; then remembering he would be gone for weeks and she was the only one he could trust with his work, he dried her eyes with his handkerchief. He said, "Come, *ma chatte*, it is not that bad. I will keep it cheap and I will write you often."

But when he had gone, she burst into tears again. She felt bound to Auguste by chains that vanquished her. She could not get accustomed to being treated as part housekeeper, part mistress. Often she had resolved to leave him if he would not marry her, yet ten years had passed and she felt no closer to marriage than before. Disgusted with herself because of her inability to refuse him, she stopped crying and decided she had not been devout enough: she should have promised the Virgin a large candle. Now only the *bon dieu* knew when Auguste would be back, and Auguste didn't even take Him into his confidence. She felt like a fish impaled on a hook. Skillful as she was at mending things, she was tired of trying to make this last. One of these days, she swore to herself, she would leave him—as soon as she had enough money saved from the francs he gave her for the house. She felt better then. She dried her eyes and added the fifty francs to her considerable hoard. She was grateful that Auguste was absent-minded, he never remembered how much he gave her. By the time he returned, if God was good and she was thrifty and able to obtain work at home sewing, she should have enough to return to Paris, without him if necessary.

II

Rheims was Auguste's first stop on his journey to Italy, and he fell in love with the cathedral. He studied it an entire afternoon. An awesome sadness hung over it. He examined with intense care the heads of St. John the Baptist, the Virgin of the Visitation, and St. Elizabeth, the best known of the many statues that ornamented the cathedral. These heads were alive. He noticed with great interest that they were carved with a look of pity, the heavy cast of sorrow. Here, somewhere in the thirteenth and fourteenth centuries, Auguste reflected, a French sculptor had individualized his art for the first time. In these statues he saw the foreshadowing of a whole race of French sculptors. He was grateful that their love of truth had not been smothered by their love of God. But he could remain only a day in Rheims, there was so much to see in Italy.

The next few days, he spent getting to Italy by way of Lausanne and Geneva. Auguste liked both cities, particularly the architectural order of Geneva, and he was delighted by the Alps. "They are incredibly beautiful," he wrote Rose in a short, cheerful letter. "Where Rheims was light and bold, the mountains are somber and powerful and enormous. Wonderful rock formations. It proves, *ma chatte*, as I have told you often, that God is the greatest sculptor of all, and you should not be offended when I say so."

III

The Italians Auguste met in northern Italy were offended, however, when he dared criticize *la bella Italia*. When he complained of the cold in Milan and Turin, he was accused of being anemic and bloodless. Disappointed because he found none of the "golden light" he had heard so much about in Brussels and Paris, there was fog and rain wherever he went, he wrote Rose, "The weather is like Belgium, bad, but the natives tell me that it will improve. I'm sure it will—after I leave."

The weather was still disappointing as he approached Florence. He wondered what had happened to the beautiful Italian winters he had heard so much about: it was still rainy and chilly. But on the train he met an Italian who was tall and handsome, and he thought, Ah! what a *chef-d'oeuvre* this fine-looking young man would make. In his mind this passionate, gesticulating youth became someone important to model.

The man, sensing Auguste's interest and that Auguste was a tourist whose ignorance could be turned to a profit, was friendly immediately. He introduced himself as Salvatore Santoni. Santoni, who knew French, having lived near the Savoy, told Auguste that he was going to Florence also. Santoni was going to Rome, actually, but he could stop off at Florence if a few francs could be reaped. He said, "Isn't the Italian landscape pretty?"

Auguste nodded, anxious to model Santoni, although he preferred the well-cultivated fields of France. The Italy he was viewing was too rugged, too barren, to suit him. He thought, mimicking Santoni, *la bella Italia*, indeed! No city could be as wonderful as Florence was supposed to be.

Santoni, hearing that Auguste was coming to see Michelangelo, exclaimed fervently, "Michelangelo, he was a great one! You are a wise man to see his work."

"Have you seen his 'David,' or 'Moses'?" asked Auguste.

"No, no, my friend, but like every good Italian, I am proud of this man. He is the glory of *la bella Italia*."

Auguste's disenchantment with Italy grew as he entered Florence. He found much of the city drab, the color of rust and yellow chalk. Yet for an instant, viewing a panorama of Florence from the piazzale Michelangiolo, he thought it a smaller version of Paris with its expanse of roofs at the foot of encircling hills; then he decided this was sentimental, for it was still rainy and cold and gloomy.

He stayed at a Swiss *pensione* on the via Tornabuoni on the recommendation of Salvatore Santoni, who told him, "It is good, the Swiss are clean, and you will not be cheated." Santoni was righteous about keeping his new friend from being cheated by anyone else. And the woman who ran the *pensione* was a friend, a Florentine, who had bought it from the Swiss owner because of its reputation for cleanliness and honesty. Auguste agreed to meet Santoni in front of the Duomo in three days. He was even more eager to model him, although he knew this was impossible at the moment, but he mustn't lose touch with such a splendid model—right out of Michelangelo, he thought.

The first two days Auguste spent sightseeing through Florence. He knew he should rush to see the art, especially Michelangelo and Donatello, but the more he saw of Florence the more he hesitated. As his disillusionment grew, he developed a reluctance to view Michelangelo in the original, certain this would be another disenchantment—one he could not endure. He did visit Dante's home, remembering that Dante had been a Florentine until exiled, but the house was nothing now and he felt betrayed by his enthusiasm.

He was surprised by the kind of enthusiasm he found in Florence. Two Florentines would fall immediately into an argument, with much gesticulating and shouting, and Auguste was sure a bloody fight would follow. Instead, once their emotion was released, they went off arm in arm. And there were the other enthusiasts, like Santoni—except they were usually short and fat—telling him how generous and hospitable they were, and, "Isn't Florence wonderful?" He strode away then.

He was growing very tired of *la bella Italia*. There was still the constant talk of the "golden light," though it hadn't stopped raining. The food was too heavy for his touchy stomach, he missed French delicacy and French sauces. There was much talk of Dante and Michelangelo and Donatello, all Florentines, but he saw no contemporary art, and the sightseers were almost all French, English, and a few Americans. But living was cheap, he thought gratefully, he would be able to see everything he was curious about, and some of the women were so handsome and voluptuous it was difficult to take his eyes off them. Statuesque women were a national virtue, he thought, and relieved the pomposity of many of the men.

The third day Santoni was at the piazza of the Duomo, as promised, with a friend, whom he introduced as Vittorio Peppino, a guide. Peppino was also tall and handsome, an even more attractive figure of a man to model.

Peppino was willing—graciously—to show Auguste about Florence, for twenty francs a day.

Auguste said, "It isn't necessary. I can find my way myself."

Peppino was furious. He shouted in clear French, "The French, they spend nothing since they lose, they give it all to the Prussians!"

But Auguste couldn't be offended: Peppino's posture was extraordinary and his pose fabulous. Then he remembered that Peppino was insulting and that to model him would be too complicated. He started to walk away, and Santone grabbed his arm and stated, "My friend likes you."

"Likes me? After that tantrum?"

"Of course. Would he waste his anger on nothing?"

Peppino said with a magnificent flourish, "I could consider your offer for ten francs."

Auguste said, "I offered nothing."

"But you must need something," said Santoni. "You are a stranger here, my friend. You want to know Florence, the art."

Auguste said, "I don't need a guide."

"Everybody needs a guide!" Peppino declared with another flourish.

Auguste thought Vittorio Peppino had the most expressive body he had ever seen.

"Do you prefer the Quattrocento or the Cinquecento?" When the guide saw the puzzled look on Auguste's face, he explained, "The Cinquecento is the sixteenth century, the time of Michelangelo, the high Renaissance."

"I will find what I want for myself," said Auguste.

"You will regret it," threatened Peppino.

"So I will regret it," said Auguste. But as he saw Peppino standing majestically in his sorrow, the guide was so striking that the desire to model him became irresistible. He said, "Monsieur Peppino, if you ever get to Paris, I would be glad to see you."

"Paris? Santoni tells me that you come from Belgium."

"I work in Belgium. But I will be back in Paris, someday, soon." Auguste gave his father's address to the two Italians.

Then Peppino grabbed him by the arm until Auguste explained that he was a sculptor. The Italian's hand fell away as if stricken with palsy. All the sculptors Peppino knew were poor.

"Oh, I will pay."

"Pay? How much?"

"Fifty francs. A hundred." Auguste felt reckless, but he liked the feeling. He could not even afford ten francs, yet at least in the gesture he would look like a real sculptor.

"How do we know you will pay that much?"

"How do I know you will be worth modeling? Either of you?"

Peppino pondered this a minute, then glanced at Santoni, who nodded slowly. Peppino wrote out an address and handed it to Auguste, saying, "My brother lives there, in Roma. We can be reached there."

With a mixture of "*Merci*" and "*Grazie*" they parted, believing they would not see each other again, yet somehow not quite sure.

Now Auguste went to the Uffizi, the Pitti Palace, the great art galleries of Florence, and though there were paintings of artists he admired: Tintoretto, Raphael, Titian, Rubens, Botticelli, he grew exhausted with the relentless devotion to the Madonna and the saints. Undeniably these were great paintings, he thought, but most of them lost their illumination in the monotony of repetition. He decided that one of the secrets of great art was variety. The very sameness of the subjects in these galleries created fatigue. He again put off seeing the "David," positive this would be the final disillusionment.

He had lost all desire to look when he came upon statues by Canova. He liked them. Canova's female nudes were plastic, alive, he thought. Suddenly he had a craving for more sculpture, for the "David," for whatever else of Michelangelo was available.

No one knew where the original "David" was. There were several copies about, but Auguste had to see *the original*. Finally, after many natives didn't know what he was talking about, he learned that the original had been removed from the Palazzo Vecchio the previous year and had been placed in the Accademia di Belle Arti.

He found the Accademia after a number of wrong directions. He paused at the entrance. It was a private world, no one else was about, but he was afraid. One more disappointment would be too much to endure. And he could not view the "David" as a *petit maître*, he had to be his own man.

He moved forward pessimistically, and suddenly the "David" loomed ahead of him and he felt a new momentum. It was not a dream, he thought, but the augmentation of the dream. No matter how good the pictures of the "David" had been, they had not been good enough. He had a sense of sheer physical delight as he viewed the figure. He savored every muscle; it was like a journey through a great anatomy lesson. His anxieties were gone. "David" was a statue where the sculptor had been in complete command.

Auguste put everything else out of his mind, studying the vitality of the figure. He examined the "David" from every position. He walked around the huge statue step by step, surveying what he called "the profiles"—each contour, surge, and definition of the stone. He ran his strong, flexible fingers sensuously and feelingly over the marble. It felt as real and alive as it looked. He was suspended in time. There was so much grandeur in the body, almost too much, he thought, yet David was heroic rather than divine. As Lecoq had said, he must see accurately. And with his own eyes.

Michelangelo had been clever, he thought: Michelangelo had made the powerful body so appealing that the viewer forgot the sling that David was holding, that it was Goliath who was the giant. And the face was too youthful, too feminine, for the mature body, but the size was just right; the amazing fact was that "David" created his own truth, his own world. He was fascinated by the size, the nudity, the flow of the flesh, the wonderful hands—he knew he would never forget the hands!

Refreshed and strengthened, Auguste returned to view the "David" the next day and the next. He wanted to see it in various lights, at different times of the day. He continued to feel that the face was vain, too pretty, but that the figure was the perfect male body.

Toward the end of the second day he stumbled upon Michelangelo's unfinished "St. Matthew" and he was stirred again. This was supposed to be one of the Florentine's lesser pieces, but there was such a concentration of energy and emotion here that Auguste was deeply moved. The very lack of finish, the writhing, tormented figure seeking to emerge from the marble, the roughness, the blend of figure and background as if the stone itself had given birth, was even more exciting and dramatic than the "David." Michelangelo was a magician, he thought; the very technique of the unfinished "St. Matthew" gave the sense of the struggle of life to emerge from stone.

During the next week Auguste exposed himself to everything he could find of Michelangelo. There were still things he didn't like, and there was nothing he agreed with completely, but he was fascinated by the four unfinished captives. He loved the rough quality of the sculpture more than the purity of finished marble; it was as if the flesh retained Michelangelo's fingerprints. As if, thought Auguste, the sculptor had fought to release these figures from the stone in which they had been slumbering. And if Michelangelo had failed in that, he *had* succeeded in giving them a Promethean ecstasy that was a grudging acknowledgment by the stone itself of the sculptor's strength.

Auguste went to the sacristy of the Medici Chapel with a new vigor. He thought the bodies of the two women, the first female nudes of Michelangelo he had seen, too muscular, with the shoulders and buttocks of an Atlas, yet he fell in love with "Dawn." Despite her muscles, or perhaps because of them, her primitive female power gave him a surge of joy.

After a quick but intense look at Ghiberti's sculptured doors, which he liked very much, he rushed off to the Rome of Michelangelo.

Yet by the time he found the Sistine Chapel—weaving his way through the horde of other tourists, priests, natives from the provinces, children chattering shrilly, he had been lost many times and was so bewildered, tired, and exasperated searching for this elusive Renaissance art his excitement and concentration were gone. There were far too many people crowded into the chapel. His neck ached as he strained to see the paintings, and he was shocked by the mixture of styles. Whatever the skill of the artists who had painted the panels beneath the Florentine's work, these panels clashed violently. Auguste couldn't remember when he had been so annoyed. He felt a victim of *la bella Italia*.

Flooded with anger, Auguste was about to stalk out when he saw several people lying on the floor to look up at Michelangelo's ceiling. Perhaps it was forbidden, he thought, but he was too disgusted to care. If Michelangelo had painted on his back, his work should be viewed that way.

He disregarded the benches, deciding he must have the best view. His eyes widened as he stretched out on the floor and looked upward. The painting was natural now, and he no longer felt trepidation. How vital a thing was perspective!

No one bothered Auguste, and he lay there and smiled to himself: Lecoq's and Barye's stress on anatomy had been right. How minutely Michelangelo had studied the position of the muscles and the veins! The figures on the ceiling and front wall were carved as if from stone.

Michelangelo had been the sculptor still, even with paint. With what concentrated energy he must have worked! There seemed to be no posture, no movement which the artist had found too difficult to draw.

Auguste didn't care for the faces—he preferred Rembrandt's—Michelangelo's were classical, idealized, perfect-featured. And as his eyes grew trained to the perspective and height, he found fault with some of the bodies, superb though they were as drawings. Many of them were the same, without variety. Many were too muscular, with their knotted legs and arms, thick, square torsos—no one had such a square torso, he thought. And the bodies were too strained and defiant, the figures more like Achilles and Hercules than Adam. But the conception of God reaching out to breathe life into Adam with a touch of his fingertips was magnificent! Auguste exclaimed. Only a born sculptor could have conceived that.

Michelangelo had created this universe like a god almighty, whatever his acknowledgment to the Bible. The chapel had become his crucible, and his figures were more furies than angels. He had transmuted his vision of life into the form that had suited him. Auguste reflected that although the artist had followed the conventions of fresco painting and the narrative of the Bible he had followed little else. He had cared only for the male nude, painting it to a degree of virility that was amazing, that made Auguste wonder. As if Michelangelo couldn't endure his own puny body, as if when the world wouldn't heed his will bronze and marble and paint would.

This artist was competing with God, Auguste's mind raced on, in his own way forcing his shapes out of his chaos. No wonder much of his work was unfinished. Michelangelo was God's rival, always striving to master the world, to impose his vision on walls and stone and life. The Last Judgment was Michelangelo's "Judgment." The Creation of Adam was *his* "Creation of Adam." If there was a divine hand touching life into Adam, it was the artist's hand.

Auguste wanted to crawl through the entire chapel to view the ceiling from every conceivable angle, but the long, oblong room had become very crowded. His fortitude was being tested as it was, braving the tourists jamming in.

Excitedly Auguste rose to his feet. He had to get to his own sculpture. Not to do it like Michelangelo, not to sculpt like anyone else:

he surged with an enormous desire to model for himself. He had been taught to have faith in his own work, but he had only mouthed the words. Now he believed.

This great wind blew the rest of his schedule to pieces. Auguste made a special point of seeing the "Moses," which he liked very much, finding it the most satisfying of all of the Florentine's works. He would never forget the hands of "Moses" as long as he lived. He spent a hectic day observing the historic Rome, the Forum, the Colosseum, but his heart wasn't in it, although he liked Roman Rome more than the contemporary city. A few hours were devoted to more museum visiting, and he saw new Canova female nudes and Bernini portrait busts, which he admired, and an inner voice kept telling him that he was using them as an excuse to avoid starting his own work. Several days after he had left the Sistine Chapel, driven by a force even more irresistible than the one that had propelled him to Italy, he arranged to return to Belgium and his studio as quickly as possible.

IV

He stood at the door in Brussels, still blown homeward by a great wind, and knocked, to give Rose warning, and hoped his studio was ready. He had been gone just a month. She should be pleased that he had cut his trip short.

She was surprised. She didn't know what to say. What had gone wrong?

"Nothing," he said, annoyed. "I've work to do."

"Oh?"

"Aren't you glad to see me, *ma chatte*?"

"Are you glad to see me, Auguste?"

"That's a stupid question," he growled. "I'm home."

Rose didn't say anything. She was determined not to complain, not to weep, but also not to praise.

Auguste pushed past her and strode around the studio. Everything was in order. She had taken perfect care of his work.

"Do you feel better, Auguste?" she asked.

"I wasn't worried," he said. "I knew you would take care of everything."

But there was a new storm within him, she could see it in the critical, harsh way he examined his old work.

"Poor," he said, surveying his last few heads. "Weak." He saw that he had neglected drawing lately. He had a sudden, passionate desire to destroy everything he had done up to now, then he knew this was foolishness. Yet he was seized with a hatred of his recent work.

She asked, "Was Michelangelo that exciting?"

"Exciting?" He wanted to tell her that it wasn't that, but that Michelangelo had made him discontented, he had to strike out more individually, but she wouldn't understand. "Not really," he added, having, however, a need to talk to someone, he was bursting so with new impressions. "In many ways Donatello's figures have more variety, more grace than Michelangelo's. Michelangelo's figures are often too similar, too athletic, too muscular, even exaggerated, distorted."

"Then why are you so excited?"

"I told you I'm not!"

"You told me."

"Yes." He glared at the small heads he had done most recently and said contemptuously, "These *rococo* delicacies, they are the sins of my youth."

"I like them."

"You would."

Her face flamed. She looked as if he had struck her.

Apologetic then, he said suddenly, "I shouldn't have left you alone, but I couldn't have afforded it if both of us had gone."

"I know. Tell me, was Michelangelo as wonderful as you expected?"

"More so in some ways and less in others." Rose looked bewildered again, and he thought irritably she would never comprehend, but he would try to explain—this once more. "There is too much striving for grandeur in his work, he is always thinking of eternity, he is preoccupied with the male nude—"

"But he is a great artist, isn't he? The greatest, you told me."

"There is no such thing as the greatest," he said angrily. "Each fine artist stands by himself. Art is not a race, not a competition."

"But he is great," she persisted.

"Great!" he exclaimed caustically. "That's a word, an unimportant word!"

"Do you love him?"

"Love? You don't love another artist. You respect him, admire him, learn from him, but caring—that's not the vital thing."

"Auguste, what did you learn from Michelangelo?"

"That emotion can be energy. That a sculptor can never learn too much about anatomy, about man in movement. Oh, I knew this before, but he made it more convincing. And that if you believe in what you are doing, allow nothing to stand in your way."

"Did you like St. Peter's?"

"The architecture is strong, but the Vatican has so much *bric-à-brac* and fig leaves it obscures the fine things, like Michelangelo's 'Pietà.' "

"You're sacrilegious."

"I prefer plain speaking to amiable gentility."

"Did Michelangelo marry?"

"No." He laughed at the naïveté of her question. "They are not even sure whether he liked women."

"But the journey was worth it?"

"I had to meet Michelangelo head on." She looked puzzled, and he explained, "I learned I had to see with all my eyes, that two are never enough," and she was more puzzled.

She said, seeking to be helpful, "But you won't worry about your work any more."

"Yes, I will worry, but from now on every time I start a statue I will believe it could be my *chef-d'oeuvre*."

"What good was it if you still worry?"

This time Auguste did not try to explain. Yet she looked so concerned, he was touched and pleased. He told her proudly, "Of course the trip was worth it. Rosette, the whole journey amounted to only six hundred francs, less than the expense of casting one bronze head." And he had gained such a renewal of energy, and he had gone looking.

CHAPTER 19

Eighteen months later Auguste stood in his studio on the rue du Bourgmestre, in Brussels, and stared at his clay figure, then at the living model, and wondered if he had made any personal contribution. He had labored on this nude ever since his return from Italy, and now, finally, it was almost completed. The life-size statue, which he had named "The Vanquished," was done except for a few finishing touches. The slim, sensitive youth stood in a gesture of anguish, with his right hand clutching his head in pain, while his other hand was braced tensely upon a staff.

"You can sit," he said to the model, Auguste Neyt, a young soldier in the Belgian Army. The boyish Neyt stopped striding about the cold studio and sat down, throwing an old blanket around his naked body to keep warm.

After many wasted weeks Auguste had gotten Neyt to be natural, to stand or stroll about the studio relaxed and graceful. But, *mon dieu,* he thought, it had been difficult from the first day he had met the soldier in the shop, looking for a miniature bronze for his fiancée, to this. Tormented by his passion to produce something that would excel, Auguste had been struck by the soldier's fine posture and natural attractiveness. He was pleased that Neyt had none of the studied artificial poses of the professional model. Whatever attitude he caught Neyt in would not be duplicated.

But Neyt, who knew nothing about art, had resisted the offer to pose, and had been offended by the request to pose in the nude. To the soldier it had seemed improper, vulgar, unmasculine, and only an offer of ten francs an hour had changed his mind. Neyt had had no idea of the magnitude of the task, and the rate had been reduced steadily as his hours had increased. Yet now, though Neyt was exhausted and the sculptor owed him for many months, he was fascinated by this replica of himself, immensely curious as to how it would turn out. Neyt couldn't believe he looked this sensuous, almost feminine; if his soldier friends ever knew about this, they would be insulting, think him insane. He told himself he was only doing it for the francs, but he hadn't known his body could be so interesting and exciting.

Yet he was very tired. This Sunday it seemed they had been working forever. It was growing dark, and he would be late for his fiancée, yet this sculptor was still working as if it were the will of God. He asked, "Will you want me to pose again, maître?"

"Perhaps."

"Is it almost done?" Neyt was beginning to think it would never end.

"Almost."

"Will it be done tomorrow? Next week?"

Auguste shrugged. It would be done when it would be done. By now he knew the calendar only by the days he worked on "Le Vaincu." Instead of the sudden departures to visit a museum, a cathedral, he had devoted every free moment to working on this male nude. He hadn't allowed anything to divert him, not even Rose, and now "Le Vaincu" was almost alive.

"Who is that outside?" Neyt asked as he heard footsteps in the hallway leading to the studio.

"My housekeeper. Now take a deep breath so your chest expands." Auguste could tell by the sound of the feet that it was Rose; he could imagine her glaring at the studio with anger and hate—as she had ever since he had forbidden her to enter this room with the arrival of Neyt as a model. He could tell from the questions she asked that "Le Vaincu" was a secret he had kept from her that she could not abide; it made her feel like an alien in her own home. She had said as much, and he had walked away. And now she prowled outside, but was afraid to disobey him and enter.

Neyt said suddenly, having to demand attention, the sculptor seemed remote once more, "You know, it is becoming more difficult for me to get away. We will be going on field maneuvers soon. Will we need any more sessions?"

"I'm not sure. Will you be quiet? But keep your hands the way they are."

Without thinking Neyt had clenched his hands because of the cold and fatigue until the muscles stood strained and ridged and tense.

Auguste modeled swiftly and surely now, having seen what he had been waiting to see. The clay responded to his touch as if it were alive. The clay gave him the sensation of flesh. He made a final hollow at the neck and on the shoulder where the body, even as it was most muscular and masculine, was most vulnerable.

Auguste saw Neyt's eyes widen with amazement.

"Yes," said Auguste, "this may be a good one, if it is ever finished."

"It looks finished to me. It's the most lifelike naked man I've ever seen."

"Lifelike, I agree, but it must also be individual."

"It's too individual. I'll be afraid to walk the streets of Brussels after you exhibit this. Everybody will recognize me."

"Good."

"I hope I won't regret having modeled for this."

"You won't."

"In the Army such things are frowned upon."

"No one will know except your superior, who has given you permission."

"Unofficial permission. Are you really going to exhibit this?"

"As 'Le Vaincu,' a soldier who could have been in any army. Now stand up. Relax. Don't be afraid. Move if it helps. This young man, Neyt, would not have developed sensitively and feelingly if you were not that way yourself."

"*Merci, maître,*" replied Neyt, but kept walking to keep warm.

Auguste's fingers felt light yet firm. This figure would not have the heroic, overpowering power of the "David"; but it would be, unless he had become foolish, *a man, a human experience,* and *every man* who had stood up to defeat in war when everything had gone wrong, as should have occurred in France in 1870 and hadn't.

Neyt asked, "What happens after you have finished with me?"

"We put our young victim in bronze."

"Not marble?" Neyt was disappointed.

"No!" Auguste was emphatic. "Marble would idealize him too much. It would become pure narcissism. He will be just right in bronze."

"Marble would be more beautiful."

"Wrong. False. Neyt, you can dress now. And *merci*."

"*Oui.*" Neyt took another last look at "Le Vaincu." "He is so naked, *maître*, something scandalous is going to happen. I can feel it in my bones."

"You're chilled, and no wonder. The next studio I have, I'll see to it that it is better heated." Neyt had such a good complexion, it took the light so well, he must use him again.

"If there is a scandal, I hope I'm not dragged in."

"There are many male nudes about. Michelangelo was always doing them, even for the Church."

"And idealized them, you said."

"Monsieur Neyt, this is the kind of male figure I have to model. In sculpture we must conceal nothing."

II

Disturbed by the model's doubts, however, Auguste asked Van Rasbourg to view the finished figure, and then as a sop to Rose invited her also. He was determined not to listen to Van Rasbourg if his partner disliked "Le Vaincu," but Van Rasbourg might say one or two things that could be useful, and if impressed, could help with the Brussels Salon.

Van Rasbourg thought Auguste had behaved like God in this matter, ignoring all other considerations when it had suited him to work on his figure, but not allowing anyone to view it. Yet now Auguste expected others to be gracious to him. Van Rasbourg had a feeling that kindness would be mistaken for weakness. But he had to see: Auguste had been so consumed, something interesting might have come forth.

Rose wanted to refuse Auguste's invitation, awkwardly given, virtually a demand. She was hurt by his barring her from the studio. In her own opinion she was not his mistress: she was *Devotion!* How could she enter his studio when she was not wanted? He must have done something blasphemous. Her curiosity grew. What could he have hidden from her?

Van Rasbourg and Rose entered together; they were friends, with just enough distance and formality between them to prevent the dangers of intimacy. He called her Madame Rose; she referred to him as Monsieur Joseph.

They stood in the doorway, paralyzed by surprise. Van Rasbourg was startled and Rose was shocked. She exclaimed, "So realistic!"

Auguste said irritably, "The anatomy is sound."

Rose asked, "This is a year and a half's work?"

"What's the difference?" growled Auguste. It had been a mistake to ask her for an opinion. But there was a strange look in Joseph's eyes, and he turned toward him, insisting on the truth.

Van Rasbourg said, "Madame Rose may be right, Auguste. It is very realistic. People may be offended."

"It is no more realistic than the 'David,'" said Auguste.

"In a way it is." Auguste didn't agree, but Van Rasbourg persisted, "The 'David' is so large it loses the sense of being a living man. We think of him as a hero, a god, but 'The Vanquished' is a breathing, living man. You have made him life size, you have put a human face on a full-length nude. It is, to say the least, unusual."

"You mean it would have been better to have made him heroic?"

"Possibly. Why, you have even—made him almost feminine. Look at those hips, those buttocks." Rose was embarrassed, but he went on. "From the rear you could think this was a girl."

Auguste said doggedly, "That's the way he is."

"I don't dispute that," said Van Rasbourg. "It is a beautiful figure."

"Beautiful?" Auguste frowned.

"Not in the obvious way, but the modeling is so plastic you want to fondle it. He may be 'The Vanquished' but he is also 'The Victor.'"

"Do you think the Brussels Salon will accept it?"

"We can try. I have influential friends." Then Van Rasbourg looked sad.

Auguste asked, "What's wrong, Joseph?"

"I'm cutting my own throat. If this statue is a success, you won't want to give even half your time to our business. You will have to be a full-time sculptor."

"No one will like it," Auguste said in a sudden burst of pessimism. "They will compare 'Le Vaincu' unfavorably to Rude or Carpeaux and say I'm not academic enough."

"Then why did you do it?" asked Rose.

Auguste answered sharply, "Why do you ask such silly questions?"

Van Rasbourg stared once more at "The Vanquished," a slender figure that stood with a delicate sensuousness, the uplifted arms in the rhythm of anguished protest, the torso and legs as smooth and graceful as the elect of Greek beauty, whatever Auguste's title. With all the realism, this was the essence of physical beauty. This was Greece revisited, thought Van Rasbourg. Auguste had striven to reach the other extreme from Michelangelo, resolved not to glorify, not to model a hero, a Hercules, even a Prometheus, a figure that appealed to Auguste, and yet he had modeled a contemporary Apollo, stricken and sad and very appealing.

When several minutes had passed without any comment from Van Rasbourg, Auguste asked anxiously, "Well, Joseph, what do you think?"

"It's a little bit in the manner of the Greeks," said Van Rasbourg.

"That's impossible," Auguste said positively. "I didn't start with a set idea. I let the model's natural, unrestrained movements create the idea."

"That may be true," Van Rasbourg said. "And if this were a Venus, there would be no danger. Everyone would assume it was a classical figure. But a male? However, we will do what we can."

Rose said, "I must admit it is convincing."

Auguste asked Van Rasbourg, "Is there anything you don't like?"

"The staff that he is holding in his clenched hand."

"I gave it to him for support."

"It is unnecessary. It weakens him."

"I don't want him to be a super man. Like Michelangelo's men."

"No one with eyes in his head will make that mistake. After all, super men don't suffer, not the way this man does. But I would remove the staff."

Auguste was impressed with what Joseph said, but he had devoted too much time to the staff to remove it summarily. He said, looking like a granite rock, "I'll see."

"Which means you won't," said Van Rasbourg.

Rose scolded, "That's not nice, Auguste. You ask Monsieur Joseph for his opinion and then you disregard it."

Van Rasbourg said with a smile, "I made my contribution. I approved. That is all Auguste really desired. And a recommendation to the Salon."

Auguste muttered, "I wanted the truth."

"Certainly," said Van Rasbourg. "Your truth. I like that you have gone deep with this figure and made us feel his life force."

"I hope the Salon agrees."

"It won't," Van Rasbourg said with a positiveness unusual for him. "You are using a new grammar of sculpture here. They will regard you as a heretic. You will see. Auguste, are you casting him in bronze?"

"Yes. As soon as—"

"I advance the money."

Auguste stood silent. What else, indeed!

A few days later "The Vanquished" was sent to the best caster in Brussels, with money advanced by Van Rasbourg, to be placed in bronze. And when it came back, precisely cast, Auguste felt every inch of it. They had made no mistakes: he could sign his name to this. He was glad the figure was stripped bare of all ornamentation. It made "The Vanquished" more vital, real, adventurous. He was not certain about the staff but he did not alter it, for it did not strike him as crucial. There was a note on his model's stand, from Van Rasbourg, informing him that "The Vanquished" had been accepted by the Brussels Salon, on Van Rasbourg's recommendation, and that Auguste should give a list of the important artists he had studied and worked with—like a *jeune maître* still, Auguste thought bitterly.

But Van Rasbourg had underlined "whom you studied and worked with," and so Auguste sat down to compose this list. He had a sick feeling that it was more vital than the work itself. After considerable deliberation he wrote, "Lecoq de Boisbaudran, Louis Barye, Albert Ernest Carrier-Belleuse, and Joseph van Rasbourg." Perhaps Carrier-Belleuse would be flattered and forgiving, and Barye's name would be useful. Barye had died last year, and now was a famous sculptor.

Then to get away from feeling like a student, which he hated, he carved *Rodin* at the base of the statue, but in the rear, so that neither the signature nor anything else could distract from the figure. It was important that the judges of the Salon see how alive "The Vanquished" was.

III

Auguste entered the opening of the exhibition at the Cercle Artistique with Van Rasbourg and Rose, who walked humbly behind him. He felt chilled and feverish, triumphant and frightened at the prospect of seeing *his* work displayed in public, but he tried to look indifferent, to saunter, although his pace quickened as he saw a statue.

It was not his. There were many statues, far more than Auguste had expected. Auguste, who had come as on a pilgrimage, was unprepared for the lost feeling that rose in him. Wherever he looked there were many statues, many rooms, but no trace of "The Vanquished."

He thought he had made a mistake, that the figure had not been accepted after all, but Van Rasbourg assured him that it had, that it must be in one of the rear rooms.

They searched and searched and finally, in the last, rear room of the exhibition, they found "The Vanquished." Auguste shuddered: the statue was placed so badly, in a dark corner, where it could be viewed only from the front. And it was creating a commotion. A crowd was clustered there, laughing and sneering at it. There was a sign hanging on the arm of the figure with the derisive comment "Cast on the flesh of the model." Auguste felt damned, a bankrupt, a pimp! However many sculptors modeled from life, it was a slander among sculptors to be accused of it.

"There, there, there," said Van Rasbourg, pulling a furious Auguste away from the contemptuous crowd. "It's the envy of a couple of idiots!"

"It's true, it's true!" they heard several spectators exclaim. "It is so lifelike it must have been modeled on the body. From a corpse, no doubt."

Auguste raised his hands hopelessly.

Rose, with sudden desperation, pushed through the crowd, ripped off the offensive sign, and tore it into many pieces. There was an abrupt silence. The spectators were cowed by her violence. She uttered a prayer that Auguste be spared further misfortune, and then with her old, proud, upright carriage strode back to Auguste. She reminded Auguste of how often men at the point of death had been reprieved. He took her hand and walked out with her and Van Rasbourg, who said, "There will be favorable opinions, too."

IV

Auguste thought it impossible to remain in Belgium, however, when the vilification of "The Vanquished" spread to the Brussels newspapers. He wrote them that their implications that the figure had been modeled from life were unfair, and the calumny grew worse. The more he protested, the more he was accused. The following week was the worst of his life. Several times he went to the exhibition, and each time he saw his figure regarded with ridicule, scorn, and only rare approval. He told himself that he must not mind, this had been the history of many artists, but he minded very much. He felt sterile, that unless he were vindicated he would never be able to sculpt again.

V

Feeling dreadfully abused, Auguste stood in his studio before the bronze of "The Vanquished" after the exhibition at the Cercle Artistique and wondered where he had failed. Everything had fused in this figure. Yet they had made a public scandal of it. Disgusted, he picked up an iron bar to smash it, then hesitated—he ached all over at the thought of destroying "The Vanquished"; it would be murder. He paced about the studio, overwhelmed with hostility and rage. They had thrown slime upon "The Vanquished" and it had stuck. Unable to endure that any longer, exhausted, ill, nauseated, he turned on the statue, not noticing Rose and Van Rasbourg, standing in the doorway. He studied the statue for a final inspection and dismissal, raised the bar. Then Van Rasbourg stepped in front of him and cried, "You're not killing them, you're killing yourself."

Rose shouted, "I told you he would do it, Monsieur Joseph! I told you to hurry!"

Van Rasbourg said, "Give me the bar, Auguste."

Auguste said, "I can't even walk the streets without being laughed at."

"Then this is a good time to fight back. And some people did like the figure."

"Some!" Auguste declared with contempt, flourishing the iron bar at his enemies. "Did they defend me? Did they write the newspapers that printed the slander? Everyone who could support me, help me, hides, even Neyt. He is away on maneuvers. Purposely, I'm sure. *Mon dieu*, why are they so envious? Is it because I am French? And I've spent all my money having it cast in bronze?"

Van Rasbourg ignored the implied plea for money and said, "I'd call it 'The World of Bronze.' "

"World? Bronze?" Auguste looked dubious.

"The figure is an age of bronze."

Auguste stared at "The Vanquished" and said angrily, "It won't make any difference."

"It might. And isn't the staff unneccessary? Doesn't it weaken him?" Auguste wavered.

"Without the staff you would have a sense of purity. All the stress would be on the figure, on this age of bronze, and his concerns."

"The Age of Bronze," reflected Auguste. He put down the bar, which was Van Rasbourg's chief concern. He visualized the figure standing alone, devoted solely to the landscape of the flesh. It would be a more lyrical mood. He smiled for the first time in weeks. He took away the staff without another word.

"He's handsome," whispered Rose.

Van Rasbourg was pleased. He said, "Feel better?"

Auguste said, "I'd feel better if I exhibited in Paris. You know, Joseph, you're right, the Belgians are jealous of me because I'm French."

"You believe that," said Van Rasbourg.

"If the Paris Salon would accept this," Auguste said with a single-minded devotion, "It would be a vindication."

"You will need every bit of influence you can muster," said Van Rasbourg.

Auguste was transformed. The thought of returning to Paris was a blessing in itself.

Van Rasbourg said, "It will mean the end of our partnership."

"I'm sorry, Joseph, but what else can I do? I've been away too long as it is."

"Suppose they reject the figure? It's—" He paused out of politeness.

"It's likely, *mon ami*; they've ignored everything I've submitted. But I have to take the plunge someday. I'll never forgive myself if I don't."

"And five minutes ago you wanted to destroy this figure," said Van Rasbourg, marveling at the inconsistency of man.

"I will call it 'The Age of Bronze.' It will reach more people."

Van Rasbourg said, "I have no objection to dissolving our partnership, but at the moment I can't give you much cash, Auguste."

Auguste, thinking that Van Rasbourg was using this to keep the partnership from dissolving, said nothing.

There was a painful pause, and then Rose asked, "Will this mean a return to Paris, *chéri*? For good?"

"Yes. Only there is no money."

"You spent all you saved on the model?" she asked.

"See here," he said, flushing angrily, "I didn't ask for your opinion."

"Excuse me," said Van Rasbourg, starting for the door.

"If you don't mind," said Rose.

"Of course not." At the door Van Rasbourg added, "It is still a fine statue, Auguste. Don't let anyone change that."

Rose waited until Van Rasbourg was out of sight, and then said as Auguste glared at her, "Could you return to Paris if you had a thousand francs?"

"Don't be foolish! Where will I get that much money?"

"But could you?"

"I could on five hundred francs."

"With me?"

"Yes! But you are talking nonsense."

Rose walked slowly to her closet, picked up an old bag as if it were holy, held it close a moment, and then with fastidious care placed it in Auguste's hand. His eyes bulged with wonder as he saw money falling out in startling profusion: dirty metallic francs, soggy bank notes pinned together, ten-sou pieces, forty-sou pieces, many so discolored he could hardly tell what they were, ancient louis d'or that were black. Bound together by her love, he thought with a sudden pang of remorse. Then he was irate—how could she have hidden this from him? "Where did you get this?" he demanded.

"I sew when you are away, and save."

"I haven't been away for over a year."

"*Chéri*, you are always away when you are modeling. I think there are almost a thousand francs here?" She put it as a question so he could decide.

"A thousand?" He didn't, he couldn't believe her.

"Nine hundred and fifty, I think. I've been saving ever since I came to Brussels. For almost six years."

He was ashamed of himself, but he couldn't say he was sorry for his rudeness. He was a sculptor, not a husband. He shook his head in amazement. "Rosette, I'll never understand you."

"Are you happy, *chéri?*"

"Not unhappy," he said. "I can submit to Paris now."

"We will move back?"

"As soon as possible." He hesitated, then suddenly gave her back the money. "I can't take it. *Merci*, but I can't. It is years of your blood and flesh, and I've given you so little."

Rose chuckled and said with peasant sagacity, "It's more becoming, Auguste, when you are stern."

"I'm always stern about what I like."

They smiled at each other wistfully. She put the money back into his hands. His fine, powerful, beautiful hands, she thought. He held her as if he would never let her go. She could feel his finger marks on her palms, callused from much studio and housework. To serve him in such a moment was such a delight. He kissed her and she thought, ah, how dearly she loved him!

He said, "You are a natural, Rosette, don't change." He was deeply stirred by her generosity, and yet, somehow, had expected it. But suddenly he frowned. Did she have to look so dowdy? He scolded, "Do you always have to wear black and gray? You know I prefer bright colors."

She cast down her eyes and blushed.

"Don't you have any *amour-propre?*" With an air of sacrifice he handed her fifty francs of her own money, then suddenly, feeling bravely impulsive, added fifty more francs with munificent generosity and said, "Get a new dress. Two."

"And a parasol? I've always wanted a parasol, Auguste."

"As a gift?" He smiled indulgently and said, "If it will make you happy. But be sure it matches your dresses, and will be bright in the sun."

"I'll get whatever colors you prefer, *chéri*."

He said wonderingly, "The things you could have done with this money."

PART
FOUR
THE
RETURN

CHAPTER 20

The day Auguste returned to Paris was a beautiful one.

He stood on the top of the Arc de Triomphe, and the moment the city spread out before him, the familiar sights he loved, Notre Dame, the Louvre, the Seine, the Invalides, he knew he was home. How grateful he felt! He thought, *Paris . . . Ah! c'est magnifique!* It was a fine winter day, crisp and clear, and perfect for visibility. All of Paris seemed to stretch out at his feet. And for the first time the Arc de Triomphe really mattered.

After Belgium, Holland, and Italy he was proud that he was a Frenchman, thankful for Napoleon, especially after the *debâcle* of 1870. He was pleased with the good taste of the boulevards, the clarity and brightness of the sun and the light. Away, he had forgotten that Paris was a painter's city, though that was a commonplace, but today it struck him as the vividest of truths and reminded him that the architecture also made it a sculptor's city.

Auguste strode down the Champs-Élysées, past the fashionable women in enormous feathered hats, the gentlemen wearing top hats and frock coats and canes, feeling uncomfortable in his plain clothes, and came to the quais, where he was more at home. Here was his favorite arrondissement, where he had grown up. And he was curious; he had heard much about the damage wrought during the Commune. He viewed the spot where the Vendôme Column had been wrecked in the place de la Concorde, where the palace of the Tuileries had been destroyed, and to his surprise, was not affronted, for the Louvre, although hurt during the ferocious civil war, appeared the same, as solid and indestructible as ever.

Then as he paused on the Pont des Arts, he felt between two worlds. On the Right Bank loomed the Louvre, long and gray and imposing as before, yet still a million miles away; on the Left Bank, within reaching distance, was the Palais de l'Industrie, the home of the Salon, the parent of the Beaux Arts, and in a sudden feeling of despair it seemed just as far away. They would not accept his "Age of Bronze," he decided; this running battle would never end.

He felt better when he saw the old barges sailing under the bridge. He forgot the tragic bloodshed of the civil war and the changes that had occurred while he was away, that the Third Republic was ruled by a President who was one of the most ardent royalists in France, Marshal MacMahon. In many ways Paris seemed no different from the day he had left, the people strolling, talking, smoking, pausing, looking, the workingmen in blue blouses and the gentlemen in frock coats, and the smartly attired girls, even the poor ones. That was what Rosette needed, he thought, the nuances of Parisian taste. She could no longer model for a Venus, but she would make a fine St. Joan, a goddess of war. Upon coming to this conclusion Auguste felt quite remarkable, almost clever.

He did not pause now until he came to what he loved. The cathedral had not changed. The stone pillars of Notre Dame still went up and up, strong and austere and straight, and the roof still seemed to float in the air. He was filled with his old wonder and gratitude. This ancient stone was alive, and it flowed into the sky. It was a treasure of medieval French sculpture.

Now Auguste was possessed with a fervent wish to absorb all of the city that he adored. He longed to look up Lecoq, Fantin, Renoir, Degas—his correspondence with Degas had died after an auspicious start—to see and discuss the latest in painting and sculpture, to hear what were his chances in the Salon. Was the Salon as benighted as ever? Had they heard anything about "The Age of Bronze"? Had the furor in Brussels reached Paris? *Mon dieu*, how exciting this part of Paris was! It gave him such will power. Suddenly he felt sorry for those who did not live here. There was an instant of great sorrow that he had been away so long, but it vanished as he resolved to work harder than ever to make up for it.

The more Auguste walked on, the more he desired to march to his old haunts, but he knew he must see his family first. They lived nearby, with Aunt Thérèse, on the rue Dauphine, and Papa would be offended if he went elsewhere first, and then there was *petit* Auguste. All at once he was nervous. It was preposterous, he thought, but he was almost afraid to meet the little one after all these years. The child was eleven, half grown-up. Would *petit* Auguste resent his long absence? Would the child still want to see him? Like him? Then he told himself this was nonsense. As he had told Rose, he was a sculptor, not a husband or a papa. Yet his nervousness increased as he approached the house.

He recognized the neighborhood from his childhood. It was not as run-down as the rue Mouffetard or as working-class as St. Denis, but it was a poor one. The iron balcony was rusty and ugly. The small stone house was cold and damp and smelled of poverty.

He knocked, not having a key although he had been paying the rent while living in Belgium, and Aunt Thérèse let him in. He realized she had been waiting for him, she came into his arms naturally and without surprise.

Rose must have gotten Van Rasbourg to write, he thought, even after they had dissolved their partnership; it was good of Joseph to do this, for he hadn't been able to—he would have become sentimental, and that would have made matters worse.

"Come," said Aunt Thérèse as she saw him waver. "Papa is waiting."

"How is he?" asked Auguste, not moving.

"As well as you can expect for his age."

But he could not ask about *petit* Auguste, it would admit his guilt and curiosity and eagerness.

Aunt Thérèse asked, "Aren't you curious about your son?"

"I never denied I was his father," said Auguste. Aunt Thérèse was even thinner than before; she walked stiffly now, like an old woman, but her eyes and manner were as bright and lively as ever.

Aunt Thérèse said, "Oh, you've supported him. That's something."

"But not enough?" inquired Auguste.

"*Mon chat*, let's not keep Papa waiting. He's very nervous as it is."

No more than I am, thought Auguste, but he followed Aunt Thérèse into the kitchen, where Papa always felt most at home, where Papa sat at the head of the dinner table, as in the old days, smoking his pipe. It smelled so vile and looked so old Auguste had a feeling it was the pipe they had quarreled about when Papa had modeled for him. Then he saw Papa jump as he neared and go quite white.

Papa's Louis Philippe chin whiskers had deteriorated into a yellowish straggly beard. His thick, heavy features had become gaunt and pinched. He sat bent over. His broad shoulders and muscular chest and arms, of which he had been proud, which Auguste had bragged about as a child, were gone and he had shrunk like collapsed clay in which the armature had failed. Old age was cruel, thought Auguste, often crueler than death.

There was a long, long pause. Papa stared at Auguste so intensely that Auguste grew embarrassed, until he realized Papa was staring this way because Papa couldn't see him. Papa was blind, he realized with a shock. He had known that Papa's eyes were bad, but this? Papa's eyes were sharp and brightly blue and saw nothing, yet they said, Why did you stay away so long? He turned to scold Aunt Thérèse for not telling him about Papa's blindness, but Papa was reaching awkwardly for him, intending to kiss him on the cheeks like a solemn ritual from childhood, and Auguste leaned forward so that Papa could do it without embarrassment.

Papa said, "That's a fine beard you have, Auguste."

Auguste said, "*Merci*, Papa. Like yours."

"You are staying home for good?"

"For good. As soon as I find a house for all of us."

"You will live with ordinary people?"

"How else do I exist!"

Papa didn't seem to hear.

Then Auguste's heart pounded like a child's. A youngster stood before him, awkwardly, self-consciously. It must be *petit* Auguste, but how the boy had grown! He noticed that the boy had the same trick of peering he had had as a child, and stood with his legs crossed, as he used to do. Nature had persisted in the boy in spite of his absence. Although *petit* Auguste's features, particularly his nose, chin, and eyes, resembled Rose's, his coloring is mine, Auguste said to himself and he moves as I do, and he has my hands, square, strong, with thick, stubby fingers—look how he presses them against his sides now, as if to make an imprint though it is probably nervousness. Yet perhaps he has some artistic ability, Auguste thought in a flash of hope. Suddenly Auguste was lonely for his son. But don't give your heart too soon, he warned himself.

Aunt Thérèse said, "Kiss your father, Auguste, like a good boy."

Petit Auguste raised his face dutifully and was as unyielding as uncut stone, and suddenly Auguste picked up the boy with his powerful hands and impulsively embraced him, and sighed deeply—this was not an easy conquest—the boy was still cold and unbending. Aunt Thérèse was concerned, afraid that Auguste would lose his temper. Then *petit* Auguste was tickled by his father's beard and began to giggle. Auguste looked confused for a moment, then began to laugh, too.

"*Mon dieu!*" cried Papa. "I haven't heard that for a long time."

"We must go for a picnic," said Auguste. "Where would you like to go, little one?"

"The Bois de Boulogne," the child suggested.

"It's far away," said Papa.

"We can take an omnibus," said Auguste. "Then walk in the Bois and on the Grand Boulevards."

The boy asked, "Can we take a big, yellow omnibus? With two horses?"

"Yes!" said Auguste, and arranged with Aunt Thérèse to have dinner after they returned. He helped Papa as they walked out the front door.

Petit Auguste wanted to sit on the driver's box with the driver, but Auguste said that was impossible. The child regarded Auguste as if he had been unreasonable, but his father remained firm.

There were many victorias, landaus, broughams, and dogcarts in the Bois de Boulogne, and *petit* Auguste wanted to know why they couldn't take one.

"We can," said Auguste. "But first, little one, we should walk."

Papa nodded, and the boy, who was attentive to Papa, subsided. Now they walked until their legs ached, but no one would admit it. Auguste held Papa by the arm and *petit* Auguste by the hand. Auguste described everything to Papa, but casually, as if it were just a conversation.

Then Papa, with some of his old vigor, declared, "During the German siege the Bois was a ruin, but when the Prussian spiked helmets marched through Paris we closed every door and shade. No one watched. But I forgot, you were in Paris afterward."

"For just a short time, Papa."

"I didn't say you were wrong to go to Brussels."

The sun dropped below the horizon, and it grew chilly suddenly. Auguste hailed a carriage. And when Papa was worried about the cost Auguste said they didn't have to economize, not on a picnic, not today!

"What did I tell you?" Papa whispered to *petit* Auguste. "Things will be different with Auguste home."

Petit Auguste asked, "Did they destroy your statue, Father?"

Auguste said, "How did you know about the statue?"

"Mama told me about it. They didn't break it, did they?"

"No, little one, no."

Papa nudged *petit* Auguste and said, "Tell your father what you are going to be when you grow up."

The child hesitated, then said to his father, "You won't be angry?"

"Of course not, little one."

"I want to grow up," the boy said with measured words, as if he had been taught to know this by heart, "to be like my father."

Papa said as Auguste was speechless, "You picked a fine carriage. This is the first decent outing I've had since Rose left."

"Why?" asked Auguste, surprised.

"We couldn't afford it," said Papa. "The cost of living keeps going up. Wine has gone up from seventy centimes to one franc a litre, sugar from seventy to ninety centimes. Coffee, which Thérèse used to get for two francs a pound, is three francs twenty-five now, and we can hardly ever afford meat. Butter, cheese, and eggs are practically impossible. After the idiocy of the Commune, I thought things would improve, but they keep getting worse. In my own lifetime I have lived through so many changes of government. I was born when Napoleon was Emperor, and then after Napoleon there was the monarchy, in 1815, and overturn in 1830, 1848, 1851 with Napoleon the Third, and then 1870. I've lived through so many different kinds of governments. You would think the people had had enough, but no, they never learn. Now there are many rumors of a *coup d'état.*"

"I thought France was prosperous."

"For the *petite bourgeoise*. But our President, MacMahon, is a royalist and a marshal. They say he'd like to be an emperor."

"You'd think, with Napoleon the Third, we had enough of emperors."

"Oh, *mon dieu*, he's dead, but the idea isn't."

"Papa, since when have you become so interested in politics?"

"What else do I have to be interested in!"

When the adults were silent, *petit* Auguste asked, "Will Mama be back soon?"

Auguste said, "As soon as we find a place where we can all stay. Now she is taking care of my work in Brussels until I find a studio to put it in."

The carriage drew up to the door. It cost more than Auguste had expected, but he pretended it was nothing. This had to be a happy occasion. And suddenly as darkness fell upon Paris, he was sad for the days he had been away from Papa and *petit* Auguste and his beloved aunt Thérèse. He was sure in a moment of apprehension that "The Age of Bronze" would be vilified here, too. Then he saw tears in Papa's eyes.

Auguste asked, "What's wrong?"

"Nothing, nothing," Papa said. "Is this a large statue you are showing in Paris?"

"A naked man. Life size."

"Ah, *mon dieu*," Papa said knowingly. "But not a Jesus?"

"Not even a saint, but a man, a young man."

"As I might have been, and you are?"

"I'm not so young any more, Papa."

"Wait until you are my age. You will wish you were thirty-five again."

"I'm going on thirty-seven. It's too late for success."

"After all the time you've spent." But Papa wore a big smile. Aunt Thérèse, to celebrate Auguste's return, had a special dinner, with *bouillabaisse*, a large roast, plenty of potatoes, vermouth, and Cointreau. "Like old times," said Papa.

Everything had to be like old times for Papa, Auguste thought sadly. And suddenly he had to say what had been on his mind for a long time.

When he got a minute alone with Papa, he reproached Papa for not telling him that Mama was dying, and Papa replied, "I didn't know she was dying—how quickly one dies! We had to bury her at once because of the contagion." Papa looked very old, helpless, and fell silent.

"But to bury her in an unmarked grave?" Auguste continued.

"Thousands were," mumbled Papa. "Even the rich. It was the time of the siege, the Commune, and you were off in Brussels."

"I didn't mean to hurt you," said Auguste.

"Why not? I can't work. I can't see. I'm worth nothing."

"You are my father," Auguste said strongly.

"Is that why you stayed away so long?"

"I had work to do."

"I know, I know. Do you really intend to stay home even if they should turn down your figure?"

"Yes. Every French artist returns to Paris. It is his legacy."

"What about the child? Will you take him now?"

"Why not? He's my son." But one thing, with all the pleasure of the day, worried Auguste. The child had held on to his hand with an intensity that was frightening, that demanded affection with a tyranny that was total. It could be too great a sacrifice, and it made him suspicious.

Papa sighed and said, "Do not be hard with him. I'm too old to train him as you were trained, and he is a little wild."

Auguste replied, "When Rose returns, she will know what to do."

CHAPTER 21

When Auguste heard, unofficially, that the jury of the Salon were divided over accepting his "Age of Bronze," he decided to visit his artist friends in the hope they could advise and help him. He learned that they were meeting now at the Café Nouvelle Athènes, on the place Pigalle.

Auguste took the Batignolles omnibus, with its yellow sides and red lamps and then climbed the Buttes Montmartre. He liked the sight of Paris spread out below him. Lights twinkled wherever he looked, as if the city had a multitude of eyes. But he found the Nouvelle Athènes only after considerable searching, on the top of a steep hill that grew into the place Pigalle. It was the last building, small and unpretentious. Auguste was amused. He stood inside the door, thinking that it was not the New Athens, whatever the owner intended. The ceiling was painted with a garish éclat, and the chef-d'ouevre was a picture of a huge rat. There was sand on the floor, and the café was divided by a high partition which separated the bistro from the restaurant.

The husky proprietor—proud that during the years of Napoleon III he had had important customers such as Daudet, Zola, Courbet, Gambetta—greeted the stocky, red-bearded man standing in the doorway. He was sure this broad-shouldered man was an artist, there was such an intense look in his eyes. He asked, "Who are you looking for, monsieur?"

Auguste was just as polite. "Monsieur Degas."

"Ah, the painter. There." The proprietor indicated a group of men sitting around two long marble tables in the corner. A cluster of blue tobacco smoke hung over the corner, and Auguste could not make out the faces.

He was self-conscious as he approached them. The years that had intervened seemed an eternity. Would they be greatly changed? Would they regard him as an interloper now?

He saw Degas, more round-shouldered then ever in his usual pepper-and-salt suit, nibbling on almonds and raisins which he didn't offer to anyone else; Manet as attractive and distinguished as ever—but much older; Renoir, still thin and straight, with the same ragged red beard and the hair casually over his forehead and not appearing much older; Fantin, with his Vandyke more carefully cultivated than before and looking sad; a Monet who had grown heavier, his big beard framing his broad, regular features, which had taken on a perpetual solemnity; and several others he did not recognize.

They were arguing vehemently, and they did not stop as he approached. Degas nodded, Renoir grinned, Monet shrugged, Manet bowed politely, and Fantin shook his hand warmly, and the discussion rushed on.

Nothing had changed, and everything had changed. Their complaints sounded the same as before, it was difficult to believe years had passed since they had seen him, and yet things were not the same.

There was a stiffness and hostility in the air. He felt remote. He thought Degas was preoccupied with Degas; Manet was tactful rather than amiable; Monet was reserved and somber. However, Fantin had retained his personal generosity and Renoir still had his *bonhomie.*

Fantin introduced him to Camille Pissarro, a middle-aged man with a long white beard and a fringe of white hair, who looked like a Biblical prophet. "A painter," said Fantin. "An open-air man, like Monet."

Pissarro smiled gently and made room for Auguste to sit down. Auguste was not introduced to the others, as if they were just hangers-on.

Degas rushed on, ignoring Auguste to attack an attentive Manet.

"We make an enormous emotional investment in our own show and you back out."

"Back out?" said Manet, a strong question in his voice. "I never said I would exhibit."

Degas said quite sharply, "But you will exhibit in the Salon."

"So will I," ventured Auguste. "If they accept me. Is that a sin?"

Degas looked contemptuous, but did not deign to answer.

"Where else?" asked Auguste.

"Where else, indeed?" said Manet.

Degas said, "You know how much we have put into this coming exhibition."

"What exhibition?" asked Auguste, feeling as if he had come from another world.

Fantin explained, "What is being called now the Exposition des Impressionnistes—the third! This April."

"A vulgar title," said Degas.

Fantin said, "It is in direct opposition to the Salon. And I think the timing is wrong."

Auguste said wonderingly, "But you were the one who was always loudest about having our own exhibition."

Fantin said, "It didn't work. We've had two, and there were a few sales, but now it is becoming a political issue. The government, being royalists, claim the Exposition des Impressionnistes is the work of the republicans."

"Utter nonsense," said Degas. "I am a royalist and I exhibit. Manet is a republican and he doesn't. But then our political life is as stupid as ever."

"Even among the royalists?" asked Auguste.

"They are most stupid of all," said Degas. "Because they should know better. They support a marshal, MacMahon, who never won a battle. He says everything must be constitutional and he sits in Versailles like a Louis XIV. He can't make up his mind, and meanwhile we are more confused than ever."

"You don't sound confused," said Auguste.

"Why should I be confused, Rodin?" Degas said with a dramatic flourish of his thin hands. "I don't intend to let the Salon get the better of me."

Auguste said, shocked, "But this sounds like a civil war."

"It is a civil war," Degas said. "The same as in the days of the Commune. Never is there such ferocity as when Frenchmen kill other Frenchmen. If we had had half as much ferocity against the Prussians, we would never have lost. And now we are being placed in the same position. The Salon, the Institute, the Academy, are making it a civil war. Our daring to have our own exhibition is an offense beyond forgiving, and they are determined to ruin us."

Fantin said, "So you have to be as fanatical as they are, insisting that anyone who shows in the Salon cannot submit with you."

"It's vital," said Degas. "They use the dry guillotine, so will we."

Auguste sighed. "An impasse, always an impasse. In Belgium they said I modeled from life."

Fantin said, "We heard."

"And here," Auguste rushed on while he had the courage to speak, "you fight among yourselves. *Mon dieu*, what can I expect from the Salon if this is the way you treat one another?"

Degas said, "Indifference at the best, contempt at the worst."

Monet asked, "Rodin, why don't you exhibit with us?"

Auguste wavered. It was tempting. But he would be the only sculptor; he would be too exposed. He said, "I've already applied. I need vindication."

Degas said, "Then you'll get what you deserve."

Auguste cried, "But I came here for help!"

"Help?" Degas regarded Auguste as if he were insane. "We are considered pariahs by the Salon and you come to us."

"How can we help you," declared Monet, looking solemn, "when we desperately need help ourselves?"

Auguste asked, "Who is showing in your exhibition?"

"In the Exposition des Impressionnistes," Fantin repeated with a mockery Auguste had never heard in him before. "Monsieurs Degas, Monet, Cézanne, Pissarro, Renoir, and a dozen others you don't know."

Auguste asked, "But not you, Fantin, or Manet?"

Fantin said, "It has been decided that anyone who exhibits in the Salon cannot exhibit with them. That's what we've been quarreling about. You see, Rodin, Paris is no more peaceful than Brussels."

Auguste said defiantly, "Paris is the place to exhibit."

"Why don't you die, Rodin?" Renoir said cynically. "Now that Barye is dead, he is a genius."

Auguste murmured, "I haven't done enough work."

Renoir added, "Then Carpeaux died soon after Barye, and now he is a genius, too. Or perhaps you could become an actress, like Mademoiselle Sarah Bernhardt. She submits regularly to the Salon. Portrait heads. And regularly they accept her."

"Is she good?" Auguste asked.

Renoir said, "There is much talk about her as an actress. Her voice is phenomenal. The Salon last year also exhibited several portraits of her."

Auguste looked sick: was even Renoir becoming malicious?

Renoir said, sensing Auguste's despair, "I'm sorry, *mon ami*, but it is the truth. I don't want you to be hurt afterward."

Auguste nodded, and saw several *lorettes* sitting nearby. As their gaze met his, they cast him an enticing smile and he had a sudden yearning. Under the gaslight they became the burning focus, not these fervid arguments that never settled anything, that only made matters worse. He wished he could be in love just like any ordinary café habitué. He noticed one girl in particular, sitting alone at a small table, sipping vermouth, dressed in a bright red costume. Her skin flamed under the gaslight, and her eyes were patches of brightness in her pale skin. Then a man sat down beside her and he was jealous. When she left, arm in arm with the man who had picked her up, he felt deserted. He heard the rumble of the omnibuses, the carriages, the cabs; he wondered what they had taken—or did she live nearby and they had gone there? Lovers filled Paris, he thought, and all he had was the naked flesh of his desire, and new disappointments every day.

"Weren't you listening?" he heard someone shout in his ear.

He turned to see Degas leaning over him. Degas' cheeks were flushed, his eyes gleamed.

Degas declared positively, "You are very *naïf*, Rodin, to think you will be noticed. Last year they had two thousand and ninety-five pictures alone, and this year there will be more. They will gape at the *tableaux de style*, the larger the better, and of course the military paintings, eternally defying Napoleon. The Salon will be full of

Gérôme, Cabanel, and Bouguereau, selling for thousands of francs, smearing their canvases with heroism and beauty and lies. Criminal aberrations, full of dead colors, and they are dead, too, although unfortunately they don't know it. Indeed, Bouguereau sold several paintings last season for many thousands of francs, so you can depend on it, this year's Salon will be full of imitations of Bouguereau."

"Yes!" said Auguste, curious about another young woman who had sat down. She was alone, but he wasn't sure whether she was a *lorette*; she was well dressed, pretty and young, without the faded look of the prostitute. But he couldn't move toward her as he desired. It was too public, obvious, and he felt clumsy. He asked, "Will there be anything in the Salon that's good?"

Degas said, "Manet, perhaps."

Manet said, "Now, let's not be patronizing, Degas. You like honors as well as the next man."

Degas replied angrily, "I'm not a *bourgeois*, like you."

Manet bent forward as if to strike Degas, who trembled but did not move. Instead Manet turned to Auguste and said, "You see, Rodin, how many Napoleons we have. Is it any wonder that *coup d'états* are our favorite form of political expression? And you expected us to be full of *esprit de corps*. Do you understand why the critics can't agree if we can't?"

Auguste was filled with foreboding. No one had asked him about his work. They were demanding recognition, but they didn't recognize him. The smoke of the café became more and more stifling. They acted as if he had accomplished nothing. The reunion, which he had gone to with such eagerness and anticipation, had become a great disillusionment.

They were still arguing when he left at midnight. The gaslight flicked off and on to warn them that the Nouvelle Athènes was closing, but they did not take the hint. Yet he was not certain they were really cold and indifferent. As he stood up and said "*Bonsoir*," Fantin advised, "Make sure they place your figure properly, it can make a great difference," and Renoir added, "So the body is not in shadow," and Degas, having to have the last word, stated, "And if it is a catastrophe, remember we warned you."

II

"The Age of Bronze" was accepted by the Salon a few days later. Auguste came to the Palais de l'Industrie with the figure, determined that it be exhibited to the best advantage. He insisted that the statue be placed in a large, light, front room, declaring that was vital, and when he had only a few francs for the attendants it was put in a small, dark, rear room. He protested vehemently, and it was moved spitefully into a corner and so high it was impossible to get behind the figure. When he complained about this shift, he was warned that worse could happen. Afraid then, remembering the tales of figures chipped and cracked while standing in the Salon, he desisted. But he felt pessimistic, sick at heart. The conditions were more adverse than in Brussels.

The opening of the exhibition was even more foreboding. The goal was reached, the goal for which Auguste had yearned, and he felt mad. He was in a civil war, in a wasteland. No one gave any attention to his statue. This was the ninety-fourth exhibit in the history of the Salon, there were over two thousand pictures on exhibition and hundreds of pieces of sculpture, and only a stray straggler got to the little-frequented room where stood "The Age of Bronze." He was in the drainage pit, as remote from the public as the sewers of Paris. And it stood so high, so out of proportion, so out of focus, its total nakedness overwhelming everything else!

Large crowds formed before a bronze and marble bust that had been executed and submitted by Mademoiselle Sarah Bernhardt, heads he had done better when he had been seventeen. Other large groups gathered before the numerous imitations of Barye and Carpeaux, now safely dead. But the biggest crowds stood in front of several ornate portraits of Mademoiselle Sarah Bernhardt, who was obviously the star of the show, and a Napoleonic battle scene by Meissonier which had been sold for 200,000 francs—several yards wide and a yard high. Auguste decided that Meissonier, the most successful painter in Paris with Bouguereau, was being paid by the centimeter. There was also the inevitable Bouguereau, a panel of nudes that was considered the masterpiece of the show, full of beauty, nobility, classic fauns, and satyrs.

Poor "Age of Bronze"! He was lost. He would never be noticed. Yet Auguste could not withdraw. He stood before the figure in a black silence, certain he would never achieve the acceptance for which he yearned.

Then suddenly, several days later, there was a reversal. "The Age of Bronze" became the most viewed statue and the most reviled.

A long article appeared in a prominent Parisian newspaper, repeating the Brussel charges that the figure was cast from life, and added, "This figure, whatever it is styled, is vulgar, wanton, obscene, *volupté* in the flesh."

Auguste immediately wrote the newspaper a denial of all these charges, but soon afterward they were repeated, with new additions that stated, "The sculptor seems to have deliberately intended to shock and offend. The figure from the rear looks like a girl, with its small waist and provocative hips. Perhaps it was not intentional, but the implication is that 'The Age of Bronze' is, in truth, a hermaphrodite."

How could they tell? Auguste thought indignantly. The figure was so high, so much in the corner, no one could see it from the rear.

But the next day Auguste was almost crushed by the mob about "The Age of Bronze," whispering, "It's immoral! See how naked it is! They're right, it's disgusting, lascivious! The sculptor must be mad!" Flustered and growing desperate, Auguste longed to answer, but where? How? He stood as if paralyzed, a terrible racket going on inside his head. He heard boos, sneers, cries of contempt. The kindest words were "So naked! My!" He wondered if there was a gallery anywhere in the world that would accept his work. Frustrated, disconcerted, not knowing which way to turn, Auguste stood all that day in a terrible loneliness, unable to flee, as if someone had to support the statue, feeling as solitary as he had ever felt, keeping his hands behind his back with a great effort of his will— or he would use them in a way he would regret later.

It was worse the next day. The crush was almost impossible. People entered the exhibition just to view this immoral figure. He was a huge success—more people stared at "The Age of Bronze" than at any other piece—and he hated it. He had yearned to achieve appreciation and he had gained notoriety. And what hurt the most in this mass curiosity was the scorn, that he was *un fourbe*, a fake, he repeated bitterly to himself.

Then there was the dignified man who came over to him, wearing the rosette of the Legion of Honor in his buttonhole, and asked, "Pardon, monsieur, you are Auguste Rodin, *n'est-ce pas?*" and when Auguste nodded yes, the man snarled, "You ought to be ashamed of yourself."

Please God, dear God, Auguste prayed, what can I do?

He was not asking for preference, not even asking for justice; he was asking for mercy. Sculpt Neyt on a crucifix and put a loincloth around his waist and he would be accepted, but now he was a madman.

Then he found himself caught in the machinery of expropriation.

The jury of the Salon, embarrassed by the stir, by the *succès de scandale*, ordered "The Age of Bronze" removed from the Palais de l'Industrie.

III

The day his figure was to be removed, Auguste thought he would die.

He had scurried about Paris, searching for a studio to house "The Age of Bronze," and had found nothing. None of his artist friends could help. They were reeling under savage attacks against their own exhibition, which had aroused unusual ferocity because they had had the audacity to hold it in direct conflict with the Salon. This bitterness had smeared even Manet and Fantin, who had not exhibited with their friends. Auguste had not seen any of the artists at the Palais de l'Industrie; it was as if this boycott was their way of fighting back.

This morning, before the exhibition opened, the attendants were preparing to remove "The Age of Bronze," and the nearby Seine seemed the only place left for it. He felt like a head without a body when he saw Lecoq standing before him. He had not even known whether Lecoq was alive, and here stood Lecoq, slim and erect, although he leaned a little on a stout cane and his hair had turned snow white. He expected Lecoq to be stone-faced.

Instead Lecoq smiled at him and ordered the attendants who

were moving the figure to wait. Lecoq said that with such eminence they halted.

Lecoq turned to a stunned Auguste and said, "You may store the figure in my studio, down the quai, until it is time to re-exhibit it, if you like."

"You care about the statue?"

Lecoq replied, "You've made a stir, even if it isn't all favorable. You've attracted attention, that's what counts today, more than your work."

"People don't understand."

"Why should they? We are all critics at heart."

"What about you, *maître?*"

"What about you, Rodin? I've retired and you're beginning."

"At thirty-six?" Auguste was very tired of this kind of encouragement.

"It happens. And there is something in your work."

"Obscenity."

Lecoq laughed. "If you want to feel sorry for yourself—"

"What should I feel—grateful for being defamed?"

"It could change. You have a boldness, yet firmness, here that is refreshing. This skull isn't just stone, it is a passionate and emotional man who is a civilized being."

"Apparently he is the only one in the Palais de l'Industrie who is."

"Rodin," Lecoq said indulgently, with more patience than he used to show, "this is a circus. In fact, they had a legitimate one here last year and it was appropriate. Our President, the Marshal, attended that."

"Whom do I protest to about this removal?"

"By law you should complain to the Under Secretary of State in the Ministry of the Fine Arts, but the real power is Eugène Guillaume. He is the head of the Beaux Arts and one of the leading members of the Institute and the Académie Française, the perfect type of academic artist, full of patriotic solemnities, who fancies himself a Torquemada, determined to devote himself to the extermination of heresy in the arts."

"And I'm a heretic?"

"He may think so."

"Then what is the use of protesting?"

"It will attract more attention."

"And the work? What will become of it?"

"Not all the artists agree with the Salon. And I'm not referring to men like Degas and Monet, who are too individualistic to become involved with someone else. Well, *mon ami*, do you want to use my studio?"

Auguste nodded and tried to find words to thank him, but Lecoq wasn't listening. Lecoq was ordering the men moving "The Age of Bronze" to be more careful. "*Mon dieu!* Don't you know a work of art when you see it?"

IV

The strength in Lecoq's voice gave Auguste the courage to protest to the Under Secretary of State in the Ministry of the Fine Arts, who referred him to the Institute, which ran the Salon. A long correspondence followed, in which Auguste was advised by the Institute in the person of Eugène Guillaume to make casts and photographs of his original model and then submit them to the Institute for examination. And though Neyt posed for these photographs in Brussels and wrote Auguste that he would like to come to Paris and testify for Auguste in person, he said that his superior officer—afraid of the scandal that would follow—would not grant him leave.

After a long wait the vital casts and photographs arrived in Paris. Auguste had them delivered at once to the office of Eugène Guillaume, and was informed it was too late, the Salon of 1877 was closing, now there was no point in looking at the casts or the photographs.

He protested again to the Under Secretary, who assured him that justice would be done. The Under Secretary appointed a committee composed of the jury that had ordered "The Age of Bronze" withdrawn, the chairman Eugène Guillaume, and several weeks later they issued a public statement:

"The committee is not convinced that there has been any falsification of 'The Age of Bronze,' by Monsieur Auguste Rodin."

A complete equivocation, thought Auguste, if ever he heard one. There was no comment about resubmission, or about an apology. Lecoq had made his studio free to work in and he had lost the power to work. If "The Age of Bronze" was a failure, it was purposeless to attempt anything else. He was told that Mademoiselle Sarah Bernhardt had won honorable mention in the Salon for her portrait bust of Victorien Sardou.

V

Amid such a chaos of emotion it was difficult for Auguste to meet some artists who wanted to talk to him. But Lecoq was insistent, and so it was arranged for a Sunday at Lecoq's studio.

Auguste got there early, hoping he could do a little work before they arrived, so the whole day wouldn't be a waste, but whatever he started struck him as stupid. After several false starts he halted. He was close to collapse, in a state of extreme lassitude. His dream had turned to dust. He had gone deeper and deeper than the scenery of the flesh, and he had been damned for it. He thought there was no emotion in flesh without intensity and no intensity without emotion, but it had come to nothing.

He was standing at the window, gazing at the Seine, at the booksellers along the quais, thinking that spring had come during the frenzy with the Salon and he hadn't noticed, he who loved nature so much, when Lecoq entered with three strangers. Lecoq was in high spirits, and he introduced Auguste to Stéphane Mallarmé, Eugène Carrière, and Alfred Boucher.

Mallarmé was a slight, slim man with fine, sensitive features, and the oldest of the three, about Auguste's age; Carrière was several years younger, with a large head dominated by a broad brow and a wide, thick, drooping mustache; Boucher, the youngest of the three, was sharp-featured, the handsome one, it struck Auguste, the *grand seigneur*, yet full of charm.

Lecoq explained, "They represent a committee for 'The Age of Bronze.'"

"Committee?" Auguste was irritated. "I've had enough of committees with the jury of the Salon."

Carrière said softly, "We admire 'The Age of Bronze.' We think the Institute has been unfair."

"Are you a sculptor?"

"A painter."

Boucher said, "I'm the sculptor, and Mallarmé is a poet."

"And schoolteacher," said Mallarmé. "But our coming here was Boucher's idea originally. When he heard that we liked your figure and thought the commotion unjust and stupid, he convinced us to come."

"Why?" Auguste looked skeptical.

"Perhaps, *mon ami*," Lecoq said with mock severity, "because Alfred Boucher is considered one of the leading young academic sculptors. He is an honored graduate of the Beaux Arts, he has won the Prix de Rome, awards at the Salon. He is the logical successor to Guillaume. He is also a sculptor of intelligence and integrity."

Boucher said, "*Merci, maître*, but it is simpler than that. Whatever my failings as an artist, I care for sculpture too much not to recognize a genuine work of art when I see it."

"And not as a competitor?" Auguste asked suspiciously, afraid to believe that another sculptor could really like his work.

Boucher said, "Rodin, we hope you won't be offended, but if you could audition for the Salon it might be helpful."

"Audition?" Auguste was ready to explode.

Boucher said, "If you could do something for the jury while they watch, you'd be able to disprove the charge that you cast from life."

Auguste was silent. This sounded like a further humiliation.

Carrière said gently, "We liked your figure very much."

Mallarmé added graciously, "That's what really brought us here."

He believed them. "Yet to audition!" he exclaimed. "I'm not a student." This proposal, so startling, so unexpected, was inappropriate, to say the least. "It's—"

"Unfair," said Boucher. "We know. But we believe it is even more unfair to allow this calumny that you modeled from life to stand."

Auguste thought of the pain "The Age of Bronze" had given him. It had caused him to be debased, castigated, locked out. He had lost weight, his clothes had grown shabby. But perhaps he should play this sad comedy to the bitter end, and he was touched by their support. He said, "I will do what Maître Lecoq advises."

Lecoq said, "I wouldn't do it, but if I were you I would thank heaven for such a chance."

Boucher said, "I will be one of the jury. And you can depend on it, Rodin, this time you will not be damned in advance."

VI

Auguste was waiting when the jury of five sculptors arrived. It was a week later, and he had thought much about the human creature he would sculpt, factual yet spiritual, and then he knew that was useless. This trial did not turn on evidence, it depended on taste. He had been indicted not for obscenity, but for originality.

Eugène Guillaume, the head of the jury, was a taut, lean, wiry man with ridged features, a long nose, sharp chin. The others, except for Boucher, were the echoes of the chairman's footfall and voice.

"Let us not waste time with the past, with recriminations," said Guillaume. "Whenever you are ready, Rodin, we are."

"*Merci*, monsieur," said Auguste. "What kind of a figure do you want?"

"Whatever you are prepared to do, Rodin," said Guillaume. "We do not expect you to be a prodigy. A simple figure will be enough."

Auguste asked, "In the style of 'The Age of Bronze,' perhaps?"

Guillaume shrugged, then stated, "We do not expect a *chef-d'oeuvre*."

"Why not?" said Auguste. "I spent eighteen months on 'The Age of Bronze.' Why shouldn't I give you a *chef-d'oeuvre* in an hour?"

Guillaume flushed, snapped, "I came only at Boucher's insistence," and the others nodded, except Boucher, who motioned for Auguste to begin.

"Yes, yes," Auguste said, as much to himself as anyone. "I'll do a body even more realistic than 'The Age of Bronze.' "

Boucher pushed Guillaume down in the chair until the latter became part of the furniture, and the others sat motionless.

For the first time in years Auguste was improvising. He imagined Lecoq standing before him, but Lecoq was too old, Boucher moved well and easily but he wasn't dramatic, then there was that Italian, Peppino, so completely without awkwardness, with a magnificent, exciting stride. He began to model now, feeling sure, seeing Peppino's walk with a clear and rational mind although years had intervened. He mounted the torso on the armature, and as the figure became real he felt in the presence of God. He made the trunk wider, stronger, more muscular, but still, at the moment, without sex.

Boucher marveled at the simplicity with which he worked, as if the structure of this figure welled up from Rodin's imagination. There was nothing abstract about this body; the concrete reality was individual. He did not use too much clay, as did most sculptors. He worked quietly, calmly, swiftly, with an ease of expression that struck Boucher as remarkable. He dominated his material.

Auguste, working with a rapidity he hated usually, had forgotten their presence. He strongly accentuated the hips—the devil with being dry, correct, timid. He was stimulated with a new enthusiasm, with a desire to do something different. Gone was the nothingness, the emptiness, the betrayal. He thought there were men like Michelangelo's and men like Donatello's and some who couldn't be labeled with anything that had been done in sculpture.

He was at the legs now. He brought one forward, then stressed the stomach muscles, which altered with the movement of the leg. He thought of the armature as a human skeleton, and he heard nervous breathing. Guillaume, no doubt, he thought, wanting him to fail. If Guillaume didn't believe what his mouth said, his hands would tell him. He lost track of time as he cut deep into the back, working in a fury now. He was grateful for the facility he had developed in Belgium. He halted when he finished the legs. Several hours had passed, but Auguste had no idea of how long he had worked. He had a sense of physical delight. He felt in a state of grace.

Guillaume's taut features grew more tense as he asked, "Without a head?"

Auguste nodded.

"And no arms?"

Boucher cried indignantly, "Does the 'Venus de Milo' need arms?"

Suddenly Auguste, disregarding them, realizing the most vital thing of all was still undone, abruptly added a penis, soft yet firm. He thought, Let them dare accuse me of making this man a hermaphrodite. He announced, "A female would have been easier, but only a man would walk this way."

"But is it finished?" asked Guillaume. There was still no head or arms.

Auguste said, "It is finished if you want to touch it."

"Touch a man?" Guillaume acted horrified.

Auguste said, "When it is a woman, you will know it."

"Nonetheless," persisted Guillaume, "is this figure really finished?"

"As an improvisation, yes," said Auguste. "As a completed work, obviously not. No decent work is done in one sitting, or even ten."

Guillaume said, "But you have such an obsession with the naked body."

Auguste said, "The heart of art comes from the human body. Bernini used the male body for the door of a palace. Michelangelo painted the male body all over the Sistine Chapel. Then there is the work of Titian, Rubens, Botticelli. Monsieur Guillaume, have you seen their paintings?"

Guillaume was affronted, but Boucher, viewing the figure, thought Rodin was right. This was a real man, quick with life, with movement, with realism and rough truth. Improvise, invent—Rodin had done far more: Rodin had created the body of a man in swift, purposeful motion. Boucher was shaken by the authority of the movement. Boucher said, "This man's technical skill is so obvious it is foolish to question it."

Guillaume said, "I grant he can improvise. But—"

"But what?" asked Boucher.

"This figure has no repose," said Guillaume.

Auguste retorted, "There is no such thing as repose in nature, not even in death. Even the decomposition of the dead body is a form of motion. Everything in existence is in motion: the universe, nature, ourselves. Even when we sleep our hearts beat, our blood moves, our minds roam far and wide."

Guillaume asked, "What do you call this figure?"

" 'The Man Walking.' What about the charges against 'The Age of Bronze'?"

"We never accused you of anything. We merely removed your work from the Salon because of the agitation it caused."

Auguste's hands tightened. For an instant he felt like strangling Guillaume; the others, except for Boucher, had not said a word.

Then he said with a merciless direct gaze, "Did I do this from life, monsieur?"

Guillaume replied, armed with self-righteousness, "I said we never accused you of that, Rodin. It was the press. And we want to avoid that this time. This inquiry must be kept secret."

"And my dirtied, reviled reputation?"

"We will admit your figure when the time is ripe."

"When will that be?"

Guillaume shrugged.

"Ten years from now? A lifetime?"

Boucher said, "I will be happy to vote for the immediate admission of both pieces to the Salon, 'The Age of Bronze' and 'The Man Walking.' We've been cut off from life, but not *mon cher maître Rodin.*"

Auguste blushed as if some outside force had done these figures.

Guillaume repeated that their decision must remain private and that the Republic of France could not be bound by any date, and the others assented. "But," he assured Auguste, to show he was a generous man, " 'The Age of Bronze' will be shown again, and if there is no agitation the State may buy it."

Auguste asked, "Then why did you attack me, Monsieur Guillaume?"

"No one attacks you, Rodin. It is your taste. You make your nude so lifelike it stirs erotic fantasies. Now if you had done *le sujet de famille* or *le sujet patriotique*"—Guillaume's eyes lit up—"or *le sujet religieux*, a *pietà*, a Magdalen, a crucifixion—"

"Or a saint," interrupted Auguste.

"Exactly," said Guillaume, looking pacific, misty-eyed. "Why don't you do a saint, *le sujet religieux*, Rodin?"

"I will. When I have reason to." Auguste stood up curtly, finished.

Guillaume nodded and walked out, the three sculptors who had not said a word following him, but Boucher shook Auguste's hand and said, "I knew you would vindicate yourself."

"*Merci*, monsieur, you did your best."

" 'The Age of Bronze' will be readmitted. Within a year, you will see."

Auguste waited for Boucher to leave, then stared at "The Man

Walking." He thought, You, alone, Monsieur Clay, make me real. Nothing else proves anything. He did not feel vindicated; he felt exhausted. Yet there was something to Guillaume's suggestion to do a saint.

CHAPTER 22

While Auguste pondered about modeling a religious subject, he settled in Paris with the determination that it must be permanent. The moment all his sculpture was safely back in Paris, he summoned Rose from Brussels and they moved into a small apartment on the rue St. Jacques with Papa and *petit* Auguste, while Aunt Thérèse went to live with one of her sons.

He chose the location because it was just around the corner from the Panthéon, within walking distance of Notre Dame, the Louvre, and the Bibliothèque Impériale, which had become the Bibliothèque Nationale. He had grown up in this arrondissement; he felt at home here. He was pleased that it was within walking distance of *petit* Auguste's school, too, and that Papa had old acquaintances in this neighborhood, living on small pensions like Papa, elderly folk with whom Papa could meet and talk. Most important, it was what he could afford. Auguste had decided to take the plunge, to be a full-time sculptor, to do nothing but his own work as long as his money lasted. If they lived economically, it might be a whole year.

He had saved half of Rose's money—he had been living very carefully since the splurge with Papa and *petit* Auguste. Van Rasbourg had made a fair settlement, giving him another thousand francs for his share of the business, with the assurance that there would be several thousand more when all of their stock was sold.

Thus though Auguste knew that Rose was dissatisfied with the drabness of their apartment, he stated it must do and refused to listen to any complaints. He didn't tell her that he disliked their bedroom as much as she did. A haircloth sofa of uncompromising severity and rectitude stood against one wall, there was a dull white mantelpiece of false marble on the opposite side, and the rest of the bedroom was crowded with a dreary chest of drawers, several uncomfortable stiff-backed chairs, and a small creaky wooden bed. But the apartment was usable and cheap, and there was a small room for Papa, another for *petit* Auguste, a kitchen and a parlor, and he intended to spend most of his time at the studio. His next *chef-d'oeuvre* must be an even greater effort.

II

No one knocked on his door to buy any of his work despite more encouragement from Boucher and Lecoq, but they continued to assure him that he had won a victory. He rented a studio on the rue Fourneaux, which was really more of a shed, but the light was good, it was spacious, and it was in the Vaugirard Quarter, where there were many sculptors.

The afternoon he went to Lecoq's studio to move "The Age of Bronze" and the improvisation which he had retitled "The Man That Walks," he found an excited Boucher and an amused Lecoq. Boucher's cheeks were pink, his eyes were bright, and he exclaimed, "I have wonderful news, Rodin!"

"So have I, *mon ami*. I just rented a studio. For a whole year."

"Fine, fine. But this is even more important."

"I'm getting a public apology?"

"Better. Much better. Guillaume has promised me that your next piece will be admitted to the Salon without question."

"I have no new pieces. What about my 'Age of Bronze'?"

"It will be admitted, too."

"When?" asked Auguste. This was the issue, he thought, not new work.

"Two years, three years, I presume," said Boucher. "When Guillaume thinks it will not create a commotion, when it will be safe to re-exhibit."

Auguste said stubbornly, "That's too late."

But Boucher persisted, "When will your next piece be done?"

Auguste answered, "In about two years." Until "The Age of Bronze" was exhibited fairly, he could not show anything else.

Boucher's face fell. "That long?"

"I haven't even begun a new piece. I don't know what I'm going to model next."

Boucher sighed. "That's too bad. There is a good deal of talk about your work at the moment. This is the time to strike." The battle over Rodin was so exciting it would be a shame to have it end now. Then suddenly, struck with an inspired idea, he felt cheerful, lively, and triumphant again. "What about 'The Man That Walks'? You've virtually finished that."

"No," said Auguste. "The shoulders are too frail, I must make the legs more muscular. There are other problems for which I've found no solution. It's not anywhere nearly done. It's just a working model."

"It's an interesting figure," said Lecoq, who at seventy-seven, having retired from the Petit École, liked reliving his old wars through Rodin, it gave him vigor. And he was determined to reduce the work of the Beaux Arts sculptors—Boucher excluded—to a grotesque heap of rubble, and Rodin was just the man to do it. "With a little more work, Rodin, it could be ready."

But Auguste refused to be moved. It gave him physical distress to rush. After the improvisation he had resolved never to work fast again. Sculpture was not born with speed, but had a tempo of its own. It was an act of many moments. It had its birth in a way of life that went on day after day. He was becoming sure that this was inevitably true. There was so much thought involved, and feeling, sensory experiment, and realization.

"If you wait," Boucher declared impatiently, "they may forget you."

Auguste felt his spine stiffen. He felt pressed in, even by his friends.

Lecoq asked, "You are going to focus on your own work, aren't you?"

"Yes."

Lecoq said, " 'The Man That Walks' could be your great opportunity."

"It is not what I want to do next. I want 'The Age of Bronze' shown first."

Lecoq sighed wearily, said, "Suppose it was a commission?"

Auguste said, "It would have to wait."

"How long?" asked Lecoq.

"Until I knew how to finish it. As you taught me, *maître*."

"All I taught you was to see with your own eyes."

"*Merci, maître*."

"And I'm not your *maître*, not any more." Lecoq abruptly left Auguste's side, strode to the window, and stared outside fiercely.

Auguste hurried after him and said, "I'm sorry, Monsieur Lecoq."

"For what? For the pupil outdoing the master?"

Auguste said, "That's not the obligation I owe you."

"What is?"

"To do my work as I see it. A figure must grow like a tree, slowly. The architecture of sculpture is not a quick bloom, but a careful growth. As it was, I was too quick with 'The Age of Bronze.' It's almost decorative."

Boucher asked, "How long did it take?"

"Supposedly eighteen months, actually many years—a lifetime."

"If you ever get a government commission, they'll not be that patient."

"But have I got a commission?" Auguste asked directly.

"Well, Guillaume did promise."

"Promise what? That they will guarantee a fair exhibit, a sale?"

"You can't expect that," said Boucher. "Still, for a man as important as Guillaume to say that your next piece will be exhibited—"

"No, no, Boucher," interrupted Auguste. "Forgive me, *mon ami*, I am grateful for your help, but I must never hurry again."

"Hurry?" Boucher was irritated. "*Mon cher Rodin*, are you going to spoil this opportunity just to gratify a sentimentality?"

That was not true, Auguste thought angrily: his feeling had nothing to do with "The Man That Walks" or doing new work. It had to do with "The Age of Bronze." He pointed to that figure with a passionate gesture of his hand and cried, "There's no use doing something new for the Salon if they don't show this. I don't want acceptance two, three years from now, I want it now! I'm willing to be reasonable, but foolish, no. I will not start all over. What's the use of doing something else for the Salon if they don't admit what I've done best—what is me? I hand them my flesh and blood and they say it isn't good enough. If this flesh and blood isn't good enough, I don't have any other. I give all that I am to this work and you want me to invest in tomorrow. Tomorrow is the next millenium! I'm tired of waiting. In three years I'll be forty—who knows how much sculpture I'll have in me?"

"Oh, many fine pieces, I'm sure," said Boucher, shaken by Rodin's emotion.

"That's sentimentality," declared Auguste. "If I do more work, it will be in spite of the rejections, not because of them. At any event," he added stubbornly, "I will not submit anything new to the Salon until they accept 'The Age of Bronze' again."

Boucher shrugged hopelessly. "One does not bargain with Guillaume."

Auguste said, "I'm sorry, but that's the way things are."

As Auguste turned to go, Lecoq said, "Keep in touch, whatever happens," and Boucher said, "You are an uncomfortable man, Rodin, but at least your feelings are your own. You are going to keep working, whatever happens?"

"I will try," Auguste answered grimly. He turned to supervise the two men who had entered Lecoq's studio to move his pieces to his newly acquired studio. It was a chore he detested, but it had to be done. He made certain each figure was packed with the utmost care.

III

To try was not enough, he discovered. Having his own studio did not prove to be the blessing he had expected. He went there every day with the sunrise and stayed until sunset, but nothing happened. The constant battling, the slander piled upon slander, had stifled his emotion. He was uncertain, full of doubt, without faith. Whenever he stared at his collected work, his dissatisfaction increased. He had not done enough, not nearly enough. The more he thought about modeling a religious subject, the better he liked the idea; it had stimulated many fine artists, yet to do a *pietà*, a Magdalene, a Virgin, a crucifixion, struck him as repetitious, a waste. When he could not decide what to do, he grew desperate. Freedom was becoming a trap. His savings were diminishing rapidly. Weeks were passing in a spreading stupor, and he was close to suffocation.

Auguste was feeling particularly desperate after another futile day at the studio when coming home to the apartment quite late, he found Rose waiting for him in the parlor. And Rose, instead of allowing him to light his pipe and gulp a little wine or serving him *café au lait* as if they were *en famille,* said before he could even sit down, "You must do something about *petit* Auguste."

"Later. Where's dinner?"

"No," she said with unexpected firmness, and put aside the sculptor's smock, which she had been mending. "Auguste, the boy is not doing well in school and I can't talk to him."

Auguste said with a gesture of annoyance, "What's wrong?"

"He goes regularly to the Little Sisters of the Poor, but he is not good. He reads badly, has trouble with his writing. I can't correct him, but you could if you would take a little time with him."

"What about Papa? Can't he punish him?"

"Papa spoils him. And he doesn't need punishment, he needs attention. Especially from you. *Chéri,* you must devote some time to him."

"Rose," Auguste said tartly, "I have to earn a living."

"He had such a wonderful time the day you came home," she said sadly. "He still talks about it."

"I enjoyed it, too. But, *ma chatte,* I don't have the time now."

"Not even one day a week? For your own son?"

Auguste was silent. He felt a sudden bitterness, so harsh it shocked him. He didn't wish to feel this way, but to accept *petit* Auguste completely, to open his arms wholeheartedly, was to make the final commitment. He said finally, "Suppose you make yourself more attractive to him?"

"For what? To sit here and mend your clothes every night? To keep cleaning your dirty blouses?" she replied, referring to the clay-spattered blouse he was wearing. "That's all I'm good for, to be your *petit* housewife, as the child is your *petit* Auguste!"

"What happened to the money I gave you for a new dress?" He was angry.

My money, she thought, but she didn't say it. Instead she reminded him, "I bought a parasol as a gift from you and I've never used it. When other people picnic or stroll on the Bois, you're always busy."

"Now, Rose, you are exaggerating." He went over to her and kissed her to show that he had forgiven her.

She poured out his *café au lait*, found several *croissants* which she had been saving for him. She uttered a heart-rending sigh.

"You're tired." He was full of solicitude now that he had his coffee.

"No." But this time her sigh was deep. She asked suddenly, "Auguste, why do you hate the child?"

"Hate him?" Auguste was startled. "I don't hate him."

"Then resent him. You do, you know, yes, you do."

"That's absurd. Oh, I resented him when he was born, but I'm not a brute. I don't resent him any more, and I have a feeling for him. I want him to grow up to be a fine boy."

"But without your help!" Rose jumped to her feet and rushed into their bedroom and slammed the door.

This was the time to walk out, he told himself sternly, it was ridiculous to endure any more. Yet at the thought of going on without Rose he felt suddenly weak. He remembered how attractive she had looked when she had stormed out: her skin like a flame, her head high like a Venus. No wonder his imagination and energy had been so laggard; they had not had one real night of passion since her return from Brussels, he had been so preoccupied with his work. He went to the bedroom door. He was grateful it was not locked, for that would have been a humiliation. He pushed it open and heard her crying. Suddenly he was by her side, soothing her, and she clutched him with an abrupt passion, immersing him in her love with an intensity that was terrifying, yet deeply satisfying.

Rose forgot her self-consciousness at the thought of Papa's being in the next room. In this house, up to now, she had held something back, but Auguste was her life, her folly, and her joy. As he responded with a vitality that threatened to sweep her off the bed, her happiness was so great and powerful it obliterated her tears, her recriminations. No longer did she feel he gave her his emotion with reluctance, as a favor. He was giving with a fullness that acknowledged her. She felt as if he were cutting a niche within her, and the more he pressed down on her the more she responded.

Afterward they were jubilant. He whispered, "I have a brilliant idea for *petit* Auguste. I'll teach him how to draw."

Rose was pleased with his interest, but disappointed with the idea. She asked, "But will it help him in school?"

"It will help him become an artist."

"How do you know he will like to draw?"

"He will like it. I will teach him. And you say he is my son."

"*Chéri*, he is your son." She kissed his fine fingers, caressed his red beard, of which he was so proud, and said, "Auguste, if we could only have a large double brass bed, with big brass knobs on the corners, it would make me very happy." And an embroidered coverlet, she thought, and tall white curtains on the windows and a crucifix and a statue of the Virgin above the bed . . . But she would ask for these later.

"Why do you want this kind of bed?" he asked, suddenly suspicious.

It would make me feel married, she thought, but she said, "You want to teach *petit* Auguste to draw, I want to learn to love you as you deserve."

Auguste was not sure what he deserved, but he said, "I'll get you such a bed when I sell to the Salon."

IV

Petit Auguste was excited by the prospect of seeing the studio. Since it had been forbidden to him up to now, yet he had heard a great deal about it, the boy was sure the studio was mysterious, fascinating, and wonderful.

And the Sunday he was to visit it, his father was waiting for him. *Mon dieu!* as Grand-père said, it was adventurous. He loved all this attention he was getting. He was accustomed to it from Grand-père and Mama, but he rarely got it from his father, and therefore wanted it from him the most. He rolled out of bed slowly, so that everybody would fuss over him.

His father said, "Hurry, little one, we don't have all day."

"Yes, Yes!" he said, seeking to imitate his father. "Will we walk?"

"Of course. You're a strong boy and it is a fine day."

Petit Auguste only nibbled at his eggs, left most of his milk— which distressed Mama, it was a sacrifice to give him eggs and milk

—but he ignored her. He had learned long ago that he could get around her and Grand-père.

He jumped up from the table when his father became impatient. They took the short cut through the Luxembourg Gardens, where they paused for Auguste to point out many of the statues. His father told him, showing him the fountain of the Médicis, "This is said to be the best example of fountain sculpture in the world."

The boy felt restless before these old pieces of stone, although he liked the bright sun on his face. Did they have to be so bulky and gray? But he asked, thinking his father expected this, "Is it the best, Father?"

"I haven't seen all the other fountain sculpture."

They went down the rue Vaugirard and across the boulevard Montparnasse until they reached the rue Fourneaux, where the studio was.

Auguste opened the door proudly, and *petit* Auguste wanted to cry. He had expected something magnificent, like the pictures he had been shown of the Louvre by his father, something worth exploring, but this drafty, shabby place was nothing more than a shed. The walls were brown with age and rust and wear. The floor was a damp, cold stone, and hard on his feet. There was nothing grand here. The studio was large and he liked the bright sunlight, but everything else was so plain: the two straight-backed chairs, the model's stand, the masses of clay, plaster, and terra cotta, the grimy fireplace. There was no fun here. It was all wrong.

But when his father began to sculpt, using him as a model for a mother and child group, he felt love in his father. His father was breathing with a strange intensity and his hands were so strong. The clay became firm, and as the figures took shape, looking like him and Mama, he was delighted.

"Can I try?" he cried. He had been told by Mama to ask, that would please his father.

"Certainly." Auguste was deeply pleased. Perhaps the child had the same appetite.

Petit Auguste was clumsy with the clay, however, and Auguste grew impatient. It was a mistake, he thought, to rush the child. There was more clay on the floor than on the figures. He halted the modeling, gave the boy paper, pencils, and crayons, and asked him to draw.

"What?" *Petit* Auguste looked thoroughly bewildered.

"Anything. Whatever you imagine."

But the child couldn't imagine anything. He sat there, on the verge of tears, all his excitement gone, until he saw his father standing over him, foreboding, gigantic. He started to draw Auguste, and it was a fair likeness.

Auguste sighed with relief. The boy had facility after all. He felt so grateful he forgot to show the boy the chores. He thrust more paper at him and told him to go on drawing, whatever *petit* Auguste imagined.

Petit Auguste shook his head. What was there to imagine? "Could I draw you again, Father?"

An intense emotional space spread between them. Auguste looked angry, disappointed.

Petit Auguste's lips trembled. He felt excluded. His father didn't understand; he could draw as long as he could see an image to copy, but anything else was unfair. In this instant he disliked this man who loomed in front of him like a large shaggy bear. He exclaimed, "How can I draw what I don't see!"

I am rushing him, Auguste thought. It took me years to draw from memory. He remembered what Degas always said: Invent, invent? It is enough to draw accurately! Auguste said, "Do what you like. You have a steady hand."

The encouragement spurred the child, and he worked hard the rest of the day, drawing one head of his father after another, and a few limbs, and some mouths, until dusk came and there was no more light. As he worked, his father talked about the might and strength of art, its pent-up energy, of its having a life of its own, and he felt stretched out on a rack. His arms were as heavy as lead. His eyes were inflamed. When they left the studio, it was as if he were stepping out of a jail.

But his father, pleased with his drawings and his industry, was unusually affectionate. Auguste was talking about learning "harmony, order, proportion," and he longed to dart into the stable they had just passed and see if it was really full of horses. He would love to ride a horse someday—that must be a great adventure.

V

Auguste's affectionate mood lasted until he assigned *petit* Auguste to perform various chores in the studio. The boy came there after school and on Saturdays and Sundays, and was supposed to do what Rose, occupied with taking care of Papa, who was ill, had done.

While Auguste worked at his modeling stand, the child was to keep the clay properly moist and make sure there was enough fresh clay with which to work, that the tools were within immediate reach, that the studio was clean—so that his father would not tread or slip on the clay that was always falling to the floor—and that the fire was kept going in cold weather. In return Auguste intended to teach him to paint and model as well as draw.

The boy disliked the chores, and evaded them whenever he could with a lazy cunning. *Petit* Auguste was untidy and absent-minded, like his father, and considered it a waste of time to put things in order.

Within a few weeks the boy, taught by Auguste, could do a Rembrandt, as he called the black and white pencil sketches, an Ingres, as he referred to the crayon drawings. He drew precisely, accurately, but never freely or imaginatively. He had no patience for painting, and modeling bored him.

Auguste felt that a cross had been thrust upon his shoulders. *Petit* Auguste, although he still had rosy cheeks and lips, was becoming a heavy, stocky boy with a round, soft face, the childish charm gone. A weaker version of his mother, reflected Auguste, without her strength or carriage; the boy had ability, but lacked perseverance and concentration. And whenever he made demands upon the child's imagination, it failed.

This afternoon, talking about the clay being flesh, he felt the boy was regarding him as a silly old fool. Auguste had forgotten the passage of time this Sunday, discussing sculpture, and the boy's head nodded and Auguste asked sharply, "What do you call the metal that is inside the clay and plaster?" and there was only the sound of a faint snore. He thought bitterly he bored his son. And *petit* Auguste's inattention was unforgivable. Three months of wasted instruction and he still hadn't found a figure of his own choosing. He dropped his chisel with a loud clatter, and the boy sat up with a start.

Petit Auguste said, "We're going home?"

Auguste shrugged his shoulders and muttered, "I've some work to do, but you can go if all the chores are finished."

The boy glanced around. There were still some tools scattered about the studio and the clay should be put away, but it was a warm, clear evening and he could hear the laughter and shouts of the children playing outside. He said, "*Merci*, Father," and rushed out.

Auguste was angry. He couldn't find several of his tools, the clay hadn't been moistened properly. The boy is like a little savage, he thought grimly, always running wild.

From then on the father gave the child more and more chores to cure him and the child became very evasive. The boy learned to slip out of the studio when his father wasn't looking, yet when caught, swore that he had been given permission. *Petit* Auguste seized every moment to run into the street to play with the older boys, or to rush to the bistro at the corner, where the patrons gave him candy and were amused by his drawings.

After a month of this irresponsibility Auguste came home one night with a new severity. Rose was mending and sewing as usual in the parlor, and he said in his most freezing tone, "I decide finally to go ahead with a mother and son group, for your sake, with the boy as a model, and he vanishes. Not only am I without a model, I am without clay. He's been using it to make balls to throw at the boys on the street."

Rose said, "It's not his fault. He's restless. Be patient with him."

"Patient? The child won't do a bit of work unless I'm at him every moment, and I don't have the time."

Rose glanced at Auguste with sudden anger. She thought, I show my age, my hair is turning gray, I have to take care of *his* papa, *his* child, *his* wants—*mon dieu!* I'm not a saint—but he looks hardly any different from when he met me except that his red hair and beard are a little darker and thicker and his features have grown more formidable with his sloping forehead, wide jaw, and prominent nose. He does not look much older, her mind ran on, full of self-pity, while I am middle-aged and tired. I need rescue far more than he does. I wish someone would look after me. But he will never appreciate me unless I leave him.

Auguste, annoyed by her failure to agree with him, declared, "It's your fault, Rose, you forced this situation on me. Teach him art?" He grumbled with disgust. "The boy takes after your side of the family, he thinks only of himself."

"He needs someone to play with."

"No. He should learn something useful. To develop strength, character."

"In the studio?" She regarded him critically. "You've said nothing about *petit* Auguste's wants. Maybe he should do nothing."

"Only daydream?"

"Didn't you, *chéri*? You told me that you were very bad in school."

"But I loved art. I would do anything to draw and paint and model."

"Give him time."

"And waste my time!" His ire rose. "Art doesn't mean anything to him!"

"He's very young."

"Going on twelve?"

"You told me that you didn't go to the Petite École until you were fourteen."

"My father was old-fashioned. He didn't know anything about art."

"Maybe he should go to that kind of school, Auguste."

"If I can't teach him, how can strangers?" Tears came to his eyes, and he cried out in anguish, "Besides, the child doesn't really care for art!" Then he regained control of himself and stated, "You'll have to help in the studio, and watch him." He would never accomplish anything with this unruly animal on his hands.

Rose, pale and tense behind her sewing, agreed to do what she could.

The truce between Auguste and *petit* Auguste lasted until the boy grew restless with the games Mama devised, became tired of his father's saying, "I don't know how you'll grow up." He didn't want to grow up. He wanted to be free. Then he would draw when he felt like it.

Now *petit* Auguste's irresponsibility became a constant irritation and it was very difficult for Auguste to keep from losing his temper. And he found Rose almost as annoying as the boy.

VI

Summer came, and Auguste was outraged by his failure to find a suitable subject. He visited the Café Nouvelle Athènes, and as he approached the corner where his friends sat he felt uneasy, realizing suddenly that he had not seen them for months. Degas greeted him with "Ah, our *maître* and *débutant!* Do you still adore the Salon?" He didn't reply. He felt like a victim. He saw no sign of Fantin or Manet.

No one offered a word of explanation. None of them said a word about his difficulties with "The Age of Bronze." Monet sat silent and glum, Pissarro looked reflective and sad, and Renoir was preoccupied with a sketch he was making of a pretty, plump, broad-faced girl at a nearby table.

This made Degas more severe. Exasperated by their lack of attention, he went off on a diatribe. He addressed Auguste as if the latter had to listen to what he was saying. "They still regard our work as a form of insanity. They continue to caricature us in *Le Charivari* and—"

Renoir interrupted, "When you would prefer to do it yourself."

Degas rushed on, ignoring him. "The bourgeois still refuse to spend their sous. At our own exhibition there were several fist fights, the public not only laughed, they jeered and snarled, and we sold virtually nothing, and then it amounted only to the cost of the frames. And naturally, we are deliberately barred from the Salon now. So what are you bitter about?"

Auguste hadn't said a word, but scowled sympathetically.

"*Mon ami,*" Degas snapped, "do you think we should jump off the Pont Neuf and drown ourselves?"

Auguste was too disgusted to answer. He wondered if there were any *cocottes* in the café.

And when Pissarro said, "Manet is suffering terribly from the constant criticisms which have been going on for years now," Degas cut in.

"Manet," Degas said coldly, "has his heart set on the Legion of Honor. He deserves their scorn."

"Yet in spite of not exhibiting with us," said Pissarro, "Manet was refused by the Salon."

Renoir said, "Manet is getting tired of the screaming. If he exhibits with us the Salon is nasty, if he exhibits with the Salon our friend Degas is scornful. Every time he paints what he sees, someone reviles him. It is making him ill."

Degas said firmly, "Manet is too weak-spirited."

Renoir retorted, "Our friend Degas thinks he is Louis the Fourteenth."

"My opinion is different," said Degas. "There is no safe passage through life, and we should expect scorn and nastiness. We live in a world of fools. I'm not so naïve as to assume anything else. Why, they call us Impressionists as if it were a slander, a vulgarism."

Auguste thought it unfair that they should be depressed when he was depressed. When he ventured to appear annoyed, Degas was sarcastic about the stir Auguste had caused. And no one said a word about the quality of his work. He felt they were contemptuous of his efforts to woo the Salon. Indignant, he turned to the door suddenly, said, "*Bonsoir*, I have to go."

"*Adieu*," Degas said curtly. Degas went back to criticizing Manet.

Renoir said abruptly, "Wait, Rodin, I'll go with you."

Pissarro and Monet said "*Bonsoir*," and lapsed into silence as the two men went out the door.

Renoir walked him to the Batignolles omnibus, and as they waited for it he explained to Auguste, "Don't be too hard on them. Monet is worse off than ever. His wife is pregnant, he has no money, no sales, he is in a vicious situation. Manet has lent him money but it helps only a little although Manet does his best. And Fantin gives Monet advice which he can't use. And Pissarro is even worse off. His wife is going to have their fourth child and he has no money or sales, either, he is even talking about giving up painting. And Degas is so bitter he says he will not exhibit again."

Auguste asked, "What about yourself?"

Renoir said, "I sell enough to eat. A few people like my colors."

"Is that all?"

"Why fool yourself? In all of Paris there are no more than a dozen people who can care for a picture without Salon acceptance. Most art lovers wouldn't purchase a five-franc sketch if the artist weren't shown in the Salon. But I'm not falling into the trap of believing work is excellent or hateful in relation to where it is shown. One does the best work one can. Everything else is unimportant, trivial. Even the front page of *Figaro*."

"*Merci*."

"Why?" Renoir was surprised.

"It's good advice, if I can live up to it."

"Who said anything about living up to it?" Renoir laughed. "*Mon ami*, I'm not an idiot." The yellow omnibus circled around the corner, and Renoir motioned for it to stop. He gave Auguste a friendly lift onto the omnibus and said, "Rodin, I'll paint you someday and that will be your immortality."

VII

Auguste decided not to wait, however. He had lunch with Boucher to ask if there was any news about when the Salon would readmit his "Age of Bronze."

They met at the Café Tortoni, on the boulevard des Italiens. It was a pleasant summer day, and Auguste at first felt fine sitting at the marble-topped table on the spacious sidewalk, but Boucher's answer was maddening.

Boucher said, "I will shake them out of their *ennui*, but it will take more time."

"How much more time?" Again Auguste had the feeling it would never happen.

"I can't say. It could do you a great deal of harm if we pushed the Institute now. They are already very touchy about your friends, les Impressionnistes. An attack from you might spoil everything we've achieved."

"I see." Auguste wondered what *he* had achieved.

"Not only are they keeping out the new men, they are keeping out the old. Millet, Rousseau, Delacroix, even Courbet, who, once he died last year, I was sure would be acclaimed and accepted, have been kept out."

Boucher sat there in his elegant top hat and fashionable frock coat, and Auguste, in his simple cloak and large-brimmed hat, felt like a workman. This sculptor, ten years younger than himself, fastidious, charming, with the air of *le grand seigneur*, had the *bon-*

homie which was essential for success—which he would never have, Auguste thought bitterly.

Boucher said, "There are several sculpture competitions under way. Why don't you enter one?"

"I don't like competitions."

"Who does? But if you won one, you wouldn't need the Salon."

"What you really mean is I should accept their indifference and try elsewhere."

Boucher shook his head ruefully. "You are a stubborn one, Rodin."

Auguste stared at this man who he had thought was going to become a good friend. He said slowly, "I should stop counting on the Salon?"

"I didn't say that. But I don't like your waiting for them, putting all your hopes on their yes or no."

How could he tell him that it had become a point of honor!

"Best of all, if you won they would have to readmit you at once."

"I won't win. I'm not museum-minded enough."

"You might. These are monuments, and you have the vigor for them."

Auguste thought Boucher sounded as if he should quit sculpture and become a simple stone carver, but he asked, "What are the competitions?"

"They are quite ambitious," Boucher said enthusiastically. "The Third Republic is planning a competition for a memorial to the national defense of Paris against the Germans, to be erected at Courbevoie."

"As Guillaume suggested—*le sujet patriotique*. What is the other?"

"A memorial to be put in Hyde Park, in London, to honor Byron."

"That might be an interesting subject. Why don't you enter?"

"It's not my kind of sculpture. My work is too lyrical for monuments. However, the winning of the Byron competition could make the sculptor well known. The judges are important, Tennyson, Disraeli, Matthew Arnold, and a couple of sculptors. Winning would be a great honor."

No one else offered help. So several weeks later, although Auguste hated rushing and had vowed never to hurry again, he found himself modeling a Byron monument with a new frenzy. If he won this, he thought angrily, he could tell the Institute and the Salon to go to the devil.

He studied Byron assiduously, and when he read the poet's lyrical description of Greece he took that as the theme for the monument, with Byron standing by the Aegean Sea. He visualized him as an Apollo, and naked—a god did not need clothes, they distracted from the magnificence of the body. But when it came time to do the clay figure, he draped it from the waist down with a simple robe. He was afraid that another "Age of Bronze" would shock the prudish, Victorian British. And he spent money lavishly, doing many figures before he decided on the final one. Eventually, still favoring the half-draped Apollo, he prepared it for casting into bronze. He placed it on a pedestal, supported on each side by smaller, symbolic figures representing Truth and Beauty. Then Rose said it was very pretty, and for an instant he wanted to destroy it. But the work had already cost half his savings. He redid the head, stressing the sadness and suffering of the poet. He worked by day and by night, by gaslight and oil lamp and candlelight.

Toward the end he showed it to Boucher, who said, "It's a splendid idea."

Stricken, Auguste mumbled, "Idea? Sculpture is not literature. What about the modeling?"

"The organization of the body is magnificent." Boucher put his arm around Auguste and declared, "This will gain you much attention. It will make you an important sculptor even in official circles."

Then why was he unhappy? Was it because the half-draped figure was a compromise? He stared angrily at the monument. The body did need more movement, agitation, tension. Byron had not been a vacuity, but a man of intelligence and perception, and a rebel, always in motion against the established order.

Auguste returned to the figure and his Byron became more muscular and powerful. He thought he must never sacrifice vigor for elegance. He had been thinking of Boucher while doing the Byron—he had almost asked Boucher to pose for him—but now he was certain that would be wrong.

He was so busy remodeling he didn't answer Boucher's "Bonsoir."

A week later the figure was cast in bronze, signed inconspicuously so that his name would not damage his chances, and shipped to London. Then Auguste waited.

There was no word about his monument, but he had a receipt that proved it had been received. Months later he read in a newspaper that there had been thirty-seven entries in a competition for a memorial to Byron, won by Richard Belt. There was no mention of his work.

He wrote to the competition and there was no answer. Finally, growing desperate, he sent a letter of entreaty to his old friend Legros, who was teaching in London. Legros investigated and informed Auguste that there was no trace of his work, and expressed the hope that Auguste would visit London soon. Despite the signature the monument had vanished as if it had never existed. He thought British prudery must have destroyed his work. Auguste thanked Legros and resolved to sign everything conspicuously from now on. He knew he should not allow the matter to drop, but he could not afford to go to London.

Then there was the "Bellona." Auguste was in such a rage over the shabby treatment of his Byron he could think of only one way to answer: work and win the memorial for the defense of Paris. Ever since the war with the Prussians he had longed to sculpt his reply to their strutting—to model Paris as he felt her, courageous, defiant, a girl from Lorraine like Rose, but in the image of Joan.

Rose was enthralled by his wish to use her as a kind of Joan of Arc. She posed gaily, triumphantly. It was as it had been when he had courted her. Her features became animated, she lost her worn look, was pretty, eager, resolute again, loving the feeling of being needed and wanted.

Auguste didn't want her happy. He prodded her into an argument, finding fault with *petit* Auguste, who had become irresponsible again—*petit* Auguste was not interested in a head of his mama, the boy saw her every day. And now Rose, defending her son like a tigress, glared ferociously at Auguste.

Just the expression he wanted, he cried to himself.

But when he finished this terra-cotta helmeted bust of her as the goddess of war—terra cotta should have more firmness than clay—he decided it was too small for a monument though he liked the head.

In the end Auguste used this head as the apex of two heroic figures, with the dominant figure a new goddess of war, rising valiantly and defiantly above a writhing soldier. He gave this "Bellona's" expression his anger and indignation, and added wings so that she would elevate the glory of France at the moment of defense. He named this monument "Goddess of War," then changed it to "La Défense" and sent it to the contest at Courbevoie with renewed hope. He was proud that he had signed it distinctly and conspicuously: A. *Rodin*.

After more waiting Auguste heard from the judges of this competition: he had been eliminated in the first round. Thirty entries had survived the initial competition, but not his "La Défense." Amid his dreadful feeling of futility there was only one consolation: this time his work was returned to him.

VIII

It had been a bad year. At the end of it he had no money left and no recognition. He felt so blank, so hopeless, that when Carrier-Belleuse offered him a part-time job in the National Manufactory of Porcelain, at Sèvres, with the proviso that he would be allowed time for his own work he accepted immediately.

Carrier-Belleuse, now art director of this famous manufactory of vases, talked not like an employer but like a teacher. He said, ignoring their past differences, "I need someone with your skill and facility and ability to improvise. I've been hearing a great deal about you lately."

"In what way?"

"As my pupil. At one time I might have been offended, but now you have a flair. I'm sure you will do beautiful designs for our vases."

"As your pupil? I never studied with you. I was an employee, not a pupil."

"You used my name when you submitted to the Salon."

"I had to give someone as reference. But I signed my own work."

"Don't be so touchy, Rodin. What you did for me has helped you with your own work. And you mustn't be impatient, your time will come."

"Whenever anyone doesn't help me, he talks about the future. I have the most promising future, and no present."

"You will do well with us. We make beautiful pottery. It is world-famous. It is well worth doing."

Auguste was surprised by Carrier-Belleuse's friendliness. They had spoken more in these few minutes than in all the days of his previous employment. And as he rose to go, the other sculptor motioned for him to wait.

Carrier-Belleuse said emotionally, "Rodin, you think it is enough to be successful, but it is not. Without energy an artist is lost."

Carrier-Belleuse sat like an old king, his flowing mustache drooping, his once handsome, full face stricken with melancholy. Auguste wanted to be consoling, but he had his own terrors. And though he was anxious about money, he had to state, "Remember, I can only work part time. Promise?"

"Before God, Monsieur Rodin."

Auguste knew the older man still didn't want him to leave, but he felt old, too. He was almost forty, yet he had not achieved any of the acceptance for which he longed. He strode out of Carrier-Belleuse's office thinking that he didn't intend to be hard and cruel but there was no choice, and there hadn't been for years. He had so much serious work still to do. The very warmth of his sturdy, mobile hands moved him with a feeling that grew by itself; the thought of clay becoming life in his hands was a gratification beyond all others. He would model vases when he was not feeling. Sculpt he must, as long as he lived. He must find better models, however, or it would be unbearable.

"Art," he whispered to himself, "*la belle dame sans merci.*"

CHAPTER 23

Peppino stood at the door. The *maître* had written him, that was enough, he informed Auguste eloquently. But the graceful Italian's face dropped as he saw the barrenness of the studio, the *maître's* surprise; but Auguste, recovering from his surprise, assured Peppino that the studio was temporary.

Auguste had not expected the Italian to respond, though he had written him several months ago, desperate for a model who would stimulate him, force him to do something that mattered. And now not only was there Peppino as if risen from the dead, there were Santoni and a young woman.

"I almost did not find you," Peppino said reproachfully. "I kept looking for Monsieur Rodin, sculptor, and all I could find was A. Rodin. You are too modest, *maestro*."

"You came all the way from Italy?" asked Auguste.

Peppino shrugged as if that were nothing.

Santoni, however, came to the point. "We were coming to Paris anyway, *signore*, and since you wrote us, and you are a sculptor, you said, we thought it would be a *divertimento* to pose. So we came to you first. But we thought you would live on a piazza at least."

Auguste felt he should hang his head in shame, but he was pleased by their appearance, and now that he was over his surprise, amused. He noticed that now that Santoni was out of Italy he became even more Italian. He wondered how much he could believe.

Peppino said fervently, "And we've done you a great favor,

maestro. We brought you a fine female model." He introduced Auguste to Annette with an extravagant flourish of his hands.

Annette, Auguste observed, was a pretty, plump, well-proportioned French girl, at least with her clothes on, who looked like the *cocottes* who worked in the bistro around the corner. He frowned, not sure what to say. He was not certain he could afford one model, let alone three.

"*Capisco*," cried Santoni, "I understand. Come, Annette, Vittorio, I told you this was a foolish thing to do."

"Wait," said Auguste. "I don't need three models, not now, but I could use one." The question was: Which one? Santoni was better-looking than Peppino, but Peppino was more statuesque and graceful and his gestures were dramatic. Auguste added, "One I can depend on. Peppino, what about *la bella Italia*? When are you returning?"

"Never."

"I thought you loved your homeland."

"I do. *Mamma mia*, I do. But I cannot make a living there."

Auguste knew it had to be Peppino now. In this moment of truth Peppino had had a look of sternness that was fine.

"*Maestro*, I do not go back. It is too poor."

"And my letter?"

"It was sent on to us. I thought if you could afford to travel to *la bella Italia* you could afford a model. But one hour in your studio —*basta!*—a man could freeze to death!"

Auguste's face turned an angry red, but as the three turned to go he said, "I will get another stove."

Annette asked, "What about money?"

Auguste said, "I need only Peppino."

Santoni asked, "How much do you need him?"

Auguste felt this was blackmail, but he handed Peppino all the money he had on his person as an expression of good faith: ten francs, fifteen sous, and a few louis. He had left himself penniless, but he said there would be more each day Peppino modeled. He told the Italian to return tomorrow, Sunday. Auguste was breathing hard as he gave Peppino the money, but the prospective model accepted it blandly, deprecatingly, and walked off with his companions, arm in arm.

Auguste wondered if the advance was a mistake. He had a feeling he had seen the last of Peppino. There had been no discussion of terms.

II

To his surprise, "the graceful Italian," as he thought of Peppino, returned promptly the next day. Then his heart sank. Suddenly he was afraid that his excitement was in vain, that the Italian—with his clothes off—would be disappointing. So often the model who was perfectly proportioned in clothes was nothing naked. Impatiently he ordered Peppino to disrobe.

"Completely?" Peppino was taken aback.

"Of course. How else can I tell whether you are worth modeling?"

Peppino looked offended, then abashed. He disrobed slowly, reluctantly, and stepped onto the model's stand as if it were a gallows.

Auguste swallowed hard at the sight of Peppino's body. It was superb, he whispered to himself, long-legged, thin-waisted, neither too muscular nor too thin, as close to an ideal body as he had seen in a man. "Move! Move!" he shouted. It was impossible to deny this body. This body was handsome enough to be an end in itself, yet he knew that was not enough. There must be an inner life as well as an outer one.

Peppino paced up and down, disappointed. He had expected to pose on the model's stand with his arms upraised like a Garibaldi or an all-conquering Napoleon. He protested, striking a pose with his arms flung out.

"No! No!" cried Auguste, sketching Peppino while the model moved. "That's a ridiculous attitude. I don't want you to pose. When you pose, you're artificial, false."

"What about money?"

"I'll give you ten francs every day you pose."

"Ten?"

"More when we work late. And we will work late often."

"Of course, *maestro*, you understand it is not the money I am really interested in. I am *simpatico* to your work. But this is not a palazzo."

"Walk about, turn, exercise, that will keep you from getting cold."

Peppino strode up and down the studio until he was exhausted, while Auguste made many drawings, capturing an enormous variety of movements. Auguste was bursting with energy, and Peppino could hardly move. Finally Peppino spread his hands in front of him imploringly and said, "*Maestro*, I am grateful for the honor you are paying me, but I am tired." He sat down, wiped his brow. He was sweating in spite of the cold.

"You will have plenty of chance to rest. Later."

"No. If I am to work this hard, it is worth more than ten francs."

Auguste felt despair, but knew better than to show it. He said quietly, "Peppino, you are going to be a *chef-d'oeuvre*. We must be patient. Both of us." He arranged for the Italian to be at his studio four days a week, and agreed to give him fifteen francs a day and to put in an extra stove.

At Sèvres the next morning Auguste informed Carrier-Belleuse that he could do pottery decoration only three days a week. He had calculated that this would give him enough money to support his family and pay Peppino.

Carrier-Belleuse thought Rodin was foolish, and said that if Rodin concentrated on pottery he might become director himself someday and grow rich, but Auguste was not interested. There was no room in his mind for anything but Peppino. He arranged to be at his studio when he was not at Sèvres. He ordered Rose to bring his meals when he didn't come home. She asked him to take *petit* Auguste skating on the lake in the Bois de Boulogne the following Sunday and he didn't hear her. And when she stated she could not serve him and an ailing Papa and a wild, unmanageable *petit* Auguste without his help, his jaw stiffened with the obstinacy she knew so well. He could no more bargain with her over his time than over money. She must manage, he told her. He had to do a figure of Peppino even if it killed him.

So Rose bowed her head in resignation and tried to appease Papa, who complained about Auguste's neglect and faded steadily, getting out of bed rarely now, and then only with great effort, while *petit* Auguste obeyed her less and less and was on the streets far more than he was at home. There were moments now when she hated Auguste, yet he looked surprised when she snapped at him. "I need you, you know," he assured her. "No one keeps the studio as well as you do."

Rose did not speak then. She had come to a discovery of her own: she could argue with Auguste until she was black in the face, but he wouldn't listen. And when he embraced her, though it was rare these days, she still couldn't resist him. She never could resist him, she thought bitterly.

Auguste could not resist Peppino. He stood in the chilly studio— the new stove had made very little difference—watching the Italian stride up and down, and the model's movements fascinated him. People took the movements of the body for granted, thought Auguste, but for him the body's movements were the most vital things in the world, and in Peppino's case quite wonderful.

With such a model, he said to himself, I am a sculptor.

He worked now as if he were in a monastery. In some ways he became as isolated as when he had begun his novitiate as Brother Augustin in the order of the Holy Sacrament. He shut out the world; he did not see Boucher or Lecoq or any of the artists. He lived as an ascetic, not a franc wasted, not a franc spent elsewhere—a litre of wine and a loaf of bread and an occasional sausage were enough to eat. He searched the Bible, Dante, Baudelaire, Hugo, Balzac, for a theme and a heroic mood. He read to the dawn by a low, flickering gas lamp.

For weeks he pondered while Peppino continued to pace about the studio. But no matter how he sketched Peppino, the model's vibrant, purposeful walk dominated, became the heart of his designs.

Peppino was intrigued by Auguste's tools. One morning, fingering the tooth chisel, the flat chisel, hammer, rasps, mallet, gouge, polishing stones, he asked, "What are these for?" He was wondering whether the sculptor would ever start on the figure itself.

"Mostly for marble."

"Will I be in marble?"

"I don't know. It depends."

"On what, *maestro?*"

"What you become."

"Have you done any marble?"

"Not for exhibition. But I will. Now don't stop, you lose your vitality when you pose. No living thing is without motion."

"Am I to be a religious subject?"

Auguste sighed. "It is what the Salon wants."

"The Salon? I've been walking up and down for weeks, and you haven't even made a toe. When are you going to start with the clay?"

"When I'm ready," Auguste said curtly. "Have you ever grown a beard?"

"No." The Italian was proud of his long, regular chin.

"Do. A small one. And let your hair grow."

"Why?"

"Because you are going to be a religious subject." Peppino let loose a torrent of emotion about how much he adored the saints, but Auguste was not listening. Now that Auguste had committed himself, he was upset. He sickened at the thought of another Madonna, Magdalen, or crucifixion to add to the innumerable ones that had been done, and it would be equally foolish to attempt a Moses or David or *pietà*. It must be a figure rarely done, or not done well enough.

But when the idea came a few days later, it struck him as so simple and obvious he wondered why he hadn't thought of it sooner.

Peppino was gesticulating with outstretched hands as he spoke; he hadn't stopped talking all day, but he looked so magnificent, so Biblical with his new beard, his longer hair, it was as if he had stepped out of the New Testament in the person of John the Baptist.

Auguste embraced Peppino suddenly.

"What's wrong?" Peppino was stunned.

"You're John the Baptist. The way you move, it is perfect. What other man in the Bible has been as active as this? As vital? None. But he mustn't be an Italian John, or a French John"—seeing Peppino scowl—"or even a Jewish John, like the rabbis in Rembrandt. When John became a saint he went beyond being an Italian, Frenchman, or Jew. It wiped out all the differentiations of nationality." Yet Auguste remembered how almost all artists created their religious figures in the image of their own nationality. "We've come halfway, Peppino—now we really have to work."

From this moment Auguste did not stop the Italian when his model began to talk. It made it easier for the model to move and it was in character with Auguste's vision of John the Baptist. His saint must be the incarnation of a faith that was heroic yet human: a man who came from nature, who was nature, yet who reached out beyond the natural life. This figure must have a greater reach than the ordinary man, striding across a vast desert to show his faith.

Peppino's powerful long stride became John moving with a proud passion to meet Jesus face to face.

Auguste, deeply involved, went into the clay easily and quickly. The figure took shape now. The clay was alive in Auguste's hands, responding to his every wish. He focused on the legs, hips, and shoulders, both hands working as one. He sculpted while the Italian continued to pace up and down, talking always. He wanted to go on all night, with no interruptions, but Peppino finally collapsed from fatigue. Auguste looked down at the reclining model without pity. But he was concerned. Would Peppino be able to work tomorrow? The statue was at a point where it could be fatal to halt.

Peppino was exhausted, but as he looked up at the figure he was astonished by what he saw. At first he hadn't liked it and had longed to shout it down with fury, but now as the figure took form he no longer thought it wicked.

"You want me to get someone else?" Auguste asked apprehensively.

"No, no, no!" cried the model. Many artists would want him after this. He stared again at the statue, wonderingly now. The sculptor had given him so many things he had never seen in himself.

Auguste worked with such a single-mindedness the weeks flew by. As he became completely absorbed, Rose could not even persuade him to come home to sleep, and he was too involved in "John" to care whether she was hurt. Whenever he worked successive days at the studio, he slept there wrapped in a blanket on the floor. He would not have eaten many days if she hadn't brought him food. His work haunted him. It would be dangerous to leave it. He would lose his conception, his energy, momentum, and continuity.

He grew more and more adroit at the pottery works. The real battle began the moment he went to work on "John." Then Auguste was charged with an abandoned, driving nervous energy that would not allow anything to interrupt him. And because he still took no time off for Papa, *petit* Auguste, or anything else in the months that went by, again Rose accused him of not caring about them, of running away from them.

But he was not running away from them or anything else, he answered her: "John the Baptist" was not an evasion but a search. He had no energy even for women. From the day he had decided on the subject, he had stopped going to his usual *maison d'amour*. What more could she expect? Yet even as he rationalized, he knew it didn't matter. Nothing mattered but "John."

"Don't blame me," he told Rose when she reproached him for not having been home for a week. "I can't help myself. I have to do it."

She nodded bleakly and said, "I understand." She had brought his breakfast over this morning to make sure he didn't go without eating.

But Rose didn't understand, he thought, and never would. She was just being unreasonable. She would assume her hurt expression, as though he was taking advantage of her. As now, regarding him with barely hidden hostility.

He felt like St. John then. He ordered her to leave, for Peppino had arrived and he had no more time to waste. Today he intended to finish the legs, the soul of the statue. He was abrupt. The model said, "*Bonjour*, Madame Rodin," and Auguste didn't bother to correct him. To get the legs, he must not allow anything else to intrude.

Rose nodded to the handsome young man and stumbled out of the studio.

Auguste wanted an even wider stride. He commanded the model to walk more energetically. "St. John" was not a figure to be stuck in a corner, to decorate a building, or ornament a wall. "St. John" must be free, vigorous, always in movement.

But it was many days later when Auguste finished the legs.

Peppino had never seen a figure with such an enormous stride. While he dressed, his body still wet from his pacing, he asked, "*Maestro*, do I really walk that way?"

"Yes—when you're John."

"Do you think they will believe it?"

Auguste stared at the earth-spanning stride, took a sip of Cointreau Rose had left for him, and offered some to the model. "Do you believe it?"

Peppino made a face as he drank the French liqueur, wishing it were Italian, and said, "I don't know what to believe any more. If anyone had told me that I would work a year for one man, work even when I am owed hundreds of francs, I would have said he was lying. But I have."

"I'll pay you. I've already paid you for your regular time."

"But I'm always working overtime. And to make me so naked!"

"Is there any other way?"

Peppino made a great flourish of his hands. "You show all of me!"

"Either you are all naked or you are not naked at all."

"What will my friends think?"

"They will think you are quite a man."

Peppino smiled. "But I'm supposed to be a saint."

Auguste smiled back. "You have been, to put up with a grouch like me."

"You're tired, *maestro*."

"And you, Peppino?"

"*Basta!* When do we model another figure?"

Auguste felt better. Peppino should make a fine Adam.

Thus they reached the final days of the modeling. Auguste, with a renewal of energy, finished the face. He sculpted carefully the grave yet proud features of a man illuminated by an imperishable faith. He gave him an open mouth and hair down to the neck as Peppino had grown his, and then a short but expressive beard. He raised the head so that John had grandeur and was possessed with the pursuit of a passion beyond himself.

Everything was done then, except the hands. Auguste worked on them for days, until Peppino's hands grew so cramped and chilled he could not move them. He got numb in his fingers and elbows. He stopped talking.

One afternoon Peppino had to stand motionless for hours while Auguste sketched and modeled incessantly. He held his hands just as ordered, although he thought they would drop off from fatigue and cold.

Auguste was mumbling to himself, "Sculpture requires love, demands love, you model a hundred hands to get two." It was growing dark as the sun dropped below the horizon. Shadows crept close to the stationary model, the statue of St. John. Auguste worked feverishly, as if he were racing the oncoming darkness. Then suddenly he halted. He circled the figure, peering at it from every possible side through the spreading darkness.

And still Peppino did not move. The model was chilled to the bone, was sure he would never be able to use his arms and legs again, but he was hypnotized by the *maestro*'s intensity.

Auguste paused when he came to the profile. He drew in his breath sharply. This St. John did matter, did stand for something, had lived for something. He gazed up at St. John with sudden devotion. He had captured what he wanted, after all. He wanted to worship at this man's feet.

Peppino was amazed by what he saw. This figure was a saint, a saint different from any that he had ever seen, rough-hewn, human, rugged, starkly naked, but a saint nonetheless, pulsating with life and movement, bringing deliverance without idealization. He felt humble suddenly. Yet he had never felt so close to the *maestro*. He had never thought he could look this noble, inspiring, strong.

Auguste caught the gleam in his eyes, abruptly embraced Peppino, kissed him on both cheeks and wiped away tears.

"It's done?" asked Peppino, feeling his flesh close to crumpling.

"It's done. And it is good." For once Auguste was sure.

III

When "St. John the Baptist" was cast in bronze, Auguste carved *Rodin* in large, vivid letters on the base of the statue and then sent it and "The Age of Bronze" for consideration by the Salon of 1880. He was stunned to realize that almost two years had passed in labor on "John" without his having any awareness of that span of time, and he was surprised to find that he was not waiting anxiously for the verdict of the Salon. Instead he resumed work on "The Man That Walks" and tentatively started an "Adam," with Peppino modeling for both pieces. He had not allowed anyone to view "John," not even Lecoq or Boucher, and he had not seen either man for over a year.

Auguste was certain they had forgotten him until Boucher appeared at his studio one Sunday while he was working on his "Adam."

Boucher said he must speak to Auguste privately, and Auguste said, "Of course," but he did not dismiss Peppino, telling the model to wait, "You are my *envoi*, this will not take long." Auguste assumed Boucher was going to tell him both pieces had been rejected but wanted to do it tactfully.

Boucher stood in the doorway of the studio, where the model could not hear them, and felt uncomfortable. Auguste did not seem glad to see him. He said, "Your new piece is a dynamic figure. The head has the look of a Dante."

"I intended it to communicate the feeling of John the Baptist."

"I know. That's clear. But I wish it were Dante."

"What's wrong now?"

"Nothing is wrong," said Boucher.

"Something is wrong. Don't deny it."

"You are a stubborn man, Rodin. You always expect trouble."

"If there isn't trouble, why are you being apologetic?"

"I like your 'John.' He has a virile Greek quality, yet is proudly devout."

"And I have been rejected again." Auguste turned toward Peppino, resolved never again to involve himself in futile quarrels with the Salon.

"No. Not really," Boucher blurted out. "But since your new figure is a saint, it is felt a fig leaf would be appropriate."

"You said my next piece would be accepted without question."

"It will be. If you add a fig leaf. Please, *mon ami*. That is not too much to ask. Michelangelo did whenever he modeled Jesus. You can do the same. It will make little difference to the beauty and power of the piece."

Auguste sighed wearily, even as he wanted to throw out Boucher as a traitor, and asked, "What about 'The Age of Bronze'?"

"It will be readmitted."

"I will not put a fig leaf on him. He is not a saint."

"It was not requested."

Auguste, in a state of cruel indecision, glanced at Peppino, waiting for him inside, reminding him of all the francs he owed the model. He muttered, "If I change 'St. John,' it could make me ill."

"Not change him!" shouted Boucher, "Drape him! Everybody does when they do a saint or Jesus. You're no different, no better. *Mon dieu!*" Boucher lost his temper and yelled, "Guillaume promises to readmit you when you do a religious subject, and when you do I hold him accountable, force him to live up to his promise, and you have to be temperamental, difficult. Three years I've waited for this chance, and now a few inches of plaster upset you."

Auguste was shaken. He hadn't been thinking in such terms. By now the impulse to do John the Baptist had become original with himself, he had come to do the saint because he had been unable to model anything else.

There were tears of rage and frustration in Boucher's eyes as he turned to go. He was on the street when Auguste halted him.

"*Mon ami,*" said Auguste, "I'm sorry. I didn't realize the trouble you went to over me."

"Not over *you!*" declared Boucher. "Over your sculpture!"

"All right, Boucher, I'll do what you want."

"What *they* want! I do not think a totally naked 'John' immodest. I could not care less what Guillaume thinks. But one does not refuse a chance to be seen. Especially when, because of 'The Age of Bronze,' many will be looking for your new work."

"I will cover 'John' myself."

"That's not necessary. The Salon has experts to do that."

IV

Auguste was startled and pleased by the placement of his two statues. He entered the Palais de l'Industrie and found them in a large, light front gallery, thanks to Boucher. They were not crowded, and could be viewed from all sides, an essential to Auguste. Many people continued to gape at "The Age of Bronze," but "St. John the Baptist," modestly covered with a fig leaf, was regarded more quietly, if not reverently.

Several critics were quick to write that "John" was incongruous with his wide stride, naked body, open mouth, and harsh, unpolished realism, without serenity, repose, or piety; but there were those who were genuinely moved and there was some public praise. Nothing was said about "The Age of Bronze"; as far as the critics were concerned, it no longer existed.

Now there was a kind of truce between Auguste and the Salon. They accepted his surrender on the "St. John" as an acknowledgment of their supremacy, and so his work, for this time at least, ceased to be indecent.

At the end of the exhibit "St. John the Baptist" was awarded the third medal for sculpture. It was unbelievable to Auguste. He had never expected it to occur, and now that it had taken place nothing was happening. There were no purchasers for either of his figures. He heard rumors that there was talk of buying the two figures for the Luxembourg, but when no one approached him he was certain it was just gossip.

However, when Auguste was invited to the salon of Madame Charpentier, where many of the pillars of French art and politics met weekly, he was surprised and bewildered. It was a sign of recognition even more eloquent than the third prize. He might meet Hugo there, or Gambetta, or Zola. Then he told himself this was a mistake.

Auguste mentioned this to Boucher over lunch and Boucher said, "You must go. It is the only way to get the good commissions."

"What about the things I'm working on? 'Adam'? 'The Man That Walks'?"

"You can talk about them at Madame Charpentier's. Many people will be interested in your new work now."

He regarded le grand seigneur suspiciously. "Did you arrange this invitation?"

"No one arranges Madame Charpentier's invitations but the lady herself."

"I am not a man of fashion. I do not even have a dress suit."

"Wear a frock coat, then. Or a cap. Renoir comes in a cap, even in the evening after he has painted the lady."

"The struggling Renoir?"

"Yes. Our colorist is becoming successful, too. Should I pick you up on my way? There will be room in my carriage."

"No." It would be awkward, he thought. He explained, "I may be late."

They parted at the Pont Neuf. Auguste crossed to the Left Bank, but for once he did not feel depressed as he approached his shabby living quarters.

He strode vigorously, a little like "John," he thought, and felt closer to a richer life. There had been a fulfillment in "John," and there was an acknowledgment in this invitation. Yet an even greater effort would have to be put forth now. Madame Charpentier's was a new and unfamiliar world. And what about Rose? He had not even taken her to the Palais de l'Industrie. He had made a John the Baptist without any national boundaries, but in everyday life there were many boundaries.

Auguste lengthened his stride as he neared the rue St. Jacques. All his life up to now, whatever he had pretended, he had lived in Paris as if it were a small village. But life was no longer that simple. He must behave as he strode, with strength.

He entered the apartment to explain to Rose what had come out of the exhibition. He had worked very hard, and now he wanted to play a little.

CHAPTER 24

The Prince Albert frock coat and gray top hat and long black scarf were hired from an expensive shop on the rue de Rivoli, and they seemed as good as new. By the evening of Madame Charpentier's *soirée* Auguste had tried them on so often he almost felt at home in them. He had had his beard trimmed and curled, and thought it looked quite handsome and strong.

He stood now surveying himself in the mirror, about to leave for the evening, and rather liked his appearance. He didn't ask Rose what she thought; she was in a foul humor because he had refused to take her, on the excuse that this was "a professional evening." *Mon dieu!* he couldn't take her, with her red work-worn hands, her untidy clothes, her poorly kept hair. All she could say was monsieur, madame, and the catechism. But he saw that *petit* Auguste, who was almost as tall as he was now, was impressed, and when the boy described him to Papa, Papa said, "You must look like a gentleman."

Yet Papa, sitting at the kitchen table with his hands and head resting on his cane, a mannerism Papa had developed since he had become totally blind, was surprised by the way Auguste was fussing. It was the first time Papa had been out of bed in weeks. Papa said, as *petit* Auguste told him about the top hat, the Prince Albert frock coat, "I never thought a son of mine would dress like this. You say the artists that will be there are important?"

Auguste said, "You are not amusing."

"I do not pretend to be amusing," Papa said critically. Feeling keenly the void of his existence, he added querulously, "Who is going to be there who is so important?"

"Writers, painters, a cabinet member or two, perhaps," said Auguste.

"Cabinet member?" Papa was interested. "Which ones?"

"Gambetta, I am told."

"Our republican lion? Our pillar of the Third Republic?" Papa asked cynically, feeling more royalist than ever, now that the republicans were in power. "Is that why you are not taking Rose?"

"Papa, for heaven's sake, it's too late to discuss it now!" she exclaimed, inevitably and automatically springing to Auguste's defense, even when, as now, she was most furious with him. She felt overwhelmed by the household: Papa had faded frighteningly the past year; *petit* Auguste could barely read and write, and couldn't wait to be old enough to leave school, to flee the studio, although the boy still liked to draw; she felt she had aged ten years in the last two, as if she had been debauched by Auguste's indifference. And yet when it came to Auguste, there was still something there. She knew it was monstrously unjust, but even when he treated her most badly she loved him. She said, "We mustn't upset him."

"No," said Papa, "I haven't much longer to live. I can say what I think."

"You have a long time to live," said Rose. "You are just depressed."

Papa heard this with a faint smile, as if he knew better. He persisted, "My son is selfish. He thinks only of statues."

"He has his reasons," said Rose. "I would have nothing to say. I am a simpleton when it comes to art. I would make him miserable. Perhaps he is right."

"He is not right," said Papa. "Look how hard he has worked. And what has he got at forty but an invitation where he will probably be ignored? Auguste, if you had only listened to me and gone into the Prefecture, you could be retiring on a pension soon."

Auguste, who had not been listening, concentrating on his clothes, said, "I really must be off. Sunday we will all go for a picnic in the Bois." He patted *petit* Auguste on the head, and did not notice the boy's drawing away. He shook hands with Papa as if Papa hadn't said a word, and told Rose, "Don't wait up for me."

II

Auguste grew excited as he approached the palatial mansion on the rue de Grenelle. It was one of the most attractive residential districts of Paris, in spite of being on the Left Bank. And then as he noticed the long line of carriages entering the courtyard he had a moment of panic. But he could not retreat, he was committed. He was glad he had come in a cab at least, and that he was wearing a frock coat and top hat. There would be people here who could spend thousands of francs on their dress alone, who lived in sumptuous mansions like this, who owned their own victorias, broughams, and open landaus.

He did not care for the sculpture on the cornices and balconies. The satyrs and nymphs bulged with flesh and had no sex. There were cupids everywhere, and a profusion of large naked women protruding from the façades and turrets—heavy, lush, overripe, and so much alike he could not tell one from another. Very fancy, he reflected, and utterly false.

He entered the lavish drawing room reluctantly. But as he saw that the long, magnificent room was designed and decorated like an art gallery, with beautiful Gobelin tapestries, glowing chandeliers of a delicate, translucent grace, and several paintings by Renoir and Manet, he smiled, pleased with the Charpentiers' taste. He realized the Charpentiers had inherited the taste of someone else when they had bought this mansion but had made the drawing room their own.

The immense drawing room was crowded with guests, and he did not see anyone he recognized. Then he saw the host and hostess greeting the arriving guests and he joined the line. The Charpentiers, who had become well known as publishers, avid patrons of the arts, and for their receptions, were younger than Auguste had expected. Monsieur was alert and pleasant-looking, and he greeted everyone with apparent gratification. Madame was dark, petite, animated, attractive, and wore her low-cut evening gown with dash and charm. Auguste felt ill at ease next to the many men and women in expensive evening dress who exuded wealth and position. But he could not retreat. He had reached the Charpentiers.

He introduced himself. "I'm Auguste Rodin."

Monsieur Charpentier looked blank, while Madame thought a moment, then remembered. "Ah, yes, you are the sculptor about whom there was so much talk about casting from life."

Auguste flushed angrily, but he had no chance to reply. Guests pressed behind him to greet the Charpentiers, pushing him away from his hosts. He turned into a corner, lonely and miserable. Uniformed servants circulated with trays of food and champagne, but he had lost his appetite. Everywhere there were movement and animation, and he felt stranded. And what had he expected, he thought bitterly, a miracle—instant recognition?

Auguste was about to leave when Boucher accosted him. Boucher said, "I've been looking for you all over. I want to introduce you to several friends of mine. Isn't it a splendid evening?"

But Auguste thought that you couldn't give a man a taste for champagne when he had been brought up on *vin ordinaire*. He said, "I don't know that I'm wanted."

"Idiot! Everyone adores Georges Charpentier and Madame, and you are offended already."

"They are still accusing me of casting from life."

"Rodin, you take everything so personally."

Auguste stood in stubborn silence.

"Come," said Boucher, "I'll introduce you to someone who admires your work." He took Auguste by the arm and forcibly led him toward a stocky, compact man whom Auguste recognized as Émile Zola.

Zola, standing by Renoir's large portrait of Madame Charpentier and her two children, was examining it carefully through his ribboned eyeglasses. He was stouter than Auguste had expected, but there was color in his usually pale cheeks. Renoir and Manet were beside him, and Zola said to Renoir, "This is a credible painting, though I disagree with the accuracy of some of the detail."

Renoir shrugged, then said slyly, "You are most generous, *mon ami*."

Zola retorted, "You are offended because I don't applaud everything you do now, as I used to. But you don't need that these days. And yet if I don't think you are a genius, you resent me."

"Not at all," said Manet. "We can benefit from criticism. But not from ridicule."

"I do not ridicule," said Zola. "Haven't I defended you and Renoir often?"

"In the past," said Manet. "However, it has been years since you've been truly sympathetic."

There was a moment of strained silence. Boucher introduced Auguste to Zola. For an instant Zola, looking as if he were being pursued, was grim. Then he relaxed as Manet said, "Rodin did the 'St. John' you liked."

"The realistic one?" said Zola. His square face lost its belligerence. He said to Auguste, "I'm glad you are a naturalist, and not a theologian."

"I'm neither," said Auguste. "I'm a sculptor."

"Well, in any case, you shocked them," Zola said with satisfaction.

"I didn't intend to," said Auguste.

"Why not?" said Zola. "Art is a battlefield, and we must recognize that. Controversy helps art, makes it more interesting."

Auguste did not answer. Zola's attitudes made him uneasy. He thought Zola was the typical writer, assuming that art was ideas, arguments, a kind of social and natural history of contemporary life resembling Zola's novels, which he liked—as novels. And now the writer was praising Degas for the latter's present devotion to pictures of Parisian life, stating that Degas was a "naturalistic painter," when Degas would be the first and loudest to sneer at this kind of praise. But Zola meant well, perhaps, thought Auguste, although the road to hell was often paved with good intentions.

Meanwhile Madame Charpentier led Zola and Manet and Boucher away to meet new, prominent guests. She wanted Renoir, too, but Renoir said he wanted to speak to Rodin. Renoir remembered the first time he had come to this salon and how uncomfortable he had been without anyone there he knew.

Renoir said, "Don't be upset by Zola. He really did like your 'John.' But now that he has become a public figure, he has to orate a little."

Auguste said, "I didn't ask for praise."

"We owe much to Zola. He supported us when practically everybody else was blind to us. We must remember that."

"And now you look to Madame Charpentier for inspiration?"

"For support, not inspiration."

"Why isn't Degas here?"

"The Charpentiers are too republican for Edgar."

"But Monet is an ardent republican, and he isn't here either."

"Have you seen Monet lately?"

"No. I've been working very hard."

"You didn't know that his Camille had died?"

"When?" Auguste was shocked. He had not known Monet's wife well, but had been aware of the painter's devotion to her. "It must have been a terrible loss."

"She died a few months ago. Monet is in a dreadful state of depression. He goes nowhere, sees no one, paints, paints, and mourns."

"I'm sorry." Auguste hated funerals, but he would have gone to hers.

"Try to see him. Perhaps you can break through his shell."

"But I don't know him as well as you do, Renoir."

"Who knows him? He respects you, Rodin. He thinks you have courage."

"Rebelliousness, mon ami. But I'll visit Monet. As soon as I can." Auguste paused, and then said with new concern, "And what about yourself, and Manet? Manet doesn't look at all well. He is limping badly—he looks like a martyr when he walks."

Renoir said sadly, "Some days Manet can hardly walk at all. Oh, I tell him it is rheumatism, which I suffer from, but Manet does not believe me and I do not believe it myself. Yet look at Hugo!" Renoir pointed to Victor Hugo, standing in the center of the drawing room, surrounded by a crowd of admirers, yet regarding them with the scornful attitude of the master, who even as he absorbed their praise avidly was above these flunkies. "Hugo is almost eighty, yet he still boasts about the women he has, the flights of stairs he climbs each day."

Suddenly Auguste couldn't take his eyes off Hugo.

Renoir said, "Don't tell me that Hugo is a hero of yours!"

"What a magnificent head!" Auguste could not resist admiring the powerful countenance of Hugo, engraved with age and toil and strength. Hugo alone, in this drawing room laden with flattery, looked his reputation. Auguste was fascinated by the full, intense lips, the mouth as expressive as any of Hugo's novels, the passionate, deeply set eyes, the Gothic ruggedness of his bone and flesh. It was a face he had to sculpt.

Renoir asked, "Haven't you met Hugo?"

"No. What a head to model!"

"I know him only slightly," said Renoir. "But Mallarmé knows him well, and Hugo likes Mallarmé." Renoir called Mallarmé over and told him what Auguste wanted.

Mallarmé said in his soft, gentle voice, "I'll introduce you gladly, Rodin, but I warn you, Hugo is not likely to pose. Hugo feels he has posed too much as it is. Everybody has wanted to sculpt him, and many have."

Renoir cut in, "And he won't like it that you spoke to Zola first."

"I was just being introduced," Auguste said, puzzled.

Renoir said, "They do not speak to each other. Zola regards Balzac as his master, instead of Hugo. And now, with Zola's books selling even more than Hugo's, the gulf between them is not to be bridged."

"Then why do the Charpentiers invite them at the same time if they don't speak to each other?"

"Rodin, you are naïve," said Renoir. "The Charpentiers adore this. Such arguments sell Zola's books, which Georges Charpentier publishes."

Mallarmé added, "And makes money, with which his wife buys your pictures."

"*Mon dieu!*" cried Renoir. "I'm not complaining. Go, Rodin, meet the great man. Perhaps he will be nice to you if you drop on your knees."

Renoir went to join Manet and Boucher while Mallarmé introduced Auguste to Hugo. Hugo, who had been speaking sternly to his admirers about the decadence of contemporary poetry, smiled gently as he saw Mallarmé and said, "Ah, *mon cher Mallarmé*, it is good to see you." He barely acknowledged Auguste, didn't catch his name, and Mallarmé had to repeat it.

"Auguste Rodin, the sculptor."

"The sculptor? Which one?" asked Hugo, frowning.

This is a waste, Auguste thought angrily. Hugo doesn't know who I am and is not interested in finding out.

Mallarmé said, "He did the 'St. John' and 'The Age of Bronze.' Remember, *mon cher maître*, the lovely poetic figure of a youth."

"Oh, the statue that was cast from life," said Hugo.

Auguste had resolved not to lose his temper, but this was too much. He almost smashed the glass he was holding, putting it down with a rude jolt.

Hugo asked Mallarmé, "What else has he done?"

"He is an assistant and pupil of Carrier-Belleuse," said Mallarmé, assuming this would help Rodin, since Carrier-Belleuse's busts were the best known in France. "You know Carrier-Belleuse's heads, don't you, *maître?*"

"Yes," said Hugo. "I don't care for them. Particularly the one he did of me."

"I'm not a pupil," growled Auguste. "Just an employee."

Hugo didn't reply, and Mallarmé hurried to say, "Rodin is a fine sculptor, *mon cher maître*. He would do a virile bust of you. Realistic. Natural."

"No!" Hugo said decisively, speaking as if Auguste weren't there. "I've had enough of busts. There have been so many done I've lost count. And the last one I sat for, Mallarmé, was wretched, a martyrdom. Imagine, I had to sit hour after hour without moving. I couldn't talk. *Mon dieu!* it was like being impotent. Yet the stupid ass of a sculptor made me look like an old satyr."

Mallarmé interrupted, "I agree, Victor Vilain's bust was incredibly bad. He was a Roman sculptor, modeling you in the stiff, formal, cold Roman fashion. But Rodin will make you live."

Hugo said, "I will live better in less clumsy hands. This friend of yours, he almost broke his wineglass when he put it down. I prefer to leave the judgment of posterity in more skillful hands. Oh, his bodies are real, but his faces are not impressive, not noble. And his 'John' is a peasant!"

"Wasn't the original John a peasant, Monsieur Hugo?" Auguste pushed himself in front of the great man so that Hugo had to address him.

Hugo said wearily, with obvious distaste for the entire discussion, "You have a strenuous manner, Rodin, but I will not sit for you." Hugo reassumed the look of indifference he had worn during most of the conversation, but suddenly was interested at the sight of a very pretty young woman who had just entered the drawing room. He stared at her intently as he motioned to Madame Charpentier that he wanted to meet her.

Madame Charpentier brought over Mademoiselle Madeleine Bufay, a young actress, and introduced her to Hugo.

Auguste did not move, although Hugo had dismissed him. He wanted to meet this very pretty young woman also. Her entrance had provoked a stir of admiration. Auguste was attracted by her expressive dark eyes, radiant smile, and fine complexion. Her shoulders were uncovered down to the cleft of her breasts, her arms were bare. He saw her white throat as living marble. He liked her graceful carriage.

And for an instant Auguste felt she preferred to speak to him instead of Hugo, then he told himself that was nonsense: Hugo was France's greatest man, poet, playwright, essayist, novelist, political hero, and exile from France as a protest against Napoleon III, inspiration of resistance against the Second Empire, the symbol of living republicanism. Wherever there was injustice to mankind Hugo protested, Hugo wrote, Hugo spoke—Hugo, who had more the air of a god than of a man, Hugo who to many Frenchmen was a god indeed!

Madeleine Bufay knew about the "St. John" and "The Age of Bronze," and the instant Hugo had finished kissing her bare wrist, since she wore gloves, she told Auguste how wonderful they were. "So vital," she said.

Hugo was glaring, and before Auguste could express his delight Mallarmé, at a signal from Hugo, led Auguste away. Auguste wanted to protest, but he couldn't; the usually gentle Mallarmé was insistent.

Mallarmé whispered to an annoyed Auguste as he pushed him toward a group in a far corner of the long drawing room, "I have a very important man I want you to meet."

But Auguste felt cheated. He was strongly attracted by this pretty young woman, and he had had enough of famous men. He said to Mallarmé, "Hugo has the manners of a dog in heat."

Mallarmé replied, "You're right to feel the way you do, but he is not interested in right or wrong as it relates to himself, but only as it relates to other people. But come, I will introduce you to Gambetta. You will enjoy meeting him. And he wants to meet you."

Auguste didn't believe Mallarmé. By now he was in a state of resistance to meeting anyone else, especially a famous man. But he liked Gambetta at once. Gambetta had an open, strong face with bright, friendly eyes. His vigorous features radiated assurance, but there was not a trace of arrogance. The terror of the royalists, this leader of the republicans who ruled the Third Republic, had a likable youthfulness in spite of his graying hair and beard. And they were almost the same age—Gambetta was just two years older—which made Auguste feel more at ease.

Gambetta seemed genuinely glad to meet Auguste and introduced him warmly to the man standing beside him, Antonin Proust, a tall, handsome man, dressed as elegantly as Gambetta was dressed plainly. Gambetta said, "Proust is our new Minister of Fine Arts, Rodin. We've been hearing a great deal about your sculpture. Manet has praised it highly, Boucher, Mallarmé. Boucher forced me to see your work. I like that 'John' is more man than saint."

Auguste said, "My religious convictions grow out of a worship of nature."

Gambetta said, "I did think that 'John' looked like a Frenchman."

Auguste replied, "He is not from any nation." He was disappointed that there was no sign of Mademoiselle Bufay or Hugo. He wondered if Hugo had made a conquest so quickly, and was sad at the thought.

"You have zealous friends, Rodin," said Gambetta. "You are fortunate."

"I learned about your work from Monet," said Mallarmé. "I was visiting him at his studio when I first heard about you. He said you did a bacchante some years ago that was one of the finest pieces he ever saw, that was broken, tragically, while you were moving. He said it was very sad. It crumpled to ashes."

Auguste was astonished. Monet had never said this to him.

Boucher, seeing Gambetta and Antonin Proust with Auguste, hurried over and said, "He has fine work in his studio that he has never exhibited."

"That has never been accepted by the Salon," Auguste said sharply.

"But I warn you, Gambetta," Boucher plunged on, "he can be an *enfant terrible* of a sculptor. When he gets an *idée fixe*, nothing changes him."

Gambetta gazed at Auguste speculatively, as if seeking to come to a decision about him. Then he asked, "Are you really so stubborn, Rodin? I've heard a good deal of talk about your stubbornness."

"Rebellious, Monsieur Gambetta, not stubborn."

"How can I object to a rebel?"

Everyone smiled now.

Gambetta continued straightforwardly, "Antonin Proust and I have been discussing a possible commission for you, Rodin. There is no question in our minds about the quality of the work you will do. But as a politician I am supposed to be practical. There are such things as subject matter, cost, how much time it will take. I am not an expert in such matters, but Proust is, and so is his Under Secretary, Edmond Turquet. Would you be interested in doing something for the Third Republic?"

Now that what he wanted fervently was within reach, Auguste did not know what to say. But he liked Gambetta. Gambetta, the most important personage here, the idol of the republican left and center, was the simplest and most courteous person he had met here. Auguste said, "Monsieur, I would be honored to do work you commissioned."

"France, *maître*, France. We are a republic now, you know," said Gambetta.

"Republic, empire, it is the work that matters."

"We had a door in mind," said Gambetta. "To be the entrance to a new Musée des Arts Décoratifs that is to be erected on the quai d'Orsay."

"It is a fine location," said Auguste. "Depending on what is done."

"A door. A door worthy of French art." Gambetta was very serious now.

"Like Ghiberti's," said Auguste, reflecting, "which Michelangelo called 'The Gates of Paradise.' "

"Perhaps," said Gambetta, "except I, personally, would prefer a more somber note. This is a time of uncertainty, of groping toward different goals. There are many wounds in France that have not yet been healed. We live, really, on top of a volcano, and sometimes I think it will consume us."

There was a heavy silence.

Then Gambetta said more cheerfully, "Think it over, Rodin. That is, if you are interested?"

Auguste gulped. Interested? He was fascinated! A monumental door showing the vast scope of human endeavor in bronze or stone. His Sistine Chapel! And Gambetta was no Pope, to demand absolute obedience. Yet how could he bargain over what he desired so passionately? He said, "As I told you, Monsieur Gambetta, I would be greatly honored."

Gambetta replied, "Of course, if you concentrate on the nude, realistically, as you have so far, you could create an enormous scandal."

Auguste exploded, "When you drape a figure, you hide the very things you want to show. Nothing is more beautiful or strong or subtle than the human figure. It conveys a multitude of emotions. Thus when you cover it, you hide, repress, distort. All genuine sculptors knew this, Praxiteles, Phidias, Donatello, Michelangelo, even though they couldn't always practice it. And this has nothing to do with obscenity, or even with sensuality, but with truth. Generally a draped human figure is a concealed one. It is usually false and unnatural. And in sculpture, as in all art, one must not conceal anything."

Boucher and Mallarmé braced for an answering explosion, but though a flush rose on Gambetta's cheeks he said quietly, "Could Antonin Proust and I look at all your work? Say this Sunday?"

"Why, certainly, monsieur," said Auguste, calming. "Except my studio is a poor place, cold, damp, small."

"We will concentrate on the sculpture," said Gambetta. "And then we can talk further about the nude."

Auguste asked, "And should I think more about the door?"

Gambetta hesitated, then said, "Let's wait and see what happens Sunday."

Gambetta was gone on the arm of Monsieur Charpentier, with Proust, Mallarmé, and Boucher following him.

Auguste had walked the length of the drawing room, not certain whether to feel optimistic or pessimistic about Gambetta's proposals, when he saw Madeleine Bufay. She was in the conservatory, off the main entrance to the drawing room.

She motioned for him to join her, and as he did she smiled and said, "That Hugo, he was like a billy goat, I had such a time getting rid of him."

Auguste began to laugh. He said, "You're positively indecent."

"Avoiding the great man? Can you imagine, he tried to pinch my legs under the table. But I have something important to discuss with you."

"What is it?"

Madeleine lowered her voice still more. "Do you model heads?"

"Not often. They are not my kind of sculpture. I do not flatter."

"How long would one take?"

"To please you? Months, perhaps."

"And to please yourself?"

"A year."

"You couldn't rush a little and do it in a month?"

"I cannot hurry. This is not a Sardou tidbit to be put on in a week."

"You are unkind. I can do anything I like with Hugo, and you refuse me."

"Would Hugo write for you?"

"A poem, he said. He was charming, quite charming. He talked all about himself. For hours, it seemed. And you never talk about yourself."

"No one gives me a chance here. Except Gambetta."

"Did he give you a commission?"

"How did you know we were discussing that?"

"Why else would he want to speak to you?"

"You're cynical, mademoiselle."

"My name is Madeleine. As for cynical, you are most cynical of all. You expect nothing, not even from me."

"I would still like to do Hugo. He has a fine head."

"Naturally. Hugo is unquestionably the greatest figure in France today."

"That's not the reason. It is the quality of his head."

Madeleine was amused. She observed Auguste's rugged head, his jutting jaw, his broad forehead, the ferocity of his expression when he was angry, and thought he had a far more interesting head than Hugo's to model. And what a rare intensity he had in his work! Madeleine became quite serious as she said, "I notice you've done no woman so far."

"Oh yes, I have, but none that really satisfy me. But I will, and not any virgins, either."

"Do you need a model?"

"To work a week? No, thanks."

"I'm serious, Auguste Rodin."

Surprised, he shook his head in wonder. He felt as if he were in a dream. And now, thinking of his studio, he felt more apprehension than eagerness. Yet her eyes shone as she looked at him and her smile was tender. He said, "I wish it were possible, but my studio is cold, I am a hard taskmaster, and—"

"There is another woman," she interrupted.

"That is not the problem," he said curtly.

She could not suppress a smile. He sounded so masculine, and Hugo had said the same thing. Then she looked apologetic, downcast.

She was so appealing now, Auguste had an enormous desire for her. Her bare shoulders attracted him sensuously. He observed the fullness of her breasts and wondered whether they were firm or soft. The thought of being with her exhilarated him, and that had not happened for a long time.

He felt she was reading his thoughts when she said, "I live on the Île St. Louis, right behind Notre Dame. Could I drop you off?"

"I'll drop you," he replied, and was exultant as he saw her lovely face light up with pleasure. Perhaps she was only flirting, but her interest made him feel fulfilled in his manhood. Beauty was the thing most worth possessing, he rationalized, beauty justified anything and achieved miracles. An artist needed beauty more than anything else. To experience and create beauty was to live.

As Auguste escorted Madeleine home, he felt he had taken a long step forward, especially when they made an appointment for her to model.

"In several weeks," he said. "As soon as I finish with Gambetta. Will I be able to reach you here?"

"Yes." She smiled to herself: Auguste was such a mixture of stubbornness and shyness. But this, she was positive, she could resolve. "Whenever you are ready, Auguste *maître*."

I am ready this instant, his body shouted, but he must get a better studio, as soon as possible. So often his friends had said he had incredible patience, but not now! He said, "I'll make a life-size statue, an Eve, a Danaïd, or something original." She indicated her pleasure with a gracious smile, and he said *"Bonsoir"* and left her at the door, knowing he would have to return.

CHAPTER 25

On the Sunday Auguste had promised to take his family for a picnic, Gambetta and Antonin Proust visited his studio to study his work. He was afraid they would be discouraged by the poverty, but Antonin Proust, the friend of many artists, and Gambetta, who had been poor himself, ignored it as if it did not exist. Antonin Proust was dressed elegantly, as always, and strode around the studio, examining the sculpture as if he were in a gallery of the Louvre, while Gambetta sat down—too rotund to walk much—and focused intently on the work.

They really did seem interested, thought Auguste. He shook off his feeling of uneasiness. He showed them all of his work, even those pieces that were unfinished. He was surprised by how much he had done. It was far more than he had realized.

Proust was fascinated by "The Man with the Broken Nose." He had a sudden sense of revelation. Despair, pain, and decay were deeply imprinted on this face. He said, "I wonder why it hasn't been accepted by the Salon."

"It was, in 1875, after being rejected in 1864. But it was ignored so then, I never felt I made the Salon until 'The Age of Bronze' was accepted."

"It's as if you were thinking of Michelangelo when you modeled him."

"I was."

Antonin Proust was pleased.

Gambetta liked "The Man with the Broken Nose," too, but was more excited by the animation and vigor of "The Man That Walks."

Auguste said, "It is unfinished."

Gambetta replied, "Life is often unfinished. This figure has great strength. Rodin, your recognition is long overdue."

Auguste thought so, too, but it made no sense praising him unless they did something about it. He waited, still skeptical.

Gambetta turned to the "Mignon" and "Bellona" busts and asked, "Aren't they from the same model?"

"Yes."

"An attractive face, strong, interesting, but not Parisian?"

"No, not Parisian, Monsieur Gambetta."

"And isn't there quite a difference in the age of the two heads?"

"Yes."

"Your wife?" asked Gambetta.

"No."

"Oh!"

"Does it matter?" Auguste asked defiantly.

Gambetta smiled and said, "Of course not. It is just that they are such fine heads it makes one curious to meet the model."

Auguste did not take the hint. He did not answer.

"I am not a Parisian either, Rodin. And I come from a humble background also. To some people it is my greatest virtue as a politician."

"It is not necessarily a virtue in a model," said Auguste. "But I would be honored if you accepted a head as a gift."

"No, no, no," said Gambetta. Then seeing Auguste's disappointment, he added suddenly, "I would be the one who is honored, but it is impossible."

"You don't really like the heads," Auguste said distrustfully.

"I do. I would prize one of your pieces. Rodin, I was one of those ambitious young men from the provinces who advance on Paris every year to gather the glorious prizes. The kind of man that Flaubert and Zola and Balzac have written about so well. Giddy—nauseating, perhaps—and unrealistic, but always yearning. I lived in the Latin Quarter, I strode about with the confidence of the conqueror. I was a lawyer, but I was also going to be the artist, like so many of my friends. Now I am supposed to please everyone, which would make me a very bad artist, and which is obviously impossible. Now while I try to be a *maître* statesman, even my weight is a source of controversy. If I grow stouter I win the bourgeois, if I grow thin I win the workers. Many say my expanding waistline is a great scandal, yet the people who criticize it the most are the royalists, who eat the most. Every move I make is watched intently. If I accepted a gift from you, it would be indigestible, and it would end whatever connection I might have with any commission you might receive."

"That's too bad," said Auguste.

"It would be even worse if it deprived you of a commission you deserve."

Meanwhile Proust had been inspecting "St. John the Baptist" and "The Age of Bronze" from every conceivable approach. Proust said, "You've placed them unusually well. 'John,' especially, looks monumental here."

"John" stood alone, yet with smaller figures within view, which made "John" appear even larger than he was and gave him a new grandeur.

Proust called to Gambetta, "Léon, from the side he's magnificent. Come, you must see 'John' from here. Here he has the look of eternity."

Gambetta rose with an effort and joined Proust. The plaster "John the Baptist" stood above them like a crag that no man could destroy. There was the wonderful stride, wild, miraculous, and true. It was a movement of exploration and liberation. "John" would make a fine outdoor figure, Gambetta thought. He said abruptly, before he could change his mind, "Rodin, there will be an offer for 'John' and 'The Age of Bronze' from the Luxembourg."

"I am very grateful," Auguste blurted out.

"Wait until you see what is offered. You may not be so grateful. No one spends more unwillingly for someone else's benefit than a Frenchman."

"How much will I get?"

"Proust's Under Secretary, Turquet, will handle the business details."

"What about the placing of the statues? It is vital, as you can see."

"I recognize that, but that is the province of the Ministry."

Auguste said emotionally, "The sculptor is rarely consulted in the placing of his work, when he should be the only one consulted. And then he is accused of arrogance, when most of the time he is the one who is never satisfied, he who is the severest critic of his work."

Gambetta sighed. "I know, I know, but we also have a bureaucracy."

Auguste said irritably, "I thought the Beaux Arts and the Salon and the Institute were being separated from the Ministry of Fine Arts."

Proust explained, "We are trying. But it is not easy. Many people would lose influence they do not want to surrender."

"What about Guillaume?" asked Auguste.

Proust replied quickly, expecting this, "Guillaume will have nothing to say about where they are placed. Just as he has had nothing to say about the purchases. And you will be consulted about the placing."

"Of course," said Gambetta, showing irritation for the first time. "We've had enough difficulty, buying your figures, let alone getting into a dispute as to where they are going."

"Where are they going?" demanded Auguste.

"Into the gardens of the Luxembourg, probably," said Proust. "You didn't expect it would be in the Louvre, did you?"

"No," said Auguste. "But I expected to be consulted, even about the price."

"You will, you will!" Gambetta said impatiently. "Who can assess the real worth of a work of art? We will give you what we can."

For an instant Auguste looked as if he were going to reject the offer. The silence in the studio was oppressive.

Gambetta flushed. All he had to do was turn toward the door and the sales were killed. He was positive that Rodin, much as the sculptor needed and craved the sales, would take no step after him. Their eyes met: Gambetta's inflexible and Auguste's immovable. Then as if each of them, statesman and sculptor, had proved his strength, the statesman smiled slightly, and so did the sculptor.

Gambetta asked, "Rodin, have you thought about the door for our proposed Museum of the Decorative Arts?"

Auguste thought resentfully, I shouldn't have, you gave me no assurance, but I have, I have thought of it walking and sleeping and working and eating. I have reread Dante and Baudelaire and Hugo and Balzac, and I find Dante's and Baudelaire's view of humanity closest to my own. But he could not speak unless it was to the point. He stood silently, waiting.

"Well," Gambetta repeated impatiently, "have you thought about it?"

"Yes. A little."

"And?"

"It should have the power and scope of the two admirable doors Lorenzo Ghiberti did for the baptistery at Florence."

Gambetta frowned and looked uncomfortable.

Auguste added enthusiastically, "Michelangelo said, 'They are so fine they might fittingly stand at the entrance to Paradise.' "

Gambetta said, "I share the general admiration of Michelangelo. After all, my parents were Italian, but we don't want a religious subject of this nature. I have just lost friends because I have insisted on the separation of Church and State. Now if I support a large religious sculpture, I will lose the rest of my friends."

"In other words, you are not interested in a door to heaven?"

"Are any of us? Are we, the Third Republic, really fulfilling the potential of man? The brotherhood of man? The rights of man? Or are we closer to hell than to heaven, Rodin?"

"To hell," Auguste said slowly, grimly.

"Yet it is not a religious hell," said Gambetta, "but a hell of our own making. We are still suffering from the corruption and decadence of the Second Empire. We, in the Third Republic, live in a kind of impotence, and will remain impotent until we recover Alsace and Lorraine. Our *via dolorosa*."

"Our shame and our cross," said Auguste.

"Yes," said Gambetta, excited by the mood he was creating. "But it is no wonder we doubt, we have lived through such troubled times. This has become an age notable for uncertainty and instability and the choosing not of good over evil, but of the lesser evils. Religion is doubted, politics is for cynics, science has not given us the utopia we desire. Is it that man is a failure?"

Proust looked solemn, and Auguste did not know what to say. Gambetta's sudden pessimism shook him, yet he could not disagree with him.

Gambetta said sarcastically, "We are in the republic backward. We are in a republic created by the royalists, who resent that we republicans are trying to govern it. It is a republic where the imperial tradition is preferred, and now that it is past, is worshiped. As every patriotic Frenchman knows, Napoleon was not defeated, Napoleon was betrayed. We live in the reflection of Napoleon's victories and ignore his defeats. We would like to have his empire at our feet, yet we have had several of the bloodiest revolutions in history to overthrow our own empires. We praise all the virtues and practice most of the vices."

Auguste asked, "And you want a door that will mirror these vices?"

"That will reflect our own," Gambetta said passionately. "Our lusts, our vanities, all the seven deadly sins. Have you read Baudelaire?"

"Many times."

"Have you ever thought of doing sculpture based on Baudelaire?"

"Yes."

"And Dante?"

Auguste said, "I prefer Dante as a theme, although I agree with much that Baudelaire wrote. Dante's hell is concrete, visual. But so much has been done. Illustrations of the *Divine Comedy* are a commonplace in art."

"Yet if you did a door which was our *vallée de la misère*," Gambetta urged eloquently, "it could be very moving. It could have great significance."

"A door to warn of doomsday," said Auguste. "An enormous door depicting a hell of punishment, of anguish and torment, of desperation and desolation. It could have a power and beauty that could be sensuous yet terrifying."

Gambetta said reflectively, "An entrance for the damned."

"Yes, yes, you may be right, Monsieur Gambetta," Auguste said, enticed more and more by the scope and vigor of the idea. "There are much confusion and uncertainty in the world. There are many of us who are troubled, groping, who believe in hell, whether it is Dante's, Baudelaire's, or our own. Indeed, there are much despair and pain and guilt in people, although many try to hide it."

Gambetta said, "There is a subterranean world in most people, a kind of hate and lust and envy which they are not always able to submerge. In times of crisis this pours out of them. And in our century we have had to endure many crises."

Auguste sighed, "I know. If it is not political, it is personal."

"Then you agree, Rodin, that this hell should be personal, human?"

"I think so."

"And if this could be put into design on a large scale, it could be quite moving. Say on the entrance for our new Museum of the Decorative Arts?"

"It would fit. Dante tells in the third canto of the Inferno of coming to a gate of hell, then entering it."

"Good, good!"

"A gate. A gate of hell," repeated Auguste, trying the idea out.

"Which my opponents would like me to walk through," said Gambetta. "I could be condemned for the gate as I was for opposing the Prussians."

Auguste, involved in the developing idea, was not listening. He said, speaking really to himself, "I will do a hundred figures on this gate. All little figures, so they can't accuse me of casting from life."

Gambetta asked the silent Proust, "What do you think?"

Proust said, "A gate depicting hell? A dance of death? C'est magnifique! But can it be modeled on a door?"

Auguste said, "It can be done. Michelangelo did that and even more in the Sistine Chapel."

"I know. But the times were different. In his day people believed more in a concrete hell," said Proust. He shook his head skeptically. "A gate of hell in sculpture. It will be a miracle if it succeeds."

Gambetta said, "It might. Sometimes I think the only place man can be respected is in the *ateliers*. If the artist is not optimistic, at least he is truthful. Rodin, when you meet with Turquet about 'John' and 'The Age of Bronze,' speak to him about a door based on Dante's *Divine Comedy*. If you two can agree on cost, something might be arranged. Yes, Proust?"

Proust nodded, although his doubts remained.

But already there was set up in Auguste's mind a magnificent door reflecting his view of hell, and Dante's and Baudelaire's and Gambetta's, too, and he knew he would acquiesce to any conditions as long as he could fulfill his own concepts and meet the cost.

Gambetta said, "The most important thing is, this door must show our deep concern about France's fate as a nation and man's fate as man."

Of course, of course, thought Auguste, but above all the figures on the gate must possess a felicity of movement and a frenzy of emotion and *volupté* that only sculpture could express.

At the door Gambetta said casually, "And there will be a state studio for you, which is given to anyone who has a commission from the republic."

Auguste was overwhelmed. "If I could only repay you, Monsieur Gambetta. Do a head of you when you are not in the Chamber."

"I would be honored, but I am so busy," Gambetta replied. "And I've had an etching done which pleases me very much. By a fine artist, Legros."

"We went to school together. He is a great etcher."

"He would be pleased to hear that. Living in London, Legros feels France has forgotten him."

"Monsieur Gambetta, I do not want to compete with my good friend Legros. But an etching and a bust each have their place. And except for Hugo, I have not asked anyone to sit for me."

"I heard about Hugo. He was foolish. Perhaps when I am less busy we could do a head." Gambetta took a last look at Auguste's work. "Boucher and Mallarmé and Monet were right. Your work is powerful and revolutionary."

"Revolutionary?" Auguste repeated, surprised.

"Certainly," Gambetta chuckled. "But I wager you don't know whether you are a republican or a royalist."

"I am whatever is good for France."

"Indeed, you will go far with such sentiments. But I am glad to see that when it comes to sculpture you are not sentimental."

II

Auguste, at home a little later, was surprised to find a storm brewing. But Aunt Thérèse's presence told him that Rose was desperate. He kissed Aunt Thérèse warmly and insisted she looked well, although he thought she had aged terribly, while Rose, full of nervous anger, talked of her grievances against him, the broken appointment to picnic, his neglect of her, *petit* Auguste, Papa, his constant absences.

"But I have good news," he shouted, irate yet exultant. "Two sales, a commission. Rose, how can you be angry? I don't understand. Now there will be plenty of time for Sunday picnics."

"Less," Rose said knowingly. "You will never be home now."

"I won't have to work so hard. I'm quitting Carrier-Belleuse. I am a full-time sculptor for good." He grabbed Aunt Thérèse and waltzed her around the room. He was awkward and she was old and they fell over each other's feet, but she was caught up by his joy. She had never seen him smile so.

Aunt Thérèse said, "Rose, things will be better now."

"Of course," said Auguste. "I'm even getting a new studio, free."

Rose said mournfully, "So you will spend the money you save on more sculpture or another studio. You will be everywhere but home."

He said positively, "I'm home now."

Rose said, "Yes. But for how long?"

"Every Sunday. I'll have six days to work for myself."

Aunt Thérèse nodded in agreement, and Rose, feeling deserted by the one friend she had thought she could trust, said, "I suppose so," and tried to make the best of it. "What statues did you sell?"

" 'St. John' and 'The Age of Bronze.' "

"To whom?"

"The Luxembourg. But Gambetta bought them himself."

"Gambetta? The great statesman? The one you met at Madame Charpentier's?"

"Rose, I told you he was coming to the studio today." He grew annoyed. She had no right to be suspicious.

Instead of answering she peered into the rear bedroom and whispered, "We'd better not talk too loud. Papa has had a bad day and he has just fallen asleep."

Auguste was disappointed. "I wanted to tell him about the sales. He's always said I would never make a living as a sculptor."

"Have you?"

"I will now."

"How much are they giving you for the two pieces?"

"It wasn't stated, but it will be a few thousand francs."

"Can they be trusted?"

"Rose, what's come over you? This is the greatest day of my life and you are full of criticism."

Aunt Thérèse said, "She's tired. Papa has been cranky, *petit* Auguste refused to come in when she called him for lunch, and she never knows when you will be home." She looked at him proudly. "So Gambetta himself bought your pieces. Soon you will be a sculptor of distinction."

"He is now," said Rose, suddenly determined not to be outdone by Aunt Thérèse. "He always was. Even when I met him. They should have recognized him years ago. When he did 'Migon,' the 'Bacchante,' when I posed for him. He never had a better model than me. Even the 'Bellona' is as good as the 'John.' But he's never exhibited them. He's afraid, ashamed of me. He's—"

"Rose!" Aunt Thérèse interrupted. "Auguste is not ashamed of you!"

"He never takes me anywhere. Never shows the pieces I modeled for."

"I showed them to Gambetta. He liked 'Mignon' and 'Bellona' very much."

"But you don't."

"I offered him one as a gift. And he would have taken it, except that it would have looked like a bribe for the commission he was giving me. I felt greatly honored by his regard for those busts. I will certainly show them if I ever get the chance."

Rose looked dazed. She didn't feel so pretty any more, but the heads were. She mumbled, "I'm sorry. I always knew you would be recognized."

"And I'm grateful for your help."

"Maybe I am stupid. But I love you. I've always loved you."

"You're a good girl, and I appreciate that."

"You're not angry with me, are you? I'm so unhappy when you're angry."

"Angry? Rosette, this is the happiest day of my life!" He took her in his arms. He said they must have a party to celebrate this festive occasion, and when he laughed she joined him, determined to share his joy.

III

But Auguste was disappointed when Edmond Turquet, Proust's Under Secretary, offered him only twenty-two hundred francs for "St.

John the Baptist" and two thousand francs for "The Age of Bronze."
With all the difficulties he had encountered in doing the two pieces,
the price barely came to the cost of casting them in bronze. Then
there was no assurance that he would be consulted in the placing of
the statues.

Turquet, who was friendly, did not even know whether they would
be put inside the museum of the Luxembourg—the honored place—
or in the gardens. But Auguste could not say no. He agreed to the
price, although his disappointment remained.

As for the use of a state studio, Turquet informed him that would
come if his plans for the door were accepted. However, Turquet was
sympathetic. "Submit your plans as soon as you can, Monsieur Rodin,
and if they don't cost too much they should be accepted."

"How much should they cost?" Auguste was embarrassed that he
had to ask.

"It depends on your plans. But if your two pieces came to four
thousand francs—"

"Forty-two hundred," interrupted Auguste.

"Let us say in round numbers four thousand. So ten thousand
should do."

"But I intend to do at least a hundred figures, perhaps more."

"Ten thousand francs is a great deal for a door ten feet by four."

"It will have to be larger. No one will feel it if it is that small.
That's half the size of Ghiberti's. His doors are at least eighteen feet
high and twelve feet wide. And they are the best that have ever been
done."

"The size can be decided later. Monsieur Rodin, there is no quarrel with your idea. But it is felt at the Ministry that it would be better
if you made it clear that your door is based on the entire *Divine
Comedy*."

"I agreed to Dante, but I had only the Inferno in mind."

"We do not object to that at the Ministry, but there will be a better
chance of approval if it is believed you will include Paradise, too."

Auguste hesitated.

"Once the commission is given, you can concentrate on the Inferno."

Auguste decided there was no time for arguing; he had work to do.
He thought there might be something devious in this stipulation but

if Balzac in creating his *Comédie Humaine* had based it on the *Divine Comedy*, so could he. Auguste said, "The door will be based on the *Divine Comedy*. I will put that in writing."

When Auguste did this a few days later, he received the money for his two statues. It was far more money than he had ever possessed. He felt rich. He quit Carrier-Belleuse at once. He resolved never to work for anyone else again, although he felt he had not lost a master but switched masters. He was surprised when Carrier-Belleuse asked, "Will you do a head of me?" There were more famous portrait sculptors in Paris, and when he mentioned them Carrier-Belleuse dismissed them. The sculptor, renowned for his own portrait busts, said, "Someday I may be remembered most for the head you did of me." Auguste pointed out that Carrier-Belleuse had done even Hugo, still smarting from that rejection, and Carrier-Belleuse retorted, "Yes, a distinguished head that no one looks at any more. I'll come to your studio, Rodin, whenever you want." Then Auguste felt immensely successful. He said he would do a head of Carrier-Belleuse when he had time. He said it with a finality that closed the discussion.

There was no time to celebrate his emancipation, for now that he was working for himself he was busier than ever. Every Sunday he spent with his family; otherwise he was always at the studio, preparing his plans for submission to the Ministry of Fine Arts.

First he had to settle on his theme; until that was decided, he could not start his architectural sketches. Whole days were spent studying the *Divine Comedy*. He bought a five-franc edition of Dante's epic poem and carried it with him everywhere. And however his mind turned, he came back to the Inferno. Inevitably and inexorably it struck him as the most appropriate and significant theme for the door. Dante's judgment on his age became Auguste's judgment on his *own* age. And the more he reflected about what Gambetta had said, the more he also agreed with the statesman politician. The deadly sins were the reality, and he must show the anguish and remorse they brought.

He thought sadly that the world was not orderly as man lived it, but a constant falling short. Man was not governed by beauty and truth, but by anxiety, doubts, sin. Even the body, so beautiful and inspiring at its best, destroyed itself much of the time with its excesses of lust, vanity, and greed. Love became a destructive frenzy. Desire often went from ecstasy to torment. Frequently the more voluptuous the body, the more it damned itself.

And Auguste realized, as if he had known this from the first moment Gambetta had proposed an expression of hell, that he must sculpt the world of the damned. Dante's "Leave all hope, ye that enter" burned itself into his brain as he began to sketch tentative plans for the door. He decided that all people, if they were honest with themselves, had known this feeling of despair, some many times. He must deal uncompromisingly with this view. He must do it with the most glorious yet most treacherous instrument of life: the naked human body.

Then Auguste, his imagination deeply stirred, plunged ahead with his architectural plans for the door. At first they were imitations of Ghiberti's doors, with a series of eight panels, four on each side, but soon he was aware that was a mistake. Gradually the separate storytelling panels became one vast lake of fire. The ten-foot-high door grew to twenty, and he had to double the width from four feet to eight. It was a gigantic conception, he knew, and there were moments when it terrified him, but he could not halt. The door became two doors, then gates as he had thought originally. The title "The Gates of Hell" became inevitable also, and his mind quickened at the vastness that suggested, and now architectural sketches seemed to draw themselves as his hands raced over the drawing paper. He didn't bother to correct now. He wanted to get all his ideas down. It was enough that he was drawing with a passion that had its own kind of ecstasy.

Many weeks later he submitted his plans to Turquet. Then he was apprehensive. The Ministry would quarrel with the scope—he could never do "The Gates" for ten thousand francs, or complete them quickly as had been recommended. His conception was too vast, once again he was taxing himself beyond reason, it would take many years to finish.

Yet when he did not hear from Turquet the next few days, he found himself cursing the Ministry. They had to give him this commission. Waiting, he sketched and modeled many torsos, limbs, and heads. The thought of not doing "The Gates" made him feel as damned as any of the people he was planning. He was fascinated by Ugolino and Paolo and Francesca.

IV

His studies of the tragic lovers renewed his desire to see Madeleine again. But he was ashamed to call on her. He had said he would get in touch with her in several weeks, and months had passed. He was certain she had forgotten him. Thus Auguste was astonished when Madeleine appeared one sunny afternoon at the door of his studio on the rue Fourneaux, in the Vaugirard Quarter. She cut short his hasty apology. She knew that he had been delayed because of the door and that until it was settled he could not think of anything else. Her understanding was so complete he couldn't believe it. He decided Madeleine must have another reason, an ulterior motive. Yet this did not lessen his pleasure at seeing her.

She said, "What must I do before you ask me in?"

He muttered, "I was going to invite you when I got my new studio." But he did not ask her in.

"You won't have a new studio until the commission is settled."

"How did you know about the commission?"

"You are well known now, Auguste. There is much curiosity about the kind of door you are going to do."

"I haven't even been given the commission. Not yet."

"You will be if Gambetta is for it. Anything Gambetta is involved in is of importance. People think he wants to be a Napoleon, or a Robespierre, especially since he is interested in a gate of hell. It sounds fascinating."

"It's going to be impossibly hard," Auguste said gloomily. "I never should have agreed to it."

"Then withdraw," she said, "before it is too late."

He stared at her angrily: was she teasing him? Or deliberately tormenting him? He had had enough of torture over the door as it was. He said, "When I get my new studio, I will do a head of you."

"While working on the gate?" Madeleine looked incredulous.

"I will. I will." But he didn't invite her in, although he did make an appointment to have lunch with her in a small café on the rue de Rivoli.

V

Boucher, hearing from an apprehensive Proust how alarmingly "The Gates of Hell" were expanding in scope, also visited Auguste at the studio. He did not stand on ceremony. Feeling very much the old friend and almost as alarmed as Proust, he got to the point at once. He warned, "You are as bad as Michelangelo and his ambitions. You will never finish this tomb either. It will end up being your own."

"I will work hard."

"But you've already planned to sculpt a hundred figures."

"They will be small figures."

"Even so, it took you two years to do 'The Age of Bronze' and 'John.' "

"I was learning."

"You are insane. You will never finish in a hundred years."

"I've promised to do 'The Gates' in three."

"Impossible. The architectural work alone should take three."

"I know. Ghiberti took a lifetime to sculpt his doors, and then he didn't finish. But I'll manage. And Gambetta will support me."

"Gambetta?"

"Proust and Turquet will support me, too."

"*Mon ami*, the only thing these people have in common is that they are French and the only thing the French have in common is that they must disagree. Otherwise they wouldn't be French. Now Gambetta is the lion of the political jungle, and at least he isn't always going back to the eighteenth century or using the name of Napoleon as if it were God. But three years from now Gambetta could be out of power and you could be without any friends in the government."

"Whoever is in power will support me. I will make the door a shrine."

Boucher looked unconvinced, but changed the subject, asking, "How much are you getting? Enough, at least, to pay for the cost of materials?"

"I don't know, but I have asked for ten thousand francs."

"Then they will give you five. They always give the artist half of what he asks, and the artist, so grateful for getting anything, asks half of what he should get. Whatever they give you, it won't be enough."

Auguste's jaw set stubbornly. Boucher was right, ten thousand francs was not enough, and it was too much to expect him to finish the commission in three years. But he would do what he could, and they would have to wait for the rest.

"Rodin, you'll regret this commission."

"I'll regret it more if I don't do it."

VI

Boucher was wrong about the money, Auguste learned. On July 17, 1880, three days after all of Paris celebrated Bastille Day as a national holiday for the first time, Turquet informed Auguste that his plans were acceptable and that he would receive eight thousand francs. Turquet kept saying that Auguste must treat the commission as a matter of business but that it was also a great honor.

Auguste was not at ease. Yet why should he be embarrassed at the thought of asking for more money? he thought angrily. He was, however. He ended by saying, "It would be impossible for God Himself to put a price on 'The Gates,' but I'll do the best I can."

"We are sure you will. We will give you twenty-seven hundred francs when you sign the agreement, the rest as the work progresses."

"Who will judge this progress?"

"An inspector from the Beaux Arts."

Auguste felt a chill of terror. He was ravaged at the thought of being in the hands of his ancient enemies.

"Monsieur Rodin, you will finish in three years?"

"If I can. I'll do my best." Auguste lost his fear. He was annoyed that Turquet should be distressed at his unwillingness to set an exact time limit when not a shovel of mortar had been mixed for the museum itself.

"Three years? No more? Promise!"

"I promise I'll do my best." *Mon dieu*, what else could they want!

A few weeks later "The Gates of Hell" became official with the following agreement: *Monsieur Rodin, artist sculptor, in consideration of the sum of eight thousand francs, is commissioned to execute the model of a decorative door destined for the Museum of Decorative Arts: bas-reliefs to represent the* Divine Comedy *of Dante.*

It took two months before Auguste received his first payment, but he was given a free studio immediately on the rue de l'Université, spacious, light, well located, what he had always wanted in a studio. Then with the money he was saving on his old studio he rented a second studio, on the boulevard de Vaugirard, also large and light, and the width of the Left Bank away from his first studio, so far apart that no one would be tempted to visit both. And with the money he expected for "The Gates," he took a third studio, just off the rue Dante, distant from his other two studios, but in the neighborhood he loved the most, where he had grown up, and close to the Île St. Louis.

He moved out of his old studio without regret. He slammed the door so hard it broke. He was delighted about the three studios. One was for "The Gates of Hell," one was for himself, and one he didn't tell anyone about.

CHAPTER 26

Now Auguste worked in three studios at the same time. He spent most of the time at the *grand* studio, on the rue de l'Université, where he labored on "The Gates of Hell." But in the second studio, on the boulevard de Vaugirard, he did portrait busts of Carrier-Belleuse, Antonin Proust, and his old friend Dalou, who in turn, was doing a head of him. Rose wondered about his sudden doing of heads, but he refused to explain. In the third studio, near the île St. Louis, he was doing a classic head of Madeleine.

When they became lovers it seemed natural and inevitable, yet a little disappointing. He had expected a spontaneous intensity, but though her body was as beautiful as he had thought, he felt that some of her passion was calculated. Yet when he went home to Rose after Madeleine, Rose seemed aging and unattractive. He put off Rose on the excuse that he was tired, and suddenly Rose got into the habit of dropping into the two studios she knew about until he forbade it, saying this interfered with his work. She was deeply hurt, but he refused to change his mind.

Rose pointed out that she was continuing to shop with economy—not a sou, not a franc, was being wasted. Even today, surveying the mound of fresh eggs in the neighborhood dairy, she carefully selected just one, the largest, from the mound, for *petit* Auguste, although the boy was no longer *petit* and most of the time refused to eat it. Only on Sundays did she buy eggs for Auguste, Papa, and herself. And though they had meat three days a week now, she was prepared to save there also.

Auguste replied, "That's exactly the reason why you can't come to the studio. You have enough to do at home, Rosette." The more involved he became with Madeleine, the more considerate of Rose he became. He assumed he was Rose's protector, that she should accept his double standard as natural and inevitable, although he had no intention of telling her about Madeleine, since that would only upset her.

II

The more Auguste used the state studio, on the rue de l'Université, the more he felt it was located ideally and the better he liked it. The *grand* studio was around the corner from his beloved Seine, close to the spacious grounds of the Champ de Mars, easy to reach from any part of Paris, yet most important, affording him solitude and quiet. The neighborhood was one of the least crowded in the city. Attached to the rear of the studio were an enormous yard, a fine garden, and two stately rows of chestnut trees. Everything about these quarters struck him as animate, sentient: the bright skies, the livingness of the soil, the rocks that circled the garden. He felt as if he were working in the country, where he could be at his best, in the middle of his adored nature. Whenever he was overwhelmed with the difficulties of "The Gates," he strolled close to nature to refresh himself.

Most of the time, however, Auguste worked. The *grand* studio filled with clay, terra cotta, and plaster working models of "The Gates." It became a great light chamber with hundreds of fragments. There were "The Gates" in miniature, in one-third final size, and life size; there were many small pieces—legs, arms, torsos, heads; there were tiny rough figures in many forms; there were endless invention, improvisation, and agitation. He was never satisfied as he designed and redesigned the architectural façade while he modeled many tentative figures, most of them based on the Inferno.

He spent immeasurable time on the individual figures. Peppino, Santoni, and Lisa, an Italian friend of Peppino's, with an unforgettable body, posed for him now. Auguste was particularly taken with Lisa. Her voluptuous figure was mature as well as warm and ribald.

He used her for a nude "Eve," and she posed with honesty and simplicity.

He was less happy with Peppino. He wanted Peppino to be the model for a nude "Adam" which was to go on top of "The Gates" as a partner to "Eve." But Peppino, in demand elsewhere since he had become known as the model for "St. John," was often late or absent. Auguste discovered that the Italian had been more faithful when he had owed him money. Yet when Auguste hired a new, French model to pose for "Adam," Peppino was hurt.

Peppino felt the *maestro* was being very unfair.

The Italian became prompt, but Auguste continued to use the new model, Jubert, a professional strong man, for Adam. Jubert lacked Peppino's animation and grace, but his huge, oversized muscles had a marvelous brute strength, just what Auguste desired for Adam.

Only when Auguste had Peppino model with Lisa for Paolo and Francesca—he was using Santoni for incidental, secondary figures—did Peppino feel human again. The Italian became reliable as long as Jubert was present and he was posing with the voluptuous Lisa.

III

Months passed, and gradually a working model of "The Gates" assumed a shape and structure Auguste could build on. He was surprised to learn they were becoming a conversation piece. And when he heard the false gossip that was spreading, that he would never finish, that he had not even begun, that he was confused, distraught, he decided to show what he had done.

Saturdays became a regular day to see "The Gates." This developed into a ritual, one of the most popular occupations among the connoisseurs. Boucher saw the number of figures increasing, over a hundred now—Boucher had counted them—and said, "Rodin can no more resist a body than give up clay, he will never finish, but 'The Gates' are incredible, they will inspire such terror."

Gambetta thought the portrait that was evolving was remarkable, it would show much corruption, and he congratulated Auguste. Proust was more hopeful than before, but still worried about how long it would take. Mallarmé thought "The Gates" were "airy." Renoir was amused by the care with which Rodin was working, as if that would matter? Even Degas stopped in one Saturday, but did not say a word. For a moment Auguste felt Degas thought "The Gates" ridiculous, then was consoled by the realization that Degas, at least, had not been insulting.

What interested Auguste the most was Lecoq's reaction. Lecoq would be utterly realistic. He invited Lecoq—the only person he had invited himself except for Gambetta—and his old teacher limped in one clear, sunny Saturday afternoon. Lecoq had been ill, and this showed in a loss of weight, but his eyes still sparkled with their usual vigor. And when he saw the working model of "The Gates," he approached it rapidly.

"How do I feel?" he said, repeating Auguste's question. "I've returned to teaching. My own school. On the rue du quai des Grands Augustins."

"I thought you were tired of teaching."

"I was more tired of being bored. Oh yes, I know, I'm too old. All my friends say so. I'm seventy-eight, the same age as Hugo."

"You don't look it."

"Of course I do. You never could lie well, Rodin." He turned to "The Gates," exclaimed, "So these are 'The Gates'? The talk of Paris?"

Lecoq is critical, thought Auguste. His heart beat quickly as he prepared for the blow. He said, "Yes. What do you think?"

"*Mon dieu, que c'est difficile!*"

"They are to be in the open air. *Al fresco.*"

"I know." Lecoq examined the work carefully. "The composition is good."

"I'm slow, too slow."

"Naturally. These are hardly figures out of *l'opéra-comique.*"

Auguste, feeling understanding from the man whose opinion he respected above any other, cried out, "Does this kind of work always have to be so hard?"

"The greater the conception, the greater the effort. And what else do you expect when you leave none of us with any *amour-propre?*"

"It will be a *debâcle,*" Auguste said in a sudden surge of pessimism.

"Perhaps," said Lecoq more cheerfully. "But think of all the individual figures you will get from the doors."

"I don't understand."

"Rodin, your doors are a laboratory of sculpture. Look at the ideas they will give you. This 'Adam,' this 'Eve,' and certainly 'Paolo and Francesca' will make fine individual pieces. Even if you never finish the doors, you will have a magnificent gallery of portraits to show for your effort."

"*Merci, maître,*" Auguste said meekly.

"I prefer you when you are not so humble."

"Oh, I'm not, I'm not!"

"Boucher says that with most people you are an *enfant terrible.*"

"Boucher exaggerates. He is nervous. He thinks I may spoil the opportunities he makes for me. But I have such a high regard for you—"

Lecoq cut him short. "If you ever decide to do Eve less than life size, I would be happy if I could buy one."

"From me?" Auguste was surprised.

"An original Rodin." Lecoq sighed. "That would call for a drink of champagne."

"I couldn't charge you."

"You can charge everybody. If you don't, you are an idiot. But I would like to buy an Eve before it gets beyond my means."

"You will," Auguste said with a new certitude. "I'll make a half-life-size Eve as soon as I can."

IV

But when several wealthy people wanted to discuss commissions with Auguste, he put them off. He still had something left from the twenty-seven hundred francs, and he was heartened by Lecoq's enthusiasm. Even with such an unreliable patron as the State, he was sure another advance on "The Gates" would be forthcoming soon. Carrier-Belleuse and Antonin Proust insisted on paying for their busts, although he didn't know what to charge, since he had done these heads as an act of friendship. Eventually he accepted five hundred francs from Carrier-Belleuse and Antonin Proust for the cost of materials, for the heads were being cast in bronze.

Then Boucher proudly brought him a well-to-do Englishman, Scott Hallam, who wanted to buy a "Bellona" in bronze. Auguste started to say no, but Boucher looked hurt and Rose would be also, he thought, and so he agreed. Reluctantly he went to work to prepare the patina on the copy.

Finished, he was dissatisfied with the accents. He did it over, found himself doing it a third time. Boucher, who felt responsible, thought the third alteration unnecessary. Boucher told Auguste, "You're the hardest man to please." And when, because of the extra work involved, Auguste requested more francs for the "Bellona" than had been discussed originally, the prospective buyer cried, "Isn't your word of any value?" and Auguste retorted, "It's not my word that's valuable, it's my bust."

The twelve hundred francs Auguste received for the "Bellona" was applied at once to the increasing cost of "The Gates of Hell." In addition Boucher wanted a copy of "The Man with the Broken Nose." Boucher was secretive about why, and this struck Auguste as a nuisance, but he gave his friend a copy for the cost of casting it in bronze.

Auguste felt better exchanging busts with Dalou.

It was Madeleine's head that was giving him the greatest trouble. He found it impossible to finish the bust, as if when he finished it they were finished. And he was not happy about the head. Madeleine had a radiant smile, but when he tried to capture that in clay only a smirk came forth. Then Madeleine herself was becoming difficult.

Madeleine, full of earnestness, was asking, "When are you going to exhibit it, Auguste? Will it appear in the Salon?"

He said curtly, "It is too late for the Salon."

"Sarah Bernhardt has entered a head."

"I'm not."

"You've been working on it almost a year."

"Almost."

"Bernhardt is leaving the Comédie Française. It's official now, and a head by you in the Salon could suggest me for the classic leads."

"I thought you preferred Sardou."

"The producers do. But at the Comédie Française I could do Racine, Corneille, Hugo."

"Why don't you speak to Hugo yourself?"

Madeleine looked at him sadly. "You know what would happen. And Hugo is so old."

"I'm nearly twice your age."

"But not wrinkled. Not an old goat."

"Hugo's wrinkles would be wonderful in bronze." He gazed ruefully at her bust, and suddenly scraped off the bony formation around her eyes.

"That's another thing," she said impatiently. "You spend hours putting a little piece of clay on my face, then spend the rest of the day taking it off."

"Your expression keeps changing."

"Auguste, you are contrary."

"I'll put you in marble. It will be my first marble head."

"Like the heads you did for Carrier-Belleuse. I heard that you did much of your best work for him."

"And my worst," he muttered.

It was weeks later when he thought the head might be ready to cast in marble. Then after it was done, the head coming out of a column in the Roman style which she had requested, he did not like it, although she did. Madeleine said, "It looks so classical," and he said, "That's the trouble." He went to work with his chisel to touch up the expression about her eyes. The marble had altered her expression, he thought, had made it too hard, unnatural, when she had a beautifully sensuous one.

He was still working like a *praticien* the following week. Madeleine thought resentfully he was as far from being finished as ever, she would be an old lady by the time this was done. Her head, when it came back in marble, had been so smooth, and now he was making it rough, even her cheekbones. She said to herself, Really, he is getting impossible.

V

Suddenly, sensing her irritation, Auguste had a great need for the company of a fellow artist. He visited Monet at the latter's home and studio, at Vétheuil, some miles north and west of Paris on the Seine, and wondered if it was a mistake. The painter, who had aged considerably, was pleased and touched to see Auguste, but Auguste's presence only seemed to add to his unhappiness.

Monet said, "I'm devoured by a hell, in spite of the good news about my painting. I'm beginning to sell now, the Salon accepts me, and I am eaten up with loneliness and loss. You will point out that my life is in my painting, all my friends do, and I still have moments, but without Camille, I am desolate. I tell myself I am a father and that should help, but it doesn't. I wanted a home and family and love, and she gave them to me. With such naturalness, no complaints, no matter how poor we were, and we were always poor, the day she died I had to pawn whatever we owned to get a doctor. And now she sleeps soundly, deeply, and my salvation is supposed to be painting. But I am lost even there."

Auguste did not know what to answer. Monet's gloom was overwhelming.

Yet when it came time to say *au revoir*, Monet begged Auguste to visit him again. "I know this must have been difficult for you, Rodin. I am not good company, but your coming has helped. I feel better after I express myself. A little less impotent, perhaps. Come back? Will you, please?"

"Yes."

Monet relaxed and said, "I hear you are becoming rather well known now, that women pursue you, people talk about you."

"A little." Auguste, who had resented Monet's indifference to his own struggles, was glad now that he had kept them to himself.

VI

Auguste returned to "The Gates" with a new intensity—Monet's situation suggested still another variation of hell. But he sank into quicksand. A year had passed since he had started "The Gates," and now it seemed to him that the more he worked on them the further away he was from finishing. Each time he completed one detail, another developed. The more figures he put in, the more had to go in.

Growing weary of "The Gates," he was delighted when he was invited to London by his old friend Legros, who was living there. He accepted at once as Legros told him that the "Bellona" he had sold to Scott Hallam and "The Man with the Broken Nose" that he had given to Boucher were to be exhibited at the Grosvenor Gallery, in London, and that he was to be the guest of honor at the private view.

London struck Auguste as a gray city, but he liked the solidity of the buildings, the stress on stone, the many examples of Gothic architecture. He went at once to the British Museum, intensely interested in the Elgin marbles and the other Greek sculpture.

He was also fascinated by Legros' etching. Legros, who had achieved a fine reputation as an etcher, spent several days showing Auguste dry-point engraving. Auguste liked the process very much—at its best it was firm, stark, and accurate. It struck him as a kind of granitic drawing, yet deft, fine-grained, and subtle. He rapidly grew skillful in it.

At the private view it was Auguste's two pieces that attracted the most attention, though there were twenty other pieces on exhibition. He heard that the "Bellona" had been sold for twenty-four hundred francs—double what he had received for it—and he was startled at the thought that he had become an investment. He knew he should resent the difference in price, but after Monet's feeling of persecution he wanted nothing of self-pity. "The Man with the Broken Nose" that Boucher had submitted was not for sale, and Auguste learned that his friend had shown it to make his work known in England.

The private view concluded with a tea, which was the British custom, and Auguste lost some of his shyness when he was introduced to several writers who wanted to meet him. He would have preferred wine, and Legros, who had invited the writers, apologized for the tea, but the warmth of the writers was reassuring.

Vital, intense William Ernest Henley was red-bearded, like himself, with a large head and strong features; Robert Louis Stevenson was frail and very pale; Robert Browning was slight, elderly, and attentive. They said *they* liked his work. Auguste was not certain he agreed with their reasons.

Browning spoke about the busts' resemblance to classical antiquity, Stevenson was enchanted with their poetic qualities, but it was Henley's enthusiasm that appealed to him the most.

Henley was excited by the realism and vitality of the two busts.

In a way, thought Auguste, this was characteristic of the writer himself.

Henley, who had had one foot amputated, who had spent two years in the hospital with tuberculosis of the bone, laughed often, swore with gusto, and insisted on showing Auguste through St. James's Park, which was blooming in the first clear day London had had in weeks. Legros, his duty done, left them at the door of the gallery, while Stevenson and Browning trailed after Henley and their French guest.

Henley declared, "Rodin, you're rather a pirate. I like that."

"Quite so," said Browning.

Stevenson nodded.

But it was Henley and Auguste who smiled at each other like members of a secret cult. Browning looked cross, as if annoyed at being left out; Stevenson's mind was elsewhere, involved in nature. Then Henley, limping vigorously, determined never to appear handicapped, insisted they walk on and on. Stevenson and Browning excused themselves, while Henley, leading Auguste to Parliament Square, showed him the Houses of Parliament and Westminister Abbey.

"The House of Commons is only about thirty years old," Henley explained. "But the Abbey is even older than Notre Dame."

Auguste nodded appreciatively, looking impressed.

"In my opinion, these buildings are among the peaks of English art."

Auguste agreed. And the discovery that they shared an admiration for Gothic architecture confirmed their earlier judgment of each other's good taste. Now they became good friends. By the time Auguste left for home, they had sworn to write each other and to see each other again as soon as it was possible.

VII

Turquet came to view "The Gates of Hell," and his politeness was ominous. Speaking with many shrugs of his shoulders, the Under Secretary said, "I'm desolated about how far you've gone, Monsieur Rodin, but the Adam and Eve on top of the doors is not what was agreed upon. It is not Dante."

Auguste tried to argue with him, and Turquet assured him suavely, "We are in complete agreement with the spirit of your work," and reminded him firmly that their agreement, which was in writing, promised to follow the *Divine Comedy*. "*Mon cher maître*," Turquet added, "we have faith in what you are attempting, greatly admire it, but Adam and Eve do not fit."

"Why?"

"Well, we prefer a less religious note. It's rather too Biblical—" Turquet halted, realizing it would be safer not to be too explicit.

"You do not recognize ourselves?"

"Ourselves?"

"We are the descendants of Adam and Eve."

"Perhaps. But I would prefer to leave that to the theologians to decide. Now, if you could put Dante on top of 'The Gates—' "

Auguste said sharply, "Everything would be solved."

Turquet started to talk about Delacroix and Ingres. "Both great artists, a credit to French art. They disagreed violently, yet in a sense one was for rebirth, the other for resurrection. Thus in the end they were for essentially the same thing."

Turquet smiled like a conspirator, and Auguste realized he might as well argue with a stone. The Under Secretary was inexorable, making it more painful because he was so polite.

" 'The Gates' must not lose the spirit of Dante, his power, his poetry. We would be deeply disappointed at the Ministry if you had to forfeit the commission and—"

"Return the money," said Auguste.

"That's what we want to avoid." Regret shone in Turquet's eyes.

"When will I get my next payment?"

"Are you ready for an inspector from the Beaux Arts?"

"Why not?"

"It might be unwise." Turquet spoke in his soft, mild voice. He sounded especially kind. "You have a remarkable talent, maître, it would be unfortunate to damage it with haste. Why don't you do the 'Adam and Eve' as separate pieces, for practice?"

The "Adam and Eve" came off "The Gates." Once they were off, Auguste realized they had been a mistake, but he still resented Turquet's approach.

He put aside "The Gates" for a few days and focused on a life-size statue of Eve, from which he would cast a miniature for Lecoq. He had Lisa walk about the studio constantly while he studied her naked body. When every detail was fixed in his mind—her wide hips, her full legs, her mobile breasts—when he was sure she was natural, he began to model. He had the proportions of her ample body quickly, but he was undecided about her pose. When he asked her to stand motionless, there was a sudden, unexpected unrest on her face. Auguste was surprised; Lisa had never been self-conscious before. He felt her stomach to be certain he had the precise curve—his hands were the best magnifying glass of all—and she instinctively covered her face and breasts with a gesture of shame.

He had no time to be annoyed. She had given him the answer he wanted. The movement was wonderful. He must capture the shame. "Perfect for Eve," he whispered to himself, "an Eve just expelled from the Garden of Eden." He insisted she hold the pose.

"It's awfully cold, *maestro*," she whimpered.

"Yes, yes." Her legs talked. Her hips were so full. The lifted curve of her knee, suggesting embarrassment, was just right. "We'll have to work late." He ran his fingers over her stomach. It was the one part of her body that didn't seem quite in proportion. He felt her stomach again and she winced. "Am I hurting you?" he asked.

Lisa, fidgeting, groaning, said, "I'm tired."

"I'll make it this time." He placed her next to the clay figure. Ordinarily he would have made many miniature models, but there wasn't time for that now. His hands went from her skin to the clay, seeking to transform her slightly bulging stomach to the statue. "Are you hungry, Lisa?"

"No, *grazie*."

"Your stomach seems large. You must be eating much pasta and sauces these days."

"It's late."

Suddenly he was sure something was missing. According to his sense of touch, the one sense he trusted almost wholly, that was almost infallible, her stomach was swollen. But it should not be, he told himself. Lisa had a perfect figure. That was why he had hired her. He ordered her to stand motionless, but automatically she assumed the pose of shame. He went over her body with both hands and she shivered. He was surprised; she should not be embarrassed; he had done this hundreds of times. The swelling was even more prominent than before. It reminded him of how Rose had looked when— But it could not be true. All at once Auguste pressed her stomach and she screamed.

"Oh!" he said, awareness dawning.

"I couldn't help it, *maestro!*" she cried. "I couldn't!"

He said, disgusted, "You're pregnant."

"*Basta*, I will marry him. I promise, I will."

"That's not the point, idiot. You've spoiled the 'Eve.' "

"Spoiled it, *maestro*? Wasn't she a mother, too?"

He studied the statue. The figure was honest and interesting and had an artful balance. He said, "When are you having the baby?"

"In a few months."

"You hid it that long?"

"You didn't look at me that way. You had your own picture of Eve."

"Who is the father?"

Lisa did not answer.

"Peppino." Suddenly he remembered how amorously they had modeled for Paolo and Francesca. His "St. John"? "It is Peppino, isn't it?"

Lisa still did not reply, but blushed furiously.

Auguste shook his head sorrowfully. "You ruined my best model."

"We can still work for you, *maestro*."

"With a child between you? I'll never be able to depend on you."

CHAPTER 27

Peppino and Lisa vanished the next day. Auguste delivered a half-life-size "Eve" to Lecoq, and the latter's appreciation made up for his disappointment with his models.

He refused to take any money. When Lecoq tried to thank him, he cut Lecoq short as the teacher always had done. He helped Lecoq place "Eve" where she would be seen in the best light, then left quickly. But the glow in Lecoq's eyes warmed him and made him glad he had taken painstaking care with "Eve."

He had no time to be reflective. He was about to interview new models for "The Gates"—Santoni had disappeared after the others had—when Mallarmé came to his studio to talk to him.

Mallarmé, his thin, long, delicate features looking more poetic than ever, said, "I hope you won't be offended, Rodin, but it concerns Hugo."

Auguste shrugged. "Why should I be offended?"

"Someone wants you to do a head of Hugo."

"But not Hugo?" Auguste was prepared to be belligerent.

"No, *mon ami*, not Hugo. That is the difficulty. It must be done in secret. Hugo is adamant about sitting. He continues to complain that it is too wearing. Actually I think he doesn't want posterity to have a record of him as an old man. Would you consider it, Rodin?"

"Who wants it?"

"Juliette Drouet. You know who she is?"

"Everybody does. But that doesn't make it right."

"It makes it right for her. I told her that you can be a tyrant, but she insisted I approach you. She's been told that you are the one sculptor who could do an honest head under the circumstances."

"Who told her, Mallarmé? You?"

Mallarmé frowned and said gently, "You can blame me if you wish, but you did tell me that you wanted to do Hugo, whatever the difficulties."

"What about Juliette Drouet?"

Mallarmé's voice took on a passion Auguste had rarely heard. "She's a great lady, Rodin, and I do not exaggerate. She has been attached to Hugo for fifty years, no matter how badly he treated her, and he has, many times with other women, although he has never deserted her. Evidently after the initial adoration wore off, he came to feel like her protector. But she always worshiped him, protected him, fought for him, from the first day she met him, when she was one of the great beauties of Paris."

Auguste was interested, but sought to look indifferent. He stared at his unfinished "Gates." Today their ceiling rose higher, the many figures extended tense and devastated. Nothing should woo him away. "The Gates" stood open, a record already on them, waiting for his hands. Yet he wanted to run to do Hugo. Run, run, he thought, run slowly, run carefully. Hugo could pull him down. But now he saw the figures without faces: it was Hugo's face before him that he had to model.

"Yes," Mallarmé said intensely, "Hugo told me that she had an amazing beauty, slender, youthful, enchanting. That her first affair was with Pradier, a sculptor, whom no one remembers now, who gave her a child, then left her. Hugo said, 'She was exquisite as few are exquisite.' Juliette Drouet was his first mistress. But she was, really, a Marguerite Gauthier. She gave up a rich, lavish life to be a penitent. She became a poor young woman, surrendering her career, her world. She became what she called "the all-but-wife" of Hugo, but never the wife. The mistress became the slave, recording his work, attending to all his wants, going wherever he desired, always praising, always encouraging, always devoted. I think, *mon ami*, she deserves kindness and courtesy."

"Should I weep for her? Didn't she know what she was doing?

Oh, I don't mean to be moral, but women always use love as an excuse when nothing else works."

"And men don't?"

Auguste knew he should be angry, but he had to laugh. And he had outdone Hugo with Madeleine; perhaps the head would be a new outwitting.

Mallarmé said, "You will probably not get another chance to do Hugo. Despite his apparent vigor, Hugo had a stroke or a heart attack a few months ago, the doctors are not sure which, since he refuses to go to them, he says he doesn't need a doctor, but at the rate he is going I doubt he will outlive Juliette Drouet by much."

"Is she that ill? I heard she was sick but—"

"She has cancer. If she lives another year, it will be a long time. But Hugo visits her every day. She feels you could model him from the alcove overlooking her sickroom. *Mon cher Rodin*, shall I make an appointment for you with her?"

Auguste nodded, although some of his doubts remained.

"Don't be shocked when you meet her. She's ill and wasted, an old lady now—seventy-six, I believe—although she hides her age."

But Auguste was shocked when he entered the Hugo house, on the avenue d'Eylau, which had been changed to the avenue Victor Hugo in honor of the great man's eightieth birthday. Hugo was out of Paris for a few days; Auguste was let in by a trusted servant of Juliette Drouet's; all the furnishings were sumptuous and elegant; he expected her to look the great lady. Instead she lay on a small couch, her head propped up with pillows, an old woman who spoke laboriously. She wore a simple black velvet dress with white lace at the open neck. There was no trace of beauty in her wrinkled, wan features, except for her beautiful white hair. Then as he bowed and said *"Bonjour"* and the servant withdrew, he saw a picture of her on the mantel. He was drawn to it by an irresistible impulse.

"Pick it up, *maître*," she said, seeing his interest.

He held it tenderly.

"I was twenty-six then," she said softly. "I had just met Hugo."

He remembered Hugo's description: "Exquisite as few are exquisite." He thought Hugo had not exaggerated. The features were perfection, the eyes lovely, the skin ivory, the smile tender.

"We were so young, Monsieur Rodin."

"Such a beautiful face—"

She blurted out nervously, "They say I'm interested only in his greatness, but it is the truth I desire."

"He's an old man now. Any head of him must show that."

"But don't be cruel with him, Monsieur Rodin."

"He was cruel to me."

"He doesn't like being old."

"No one likes being old. I'm past forty."

"Past forty." She smiled wistfully. "You're a young man compared to him. And I no longer tell people my age. Do your best, will you, maître?"

"I will do my best."

She halted him at the door. "Remember, he must never know."

"Never?"

"He would not allow it."

"Then why do you want the head?"

"He is here every day. But the evenings grow lonely. I will feel as if he is here when the bust is done." She leaned back on the propped-up pillows, exhausted by this exertion yet determined not to display any weakness, not permitting herself to lie in bed, to admit the severity of her illness, although it was apparent she was very sick. "It is a risk, Monsieur Rodin, but Mallarmé said you wanted to do a head of Hugo."

"I do! I do! I do not like his manner, but his head has grandeur."

"If it is successful, you will be paid well."

For an instant he wanted to throw the entire scheme in her face. His features grew rigid, flushed. There was a moment of heavy silence.

As she saw his irritation, she hurried to explain, "I meant in many ways. The prestige, the honor, your own gratification. You must forgive me, maître, but when one gets ill one becomes mawkish. I will try to keep him occupied. Please! You will do it?" She reached for his hand imploringly. "Mallarmé says you will do a fine head." She was as white as marble, and he thought she would faint. "We must not delay. We do not have much time."

The next day, surprised at his own impetus, Auguste made the necessary plans with her. It was arranged for the sculptor to be admitted secretly at the rear of the mansion, and to go up the winding stairway from the kitchen—Hugo always went up the fashionable front staircase, which was a miniature of the Opéra's, so there was little chance of their meeting. Then Auguste set up his studio in the alcove which overlooked her room. Hugo never went to this alcove —it was her dressing room—and Auguste placed in it clay, armatures, stands for several heads, and sketching material. Heavy drapes were hung between the dressing room and the sickroom to veil Auguste, and they were drawn tight while he worked, except when he wanted to observe Hugo, and then he opened them as much or as little as it was safe.

Auguste resented all these difficulties, yet once he started he could not stop. Juliette Drouet was right. There was very little time. It was obvious she would not live much longer—a few months at the most.

He put everything else aside. He closed down his studios for the time being, and that created a new difficulty. He asked Madeleine to interrupt their sittings for a short period while he did a special commission that had to be done urgently, and she looked annoyed and asked, "How long will it take?"

"Several weeks."

"Is it *that* important a commission?"

"I suppose so."

"It will take you months," she said pessimistically. "Who is it?"

"It is a secret, *chérie.*"

"A secret, *chérie,*" she repeated, mimicking him sarcastically. "It must be an important personage for you to put everything aside, even 'The Gates.' "

His face grew red, like the color of his beard, but he did not answer.

"Who is it, Auguste?"

He said curtly, "I told you it was a secret. I cannot tell you."

She looked beyond him to her unfinished marble head. He had sculpted a gentle, mobile face, and not a *femme fatale,* as she had expected, but she felt humiliated. She said, "You will never finish me. I'm not important enough."

"It isn't that," he replied angrily, "but I have to do this commission now, for I won't get another chance."

He made a gesture as if to say he had no alternative, and then she knew. "It's Hugo," she declared. He was evasive, but he went white, and now she was positive. She said, "You don't have to try to deceive me."

"It is not a question of deception. I gave my word not to discuss it."

"Does Hugo know?"

Auguste was silent, but his hands shook with anger.

"So it is a secret from him also."

"You won't tell him, will you? You won't, Madeleine?"

She was furious. To have Hugo as a rival was especially exasperating. She resented this rival more than a woman. She said, "At least another woman would give you something, but Hugo, like most famous men, will take, not give."

"He will give me a fine head. Madeleine, I care for you very much."

"You do? You really do?"

"I'll finish your head. I promise."

"When?"

"Soon. When I get the time."

"After Hugo?"

He shrugged.

"You mean I should wait until you finish the great man?"

He nodded vigorously, without hesitation.

"No! That patient I am not." Madeleine picked up her bust and carried it to the door. It was heavy, but Auguste did not offer to help her or try to halt her, as she half expected and hoped. She felt like a stranger to him, embarrassed in a way she had never been before. She said, "I never thought I would have Hugo for a rival."

"You don't."

"Will you give up Hugo? For me?"

He threw his hands up in despair. "I can't. I gave my word to do him."

"*Bonjour.*" She turned toward the rue Dante.

"You won't tell anybody, will you?" He was frantic in his entreaty.

"That I lost you to Hugo?"

"Madeleine, that is not true. I do care for you, I do!"

"No doubt. When you need me." Madeleine held her bust close to her, like a beloved child, and said, "You certainly don't make life easier for yourself, the way you work. Doing Hugo without his knowing it." She sighed, "It will be a miracle if you succeed." She walked out decisively.

II

Suddenly with Madeleine's absence, Auguste had a need to tell Rose about Hugo. He knew he could trust Rose. She would be proud of him. Then the closing of his studios would make her suspicious, and he wanted to avoid that; her recriminations would be too distracting.

Rose was pleased that Auguste confided in her. *Petit* Auguste had told her that the two studios were being closed, and she had been afraid that the thing she had always dreaded—another woman in Auguste's life—was coming true. But now that he was reaching out to her, she felt like a new woman. She liked the idea of secrecy, as long as she was a part of it. And she was fascinated by the devotion of Juliette Drouet to Hugo.

Auguste told her, "They have been attached to each other for fifty years."

"And he never married her?"

"That would have spoiled it."

"How?" Rose flushed, but tried to look calm.

"He would have felt tied down. It would have made him resent her."

"Yet you say they have been together all these years. Why couldn't he have married her?"

"He was married."

"But he could now. His wife is dead."

"Nothing is as enduring as an emotional attachment, while one can have a legal attachment and not be attached at all. Paris is full of both."

Rose, sensing an irritation developing in Auguste, changed the subject. She kissed him and said, "You are becoming important, *chéri*. The head of Hugo will do you good. Now you won't have to worry about the Salon."

III

The next few weeks nothing but Hugo mattered. Juliette Drouet's huge second-floor room became lounge and drawing room, bedroom and sickroom, and artist's studio. She placed the couch as Auguste ordered, where he could see Hugo best. She refused to lie in bed, determined not to depress Hugo. Many pillows propped her into a sitting position on the couch, and she was always dressed, although she was failing daily.

Hugo visited her at least once every day no matter how busy he was elsewhere; the only exception was an occasional day he spent out of Paris. Auguste sensed that Hugo traveled out of Paris for a romantic attachment, and sometimes went from Juliette Drouet to a *maison d'amour*, but when Hugo was with her the poet was devoted. Most of the time Hugo wore a frock coat with a velvet collar and a blue silk scarf, although there were days he donned a simpler black alpaca coat—generally when they were alone. And often he went without a hat, proud of his still thick, close-cropped hair.

To make matters easier for Auguste, Juliette frequently had guests, for Hugo's hearing was faulty, which Hugo would not admit, and when they involved Hugo in loud conversation they hid the noise of Auguste's work.

But Auguste preferred the times Hugo was alone with Juliette. When others were present, Hugo was quite hopeless as far as Auguste was concerned, posing while talking or being moody and impatient, but when he was alone with her the poet dominated and he was tender and solicitous and natural.

Then Hugo read to her, putting on his spectacles, which vanity kept him from wearing at any other time, or he helped her with her medicine, admired her courage, measured her temperature, ate with her to encourage her poor appetite with his still hearty appetite, or did what she liked best: read her reviews of his work, which continued to arrive, mostly from abroad.

Auguste liked his model best, however, when Hugo told Juliette about the world outside. Then Hugo paced up and down, animated and vital, and always in motion: Hugo denouncing the *petite bourgeoisie*; Hugo criticizing Gambetta for not including him in

Gambetta's cabinet—although this cabinet had fallen, Hugo quoting Aristotle that it was not life itself that had value but life made noble by heroism. At such times Auguste sketched furiously. He was grateful for his habit of making models move, for Hugo was most expressive when in movement. Hugo's face was especially animated when he spoke. Auguste distrusted the quick first impressions, but he did preliminary drawings of the strong jaw, the severe lines of the cheeks, the powerful brow, the sensuous lips, the firm beard and mustache—still carefully kept—the passionate eyes, the close-cropped hair of which Hugo was so proud.

As these features became individualized, Auguste blocked out the head in the dry-point etching he had learned from Legros. He made many such etchings so they would be a permanent record in case he could not finish. Juliette was growing perceptibly weaker, although she still sought to hide that from Hugo, refusing to take to her bed. And Hugo himself insisted on her believing that she would get better. Hugo made this a kind of exaltation, as if any other belief would be a betrayal of all that Hugo had preached.

Auguste was resolved not to be oversympathetic to Hugo, but gradually Hugo's spirit pervaded the clay models, the spirit that never admitted defeat, that had to see nobility in humanity, even if Hugo rarely saw it in individuals. The head became a statement of Hugo's faith.

The drapes remained tightly closed except for the occasional moments Auguste opened them an inch or two to capture a glimpse of Hugo. It was the most difficult sculpture Auguste had ever attempted, for he rarely got a clear or thorough view of his subject. And to work in silence was very hard, but hardest of all was the inability to touch the subject. He yearned to touch Hugo's face, as he touched all his subjects to verify their bone and flesh structure. He hadn't been so aware of his nearsightedness for years.

He worked in a silent fury now. After a month he completed one rough, tentative head of Hugo in clay, finished most of a second one of Hugo bending over Juliette, but he knew he would not be able to finish a head in bronze while his subject was still available—Juliette was failing so rapidly—he would have to depend on his etchings and clay masks.

These days Hugo rocked her back and forth to comfort her and to ease her pain. She refused to cry when Hugo was present, and that was the worst of all.

Yet when Auguste suggested he stop, when Hugo was not present, she would not hear of it. She murmured, "*Maître*, there's no need to stop."

He could not argue with her; he could not tell her that she was dying.

She asked, "How are the heads progressing?"

"Splendid, splendid," he lied. "We will have a fine, strong head."

A little color came into her white face, and she struggled to a sitting position. She said, "Show it to me."

He carried in the clay model he liked best, although suddenly he was not sure he liked it at all, he had done it so hastily and imperfectly. Just yesterday he had altered the nose, and now he wanted to scrape off what he had done then. He had to fight with himself to keep from touching it. He expected her to shake her head at it or scowl, but she only smiled.

He was at the door when she asked, "You will finish it?"

"Of course. It will be at your side, as you wished."

"I would like to think so, *mon cher Rodin*, but the facts are against me."

He moved to her side, but he didn't know what to say.

"No medicine, please. I'm sick of medicine." She said suddenly, "You have given him an unusually thick head."

"That is what makes his head so exciting," Auguste said enthusiastically. "The size of it, especially in length and width."

"I like the expression. It is heroic, virile. That would please him."

"The head will be in bronze in a few weeks."

"A few weeks?" She smiled wearily, as if that were an eternity. "Keep working, *maître*, will you please, as long as you can?"

Auguste promised.

Several weeks later Auguste entered her room to find her sprawled unconscious outside Hugo's bedroom. He picked her up tenderly, carried her to her precious couch, and called her personal maid. Smelling salts brought her back to consciousness. She thanked Auguste for not telling anyone else and refused to call a doctor.

But the next day she had to take to her bed. It was at the far end of the huge room, and Auguste had difficulty seeing Hugo, who sat by her bedside.

Hugo was full of distrust now. He felt betrayed by Juliette's refusal to get better despite his exhortations. He was horrified at the idea that she was dying and leaving him.

Then Hugo grew concerned about himself. Gambetta, apparently in the prime of life, accidentally wounded himself in the hand while testing a gun for the Army and died of blood poisoning on December 31, 1882. This worried Hugo, who was almost twice Gambetta's age, while Auguste felt he had lost a good friend, a necessary friend. Gambetta's sudden, unexpected death reminded Auguste that there had been no further payments for "The Gates," although they had been promised, and Auguste had a feeling there would not be any more. And now Juliette, for all of her resolve to spare Hugo her pain and suffering, grew critical. At the mansion on the avenue Victor Hugo there was no more sculpture. The sickroom filled with nurses and doctors, and there was no place for anything else.

Auguste had to remove his unfinished work to the studio just off the rue Dante, where he could continue the heads in secret. He tried to finish Hugo from memory; he recalled Hugo sitting lovingly and consolingly beside Juliette, but he could not concentrate when he heard that Manet was dying also.

He and Manet had never been intimate, he reflected, but Manet was too young to die, just fifty-one, in his prime, his best work ahead of him. Death would be absurd, Manet had just received the Legion of Honor, which Manet had coveted. Manet should have time to enjoy it; it was the wrong time to die; it made no sense. When Manet died several months after Gambetta, Auguste felt it was a treacherous trick of fate. He was deeply shaken.

There had been state mourning at Gambetta's funeral, but Manet's was private and personal. Auguste could not endure funerals —he avoided them whenever he could—but it was incredible not to honor Manet.

He saw many old friends at the funeral, Degas, Fantin, Monet, Pissarro, Mallarmé, Boucher, and acquaintances like Antonin Proust, Cézanne, and Zola.

Degas, standing at the grave, cried out, "Why did I quarrel with him?" Degas looked ill. "He had so many paintings within him."

Auguste forced himself to nod. He remembered the days at the Café Guerbois and the Nouvelle Athènes as happy times now, though he had not felt happy then, and none of them frequented these cafés any more. He asked Fantin, "How are you, *mon ami?*" It was the first time they had met in a long while. Fantin, once so cheerful and convivial, looked aged, the recluse now, stout, without his old bubbling grace, his paintings smelling more and more of the Louvre, as Degas had warned years ago. "Working hard, Fantin?"

Fantin shrugged and said sadly, "No more impressionists—we have dissolved like the dust."

A week later Juliette died. Auguste had expected this, yet he was shocked. He had come to care for her in the time he had worked on Hugo. He didn't know what to do with his unfinished, unpaid heads. Hugo was taking care of her affairs, and he could not approach Hugo. He threw moist cloths over the two heads he preferred, to keep off the dust.

IV

Before Auguste could decide what to sculpt now, Papa became very ill. The doctor said it was only a matter of days and that all they could do was make the dying man comfortable.

The doctor asked Auguste, "How old is Jean Baptiste?"

Auguste thought back: Papa had been born in 1802, the same year as Lecoq and Hugo. He said, "Eighty-one."

"It's as I suspected," said the doctor. "He's dying of old age."

Auguste, who had spent very little time with Papa the past few years, was with him all the time now. He started to paint Papa in oils so that he would have a permanent picture of him and because it would not disturb Papa as sculpture would. Most of the time Papa lay in a coma, and Auguste painted his strong nose, small white beard, clear blue eyes—now sightless—and gave him the ruddy skin of the Papa he remembered as a child, although Papa's was as pale as wax now. Auguste concentrated on the expression, without sentimentality, seeking to be precise, natural. He was surprised at how well the painting was going; he longed to caress the canvas as he caressed his sculpture.

Then one afternoon, just as Auguste was thinking that Papa was sinking into death without a sound or a struggle, Papa recovered consciousness and in a heavy, urgent voice wanted to see everybody.

Rose brought in Aunt Thérèse and *petit* Auguste, who had become a plump, medium-sized young man of seventeen. They spoke to Papa so he would know they were there, and when he heard *petit* Auguste's voice his face lit up.

Papa said, "Listen to Mama."

Petit Auguste said, "Yes, Grand-père." His voice broke a little.

"Don't cry," said Papa. "It's not grown-up."

"I'm not crying," sobbed *petit* Auguste. "I'm glad you're getting better."

"*Mon dieu!*" cried Papa. "You don't lie any better than your father. Come close, so I can touch you."

Petit Auguste did, and Papa, finding his face with his hands, kissed him tenderly on both cheeks. Then he reached for Aunt Thérèse.

Aunt Thérèse said, holding his hand, "You will fool them, Jean, you will see."

Papa, smiling feebly, replied, "As long as I have my health, Thérèse."

"You will be yelling at all of us yet, like old times."

But suddenly Papa looked ghastly, coughed violently, and whispered, "Let me talk to Rose and Auguste a moment."

Aunt Thérèse took a weeping *petit* Auguste from the room.

Papa said, feeling Rose's arms around him trembling, "What's wrong? Is he neglecting you again?"

"No, no, Papa," said Rose, fighting to hide her tears. "Auguste is working very hard. He's painting a picture of you now."

"A picture?" grumbled Papa. "He's a sculptor."

"A fine one," Rose said proudly.

"Is he making a good living?" Papa said sharply, with a flash of his old vitality. "Has he gotten another payment on those monsters, 'The Gates'?"

"Not yet," said Rose. "But he will, *mon cher papa.*"

"He will not get another payment," Papa said positively. "He never will."

"Now, you mustn't talk any more," said Rose. "I'm sure the doctor would say you've talked enough."

"The doctor?" Papa looked surprised. "It's too late for the doctor.

Auguste, I told you that you would never make a living as a sculptor."

"Of course, Papa, of course," said Auguste, trying to humor him.

"If you had only listened to me when you were younger and had gone into the Prefecture, you would be retiring on a pension soon."

No one replied.

"Oh, you don't have to answer," said Papa. "Where's your hand, Auguste?"

Auguste placed his hand on Papa's, and Papa got a firm grip on his fingers and would not let go. He pleaded, "Be good to Rose. She's been good to me, like a daughter."

Auguste said, "I'll do my best."

"That isn't a promise." Papa grasped Auguste's fingers so hard that the bones cracked. He glared at where Auguste's voice was and declared, "Your best isn't good enough!"

"Please, Papa," cut in Rose, "you mustn't—"

"No, you can't stop me." Papa, pulling himself up with his clutch on Auguste's fingers, raised his body to a sitting position. "Auguste, promise me, you will marry Rose?"

"I can't promise that," Auguste said slowly, painfully. "But I promise to take care of her." How could he forget that Rose had given him his first studio, his first opportunity to work for himself, to be himself? Everybody else had taken away.

"That's not enough," Papa persisted. Papa held his sitting position with a tremendous effort of his will, breathing heavily, as if struggling against an enemy. "No excuses. Promise me, Auguste, you will marry her."

"I'll get the doctor," cried Rose, alarmed by his heavy breathing.

"No. Promise, Auguste, promise."

"Well . . ." mumbled Auguste.

"I won't stop until you give me your word. Promise!"

"I said I would take care of her."

"You'll forget unless you give your word."

"You don't understand."

"Promise, Auguste," Papa persisted. "Promise."

"Someday," said Auguste with a sigh. "Someday."

Papa's sightless eyes stared at Auguste suspiciously, and then Auguste said, "I promise—someday," and Papa smiled slowly and said,

"*Mon dieu*, you are stubborn, it's your blood." Papa sat proudly another moment and then slumped backward on the bed.

Auguste's powerful hand held on to Papa's while Rose cried and prayed and then went for a priest, but by the time the priest arrived Papa was dead.

V

After Papa was buried in a family plot which Auguste bought and made sure was large enough to include himself, Rose, and *petit* Auguste, he took Rose to see a house on the rue des Grand Augustins.

Since Papa's death Auguste had not said a word about marriage, but Rose was grateful for his including her and the boy in his burial plot. She felt a new consideration in him; but when she tried to thank him, to tell him that this would give her eternal peace, he was gruff and changed the subject.

Auguste was astonished at how much he missed Papa. He remembered how Papa had scolded him for drawing, painting, for untidiness, absent-mindedness. But now these memories made him smile, although he still felt pain. Papa had had his own mind, he reflected. He had inherited that at least.

Auguste came out of his reverie as they turned off the quai des Grand Augustins on to the rue des Grand Augustins, a short, narrow street between the Pont Neuf and the Pont St. Michel. He pointed to a large old house which had an *ancien régime* style and distinction and which was not far from the Seine. He turned to Rose, asked, "Do you like it?"

"A whole house?" Rose said in wonderment. "Are you thinking of renting it?"

"I've bought it." The sun glinted on the black mourning band he wore for Papa. "It's a fine house, isn't it?"

Rose knew better than to argue with him. The house was almost a mansion in size and of a style she liked, but it would be difficult to heat and clean. She nodded slowly.

He said excitedly, "There's a garden, with flowers, trees, sky. You'll think you're back in your beloved Lorraine."

"Can we afford it, *chéri*? You haven't gotten any more payments for 'The Gates'? Or anything for the Hugo heads?"

"They'll pay me for 'The Gates.' An inspector is coming to judge them as soon as I'm ready. And I can always get commissions now. I've become a vogue. I've had a number of requests in the past few months, but I've had so much on my mind, with all these deaths—" He gulped, not wanting to show the sadness that sometimes threatened to overwhelm him. "But I hope to start work soon, as soon as I get you and *petit* Auguste settled."

"*Petit* Auguste?" Her face lit up.

"*Yes.* Do you like our new house?"

"If you like it, *chéri.*"

He looked disappointed. He said, "I got it for you."

"Without asking me?"

"It was to be a surprise."

"It is." She asked warily, "We are going to live in all of it?"

"Whatever we need," he said proudly. "We won't live like Louis the Fourteenth, but things should get better now, little by little."

"What about the boy? He's stopped going to school, he's always on the streets, and now, without Papa, whom he listened to at least once in a while, I don't know what we will do with him."

Auguste's face took on a rare look of triumph. He announced, "I'm taking the boy into the studio." This was the biggest surprise of all.

"To do more chores?" she asked skeptically.

"No," he said positively. "I will not drive him to be an artist, but he can work as a model—he's already shown some ability there—he can keep the accounts, buy materials—"

"Manage your studio?" she asked eagerly.

"Eventually. If he is competent."

"Oh, Auguste!" Rose threw her arms around him, and for the first time in a long while, although they were standing on the street, he did not withdraw. "I'll save, save, save." Then she paused, not certain she should be happy, with Papa dead so recently.

Auguste, sensing what she was feeling as tears came to her eyes, pointed out, "It's what Papa would have wanted. He was very fond of the boy."

"He loved him." When Auguste did not correct or criticize her, she regained her enthusiasm and said, staring at the large, old house on the rue des Grand Augustins, "This is what I've always wanted, a real home, just as you wanted a real studio. *Chéri*, you must not give up sculpture. I know you've been upset by all the deaths, Gambetta, Manet, Papa."

"And Mademoiselle Drouet. I liked her, too. Very much."

"I did, too," Rose said earnestly. "She was so faithful. But you have to stop mourning, Auguste." She went on, with a naïveté that made him smile, "Everybody dies, but art lives on. Good art does. Like yours."

"Perhaps."

"Of course it does. You're going to become the most successful sculptor in Paris."

Auguste didn't answer. He was thinking that Rose meant well but that it was useless to discuss his work with her. The house was her proper sphere of influence. He led her into the parlor of their new home and showed her where to hang his portrait of Papa.

PART
FIVE
THE
PASSION

CHAPTER 28

The morning Auguste waited for the inspector from the Beaux Arts was an anxious one. A year had passed since Papa's death, and he had worked in a frenzy to complete "The Gates of Hell," but they were as far from completion as ever. Yet some things had been accomplished. He had decided on their final form and he had done many individual figures.

He stood at the door of the large studio, on the rue de l'Université, where he had the best view of "The Gates," and as they towered above him with the finished figures of Ugolino, Paolo and Francesca, the Prodigal Son, and many struggling, contorted lovers, he knew, whatever the inspector might say, it had been a fertile year. He had achieved a new excitement in these naked bodies. The nudes that satisfied him now were creatures of the underworld, possessed by a demonic anguish and ferocity, flesh devouring flesh.

Then he was sad. His apprehensions grew. He was certain now that the inspector would be harsh. The Beaux Arts was his ancient enemy, and in spite of the passing of time had remained a citadel of classicism that clothed nudity in an air of unreal refinement, but "The Gates" were an orgy of sensuality. He glanced at the tympanum at the top of "The Gates." The figure there, which he had modeled after Dante and called "the poet," was wrong. There was no tension in the sitting figure with his elbow on his knee and his hand at his chin. The man was thoughtful, yet something was missing. But it was too late to alter it for the inspector.

It was the fault of being too busy, Auguste reflected. In the last year he had moved into the new house and Rose had furnished it simply and austerely, with his advice and approval; *petit* Auguste had joined him full time in the main studio, and had been given important duties, such as buying clay, plaster, other materials, supervised by Auguste. His "St. John" was now in the permanent collection of the museum of the Luxembourg, and "The Age of Bronze" had been placed in the gardens, though without consulting him, in a remote section where he had played as a child. He had done heads of Henley and Legros and several private commissions to support himself, turning down others as soon as he had made enough money to pay for the growing expense of "The Gates."

Most unwillingly and yet most necessarily Auguste had taken in student assistants such as Robert Browning, Jr., the son of Robert and Elizabeth Browning, who by inheritance had to be an artist, but writing having been pre-empted by his parents, had chosen sculpture; Baden-Powell, the son of the famous English scientist, a brisk, no-nonsense student; Jules Desbois, in his early thirties, who had become the first assistant and had achieved recognition, his work resembling the *maître's*; and a number of other students whose main activity was to perform the many chores.

The studio on the rue de l'Université had grown crowded also with models as Auguste had sought the exact bodies for "The Gates." Most of the women were voluptuous, while the men were chosen for the energy yet pathos their bodies suggested. Auguste had not employed any new Lisas, Peppinos, or Santonis, but French models, not because he thought the French more reliable or attractive, but because they were thriftier and thus less likely to leave a well-paying job. And it became the custom at the start of each day for the *maître* to line up the naked female models in a single line and have them walk by him. He did not glance at their faces, but when he was satisfied with their buttocks and breasts he patted them on their bottoms, and then they knew they were to work that day. The men were chosen for the way they moved. All the models were expected to walk about the studio naked, without self-consciousness—it was the only way the *maître* could model them. Often the studio was quite cold and there was no place to sit or rest, but very few quit, for they were paid well if they were patient and co-operative.

Auguste, reviewing all this as he wondered uneasily if the inspector would ever come, knew he should feel successful—he had one of the most active studios in Paris now. But he did not feel content. The heads of Hugo, under cloths in the small studio, off the rue Dante, were still unfinished. He could not tell how long it would take him to complete "The Gates." The more he stared at them, the more he saw other things that had to be done.

He started to dictate his corrections to *petit* Auguste, who fell hopelessly behind him in the next few minutes. The boy was poor with words, spelled badly, had no sense of punctuation, and was easily distracted—especially when a young, pretty model sauntered by. Auguste sighed and halted. He would need a secretary soon, he thought worriedly. His life, instead of becoming simpler, was growing more confused. If only there were one person he could depend on to integrate all the various activities of his studio.

Petit Auguste asked, "May I leave now, Maître Papa?"

Auguste regarded him suspiciously. "You know this is an important day. I'm expecting the inspector. Everything should be in order."

"It is. I had 'The Gates' placed just where you ordered."

"Why do you have to leave? Is it a girl?"

"No, Maître Papa."

"A model?"

"No, no! Mama wants me to help her choose furniture for the parlor."

Auguste didn't believe him, but he said, "You know I said we had enough already. I do not intend to live like Louis the Fourteenth."

Petit Auguste shrugged, evaded his gaze, and a few minutes later, when his father was occupied shifting "The Gates" into a better light, was gone.

The boy was useless in the studio, Auguste thought pessimistically. The boy who had been bored at school was even more bored in the studio, always looking for an excuse to be somewhere else. It was depressing and disturbing. The only time *petit* Auguste wanted to remain in the studio was when an attractive female model was posing. He had forbidden the boy to have anything to do with the female models. The boy was only eighteen—still a child!

He came out of his reverie when Jules Desbois, his favorite assistant, informed him, "*Maître*, the inspector is here."

The inspector from the Beaux Arts, Monsieur Gabriel Pantin, introduced himself and waited for Auguste to make the next move.

Auguste saw a slim, dark man, much younger than he had expected, young enough to be a student, but with intense brown eyes that seemed to be observing everything. Auguste led him over to "The Gates."

There was a long pause while the inspector stared at them so intensely that Auguste became anxious again. Then he said, "This is not finished, is it?"

"No. This is my working model." Auguste was bitter at the thought of being in the hands of the Beaux Arts once more.

"How much longer do you think it will take?"

"A year. Two. Three, perhaps."

"You said that three years ago," the inspector reminded him.

How could he tell the inspector he was full of such good intentions, but that he was still groping in the dark, in his own hell? "Several more years shouldn't matter. The Museum of Decorative Arts isn't finished either."

"The Beaux Arts feels a definite date should be agreed upon, once and for all time, definitely."

"But I haven't received any more payments. You are behind schedule, too."

"Really? Indeed!" The inspector had the good grace to look surprised, even a little embarrassed. "There have been so many changes of cabinet in the last few years, that must be the reason for the oversight."

"I've gone into debt on account of 'The Gates.' "

"That's unfortunate, but you shouldn't let it bother you."

For a furious instant Auguste longed to tell the inspector and all of officialdom to go to hell—that he would find another way to survive. But the thought of giving up "The Gates" was beyond enduring, and he could not do them without state approval. He groaned. What had he gotten into? He was not a politician, not even a tactful man. He stood silent, tense.

The inspector surveyed the rest of the studio, the ceaseless activity, and asked, "You are doing other work here?"

"Yes," Auguste said curtly. "But 'The Gates' are the pyramid."

"If you got another payment, say, in a month, how long would it take you to finish them?"

"Three years. No more. If I am paid in full. I promise."

The inspector relaxed, smiled, and said, "Your individual figures are superb. They are a welcome change from the cold classical nudes that you see everywhere. When you enter through your 'Gates,' you feel in a real hell. There is a grim, awesome air about them, and your conception is magnificent. I don't care for the sitting poet on the top, but the Ugolino with the hollow eyes is frightening and fascinating."

Auguste stammered, amazed, "But I thought the Beaux Arts, their views—"

"I was appointed by Antonin Proust."

"Oh!"

"I was afraid, before I came, that you were making a vast fresco, full of innocent Venuses and Apollos, betrayed by their innocence. Instead, as Boucher said, your nudes are naked. Not tranquil, pure, academic, but abandoned, free, sensual. No wonder the provincials are shocked. Your hell is a whirlpool of anguished, writhing carnality. It will surprise, but no one will be able to ignore it."

"And the payments?" Auguste murmured.

"It is a work of art. I will recommend extra payments at once."

II

Inspector Gabriel Pantin was as good as his word. Soon afterward Auguste received another payment, of three thousand francs, and when this was followed by a third payment, of four thousand francs, and he was assured there would be more money forthcoming, although already he had received more than the amount originally agreed upon, he prayed, "Please, God, give me the energy to justify this faith." He was puzzled by this unexpected generosity until Boucher told him that there were rumors about Paris of a royalist clerical plot to destroy "The Gates of Hell" and that the stories had aroused a wave of public opinion in its favor. Boucher said he had no idea who had started these rumors, though there was a twinkle in his eyes as he told Auguste of the new interest in the completion of "The Gates."

"Now you can take your time," said Boucher. "I am sure there will be further payments, and you can make 'The Gates' as painstakingly as you like. You can take forever, as you would prefer. You can embark on four times the amount of work you should."

Auguste retorted angrily, "*Mon dieu!* Do you think I'm enjoying myself?" With a wild sweep of his hand he pointed to "The Gates" and the many figures littering his studio. "Do you really believe I like working myself to death?"

"You actually do feel oppressed," Boucher said, amused.

"By myself, I admit, *mon ami.* But that's the worst kind of oppression."

"Are you too exploited to exploit someone else?"

"What do you mean?"

"I have a student who wants to study with you. A young woman, Camille Claudel, talented, ambitious, hard-working, and—"

Auguste cut him short. "I don't want any female students. I've had enough trouble with my female models. Lisa, others. And now *petit* Auguste and some of my younger students are casting sheep's eyes at them."

"You shouldn't let them walk around naked."

"How else can I catch them in natural movements?" Auguste was distressed. "No, Boucher, I know you mean well, but I do not want any female students."

"She is very talented."

"Why doesn't she continue with you?"

"She says she must work with Auguste Rodin or no one."

Auguste grumbled, "I've no time. I've too many students as it is."

"She can also pose for you. She is very attractive. I think you will approve of her figure and head."

"We'll see," Auguste said impatiently, finding no other way to be rid of Boucher. "What did you say her name was?"

"Camille Claudel. She has been studying with me, but since she has seen your work she regards my sculpture as just so much *pâté.*"

"I could use a secretary. I'll see her tomorrow. For five minutes. Is she well educated?"

"Unusually well educated for a woman, especially such a young woman."

"A good secretary would be indispensable."

"Perhaps she will help you there, too, in return for studying with you."

Auguste shouted, "I make no bargains. I have too many pupils as it is." Suddenly he saw what had dissatisfied him with "The Gates." "I have no time. Five minutes tomorrow. Remember, that's all." He turned to the figure of the poet sitting on top of the tympanum. The man was too fragile. And he needed powerful, tragic figures on top of "The Gates" to set the mood. He cried, "Where is *petit* Auguste?" but no one knew. If only he had Peppino and Santoni now. What he needed more than anything else was good models. He grew so preoccupied he forgot to say *au revoir* to Boucher.

III

Auguste was startled when Boucher brought Camille Claudel to his studio the next day. He had forgotten about her. He was laboring on the figure of the poet, with *petit* Auguste posing for it, but the boy was too weak, too immature. Worse, the boy had been late for the sitting, and now was not concentrating, staring at several new female models. And he didn't like being interrupted, irritated already, but he was caught by her appearance.

She was beautiful, he realized, with a sudden surge of emotion. He had known several women since Madeleine and they had been attractive, but suddenly they seemed drab beside this young woman. How gracefully she stood, he thought. How elegant she was. What a fine carriage and head. Her features had a harmonious flow of line. She had light gray-blue eyes in a perfect Botticelli face. Then he felt a profound apprehension. The past few months he had been toiling like a crusty, deprived hermit in a provincial cave, with an occasional release with Rose—the other women had been like taking medicine once a week to stimulate his circulation and energy—but this young woman reminded him that he was still a man with many longings.

Yet when Boucher introduced her, he nodded curtly, said, "Bonjour."

Boucher said, "Rodin has bad manners, Camille, but he is quite busy."

She said in a clear, incisive voice, "I am not interested in his social behavior. I want to study with him."

Petit Auguste was regarding her with widening, fascinated eyes, and Auguste, annoyed, dismissed him, ordering him to check the amount of marble in the yard. Auguste said, "Mademoiselle, how do you know you should study?"

"Isn't that a little absurd?" she said. "Would Monsieur Boucher have brought me here if he thought it a waste? He's a busy man, too, monsieur."

Boucher nodded, and Auguste said, "Perhaps, but I have enough pupils. Can you work as a secretary?"

"But that's wicked!" she exclaimed.

"Wicked?" Auguste was confused.

"You make beautiful, free women in your studio, but when a woman wants to be free in life you are against it, Monsieur Rodin. I am a sculptress, not a secretary. Didn't Monsieur Boucher make that clear?"

"I need a secretary."

They stood staring at each other. She was far too beautiful to be a sculptress, he decided, and too patrician to be a model, or even a secretary.

She saw a stocky, vigorous, middle-aged man in a long white sculptor's smock who reminded her of a medieval stone carver at work on one of the great cathedrals. She noticed his broad, muscular shoulders, his heavy, brawny arms, his large, thick hands with their life-giving fingers and their huge square-nailed thumbs. His gaze was stern, but his hands, though she had interrupted them, continued to caress the clay he had been working on. They wandered over the unfinished figure like a lover's. They made her think of the hands Michelangelo had given his "Moses" and "David," imperious, heroic, powerful. Then as his hands clenched involuntarily, hard, as if against something, she visualized him working naked to the waist, a Vulcan bringing fire to the forge. But no, with his thick red beard he was actually a Mephistopheles glaring at her contemptuously, determined to reduce her to ashes.

She said, resenting that he made her feel defensive, "I started working on clay when I was thirteen."

He replied, "My studio is not for dilettantes, it is a serious business."

She became aware of his high sloping forehead, his thick red hair with a slight touch of gray, his clear blue eyes, the way he leaned his head forward because of his nearsightedness. She had a sudden wish to model him. She said, "Monsieur Rodin, I'm very serious. I would love to model you."

He said, "There is no such thing as love in sculpture, only hard work."

"And you must assassinate me," she said angrily. Her eyes flashed, her delicate face grew firm. "Certainly, maître, I could help as your secretary, but I must also work at sculpture."

"And sweep out the studio if necessary," he added.

"If necessary," she said.

"And clean up the clay, plaster, and all the debris made by the others?"

"Yes."

"And never complain?"

"Never."

"Work long hours. Into the night sometimes? And on Sundays?"

"As long as is needed."

"You mean, mademoiselle, there are no young men?"

She flushed angrily, started to say, "That is none of your business." but Boucher interrupted, "Mon cher Rodin, aren't you being unusually severe?"

"No. I don't want to bring a woman into my studio and then lose her to a romantic impulse just when she can begin to help me."

She said quietly, "You won't have to worry about that, monsieur."

But now Auguste was filled with panic. The longer she stood here, the harder it was to keep his eyes off her. Camille's delicately curved features were a miracle, what he had always dreamed of possessing. How joyful he felt when she smiled; it made him marvel at the excitement that surged through him. Yet this was absurd. He was much too old. He was becoming a family man. He said, "In addition to a hundred chores you will have to do your pieces over and over again."

She said, "I expect to do what everybody else does, maître."

"Very well. You can start next week. Report to *petit*— No, come to me first, I'll tell you what to do."

"*Merci, maître.* I am very grateful. I—"

He cut her short, warning, "This is just a trial, mademoiselle. Frankly, I do not think any woman has the strength to be a first-rate sculptor. Especially a young woman." But as he saw her dismay, he added, "Well, at least if you try, if you are prepared to work hard . . ." She nodded eagerly, and he said, "Remember, as I said, sculpture is work, hard work, not love. Love in art is for dilettantes. Nothing distresses me more, mademoiselle, than dilettantes in my studio."

He did not bother to escort Camille and Boucher to the door. He wished she weren't so beautiful. And so young, less than half his age. Then he assured himself that her loveliness was incidental, that the emotion that rose in him when he was close to her was simply a desire to model her.

IV

Camille worked twice as hard as any of the other students to prove her worth. She did whatever Auguste requested: she swept and she cleaned and she sketched and she sculpted and she built armatures and scaffolding. There was one restriction. Camille did not pose, and Auguste did not ask her to, and she was grateful, for the thought of it made her self-conscious, since much of the posing in the studio was in the nude and that advanced she was not.

Most of the student sculptors posed, to learn how it should be done, but Auguste justified his avoidance of it for her on the grounds that she was not a professional model like the other girls in the studio.

Otherwise he ignored her except to give her an occasional order, yet she had a feeling he was watching her much of the time. Often she was very tired, for the hours were long and it was assumed she would do whatever the men did, whether it was to carry a head, climb the rickety, precarious scaffolding, or hand the *maître* his tools.

Hardest of all was the solitude. Everyone was very polite and very formal. It was accepted that a pretty young woman would model, but it was unusual for a well-bred girl like Camille to sculpt seriously. She felt that subtly she was being driven out. As she toiled in the untidy, disorderly studio she was full of an angry despair. Why should she permit this to happen to her? Auguste Rodin's studio, which she had expected to love, was drab, imprisoning, without understanding. Instead of becoming the center of her universe, it was merely a place to be lonely in.

One day, on a desperate impulse to give her studying some meaning, Camille began to model a head of Rodin as he worked on "The Gates." At first she had no thought of showing it to him—it was simply that she had to work on something she saw with her own eyes and emotion—but gradually as the head took shape she became absorbed, even hopeful that he might not be too displeased. The *maître* had just found a concept for the top of "The Gates," three male figures which he called "the three shades," and as he planned to bring them to the fore he worked with a fierce focus and his disposition improved.

Camille, pleased that the *maître* was preoccupied and leaving her alone, was working intently one morning to finish the head when she heard a violent cough. She turned, to see him staring at the bust. She expected to be castigated, but he said, "You've made the nose too prominent and the mouth too thin and the eyes are nothing, but you are young—you will learn not to confuse truth with unkindness—and your touch is good."

From then on he gave her individual attention. He encouraged her to finish the head. The few minutes he spent with her each day became the most fruitful of her life.

Yet the afternoon she thought she had finished, after several weeks of the hardest work she had ever done, he said, "It's not right."

"What's wrong?"

"Study your subject more closely."

"I have."

"Perhaps, mademoiselle, but you haven't captured his inner necessity."

Discouraged, Camille wanted to quit, but now he wouldn't let her. Yet when she asked to work on "The Gates," as most of the other students did, he refused her. He also suggested that she withdraw from the group of students who were working in the life class with the naked male and female models.

As she looked disheartened, he said, "You are developing a flair for heads. They could be your *métier*. You should concentrate on them."

"But you are never satisfied with what I do!"

"I am never satisfied with my own work."

Camille did not believe him and her sharp glance said so.

"It is true, however," he said. "Have you seen my heads of Hugo?"

"No. I didn't know you made any, *maître*."

"They are in another studio. They are a secret. Done without Hugo's knowledge. But they are not finished. Because I am not satisfied with them. Would you like to see them?"

"I would be honored."

He smiled wryly. He gave her the address of his third studio and said, "Don't tell anyone. This is my private studio, and no one knows of it."

She was a little frightened, yet excited. This was the first time the *maître* had indicated he was also a man. She promised, "No one will know, monsieur."

"It's not what you think. How old are you, mademoiselle? The truth!"

"Twenty."

"I could be your father."

But you are not, she thought, and she was glad he was not. "Will we work there, Monsieur Rodin?"

"It depends."

V

Camille was surprised and disappointed by the run-down condition of the third studio, near the Île St. Louis. She liked the location, but disliked the yellowish-brown walls, the blistered paint, the faded curtains, the cracked slats that were supposed to serve as shutters, the clutter and the debris, and the dust that was everywhere. This *atelier*, instead of being picturesque, as she had hoped, looked ready to fall to pieces.

Auguste smiled at her dismay and said, "I'm getting another."

"But you have three already?"

"So I'll have four. I've always wanted a studio near the place d'Italie. It is an interesting part of Paris. And very good for privacy."

"You could have this cleaned. It could look presentable."

"I'm not concerned how a studio looks. That's vanity."

"And four studios are not?"

"I need space to move around. I'm too crowded in three."

"But this is such a good location, *maître*."

"Oh, I will keep this, for occasional work." He dismissed her objections with an abrupt wave of his hand. "The next studio will have a courtyard. I've always liked courtyards. Wait, I'll show you the heads."

Camille had started for the door, offended by his curtness, but she paused, attracted by a female head in the corner. It was a plaster cast of a very pretty young woman, and her curiosity was aroused. She asked, "Who is this?"

"None of your business, mademoiselle."

He was a tyrant, she thought furiously. Yet she felt she would die of humiliation, she felt so gauche for asking. And feeling foolish and therefore revengeful, she snapped caustically, "It's so classical. Almost Roman."

To her surprise, instead of being offended, he said, "You're right."

"You don't like it?" Camille was amazed.

"Not much. I was being influenced by Carrier-Belleuse and thinking of Marie Antoinette."

"She has an unusually pretty face."

"Anyone can model a pretty face." He made an impatient gesture, pushing this bust out of their conversation. "But never mind about that. Here are the Hugos." He took the cloths off the two heads. "Now the truth, mind you. Be merciless, if necessary."

"Of course," she said. She would be as harsh as he was. But suddenly Camille could not speak. It was as if Hugo were facing her. Le Père Hugo, watching over his beloved France, the eternal yet the personal Hugo. She was surprised. The *maître* had said they were unfinished—yet she could feel the veins throbbing in Hugo's forehead. Each feature was vivid, a part of the rhythm of the whole. The surfaces of both heads were rugged, two human crags cut with many crevices. Gone was sentimental smoothness. Gone were round, glossy surfaces. Gone was the artificial modeling, she thought, that had prevailed in French portrait sculpture for centuries, even in Houdon. In this moment of aesthetic ecstasy she wanted to give him her heart. How could she dislike such an artist! And because she felt so vulnerable, she tried to hold herself aloof. She stumbled to the one chair in the studio, sat down, and fought to look remote as she tried to control her emotions.

"You don't like them, mademoiselle?"

Was there any choice? she cried to herself. He did care what she thought. He looked unexpectedly vulnerable, too, waiting for her verdict.

He said pessimistically, "I told you they were unfinished."

"No, you're wrong. They are finished."

"But the expression, I find myself always having to change it."

"Because his expression always changes."

"Hugo's?" He looked at her intently. Why hadn't he thought of that?

"Yes. And yet," Camille said as carefully as she could, considering that her heart was pounding furiously, "each head has an expression that seems completely characteristic of Hugo."

"Do you know him?" Auguste asked, suddenly worried.

"Only by reading. Do you, maître?"

"Slightly. Do you like him?"

"His poetry is too romantic for me, but I like Les Miserables, I think it is a remarkable book. Have you read it?"

"Not all of it," Auguste said regretfully. "It takes leisure to read."

"But I prefer Zola, Daudet, and this new writer, Maupassant, though I don't like his views of women."

"I could introduce you to Zola and Daudet if you like."

"No," she said with sudden decisiveness. "They will disappoint me, I'm sure. Most important people do."

He smiled slightly, but she didn't continue on this note.

She asked, "Whom do you prefer, maître?"

"Rousseau, Dante, Balzac, Baudelaire—"

"Baudelaire? He's making you change 'The Gates,' isn't he?"

"I keep him at my bedside, with Dante, but there are enough figures in Paris alone to keep me busy on 'The Gates' for the rest of my life." He was silent then, as if he had exposed more of himself than he liked. She said nothing either, and he studied her as she sat there, her lovely eyes downcast. He was taken with her wistful quality, which he had not seen before. He could model her just in the position she was in now.

She raised her eyes to him. Their gaze met, then fell away.

"I would like—" He paused.

"You want me to pose?"

"I'm not sure. You are very young."

"Youth is a state of mind. I was the one in my family who got us to move to Paris from Champagne. I am the one who will be an artist no matter what they say."

"Oh, I grant you are mature in some ways, mademoiselle," he said, pleased yet confused by this young woman, different from any other he had ever known. Her ability to respond, to communicate, warmed his heart like a caress, but she was a bud still to bloom while he— *Mon dieu*, he felt old suddenly!

"You worry too much about youth," she said. "Does Hugo?"

"Hugo!" Their eyes met again and held, particles of light lifted from a deep darkness. "*Merci*, mademoiselle, you were helpful. We will work in my new studio. As soon as I get it. One day a week. Saturdays."

CHAPTER 29

Saturday came, and Auguste was at his new studio promptly, eager yet nervous, and when Camille was prompt also, he sighed with relief.

Camille noticed that this newly rented studio, near the place d'Italie, at the junction of the rue Rubens and the rue Véronèse, was smaller than she had expected but fastidiously clean, with good daylight, a sense of intimacy, a large courtyard in the front, and a tidy garden in the back. She was disappointed by the austerity of the studio; there were no furnishings except what was necessary for sculpture. But she liked the iron gates set in a high archway, the marble fountain in the center of the cobbled courtyard, and the high walls that enclosed it.

He said, "The studio is part of a complete three-story house. I rented the entire property so that I would not be disturbed."

"There are living quarters above?"

"Of a kind. I have a bedroom on the second floor should I want to stay over, and a storeroom on the third floor for my materials."

"It must be quite expensive."

"As studios go. But it is worth it, mademoiselle."

"If you think so, *maître*." She didn't have the heart to disagree with him; he was as proud of the studio as a child with a new toy.

"I spent an entire day finding it. I looked at many studios before deciding on this one. Do you like it?"

She smiled, pleased that he was interested in her feelings after all. "Yes, yes. It is an improvement on the others. Quiet. Restful."

"I hope so. I have much work I want to do."

"What shall I do, *maître?*"

"Just walk about. Naturally, as the models do in the big studio."

She felt she had walked miles before he put a line to paper. Then he hardly looked at her as he made many sketches. He spent the whole first day planning a head of her. There was nothing else, yet when he said, "Next Saturday—yes!" she was gay suddenly.

Everything seemed to move so slowly the following week, though she was quite busy in the big studio. The *maître* had her work on pieces for "The Gates," female figures chiefly, in addition to the head. He gave her fewer chores and more sculpture to do.

At the new studio on Saturday he worked unexpectedly on her hands. "Your hands are lovely," he blurted out abruptly, then was silent, as if ashamed of what he had said. But he sculpted them with even greater care now.

No one had to say a word about the following Saturday. It was raining heavily, but both of them were prompt. He said curtly, "Since we've known each other for some time, I think we might stop using *maître* and mademoiselle and call each other by our right names."

"As you wish, monsieur."

"No, no, I'll call you Camille and you call me Auguste. But not in the main studio. It would be wrong there."

She nodded, but as always they stood far apart. The rest of the day passed in work. He did not ask her whether she was tired, but halted when his own energy ebbed. Then he escorted her across the cobbled courtyard that was surrounded by the high walls. She had been excited by the marble fountain, but now it made her sad. He left her at the iron gates with a brief *"Au revoir,"* as if anything else would choke him. Neither of them had been able to call the other by the first name.

II

It seemed to Auguste that the next few weeks were devoid of people, a life of complete absorption in his work, with Camille simply part of this work. He wondered if she was relieved or regretful. For himself he could endure anything, he assured himself, if his sculpture was going well, and it was now. He was modeling her head, her hands, and her arms, all as separate pieces. She stimulated him to do hard, good work. He tried not to be rude, as his friends accused him of always being with his female models, but he was curt to Camille. He was outraged that he felt self-conscious in his desire to see her body—that had never happened before. It was unfair to be so tempted and so frustrated. He was positive she had a model's body.

One Saturday, instinctively, he started to stroke her arms to make sure they had the proper contour. She grew rigid. How could he tell her that he couldn't help himself? He was only doing what he did with all his models. He gazed at her a moment with an irate, puzzled expression and then snapped, "A sculptor has to make his own rules, according to his nature."

She was not concerned with what he was saying. All that mattered was the fear that went through her, and the desire.

He said indignantly, "I am not a *boulevardier.*"

She didn't say a word.

He said, "You may go, mademoiselle. *Mon dieu,* I do not want a model who worries about the dinner on the stove or can't forget her sheltered life."

She didn't move. She asked suddenly, "Do I have a model's figure?"

"Probably."

"Will it help if you see my body?"

He shrugged—but naturally! A body was a body, his shoulders said.

"You want me to model for 'Eve'?"

"*Merci*—no! I've had enough of Eves!"

"What do you want?"

"It will depend on what you suggest."

She hesitated, then said, "Will you turn around while I undress?"

For an instant he wanted to shout that this was absurd, but as she smiled shyly at him he knew without words that she was placing her future in his hands. He turned his back on her obediently.

Several minutes later Camille whispered, "I'm ready, Auguste. I'm by the model's stand."

She was as perfectly formed as he had thought, her body as lovely as her face. He told himself jubilantly that she had the ideal model's body—what he had always looked for to sculpt: virginal white shoulders, a long, graceful torso, a tapering waist, fine hips, pliant, well-developed legs, small yet precisely formed buttocks, and most exciting of all, swelling breasts. *Mon dieu!* what magnificent, thrusting breasts! They were even more superb than he had imagined, high, Egyptian, full yet firm. And he was delighted with the rosy freshness of her skin. The texture would take the light wonderfully. Now, finally, he had a subject worthy of marble.

Camille could hardly recognize the *maître*. His eyes sparkled, his cheeks were red, he moved toward her with an urgent spring in his step. Then suddenly he halted.

"What's the matter?" she murmured. "Have I done something wrong?"

Camille's face was the whitest he had ever seen. She was terrified. "It's your fear. You must not be afraid."

"I'm not." But she shivered.

He threw one of his smocks over her shoulders, lit the fire, and when she stopped shivering and looked warm, her skin a rosy pink, ordered her to discard the smock and stride up and down the studio. At first she was awkward and stiff, but when he said impatiently, "Don't be so clumsy, time enough to be that way when your buttocks have fallen and your belly is gone," her pride overcame her self-consciousness and she strode proudly and color returned to her face.

Auguste drew her in a hundred movements. He started a number of nude figures, but none of them satisfied him. It was nightfall when he ordered Camille to halt. She was exhausted, but he had not finished. He told himself that she was too refined. He was positive he was regarding her with professional detached candor; but when she smiled at him apologetically, facing him with her sensuous body, he knew he had been fooling himself. He was intensely involved. The sight of her naked made him exultantly alive. He desired her as he had never desired anyone in his life. He was annoyed by this, as if driven by a force he could not control, and he said sharply, "You're still too stiff."

There was a long silence while Camille stood with her head bowed. She was hurt by his anger, yet she knew, without a doubt now, that she had to have this man. As she felt his disapproving eyes on her, she could not endure that, he was so masculine, as a man should be.

He said curtly, "Walk in front of me."

She did so, slowly, hesitantly.

Suddenly he halted her. He had to feel her body to capture its flow. His hands stroked her waist to catch the exact contour, the palpitant flesh, the subtle flavor of her skin. She was different from the models. Her nearness gave him an overwhelming need to possess her.

The touch of Auguste's superb hands sent a wave of turbulent feeling through Camille. Her flesh throbbed under his touch. He was taking possession of her, and she would hate him if he didn't. Her fears died in her love. She clung to him as if shaken by a convulsion.

Auguste led her upstairs with a new assurance. Romantic love was the most dangerous of all, he knew, and he was beyond caring. He said to himself, how remarkable that they could communicate on so many levels, but what really mattered was that she made him feel like the being he wished to be.

Then nothing mattered but their pairing.

Camille was grateful afterward that in love Auguste was not rude or curt or brief, but led her through the shoals of her ignorance and innocence with a consideration he had never shown before. She lay beside him, feeling a wonderful richness. She pressed his strong hands to her soft cheeks, kissing them, fondling them, holding them close to her breasts, seeing herself as the inspiration for his art. She was shocked when suddenly he pulled away. Before she could ask what was wrong, he lit a candle, threw a smock over his shoulders, and hurried downstairs, muttering to himself.

He felt like such a fool. He stood by the last figure he had started of her, and now he knew he was wrong—he had been making an idealization rather than an individualization. He was embarrassed. His approach had been false.

There was a knock on the door. Startled, wondering who could have trailed him here, he was relieved when it turned out to be the concierge, awakened by the light.

"I'm working," Auguste said.

"I'm sorry, monsieur," said the concierge, a dark, stout, elderly man.

"*Bonsoir*." Auguste closed the door in the concierge's face.

Auguste was working so hard on the figure he was not aware of Camille standing at the foot of the winding staircase and watching him, a blanket around her—she hadn't been able to find anything else to put on quickly. She had to cough loudly, several times, before he noticed her presence.

Then he said angrily, "I was an idiot!"

"An idiot?" She felt sick; had she been just an experiment? She asked, "What about me?"

"What about you?" he repeated. "I was a fool, but you weren't much better."

"What else could I have done?" Her eyes filled with tears. He was her first, yet she had reacted as if he had been irresistible, which he was. "I did the best I could." In this instant she hated him.

"Yes, of course. But it was not good enough." He scowled at the figure.

"I didn't mean that. I meant—upstairs—us."

"Oh, us." He said abruptly, "You look lovely with your hair down. I didn't know it was that long. Stand there, with it around your shoulders."

"Where?" She felt utterly confused.

"By the model's stand. Why else do you think I came down?"

"Then you weren't unhappy upstairs?"

He looked at her as if she were crazy. "*Chérie*, do you have to ask?"

"But I thought—" Now she could not tell him what she had thought.

He was not listening. He was staring at the figure he had been re-working when she had interrupted him. "It's very embarrassing. I made such a terrible mistake. How could I be such a fool? And you didn't help any."

"Auguste, that's not fair." He was making her feel like a child.

"Fair?" He laughed curtly. "There is no such thing as fairness in art. But it was my fault, too. I saw you as an ideal form instead of an individual form. I wasn't positive, concrete enough, modeling you. It is not enough to make you Springtime or a Danaïd, I should have seen you as you really are. But I was a slave to what I was feeling instead of being the master."

"What should I have done?"

"Been more individual, personal, in your modeling. You should have made me feel Camille, not just another body."

Panic touched her. She would never satisfy him, least of all as a model or as a student. Camille tightened the blanket around her, started upstairs, and he halted her.

He kissed her and said, "Camille, *ma chérie*, I cannot help being rude, I come from peasant stock, I am not good with compliments, I—"

"Oh," she interrupted suddenly, "you taste of clay." He backed away, and she was sorry. Much as he had hurt her, she did not want to hurt him. "I'm sorry, Auguste, it's just that I don't always understand you."

He said quietly, "A while ago you stood here and I said to myself, *Nom de dieu*, she is unapproachable, and so now I still cannot believe what has happened. But when I work on your figure it is real. It is the best way I can talk to you. Could you model a little now?"

"Of course!"

"It will only be a few minutes."

They worked almost to dawn.

CHAPTER 30

Every day now Auguste spent some time working with Camille on her sculpture. Moreover, he allowed her to work on his own rough statues—a thing he permitted no one else—and he entrusted her with modeling the heads, hands, and feet of many of his figures. And now he spent Wednesday as well as Saturday at the new studio with her.

For Auguste, Camille's presence was a delight he had never known before. She became the image of beauty, the embodiment of all the things he had desired in a woman. She made him feel young just with her smile: she had the loveliest smile he had ever seen. She was like a first love, he thought, and perhaps she was. Wherever he was with her, Paris became *la belle Paris*, romantic, gay, animated. Whether they strolled in the place de l'Opéra to admire Carpeaux's sculpture of "The Dance," or studied the statue of Henri IV on the Pont Neuf, or discussed the many statues in the gardens of the Luxembourg, including his own, he saw *la belle Paris* with new eyes.

From the start of his head he had recognized her innate ability as a sculptress, but he had never expected to find a love with whom he could share his thoughts. Her ideas were a miraculous thing to him. She was well read, well educated, yet never *bourgeois*, never conventional in her thinking.

Camille told Auguste that she could manage her mother, but that she was always quarreling with her father, who had reared her in a freethinking atmosphere. Yet though she shared her father's skepticism about religion, there were moments when she had an intense need to go to church, to believe in the doctrine of original sin, even as the next instant she was declaring religion was a fraud. She was the oldest of three children: her younger sister, Louise, was as determined to be a great pianist as Camille was to be a great sculptress, and her brother, Paul, had dreams of becoming a noted poet-dramatist. She lived on the rue Notre Dame des Champs with her mother, sister, and brother; her father, a civil servant, had remained in Rambouillet. But she listened to no one, she declared proudly to Auguste, except herself and Auguste. When her mother reproached her for the nights she did not come home, she said she would leave for good, and then her mother was quiet. She sensed that her mother prayed desperately for the salvation of her soul, but she pretended to be unmoved. Yet there were times when Camille felt guilt, as if she had not quite departed from her brother's Catholicism, which she now abjured. Then she stopped seeing everyone but Auguste, and was at his studios always, devoting herself exclusively to work, as he did. At such times she worked very hard, as hard as Auguste. She felt relieved that she was willing to give up everything for Auguste, as if a touch of martyrdom would ease her guilt. And as the weeks passed this way, she was sure she was happy, studying and working with him, posing for hours, and being shouted at when he was dissatisfied.

These days Auguste spent more time on his toilet. He trimmed his thick beard with great care, proud of its redness. When he saw a gray hair, he pulled it out at once. He cut his nails after she said they hurt. He took to wearing cleaner smocks.

There was no question about what he preferred to do any more. Though he continued to work on "The Gates" and other commissions, her rare chiseled beauty stimulated him the most. She became his favorite model. Now his other, professional models struck him as tarts or Montmartre *midinettes* or café *lorettes*, but he found her aristocratic features perfect for marble. He did busts of her which he called "Dawn," "Iris," and "Thought," then put them in marble. He was particularly interested in "Thought," where her head emerged from a block of marble as if newborn.

Camille was surprised by his dissatisfaction with this piece—she thought "Thought" a lovely, reflective head, and truly original—and he replied, "There must be more vitality in the head, so that it gives vitality to the marble underneath the head, which, in a sense, is earth. When you feel the blood from the head circulating into the marble underneath, I will be satisfied. But you don't have to pose for this any more. I can work on the marble without you."

"But isn't it finished now that it has come back from the marble caster?"

He regarded her as if she were a child. He explained irritably, "I am not a marble carver, like Michelangelo. There is no need for that any more. Yet there is much I can do with my chisels, rasps, polishing stones. If I didn't touch up my marbles, they'd just be blocks of stone, imitations of a model. Camille, each material creates a different result." He looked up at the marble as if looking up to God, and returned to work.

No matter how much Auguste labored on everything else, he kept coming back to one other piece which he thought of as a Danaïd. At first in his joy with her passionate body he yearned to model her as Venus. Then he decided that this subject had been exhausted. And the concept did not stimulate him. His illumination came when he remembered her moment of panic their first night, when she had doubled over in a crouching, panic-stricken position to hide her embarrassment from him. He had never forgotten it, or quite forgiven it, yet he had treasured it as a dramatic emotion in movement to model.

This morning he could not think of anything else. It was a week after their disagreement over "Thought." She arrived at the new studio prepared to pose for a new head, and he said only one word, "Undress."

She did not dare argue, although her mood was different.

"Good!" he said when she was completely naked.

She asked as he ran his hands over her back, "Do I meet with your approval?"

"You could be better, but you are learning. Bend your body more. All the way over. Cringe!"

"Cringe? The floor is cold."

"The marble will be, too, if you don't." He pushed her down until her head touched the floor. As she shivered her flesh grew tense, and he sketched that rapidly. His loving and searching eyes sped over the soft contours of her back and buttocks, capturing the shape and droop of her shoulders, the partition of her buttocks and the curve of their cheeks, the slenderness of her hips, and the trembling sensitiveness of her skin.

He was working so hard she was afraid to breathe. She thought not even God would dare to interrupt him now. She bent in this position until she was afraid her back would break and her muscles ached.

All he said was, "Lift your shoulders more—your hips are too high! Can't you keep still a minute? *Mon dieu!* Don't keep shifting sideways!"

Camille thought there was nothing more difficult than to be a perfect model, except, perhaps, to be a perfect companion for Auguste. The blood rushed painfully to her head and she waited for praise, but after several hours he said only, "You may stand."

"Was I satisfactory?" She was so stiff she could hardly stand.

"You were patient."

"*Merci*, Auguste, you are so kind."

He frowned. Why did she have to divert him with this need for praise when he had begun to think of her for an amorous pairing?

But when Camille saw his preoccupation, she was positive he was thinking of his family. She asked suddenly, "Don't you ever miss your family?"

She had learned about Rose, to his annoyance, though this was the first time she had mentioned her. He wondered angrily who had gossiped in the studio. He had caught *petit* Auguste eying her often, but *petit* Auguste kept to himself these days when he was at the main studio. Auguste muttered, "You shouldn't ask me."

"I should be grateful and just take you as you are?"

"I can't be any other way."

He sat down, looking a little desperate, and she took his hands in hers, gripping them tightly, and said, "I don't want to ruin your life, Auguste, I want to inspire it."

"There is no such thing as inspiration," he replied sharply. "Just work. Hard work." He got up suddenly, pulled away from her, and went to the "Danaïd."

He stared at the figure. It had been a good day. The "Danaïd" was taking on the freshness of morning dew, yet even as it pulsated with life it retained a subdued pathos. He felt fruitful. This could be a memorable piece after all.

That evening Auguste came to Camille with such feeling she sank into his embrace as if they were one. The next few weeks there was no further discussion of their feelings, but many evenings of making love.

II

Rose, seeing Auguste only when he came home to sleep, and many nights he did not even do that, suspected he was interested in another woman, but had no proof. When she questioned his increasing absences, he said he had gone to Chartres and Rheims to study the cathedrals. He started to explain, "The old Gothic cathedrals are sculpture at its best," then broke off, thinking she wouldn't understand. And when she pressed him, he lost his temper.

This distressed Rose. All she desired was kindness, yet she had made him angry.

At bedtime she snuggled close to him, and his coldness made her feel ashamed. He turned away from her and went to sleep.

Other nights when she grumbled about this, he muttered, "I'm tired, very tired, I'll never finish 'The Gates,' I've too many commissions. Tomorrow, Rose, tomorrow."

Suddenly one evening when Rose and Auguste were preparing to go to bed, Rose—who always came to bed in a proper nightgown and in darkness—left the gaslight on and stood before him naked, seeking to be seductive and voluptuous in a manner she had never assumed before.

Auguste was astonished and shocked. He sat up in bed abruptly. Mon dieu! What did he have to cope with now? Couldn't she control herself? What was wrong with her? She was behaving ridiculously. She was bare-breasted, like a whore. The wrinkles in her flesh were an obscenity. How old she looked! Every day he saw such beautiful bodies, and she showed only the brutality of age. Twenty years had wrought harsh changes. She still moved gracefully and had retained her fine carriage, but she was forty. Then he felt sad, remembering how young and attractive she had been when she had posed for the "Bacchante." He said, "You'll catch cold. You had better put a robe on. Here, use mine." He handed her his robe.

"Did I do something wrong, *chéri?*" She did not take the robe.

"I haven't time to talk about such things."

"Am I so ugly?"

"Rose, it's not becoming!"

"That I love you?"

"You're not a ten-franc tart, an old whore who would do it with anyone."

"What am I? Your housekeeper? Your servant? A domestic?"

He shrugged, and embarrassed, felt like a stranger. A veil dropped over his eyes. He turned his head away, pretending to dismiss this aberration from his mind, and grumbled, "I had a terribly hard day at the studio, I had to do all of your son's work, he was nowhere around when I needed him, I'm exhausted." And as she stood there looking stunned, he put out the bedstand light and sank back in the large double bed, apart from her, to punish her.

III

Now nothing was as it had been. Rose began to watch Auguste like a hunter in an ambush, observing, analyzing, interpreting every move, look, and word. She was almost sure he was guilty, he was so preoccupied these days, but she was still not quite sure of what. And when her uncertainty became too much to bear, she went to the big studio, on the rue de l'Université.

Rose entered as if by chance, and thought she had never seen such pandemonium. Everyone was so busy no one noticed her. It was the first time she had been here in a long while, and she was amazed by how much the activity had increased. Wherever she looked there were students and models and sculpture in work: hands, arms, legs, torsos, heads, fragments, statuettes, masks, complete figures, groups, most of them in clay and plaster, but some in terra cotta and several in bronze and marble. But "The Gates" still dominated, Rose saw, towering above everything else like the side of a vast mountain, with more figures on the main model than she could count. There were many attractive women among the models, and she did not know whom to focus on. Then Rose saw

Auguste standing at the foot of "The Gates" with two assistants, one a young man and the other a young woman, commanding them to climb the ladder to the top of the scaffold and alter the figure sitting above "The Gates" while he surveyed the changes.

Rose, deeply resentful—he never consulted her any more about his work—hurried over to him.

Auguste looked startled for a moment, then grew angry. "*Mon dieu*, Rose!" he cried. "You've come to spy on me!" He led her to the door, ordered her to stay away. When she reminded him of how she used to help him—no one could keep the cloths damp the way she could—he cut her short, saying, "That's not necessary any more. If you come here again, I'll lock the door on you."

It was a dreadful humiliation, but she realized that to argue with him in front of everyone else would be an even greater one. She had no choice but to leave.

Several days later, however, when she was alone at home with *petit* Auguste—who was seldom home, the young man said it was too lonely at home—she asked him, "Is your father interested in—someone else?" It hurt horribly to ask, but she had to know. Anything was better than not knowing.

Petit Auguste wanted to be delicate. He shrugged.

"I see that he is involved," she said, positive in her despair.

"No, no, no, I'm not sure, Mama, he is a connoisseur of beautiful women now with all the nudes he is doing, but everything in this studio is work."

"In this studio? He has only one other. Doesn't he, *chéri?*"

There was silence. It was complicated, thought *petit* Auguste. He didn't want to hurt Mama, yet the old man deserved it, running everybody with an iron hand. He said as if tearing this from his very roots, "The *maître* is never at the rue de l'Université on Wednesdays and Saturdays."

She said unbelievingly, "You mean every Wednesday and Saturday?"

"Every. And I've noticed," he said proudly, "that one of the students is always absent those days, too. A Camille Claudel. She is quite pretty."

"Oh!" Her face turned gray. "Do you know where he goes?"

"It's not the studio on the boulevard de Vaugirard. But there are rumors among the students that he has several other studios that no one knows about."

"But that's extravagant!"

"Please, Mama, you must not get upset." After all, an extra woman here and there was hardly heinous. It was the one advantage of being an artist.

But Rose's resentment increased. And when Auguste did not spend the next Sunday with her, as if to punish her, she had no hesitation about what to do.

The following Saturday morning when he left the house after breakfast, she trailed him, unobserved. She paused outside the new studio, near the place d'Italie, for a few minutes, to give him time to become involved with whoever was there, then knocked on the door, prepared for the *coup de grâce*.

A beautiful young woman opened the door, her head tied up in a duster, a brush in her hand.

This was the most infuriating of all, thought Rose. No one else could serve Auguste as she could! The two women stared at each other, face to face. The door was only partially open, and Rose could not see Auguste but she could hear him discoursing on his favorite subject, Gothic architecture, absorbed in his work and unaware that anyone was at the door. He was muttering, "No one understands me as you do, Camille," and Rose's fury rose.

Rose pushed her way in, past a white-faced Camille, who, having lived at this studio for the last month, was saying, "I came to Monsieur with the best of intentions."

Rose replied, "That is what they all say at the beginning."

Auguste, his attention aroused, interrupted, "That's not true."

Rose announced, "I'm Madame Rodin."

Auguste said, "Rose, you are making a fool of yourself. You and I are not married." He wondered if his voice sounded as unnatural to Camille as it did to him. He felt strangely shaken. But he must impress upon both of them that *no one* ran his life.

She hates me, thought Camille, she would kill me if she could. Panic filled her, and Camille wanted to flee, but Auguste motioned imperiously for her to continue her work. Camille retreated behind the many pieces of sculpture, dusting them frantically in her agitation.

Rose went to follow Camille, but Auguste halted her. He said, "I warned you not to spy on me."

"And I am wrong?" Rose cried. "I am not Madame Rodin?"

"You are not married to me," he repeated, sharply this time. "Why shouldn't Camille and I live together if we choose?"

"What about me?"

"Well, of course, Camille and I are not engaged. Everyone knows that you are my companion, except we are not married." But Rose was not satisfied, and he was baffled. He failed to see why he should change anything . . . "if I support both of you and put up with the atrocious scenes you are making." Rose turned white, and he said angrily, "Don't fall into the Seine."

Rose stared at Camille, who was trying to hide in a corner of the studio behind a crouching nude marble for which she had obviously modeled. Rose visualized Camille's perfect and youthful nakedness under *her* Auguste and the thought was too much to endure. She felt withered suddenly, though she still saw herself as a strong, good-looking woman, but not as attractive as this one, who was half her age. All at once she was crying bitterly, her face buried in her hands.

"Please, Rose, let's not be stupid, let's not—"

"I don't understand. What did I do wrong?"

Auguste was very cross. He wanted to shout, "Shut up, you idiot," but she looked in a state of shock. He handed her a hundred francs. "Here, get the chairs you wanted."

"Don't send me away!"

"I'm not sending you away. You have your place in the home and —" He halted: he could not tell anyone else what pure enjoyment Camille gave him. Rose was a woman to protect, but Camille was a woman to cherish. Rose was dependable, but Camille was the sunlight, Camille had style, poise, elegance. How could two such different people compete? It was incomprehensible. Then suddenly he was in a rage. Who had told her about this studio? He demanded to know how she had found out about it.

Rose blushed, and now he knew.

"*Petit* Auguste!" he shouted. "The spy! The cheat!"

Rose shook her head, but Auguste was sure—Rose never could hide anything from him.

He felt an extreme bitterness, as if he had been betrayed. He declared, "It was a great mistake to bring him into the studio."

"You're not going to dismiss him, Auguste? Please, don't," Rose pleaded.

"I hardly have to dismiss him, he's there so seldom."

"He means well."

"Like telling you about this?"

"I would have found out. Someone else would have told me."

"No doubt. Though it is none of their business. It is nobody's business. I want to see the boy when I come home tonight."

"You won't be hard on him? He's all I have left."

"That's nonsense." But his voice softened. He put his arms around her and guided her to the door. "*Ma chatte,* you know I couldn't manage without you. Nobody takes better care of me than you."

It was incredible, Rose thought sadly; no matter how badly he treated her, she could not argue against his arms. At the door, when he repeated, "Remember, I want to see the boy tonight," she nodded. She had achieved her aim, which was to catch him with his *amour,* and he made her feel guilty. What he had done was unforgivable, yet he assumed that she was in the wrong. She resolved not to let him forget his guilt quickly, though she answered his *au revoir* with a *bonjour.*

Camille, emerging from the protection of the statues after Rose left, said, "I cannot stay. It's too uncomfortable."

Auguste retorted, "You have to stay. We haven't finished the 'Danaïd.'"

At that instant Camille wanted to slap him in the face, but he was out of reach, at the model stand, working.

Then he said almost apologetically, "She's a savage, a peasant."

"And I, Auguste?"

"Come, we are wasting time."

"You can go on working? After this!"

"I keep saying that you don't work hard enough, but you don't believe me."

"Did you ever say you loved me?" she cried, angry with herself for being driven to say this, and thus even angrier with him in this instant.

"I'm not a *grand seigneur.* But as long as I model you as *une femme parfaite,* my dear Camille, you have nothing to complain about."

"Such arrogance," she stormed, but she did not leave. She was unhappy when he could not stay the night—he said he must speak to *petit* Auguste—but she agreed to remain, for she had moved all her things in, and he promised to return tomorrow, though it was Sunday.

At home Auguste was surprised to find the boy waiting for him with a defiant smile on his face. And when he started to berate *petit* Auguste for treachery, the young man grinned and said, "I'm going into the Army."

"Tell Papa why," said Rose.

Petit Auguste could not do that—Rodin was not his father, not really, whatever Mama said. He couldn't call him Papa, he wouldn't dare. And he was afraid that the *maître* would guess the truth, that he was fleeing from the studio, and not because he wanted to be on his own, as he had told Mama.

Auguste said, "Well, perhaps it is the first sensible thing you've done. There you will have to listen to authority."

Rose said, "Aren't you going to give him your blessing?"

"I'll give him some advice," said Auguste. "Acquire some rank, and perhaps in the Army, at least, you may have a career." He turned away to hide his deep disappointment.

"I'll do the best I can," said *petit* Auguste, then started to laugh.

Auguste swung back to face him. "What is so amusing?"

"The studio was supposed to be l'Académie. But in the Army it is *la vie et la mort*—the real thing."

"Yes," Auguste said slowly. "The real thing. *Bonne chance.*"

Rose felt better now. When Mademoiselle Camille ages, she thought, it will not be so unequal. She must wait. Besides, there was no other choice.

Rose cried, however, when it came time for *petit* Auguste to say good-by. Her baby was leaving her, she sobbed, and Auguste had difficulty quieting her. She stopped only when father and son shook hands.

As they left *petit* Auguste at the railroad station and walked home, she said, "Believe me, *chéri,* the love of a good woman is a precious thing, you don't need any *cocottes,*" and Auguste cut her short.

"I refuse to discuss this matter any further," he said positively.

Rose felt faint, but he did not relieve her of his overcoat, which she was carrying. He had started a drawing of *petit* Auguste waving *au revoir* and he had to finish it.

CHAPTER 31

The next few years were a time of feverish activity. While Camille and Rose shared Auguste with a kind of suspended hostility, as if each woman understood her place, he threw himself into a profusion of work. There were so many commissions now that Auguste had difficulty sorting them out in his own mind, but he could not give up a single one of them. Day after day he planned, sketched, modeled, cast and recast. There was always some time spent on "The Gates" and the figures it depicted: Paolo and Francesca, the Poet sitting reflectively on the top, lovers paired in writhing, tortured embraces, and single figures and heads. But it was the new concepts and commissions that absorbed him the most. Constantly searching to express his new vitality, he modeled a crouching, weeping lion of which he thought Barye could have been proud. He labored on Ugolino devouring his children until the figure became a cadaver in plaster. He could imagine the cries of disgust as he created the corpses of the children; with a grim humor he placed the entire study next to a marble nymph in the embrace of her lover.

But his favorite became an amorous study in white marble which he called "Eternal Spring." Refusing to make any concession to convention, he designed a huge rock upon which the lovers reclined. Then as the rock formed a frame for the figures, he modeled a sunlit Adonis embracing a glistening nymph who knelt in a pulsating curve against her lover's body. He thought of Camille and himself, and made both bodies vibrate with sensuality.

Yet all this work was minor compared to the importance of his commissions, especially the monuments. One after another they came: a monument to General Lynch of Chile, his first equestrian statue, for the Republic of Chile, to be erected in Santiago; another to the romantic French painter Bastien-Lepage, a personal friend, who had just died tragically at the age of thirty-six, the figure commissioned by the painter's birthplace, Damvillers, for its cemetery; a third to honor the great French landscape painter of the 1600's, Claude Lorrain, ordered by Nancy, to be placed in the central square of the city; and two commissions Auguste especially prized.

The first was a monument to Victor Hugo for the Ministry of Fine Arts, to be placed in the Panthéon. Hugo had died on May 22, 1885, two years after Juliette Drouet, and had been buried in the Panthéon, not beside Juliette, as she had wished, after a magnificent, Dionysiac funeral which had been followed by two million Frenchmen.

The second, which he considered the most exciting commission of all, was requested by the town of Calais. Auguste, after competing with many other sculptors, was chosen to execute a monument in honor of the heroic burghers of Calais who, in 1347, had given themselves up as hostages to Edward III of England to prevent with their sacrifice the massacre of the rest of the inhabitants of the besieged city. It was one of the most dramatic of French historical incidents. After a heroic defense lasting nearly a year against the power of Edward III, lack of food had forced Calais to surrender. Then when the English king had threatened to raze the city and kill all the citizens, six of the burghers had offered themselves to Edward III, with nooses around their necks and carrying the keys of Calais, as the price for the lives of their fellow citizens. The story stirred Auguste as he had been rarely stirred. "The Burghers of Calais" became his chief love. He went to work on this monument with a fervor that was fanatical.

II

Boucher thought he was insane. This did not surprise Auguste, but he was displeased when Camille agreed with Boucher.

Auguste stood before the working model of the Calais commission, Boucher and Camille behind him, and he wanted to dismiss both of them. But Boucher had come to this out-of-the-way studio on the boulevard de Vaugirard, in Montparnasse, to be helpful and Camille had worked very hard.

It was midnight, and Auguste and Camille had been laboring since early morning, without anything to eat but a little veal, a bowl of cabbage soup, and some sips of Cointreau, and she was ready to drop; but Auguste had not finished. As if to show them that they were wrong, Auguste paced around the figures of the burghers in his carpet slippers while Camille followed him, awaiting his instructions but looking as if she were walking in her sleep.

Boucher repeated, "Not only are you insane, enlarging the Calais commission, but the hours you work, you will give yourself a heart attack."

Camille added, "He gets up at six in the morning, he's at the studio at seven, he never stops working except to eat. He works even by candlelight, night after night, like now, and the studio is so damp, if he doesn't get a heart attack he'll catch his death of cold. And he's having trouble with his hands. He's getting rheumatic pains in them, though he won't admit it. He'll have chronic rheumatism if he isn't careful, like his friend Renoir."

As Auguste paused in his pacing, apparently half convinced of his present folly, Boucher said, "And you work so oddly. You don't start one work any more and carry it to its conclusion, then do another. Instead you work on so many at the same time. No wonder you don't finish the big pieces, such as 'The Gates.' "

Auguste said, "I have to explore, and that takes time and variety." He had been working on the walls of the studio, stuffing the cracks with clay and old rags to keep out the cold, but his hands were getting numb.

Boucher said, "Camille, you talk to him, I can't. Originally he was supposed to do one burgher, now he wants to do six. *Mon dieu!* By the time he has finished who knows how many figures he will want to do?"

"Six," said Auguste. "I'm sure. No more, no less."

Camille said, "He will stick to his word. He has to. There is no more room on the stand."

"It has to be six," said Auguste. "Six surrendered as hostages."

"But Calais asked for only one," insisted Boucher. "Eustache de Saint-Pierre, the leader and the most famous. I know Calais is unhappy about your decision to do six. The citizens say you are crazy, the mad Rodin."

Auguste said stubbornly, "Froissart, the greatest historian of the age, said it was the act of six men, not one."

Camille said, "But six are so expensive, Auguste."

Auguste recited Froissart's description of the act: " 'The six burghers, bareheaded, their feet naked, with halters around their necks and the keys of the town and castle in their hands, said good-by to their loved ones, sure they would never see them again, shivering with fear, cold, and anguish.' "

"Oh!" cried Boucher. "I agree it is touching. But not sensible."

Auguste brooded. "How can I compromise? The six burghers didn't."

Camille said, "But Calais is offering the same fee for six as for one."

"I know," Auguste said gloomily. "What Calais has offered for the entire project will barely cover the cost of one figure."

Camille reminded, "You will have extra costs for the stone, the foundry, the casters, the architect, trips to Calais. Even for one figure you will not make any money. For six, Auguste, it could cost you thousands of francs."

Boucher said, "And Calais has been negotiating for years. Since 1845."

"Eighteen forty- seven," corrected Auguste. "But you are right about one thing, Boucher. There are so many negotiations I think I will go crazy. They argue about everything, date of delivery, size of the figures, where they will be placed, final costs. Then one moment they say yes, the next no. It is like a seesaw, and meanwhile I will fall off."

"Yet you work on it harder each day," said Camille. "Why, Auguste?"

Auguste ignored her, muttering, "All they have given me is promises, promises. No wonder I make such slow progress. What a difficult group! Groups are so complicated!"

"But you persist. Why?" asked Camille.

Auguste said, "It is a great opportunity for a sculptor. It could be a monument different from all others."

Boucher said, "At least with 'The Gates' it is definite, if you ever finish."

Camille said, "And we've such trouble with models—no one satisfies him."

Boucher asked, "Not even your son?"

"*Petit* Auguste," growled Auguste. "I use him when he comes home from the Army on leave, but he poses only for the francs I give him."

"He is good for one of the burghers," said Camille.

"I may have to use him because I cannot find anyone better. But good? No." He still could not forgive *petit* Auguste for telling Rose about Camille, though he knew Rose would have found out eventually. And the boy considered his generosity charity, which was most insulting of all.

"What about Peppino?" asked Boucher. "I hear he has returned."

Auguste smiled for the first time tonight. "Yes, without Lisa. When I ask him what happened, he looks so old, tired, and says, 'I was not meant to be a father, *maestro*. *Basta*, that's hard work.' Peppino was so unhappy, what else could I do?"

"He must have been out of money," said Boucher. "Is he still a good model?"

"When he's interested. But he is not right for 'The Burghers.' He is too noble-looking. He has the quality for a Christ. The burghers were not noble." Auguste was struck with a sudden idea. "The *grand seigneur!* Boucher, be quiet, look sad, dejected."

Boucher said, "I am sad, dejected, at the way you are wasting your energy."

"More dejected." Auguste held up his candle to observe Boucher, told Camille to get several more, and walked around Boucher so that he could see how the light fell on him from all sides. He studied Boucher intently, then said, "No, you are too effervescent." Stimulated, however, he resumed work.

Camille didn't join him, as he expected. She said hesitantly, "Auguste, I'm tired." She didn't dare say *exhausted*.

Auguste didn't answer.

But his severity made her feel guilty. She hastily picked up a candle, asked, "What do you want me to do?" angry with him for making her feel guilty.

Camille has her hero and she may live to regret it, Boucher thought sadly, Auguste can be a stone wall. Sorry for her obvious embarrassment, Auguste was so plainly disregarding her wishes, Boucher hurried to ask, "Has Calais settled anything?"

"I have the commission. That's official."

"What about the money?"

"When they raise it, they will give it to me. They are getting it by public subscription."

"You will never see a franc."

"I'm going ahead. Camille, show Boucher the figures. And look closely, Boucher. Remember, I want the truth."

Camille slowly and silently led Boucher around the six burghers, her candle lighting the way. Whatever she was feeling, she was careful to show them to the best advantage. No one said a word.

Mon dieu! thought the younger sculptor, the older man was right: Auguste had brought the burghers back to life in all the harshness of facing impending death. Yet there was also a feeling of grandeur, this was their own choice. The burghers were naked except for mourning shrouds which draped their sorrowful bodies. They were human sepulchers in stone, reflected Boucher. What a wonderful group! But I must not tell him, for then he will never listen to reason. Boucher exclaimed, "Why, you are making six Christs, when one would be difficult enough, and all of them different!"

"They are not Christs. They are human beings, like any of us."

"Not like any I've ever seen. And you've made them naked under the shrouds."

"Smocks. But I should have used sackcloth."

"I don't know."

Auguste sighed. "I don't know either. I don't want a cardboard effect, yet sometimes I think they are mediocre."

"They are not mediocre. Grotesque, perhaps, and Calais may be shocked by your harsh appraisal of suffering. Particularly since they probably expect something sentimentally beautiful. Have they seen this group?"

"No. This is the first time I've made them final size."

Camille said, "Auguste does his tentative models one-third or one-half final size. Do you like them, Alfred?" She looked as anxious as Auguste.

"It is not a question of liking," said Boucher. "One is moved or not moved."

Auguste, suddenly sure that Boucher was being evasive to avoid being painful, grew bitter and hostile. He stood there wishing he could turn into a block of stone and muttered, "It's not finished."

Boucher asked, "When will it be finished?"

"Who knows? I've much work ahead of me."

"Come now, Alfred," pleaded Camille. "The burghers are true, aren't they?"

"Keep out of this, Camille!" cried Auguste. "Keep out! He is against them on principle, whatever I model."

"That's so," said Boucher. "But you don't need me for Saint-Pierre."

"Thanks for the advice."

"Which you won't take."

"I asked you here, Boucher."

"Why?"

"You are as bad as Camille, you always want answers. You can't have profound thoughts if you are talking all day long."

"What about Camille? She is exhausted, Auguste."

"She can stop any time she wants."

"Then you will say there never have been any good woman sculptors."

"Do you know of any?"

"Camille speaks your language."

"Occasionally." Suddenly Auguste spoke with finality. "Everybody questions their dejected attitudes, most people would prefer drama à la Marseillaise, but it is true." He was immovable now. "I will remove the burghers before I change them."

"Will you stop working on the burghers then?" asked Boucher.

"Stop?" Auguste glanced at Boucher as if the latter were insane. "After all the work I've done? No!"

III

But when financial difficulties in the city of Calais held up payment of the fee, he began to spend more time on the Victor Hugo monument. He still worked on "The Burghers," "The Gates," and his other projects, but he attacked the Victor Hugo with a new fury, resolved to show Calais that the greatest French city of all, Paris, was waiting eagerly for his work.

A number of irritations drove him. He was furious when Dalou was selected by the Hugo family to make the death mask of the poet instead of himself. "Dalou is a traitor," he cried angrily to Mallarmé, who knew all the parties concerned. "I introduce him to the family, and then my good friend Dalou, behind my back, without saying a word, takes the commission away from me by telling the family that Hugo didn't like me. My friend, Dalou?"

"Hugo didn't like you," Mallarmé reminded Auguste.

"I didn't like Hugo," Auguste said sharply. "But that has nothing to do with it. I knew Hugo better than Dalou did. I saw Hugo under the most exacting circumstances. I would have made an accurate death mask of him."

Mallarmé said consolingly, "It is really not that bad. You will show the true Hugo in your monument and your busts."

That was another thing. Auguste was bitterly disappointed and very angry that the Hugo family had refused to accept the busts. They had said the busts belonged to Juliette Drouet and she was dead. But when he complained about this to Mallarmé, adding, "It is true I'm still not satisfied with the heads, but Camille says they are strong," Mallarmé replied placatingly, "The family thought you made Hugo look too old, undressed, without a collar or tie. But their opinions don't matter. They don't understand sculpture."

"Stéphane, tell that to Dalou, who's trying to do a second Hugo monument."

"I don't blame you for being annoyed. But remember, Dalou, though he is a fine sculptor, wants to be an *official* sculptor. I'm sure that when your Hugo monument is done no one will look at any other."

"I'm not so sure," growled Auguste.

Yet now, whatever he had thought of Hugo as a man, he was determined to show the poet at the height of his powers. As he told Camille, "No matter what I experienced, the people of France regard Hugo as a great hero, second only to Bonaparte."

The next few months Auguste buried himself in Hugo lore. Evenings he read everything he could about the poet; the following days he transmuted this into energy. He toiled intensely, with Camille at his side, often stripped to his waist to show that he was still youthfully strong. He thought how odd that anger could create such vigorous sculpture; the man he had disliked he was making godlike. For the head he used one of those he had modeled for Juliette, of Hugo bending over her tenderly—the world would accept it if the family hadn't! But the body was that of a younger man, with a feeling of illumination about it. Then he placed Hugo on a rock by the sea, choosing what he considered the peak of Hugo's life, his rebellion against Napoléon le Petit and his exile in Guernsey, where he had stayed like Bonaparte on St. Helena.

He lost track of time. All that mattered was how the work went. Boucher said that Hugo should be monumental, heroic, standing —it was expected—and he modeled Hugo sitting before the sea, part of the rock that had withstood the sea for centuries. He told himself he was inventing nothing, but expressing nature. He felt a glorious freedom as he modeled a naked Hugo, a Hugo who, whatever his flaws, had been always free. He stressed Hugo's nakedness. Naked because the sea and sun were naked; nature did not drape a natural element, and neither would he.

Mallarmé, invited to view what he had done, was surprised by the drive of the body and afraid that the public would be shocked by Hugo's nudity. But Camille agreed with his conception, and so, despite Mallarmé's fears, he refused to alter Hugo, except to improve him as he thought he should.

He was afraid he would never finish. The more he read about Hugo, the harder he worked on the monument, the vaster grew the difficulties. Each detail suggested a new detail. Like everything else he did, he groaned to himself, the more he desired for his work the less he was satisfied.

IV

It was 1888, and he had been laboring on Hugo for many months when Turquet came into his studio on the rue de l'Université to find out, once and for all, when "The Gates" would be finished. With Rodin's growing renown there had been more payments, totaling

25,700 francs. Enough to finish many "Gates," thought Turquet, but he must move carefully, Rodin was easily offended.

Turquet was surprised by the hundreds of pieces littering the studio, and annoyed that the sculptor was working on the Hugo monument. "The Gates" had been commissioned first; if it had not been for "The Gates," the other commissions might not have followed. Then Rodin was frowning, irritated at being interrupted.

Turquet decided not to waste any more time. He announced, "The Ministry wants 'The Gates' finished by next year, 1889."

"Impossible."

"We've given you the money requested. How many more figures must you do?"

"It's not a question of quantity. 'The Gates' move slowly, but the quality of the work will be good."

"That's why we want to exhibit 'The Gates' at the Exposition Universelle."

Auguste's eyes lit up. Then he grew sober again. "*Merci, mon ami,* it would be a great honor, but 'The Gates' will take a few more years."

"A few more years?" Turquet sighed sadly. "You will never deliver them."

"They are not right. They are close, but not right."

"If you show them at the Exposition, the whole world will learn about your work. There will be thousands of foreign visitors."

Auguste stopped work, turned, and faced Turquet. "Yes, it could be a great opportunity. But if 'The Gates' were wrong, I would never forgive myself."

"This Exposition will be the finest in our history. We are dedicating the Eiffel Tower; it is the hundredth anniversary of the revolution and the storming of the Bastille. 'The Gates' could become a patriotic monument."

"Don't you think I am interested? Do you think I like taking so long? Missing this opportunity? But I cannot show work that does not satisfy me!"

"Rodin, you are too critical, too hard to deal with. If you push us any more, you will lose all."

Auguste did not reply. But after Turquet left, he could not work. He stood in front of his plaster Hugo, eye to eye. Whatever his differences with Hugo, he respected the poet's refusal to compromise. Yet as far as his commissions were concerned, Calais, Nancy, Damvillers, the Ministry of Fine Arts, he was taking advantage of them—they took advantage when they could. Until he delivered the commissions, he had not earned what he had been paid. He thought the artist had no real capital, property, or security in worldly terms, only energy. Perhaps there was no such thing as security.

V

This feeling drove him back to his private work. At least there, he assumed, no one would press him. But now Camille became difficult.

It was one of their regular Saturdays at the intimate studio, near the place d'Italie, a clear sunlit morning, perfect to capture the contours of her lovely white skin. He was preparing to start a new nude of her, and she was objecting. Camille agreed that the burghers should be naked except for their smocks, that Hugo—as a French god—had to be totally naked, no one dressed a god, that the many nude figures on "The Gates" were essential—she accepted without question the nudity of the Adam and the Eve. Yet this morning when he ordered her to model for a romantic pairing, with the woman sitting on the man's lap, legs entwined, in a passionately sensuous kiss—the pairing to be called "The Kiss"—she refused. She said, "It is too revealing, too embarrassing, to be depicted in the arms of another man."

He could not admit that he had no intention of using her with a nude male model in the same studio—it would be a concession of weakness. He retorted, quite annoyed, "This sudden attack of modesty, mademoiselle, is unforgivable in an artist. You sound like the *petite bourgeoisie*."

For an instant Camille was amused—Auguste had called her an artist—but then her irritation increased, he had no right to be rude. He was a mule, she thought angrily, he hadn't paid attention to a word she had said.

Auguste, meanwhile, delighted with her animation when she was angry, ordered her to undress. When she still refused, he was irate. He was not going to involve her with another man; he merely intended to make her beautiful body an expression of love. She was being a prude, a fool. But he was attracted by the proud way she stood. Like Sarah Bernhardt in *Phèdre*, he thought, a tragic queen, determined not to submit, whatever the indignity.

She said, "Why don't you finish what you are doing?"

"You, too!" He was shocked. His voice grew harsh.

"Yes, monsieur."

He glared at her, thinking, This is dreadful, this girl will be my ruin, and muttered, "You don't have to stay."

She looked surprised now and said sharply, "You mean, *maître*, I am merely a model to hire or dismiss as you see fit?"

And Auguste could not explain. Every day Camille grew more beautiful and gave him such a desire to sculpt her, yet it was becoming increasingly difficult to do so. He had trained himself to create what he saw—he liked to say, "I invent nothing, I only rediscover what is in nature"—but she made him so full of feeling it distorted everything about her. Close to her, he could not be coldly observant, reflective.

When Auguste did not reply, his face expressionless, she said haughtily, "I'm not a *cocotte grande* or a *cocotte de luxe*, and don't tell me how much I mean to you. It is not enough to be told I am beautiful, that I make this studio attractive, it is still a *maison d'amour*."

Auguste, much as he desired her, could not endure her complaints any longer. He said curtly, "You don't have to remain. I'll get another model for 'The Kiss.' Margaret."

"She's too cold, too English!" Camille was horrified by his bad taste.

"Renée?"

"She's provincial. And she has such a petulant expression."

"Yvette?"

"A born housekeeper. Wait!"

"For what? For you to change your mind? I don't work that way."

"Please, Auguste." Suddenly, winning this point became more vital than anything else. If he gave in on this, she would be certain he loved her. It would be a sacrifice worthy of a true love. "Do something else, a head, a single figure. I'll pose for you nude then.

You can do a bacchante, replace the one that was broken so tragically years ago."

"No." That was Rose.

"Then a Madonna."

"Naked?" Even Auguste was shocked.

"Why not?"

"It would be wrong. Particularly for a Madonna."

"Yet you want me to embrace with another man."

"No, no, no!"

He was so possessive in his denial she suddenly glowed. "Oh, Auguste, why didn't you say so?"

He had said so! For an instant he wanted to spank her as a father did a child, she was so contrary. But he did have an extraordinary working compatibility with her, especially when his work was important. And he rationalized that she would be hard to replace. He stated abruptly, "We will do a new nude. I will decide on the setting as I work."

"You will not pair me later?"

"I said *no!* *Mon dieu*, she was becoming difficult!

"You did for 'Eternal Spring.' You modeled me as a single piece, as another version of the 'Danaïd,' and then paired me." She made that sound like a betrayal. "Auguste, you are not exhibiting 'Eternal Spring,' are you?"

"I've already sent copies to Henley and Robert Louis Stevenson."

"Will they recognize me?"

"No one will."

"Everybody will," she said pessimistically. "Don't you realize you will discourage the collectors if you keep doing these nude pairings?"

"I didn't ask you to study with me. 'Eternal Spring' will be exhibited as I see fit."

"It is so sensuous it frightens me."

"Good. Now I know I'm on the right track. Now we can concentrate on getting it ready for exhibition."

"Exhibition?" Camille looked bewildered. "What exhibition? You haven't mentioned a word about that to me."

He shrugged: why should he tell her? It was his decision, his freedom.

Furious with him for being secretive, she cried out, "One of these days you will have an exhibit under my nose, and I won't know a thing about it until the concierge tells me."

"Well, we are considering an exhibit in Paris."

"We? Who is we?"

"Claude Monet and myself. At the Georges Petit Gallery."

"The fine, large gallery near the Champ de Mars?"

"Yes. Georges Petit thinks it would be good to have it open next year, in 1889, to coincide with the Exposition Universelle."

"Such a great opportunity! And you kept this a secret from me?"

Auguste shrugged again. He hadn't told her the worst of all, that if the exhibition took place he had no intention of inviting her or Rose to the opening, it would be too embarrassing.

"Is the exhibit definite?"

"I will decide when I see how much work is ready."

"I will decide," she mimicked. "The new Louis the Fourteenth. What about Monet?"

"He is agreeable. We will not compete against each other."

"The Georges Petit Gallery is quite important."

"We will see."

"Are you showing 'Eternal Spring'?"

Auguste didn't answer.

"If there is an exhibition?" she prodded.

"Yes."

"Rodin, *père*, says yes, and I am supposed to be content."

"Yes."

"And 'The Burghers'? Are you showing them?"

"I'm not sure."

"They are practically finished. You have them in clay, terra cotta, and plaster now. They are definite enough to be shown."

"I said I'm not sure." He added quietly, "*Chérie*, we haven't much time left. I have to see how many of my pieces are ready for exhibition, and I need your help."

"What about the nude you wanted me to model for now?"

"I will do it later." He took her hands in his, held them caressingly, and said affectionately, "Camille, you are an intelligent and beautiful artist, with genuine emotion and understanding. We mustn't spoil that."

She stood bewildered, wishing he didn't hold her so tightly.

"After we see what is ready for exhibition, you can finish the head of me that you were doing. And if you like it, I will show it. I promise."

Proud suddenly, and ashamed that she had doubted him, she said, "I will work on it every free moment. So if you decide to have the exhibition, it will be ready, too, Auguste."

"Thank you." Until this moment he had hesitated to accept this invitation to exhibit his collected work. But now he knew he had to say yes. Camille's enthusiasm had convinced him.

CHAPTER 32

To Auguste the joint exhibit with Monet in 1889 at the Georges Petit Gallery became, as he told Monet, "the first one that could really matter."

The Georges Petit Gallery was gaining genuine prestige. It was getting high prices as well as selling frequently. And it was strategically located. The gallery was next to the newly opened Exposition Universelle, the largest in the history of Paris, erected to make everyone forget the humiliation of the Franco-Prussian War and to attract visitors from all over the world. It was close to the Eiffel Tower, dedicated a few weeks ago in a patriotic frenzy by a million Frenchmen, proud that it had cost fifteen million francs to build. And many distinguished guests had been invited to the private view.

Yet there were moments when Auguste could not believe that this exhibition was happening to him. Much of the time, even now at forty-eight, he felt he was just a brawny, barrel-chested workman who still got up with the dawn each morning for a full day of labor at one of his four studios. But when he said this to Monet at the gallery—where they were placing their work—in a moment of doubt about the wisdom of their joint exhibit, adding, "Our work is so different, Claude, this could be a *debâcle*," Monet replied, "We will survive. Both of us. And it is about time, for both of us."

"Seventy paintings by you, thirty-six pieces by me. It is much work."

"A lifetime. A truly retrospective show. And the first I'm truly satisfied with—that is being properly prepared."

"But if we fail?"

"We will try again. It is the only way to overcome the Salon."

Auguste was silent then, recalling his own bitter battles with official French art, and watched Monet as the latter continued to arrange his paintings. Monet's large body had grown sloppy with middle age, but he still looked immensely strong, a bear of a man who painted such fragile pictures. Monet's paintings were blessed with luminous colors that captured the quality of sun and air, thought Auguste, paintings that searched for the infinite nuances of light. However, the sculptor was sad at how much his friend had aged: the painter's broad, handsome features had become lined and careworn; his striking black hair and beard had turned a somber gray; his brown eyes, once so bright, were bitter now; his expression, formerly good-natured, had grown curt, rude, especially with prospective buyers. Yet this trait heartened Auguste now. For it occurred to Auguste that Monet, who had suffered dreadful privation for his painting—his beloved wife had died for lack of money, he had starved and frozen and been forced to beg, he had been ridiculed, scorned, rejected time and time again, but he had never halted, never changed, never flattered or compromised—must like his work, or he would never have invited him to exhibit with him. Now Monet needed no help to sell, he got a thousand francs a picture, he sold as much as he wanted to.

What pleased Auguste the most and confirmed Monet's assurance was the fortuitous circumstance that they had been born within forty-eight hours of each other.

At the private view they stood side by side at the entrance to the spacious gallery, greeting the distinguished visitors as one.

It was mad, thought Auguste, the world had turned upside down, this show might not be a *debâcle* after all. He stared incredulously as he saw Sadi Carnot, the President of the republic, who had been on the front pages of the world press when Carnot had opened the Eiffel Tower a few weeks ago, enter with Edward, Prince of Wales, who at forty-seven, bohemian and British in the same breath, was the ideal of the republican French *bourgeoisie*. Behind them was Georges Clemenceau, the doctor turned potent radical politician journalist, determined never to forgive Germany as long as there was a vote left in France. Clemenceau was joined suddenly by Eugène Guillaume, still director of the Beaux Arts and the ruler of French official art. Guillaume knew that Clemenceau could be Premier someday, though the royalists called him an anarchist. The line of visitors grew more interesting to Auguste as he saw Degas and Henley, arguing vigorously; Renoir, limping a little from his chronic rheumatism, with the usually shy, withdrawn Cézanne close to him; Daudet and Zola and Goncourt, together, and yet somehow quite apart; Pissarro, Mallarmé, and Huysmans, observing the exhibit carefully; Boucher and Carrière, coming to him directly with their enthusiasm; Turquet and Antonin Proust, looking like ambassadors from a royal court; the quiet, scholarly César Franck and his pupil-protégé, Vincent d'Indy, talking to Jules Massenet; his new friend, the dignified Puvis de Chavannes, examining every detail of his work; and the flamboyant Sarah Bernhardt, accompanied by Victorien Sardou and chatting loudly with Madeleine Bufay and Anatole France.

This was like nothing Auguste had expected. Overwhelmed at first, gradually—remembering his past—he found himself greeting the visitors with a wry amusement. A clean tricolor waved outside the gallery in honor of the President of the republic, the Exposition, and the exhibit.

The Eiffel Tower could be seen from the windows of the gallery. Paris was full of people from all over the world, and many were here, Auguste noticed. The gallery filled with top hats, frock coats, canes, beards. There was much leisurely strolling about, and a constant buzz of conversation. He could hear the clatter of carriage after carriage on the cobblestones outside.

Auguste whispered to Monet, "Such interest, Claude. I am surprised."

Monet whispered back, "Not interest, Auguste, curiosity." But Monet, for all his skepticism, looked pleased. There were some guests who were actually looking at the paintings and the sculpture.

Boucher, as excited as if it were an exhibition of his own work, exclaimed to Auguste, "Everybody is here!"

Everybody but Camille and Rose, Auguste thought unhappily. He tried not to think of the scenes they had made when he had told them he could not invite them to the opening—that it would be too difficult. The thought of their behavior agitated him too much, yet he could not get them out of his mind.

Rose had wept though he had informed her that all the pieces for which she had modeled would be shown, and Camille had stormed and taken to bed even when he had assured her that her bust of him would have a place of honor.

Didn't they realize how much he was giving them? The jealousy of women, he thought ruefully, was like nothing except the ferocity of the tigress. This exhibit was just part of his work, and it had brought them to tears. Yet neither had left, though Camille had threatened to. For the moment she was too ill to leave the studio on the place d'Italie, she said, but she would go as soon as she was well enough to pack. He didn't believe her, yet her threat worried and upset him.

As the world of art and society kept growing, he wondered whether the two households were worth the difficulties: the tense, self-pitying one on the rue des Grand Augustins, and the passionate, resentful one at the place d'Italie.

He felt better standing close to the plaster cast of "The Burghers," as if to protect them in their first public showing. He noticed that those guests who looked at his work looked most at "The Burghers," Ugolino devouring his children, his nude pairings, and the unfinished terra cotta monument of Hugo, and not at the "Danaïd" or "Thought," for which Camille had modeled, or at her head of him, which had the place of honor, with her name conspicuously underneath it.

He came back to the present with a jolt. Sadi Carnot, the President of the republic, was saying admiringly to him, "What an abundance of work!"

He noticed that the President was immaculately tailored, his square-cut beard perfectly barbered, that they were about the same age. He recalled that Carnot, an eminent engineer, had been chosen President because his father had been a hero of the republic, and his grandfather had been famous as the "Organizer of Victory" of the Revolution, and because as a middle-class republican he was expected to offend no one.

Antonin Proust, a special representative of the Ministry of Fine Arts with the return of a liberal government to the republic, hurried to explain as he saw Auguste hesitate. "A remarkable exhibit, Monsieur President. Thirty-five pieces by Rodin and seventy paintings by Monet."

"Thirty-six pieces," corrected Auguste.

"Prolific," said the President. "The two exhibits go hand in hand."

Auguste thought, I could be vengeful, I could write under many of my pieces "Rejected by the Salon," and so could Monet, but Carnot, staring intently at "The Burghers," had him by the arm while everybody else drew aside to permit the President to view the work unobstructed.

How long they stood before the six burghers Auguste could not tell. He had wondered about giving them such a prominent focus in the center of the gallery, but now he knew he had been right.

Carnot expected to glance quickly at "The Burghers," say, "How interesting!" as he did so often in his official role. Instead he stood transfixed, as if there were no sight in all of France but these citizens of France. He reflected gratefully that none of the burghers were dangerously republican or threateningly royalist, but in their anguish and courage simple Frenchmen who expressed what many felt yet could not say. And he liked the engineering, the way they had been grouped. He said softly, "How moving they are, Rodin, and so appropriate for the anniversary of the Revolution. Calais should be greatly pleased."

"I'm not so sure, Monsieur President," said Auguste, "but I appreciate your feeling."

"It is a superb evocation of one of our proudest moments. The air of sacrifice is heroic. Your doubts about Calais' enthusiasm must be a mistake."

"It is no mistake. Calais has paid me only half of what they promised. And even what they promised won't cover all the expenses."

"Is that why they are in plaster instead of bronze?"

Encouraged by the President's interest, Auguste gave vent to his grievance. "Yes, Monsieur President. Calais hasn't even money for the casting and the erection of 'The Burghers.' " His voice grew scornful. "Calais' Municipal Council would prefer one burgher, not six. I've so much other work they've gotten in my way, I've had to put them in a stable while Calais makes up its mind."

President Carnot looked shocked, but Auguste had to say what was on his mind, thinking he might never have another opportunity.

"Monsieur President, I take private commissions so I can afford the public ones."

Antonin Proust sought to divert Carnot, for the President looked angry now, but the President was not to be distracted, asking, "What about 'The Gates of Hell,' Rodin? You've been paid for them."

"They are unfinished."

"Most of your work is unfinished. 'The Man That Walks,' the—"

Auguste interrupted, "That is finished."

"And 'The Burghers,' the Hugo monument, 'Claude Lorrain,' are they finished?"

"Is nature ever finished, Monsieur President?"

"I am an engineer. I finish what I start."

Auguste bowed slightly, said, "That is the difference between us, monsieur."

Antonin Proust thought bitterly, Rodin is destroying this wonderful situation I was creating for him. The President's face had turned a flaming red. But before Proust could change the subject, they were joined by the Prince of Wales, who had overheard the discussion about "The Gates." He said, "I hear they are the talk of Paris. Everybody wants to see the victims, the punished. And they were my old friend Gambetta's favorite project, weren't they?"

"Yes, your Highness," said Auguste. "He was a great man."

"Did he ask for a time limit?" asked the Prince of Wales.

"It was discussed, your Highness. But do you tell a tree how many years it needs to be full-grown?"

"Trust an artist to have an answer for anything he does."

"Am I wrong?"

"I wouldn't quarrel with a man's art any more than I would quarrel with his taste," the Prince of Wales said hurriedly, to show that he had taste, too.

"Then you don't resent what the critics call my 'unfinished sculpture,' Monet's 'pictures of nothing'?"

"I am not a moralist, as you may have heard."

"Stone has no morality either."

"Oh, I have morality, which is a different thing. To be a ruler one must have morality, so that the people will respect you for the virtues they do not have."

"You sound like a Frenchman, your Highness."

"And was born an Englishman whose blood is mostly German. Rodin, you are fortunate, you are doing what you want to do."

President Carnot grumbled, "With official money."

The Prince of Wales said jovially, "But, Monsieur President, aren't you fortunate also? Here in France, unlike my mother's England, it is considered not only appropriate but admirable to like beauty, wherever you find it, and to support it with government approval and funds."

Disarmed, President Carnot nodded agreement and joined the Prince of Wales, who was greeting several women who looked beautiful enough to have modeled for "Eternal Spring."

Monsieur le Préfet de Police, close behind the President and the Prince of Wales, congratulated Auguste and told him that he remembered Monsieur Rodin's father very well. Auguste knew this was not true, but he nodded politely and moved over to chat with Sarah Bernhardt. She wanted the *maître's* opinion of her latest sculpture, which was even more awkward, and Auguste wished he were alone, while she wondered why he was so nervous and attributed it to overwork.

He tried to hide in the crowd, but that was uncomfortable, too. The gallery was full of voices whispering, "'The Burghers' are decadent . . . 'The Burghers' are ugly . . . Look at 'Eve's' *derrière*, and such a bulging stomach, she must be pregnant, how could he! He is worse than Zola!" He backed into a corner, but all he could hear was, ". . . and his nudes? He has gone too far!"

Then Guillaume angrily pulled Auguste to the front of the unfinished Hugo monument, where Clemenceau was standing, and expressed shock that the great poet was being shown completely naked.

"But we are all naked," Auguste said wearily. "'Naked came I into the world, and naked must I go out.'"

"Monsieur Clemenceau, this is blasphemous, to treat a genius this way," growled Guillaume.

Auguste disregarded Guillaume and asked Clemenceau, "Did you know Hugo?"

Clemenceau said, "For a few years. Until I disagreed with him."

"Isn't this the proper way to show him?"

"Proper? I would hardly say that."

Guillaume said, "The amount of nudity in your sculpture is revolting. If you persist in doing these nude pairings, you will never be bought by the Salon."

"Monsieur Clemenceau, what do you think?" asked Auguste.

"Do you care what I think?"

Auguste thought, Not really. He loved the body for the body's sake, not for sensuality—it was for him what the human face was for Rembrandt—but this was very personal. He said, "Clemenceau, you knew Hugo, the good and the bad."

Clemenceau said, "So, Rodin, your flesh tones have eluded the Academy. You are not the only one." He strode away, Guillaume trailing him.

Before Auguste could flee, as he longed to, Boucher was congratulating him on the success of "The Burghers," delighted that he recognized *petit* Auguste in one of the figures. "You were right to make six after all. Each one has a distinct character. I see *petit* Auguste in the one that has his and your nose. Yes?"

"Does it matter?"

"Of course. This is the peak moment of your life. Look, Degas and Henley are quarreling about your work as if it were their own." Boucher pointed to the painter and the writer, standing in front of "The Man That Walks." They were so vehement it seemed as if they would come to blows.

Auguste knew Degas was expected to be violent in his opinions, but he was surprised by Henley—Henley usually was gentler. He was curious as to what had provoked the Englishman.

He allowed Boucher to lead him to where the two men were surrounded by an eager circle of admirers, waiting greedily for the newest *bon mot*, for the taste of blood. Auguste became uncomfortable. He felt he should stop this argument before he became the chief target, but he hesitated. He was disappointed to discover that they had wandered far from the exhibition.

Degas' slightness had become stoutness, but his voice was as sharp as ever. Henley was still the hearty-looking male—determined, as always, to overcome his crippled body with the vitality of his manner—but Degas seemed determined to strip the writer bare because the latter had dared disagree with him. He snapped, "Henley, your judgment is appalling. As if anyone with taste would really want to agree with our *haute société protestante!*"

Auguste translated, "The Protestant upper class."

"I know, I know." Henley was proud of his fluent French. "Degas doesn't realize politicians get elected so nothing will be done."

"I resent that republicans have an obvious lack of *bonhomie*. Take Clemenceau!" Clemenceau had left a minute before. "He is a formidable speaker, a ruthless duelist, but like most rebels, he listens to no one but himself."

"Like yourself, Degas."

"But I am not a politician, I am an artist."

"Clemenceau thinks he is an artist, too."

"Henley, you know better than that. You don't care who rules, you don't have a political idea in your head."

"And you, Degas, have only one, that every republican is a Protestant or a Jew, and therefore a heretic at heart."

"Isn't he?"

Henley shrugged as if to say did that matter? Then he added caustically, "You believe this exhibition is political?"

"Of course. After this exhibit Rodin will be equally at home in the royalist salons and the republican ones and pretend to be neutral."

Auguste cut in, angry, yet determined to create a calm in the midst of all this quarreling. "Well, I do not agree with the republicans that French history really started with 1789, but I also do not believe we should return to Louis the Fourteenth, or even to Bonaparte. Things are not that simple. I do not like to be called a royalist because I care for Notre Dame and Chartres, and then on the next day be accused of being a revolutionary because I make the burghers humble men except for Saint-Pierre. I intend neither to degrade nor worship, but to observe." Auguste halted abruptly, as if he had said too much already; if his work didn't speak for itself, anything he added was only an admission of failure. Then Degas was not listening.

Degas said, "The Exposition is celebrating how wonderful the republic is, now that it is an empire. We have Tunisia, Algeria, Timbuktu, Madagascar, and soon Indo China will be ours. We won't need Alsace-Lorraine back."

"You mean that is what is wrong with this sculpture?" Henley said.

"I didn't say that."

"You know, Degas, Rodin's attitude that nature is right is artistically true."

"For you."

"And for Rodin. Reality is what the artist sees. You should know that, Degas. Rodin has imposed Rodin on his reality, just as Monet's reality is different from anyone else's reality."

"Oh, I like Monet's work," said Degas, "but all he can do is see."

"Yes? All he can do is see? Monet is only an eye, but what an eye!"

Degas asked, "Do you like 'The Man That Walks'?"

Henley said, "It has wonderful movement."

"Without a head?"

"Does one walk with one's head?"

As Degas for once looked disconcerted, Auguste—pleased with Henley's defense of his work—took the writer's arm to talk to him privately about the Hugo monument. He was disappointed when Henley did not share his enthusiasm for it, saying, "If you were modeling Shakespeare, Corot, or Delacroix, it would be worthy of your ability, but Hugo, I can't share your regard for him as a poet, he was so selfish, amoral, vain. Yet your 'Burghers,' they are a rock of Gibraltar, really splendid, splendid!"

"Would you prefer I do another Joan of Arc or Napoleon, when they've been done many times already?"

"I'm sorry, Auguste, but you say you always want to hear the truth."

Whose truth? thought Auguste. He wondered if any two people ever agreed on a work of art.

But now all eyes were on Zola, Goncourt, and Daudet, who were approaching him. He felt that this gesture by the three writers, once inseparable but today reputed to be friendly only in public, was just a wish to gain more attention and thus more adulation. The elderly Edmond Goncourt was still a handsome man with his shining brown eyes and striking white hair, but it was Alphonse Daudet who fascinated, bursting with vitality, charm, and victories. Daudet was the brilliant talker, while Goncourt was the great listener. Yet for all this, most of the attention focused on Zola. Perhaps this was why they were no longer friends, reflected Auguste. Zola had become the first writer of the Third Republic; the forty pounds Zola had lost for love of his mistress was talked about more than a cabinet crisis.

There was a limp handshake from Goncourt, a vigorous one from Zola, and an almost mocking one from Daudet, whose interest was elsewhere.

Auguste was aware that he didn't really know any of these men, though he had met each of them a few times. Zola looked gratified, saying, "I hear they are calling you the Zola of sculpture because your work is so realistic."

"Isn't it a little too realistic?" said Goncourt. "Oh, I know you are poetically inclined, too," he hurried to add as he saw Auguste frown, "but you seem excessively preoccupied with pairing—perhaps it is an unconscious salaciousness. Whenever I've gone to your studios, you were doing nudes."

Zola said, "But look at Ugolino. You can feel his hunger, despair. He is right out of Dante."

Auguste said, "Dante is literature. Literature in sculpture is a mistake."

"But you are a realist," said Zola. "Like me a little, perhaps, but more like Flaubert. I see it in your 'Burghers,' 'Adam,' the realistic 'Eve.' "

Yet others had called him a naturalist, like Zola, reflected Auguste, and some had called him a romantic, like Hugo, when he was neither, he was Auguste Rodin, observer, workman, sculptor. He muttered, "What does it matter what you call me? Sculpture is in everything if you look at the world that way."

Goncourt asked, "Which of your works do you prefer?"

Auguste replied, sensing a wish for gossip, "I like all my children."

"Even the ugly ones?"

"Even the ugly ones."

There was an awkward silence, and then Zola said with hearty approval, "The important thing is, the Academy hates and fears Rodin's work as it does our own. We must support his work, as I've supported Monet's."

There was another pause, and Zola left to talk to Monet and President Carnot, Goncourt and Daudet accompanying him. Not as friends, Auguste was more certain than ever, but to prevent anyone from obtaining an advantage.

Suddenly now Cézanne rushed over to Auguste, once he was sure his ex-friend Zola was gone, dusty and disheveled, looking as if he had traveled all the way from his refuge in Aix on foot, declaring in a quick spurt of emotion, "At least your work is not of some damned bourgeois!"

Renoir joined them, one of the few people Cézanne could feel at home with. There was a moment of silence, and then Renoir grinned and said, "Well, *mon ami*, you are part of the great world now. I hope it doesn't ruin you."

"It won't!" Cézanne declared. "He'll keep working. You'll see."

"I'll try, Paul," Auguste replied, thinking this one of those times when a bath would have made Cézanne a little more appealing. The painter's ancient black frock coat and trousers were caked with mud and dirt.

The three of them were watching the progress of the President through the crowd with Zola, Goncourt, and Daudet by his side, when Auguste had a shock. Lecoq stood in the doorway, all alone, very thin, very aged, yet trying to stand straight even as he leaned heavily on his thick cane.

Tears came to Auguste's eyes. He blinked them back. Tears were for children and women. But he longed to throw his arms around Lecoq, embrace him, kiss him on both cheeks. He excused himself. He was grateful that Cézanne, who could regard an innocent *au revoir* as a declaration of war, understood and was not hurt.

He offered Lecoq his arm and Lecoq refused. Lecoq snapped, "I can walk."

"But to come alone, *maître?*"

"Boucher offered to escort me, and Carrière. Fools! If I needed help, I wouldn't have come. But *voilà*, you see, I am here."

"I am deeply pleased."

"Where's the work? I came to see the work. Not a lot of parasites who belong on the Faubourg St. Germain."

Auguste showed Lecoq all of his pieces, slowly, carefully, ignoring everyone else. He sensed that this took an enormous effort of Lecoq's will and limited energy, but Lecoq refused to halt or sit down. Lecoq remembered "The Man That Walks" and was glad it had not been altered, grunted approval of the "Adam," said he preferred his "Eve," and said of "The Burghers," "The proportions are good—oh, you will finish it, whatever Calais does." He paused longest before the Hugo monument and observed, "You've made the old man naked. Good. He always was, really. Do they approve?" Auguste frowned. "No. Fine. You are on the right track."

"Do you want to sit, *maître?*"

"No, Rodin, no! Soon I will have all of time to sit."

"You are not amusing."

"*Mon dieu,* I do not intend to be amusing. I am eighty-seven. Did you know that I was born the same year as Hugo?"

Auguste looked surprised.

"But you thought I was dead."

"Busy, not dead."

"At my age?" Lecoq laughed. "But I have outlasted the old man. Hugo was always boasting about his circulation, his vitality, but I'm still here."

"And will be for a long time yet."

"You never could lie well, Rodin. How is the exhibition going?"

"The guest list is distinguished, I presume, but there are much jealousy and criticism. Everyone thinks himself a critic and has to find some flaw."

"Naturally. At the private view the guest has to prove that he belongs there, which means as a critic—having to be harsher than anyone else, showing that though he worships art he detests the artist."

"I am not sure I will exhibit again."

"If I had continued to exhibit, I wouldn't be alive today."

"You're teasing, *maître.*"

"No, I'm quite serious. If I hadn't stopped exhibiting at fifty, I wouldn't have lived this long."

"I'm forty-eight."

"But you are a better artist. And remember, when the criticism grows especially jealous and harsh, that of all the sins we commit, pre-eminent ability is what our contemporaries least forgive."

"*Merci.*"

"Besides," Lecoq said with satisfaction, "it's no *debâcle* this time."

"Perhaps."

"I am sure. They greatly underestimated you, but I didn't. You and Monet will do more to bring down the Salon and the Institute than all the shots I fired, and neither of you belongs even to the *grande bourgeoisie.* You will end by being invited to the presidential shoots at Rambouillet, the dinners and receptions at the Élysée, the race meetings at Longchamps—everywhere."

Auguste was skeptical, but too pleased with Lecoq's presence to argue.

Lecoq was thinking that this man had practiced the virtues which he had been content to praise. Then suddenly Lecoq was very weary.

Auguste escorted him to the door and waited until a comfortable carriage was obtained, not noticing that the President was leaving and that Proust wanted him to say good-by. He was still standing at the door, looking nostalgically after Lecoq, having promised to visit him as soon as the exhibit ended, when he was reproached by Proust for having neglected the President.

"Neglected?" Auguste was indignant. "He was impolite first."

"It doesn't matter," interrupted Monet. "Carnot won't buy any work, whatever you say, Proust. Come, a few of us are having drinks in the rear."

The few turned out to be a relaxed Renoir, an uneasy Cézanne, and a haughty Degas, who ignored Carrière, sitting quietly with Boucher and Proust, who seemed to have been invited as an afterthought.

"Only artists," Monet said to Auguste. "Except Proust."

"*Merci,*" Proust said sarcastically, but he didn't depart, as Monet appeared to wish. As Auguste muttered that the private view was a waste, perhaps even a failure, very few people had really looked at the work, Proust cried, "A failure?" Why, you attracted the most distinguished list in years! You outdid the Salon, you and Monet are the talk of Paris. This exhibit is a front-page story. And despite your bad manners, Rodin, I have news for you."

"What?" Auguste braced himself for a further annoyance.

"You will be nominated officially Chevalier de la Légion d'Honneur."

Stunned, Auguste could say only, "Like Manet—like Manet?"

"Yes. But first we want your permission. It would be embarrassing if you refused after we went to all this trouble."

"You will be nominated, too, Monet," cried Proust.

"I refuse," said Monet. "As Manet declared, it is too late."

Proust said, "But Manet did accept."

Monet said, "Manet was dying. No, I will decline it if offered."

Cézanne said hurriedly, "I would accept, Monsieur Rodin."

Auguste was astonished by Cézanne's desire for official honor, the painter was such a recluse.

"It is official recognition for all your struggles," said Cézanne. "But what about Renoir, Proust? He should be nominated, too."

"He will be. But it is going to be by the Department of Commerce, to avoid the hostility of the Institute. That is, if he accepts."

"I accept." Renoir smiled. "I am not so proud as Monet."

"What about you, Rodin?" asked Proust. "We are showing pieces of yours and of Monet's at the Exposition after this exhibit is over, as representative of the best of contemporary French art."

"So now I am a French artist? And not obscene?"

"You are the first sculptor of Paris."

"Of course," said Degas. "Now it will be official." He glared at Proust. "I wouldn't take the red ribbon if the Pope offered it to me. Whatever you say, Proust, it has the stench of the Salon. This desire for official approval is a disease that will destroy all of us if we let it touch us."

Carrière said softly, "I would take it. It is a great honor. And most important, Auguste, you deserve it."

"Thank you, *mon ami*. And you, too, Cézanne. Eventually you will get it also."

Carrière shrugged, and Cézanne blurted out, "No, not me, they would feel they were going too far. But I would like official recognition, just once. So they know I am alive."

Boucher asked Proust, "What about Degas?"

"He has declined. Several times."

Degas snapped, "I threw it back in their faces. Rodin, you are a traitor."

"I didn't ask for it. Why don't you blame Proust?"

"Because you will be the one who will be getting rich now."

Auguste flushed and said, "I'm still as poor as I ever was."

CHAPTER 33

Camille was gratified by the Legion of Honor, but not appeased, for it was Rose who sewed the red ribbon on the lapel of Auguste's frock coat.

Rose was proud, and for a time stopped feeling sorry for herself, while Camille felt better when Auguste asked her to help him choose the pieces for the Exposition.

He listened to her attentively, and Camille was pleased when he exhibited "The Age of Bronze," "St. John," and "The Burghers"— not even suggesting a pairing—and the heads of Proust, Hugo, and Dalou. She was amused about the Dalou bust, and attributed it to his need for revenge, for he and Dalou were no longer on speaking terms as Dalou persisted in his efforts to obtain a commission for a new Hugo monument and there were rumors Dalou would get it.

She was not amused by his preoccupation with his work. He was absorbed totally with sculpture, full of a nervous energy which drove him to many private commissions, to striking out in new directions for the sake of sculpture alone, and which made him impatient with anything else. Despite some negative criticism, many of his pieces had been lauded. "The Burghers" had created a furor. The press called it "a splendid depiction of our heroic history that should reach the heart of every loyal Frenchman."

Yet there was still a crisis. Calais was still without the money for the casting and erecting of "The Burghers," and they remained in the stable while there was discussion in Calais of raising the money with a city-wide lottery. His friends told him that "The Burghers" were too necessary to French patriotism to be discarded, and the waiting made him more impatient and suspicious.

Boucher invited him to lunch and informed him, "Now that you've had a major showing of your work, with the stir over 'The Burghers,' you are an important artist, a success, everything you do will be watched," and Auguste cried out angrily, "Is that why there is so much agitation over the Hugo monument? Showing it too soon has done me much harm. All they talk about now is how I made poor old Hugo naked, as if he weren't always. If this is success, I'm not certain I want it."

Then Camille and Rose didn't seem to understand his situation. He had settled into what he considered a permanent situation with them—there had not been any other women in his life since Camille —and he was proud of his faithfulness. He thought both women should be content with this, yet whenever he set foot in either's house he felt in enemy territory. Their discontent often made him violently ill.

The number of evenings Camille spent alone had increased at an alarming rate. She thought, Because I accepted him, he thinks I will accept anything. The idea of giving him up to another, even for only several evenings a week, brought a rush of tears. Then though he insisted that she was becoming a fine sculptress and that he would help her exhibit when her work was ready, she was coming to feel that nothing mattered to him actually but his own work.

One evening she accused him of that. Auguste looked shocked.

Suddenly he said, "How can you think that, *chérie?* I gave the place of honor to your head of me. Everybody saw it. The piece was much admired."

"And 'Danaïd'? 'Thought'?"

"They were admired, too. The 'Danaïd' created a sensation. If ever you wanted to make a reputation as a model, I would have a difficult time keeping you."

She didn't reply. She couldn't express the feeling that it hurt even more when he praised her as a model, as if her sculpture amounted to little.

"I'm sorry I'm so busy, *chérie,* but I can't refuse my own country."

"They will reject you if it suits their purpose. As they already have."

"That's unfair. Cruel."

And you haven't been! she cried to herself. She longed to tell him of the bitterness spreading in her because he refused to leave Rose and admit that she was the sole object of his affection. Yet she sensed that if she suggested permanence at this moment, he was so irritable over his difficulties with the monuments, he would allow her to depart rather than give in to her, however much it hurt him. If he would only give in a little, get rid of Rose . . .

But when she suggested that he leave Rose, he didn't respond. She flung her arms around him to persuade him, and he stood colder than any of his statues. "What's wrong?" she cried. She could feel her heart beating wildly against his.

He said, "I don't expect you to help me with my work, because no one can. But I did hope you would understand me."

"I do! I do!" But he should understand her, too.

"I can't change the way I am. It's me, that's all."

After Auguste was gone, after a night of love with the excitement of a reconciliation, she visited Boucher at his studio. Boucher was not surprised to see her, and he got to the point at once, hiding his annoyance at being interrupted in the middle of an important commission. "Rose hasn't got a chance. You are far prettier, half her age."

"Far prettier? I've seen her. She is still a good-looking woman."

"There's no comparison. Oh, Rose might have been a fine-looking woman at one time, to judge from the heads she modeled for, with a splendid posture, which always appeals to Auguste, but now, compared to you, she's almost ugly."

"Ugly? Then he will never leave her!"

Boucher was surprised.

Camille said, "Don't you know that pity is more compelling than love?"

Meanwhile at the large, gloomy house on the rue des Grand Augustins, Rose tried to pretend that part of Auguste was better than none. But as months passed after he had had her sew on the ribbon of the Legion of Honor and he did not invite her whenever he wore it, she grew afraid that he would never keep his promise to Papa. If le bon dieu didn't perform a miracle soon, it would be too late. And as he was home less and less, often skipping Sundays now, these became tense, furtive days for Rose. She was always watching him when he was home. He kept saying, "Rose, there are some things you don't understand," but she understood very well that there was this other woman, and how much longer could she wait for him to become bored with this affair?

Rose knew her love was indestructible but life wasn't.

He did remember her birthday, had dinner with her then, and gave her a hundred francs as a present, telling her to buy a new dress. But instead of feeling happy she was sad. The birthday made her feel old. And did he have to remind her, punish her? It wasn't her fault she was older than Camille.

But she said, wanting to be a good spouse, "You've sold a good many pieces, haven't you, since the exhibition?"

"A few."

"At better prices?"

"A little. But don't get extravagant because I gave you a hundred francs. As I told Degas and Proust, we're still as poor as we ever were."

"With all the studios?"

He gazed at her sadly. Poor Rose, she didn't have the slightest idea of what he needed. She was so distraught about what she considered his sinful life with Camille she had no awareness of how foolish her jealousy was.

"I hear that you could make more money if you weren't so stubborn."

"Who told you? *Petit* Auguste?"

"No. *Petit* Auguste doesn't go to the studio since you told him not to."

"I didn't tell him that. I told him that if he comes he must work like everybody else. But your son doesn't like to work. Even in the Army he didn't become more than a private. And since he has come out of the Army, he has been living on what you give him."

"Because you don't give him anything."

"Because he drinks it up, or tries to bribe the pretty models to go out with him. I'd be glad to give him a regular salary if he would work. He doesn't have to be an artist, though he draws well. But he prefers to be irresponsible, it's easier. He can't even stay here, he has to live in Montmartre. But think, Rose, if he worked in the studio and lived here, you wouldn't have to pay the help to spy on me, he would keep you informed."

Rose started to weep then, which infuriated Auguste—it made him feel helpless. But there was no change in any of the arrangements. She did not dare ask, and he would not have agreed in any case.

II

A few days later the Ministry of Fine Arts was ordered by the Commissioner of Public Works to place a copy of the Hugo monument in the Panthéon to see if it fitted their specifications. The Commissioner of Public Works, representing the city of Paris and thus being a natural enemy of the Ministry—which represented France—didn't say what the specifications were.

And the Ministry—instead of placing the plaster cast that Auguste had shown at the gallery as he suggested—ignored him and had a Beaux Arts student paint a replica of the monument, with Hugo standing on a mountain of rock. Then Auguste was invited to view it with a committee from the Ministry and the Commissioner of Public Works.

Auguste stood at the entrance of the Panthéon and couldn't believe his eyes. The Beaux Arts student's copy of the monument was a huge mass of papier-mâché and cardboard. Hugo himself perched on the summit of the rocks like a shop window dummy. The model was placed too high, without perspective. And the painting itself was an obvious copy of Bouguereau, the idol of the Beaux Arts, glossy and superficial. Auguste thought he had never seen anything so revolting in his life. He grew violently ill. They had desecrated the Panthéon and his work.

Absolute silence prevailed for a moment. Then the chairman of the Ministry apologized to the Commissioner of Public Works, "It is not quite done, but the finished copy will be fine."

The Commissioner said, "There may be other difficulties," and Auguste blurted out, "This is impossible." He wanted to shout this was a vulgarity, an obscenity, but they would be shocked. He said, "This student's work is too obvious, too decorative, like a gigantic poster. It might be right for the Moulin Rouge, but for the Panthéon, impossible! And it is too high!"

"Too high?" repeated the Commissioner of Public Works. "It fits the ordinance for public monuments. But will it be understood?"

"Of course not," said Auguste. "Sculpture, unlike painting, must be seen in the round, from every conceivable side, since the sculptor creates as much with the back and the profiles as the front. But this is painting."

The Commissioner said, "I agree. This is wrong. There are many pieces by Monsieur Rodin I should like to own, but this clashes with the Panthéon."

Auguste waited: perhaps the Commissioner understood after all.

The Commissioner said, "Monsieur Rodin, your rendition of Hugo is dramatic, but no one will be relaxed looking at him. Hugo is too intense, too naked. It is not appropriate. We admire your seriousness, but we want something our citizens can look at without embarrassment."

Auguste was silent. He stared at his hands as if they had betrayed him. The Panthéon was a morgue. Before anyone could comment further, he fled. It had started to pour, but he could not return to his studio. He paced along the quais for hours, getting soaked to the skin, aching all over. The wind grew icy and cut through to the bone, but he could not stop. He knew this arrondissement by heart, yet there was nowhere to go. He stared at the familiar barges anchored under the bridges to escape the pelting rain. No one was fishing today, even from the Pont Neuf.

He ought to store the Hugo monument in his concierge's damp cellar, where it would rot away like a cadaver. He walked on and on.

III

Auguste was pale and listless when Proust came to his studio on the rue de l'Université. It was a week later, and he had been unable to concentrate on anything since the distortion of his work.

Proust said, "You know I am your friend, *mon cher maître*."

No greeting could be more flattering, thought Auguste, and more deceiving. He said, "I know, Antonin. You are quite sure of it."

Proust ignored that, hesitated a few seconds, as if it took an enormous effort to go on, then asked, "Has the viewing committee written you?"

"About what?"

"Hugo. They are unhappy about the viewing last week."

"Unhappy? What about me? The model they made was dreadful."

"I know. It was not your fault. Believe me, they sympathize with you. But the fact remains, they have decided that to put a naked Hugo in the sacred Panthéon is unthinkable. The Commissioner of Public Works, who has the final word, says it is not fitting and has refused it."

"It must be Guillaume again."

"It is many people. The Commissioner heard there were many protests about the way Hugo was shown at the gallery."

"Hugo was not a chaste man."

"But people were embarrassed in front of your visualization of him."

"I was embarrassed in front of the real Hugo. But that is irrelevant. Are people embarrassed looking at the 'Venus de Milo,' the other Greek nudes?"

"We don't know them as real people."

"But an unclothed Hugo is shameful?" cried Auguste. "Yet Hugo was proud of his virility. Did he make love with his clothes on?" Before Proust could answer, he pointed to the plaster cast. "Look, his torso is as flat, as hard as a rock, his body the essence of human strength. Hugo would be pleased."

"It is a fine figure. But they want you to represent Hugo more closely."

"Representation isn't art, it's literature."

"*Cher maître*, it was you yourself who said Hugo is an outdoor figure."

"So you deliver me into the hands of my enemies by having the Beaux Arts reproduce my plaster with a cardboard mess. Monet was right to reject the Legion of Honor. You only gave it to me to obligate me, to make me obey."

"I am your friend, but the Institute still rules official French art, and we at the Ministry must move carefully."

"How did I get the Legion of Honor? It must have been a mistake."

"That's what they are saying at the Institute and the Beaux Arts. As for the Academy, they say it is a disaster. We have to prove they are wrong."

"Prove? That's nonsense. Lecoq said that Hugo was always naked, really, and that I am on the right track."

"Lecoq was a fine teacher, but they do not listen to him in official circles."

"Lecoq was right. We should send our student sculptors to schools of taxidermy to fit them for the exact iconography you want."

"Not what I want. As it is, it is a battle to get you a second chance."

"A second chance?" Auguste was deeply offended.

"They are quite touchy at the Ministry over 'The Gates.' There is talk of asking you for the money back if it isn't delivered soon."

"I've spent more money than they have given already."

"They want 'The Gates.' "

"Is the Museum of Decorative Arts started yet? A foot of soil dug?"

"The Ministry says that is not the point, that an agreement is an agreement. But I have a proposal that should satisfy everybody. Clothe Hugo, and have him standing, and it will be acceptable. They've told me so. And if you satisfy the Ministry with Hugo, they will be more patient about 'The Gates.' "

"I'll drape him around the waist. Like a Jesus. But no more."

"That's not enough. *Maître*, you are difficult!"

"Difficult? What about this?" He indicated his monument, which he had been unable to touch since the viewing at the Panthéon. "Is it to be left on my hands? *Mon dieu!* I had enough trouble with Hugo when he was alive!"

"If you drape him, it will be put in the Luxembourg Gardens. It is felt that would be more suitable for an outdoor setting."

"No."

"Reflect. Don't be hasty."

"No." Hugo had not compromised: how could he?

"Please. There is talk of Dalou."

"To do the Hugo monument in my place?" Auguste was shaken.

"It is possible. Dalou cultivates important officials, he has friends at the Beaux Arts—he went there, you know. Think it over. I am sure you can find a new concept for the Panthéon. I can persuade the Ministry to wait a little, but not too long. It is difficult enough with 'The Gates.' "

"The Gates"! How could he tell anyone that no matter how many figures he sculpted he required more? Hell had been immense to begin with, and now as he grew older it became enormous, a dissection that must go as deep as he was capable. But to be a state sculptor one had to be a whore, a slave, he thought bitterly, and a *bourgeois* with relatives in the bureaucracy. He should never have taken these state commissions, but remained obscure, working in solitude and peace, sculpting as he had to sculpt and should sculpt, away from interference, away from dictation and reproach, responsible to no one, to nothing but himself. He picked up an iron bar to smash the Hugo monument, and Proust grabbed it away from him as he cried, "You want Hugo altered, this is the quickest way!"

"No, no, Auguste. Modified. Impulsiveness will only help Dalou."

He did not wrestle away the iron bar from Proust, as he had intended. His flash of fierce, vigorous strength was gone. He escorted Proust to the door and said, "I will think over what you suggested."

IV

That evening he asked Rose what he should do. Rose said that he was not a rich man and that he could use the money, but she had some francs saved from her household money and if he needed it she would give it to him and he could do the work he wanted to do. He was annoyed at her for again hiding and hoarding money. Yet he was also pleased. He thanked her and told her to hold on to the money until he made up his mind.

The next day he told Camille about Proust's proposal. Camille was furious with the Ministry, but she said that he should attempt a new Hugo. "With your skill, Auguste, you can do anything." He told himself that he was not flattered, but that she was right, there was common sense in her when she added, "Does it make any difference to dead people where they lie?" for when he replied, "It would to Hugo," she pointed out, "Then you will have him in two places and Dalou will be defeated on both fronts."

Some strength returned to Auguste. A few days later he informed Proust that he would try to do a monument of Hugo standing, fully clothed, for the Panthéon. Proust was enthusiastic, and embraced him warmly.

Now negotiations began with the Ministry for two monuments, the new one for the Panthéon and the old—partially draped—for the

Luxembourg Gardens. There was the usual delay over terms, but Auguste went to work.

He had no feeling for a clothed, standing Hugo, however. He found himself returning to the original monument. He draped Hugo around the waist so the flow of line suggested the contours of an ocean wave that blended into the stone and the body. Then he asked Proust to view it.

Proust said, "It is solid, feasible, it should fit the gardens. How is the new work proceeding?"

"It isn't," he said gloomily.

But Proust insisted on looking at the new Hugo.

Hugo stood fully dressed on a traditional pedestal, fully recognizable. Proust examined the figure carefully and said, "Hugo is more than just an artist, he is a symbol of a France that was undefeatable and heroic," and Auguste wondered if the entire truth about any man could ever be known, since the memory of man was not only unreliable but preferred to encourage vanity.

"It's very bad, isn't it," said Auguste.

"Not too bad," said Proust. "It has a nice feeling of nostalgia. Keep working and you will find what we all want."

It was a relief when Claude Monet visited him. Monet was on a special mission. "Auguste, I'm organizing a subscription to buy Manet's 'Olympia' from his widow so that it can be offered France through the Louvre."

Auguste said pessimistically, "They won't take it. It's a realistic nude."

"We have to try. Many have subscribed, Degas, Pissarro, Fantin, Lautrec, Proust, Henley, Carrière, Renoir, Huysmans, Puvis de Chavannes—"

"And Rodin," Auguste interrupted, with his first smile in weeks.

"How much?"

"Twenty-five francs. It is not enough, but I want my name on the list."

Despite his own struggles with poverty, Monet was surprised and showed it.

Auguste explained—Monet, at least, would understand— "It is all I can afford. I may lose the 'Hugo,' I am in debt already with 'The

Burghers,' 'The Gates.' If I ever do another public monument, I am
really insane."

"What about the 'Claude Lorrain'? He was the first painter I really
liked."

"It's almost done. But you will see, my patron, the city of Nancy,
will find something to complain about and become difficult. It's inevitable."

"I like your 'Claude Lorrain.' It is of a painter in the act of painting, and painting what he loved, sun and light and air. It's true."

V

That was the difficulty. Lorrain had been a small, thickset man, with
round cheeks and prominent eyes, always searching the horizon, always striding into it in search of new vistas, and Auguste depicted
him this way and the citizens of Nancy were displeased. Carnot, still
President of France, dedicated the statue in June of 1892 before a
large crowd in the main public square of Nancy, and while he spoke
of Claude Lorrain as "one of the natural glories of France and one of
Nancy's greatest sons," the crowd listened respectfully and applauded
loudly. But the moment the President was gone the crowd jeered the
monument and threw stones at it.

The criticism went on after Auguste was back in Paris. He was accused of having slandered French art by making Claude Lorrain
homely, short, when as a French genius—though the painter had
spent all of his adult life in Italy after growing up in Nancy—Claude
Lorrain should have been modeled heroically and monumentally.
There was talk of having the commission done over, by someone
else, if Rodin would not alter it. So Auguste, to prevent the "Claude
Lorrain" from being destroyed or completely distorted, agreed to
redo the horses, to bring them more distinctly out of the marble pedestal. He was angry with himself for giving in, but he felt he had no
choice.

This did expedite the negotiations over the Hugo monuments, as
he had hoped. Shortly after he agreed to redo the base of the
"Claude Lorrain," the Ministry of Fine Arts informed him that the
Commissioner of Public Works had approved his clothed, standing
"Hugo" for the Panthéon, and sent him a thousand francs as an ex-

pression of their good faith. The Ministry also gave him another state studio on the rue de l'Université, larger and better located, and there was talk of another award of the Legion of Honor.

Auguste wanted to refuse the new studio—it struck him as a bribe to make him submissive—but a studio was the one thing he could not resist.

And it was easier to accept when Proust reminded him, "We live in a world where men are frail, contradictory, fallible. You must do the best you can with capricious institutions constructed by capricious men. There is no substitute for a good commission, however imperfect some of the commissions may be."

Auguste nodded, and resumed work on the new "Hugo" at his new studio. He labored so hard he got blisters on his fingers.

CHAPTER 34

He was still toiling at this feverish pace in his new studio on the rue de l'Université when Camille stormed in. It was quite late, even for him, almost midnight, but he was astonished by her rage. It was true he had forgotten to meet her at their studio at the place d'Italie, as he had promised, but he thought that did not justify her fury; he had become involved in his work and as a sculptress she should understand. He stood behind a plaster cast of a standing "Hugo," whom he had clothed in a flowing cape and large-brimmed hat, and gripped his chisel hard with his powerful hands. In the fitful light of the candles by which he was working, his face was rigid shadow and burning eyes.

She announced angrily, "I'm leaving. It's better that you know."

He stared uncomprehendingly, then looked incredulous.

"I'm not going back to the studio after this."

"Why?"

"You've fooled me. You promise, promise, and never keep your word."

He stood motionless, still gripping his chisel. Then suddenly he was scornful. "If you want to desert me when the ship is sinking, I cannot stop you."

"For ten years you have held me in a vise."

"Eight. And the vise is your own."

"That doesn't matter. No passion can last without fulfillment."

"If you wish." He turned back to the new "Hugo."

Camille had expected him to halt her, plead with her. His indifference was a shock. She wavered.

He said, "I warned you romantic love is like gunpowder and as unreliable."

"If you could only—"

"I made you no promises. You know the nature of my work. It is my life, sometimes holy and usually desperate."

"Because you are mad and must make everything nude."

" 'Claude Lorrain,' 'Bastien-Lepage,' 'The Burghers'—nude?" He stared at her with naked force, and again she was strangely moved. He said abruptly, "I'm being offered another award of the Legion of Honor. Should I accept it?"

"Don't ask me." This time she was not going to be appeased easily. "Besides, you will do what you want in any event."

"Do you like this 'Hugo'?"

"No." She had not even looked.

"It's this damned 'Hugo.' It's destroying everything in my life."

She was surprised by the sudden, unexpected note of self-pity in his voice. It was not like Auguste to reveal this to anyone, even her. For an instant she longed to console him, then thought, no, this was another of his traps. Yet she wondered if he really desired her sympathy, and if she had been too harsh, announcing her departure, but she could not retreat now unless he gave in first. She started for the door, wishing it didn't hurt so much. At the door she paused, said, "I'll leave the key with the concierge."

Her voice had softened, and his metallic mood melted and he came to her swiftly and said in his gentlest way, "I'm sorry I kept you waiting. I didn't think you would mind this much. But if it has really upset you, chérie, it was wrong of me."

Still overwrought, she repeated, "I'm leaving," though she was moved by his tenderness and this time looked at the candlelit "Hugo."

"What do you think of this 'Hugo'?"

"Don't bully me."

He said austerely then, "I thought you would say something special."

"You expect too much. Everybody will recognize Hugo. Isn't that what they want?"

"Yes. And nothing is more foolish." He looked as depressed as she had ever seen him; then abruptly, with a burst of revitalized energy that amazed her, he said, "I have been offered a commission to do a statue of Balzac, to commemorate the hundredth anniversary of his birth."

"You said you would never do another public commission."

"This is not a public one. It is being given by the Société des Gens des Lettres de France—Balzac was one of their founders—and it has been suggested to me by their president, Zola, who has recommended me for the commission to the Société, the leading group of writers in France." He saw her frown and asked, "Am I such a monster, Camille?"

"You are the only person I've ever—"

"Should I take the Balzac?"

"Why ask me?"

"I've asked no one else."

"You want to take it, don't you, Auguste?"

"Want to!" It was frightening how much he wanted to. "No writer appeals to me more. He is the greatest writer for me, not Hugo, not Flaubert, or Zola or Goncourt or Daudet, whatever they think of themselves. He was the first writer I read who wrote about a world I knew, that I and my parents could have grown up in. No one could read in my family except my aunt Thérèse, and when Balzac died I didn't know anything about it, I was only nine, but when I discovered him a few years later at the Petite École, thanks to Lecoq, I began to understand what Lecoq meant when he said, 'Do not invent, observe.' No one observed better than Balzac. La Comédie Humaine became my Bible." Auguste's excitement changed to sadness. "But they will never allow me to make Balzac as he was, really, more fascinating, interesting, and dramatic than any of his characters in La Comédie Humaine. He was obese, with a protruding stomach and short stubby legs, thick heavy lips, and ugly oversized features. He was gross yet full of sensibility, a royalist who wrote about republicans more accurately than anyone else, enormously complicated and difficult. And there has been so much trouble over this monument. Dumas, the day after Balzac died, started a national subscription for a monument to Balzac, and now, over forty years later, it still hasn't been done. Dumas ended in a lawsuit because of his efforts, and there is a statue to Dumas now, but none to Balzac. And Chapu, just a few years ago the best-known sculptor in France and a leader in the Institute, was given the commission, only to die before he could finish it. Now everybody wants it, Dalou, my friend Falguière, even my assistant, Desbois. If I take it, most of the sculptors in France will be jealous and hate me. It would be insane to attempt it, and yet . . ." His eyes lit up with a brilliant gleam.

And she was not deceived. Nothing would stop him from doing Balzac but death.

"Camille, if I take it, I will need all the faith I can muster. You cannot leave me now." He embraced her, kissed her eyes, her cheeks, her mouth. "We mustn't quarrel. I need you as my assistant, my first assistant."

She stood stiffly, as if he had not touched her, though the yearning to respond was almost more than she could endure. She tried to sound cold as she said, "You mean you will give me preference over Desbois, Bourdelle, Maillol?"

"When you deserve it."

"Do you think I am better than they are?"

"Each of my students has his own virtues."

"But we are not students. Maillol has exhibited and so has Bourdelle, and Desbois is one of the best-known sculptors in France. I am the only one of your first assistants who has not been exhibited properly."

He looked solemn, and just as Camille thought he was going to lose his temper because of her criticism he smiled and said, "I will arrange an exhibition for you. Puvis de Chavannes, Carrière, a few others, and I have organized our own Society and Salon, independent of the official one, and we will exhibit you. Oh, not because of any personal relationship," he added hurriedly, seeing her cheeks grow flushed again, "but because your work should be seen. You are ready now."

Give him up, a voice cried within her, he is not a true lover, whatever he professes, but a pitiless element susceptible only to sculpture.

Then as he said, "I have no one else I can trust," she replied even as she told herself she mustn't, "You can trust Boucher."

"As I can trust Proust?"

"You can trust him, too. They are both your friends. Like most men trying to bring opposing sides together, they are the most vulnerable, apt to lose both sides as friends."

"That's what I mean. I can't do without you. Your common sense."

Give him up, the voice repeated, give him up, this will not last, all common sense is against you, he will never leave Rose, never . . . !

"I will move Rose to the country."

"When?"

"As soon as I find a place. Then we can concentrate on the Balzac."

Auguste stood before her, as eager to model as she had ever seen, and his urgency filled her with an overpowering force. He was a fundamental element, like Balzac, she thought, his was the magnificent energy of nature. Now, at last, she understood him. His intolerance was for trivial things; he rejected comfort and ease so that he could find beauty and truth and expression.

"And if you like, *chérie*, we can go to Tours, to Balzac's birthplace. I will have to go there if I do the statue."

"If? How can you refuse?"

"It will be a kind of vacation for both of us."

"A kind of honeymoon?"

"In a way. We will think of nothing but ourselves and Balzac."

Camille felt strong again as well as clever then. She said, "Let us go as soon as we can." Before either of them could change their mind.

II

Now Auguste assumed they had solved everything, but Camille— when he did not move Rose out of Paris or take her to Tours the next few weeks—was not sure they had solved anything, though he applied for the Balzac, as she had advised, and obtained the commission. In return for thirty thousand francs—ten thousand to be paid in advance—Auguste agreed to complete the "Balzac" in eighteen months, and to do a statue ten feet high on a pedestal to match for the place du Palais Royal. And every time she asked him about his promises he assured her that he would keep them, but he was too busy at the moment. "Later, later!" he cried.

The eighteen months was risky, he thought. All his vital work had been done very slowly, and this was the most vital of all. The more he went on with his study of Balzac, the more he realized the vast task ahead of him and the more determined he became that his figure would be characteristic of a writer unique as well as extraordinary and complex.

He longed to go to Tours as much as Camille, and he intended to move Rose out of Paris, but there was so much to do first. Balzac had lived most of his life in Paris—eight years at 47 rue Raynouard, in nearby Passy—and the immediate urgency was to observe this world and then do his preliminary sketches. Moreover, there were other reasons he had to be in Paris at this time. The Commissioner of Public Works had refused his "Hugo" again for the Panthéon, declaring his new statue was sullen, and he was modeling a third interpretation. Then the Mayor of Calais had approved of his final cast of "The Burghers" and had assured Auguste that if the city-wide lottery did not raise enough money other means would be found, and would the sculptor please touch them up—they were still too tragic, unheroic. So Auguste, though he did not believe "The Burghers" would ever be erected at Calais, found himself making them more tragic and human. But also "better," he assured the Mayor of Calais. The Balzac gave his energy such a thrust he wanted to work on all his sculpture. He was able to work on the "The Gates" with a new vigor. He took several private commissions for portrait busts to pay for the trip to Tours and the move to the country. And it caused him to review the "Claude Lorrain."

He went to the Louvre to re-examine the painter's landscapes, to make a fresh and final judgment as to whether his monument fitted their mood.

It was the first time he had been in the Louvre in years. It reminded him that Monet's efforts for Manet's "Olympia" had been only half successful, the painting had been refused for the Louvre but accepted for the Luxembourg. And as he studied Claude Lorrain's landscapes, he realized how far Monet had come from this seventeenth-century painter, no matter how much Monet admired him.

In a sense, reflected Auguste, it marked how far he had come from the Louvre. What he had worshiped once was now a memory only of growing up.

The sculpture rooms still fascinated him—he had begun to collect Greek and Egyptian sculpture whenever he could afford it—but the students copying masterpieces as he and his friends had done years before struck him as provincials. When he left the Louvre, he strode slowly to one of his favorite bridges, the Pont Neuf, rested his arms on the parapet, and gazed at Notre Dame, which had given him so much sustenance in the past. In the dusk he could barely make out the cathedral's magnificent west front. He wondered if that was his difficulty with the "Claude Lorrain": he was too removed from the feeling that had created it. Then a young couple standing close to him in a passionate embrace, as if he weren't there, suddenly stopped laughing and began to quarrel until the girl wept and the man fled. Auguste decided he would not alter "Claude Lorrain" any more. He wished the girl would stop weeping; he hated tears.

III

Camille, after waiting months for Auguste to keep his promises, went to bed with nervous exhaustion. Auguste didn't know which way to turn. She had been helpful on his preliminary work with Balzac, doing willingly whatever he requested, their nights had been more emotional and amorous than ever. Yet now when he answered her demand, "When will we go to Tours?" with a "Someday—soon," she was not satisfied. He sat by her side and she insisted she didn't want medical attention. She lay on a cot in the studio at the place d'Italie, her head turned to the wall, and acted as if she wanted to die. She seemed on the verge of a nervous breakdown. He showed her new sketches he had made of Balzac and she refused to look at them.

This annoyed him: he was not a husband; besides, why did he have to be forgiven? Yet he took her hands, kneaded them gently, said, "I must do a statue of you as a convalescent." Suddenly he was absorbed. "I will do your hands. You have such unusual hands, like Balzac."

But she lay on her face now, hiding her hands from him, refusing to talk to him, to eat, to sleep, to weep, to do anything but lie there.

She looked so wan and exhausted that he said softly, "You need a rest. Would Tours do?"

She murmured, "Yes, but we will never go."

A few days later Auguste informed Rose that he was visiting Tours to study Balzac's birthplace. He told Rose decisively, after she had finished serving him breakfast, as he was about to depart, so that she would have no time to argue.

Then as she stood at the other end of their bare breakfast table, looking stunned by his sudden announcement—there wasn't even time to help him on with his boots or give him more coffee and eggs, he never ate properly when he was away—he kissed her on the brow and said, "I will be back in a week or two," and was gone, certain she would be here when he returned.

The studios were left in the care of his assistants. He did not tell them about Camille either, but simply that he was going to Tours for several weeks and that no new work should be accepted until he returned.

IV

Camille found herself in a large bedroom in an old provincial inn on the outskirts of Tours. Camille, elated when they had left Paris, yearning to view these quarters as a bridal chamber, was dismayed that the furnishings were shabby, with faded curtains on the window and a metal bed that creaked at the slightest touch. But Auguste surveyed the surroundings casually: as long as they had a spacious bed, and a window with good light so that he could sketch, it would do. He said the room was comfortable, and was satisfied. So Camille, not wanting to spoil his holiday mood, hid her irritation, though there was so much dust in the room she could not stop sneezing.

He registered as Monsieur and Madame Nerac, of Paris. "To observe the proprieties," he told her. "They will know I am from Paris by my accent." But he reassured her, "No one will know us here, however." And before she could take off her new, stylish flowered hat, purchased for the occasion, and settle into his arms, he insisted they visit Balzac's birthplace.

Wondering if *he* would ever understand *her*, she followed him down a narrow, winding staircase and into a feudal courtyard. He paused there to point out that the inn was attractive from the outside, in the style of a Louis XIV château. He liked the Gothic turrets, the stone balconies, and the delicate female statues in niches over the entrance. He said, "It's restful."

Camille, even as she seemed to agree, thought, Enough, enough! When is he going to really love me? The inn's architecture doesn't matter a damn if he doesn't marry me. But she cried, "Auguste, it is lovely!"

"I hoped you would like it. Monet recommended it. He comes here to paint occasionally."

"Did you tell him about us?"

"I don't discuss my private affairs."

"*Chéri*, I wasn't criticizing you. Where is the Balzac house?"

He led her through narrow little alleys and streets that dated from the Middle Ages until they came to a bridge, and there on the other side was the small house where Balzac had been born. They were disappointed to discover that it was a house without distinction. They did not enter it, but hurried to the public square, where they saw marble statues of Rabelais and Descartes, who had lived in Tours, but none of Balzac. Auguste didn't like these statues, and told Camille indignantly, "Rabelais would have laughed himself to death if he had seen himself so solemn and pompous, and Descartes would have said, 'How illogical and ridiculous!' "

No one was looking at these statues. When he asked natives if there was any of Balzac in Tours, they didn't know what he was talking about—they had never heard of Balzac. Finally an old priest, hearing Auguste's questions, said, "Honoré Balzac is in the museum," and told them how to reach it.

The museum was gloomy, depressing. Again they were the only ones there. The bust was high on the wall, almost out of view. Auguste disliked it on sight and said, "It is obvious, stupid, not even a good reproduction."

Camille nodded. The museum was a crypt, and she hated it.

But they loved Tours and the country around it. The rest of the day they strolled about the town and the countryside. The sun was warm and genial, and the light was bright, yet gentle. The land was a vast cultivation, a profusion of gardens and vineyards, dazzling flowers in bloom and shining green fields, orderly woods and carefully kept meadows. Camille suggested gaily, "Let's stay out all day," and Auguste smiled his assent.

Bathed by the splendid sun and the tranquil air, they paused before what Auguste loved, a real château with beautiful medieval arches, soaring buttresses, cornices and façades adorned with sculpture done in a delicate and subtle relief. Auguste was enchanted by the skill and grace of these anonymous Gothic sculptors. They gave him a new buoyancy.

I love him, thought Camille, when he is like this. I will always love him if he stays like this. They went back to the inn drawn deeper to each other.

That evening when it came time to go to bed, she put on a lovely white silk nightgown that she had been saving for this occasion.

He was impatient with it. He wanted her to take it off. He had caught a glimpse of her naked in a corner of the room and suddenly had grown conscious in a new way of her beautiful bare breasts and fine long legs. He sat on the edge of the metal bed, bare to the waist, halted in his undressing by the sensuous delight of her body. He pointed at her breasts with his sketching pencil and said, "You shouldn't cover them. I'll never see them properly then. You're a wonderful nude. Especially in this mood."

For an instant Camille was furious, but when he said, "You move so gracefully when you are naked," she had to laugh and say, "Can't you ever stop being a sculptor?"

He was amazed. If she gazed into a mirror, she would comprehend what he meant. However, she did what he asked and discarded the nightgown. Then perversely, he was sure, instead of striding about the room as he requested, she came to him swiftly and perched upon his lap in the pose he wished for the unfinished "Kiss." But he could not draw her now. Blood rushed through his body, he tingled with desire. She sat against him, kissing him with warm delight, and he could not resist her. He pulled her close with a physical passion that became rapture.

That night was the most passionate of their lives. The more virile he grew, the more sensuously she responded. Toward sunrise, when they fell asleep, they held on to each other as if they would never let go.

Camille was so happy she did not dare risk this joy by suggesting marriage. And Auguste, with Camille by his side, found everything in Tours beautiful. They strolled everywhere with a new zest. Eating, drinking, viewing a tree, a rock, a flower, sculpture, a landmark of Balzac, Rabelais, Descartes, whatever they did gave them an extraordinary sense of well-being.

The vicissitudes of life seemed far away. Paris grew remote. Here in the gardenland of France the disasters of state commissions, the fear of possible difficulties to come, vanished in a pervading joy.

Auguste, who had felt old in Paris, vibrated with the vitality of youth now. And this vigor was highly pleasing to Camille. She appreciated his strength; she was grateful for his deft, yet potent thrust, and his gentleness afterward.

In their elation they came to love with a new excitement. Never had Auguste felt better, and Camille prayed that it would never end.

Auguste was positive he would benefit from this renewal of his energy. He began to imagine Balzac as he thought Balzac had imagined *La Comédie Humaine* before writing it. When the time came to return to Paris, he was filled with a tremendous desire to start his rough models of Balzac. He felt a closer identity with the writer. It was time to work again.

Camille was sure he would move Rose out of Paris now, and eventually leave her. She knew her ideas of love were more practical than his, but this should not offend him—he had his work to occupy him. She thought, How wonderful it is that we love each other so much! How fortunate he is that I am here to help him! For all his strength, he would be helpless without me.

They arrived in Paris a month after they had left. Auguste had stayed twice as long as he had intended, but it had been worth it. What a fool he had been to worry whether Camille really cared for him, he thought. He left her at their studio at the place d'Italie, promising to be back that night.

CHAPTER 35

Auguste had reckoned without Rose. She was at the house on the rue des Grands Augustins, but Auguste, having stopped off first at his main studio, on the rue de l'Université, learned that she had been there, indignant and righteous, demanding to know whether they had heard from him. By the time he got home, he was in a temper. However, she matched his shouting until he thought he would go out of his mind. She announced that she was leaving. He had said he would be away a week, and he had stayed away four.

He felt his spine stiffen. He had an impulse to let her go, to be done with her forever. Then he moved quickly to the other end of the kitchen to protect her from himself. One day he would let her go, but now, alone, without him, she would become a ruin.

Rose said, "Why did you come back at all, Auguste? You don't love me. I don't think you even care for me, you never show any real affection any more."

"I do care for you. But you want too much."

"You need change. Always change."

He was not sure what he needed, but he was sure Rose needed him. She would be lost without him. "We'll move to the country. You'll like that."

"And never see you there? No!"

But when he turned his back on her as if to depart, she darted after him angrily, careless of her feelings, shouting, "Where are you going now?"

"Where should I go? You don't want me, *ma chatte*."

He looked so wronged she could only stare at him in surprise.

"Scold, scold, no wonder I don't want to come home any more."

"Really, Auguste . . . ?" She felt confused, dizzy.

"I'm not going to stand it." He was at the door now.

She knew she should let him depart, but where would she go? She started to cry, imagining herself in widow's black, woebegone, alone.

He moved to her side and she tried to repulse him, but when he put his arms around her consolingly she could not resist him. An immense emotion seized her. She was again the young woman who, when he touched her, craved him wildly, carried away by his strength, dissolving her will, her anger. She was glad he did not try to make love; she did not know how she would have handled that. He put her to bed, saying, "Rose, you are overworked, nervous. You need rest and country air." She did not argue. She appreciated his solicitude as he tucked her under a quilt and made sure she was warm and comfortable. He did not leave her that night, as she had expected and feared.

He told himself that he could not leave her, she looked so helpless. Camille would understand, and be amused.

Camille was not amused. When Auguste did not appear that evening, as he had promised, she felt ill and was filled with loathing for her situation. Only his pledge the following day that he was moving Rose immediately to the country appeased her at all. But she was impatient and said so.

He kept his word. Soon afterward he was able to announce to Camille that he had found a residence for Rose in Bellevue, a suburb of Paris close to Sèvres, where he had labored once in the pottery works. It was 1893, he realized with surprise, almost a year since he had agreed to this move. But now he assured Camille that she would have all of him—when he was in Paris.

The day of the moving Auguste stood outside the ancient, drafty house on the rue des Grand Augustins and felt as if a vital part of his life was ending. Virtually all of his life, except for the years in Belgium, he had lived within walking distance of this part of old Paris, so centrally located for an artist, and now he felt pulled in opposite directions, drawn one way by his love of nature, the other by his love of Paris.

Then as Carrière, who had become a close friend, supervised the movers he had hired, he recalled the day his friends had been the movers: Fantin, the leader, with his youthful vitality, his desire to be helpful, and thinking himself a new Villon with a touch of Delacroix; the easygoing Renoir, with his sly humor, serious only about his painting; the earnest Dalou, with his already gaunt features and determination to be the official sculptor of France; the proud, somber Legros, saying little but always dependable; the sturdy Monet, saying even less, but also generous and reliable; and Degas, inevitably doing the least moving and criticizing the most, yet for all his cynicism as distressed as everybody else by the accidental destruction of the "Bacchante."

The memory made Auguste sad. So much had changed. Fantin had grown disenchanted, a recluse, barricaded in his studio from human involvements; Degas, troubled by his worsening vision, had become more misanthropic, saying he would never exhibit again. Monet was less satisfied with his work, though he could sell whatever he did at high prices; Renoir was still amiable and retained his sly humor, though there were moments when it was cruel, and he was in Paris just for his exhibitions, living in the South of France for his chronic rheumatism. And Legros was always bitter these days, feeling he had not achieved the kind of recognition he had desired, though he was considered one of the world's best etchers; while Dalou, Auguste thought unhappily, was his most savage competitor and they were no longer speaking to each other.

No wonder Carrière was such a relief, Auguste reflected. The painter was without malice in a malicious world, though he was very poor because of his ailing wife and five young children. When he got a patron, he introduced this patron to other artists; he exhibited his friends' work in his own studio; he insisted on all his patrons seeing Auguste's work. The square-faced painter with his wavy brown hair, thick brown mustache, and gentle brown eyes was a man of unusual sweetness. Yet he worked as hard as anyone on his paintings, and was inflexible about his portraits. Neither Verlaine nor Daudet nor Zola, who had sat for him, had been able to influence him.

Now, however, Carrière—realizing that Auguste was too emotional to supervise the moving properly—was quietly but firmly making sure that everything was being handled carefully.

The moving was almost finished when Auguste's thoughts were broken by the sight of Rose standing in the doorway. She tenderly held a statuette he had modeled many years ago of her with the infant *petit* Auguste in her arms, not trusting the movers. She was smiling, pleased with Auguste's consideration, believing this move to the country could be a convalescence, as he had said. Rose had never cared for this house, hot and airless in summer, raw and chilly in winter, with very little sunlight and no feeling of being home, but she had not said so for fear of offending him. Yet when she saw Carrière, she paused and regarded him as if he were a dangerous animal, until Auguste introduced her as "Madame Rose," and then she blushed.

Carrière gazed at the piece she was holding and said softly, "A fine work, Madame Rose. I love doing children. I am always doing my own."

Rose turned pink, looking younger than she had for years, and said, "Do you hear, Auguste? I always said you should do more children."

Auguste did not answer.

There was an awful silence. Was he going to chastise her publicly? She held her breath. Then Carrière said, "Auguste does lovely children," and Auguste smiled and she sighed with relief.

Auguste said, "It's late, *ma chatte*."

"I'm ready."

"You will like Bellevue."

"I'm sure I will."

Carrière said, "It is pretty country, Madame Rose. The house is on a hill with a fine view of Paris. Auguste showed it to me before he bought it. You should get better there."

"*Merci.*" She felt better already. Auguste had finally introduced her to one of his artist friends. "Monsieur Carrière, I'm sure I will love Bellevue."

II

The house at Bellevue was "almost Louis the Thirteenth in style," Auguste informed Rose, "but actually Paris suburban." It was larger than any residence they had known, with three floors and many rooms and abundant sunlight. She agreed with Auguste that it was beautifully located, overlooking Paris and the Seine, and surrounded by meadows, orchards, and fresh air. She liked the countryside, the spaciousness, the air, the flowers, and Auguste praised Bellevue so much she was sure he would be home often.

Her enthusiasm gratified him. He felt he had made the ideal compromise.

Instead his life grew more divided. He came to the conclusion that there was no such thing as an ideal compromise. At his studios in Paris he devoted himself to Camille and Rose was excluded from his life, at Bellevue he tried not to think of Camille and took Rose for walks and tried to rest, and neither woman was appeased. He was proud that he had shown great consideration for each of them by moving to Bellevue, and Bellevue made each woman feel he preferred the other. No matter where he was one moment, inevitably he was going to the other place the next. And they had no desire to share.

He was given a second award of the Legion of Honor—where it had been the cross of knighthood, now it was the rosette—and while he wondered whether it was a bribe, for Guillaume was a member of the French Academy but he wasn't, he accepted it, but neither Rose nor Camille seemed to care.

The day he told Rose about the new Legion of Honor award she retorted, "You never use the word *love*. Is it so hard, Auguste?"

"Then don't sew the rosette on."

"You mean she can sew?" Rose laughed incredulously. "Of course I will put it on your lapel. You want it to stay, don't you?" When he did not reply, she glanced at the painting he was holding and asked, "What's this for?"

"It's a portrait of me. By Carrière. I thought you would like it, as a present, to hang here."

"It's a good likeness. But gentler than you are usually. What about this other portrait you've sat for, by this American, Sargent?"

"I'm hanging it in the studio."

"For her?"

"Do you want this one? I won't ask again."

"We've been together thirty years, and I have to beg for a kind word."

"Twenty-nine. And maybe that's been too long." With a flourish unusual for him he swung the picture about as if to destroy it against the wall.

Rose, horrified by his violence, grabbed the portrait then, but said he should place it—he would only disagree with her taste if she did. When the portrait was safely hung in the dining room, she detested herself for giving in. She knew she should hate him, this other woman was such a humiliation, but that would only make him indifferent, and that was worse. But as she sewed the rosette of the Legion of Honor on his favorite frock coat she kept sticking her thumb with the needle.

Camille had been hearing much in the last few months about Sargent's portrait of Auguste, and she was pleased when he insisted that she hang it in *their* studio, though she was determined not to give him any satisfaction until he left Rose entirely. She told Auguste as she placed it, "Sargent's is an effective interpretation." Her voice grew spiteful. "He made you look like Mephistopheles. Selfish. Cruel."

"Give it back then." His skin grew as red as his beard.

"No. I appreciate the truthfulness of the portrait. At least someone has kept his word."

"I moved Rose. I got you an exhibition."

"It did me more harm than good. Everything was placed so badly."

"That was Dalou. He managed the showing and I couldn't say anything, I would have been accused of being prejudiced."

"And tomorrow you will tell me that I don't work enough."

"You don't. Some of your pieces were admired, several bought, but—"

She cut in, "As long as I work with Rodin, I will be compared with Rodin."

"Not necessarily. Maillol has his own style, and so has Bourdelle. I've never told you what to do. Only how to do it. You have a remarkable talent, *chérie*, you are the first woman sculptor whose work I could admire, but you waste energy worrying about personal things."

"You don't?"

"I don't allow that to stop me from working." To prove his point, he went to his preliminary sketches of Balzac—he had done several hundred—and said, "I need models. Will you help me find them?" And though she knew she should feel honored, she also felt discontented and unfairly diverted, for he was pushing her into the Balzac with such force. She found herself fascinated by the way he was working as she helped him select the best sketches. He was examining them with an emotion amazing even for him and stating, "Lamartine described him best. Listen!" Auguste quoted, " 'Balzac had the face of an element; enormous head, hair disheveled over his collar and cheeks, like a man which the scissors never clipped; very obtuse, eye of flame, colossal body, joined to the head by a huge neck, short legs, and short arms. He was thick, square at the base and shoulders, but no heaviness, there was so much soul that it carried the weight lightly; the weight seemed to give him force, not to take it away from him; his short arms gesticulated with ease.' "

Camille cried impulsively, "A remarkable description! Can you fit it?"

"I have to," he said without looking up from his sketches. "I'll find it in the models we get. Middle-aged men. Not handsome, yet impressive."

CHAPTER 36

Now the call went out. Maître Rodin was looking for a Balzac. His first assistants, including Camille, scoured Paris for all the fat-bellied, short, stubby-legged models they could find. For none of the models available in the studios fitted. Peppino was too noble-looking, Jubert was too tall, and Auguste's other models were either too young and attractive or too muscular and well built.

None of the models his assistants found satisfied him, but he kept some of them, for now he had to sculpt. He cast the Balzac models in many poses, but continued to return to one basic conception: the head massive, yet unsymmetrical and too large for the body; the torso dominated by a stomach so fat it was a great protuberance, and too big for the short stubby legs—altogether a conglomeration of disproportionate elements. His assistants had searched all of Paris without finding this unharmonious mixture, but from some of the models he hired he got an arm, a leg, a torso, a belly. He thought he would have to come to this realization by many devious roads. After he had designed seventeen different clay versions of Balzac, all standing and all nude, he called in his first assistants to view the figures.

They filed in slowly, almost timidly, led by the intense, diminutive Antoine Bourdelle, a romantic from provincial Montauban, who loved to do large monumental figures, the soft-spoken Aristide Maillol with his Catalan accent, who had just turned from painting to sculpture and who had come to study with the *maître* because of his worship of the female nude, and Camille, wishing he hadn't involved her. They viewed with caution and deliberation. One careless, ill-advised word could infuriate the *maître*, yet criticism intelligently thought out and honestly stated—no matter how severe—could bring a quick nod of approval and even a slight smile.

The seventeen "Balzacs," on their temporary bases, each stood twenty feet high. Contrary to his usual custom, Auguste had not made his first figures one third or one half the final size, but seeking reality, had done them to the specifications of the monument, though this had meant a vast amount of extra work and the studio was so crowded there was barely room to breathe.

He said deprecatingly, "I'm just beginning. These are first drafts."

There was a hush. Then Bourdelle, generally the leader, pointed to the "Balzac" standing astride a huge, thick tree trunk, as if being born from it, arms akimbo, belly projecting, the legs thick and short but very powerful, and said, "This looks the most developed, *maître.*"

Displeased with their hesitation, Auguste asked, "Any more opinions?"

Maillol, who preferred work to talk, said reluctantly, "I like the satyr. The curves are perfect. And he was a little of a satyr, I believe."

Auguste turned to Camille. "Mademoiselle, which do you prefer?"

"Each has its own quality," she said.

"Seventeen?" He looked incredulous.

She nodded, hoping this would make him angry. If he was quiet he was indifferent, but if he was angry he cared.

But he was not satisfied with any of the figures, he knew suddenly. And his first assistants were not either, whatever they professed. He could tell by the way they shuffled their feet, coughed before they spoke, had to be prodded to volunteer an opinion. He felt smothered to extinction by their politeness. He said, "In art there is no kindness, only truth," but still no one spoke. Abruptly he dismissed them with a curt *"Merci. Bonjour."*

Yet nothing was ended but only begun. He could not lie to himself: the real battle was his. He studied the figures all that night, and by dawn he was working on seven of them. But he knew this was still an evasion.

He summoned Camille to help him decide which of the figures to concentrate upon, and he was disappointed when she said she preferred Balzac clothed. Now he knew why she had been evasive. "Clothed?" he repeated. "Perhaps." All seven figures he had chosen were still nude. "But first I had to make him nude, to get his body right. You don't make the clothes first, then the man."

She shook her head in despair, said, "Why ask, then? You never listen."

"Does anyone really listen? After all, when does one hear common sense?"

"But you are full of it," she said sarcastically.

"I? I am mad. To carve ugliness and at the same time make it magnificent is impossible."

"Yet you try? Why, Auguste, why?"

"You are no comfort." Now all the figures he had chosen seemed artificial and superficial. He went to destroy them and she halted him.

She asked, "What do you like?"

"None when I am this tired."

"When you are not tired?"

He pointed to the "Balzac" growing naked out of a tree trunk like a Hercules, the one Bourdelle had chosen.

"Then do it. You always tell me to follow my own instincts."

He did, but it did not end his difficulties. He focused on the figure projected from the tree trunk and found himself doing many variations of this "Balzac" without settling on one. He felt that these figures captured the fertility and vitality of Balzac, but not his grandeur. Many months passed as he studied numerous models, but none had the quality he wanted. There was no other income as he did nothing else. The ten-thousand-franc advance dwindled, but he could think only of Balzac. He read and reread him. He became Père Goriot and Rastignac and many more of the two thousand characters Balzac had created. He hunted Balzac as Balzac had hunted his characters. He had always loved the writer; now he came to love the man and his insatiable curiosity. And he had to express Balzac's enormous energy even if it took him the rest of his life. That was the secret—Balzac's energy! Once he found that in a model and translated it to clay, they would be brothers.

II

The Société des Gens des Lettres was proud that it was businesslike and practical as well as literary. When the "Balzac" was not delivered at the end of eighteen months, as Auguste had agreed, the Société informed him that this was a breach of contract and that they expected the statue to be delivered at once or they would revoke the contract and demand the return of the ten thousand francs. The Société added, would he please stop procrastinating by doing other work.

Auguste was shocked by their accusation. He wrote back that as far as the "Balzac" was concerned, he had been doing nothing else. He demanded an extension of eighteen months. He pointed out that the centenary of the birth of Balzac wasn't until 1899 and then the Société would have a statue worthy of the occasion.

He thought his logic irrefutable. Thus he was surprised when the Société said they must see his "Balzac" before they could grant him an extension, adding, "Monsieur Rodin, you do have a reputation for not finishing. Witness 'The Burghers,' 'Victor Hugo,' 'The Gates of Hell,' and 'Claude Lorrain.' "

He was indignant. "The Burghers" and "Claude Lorrain" were finished. His impulse was to crush them with his anger. Yet on the advice of Mallarmé, Boucher, and Proust, he replied in what he considered a conciliatory manner. He wrote politely that he appreciated the Société's concern for the statue, which he shared; therefore to make sure they would be satisfied, he needed more time. Then he would be pleased to show the Société the finished work. He ended his letter, "Sincerely and cordially, Your friend, Auguste Rodin." He was pleased with the way he had handled the situation. He was certain this was the end of the matter.

III

Thus Auguste was irate when a committee of five from the Société surprised him at work on the naked "Balzac," bound at the genitals to the trunk of a tree. He did not ask them to sit down or to stay. He stood apart from them, as if they were enemies.

Zola, still robust at fifty-three, the same age as Auguste, introduced the others: André Cholet, a successful playwright with an elegant style and a gentle manner; Victor Pisne, a noted military historian, a tiny man with a face like a hawk; Robert Berard, one of the many third-rate writers who made up the bulk of the membership of the Société; and Henri Rieu, biographer, who was determined to outdo Goncourt in smelling out scandal.

Auguste sensed that when Zola's term as president ended Berard and Rieu would follow either Cholet or Pisne, the two strongest members of the group. He saw that they were all shocked by the figure, even Zola; it was worse than they had feared, for when Cholet said, "Monsieur Rodin, we come with the best of intentions," Auguste felt instantly on guard. He asked, "What's wrong?"

"His belly?" Cholet looked baffled now rather than shocked.

"It hasn't fallen," Auguste said defiantly. "And his legs are powerful."

Pisne said, "But Balzac looks like a fat satyr on a gross picnic."

Auguste said, "Rarely does a statue succeed if it seems right at once." But he could feel that the others on the committee agreed with Pisne, offended because he refused to be apologetic. He added, "In sculpture I remember Rousseau and conceal nothing." He was very angry with them for forcing him to explain; the instant he started to explain his work he was finished.

Pisne retorted, "Did you have to make him so obese? Ugly?"

Auguste said, "If he is ugly, it is because you see him that way."

Pisne said, "Nonsense. You have a morbid, salacious mind."

Auguste turned to Zola and addressed him formally, though he knew him better than that, "Monsieur, why is it the sight of the human body gives so many people a feeling of shame when the Greeks were matter-of-fact about it?"

Zola said, "Perhaps because they are ashamed of their own, maître."

"This is irrelevant," said Pisne. "The statue is inexcusable. We must reject it."

"But I've invested all my money in it, all my time," cried Auguste, alarmed. "Everything I've been building would be ruined."

Pisne said, "Between ourselves, you've already ruined 'Balzac.' "

Auguste replied, "I admit I do not work swiftly, but the effect of the 'Balzac' should mount, like Balzac's own work."

Cholet asked, "How much more time do you need, *maître?*"

"A year, two. What does it matter? It will be done for the centenary."

Pisne said, "Suppose you become ill? Die? No, we can't give you any more time."

Auguste said with sudden fury, "I am not going to fail. This is what I have been waiting for all my life. I cannot fail."

"Everybody can fail," said Pisne. "Even a Napoleon."

Cholet said, "*Mon bon ami Pisne* is a military historian, perhaps, but art is creative, and cannot be measured in days and weeks and campaigns."

Pisne flared. "Anyone can see, even a Monsieur Cholet, that this will never be finished. And this figure—why, it is all phallic symbol. The trunk is just an elongated penis. All he has represented is the Balzac of *Contes Drolatiques*, Rabelais in the flesh. It is revolting."

Now Zola grew offended. He declared, "Pisne, I've always been fond of you for your analysis of Sedan, but now you are being silly."

Pisne retorted, "Zola, do you want this 'Balzac' to stand at the place du Palais Royal? In the heart of Paris, with the Société's name on it?"

Auguste said urgently, "This is not the final 'Balzac.' I may clothe him when I get the body right. But I have to decide. And that takes time." He turned to Zola. "Would you invite this committee to judge your unfinished book?"

"I want to give you free rein, but I won't be president much longer."

"How much longer?"

"A few months."

"I'll try to finish it by then. Give me six months."

Auguste saw a look in Zola's eyes that said, "I don't believe you," but Zola nodded assent, and the others followed, except Pisne, who said, "This is wrong. He will never finish. The sooner we revoke the contract, the better. I doubt he can even make a statue that resembles Balzac." But the others, still accepting Zola's judgment, were quiet, while Zola regarded Pisne as a nuisance and nothing more, thanking *"mon cher maître* for your courtesy and time," and then led everyone out so the sculptor could finish within the time agreed to.

IV

For a few months Auguste was left in peace. But this was a postponement, not a settlement. Six months after the surprise visit of the committee Zola came again to Auguste's studio, this time alone, and said, "With my term as president ending, *mon ami,* the doubters are growing loud in their demands that the Balzac be canceled. This matter will come to a head when a new president is elected. Then they may be able to get the Société to officially and legally demand the delivery of the statue or—"

"Or what?"

"They will want the ten thousand francs back."

"Are they artists, or fools?"

"Artists. If they weren't, they wouldn't be so difficult."

"It's not ready yet."

"*Mon ami,* you said in six months—"

"I was wrong. Isn't it better to be wrong about that than about the work itself?"

Zola shrugged. He thought, I have a reputation for being difficult, but Rodin is worse. And though he liked Rodin's devotion to his work, the *maître* was being unrealistic. Now Zola was certain a storm was about to break.

V

Several weeks later Proust, Boucher, and Mallarmé approached Auguste with trepidation. The door of the studio where he was working on "Balzac" was locked despite the heat which hung oppressively over Paris, and only their loud knocking brought him to the door. He didn't ask them in, as he usually did, though they considered themselves good friends, but he didn't halt them either as they pushed their way inside. They noticed that his eyes were bloodshot from lack of sleep, there was gray in his red beard suddenly, his thick hair was heavy with dust, as if he had been toiling alone, and he was wearing a houppelande, which resembled Balzac's Dominican writing robe, and that he had been modeling "Balzac." A new conception, thought Boucher, getting just a brief glimpse of it as Auguste covered it hurriedly to prevent them from seeing it. Boucher was hurt—Auguste had never done this to him before—but Proust got to the point of the visit so there would be no misunderstandings. Already Auguste looked ready to explode with anger.

Proust said, "*Mon cher ami,* we've come because we are your friends."

Auguste thought bitterly, Everyone is so polite and friendly, so full of *mon cher ami,* I can't trust any of them, not even Mallarmé. He flushed fiercely and regarded them suspiciously, not saying a word.

Proust said, "The Société has asked us to speak to you about the 'Balzac.' "

Auguste asked caustically, "As their representatives?"

Proust stressed, "As no one's representatives. But as mediators."

Auguste did not answer, looking haughty and distrustful.

Proust explained, "Zola is in Italy, preparing research on a new book, and Cholet is the new president. And while he is your friend, Pisne now controls the Société. And Pisne has always been for revoking the agreement."

Auguste began to roll balls of clay with his large palms, and in an instant had a fist. The fingers were tightly clenched, their severe curl showing anger. Then he opened the fingers slightly, and now they were talons, fierce and defiant. And the soft clay seemed to take on the strength of stone.

Proust went on, weary suddenly, feeling that he was trying to penetrate granite. "Pisne got the Société to pass a resolution that you must deliver the 'Balzac' at once or they will cancel the contract and force you to return the ten thousand francs, with damages."

"The whole Société agreed to this?" Auguste asked incredulously.

"Unanimously. Cholet, as president, couldn't vote. Then he is not Zola."

"And you are doing the devil's work," Auguste said scornfully.

Mallarmé said softly, "The original resolution was to give you only twenty-four hours. We got them to extend it a month."

"I see." Auguste respected Mallarmé—Mallarmé had never compromised his poetry despite the violent attacks that had been made against it. And the poet blended gentleness with firmness better than anyone else he knew. "What do you advise, Mallarmé?"

"Try to give them a working model, if you can."

"Within a month?"

"Yes. They insisted they would give you only a month, no more."

"Then this proposal you bring me is not a compromise but an ultimatum."

Proust said, "Let's not go backward. The future is difficult enough."

Boucher said hurriedly, "And I'm sure your new model will please them, if you clothe him and—"

Auguste interrupted. "And make Balzac heroic, handsome, a super man."

"Not completely," said Boucher. "But a little of that will help."

"No," Auguste said decisively. "Balzac was a great writer, but he was also very human. I will not humiliate him by putting him in a posture of heroic attitudinizing. Balzac would be the first to deplore that."

Boucher, still hurt by Auguste's refusal to show them his present work, said entreatingly, "Let us see what you are doing. Then we can tell the Société that you are doing your best to fulfill the contract."

Auguste said, "I will fulfill the contract by giving them the best 'Balzac,' not the quickest. But no one sees my unfinished work from now on. You saw what a disaster it was when the Société did that with their committee."

Proust asked, "Then what do we tell the Société?"

"That I am using the best armature with the strongest iron. That it will stand a long time."

"And when will it be done?"

Auguste paused, took in their intent faces one by one, and now, speaking with great deliberation, said, "I don't know."

"But not within a month?" asked Proust.

"Not within a month," said Auguste.

"And your promise to finish in eighteen months?"

"It was a mistake. It is always a mistake for me to put a time limit on my work."

Boucher cut in, "And they are worried about your health."

Auguste smiled as he said, "Do they want to put me in a hospital?"

"It isn't that," said Boucher, "but there have been rumors that you have been so tired and ill you will never be able to finish the 'Balzac.' "

"So they are concerned about their ten thousand francs," Auguste said sarcastically. "Not about me?"

"Yes," said Boucher, having the grace to look embarrassed.

"Well, I've been very tired many times, often to the point of exhaustion," said Auguste, "but they will not lose their money."

Proust said, "Then you will agree to return it if you don't finish."

"No!"

Proust was shocked. "But you said—"

"I said they will not lose their money. I will finish, whatever you think."

Mallarmé said, "I think you will," and Boucher nodded assent, but Proust—the memories of the difficulties over "The Gates of Hell" and "Victor Hugo" still painful in him—said, "I hope so, but I am not as positive as you are."

"It's the conception," cried Auguste. "Once I get that—"

"Suppose they sue?" asked Proust. "The Société says it will if you do not deliver the statue or the money within a month."

"Then they'll sue," said Auguste, controlled again.

Boucher said wonderingly, "You act as if it were a small matter."

"It is a matter of the utmost consequence to me. It could ruin me. But I can't give in. Mallarmé, you understand, don't you?"

Mallarmé said softly, "I think so."

Auguste said passionately, "It is not a question of integrity, or having to be brave. I am weak in many things, often cowardly. But don't they realize I must do it my way, that everything else is futile, a waste?"

A dead silence followed.

"Then you are against me, too!" Auguste shouted.

"We wouldn't be here if we were against you," Mallarmé said, and Boucher and Proust concurred. "We will ask the Société to give you another year at least, and maybe two. Yes, Proust, Boucher?" Again they agreed. For an instant everyone smiled. Then they grew solemn as Proust, always the official, asked, "What will you do, Auguste, if the Société does not give in?"

"What I learned a long time ago. Never hope. And do not hurry. Nature takes her time, and so must we."

VI

After this visit Auguste, though he had promised Camille that he would spend the evening with her, walked over to the Bois de Boulogne to absorb the stimulating scent of nature and sat there until the stars came out.

When they grew dim before the full moon, he strode over to the Arc de Triomphe and stared at the sculpture commemorating the victories of Napoleon.

Was this what he should have done? he asked himself. It would have been easier. It would have made more people happy.

And now instead of strolling down the Champs Élysées, as the crowd was doing, he turned off at the avenue Kléber toward Passy and the rue Raynouard, where Balzac had lived. At first the neighborhood was fashionable, but as he approached Balzac's longest-lived-in residence in Paris, where Balzac had spent the days dodging creditors and the nights writing feverishly to pay these creditors, the streets grew poor and run-down. The rue Berton, behind the Balzac house, was the old Paris, the Paris that Balzac had known and written about, a narrow, winding lane with heavy cobbles and ancient trees.

Auguste surveyed the surroundings as he thought Balzac must have done many times when the writer had been exhausted or needed a change and even the endless pots of coffee had not sufficed. Energy returned to Auguste then. He smiled at the vision of the stout Balzac, hurrying out the back door onto the rue Berton in his Dominican gown when his creditors had rung the front doorbell on the rue Raynouard. What a queer sight Balzac must have seemed to his neighbors, with his bulky body, short legs, and massive head, as he rushed down the street in his long, flowing gown. No wonder legends had sprung up about the clothes Balzac had worn! Then Auguste realized that at such times no one had seen Balzac's stubby legs and bulging stomach, the gown had covered them.

This made Auguste very thoughtful. Perhaps this was what his "Balzac" needed, a flowing Dominican robe from head to toe.

He was still contemplating this possibility when he arrived many hours late at the studio on the place d'Italie, where Camille was waiting. She had gotten the concierge to start a fire in the fireplace—the heat of the day had gone with the coming of night—and Auguste loved to sit before the fireplace with her, a screen at their backs to keep in the heat. She had also placed his carpet slippers by his chair —though she never helped him put them on, as Rose did—but he was pleased with her thoughtfulness.

Yet before he could tell her of this new conception of Balzac, she was grumbling, "Balzac, let the Société look for him in the Bibliothèque Nationale, you will never execute him to satisfy the Société."

This rebuke sent him angrily to his feet. Suddenly the studio was chilly even by the fire, and barren. He did not tell her about the ultimatum; she would only advise him to give in. But she knew about it—through Boucher, he guessed—and wanted to know what had happened, and when he told her she said, "You can't defeat them, Auguste, they are too powerful."

He was grateful, however, that she did not pursue the matter. She had a sudden desire for immediate affection, as if to prove that his lateness had been because of work and not another woman. And though he was still irritated with her, he could not resist her when she was loving. In the passion of the moment all the energy and intensity he had repressed this difficult day poured out in a great release, and their love-making rose to a new pitch.

VII

The next day Auguste felt there was only one person he could go to for advice. But Lecoq at ninety-two was in bed, feeble, and living in the past. It was as if the teacher remembered vividly everything that had happened to him as a young man and nothing that was occurring now.

Lecoq kept repeating, "Titian, who was one of my favorites, kept saying to the end of his life, and he lived to be ninety-nine, that he was just starting to learn his trade."

Auguste brought the subject back to the "Balzac"—what should he do? Give in or fight it through? And Lecoq murmured, "Yes, yes, I'm a contemporary of Balzac's, you know, born just three years after him. And Hugo, I'm glad you made him naked." Lecoq's voice faltered, and the housekeeper-nurse interrupted them and said it was time to go.

Auguste held out his hand in a gesture of *au revoir* and Lecoq clutched it grimly, as Papa had done years ago. But Lecoq had no admonition, no advice really, thought Auguste. Lecoq had aged terribly these last few years. The old man lay with his eyes closed, the sheet drawn up to his white beard, looking like a corpse. And Auguste was shocked at himself—he had never thought of Lecoq as an old man before, even at eighty-seven. He was at the door when Lecoq stirred, opened his eyes, and suddenly, fully conscious, said, "They can't ignore you now. You have no need of advice, Rodin. *Bonsoir*."

VIII

He heard the news about "The Burghers" several weeks later, while he was still waiting for the Société's next move. Proust had warned him that the Ministries of Fine Arts and the Interior were meeting to discuss "The Burghers" with the Mayor of Calais, yet he had not believed anything would come of it. But now the news that the Ministry of the Interior was having a national lottery throughout all of France to raise 45,000 francs to cast the group in bronze and to erect it in Calais, at one franc a ticket, drove away some of his anxieties about the Société. He did not like all the details, however, when Proust gave them to him.

Proust said to Auguste, standing before "The Burghers," which had been removed from the stable though the sculptor was still working on "Balzac," "The lottery will be for things people will buy. Wines, slippers, baskets, soap, lamps, pottery, all sorts of odds and ends." Auguste didn't say a word, motionless before a draped, damp "Balzac." The sculptor's fingers were still wet from the clay, the studio dark except for a flickering glow in the fireplace, and his eyes were focused on the statue.

"Everybody in France will contribute. Your name will be all over."

"On every kiosk and *pissotière?*"

"Why not," Proust said defiantly, "if it will get 'The Burghers' erected!"

"I don't know," Auguste said somberly. "I've seen some of the posters they've placed on the *pissotières* advertising the lottery for 'The Burghers.' It makes 'The Burghers' sound like a cabaret act at the Moulin Rouge."

"Just the same, it could help you with the Société."

Auguste was surprised and interested. He paused in his denunciation of the use of the *pissotières* for the lottery.

"If the lottery is successful, and it is likely to be—for a franc everyone should be willing to subscribe—'Rodin' will be on everybody's lips. Then the Société could get a black name if they press France's best-known sculptor. It can be pointed out that if 'The Burghers' took almost ten years you can take another year or two for 'Balzac.' Already, with the present interest in 'The Burghers,' the Société has second thoughts about suing you."

"They were going to sue me?" Auguste was stunned.

"They have been talking about it, as I warned you before, but now they are hesitating. But that happens sometimes. One work helps another."

But Auguste was disgusted suddenly by the lottery, and when Proust handed him a hundred lottery tickets, saying that if he sold them it would help the cause, he wondered, Whose cause? When Proust wasn't looking, having walked over to "The Burghers" to see the group better, he threw the lottery tickets into the fireplace.

The six burghers were gray in the dim light. Yet the very dark made the group more dramatic, thought Proust. The figures were impregnated with sacrifice. They affected Proust with sudden emotion. He felt they were fragments of the French earth. He said with a passion rare for him, "Auguste, they must be seen!"

"Yes," Auguste said.

"Then you consent to the lottery?"

Auguste hesitated, then nodded. Sculpture, when it was good, brought order even to a chaotic world.

IX

The lottery was a success. On June 3, 1895, almost ten years after "The Burghers" had been commissioned by Calais, they were dedicated there in a ceremony celebrated by the entire nation.

Auguste sat on the platform reserved for the honored guests and wished it didn't hide the group from the growing crowd. He was unhappy about the location of "The Burghers"—he had wanted them in the heart of the city, before the ancient Town Hall on the place D'Armes in the old town, which fitted the group's mood of martyrdom—but the city had insisted on putting them at the place Richelieu, in front of a new public park. And he was dissatisfied with the height of the group. He had modeled "The Burghers" to be just a foot above the ground, so that the citizens could feel at home with their predecessors. Instead Calais' Municipal Council had put them on a five-foot pedestal as a compromise, informing him that no one would see them on a one-foot base. Then he was displeased with the ornamental grille that the city had built around the group. And now that all the work was done, he realized that Boucher was right. "The Burghers" had cost him a considerable amount of money.

Proust whispered to him, bringing him back to the present, "The lottery has been a great success. Calais and the Ministry had to add only a few thousand francs to get the group properly cast and placed. And the Société has decided to wait a little while longer for the 'Balzac,' a year probably."

And Calais was treating him with respect. He had been made an honorary citizen of the city upon his arrival the night before; they were circulating a *Golden Book* at this moment, devoted to the history of the six burghers and to the work of Auguste Rodin.

But he felt frustrated sitting on the platform. He could not tell what the citizens felt. The onlookers were chiefly family groups, the children hushed to silence and looking bored. He longed to explain the burghers to the children; he felt that the officials, with all their pomp, were destroying the children's interest with a Machiavellian inspiration. But gradually when the glowing words of appreciation ended, a strange silence fell on the crowd. It was as though no one wanted to disturb the ghosts of their onetime citizens, reflected

Auguste, but as he eased off the platform and blended into the crowd he realized it was something else.

They were regarding the group as their own. The burghers were simple, plain men, men they understood and knew, as they knew themselves. Yet each burgher was lonely and apart, each one given life by his own particular breath and style, each cast in a mold different from the others. And as the crowd pressed closer, hushed and intent, the burghers became fellow citizens who had yielded, yet not yielded, who were suffering, yet would endure, who expected to be crucified, yet had come to that of their own free will.

A curious child reached out to touch the leader, Eustache de Saint-Pierre, to see if he was real, and could not because of the grille. Auguste longed to embrace the child and was furious at the grille.

Another child wanted to feel the knotted muscles, the taut hands. But what moved Auguste even more was when a child climbed over the grille and onto the base, gazed into the eyes of the burghers, and began to cry.

And as he walked toward the group, the crowd parted to allow him through. No one said a word. He stood before the sacrifice of the humble and felt their regard and respect. In this moment they were all part of the same: they were French, and proud of it, and something else, part of the human race.

What finally shattered Auguste's reverie was the screech of the train whistle returning to Paris. The train was waiting for him, he realized, a special wait, just for him. He was pleased and touched when Carrière said as they hurried to the railroad station in the Mayor's official carriage, "One has to see 'The Burghers' in the open to realize what you have done, that you have planted their roots in our earth."

CHAPTER 37

Auguste was still bathing in the consummation of "The Burghers" when he had a visitor who stunned him. He had returned to a clay study of a Balzac head, working alone this June Sunday in his studio on the rue de l'Université, and his half sister, Clotilde, stood in the doorway. He would not have recognized her if she had not told him who she was. She had aged so; not a trace of the very pretty girl remained; she had become a hag. But now she approached him with an air of defiance, which he sensed was actually an act of desperation. She wore a thick coat of rouge, arched eyebrows, hair that was not her own, and a hideous zebra-striped hobble skirt. He was sad, remembering her beautiful dark complexion and black hair.

And while he was still recovering from his surprise and trying to hide his shock, she blurted out, "I saw your name on a kiosk near the place du Carrousel. In big letters. At first I couldn't believe it was you, this advertisement for a lottery. Then I remembered that as a little boy you liked to draw, so I took a couple of tickets. They were only a franc apiece, you know. But I didn't like the wine I got. It was poor, mostly water."

He didn't ask her what she had been doing. Whatever it was, it had not been good for her.

Then she said, "You look so much older than I expected."

He never told other people they had aged. He said nothing, but continued to look startled.

"Oh, I know it's a surprise. I've had a hard time. I've been in St. Lazare. Several times. Elsewhere. They took my card away."

So Papa had been right, he thought sorrowfully. He said, "I'm sorry."

"Don't be sorry. Papa predicted it, didn't he?"

Auguste didn't reply.

"But if Gaston hadn't deserted me when I walked out—" She shrugged. "It's too late now. How's Marie?"

"Dead. She's been dead many years. She died soon after you left." And though it had been a long time ago, his eyes began to mist.

"She tried to keep in touch with me, but it became impossible."

"Yes." He could still remember Marie's small oval face, her reddish-blonde hair, her simple dark dresses with her preference for white collars and her love of lace, but then they could not afford lace. He choked up.

"And Mama?" Mama had been her stepmother.

"She died when I was in Belgium, twenty-four years ago."

"You won't mind if I visit her grave?"

"There is no grave. They had no money when she died, and many were dying—it was the days just after the Commune. Do you want to see Papa's?"

"No."

"Papa was your blood relative."

"Not really." For the first time she actually gazed at the studio and the vast amount of sculpture that filled it. "Are you truly so successful now, Auguste, my little brother, Auguste?"

"It's a matter of perspective. People talk about me, order my sculpture, but I'm still in debt."

She paused, then asked, "Do you have a family?"

"I have obligations, responsibilities."

"Children?"

"None that I want to talk about."

"Are you really still poor? With all the money that came from the lottery?"

"I got none of it. It went to the cost of erecting the figures, the casting."

"How much money do you have?"

He answered abruptly, "How much money do you have?"

"Ten centimes." She said suddenly, "You're judging me."

"Of course not." He handed her twenty francs.

She said, "Mama would have been proud of you."

"I doubt it. She didn't know anything about sculpture."

"Do you have many famous friends?"

He handed her twenty more francs, all that he had left in his pocket. He said, "Come again if you need help." He had a feeling that she wouldn't.

She hesitated, then asked, "Is Aunt Thérèse alive? I liked Aunt Thérèse."

He was full of guilt suddenly. He hadn't seen his aunt for a long time. He said, "She is alive. But not well." He looked grave.

Clotilde was amazed by the fervent way he regarded his statues, as if he were in a church, receiving a benediction from them, and she had to ask, "Are all these pieces yours?"

"Yes." He moved closer to them, until he was surrounded by them.

"Really!" Now that she had what she had come for, she felt more at ease. But she was surprised by the number of pieces, and their nature. There must be several hundred here, she thought, heads, torsos, legs, arms—and nudes, so many nudes. She had never seen so many different versions of the naked body, male and female, even in her own work. She was shocked that her little brother had come to this. "You made all these naked people?"

He nodded casually, picked up a huge clenched hand he had been modeling in plaster, and said, "I could give you this."

"But it is so ugly," she burst out. "I'm sorry, I didn't mean to offend you, but it's not my taste. Yet I'm sure it has some value."

He flushed, but said quietly, "Nothing is ugly in sculpture unless we see it that way. Clotilde, what should I tell Aunt Thérèse?"

"Don't tell her that you saw me." When she saw him look critical, she hastened to add, "Oh, she would want to help me, and I don't need help, not a sou. I'll return your francs. Soon. You'll see." She was grateful that he did not attempt to disagree with her.

They exchanged *bonjours*. He watched her walk away defiantly, though age and fatigue lay heavily upon her. He thought the years apart had created too wide a gulf. Her last sight of him was of a stocky, wide-shouldered man whose thick red beard and heavy hair were turning gray, but whose hands were lively, remodeling a huge clay head with an authority that amazed her.

II

The next Sunday, Auguste went to see Aunt Thérèse. It was the first time he had visited her in years, since Camille had become a part of his life. But he had kept himself informed of her circumstances through her son, his first cousin and a good friend, with whom she was living in a working-class district.

He entered the small stone house with apprehension, afraid of what he would find. Aunt Thérèse was going on eighty; she had been ill often the past few years, and he expected to find a bedridden invalid. Instead, though she seemed to have shrunk to half the size he remembered as a child and looked very old, her face deeply lined, her hair completely white, she rose out of her rocking chair the instant she saw him. She insisted on serving him wine, coffee, and *croissants*, proud that she could still do things by herself. She knew about his work—she had newspaper articles pasted on the walls of her living room, describing his commissions and achievements, with the prominence given to articles on "The Burghers," the "Balzac," and the "Victor Hugo"—but she didn't want to talk about them, regarding them as accomplished.

Family was her concern. She was afraid that this unexpected visit was because he had to tell her about a new woman, another child. When he assured her that he was still living with Rose, she sighed with relief, though she was disappointed that Rose never visited her any more. He didn't tell her that Rose wanted to visit her, but he had forbidden it, fearful that Rose would talk about Camille. And that was his business, no one else's.

Aunt Thérèse asked in a sudden explosion of emotion, "How is Rose? The boy? I miss Jean so! The stubborn old man! If he were alive, he'd visit me."

Auguste assured her, "Rose and the boy are satisfactory, and I keep fresh flowers growing on Papa's grave. Aunt Thérèse, do you need any help?"

She looked insulted and said tartly, "I'm past that." Then her tone softened, "You ought to legitimatize the boy."

Color deepened in Auguste's cheeks, but he did not retort angrily, as was his impulse, for he saw how proudly she wore her wedding ring—achieved finally, long after her three boys had grown up.

She said, "You won't desert them? Many women must seek you out now."

"That's exaggerated."

"Rose is a good woman. You can trust her."

"She doesn't have to worry. I said I would take care of her."

"Is that all?"

He fondled the rosette of the Legion of Honor, which he had worn because he had thought it would please her. But she had not even noticed it. There was a moment of silence, and then she came to his side as she had done when he had been a child, took his hands in hers, and brought them to her lips.

And now from her small height she looked up into his blue-gray eyes and said softly, "I know I sound like an interfering old lady, chéri, but you have such fine hands, they do so much, sometimes I think they were given to you by God, is it too much to ask this of them?"

She clung to him with emotion, and he recalled how she had always defended him; of all the family she had understood him best. He took his hands out of hers but did not withdraw them, as she feared, but embraced her with an expression of feeling rare for him and said, "I will do the best I can, Aunt Thérèse, as I promised Papa."

That evening he went directly to Bellevue, told Rose that he had just seen Aunt Thérèse, and suggested that she visit her, too. Rose was delighted. When he got petit Auguste's address from her, saying he wanted to bring the boy back into the studio, she was happier than she had been for a long time.

It was like a sign from heaven, she thought, though she knew it didn't mean everything would happen as she desired—there were too many irritations between father and son for that. But all she said was, "Don't be too hard on him, Auguste, he's had some hard times," and he surprised her by not resenting that, saying, "We've all had hard times, ma chatte, especially Aunt Thérèse. I wouldn't say anything that would upset her." And Rose promised to be cheerful and hopeful, and to say nothing negative.

It was almost a week later before Auguste could visit *petit* Auguste. He thought the boy made a poor figure, unshaven, almost in rags, living in a hut in Montmartre, just around the corner from the newly erected Sacré Coeur.

After an exchange of greetings the son waited for the father to speak—it was the custom. He didn't invite Auguste in, and Auguste didn't suggest it.

He got to the point quickly. "Would you like to return to the studio?"

Petit Auguste was surprised. His father's tone was unusually soft. His father almost looked guilty. He said, "It depends."

"On what?" Auguste's voice sharpened a little.

"On what I am to do."

"You will do what everybody does. Work."

"At what? Sweeping, cleaning, being no more than a concierge?"

"I still need a good secretary. But you would have to shave, comb your hair, wear clean clothes, stop playing the bohemian."

"And be your son?"

Was *petit* Auguste taunting him? Auguste said carefully—they had never actually discussed this before—"You are my son. There's no doubt about that."

"But have you accepted that? Acknowledged that?"

What was the boy driving at? Suddenly Auguste had a feeling he was getting into serious trouble. Yet he could not retreat, he had gone too far. He said, "I've given you work whenever you were willing. I brought you into my studio." And now he felt righteous. "And I'm asking you to return, despite the irresponsible way you have behaved."

"As an obscure employee?"

The boy was prodding him with unusual shrewdness. *Mon dieu*, what was he up to? Auguste wondered. He said, extending himself further than he had done for a long time, "Behave yourself and you can meet the world there if you want. It's up to you."

"With whose name? Yours?"

Auguste was shocked out of his self-control. The blood rushed to his face. He wanted to stride away without another word. But he had promised himself to see this matter through. Yet there was anger in his voice as he said, "What do you mean, *petit* Auguste? You have my name—Auguste."

"I want something more important." The son was frightened; he was speaking more daringly than he had ever done before, but he was also desperate. "I want the name Rodin. I am your son."

"Yes. I've never denied that."

"But my name is Beuret, Mama's name, not yours. Why haven't you legitimatized me? Why have you treated me as a bastard?"

"You are a bastard."

There was a heavy silence. *Petit* Auguste's face flamed, even under his unshaven stubble, and he looked his twenty-nine years.

Now that he had said it, Auguste was not sure he should have. But it was the truth, he thought. And because he was proud of his ability to be precise, whatever the circumstances, he was sure he was right. Yet since he was also proud that he was a fair man, he felt in a dilemma, not certain he had been fair with the boy. But as his confusion grew, so did his indignation, thinking his son should not have put him in such an embarrassing position.

Petit Auguste, who had regained his presence of mind and who had to press this home, feeling that never again would he have this much courage, asked, "Is this why you haven't given me your name? Legitimatized me?"

Auguste didn't answer. He honestly didn't know. As he thought back through the years with Rose, he remembered how he had resented the coming of the boy—he had assumed it was a device to trap him. Nonetheless, he had called the boy Auguste, he had wanted him to be his son. And since he took such pride in his honesty he asked himself, Is it really that I have been ashamed of him, that the boy hasn't been even a competent workingman? Or that I didn't want to make this final commitment? Or make him my heir? Especially with his growing irresponsibility? Even now the boy is living barely better than a derelict. Or is it for a reason I do not understand myself?

Petit Auguste said, his voice quivering with emotion, "It may be easy for you to call me a bastard. It is not easy to live with."

"I never thought it was."

"But I've had to live with it," *petit* Auguste said bitterly.

"You're my son. Everybody in the studio knows that."

"Not the world, though. You always introduce me as Auguste Beuret."

"As *petit* Auguste."

"That's even worse."

For an instant the father wanted to cry out, "What do you want?" But he couldn't, knowing it would give the boy an advantage he could not endure. Yet they must shed their animosities—for Aunt Thérèse's sake, if no one else's. He said, choosing his words carefully, "Come back to the studio and we shall see what we shall see."

"I will not be just a servant."

"I don't want you to be a servant!" *Mon dieu*, the boy was difficult. "If you can't be a secretary, we will find something else."

"It isn't a question of *can't*," *petit* Auguste said with sudden pride, looking very much like his father now with his prominent nose and wide, sloping forehead. "But what I want. You have never considered that."

"I, I, I!" Auguste cried. "Is that all you are interested in?"

"Aren't you?"

Auguste paused. He thought a reputation seen from close up must seem selfish, cruel, even trivial. A child could not live in a shrine. Just as he could not live as Papa had wanted him to many years ago. And the realization that he was behaving like Papa made him shudder. He said quietly, "We will try to find something in the studio that you will want to do."

"What about my name?"

"If you've set such value on it, you should be willing to work for it."

Petit Auguste hesitated, but his father—though offering little, he felt—had never lied to him. He said, "If you promise . . . ?"

"Will you promise to work hard?"

The *maître* was a shrewd one, *petit* Auguste thought admiringly. One would have to be smart to get the best of him. He said, "I'll try."

"And I'll try to act like a father. But I'll need a little help. Yes?"

"Yes."

They shook hands on that. Then suddenly and abruptly Auguste lunged forward and kissed his son on both cheeks. And he handed him a hundred francs to buy new clothes. But only after *petit* Auguste promised to be at the rue de l'Université the next morning.

CHAPTER 38

When his son did not appear the following day, Auguste was certain the boy would not keep his word, and he was disappointed. However, *petit* Auguste did appear several days later.

He did not offer any explanation for the delay, but he looked clean and tidy in new clothes. After a short discussion it was agreed that *petit* Auguste would supervise the purchase and distribution of materials—it was the son's idea, but Auguste, though some doubts remained in his mind about the boy's seriousness, liked the idea of his son assuming such responsibility.

Auguste seemed so deeply involved in making this reconciliation work that Rose resolved to do her best to help it flourish. She visited Aunt Thérèse, as he had suggested; she told her that Auguste was showing a special interest in the boy since he had seen her—she didn't mention Camille.

Camille was disturbed by the re-entry of the son into the main studio, but she was too busy to do anything about it. Auguste was sculpting with an intensity unusual even for him, and always involving her. And at the slightest criticism from her he accused her of wanting to desert him. How could she at this greatest crisis of all: the "Balzac"?

Before she could recover from her surprise—she had no intention of deserting him—he was arranging for her work to be shown by the society he had helped form. He told her that for whatever commissions he could not do himself he would recommend her or

Bourdelle, whoever was better fitted. Since he thought Bourdelle was the finest young sculptor in France, she was elated. She felt she had graduated finally: she was no longer the student, but the mature artist.

"I need you more than ever," he went on to say. "You have that marvelous thing, dedication with enthusiasm. Who else can I discuss my artistic problems with? You have a fine future. I am very optimistic about your work." She could not be cynical or think of leaving him now. She had never heard him talk like this. And when he said, "After I finish the 'Balzac,' whatever you want to do, we will concentrate on that," she felt a new joy.

As soon as she awoke these days, she had to get to the "Balzac" with him. She thought with exultation, When it is finished, all the long and difficult years with him will be worth while. Then he will realize I am the only one.

The Société had given Auguste another year because of the applause for "The Burghers," now spoken of as "a great sculptural group commemorating French spiritual dignity and heroism in the face of tragedy," but he had been warned he would get no more. The Société regarded the extra year as a special favor.

But again a year passed and there was no completed "Balzac" or "Hugo." He did many new versions of each figure, but none satisfied him. And to afford this work—long ago he had spent the advances for these commissions—he took new work. As he was fond of repeating to Proust, "I take the private commissions to afford the public ones."

Camille resented much of this other work as diversions delaying the "Balzac" and his promises, but she was pleased with his strong, dignified head of Puvis de Chavannes, which she thought as fine a portrait bust as she had ever seen and which he gave to Chavannes as a gesture of friendship.

She was angry about his portrait bust of Henri de Rochefort, for this potent radical journalist, after ordering it, had sat impatiently for it and then refused it, disliking it, for instead of being portrayed heroically, as he had wished, he had been shown as an ambitious, shrewd figure, which he was.

She was most engaged with Auguste's head of Baudelaire. Baudelaire, in spite of Auguste's admiration for the writer's poetry and art criticism, was, in her opinion, depicted with a precise realism: somber, intense, suspicious, with a prevailing air of corruption, but also as a unique individual whose extraordinary taste had condemned him to cultivate his bitter sensibility even at the cost of his own career and life.

Most of all she was amazed by Auguste's energy and accomplishment. Outwardly she reproached him for attempting so much, inwardly she was proud of him. She thought "The Crouching Woman" and "The Old Courtesan," which he had done with Clotilde in mind, dramatic and touching. She saw his nude pairings of Orpheus and Eurydice, Adonis and Venus, Cupid and Psyche, as lyrical and tender. And though she was embarrassed by the frankness of "The Eternal Idol"—a naked youth knelt before a naked maiden, passionately kissing her over her heart—for she saw herself as the model for this pairing, she was moved by the devotion with which he used her body.

And when he did a noble helmeted head of her which he called "France" and said she was his Joan of Arc, she gave in to his repeated pleas and agreed to pose for the female figure of "The Kiss," though reluctantly, and then only when he promised to use her alone—the male figure to be done from memory.

He resolved that "The Kiss" must express the beauty of marble, and he shut out everything but this romantic pairing, the Hugo monument, and "Balzac." He was teeming with a new strength and sensuality. Everything was going so well he could hardly believe it. Rose, gratified by his interest in *petit* Auguste, had stopped complaining and seemed interested only in making him happy. *Petit* Auguste was satisfied, apparently, and there had been no further discussions about legitimacy—as if that was an embarrassment to both of them— but Auguste had been careful not to criticize the boy while *petit* Auguste had been respectful and absent only occasionally. And Camille's love had a compelling passion that heightened everything around him.

Thus he was surprised and upset when Cholet, his best friend in the Société now that Zola was out of it, came to the rue de l'Université and said, "*Mon cher maître*, the Société has decided that the 'Balzac' must be exhibited in the Salon of 1897 with the 'Hugo.'

They will wait until then, but if you break your word this time, it will be impossible to hold off the wolves."

"But I did not promise that, monsieur," Auguste protested. How could they distract him when he was so busy!

"The contract specified eighteen months. You've taken twice that, and still there is no sign of the 'Balzac.' I cannot hold them off much longer."

The pleasure went out of Auguste as he saw Cholet's grave expression. He said bleakly, "I have nothing to debate."

Cholet was not to be put off so brusquely. His own prestige was at stake, too. He said, "They are saying at the Société that you will never finish the 'Balzac,' as you have never finished 'The Gates' or the 'Victor Hugo.' "

"That's not so! I will show something in 1897!"

"Eighteen ninety-seven? It is almost that now."

Cholet looked so dubious Auguste found himself swearing that the Hugo monument, at least, would be ready, even as he was disgusted with himself for allowing anyone to push him into such a statement.

Cholet asked, "What about the 'Balzac'?"

"I'm working on it."

"May I see it?"

"No." When he saw Cholet's dismay, he said, "It's not ready."

"Will it be ready for 1897?"

"I don't know."

Cholet shook his head in bafflement. "*Mon cher maître*, you are forcing us, your good friends, into the most desperate circumstances. Proust, Boucher, Mallarmé, myself, we've gotten one delay after another for you, yet you continue to refuse to give us a specific date, even to allow us to see the work. Believe me, we want the 'Balzac' to be a success, but you make it hard to have faith sometimes, you are so stubborn."

Auguste said wearily, "Maybe all that is true. But I cannot give a promise I am not sure I can keep. I said the 'Balzac' would be ready for the centenary in 1899, which is what you wanted it for. Beyond that I do not know."

Cholet answered, "I will try to hold them off. But if there is nothing in the coming Salon, they will sue. They are very angry as it is."

II

Six months later a large crowd gathered in the dissident salon, which had been formed by Chavannes, Carrière, and Auguste, and which included many well-known artists. Important works were scheduled to be shown, but everyone was waiting to see the "Balzac."

There was no "Balzac." Auguste had decided not to exhibit the naked "Balzac" since he was certain now that it was not his final conception. But as he entered the gallery he felt he had kept his word, the Société could see how hard he had worked by his "Hugo." Then he felt ill. He approached the seated, clothed "Hugo," which he had altered at the last moment, dissatisfied with the standing figure, and he knew it was a disaster. He wanted to flee, but Camille joined him, delighted with the prominence he had given to her work and having to thank him. Boucher hurried over, embracing him as he exclaimed, "Camille's modeling is so graceful, so elegant. I certainly made no mistake, did I, Auguste, when I brought her to your studio!"

Auguste nodded, thinking bitterly, In compromising I lost whatever strength the original "Hugo" possessed and gained nothing. I was too careful, this "Hugo," supposedly sitting in a mood of reflection, does not grow out of the rock, as I wanted, but is pressed in by the enclosed plaster, tight, constricted, obvious.

III

Auguste was not disappointed, but relieved, when the Ministry of Fine Arts informed him that this "Hugo" was not suitable for the Panthéon or the Luxembourg. But they appreciated his efforts to please, they added; as long as he tried to please, they could allow him more time.

He was too tired to be grateful, as Camille thought he should be for what she called "your reprieve." She was happy that she had sold several heads, and that her work had been favorably reviewed, almost as well reviewed as Bourdelle's. Auguste was pleased for her, but it did not end his depression.

There was no word from the Société as yet, but he was sure there would be. He could not model anything after what he thought of as the "Hugo *debâcle*." Insomnia dominated his nights and rheumatic pains his days. His hands were often stiff, numb. It was terrifying. He wondered whether Balzac, writing so much, had had the same numbness.

Then Camille felt marvelous, and that made him very uncomfortable, as if the difference in age had become the difference between a young woman and an old man. In her enthusiasm she was getting younger while he was growing older. But he could not reveal that: he had to hold her by his strength, not weakness. When she asked him why he was not working—it was so unlike Auguste to be sitting before the fireplace day after day, warming his hands, his body—he said it was the weather, this continual rain and fog that had settled over Paris. She did not think the weather was that bad, but she did not argue—he looked too miserable. He was despondent. Every time he thought of the clothed "Hugo," he was filled with loathing for what he had done. He wondered whether he could ever do any more work; there were moments when he wanted to shatter all the "Balzacs." Yet when Camille suggested that they visit his old friend Renoir, who was still living in the South of France for reasons of health, he regarded her as if she were insane. He shouted that he couldn't go anywhere until he finished the "Balzac"!

She was shocked, therefore, when he informed her a few weeks later that he was moving his home from Bellevue to Meudon, at Val Fleury.

He said, "This will get me started again. It has fresh air, ample sun, gardens, fine trees—you know how I love trees—and it is on a splendid height commanding a fine view of the Seine." And she thought unhappily that he was moving farther away. But when she said that, he regarded her as disloyal. His face took on the texture of stone. He stated conclusively, "The move is settled. I've bought the place. It's called the Villa des Brillants, though it is hardly that, but a modest house and grounds."

"Grounds? An estate?"

"A few acres. Nothing much. I must get away from the Ministry, the Société, their gossip that I won't finish, can't finish. I must have some rest or I will never finish the 'Balzac.'"

He made it so obvious that there was no disputing this move she walked out of the studio. He did not follow her, certain she would return.

She did, after he was gone. And that night, alone in the cold, empty studio, hearing only the stir of the concierge across the court-yard, she wondered what to do. Distraught, unable to sleep, shaking with frustration and rage, the more she thought about his behavior the worse she felt.

When he did not come the next day, she went to see Boucher. Boucher knew why Camille was visiting him. He had seen the new home at Meudon. He got to the point at once. "Meudon is lovely —oh, not the house but the country. The main house is somewhat like Bellevue, but larger. It is the rolling countryside that attracted him."

"Do you think it is permanent?"

Boucher did not reply.

"You do."

"Well, it is a considerable investment. I'm surprised he found the money to buy it. He is always complaining about how poor he is."

"He must have borrowed."

"With all the agitation over the 'Balzac'? He wouldn't get the credit."

She thought bitterly, didn't Auguste feel anything for her situa-tion? Didn't he realize it couldn't go on forever, didn't he know each time he moved away from her, inevitably they lost something? That she could only truly live in his studio when he was there? And she could hardly endure that now.

When Auguste arrived at their studio the next afternoon, even as she was glad, she shouted, "Go away, go away! I can't go on this way any longer!" She burst into tears. She felt he had come only because of Boucher.

"You must be brave," he said. He sought to dry her tears, though he believed she was exaggerating her pain. "You won't have to worry about Rose at all now. She is far away."

"Do you think there is a chance, a tiny chance, you will ever leave her?"

He stared at her harshly, but he didn't answer.

"No," she said. "You will never leave her. And we are doomed."

He turned away abruptly, but he did not walk with his usual vitality.

She noticed that his shoulders sagged and he looked aged. And though she had resolved not to be sympathetic, she murmured, "Where are you going?"

"Where should I go?" he asked mournfully.

They stood staring at each other a moment, then came together in a ruthless, straining abandonment that was the more sensual for the nearness of their parting. Afterward Camille realized they had made love naked in the sunlight for the first time. She stared out the window and across the blue horizon of Paris and felt part of a great plan.

He stroked her with his hands, and she whispered, "Do they feel better?"

"Much better," he replied.

"Because of Meudon?" She couldn't resist, then was sorry and afraid.

He frowned, but his voice was gentle. "Meudon is peaceful, but I had to borrow to buy it. I got the money from two bankers when I pledged my work as security. Forty thousand francs. More than I am getting for the 'Balzac.' It's a great risk, I'm not sure I'll be able to keep Meudon."

She didn't know whether to be glad or sorry. But as she felt the power of his hands, she felt that God had created a great man, it was enough to have ecstasy if not happiness. As he said, "Meudon could be another *debâcle*," she replied, "What does it matter? You must finish the 'Balzac,'" proud that her arms would be his haven, though some of her disquiet remained.

IV

Auguste had another visit to make, to *petit* Auguste. He had several things to discuss with the boy, and the longer he waited the harder it would be.

But *petit* Auguste was absent from the rue de l'Université and it was a week before the boy reappeared. Then *petit* Auguste looked uneasy as Auguste approached him, which made Auguste, already irritated by the boy's absence and bills incurred without his knowledge, angrier. He was upset about his son. No matter how much money he paid him, and he was paying him more than anyone else in the studio, the boy never seemed to have enough. These wine bills he held in his hand, signed *Auguste Rodin* by *petit* Auguste, were a shock. Still, if the boy would live at Meudon, he would overlook this.

Auguste said quietly, "Your mother and I have moved out to Meudon, and we would like you to live there with us."

Petit Auguste did not wish to live at Meudon. It was too far from Paris, ten, twenty miles at least, difficult to reach, no women, nothing to do. But he knew he must find another excuse. He said, "I would like to, *maître*, but it would be impossible to live there and be here on time."

"Are you ever on time?"

"I try. I didn't feel well the last few days."

More likely drunk, Auguste thought contemptuously. Then he remembered how much *petit* Auguste could help Rose and quiet her complaints about being lonesome. He said, "You can save money. There will be no room and board." He felt magnanimous; it was more than his own papa had given him. "Your mother and I are living in the main house, the Villa des Brillants, and there is a nice white cottage for you, clean, heated, comfortable, all your own."

"*Merci, maître,* but—"

"But what, *petit* Auguste?"

"What about my name?"

Auguste wavered. If he legitimatized the boy, he would be acknowledging Rose as his wife, even if he didn't marry her, and thus lose Camille. And if he allowed the boy to push him into this, he would be pushed into worse things.

"You promised."

"I said I would see how you behaved. What about these wine bills? And the way you signed them, *Auguste Rodin?*" Suddenly Auguste felt wronged.

Petit Auguste shrugged: it was easy to arrange in Paris. Everyone knew Auguste Rodin now, so he charged his wine, telling them he was Auguste Rodin's son. His credentials were good. All the shopkeepers knew that Rodin was his father. The francs could be paid later.

Auguste said, "I don't expect any thanks for what I've done for you, but when I was your age I wore paper collars and cuffs to save money. And when I could no longer wear them, I sketched on them to save sous."

"Do you want me to wear them?"

"I want to be able to depend on you. Know that you are not wasting money."

"With your name?"

Auguste did not reply.

Petit Auguste exclaimed, "You won't trust me with your name, yet you expect me to trust you! It's not right, not natural."

And now there was a fierce, hopeless quarrel: Auguste swore that *petit* Auguste must live at Meudon with his mother, and *petit* Auguste cried that he could not live any longer as a bastard. This was followed by misery, for neither of them was listening to the other. The boy strode about with a flushed, defiant air, while the father went from anger to disgust to rage. But Auguste didn't order *petit* Auguste to leave, as the boy expected and half wished when he refused to move to Meudon or pay the wine bills, and the boy didn't walk out, as Auguste feared. Instead when *petit* Auguste realized that his father wasn't even listening to him, he shouted, "I have a message for you! Somebody was here from the Société with an ultimatum for you!"

Suddenly Auguste was attentive, asking in a worried voice, "Ultimatum? What about? The 'Balzac'?"

"Why ask me? You can't trust me," *petit* Auguste said with a burst of self-satisfaction. "But they were upset and angry, even more than you are."

CHAPTER 39

The ultimatum was clear: "*Give the Société the completed 'Balzac'* *at once or return the ten thousand francs received, and one franc* *for damages.*"

Auguste heard this shocking declaration from Pisne the next day when he hurried to the office of the Société to find out about *petit* Auguste's news.

Pisne stood hostile and arrogant in front of a daguerreotype of Balzac, and Cholet, standing behind Pisne, squirmed uneasily and wanted to say something to help Auguste, but what? The ultimatum had been passed by a majority of the Société. And when Auguste looked incredulous, Pisne repeated the ultimatum with a brusque, malicious gratification.

"It's impossible!" Auguste exclaimed. "I'm not finished!"

But the savagery in Pisne's voice increased. "Everything is impossible, Rodin, especially for you. But we will not wait this time. We have already consulted our lawyers. If you do not give us the statue or the money at once, within twenty-four hours, we will institute legal action."

Auguste pleaded, "Suppose I deposit my ten-thousand-franc advance with the government as an expression of good faith?"

Pisne looked indifferent, but Cholet said, "That's a valid suggestion."

"Delay!" Pisne cried in his harsh voice. "Delay, always delay with Rodin! I agreed to that once. But not now."

"Yes, you will," said Cholet. "You don't speak for all of us."

"Keep quiet," said Pisne.

"I can say what I think," said Cholet, gathering courage. "You outvoted me in committee, but there are still newspapers that will print what I say."

"Keep quiet," said Pisne, looking ready to strike Cholet.

"No, Pisne. I will write to *Figaro* that you are so against Rodin you won't even allow him to put the ten thousand francs in escrow as an expression of good faith. It will become a national scandal. It could destroy the Société. Most of the artists will turn against us."

"How will they know? Not everything you write is printed in *Figaro*," Pisne said contemptuously. "And then it will appear only on a back page."

"Not if I resign as president because of your spiteful treatment of Rodin, our greatest sculptor," Cholet said, as arrogant as Pisne suddenly.

"Greatest?" Pisne sneered. "Falguière, Dalou, Boucher, are better."

"You may think so," said an aroused Cholet. "But Zola, Mallarmé, Monet, even Boucher, prefer Rodin. And so do many others. If I resign, I will take many members of the Société with me. Enough, believe me," Cholet said with a new excitement, "to start a new Société."

The two writers stared at each other, and Auguste said, "I will deposit the ten thousand francs in a government office tomorrow. And show a finished 'Balzac' in our salon next year. I promise."

Pisne turned his back on Auguste and went out of the room without another word. Cholet said, blushing, "He doesn't matter really, *mon ami*. The vital thing is to give you time to finish. You must deposit the money with the government. That is what they are worried about, that you will fall ill or die before the statue is finished and then they will lose the money."

Auguste could not speak; he could only nod and tighten his lips to prevent himself from denouncing all of them. He was in service to still another master, the Société was no better than the State, and he hated masters.

Cholet said, "My threat to resign should halt the ultimatum."

"And if it doesn't?"

"Announce your willingness to return the money if you don't finish."

"But I will finish."

"I know. But the public and the Société don't know."

"I will keep my word," Auguste said with growing pride.

"Splendid." Cholet smiled for the first time. "We will put an end to Pisne's arrogance yet. I will enjoy that."

The next day Cholet came to Auguste's studio and informed him that the ultimatum would be postponed—if the money was deposited as agreed.

Auguste tried, but the government refused to hold his ten thousand francs in escrow. They stated that it was an artistic matter and that they never interfered in such things. And now while Cholet still cried for compromise and delay, Pisne got a majority of the Société to pass a new resolution to put the "Balzac affair" in the hands of their lawyers. Cholet replied by resigning from the Société, followed by six members, and wrote an eloquent letter to *Figaro* explaining why. This was printed on the first page of the newspaper, next to the announcement that the Société was bringing suit against Rodin for the return of the money paid on the "Balzac."

Suddenly the "Balzac affair" was on the front page of all the Parisian newspapers. Protests against the Société's scheduled lawsuit appeared from Zola, Mallarmé, Proust, Chavannes, Monet, Carrière, Boucher, and Henley, and were reprinted in the newspapers. Not all of those protesting cared about the "Balzac," few of them had seen even the early, rough copies of the "Balzac," but they resented the purchaser forcing the artist to sacrifice his convictions to the power of the franc. Many of them felt that if the artist was forced to conform to the Société's bourgeois sentiments and taste, this principle would be established and they would all be in jeopardy.

Auguste himself was not concerned about principles: he was concerned about the "Balzac." He was beginning to feel within sight of completion, and everything else was a distraction, and thus an annoyance, which made him very angry. He went to his lawyers, demanding that they end this annoyance. He wanted to answer the Société's threatened suit with a countersuit, but his lawyers advised him to wait. They said that since the suit had not been filed yet, it was possible, even likely, that the Société was impressed with the public protests and was having second thoughts on the matter. And so, though he was irritated by their caution, he agreed to wait if the Société did.

A few days later while Paris watched intently to see who would attack or retreat first, the Société or Rodin, Cholet came again to the studio. He announced jubilantly, "The Société has asked me to withdraw my resignation."

"Are they withdrawing the suit?" asked Auguste.

"Not yet. But they will, *mon cher maître*. They want me back."

"Are you going to return?"

"No. It is a matter of principle now. Don't give up, *mon ami*, and I won't."

Auguste didn't answer. He thought wryly that Cholet was proud of their alliance, as if it brought honor to both of them, but he wished they would let him alone. He would never finish this way.

However, Mallarmé, approaching him a week later as an unofficial mediator, was like an ascent from a squalid prison into sunlight. Auguste thought Cholet a bit of a bore, forever busy with details and self-congratulations, though a decent man, but Mallarmé understood his artistic problems—the poet was striving to shatter syntax as he was seeking to shatter stone. Mallarmé was one of the few artists he knew who did not function chiefly from self-interest.

Mallarmé said, "The Société is talking about giving the Balzac to Dalou, or Falguière." He was determined not to spare Auguste, but not to lie either.

"But Falguière is my friend." Auguste was surprised and hurt.

"They even suggested that Boucher or Desbois do it."

This was an even worse shock. Auguste went white.

"Boucher admitted he was tempted. Desbois was outraged."

Auguste found his voice. "Desbois should be. He is still working with me."

"Would that stop Dalou? Auguste, this Balzac has become a prize."

"So if they win the suit, someone else will do it."

"If they sue." Mallarmé's heavy tone lightened. "They have had a new vote by the Balzac committee. In spite of Pisne's hostility and insistence, they have decided, thanks to the agitation started by Cholet, to hold off until the next Salon, but no longer."

"The next Salon! That's less than a year away."

"A little more than six months if it is held in the spring, as usual."

He could feel Mallarmé's concern, but he didn't know what to say. A few days ago, facing the critical moment of a lawsuit, six months would have been a great relief, but now, facing the finality of it, he wavered.

"Auguste, it is the weight of public opinion that is getting you one last chance, but if you don't take advantage of this it could turn against you."

"Yes," he said. Deadlines were dreadful things, and never again must he allow one to oppress him, but he had to finish the "Balzac" and he was grateful for Mallarmé's support. "Tell them I will show a finished 'Balzac' in the Salon."

"The next one?"

"Stéphane, do you have to press me, too?"

"This is not one of my favorite tasks. But I have to satisfy them also."

"They will give me six months?"

"Not in writing. But they will hold off their suit, withdraw their ultimatum, if you give me your word there will be a 'Balzac' by 1898."

"So they can decide whether or not to accept it for the centenary? Then if they don't like it, they will still have a year to get someone else to do it."

Mallarmé shrugged. "Perhaps. But you have no choice."

"What brought on this new attack?"

"I'm not sure, but it is rumored that members of the Société resent your purchase of Meudon. They feel you used their money to buy it. And that if you could afford Meudon, you could afford to return the advance payment."

"Idiots!"

"You say you always want the truth."

"Yes. And they will get it. All right, Stéphane, you can tell them that I give my word that there will be a 'Balzac' in the Salon of 1898." As Auguste stated this, he knew he had come to a decision about the "Balzac" for himself and for the first time. And he felt a strange peace.

II

The Société withdrew its suit, for the time being, on the understanding that Rodin would exhibit the "Balzac" in the next Salon, but the peace did not last. A month passed, and Auguste was as far from finishing as before. Though he hungered for the "Balzac," it seemed spoiled by the controversy. It appeared as if this year, 1897, was going to be the most difficult of his life.

He decided to visit Lecoq, only to be told by Bourdelle that Lecoq was dead. He exploded in a terrible rage. He castigated Bourdelle, everyone in his studios, even Camille, for not telling him about Lecoq—at least he could have gone to the funeral to pay his respects. He brushed aside Camille's reminder that he avoided funerals whenever he could. She explained that Lecoq had died while he had been fighting over the "Balzac" in the press, when no one in the studio had been able to talk to him, and he was stricken with a deep gloom. Stevenson had died a few years ago in Samoa, and now Lecoq—Henley was ailing, and Mallarmé had become ill also. Suddenly he had a feeling of waiting for who would be next.

Lecoq had been buried in Père Lachaise, where Balzac was buried, too. The Saturday after he heard about his teacher's death— it was no consolation to realize that Lecoq had lived to be ninety-five —he insisted that Camille join him in a visit to this cemetery on the heights above the avenue de la République. It was a gruesome chore for Camille; she hated cemeteries even more than Auguste did; it was not memorable to her that Chopin was buried here, and George Sand and Molière, in addition to Balzac.

But Auguste said it was cowardly for her not to go with him, and so she trailed along, complaining, falling behind, footsore and tired. The cemetery was so vast, she cried, but he didn't hear her, far ahead, seeking the grave of Balzac now rather than that of Lecoq. She dragged up a steep road after Auguste, under trees so heavily leafed the sun could not penetrate, and it was as if she were entering an earthy hell. A thunderstorm developed overhead, dark and threatening, and she was terrified at the thought of being caught under a tree. She wanted to flee, but there was no refuge within view, only one house of death after another, and foreboding trees.

Then suddenly she couldn't be critical. The storm passed over without striking. There was the glint of sun on marble tombstones. And Auguste had found Balzac's grave.

Auguste stood in a silent reverie until Camille joined him. Then he cried out, "It's a crime! Balzac has barely six feet of soil, and a small, ugly monument, and Napoleon is buried in splendor."

Camille shrugged and said, "Balzac is less fashionable."

"But Balzac was France, not the Emperor."

"That is not what most people feel, Auguste."

"And look at this head on top of the monument. Have you ever seen anything so obscene, vulgar, fatuous? It is ridiculous!"

III

After this pilgrimage he resumed work on the "Balzac" with new energy. He talked Cholet into lending him the daguerreotype of Balzac hanging in the office of the Société, though Cholet was reluctant. He told a puzzled Cholet, "Not to copy, not even to use slightly." He added scornfully, "I don't want to make Balzac like that, with an open collar and flowing necktie, looking Byronic, superior, handsome, but the neck is good, strong and muscular."

He was especially encouraged when he found an aged tailor who had fitted Balzac with trousers, waistcoats, and Dominican robes made to order.

Jean Gueret was very old, almost fifty years had passed since he had fitted Balzac, but the tailor kept repeating proudly how well he had fitted Balzac's odd body, so unusual and grotesque that he had held on to the exact measurements to prove his accuracy, and that the writer still owed him money.

Auguste carefully wrote down Balzac's waist, seat, leg length, shoulder width, chest span, neck size, to the inch. Despite all he had learned, he was amazed by the disparity of Balzac's dimensions. Once more he was struck by the contrast between the circus-strongman chest, shoulders, and neck and the short stubby legs. And Balzac, though his bulk had given the impression that he was a large man, had been only five feet two. He thought that to put these incongruous dimensions into a conventional waistcoat and trousers would be as misleading as to show the writer naked, for they would not give any sense of the dominating vitality of the man. This spurred him to take the precise measurements of the Dominican robes. Then with a warm "*Merci*, Monsieur Gueret," and a generous tip he rushed out of the old, retired tailor's house with a new conception burning within him.

And again the call went out for a model, but this time Camille went to the arrondissement of Paris where provincials from Balzac's native province of Touraine settled. She didn't look for a *grand seigneur*, but searched on the streets and in the shops and found a peasant from Touraine who had the dimensions of Balzac and whose features resembled the writer's.

Pierre Ralle had become a butcher upon his arrival in Paris because of his great strength. At first Pierre thought Camille and Auguste, who had come quickly at her request, crazy at their insistence he model for them.

When Pierre heard the fee, however, five francs an hour—though he still thought the sculptor crazy, and Camille was amazed also, this was a fantastic rate, which could ruin Auguste with his endless hours of work—Pierre wiped the blood of the horse meat he was carving off his thick, strong hands and shook Auguste's hands in agreement.

Auguste liked the butcher's grip, it was muscular and powerful, like his own. The thought of modeling these hands as Balzac's hands gave him great pleasure. But when he put the butcher on a ten-foot stand, as had been agreed to in the contract, he winced. Despite the massiveness of Pierre's shoulders, chest, and neck, the height of the stand made him look like a dwarf.

Camille, seeing Auguste's doubts, stopped preparing the clay for him—she was upset as it was, for *petit* Auguste, absent often now, had failed to order as much clay as had been requested—and asked, "Is the pedestal too high?"

"Far too high." He sighed, "It's depressing, there is still so much to be learned." He stood bowed as if under an unsupportable weight. Then as Pierre shifted uneasily, saying, "Monsieur, it's so high I feel like I'm going to fall off," Auguste's face lit up. Suddenly he knew what had to be done. He ordered Pierre to wait on the pedestal, to sit if uncomfortable; he shouted down the butcher's protests with "I'll be back soon, monsieur," and handed him twenty francs, though

Pierre had stood only a few minutes, and added, "There will be more when I return," and hurried over to the place du Palais Royal, where the statue was to be placed. It was within walking distance, and he didn't say a word to Camille, assuming she was following him. She was, grumbling, yet compelled by the force of his energy.

His first clear view of the place du Palais Royal confirmed what he feared. A ten-foot pedestal, whatever the Société thought, was too high. Balzac would be dwarfed by the height of the pedestal and the size and importance of the buildings around him, when Balzac should dominate. But he did not hurry now. This was a matter of the utmost consequence. The Palais Royal, which would loom behind the statue, the Louvre, which would be in front of it, and the Théâtre Français, which would be on the side, were all landmarks in Paris. This was dangerous. Balzac would be surrounded by so many historic sites that he must be located dramatically to capture attention. Auguste moved quietly and deliberately about the square until he was sure of his conclusions, while Camille followed him silently.

It was hours later when he returned to the studio. Pierre was still waiting. At five francs an hour the butcher was willing to wait forever.

He took Pierre to the best tailor he knew, and had him fitted for trousers, waistcoat, and Dominican robe in the exact style and to the precise measurements worn by Balzac. The tailor was one of the most expensive in Paris, but Auguste waved away Camille's protests. He informed her that he had gone to this tailor because he wanted the best. She thought he was as extravagant as Balzac now, insisting that the clothes be in the style of Louis Philippe, which Balzac had favored, for these clothes had been out of fashion for many years and were costly to duplicate. He ordered Pierre to return the next day and paid him for a full day's modeling, though he had used Pierre for only half a day. Camille pointed out that the clothes would not be ready for several weeks, to use the butcher until then was a waste, and he replied, "I will keep him occupied. I don't want him to think of anything else."

When he had to wait for the clothes, as she had predicted, he went to work on Pierre nude. Upset by any interruption, he moved all his Balzac material to his studio on the rue Dante. Then finding this too small, he rented a new studio on the rue de l'Université—his third on this street and his sixth in Paris. He was gratified by this move. He was nearer to the place du Palais Royal, and here he could have absolute privacy.

But Camille was furious when he closed his new studio even to her. He didn't want her in the "Balzac studio" while he was modeling this nude, in a sudden mood of modesty, but he repeated that he must have absolute privacy. He added, seeing her anger, "But you can handle the materials." *Petit* Auguste was increasingly undependable, and he needed someone reliable.

IV

Several days later, when Camille's ill temper continued and no material for the "Balzac" arrived at the new studio, Auguste decided to be stern. He was not certain whether this delay was her fault or *petit* Auguste's, but he was angry, positive she could have rectified this delay.

He went to his main studio, but she was not working there, as he expected. Alarmed—he had told her to work on one of her own pieces until he was ready for her on the "Balzac"—he hurried to their studio, at the place d'Italie. He was relieved to find her there— for a dreadful moment he had feared she left him. But it was no relief to see her sitting as mournfully as he had ever seen her. He could not bear that she should be in so sad a state when he was bursting with enthusiasm. He announced, "I'm completing 'The Kiss.' I'll need you again as a model."

Camille, instead of becoming cheerful, as he expected, frowned and said, "You must continue on the 'Balzac,' you are so much in it."

"I'm in 'The Kiss,' too. I'm ready to do the final figures."

"What about the male figure?"

"I've done him from memory." He didn't tell her that he had given the lover the figure he would have liked to have—lean, tall, lithe, with wide shoulders and a tapering waist and long legs. He had always resented his short legs, not as short as Balzac's, but too short for the desired image of himself.

She was not satisfied. She asked, "What about Pierre? Will he wait?"

"Of course. He will never earn as many francs again in his life."

Moreover, he wanted the "Balzac" to gestate a little longer while he relaxed by completing "The Kiss," which was simple compared to the "Balzac." He said decisively, "We will start tomorrow morning in this studio, our studio."

V

The next few weeks he kept paying Pierre; he had the clothes altered until they fitted exactly; otherwise he modeled Camille for the final version of "The Kiss." He had her walk, sit, and recline in many positions while he studied the variations of light and shadow on her lovely naked body. He had done many modelings of this pairing, some that went back to the time he had fallen in love with her, but now the pairing struck him as right for the first time.

He brought the man to completion first, placing him seated upon a rock whose curved contours embraced the lovers suggestively. Then he modeled Camille with the delicacy and care of a lover. As his strong, sensitive fingers set her in place, he felt like a young man again. Often he had said to her, "All emotion is in the human body." And though she had not agreed, now, more than ever, he had to make that true. Her face would be partially hidden; it was her beautiful body that must convey the emotion, focus the attention.

But one day he paused in exasperation. The result was not coming up to his conception. He stared at her critically, and suddenly he realized he was modeling her as she was, not as she had been. She was thirty-four now, he noted, and a little heavier than when he had met her, though she still had the slim, supple body that had always been his favorite body, with her full, high breasts, her fine thighs, her delicately formed buttocks, and her slender waist. But not perfect, and she had been perfect, he thought angrily.

From then on Camille had to diet. She protested, she resisted—the idea threw her into a state of panic—it reminded her of the many years that had passed since she had met Auguste. But his urgency forced her to surrender. When he declared, "I can't do without you, chérie," and demonstrated that by the passionate way he modeled her and made love to her and even was devoted to her, she could not resist him. He ate, slept, and toiled at their studio, going to his main studio only to keep his affairs in order and to pay Pierre. He had not gone to Meudon since he had started this final draft of "The Kiss," and Camille blossomed with the hope that at last he was leaving Rose.

He did not tell Camille that he had heard that Rose was complaining bitterly about his absence, the longest one she could remember, or that Rose had spies among the workers in his main studio whom she paid to keep her informed. He assured himself that he didn't care. All that mattered was finishing "The Kiss" and the "Balzac." He expected Rose to accept what he had told her when he had moved her to Meudon: "*Ma chatte,* you shouldn't be lonely when I'm in Paris. You will have sun, fresh air, you will be free of drafts and dampness, you will sleep better—you always say you are a farm girl at heart."

He was certain that took care of Rose, and yet as Camille dieted and came to resemble more the girl he had met years ago, he was reminded that Camille was only a year older than *petit* Auguste. Shaken then, he knew only one solution and followed it: work, work, work. Whether it rained, or the sun shone, or the wind blew, or it was a mild day, he never knew these weeks, he worked so hard.

And when Camille complained that he would never finish, one day he added, the next he took away, he retorted, "Your expression keeps changing."

"My expression? You're doing my breasts."

"Of course. They are never the same two moments in a row." Ignoring her irritation, he tied a blue ribbon around her breasts to capture their exact swell when she was agitated, as when making love, as now. "What a curve they have!" he cried, and when they bulged out in anger he said, "Don't be a cow!"

She shouted, "You would be critical of Venus herself!"

"No doubt, but now I'm doing you." He cupped his hands over her breasts to feel their contour, and then—while she still tingled from the passion of his fingers and longed to take him in her arms— he hurriedly transferred the warmth of her flesh to the clay. Next he felt the ripple of the muscles along her legs, the hollow of her neck, the roundness of her buttocks. She stirred suddenly, unable to contain the waves of desire surging through her, and he was annoyed. As she wondered how he could stand this, he tied a cloth around her breasts until they were hidden and said, "I don't want to be distracted. They are no more important than the rest."

But when he finished this day, he satisfied the desires he had aroused.

The next day, however, he was more difficult than ever, she thought. To make sure that he captured the contours of her back, he forced her to lie on the cold, hard floor, not on a couch, as she pleaded. It would be artificial, he retorted. Then with her face on the floor and her body between his knees, he modeled her back with his thumb, touching her flesh and then the clay while his thumb was still warm from her skin. She cried, "You will never finish!" and he said brusquely, "Yes, I will, if you co-operate."

But Camille was surprised when it happened. The pairing looked complete to her, but he was working on the hands several days later, muttering, "You are too rigid, time for you to be upset when your breasts have fallen and your buttocks are gone," and suddenly he paused. He grumbled, "This clay is like dough. It's a pity."

"What's a pity?" Today he was allowing her to sit, which was a relief.

"Clay. It doesn't do justice to the work."

"Then why leave it in clay?"

"I don't intend to. I've always planned to put you in marble. Women are better in marble, men in bronze." He gazed at the couple kissing passionately, yet tenderly, then said, "Come here."

She moved to his side, her naked body as slim as when he had first known her. "Yes, Auguste?"

"What do you think?"

"Do you really care what I think?"

"Of course I do!" he said impatiently. "You're a sculptress, aren't you?"

She was startled; she had almost forgotten.

"A good one, too. If you can't judge, who can?"

She had a sense of physical delight as she examined the lovers, but she was annoyed by his curtness. She didn't say anything.

"Well?" All at once he looked stricken with self-doubt. He said, "The two figures are not bad, are they? At least they are alive?"

"Yes," she said mockingly. "They have the hideous appearance of truth."

He stared at her as if she were insane, then realized that she was teasing. He said, "Yes, they will probably be a scandalous success. What day is this?"

"Does it matter? You have less than six months to do the 'Balzac.' "

"It will get done in time," he stated with a new certainty, then returned abruptly to the work before them. "The girl leans too much." But as Camille frowned as if this were a criticism of herself, he added, "Isn't love always a leaning?" And when he put his arm around her and said, "You are right, *chérie*, they will look fine in marble," she answered his embrace with passion.

That evening they were pervaded with an amorous warmth which was a happy blend of joy and gratitude for what they had wrought. But Auguste could not fall asleep. Long after Camille had drifted into peaceful slumber, he lay awake. "The Kiss" was felicitous, truly an expression of their love, but "Balzac" had to be more. And he was going on fifty-seven, already he had outlived Balzac by six years, and this revival of energy might not last much longer, though tonight he felt half his age.

VI

Auguste returned to the "Balzac" and again made himself inaccessible to everyone. When Cholet came to the studio, saying, "*Mon cher maître*, you might at least let me, your friend, see the 'Balzac,' " he retorted, "No, you won't understand it, a work shouldn't be seen by anyone until it is finished," and shut the studio door on Cholet before it could deteriorate into an argument.

Unfriendly newspapers were slipped under his studio door with their savage criticism underlined: "*Monsieur Rodin is modeling a corpse . . . he will never finish because he is afraid to finish . . . he will get what he deserves, not a sou,*" and Auguste regarded this as nonsense and tore them up, and then ignored the newspapers that continued to be slipped under his door.

The days of modeling sped by in a flowing stream. Pierre was responsive, and Auguste placed him on a one-foot pedestal, though he knew this would not be the final height. He decided to fit the base to the figure, and now as he designed the "Balzac" he knew irrevocably that Balzac himself had to be ten feet tall.

He made many sketches and rough clay models. The cost doubled, tripled, but he interrupted himself only to view the "Victory of Samothrace," in the Louvre, and was struck forcibly by the purposeful projection of the body, the vitality of the legs. He studied rocks, then trees, and came to think of Balzac as a giant oak standing on a hill, dominating, yet leaning back slightly so as to not appear to need this domination. Balzac became a large figure, tall, broad-chested, with heavy features, a great mane of hair, and deep eyes. His stomach remained fat, the legs short and stubby, but that no longer worried Auguste; Balzac's massive head showed his energy and vision.

The Salon was approaching; Auguste's supporters grew as impatient as the Société and began to ask, "Why does he still delay?" There was no word from him. No one knew the state of the "Balzac." He remained unapproachable.

Then a few weeks before the opening of the Salon of 1898, Auguste asked Camille to examine what he had done. She was surprised by the starkness and severity of the design, by the bare and austere quality of the completed body; despite its nudity it had none of Auguste's usual sensuousness. And the head was magnificent.

She asked, "You are clothing him?"

"Yes." He was curt. Her expression told him what he wanted to know. "*Merci.*" He dismissed her without another word.

Before she could get angry, he asked her to return a week later to view the clothed "Balzac." She was surprised by his fixing a date.

But Balzac was clothed then. Camille thought the trousers and waistcoat handsome, but somehow disappointing. Balzac had lost his power and starkness, which had been so impressive. Yet she mumbled, "It is authentic."

"Say what you mean." He disliked her uneasiness.

"You won't be offended, Auguste?"

"Yes, but I will be more offended if this is a failure."

"It is not a failure. I like the modeling—"

"Like?" He cut in abruptly. "Stop finding excuses. Who cares about that? It's the clothes, they make him look stuffed."

"But he was a gourmet, wasn't he?"

"A glutton, according to some. But also a glutton for experience, who in his work never allowed anything to blur his vision, however he lived."

"What about this Dominican gown? You said you were going to use it."

"Yes, but—" He looked hesitant.

"It doesn't fit over the waistcoat?"

"No."

"Then why not discard the waistcoat?"

He regarded her as if she were crazy.

"Do you think Balzac wore the waistcoat when he worked in his Dominican gown, or when he was fleeing his creditors?"

And even as he started to disagree, he had to laugh, and knew she was right. He said, "It's often the simplest ideas that are the most difficult."

The following morning Auguste insisted that Camille fit the Dominican gown on a Pierre wearing trousers and a shirt but no waistcoat.

"You know more about clothes than I do," he said. "You are a woman."

While she fitted Pierre to the fraction of an inch with a flowing Dominican robe that covered him from his neck to the tip of his toes, Auguste tore down the entire figure and made plans to rebuild it without a waistcoat. When she questioned this—pointing out all the work he had done on the figure he was destroying—he retorted, "Like an iceberg, seven eighths of what I do is hidden."

Pierre, braced by the grandeur and warmth of the Dominican gown, stood with a new dignity and strength.

Auguste said, "It is gratifying. The gown holds everything together."

Camille said, "Oh, I like the gown, but I still think it hides his body."

Auguste exclaimed, "And reveals him in a different way! Who would have thought a gown would give him such a sense of soaring!"

VII

The completion of the "Balzac" became a dance for Auguste as his hands moved with a fresh swiftness and certitude. The shapeless mass became feet, then thighs, and the torso grew to a masterly climax in the great head and huge mane of hair which took on the majesty of a proud lion. And now Auguste's hands swung about the figure, and dancing again, subtly interwove the Dominican robe until it and the figure were one. He felt a sensuous joy in the joining of the gown with the body, movement within movement, rhythm within rhythm. Each fold was another dance approaching and arriving at a new climax. No detail was too tiny to escape his dancing hands. He made all of Balzac palpitant. The body which so many had ridiculed, the robe made magnificent.

Then began the final days of work on Balzac's hands, which had to compress in one feature Balzac's vitality, courage, industry. Day after day passed while Auguste modeled what became a hundred hands before he found the essential sense of illumination. To achieve this, he brought the hands across Balzac's stomach, the hands holding the gown to the stomach. They were strong hands, Auguste thought proudly, hands which Balzac, with his respect for strength, would have liked. Auguste found himself spending more time on them than on any other feature.

It was not until he placed Balzac on a five-foot pedestal, however, and did the final figure at double life size, and then had him cast in snow-white plaster, that he was prepared to show the work to anyone else.

He called in Camille, Bourdelle, and Desbois—Maillol was no longer in the studio—and waited for their reaction. They stood transfixed. The great ten-foot figure atop the five-foot pedestal was impressive even without the drama of the robe and the lift of the head. But though it was very heavy, the white plaster gave Balzac an amazing lightness.

Auguste asked, "Nothing wrong? Your own judgments, please?"

Camille whispered, "It's wonderful." Tears of joy came to her eyes. He had found a solution after all the years of stalemate.

Desbois was glad that it was over. Now at last the *maître* would return to profitable work and allow him to do more of his own work. But it was a remarkable experiment, thought Desbois, and then recalling how he had been considered for this commission, he was not certain he liked it.

Auguste said, "No opinion, Desbois?"

Desbois said, "Didn't the Société want a ten-foot pedestal, maître?"

Auguste said, "It was wrong. What do you think of the figure?"

"It has enormous power," said Desbois. "But it could be misunderstood."

Bourdelle had said nothing. Bourdelle was staring, not at the head, as were the others, but at the hands, at the days of the most intense effort.

Auguste asked, suddenly anxious, "You don't like them?" Bourdelle was his best pupil, and already an outstanding sculptor in his own right.

"Oh, I like them," said Bourdelle. "But—"

"I've failed?" questioned Auguste. Bourdelle would be honest.

"No, no," said Bourdelle as the maître picked up his chisel. "The head keeps the focus, the drapery creates its own harmony, the hands are fine, powerful, but—"

"They are too powerful," said Auguste.

Bourdelle hesitated, then nodded slowly and said, "I believe so."

Auguste walked completely around the "Balzac," and then in front of it again, stopped and stared at the profile. Bourdelle was right, he thought sadly, the hands were too dominant, and there was only one solution. With a sudden gesture he cut off both hands.

Camille shuddered—weeks of work smashed in an instant, and Desbois was shocked—the hands had been superlatively made.

Auguste asked Bourdelle, "The figure is finished now, monsieur?"

"It is finished," said Bourdelle.

"Good," said Auguste. "We will prepare it for the Salon. As I promised."

CHAPTER 40

The Balzac salon became the thing to see. It was as if everyone in Paris were a connoisseur now, and the scramble for tickets for the private view was frantic. There were other provocative works on exhibit, by Besnard, Carrière, and Chavannes, the organizers of the salon with Auguste, but within a few minutes of the opening, on April 26, 1898, several thousand spectators, many of whom had not been invited, jammed into the Galerie des Machines, on the Champ de Mars, and focused on the "Balzac," "The Kiss," and Auguste Rodin.

Auguste stood between his two pieces, quiet and stationary, striving to look as impassive as rock, apparently favoring neither piece, though his heart was in the "Balzac" and he seethed inside. Viewing them in the gallery, he thought "The Kiss" attractive and effective salon sculpture, but the "Balzac" struck him as the peak of his effort. There was a stir as Pisne, Cholet and Zola approached him. The crowd formed a circle around Auguste and the others, eagerly expecting an explosion. Then Carrière stood by Auguste's side for support.

Auguste could see Degas in the crowd, and Monet and Henley and many others he recognized, but there was such a crush about him that he could not move. The pressure of the crowd, the heat, the avid curiosity, so irritated him that he cried out in pain. Once again no one was looking at his work but at him, as if he were some kind of a strange creature.

Then all eyes turned on Pisne, Cholet, and Zola, viewing the "Balzac."

Zola said abruptly, "Cholet, you remember, when I asked eight years ago in *Figaro* for a statue for Balzac, I declared I would give a thousand francs for it. Well, here they are." Zola handed Cholet the money.

Cholet said, "I have no official position any more, Émile, I—"

"Take it unofficially. I'm sure you can get it into the right hands."

Cholet didn't know what to say. The "Balzac" was different from what he had expected, a tall sheath of white plaster, and he preferred "The Kiss," which he thought was lyrical and human. Then Zola was in trouble himself because of his involvement in the Dreyfus affair. But he had supported Rodin so fervently that he couldn't back out now, it would be a confession of defeat.

Pisne hadn't said a word. Now suddenly he snarled, "It makes me ill."

Auguste said, "I don't criticize your histories."

Pisne shouted savagely, "My histories are finished!"

Carrière said, " 'Balzac' is a great statue—if you would look at it, Pisne."

Pisne snapped, "Keep quiet, Carrière, no one asked you."

"No one asked me either," said Zola. "But Carrière is right, Pisne. You should open your eyes when you look at the 'Balzac.' "

"That snow man? That plaster seal? That sack man?" Pisne said contemptuously. "We didn't order it in white or to be clothed in a sack. Or to be placed on a small pedestal and in plaster."

Auguste said, "I put it in white plaster because you didn't pay me to cast it in bronze."

"Thank God!" cried Pisne. "We didn't waste that money."

Cholet said, "You don't speak for all of the Société."

Pisne said, "I speak for enough."

"We will see," said Cholet.

"Yes, we will see," Pisne said mockingly. "Whoever was doubtful before won't be any longer, now that he can see this snow man for himself." As he saw the crowd listening intently, Pisne grew eloquent. "This piece is not a proper figure at all, but a monster. From the front it is a snow man, from the side it is a seal, from the back it is nothing. And the thick lips, the fat cheeks, the excessive hair, the whole head is a gross travesty of a great writer. He doesn't even have hands. How did he write his books? With his toes, the only part of his body we are allowed to see?"

Auguste replied, "I didn't want Balzac to look like a stage lover, an opera tenor. I wanted him to be a deeply thoughtful, observant man."

There had been laughter, however, at Pisne's last gibe, and Pisne, encouraged, ignored Auguste and rushed on. "I cannot see anything human coming from this figure. If I met him on the street, I would flee from him in disgust. No wonder he is so revolting to behold. He is an insult to human dignity. The work has been done by an artisan who despises humanity." Hisses and boos rose from the onlookers, and Pisne, close to hysteria, declared, "When the papers finish writing about it, it won't have a worth-while friend in Paris. 'The Kiss,' is pretty, at least, but this isn't even an *objet d'art*." Pisne strode away, a confident smile on his face, a coterie trailing him.

Cholet tried to be consoling, but this only made Auguste feel worse; Zola said that many would support Auguste, and Carrière agreed, yet the next instant they were discussing Alfred Dreyfus.

Auguste blurted out, "Everyone is discussing Dreyfus. Is it so vital?"

Zola looked somber, but said quietly, "They are also discussing Auguste Rodin and his 'Balzac.' "

"I wish they weren't," said Auguste.

"And I would have preferred to avoid getting involved with Alfred Dreyfus," said Zola, looking old and tired now. "But I am."

Auguste said passionately, "The two things have nothing in common. Dreyfus has been found guilty, but I—I've done nothing wrong."

Zola said, "Dreyfus isn't guilty either, whatever the courts have found. Have you signed the petition we are getting up to support Dreyfus?"

Before Auguste could reply, the others, seeing Degas approaching, moved away, obviously determined to avoid Degas. But Auguste caught Carrière by the arm, even as he thought *mon dieu!* he didn't want to get involved in the Dreyfus affair, he was having enough trouble with "Balzac." Degas had been stopped by Henley, and Carrière paused.

Auguste pleaded, "Will you stay, Eugène? Please?

Carrière said, "I would like to, but Degas regards anyone who supports Dreyfus as a traitor. He isn't speaking any more to Monet because of that, and he never really liked Zola or me. You know he detests my painting."

"And my sculpture."

"He respects your industry."

"That's all Zola cares about, actually. It isn't that he likes 'Balzac' as sculpture, but that I am another cause to be supported. Like Dreyfus."

"Do you really believe that is why he is involved in this bitterness?"

"Of course." Auguste was positive.

"Despite the fact that Zola, because of writing *J'Accuse*, which is probably right, has been found guilty of libel and has been sentenced to a year in jail and has been fined three thousand francs, and that he is out of jail now only because he is appealing, an appeal he is not likely to win, considering the present state of the country. He is even in danger coming here." When Auguste looked surprised, Carrière cried, "Didn't you know?"

"I knew that he had been found guilty and that he is appealing. But I've been so busy with the 'Balzac' and 'The Kiss,' I've been out of things."

"It goes far deeper, Auguste. Many threats have been made against Zola's life because he has created doubt about Dreyfus' guilt. It is as if he is doubting the patriotism of the Army, of the hierarchy. If Zola hadn't been found guilty, I believe some enraged would-be patriot would have killed him. Now, however, he is regarded as a failure. But the mass hysteria remains, and anything could set it off. People like to make fun of Zola because he has such a high opinion of his own work, but he also has great courage, as now, coming here to support what is, in many quarters, another unpopular cause."

"I'm grateful."

"What about Dreyfus? Are you going to support him?"

"*Mon dieu*, don't I have enough trouble?"

"You won't be able to keep out, no matter how you try."

"Oh, he is probably innocent, but how many battles can I fight? I was given a genius to depict. That's enough responsibility for one man."

Carrière didn't answer, retiring as Degas came up to Auguste.

Degas said, "You are not going to help *his* cause, are you, Rodin?"

"What cause?" Auguste was confused.

"Dreyfus. The Jew."

"I haven't thought much about it. I've been very busy."

Degas declared, "Of course Dreyfus is guilty. He is a Jew."

Auguste said mildly, "Pissarro has Jewish blood, and you are friends."

Degas said curtly, "Pissarro is a painter."

"And I have a number of students and workers who are Jewish. Some good ones. Should I dismiss them because they are Jewish?"

"I don't run your studios."

"No—fortunately. The Army versus Alfred Dreyfus. Aided by Edgar Degas. You are so angry it almost convinces me that he is innocent."

"Aren't you going to take sides?"

"Does one have to take sides? I'm a sculptor, not a politician."

"They won't allow you to stay neutral."

Auguste stared at Degas, who in his sixties had become a plump, yet shrunken, aging man with eyes he complained about, a present he despised, a future he resented, and a past of which he approved, now that it was the past.

Degas said, "You mean you like everybody?" Good God, what could be worse!

"Of course not. But to dislike a man because he is a Jew, that's like an oak tree looking down on a birch because the birch is thinner. It's not common sense."

"Trouble with you, you have no religion, you are not even a Protestant."

"Because I still admire Rousseau?"

"You'd admire anybody that praised nature."

"I was born a Catholic. I'll probably die one, if they will allow me a few journeys in between."

"You want the best of all possible worlds."

"Like the Société?"

Degas, in spite of his annoyance at Auguste, had to smile. Degas said, "The Société is composed largely of fools, but what did you expect, artists are always at their worst when they try to work together. But they have created such a commotion about your 'Balzac' that people are squabbling about you as much as they are about the Dreyfus affair."

"And those who complained about Hugo naked now complain about Balzac dressed."

Degas glanced at the "Balzac," said, "It looks harmless, an impressionistic version of the writer. Bigger than most. And you've established who it is."

Before Auguste could decide whether this was reproach or approval, they were interrupted by the arrival of the President of the republic and his entourage. A hush fell on the crowd as the President approached Auguste.

Auguste bowed to the President, though he resented doing so, thinking Félix Faure was an ideal politician, a self-made republican who was as *bourgeois* as the most accessible Bourbon, a Roman Catholic who had been born a Protestant, and who was expected now to keep both sides happy in the unhappy Dreyfus affair that was splitting France. Faure was for justice for the Société, for Rodin, for the Army, for the Dreyfusards, for anybody who could vote.

Everyone was watching, and when President Faure told Auguste that "The Kiss" was charming and then went by the "Balzac" as if it didn't exist, his disapproval plain, a new storm broke. The figure became an irresistible attraction for the haters, the butt of loud gibes, people crying out, "You ought to be ashamed . . . It should be ripped down . . . It is vulgar . . . A disgrace to France."

Auguste longed to flee, but he couldn't retreat; it would be an admission of defeat.

A reporter from *Figaro* asked, "How do you feel?"

"I have nothing to say."

"Will you answer your critics in the Société?"

"First there must be something to answer."

"Can you tell us about this work?"

"The work of ten years cannot be described in a few sentences."

"Why didn't you give him hands?"

Auguste broke off, walking toward Camille, who was examining "The Kiss."

Camille stared at "The Kiss" in marble and thought Auguste had done his perceptions of her with love. He had used the polish and finish of marble to give her a lovely naturalness. His eyes had absorbed all of her body and put it together as a caress in stone. He had modeled her without myth, reticence, modesty, or shame, the two bodies entwined directly yet tenderly. He had subtly stressed her silhouette, so the eye would linger longest on the loving, intense joining of body with body.

She whispered to Auguste, "It's beautiful." She realized with a flush of joy that he was glad to see her, though he had not invited her. "I love it."

"Yes." He wanted to say "The Kiss" was satisfactory but much like his other pairings and he had not found anything new in it, but the "Balzac" had been a discovery. He did not argue with her enthusiasm, however; she was a buffer against the intruders. He said, "I made it for you, *chérie.*"

Now Camille felt truly acknowledged; he would leave Rose after all.

But she was upset when he muttered, "I'm competing with the Dreyfus affair."

"Auguste, you mustn't get involved with that!"

"I don't want to."

"Besides, he is guilty."

"I wonder."

"Of course he is guilty." She was proud of her aristocratic principles. "But you must keep out of it, you are an artist, not a politician."

"Do you still like 'Balzac'?"

"I always did," she said loyally. She would prove to him that he could depend on her in the worst adversity. Whatever happened to the "Balzac," he had done too much fine work to be dismissed because of one piece. "But it is the eyes that communicate the most." He was vulnerable to praise of the eyes he modeled. "As you always say, no good statue comes at once, and you have made the inner modeling so vital it makes the outer firm and lasting."

Monet came over to congratulate Auguste, accompanied by Henley, the latter gloating. "Auguste, you certainly set them on their ear! Your 'Balzac' is the center of attention!"

II

The "Balzac" was all Paris talked about. It pushed the Dreyfus affair off the front pages. For many years Auguste had read several shades of opinion impartially, considering himself nonpolitical. One day he read the left-wing *L'Intransigeant*, the next the right-wing *La Patrie*, the next the center *Le Figaro*. But now he could not be casual about the press. Wherever he looked, the criticism was caustic, and often worse. He was nauseated as he read:

"The Société asked for a 'Balzac,' and was given a wasteland."

"A slur on a great writer. It is a monstrosity, as we expected."

"The figure is a scandal, it has no moral value."

"When one considers all the effort, one might well say a mountain labored and a wretched little mouse was born."

"The 'Balzac' is grotesque, obscene—why did he have to be dressed so—absurd! absurd! absurd! He is indeed a snow man!"

What angered Auguste the most was the words "Poor man! Did he have to remind us with this vulgarity of his other misfortunes, the 'Claude Lorrain,' 'The Gates of Hell,' the monument to Victor Hugo?"

He could not sleep. He could not work. Friends assured him that he would still win, and came to his defense with articles in the press, some in the newspapers that had attacked him most ferociously, praising "the majesty of Balzac's head," "the masterly modeling," "the wonderful flow of the robe," and his insomnia lessened, but he still could not work.

Interviewed, he said, "I do not expect everyone to find things in my 'Balzac' that will give them pleasure, but Balzac would not have resented it."

Yet the criticism spread to the streets of Paris and peddlers did a flourishing business vending malicious copies of the figure: tiny sacks of flour, imitation seals perched upon their tails, and small snow men which were obvious mockeries, called "Balzac, by Rodin."

Meanwhile the Société met in a series of sessions that were bitter and tumultuous. Many feelings were bruised, but Pisne, with most of public opinion behind him, won. The Société voted eleven to four to refuse the "Balzac." Proud of their tact, they presented their resolution to Auguste and the press simultaneously:

"The committee of the Société des Gens des Lettres finds itself regretfully obliged to protest against the unfinished work exhibited by Monsieur Rodin at the salon; it cannot regard this as a statue of Balzac."

Auguste, in spite of the torrent of abuse, had not expected this. Yet the resolution said nothing about a final rejection of the statue.

He consulted Cholet, who replied, "It is final, maître, however they say it. They regard the statue as unfinished, and your placing it on a five-foot pedestal instead of a ten-foot pedestal as a violation of the contract."

"Unfinished?" Auguste recoiled, finding it difficult to speak.

"They want the ten thousand francs back."

Auguste found his voice. "Then they do know what they want!"

"They don't want your 'Balzac.' Are you going to fight?" Cholet liked the idea; he would defeat Pisne yet. "You would have a good case in court."

"Like Alfred Dreyfus?"

"You will have as many supporters. Many of his supporters."

"I don't know." He didn't want to be a martyr; he wanted peace.

"You can't give in now."

"I suppose not." He stared at Cholet uncertainly.

Cholet dismissed Auguste's hesitation, declaring, "We will win. We will show the Philistines they cannot control French art."

However, it was another blow to Auguste when a few days later the Paris Municipal Council, which had the final right to approve or reject the placing of the statue at the place du Palais Royal, or at any site in Paris, announced that the "Balzac" was a "monstrosity," and refused to allow it to be erected at the place du Palais Royal or anywhere else in the city.

Auguste heard this news at his main studio, on the rue de l'Université, where every day more people were coming to tell him that he must fight back. He listened in what seemed a stubborn silence to Cholet, who was telling him about the Municipal Council. He was so tired, so tortured with a frightening impotence. If he could only think of a formula which would halt this fighting! The one thing he longed to do—to work—was the last thing he was being allowed to do.

Cholet was speaking about "this unspeakable affront to French art" when Carrière entered with more news. Carrière said, "Some of us have gotten up a statement criticizing the action of the Société."

Auguste said abruptly "I don't want the Société to have the 'Balzac.'"

"*Mon dieu!*" cried Cholet, looking shocked, but Carrière nodded and said, "We don't either, Auguste, but we want the Société to know that they speak only for themselves, not for anyone else."

"Eugène, I can't take any more fighting."

"We'll do the fighting. Listen to who has signed the statement denouncing the behavior of the Société." Carrière read with a pride unusual for him, " 'Zola, Monet, Vincent d'Indy, Henry Becque, Maillol, Anatole France, Claude Debussy, Pierre Louÿs, Bourdelle, Desbois, Toulouse-Lautrec, Mirbeau, Geffroy, Albert Besnard, Georges Clemenceau, Lucien Guitry, Catulle Mendès, André Berthelot, Lugné-Poë, Constanin Meunier, Paul Fort.' "

Auguste was deeply moved, but all he said was, "How long has this been going on?"

"Ever since the Société refused the 'Balzac.' And we are taking further steps."

"What steps?"

"We'll tell you when they are completed," said Carrière. "Come, Cholet, Auguste has to work." He took Cholet by the arm and led him out.

It was a week after this meeting that Carrière returned to tell Auguste that the statement criticizing the behavior of the Société had been greeted with such approval that a committee had been formed to raise thirty thousand francs to buy the "Balzac" and place it in a public square of Paris. When Auguste was incredulous, Carrière said, "It's being done by subscription. We've already raised half the money. Mallarmé, who has been ill, is heading the committee. We've even gotten money from Paul Roye, a member of the Société, from Turquet, who negotiated with you for 'The Gates,' and from Sisley. Sisley is very ill, impoverished, but he gave five francs. And that's typical. Even Madame Carpeaux is giving the Rodin subscription an original work of Carpeaux's, the money obtained from it to go to the fund."

Auguste was especially pleased by the donations from Carpeaux's widow and Sisley. He had never known Sisley well, and Sisley's life had been such a struggle, and Carpeaux had been one of his idols.

Thus he was startled several weeks later when many of the people supporting him suddenly accused him of betraying them. Clemenceau, one of his most vital supporters, asked Auguste to sign a petition demanding that Dreyfus be given a new trial, and he refused. He cried to Clemenceau, "How can I be involved in a new battle? It takes all my strength to fight for the 'Balzac'!" But Clemenceau, offended, strode away without another word.

And Auguste, instead of becoming less involved, found himself more deeply involved, for most of his supporters were defending Dreyfus, too. Camille agreed with his decision, Degas congratulated him on his good sense, but many withdrew from the Rodin subscription. Clemenceau ordered his name removed; Zola did, too, and withdrew his donation of a thousand francs; others followed their example; many of the Dreyfusards who had been supporting Auguste now stated that they had been wrong, that Rodin was a "coward and a fool," while Pisne, an ardent anti-Dreyfusard, said publicly that Rodin was trying to appease him but that neither he nor the Société would change.

Auguste thought a man was lucky if he only got himself hated. He didn't know how to answer the charges that were coming at him from all sides. Perhaps he had been wrong about Dreyfus, but to be despised for it—this was horrible.

One good friend stood firm. Carrière, who was a dedicated Dreyfusard and socialist, came to the main studio, on the rue de l'Université, with new plans for the "Balzac." Carrière didn't chide him, didn't want to talk about his refusal to sign the petition supporting Dreyfus, but said simply, "We must attack on another front."

"*Merci*," said Auguste, and cried out, "I am not a political man! How can they accuse me of anti-Semitism, of royalism?"

"It will pass," said Carrière. "We must save 'Balzac.'"

For a moment Auguste could not answer. Carrière stood silently and patiently, and suddenly Auguste exclaimed in a great burst of emotion, "Yes, it was a mistake, I should have supported Dreyfus, but they expect too much, too much, Eugène, I'm only one man, one man, and I was blind with fatigue!"

Carrière said, "Sometimes I think this Dreyfus affair will blind everyone. It has created such a convulsion I don't think France will ever be the same." Then his voice lightened. "But we have other work to do. There is still fifteen thousand francs in our fund. It will take just a little longer."

"No," Auguste said harshly, "I don't want the subscription to continue."

"You must. For everyone who has withdrawn I will get two new members."

"Even if they are against Dreyfus?"

"That is not the issue. You have been treated unfairly, and we must rectify that." Carrière went on quickly, urgently. "We must show that there are artists willing to fight for art, to do more than talk."

"Eugène?"

"Yes?" Carrière paused, Auguste looked so intense.

"I've been offered twenty thousand francs for the 'Balzac' by Monsieur Pellerin, a wealthy manufacturer and art collector."

"It is the least you deserve."

"And a London group of artists led by Henley want me to show 'Balzac' in their salon."

"Fine. You are being vindicated already."

"And Belgium's official art society wants to buy it and put it in a public square in Brussels."

"You are not letting it go out of the country? That would be a disgrace."

"No."

"Good. As I told you, we are getting many new people, and Monet has repeated his regard for the 'Balzac,' for all your work. He is writing you himself to tell you how much he likes the 'Balzac,' and he said I can quote him. Monet will influence many fence-sitters."

"Isn't Monet one of the strongest supporters of Dreyfus?"

"What has that got to do with it?"

"Several of the people who want to buy the 'Balzac' are against Dreyfus. Some of the new subscribers are also."

"You are obstinate. Don't you want Monet's support?"

"I am very grateful."

"And others are still for you. Pierre Louÿs, Toulouse-Lautrec, Lugné-Poë, Constanin Meunier, Desbois, Maillol, Geffroy, Mirbeau, Bourdelle, Mallarmé—"

Auguste halted him. "It is encouraging to know some people are constant."

"And there will be others."

"No doubt. But as I said, the subscription must end."

"Yet you just told me that you are not selling the 'Balzac' elsewhere."

"I'm not. I'm keeping it myself."

Carrière could not speak.

"My lawyer says I could force the Société to live up to the contract, but that it would take an enormous amount of time. I must get back to my work. I've wasted too much time as it is."

"I still think you could win."

"Has the government of France or of Paris said one word for the 'Balzac'?"

"No, but we can override the Municipal Council if we persist."

"And waste more time?" Auguste grew more positive. "Impossible!"

"You could take one of the offers."

"And see the statue used as a political issue? That's impossible, too!"

"What about the money?"

"I'm returning the money. Ten thousand francs and the interest, three hundred and twenty francs."

Carriére felt sick and abandoned, and thought desperately, Nothing will change him, but he said, "We could still win, Auguste."

"No, Eugène, no! As it is, I've given too much of myself to being a politician." When he saw Carrière's chagrin and sadness, he put his arm around Carrière's shoulders and said, "All I ask of you now is that you give me the list of those who have contributed to the 'Balzac.' Their generosity and faith have made it possible for me to continue to do sculpture." Unexpectedly and emotionally he kissed Carrière on both cheeks.

CHAPTER 41

Auguste moved the "Balzac" to Meudon and placed it in his garden, where it stood with a ghostly splendor. He liked this so much he decided to have another studio there.

Camille was stricken with pessimism when she heard that he had placed the "Balzac" at Meudon and was opening another studio there, for his country home was forbidden to her. He was being selfish once more, she thought. When she did not see him for several days, she started to pack.

He was surprised to come upon Camille preparing to leave their studio at the place d'Italie. He had been delayed at Meudon by the difficulties of placing the "Balzac"; the base had to be improvised and it had taken a long time before he had found the right site, and he was still not sure it was final. Then Rose had begged him to stay, and when he had refused she had been difficult and it had taken more time to quiet her. And there had been other things. He kept recalling what Rose had said even as he faced an irate Camille. Camille was packing feverishly, and he remembered Rose staring at the "Balzac" with a hypnotic intensity.

It was the first time he had seen Rose gazing at the "Balzac" since he had placed the statue at Meudon, and he was drawn by her fascinated interest though he pretended to be indifferent. He was convinced that Rose did not know what she was looking at.

Mon dieu! she thought. What an odd but powerful peasant's face it has! The body didn't matter, but "Balzac" was no corpse. She stood a few feet away from the statue, having learned long ago from Auguste to regard outdoor sculpture from a distance in proportion to its height. She was hurt that he had not asked her to look at it, but she sensed she had his attention now, though he was completing the placing of the figure.

Rose had been astonished by the commotion over the "Balzac"— she had heard about this from the neighbors and her friends in the studio; it was all they had talked about. And when Auguste brought the statue to Meudon, she had thought, What a miracle—he is going to stay! But the moment she asked him how long he was going to remain he had walked away quickly, before she could say another word.

And now, she felt, he was regarding her opinions as pathetic, though he was watching her. She said, "It looks fine here," and he did not answer. "Are you going to keep it here?" she persisted, even as she wanted to protest angrily against his rudeness, and she turned red.

"I don't know. It depends."

"On what, Auguste?"

"It doesn't matter." He dismissed her concern with a wave of his hand.

"Is it money? You should keep the statue here. It fits here. If you need money, I could go to work."

"At what?" He looked cynical.

"Sewing. I used to sew very well, and still could if I had to."

He did not comment, as if this suggestion were too absurd to consider.

"I don't do anything here," she said, aggrieved, "except to wait for you to come home. When you do. Which isn't often."

His gesture of irritation warned her not to pursue this thought.

"Will you be able to manage, Auguste? Returning the money to the Société, wasn't it dangerous?"

"Perhaps. But it was more difficult not to."

"I've saved a little money. From what you've given me for the household. If you need it—"

"How much?"

Her face brightened. "Over five hundred francs."

He smiled contemptuously. "That's nothing compared to what I need."

"But five hundred francs used to be enough to live on for months."

"I have many studios, many expenses, many—" He halted abruptly. It was useless: she didn't understand and never would.

To Rose, however, it seemed clear that to ignore her generosity, concern, and love was selfish of him. But before she could express her affection, he moved away. She cried, "Where are you going?"

He answered, "How did you save five hundred francs? It takes that to run the house." Now he was suspicious, too.

"I'm careful. Are you going to see her?"

"I told you never to mention her name."

Rose turned pale, but she couldn't stop. She said, "I hear that Mademoiselle is still beautiful."

"Don't you understand anything?" he said angrily.

"I understand that you prefer her," she said sadly.

"You have no idea of what I need."

"Is she ever lonesome?" When Auguste was silent, she said, "She must be. You're not always there either."

He changed the subject. "How did you know about the Société?"

"Everybody has been discussing it."

"And Dreyfus?"

"Poor man. Do you think he is guilty, Auguste?"

"How should I know! I'm not a politician!"

"Don't get angry. I'm not taking sides."

"That's the trouble. I would have been better off if I had."

"You have had a difficult time, haven't you?"

But he didn't want her sympathy—it made him feel guilty, and he hated that. He attacked on another front, one which affected him deeply. He said, "Yes, everybody has been arguing about the 'Balzac' except your son. I haven't seen him for weeks. Do you know where he is?"

Rose blushed. She didn't know where *petit* Auguste had vanished to, except that he had stopped going to the studio soon after the Société had refused the statue. At that time he had come to her for money, which she had given him—fifty francs, but no more, to make sure he would return when this was gone. She had been concerned about his shabby appearance and his alcoholic breath, but she had not criticized him, for then he would stay away. But as it was he had not returned, though a month had passed.

"I undergo the worst crisis of my life and he disappears at the height of it. Sometimes I think we would have been better off if we hadn't had him."

Rose did not agree—she knew *petit* Auguste's faults, and very little he did surprised her—but he was her son and Auguste's. How could Auguste reject him under any circumstances? She knew the boy could do strange, even destructive things, but Auguste himself was not a moral man. She said, "He must have been upset because you didn't confide in him."

"He was upset?" Auguste laughed bitterly. "What about me? How can you confide in someone you can't trust! I was wrong to ask him to return to the studio. During all this agitation over the 'Balzac' he didn't support me in any way. As I said before, we never should have had a son."

Rose turned from him, numb. She could not bear to argue any longer. She could not bear anything about him. Even his work was suddenly repulsive to her. She didn't care any longer. She wanted only to be left alone.

But he could not endure to see Rose so stricken. She was wrong about Camille, he repeated to himself, and he was right about the boy. Yet however little she understood him, she had not failed him. He was grateful. He caught her by the arm as she reached the gate of the hedge that framed the "Balzac" and asked, "Does he look like an ape?"

Shocked—was he crazy? Rose blurted out, "He looks like a Rodin!"

"Good!" If she were only not so jealous.

She opened the gate for him. She said, "*Bonsoir*."

He said, "I'll be back."

She did not ask when, but watched him go toward Paris, into the valley, which was hidden by mist, walking with what she thought was a devilish self-sufficiency.

And now Camille was reproaching him with her packing, answering his protests with a distraught outburst. "I have to move. I can't sleep here. I had a wretched night. I'm always waiting for you."

He thought angrily, sometimes the two women sounded so alike. He said, "I don't know what's wrong, but I'm not guilty."

"No, you never are," she said, convinced of her superior virtue. "But I'm simply a *divertissement* for you, a sport. We have no private life, your work always comes first, and now so does your housekeeper."

"She is not my housekeeper," he said severely.

"What then? Your mistress?"

He did not reply.

"If she is your mistress, monsieur, what am I?"

"No one is my mistress."

"Or your wife?"

"You are jealous. That's the trouble."

Her clothes were piled high upon her trunk, and she looked desperately wronged even as her pulses hammered and she wondered if she was acting insanely. This had become a much lived in and deeply loved studio, book-strewn and crowded with clay and plaster and terra cotta, but she could no longer be calm. His constant absences had ground her to a harsh edge. She cried, "We live in different worlds. You are a mixture of *bourgeois* negligence and Mephistophelean selfishness, and if I stay it will kill me!"

She grew white with anger as he did not answer. Then amid a terrifying silence she resumed her packing, her head held high, her motions resolute.

"Come, *chérie*," he said in a sudden wave of emotion. "I'm just a man. You expect too much from me, far too much."

"I don't want your apology!" she cried, and hurried on with her packing.

Abruptly, however, without heeding her show of indifference, he pulled her close, holding her with his powerful hands. She was unable to resist, yet unable to respond. He said, "I tell you what, we will go on a holiday to the south. We'll visit Renoir, who is living on the coast at Antibes, not far from Nice. We'll stop at Nice, Cannes, wherever you want to go."

"What about money?"

"I'll manage."

"And your work?"

"I need a rest."

She paused, then asked slowly, "Tell me, are you still in love with me?"

He bolted the door. He kissed her passionately. He declared, "To-night when I thought you might really leave me, I could not bear it."

She came to him then to be loved. He felt she yearned to be compelled and subjugated. More than ever he satisfied her, while she gave him the feeling he was the only man who could. He assumed this ended their difficulties.

II

He left his studios in the care of Desbois and Bourdelle, he did not return to Meudon to say good-by to Rose or tell her where he was going or when he would be back, he spent a month taking Camille wherever she wanted to go. Yet this did not satisfy her and the irritations remained.

She wanted to think of their holiday as a honeymoon, and he regarded it as a walking trip. He had never taken Rose on any of his holidays, and he felt noble, a true lover, and Camille wondered if he would propose. He was fascinated by the medieval sculpture they found in the South of France, and her only interest was that he marry her. He was happy to be away from Paris, which was rainy and dreary; he said it was weather fit only for concierges, but he was not penitential, as she desired.

And visiting Renoir, who was hospitable and cheerful despite the pain of his rheumatism, which was making it very difficult for Renoir to paint, Camille did something that puzzled and troubled Auguste.

Renoir was showing them his birds, of which he was proud, when Camille suddenly and emotionally threw open the door of the cage, crying, "They should be free!" and would have opened all the cages if Auguste hadn't halted her.

Renoir was amused, but when Auguste scolded her after they returned to Nice, she accused him of bullying her, repeating passionately, "Yes, that is what your love has meant, bullying and denying, that's all!"

Then on the way back to Paris he was shaken by her attack on him through Zola. Zola, when his appeal from his conviction had been rejected, had fled Paris for London to avoid being put in jail. His supporters had insisted that Zola would do Dreyfus more good out of jail, where Zola could write.

But Camille was outraged. "See!" she declared. "This proves he is guilty!"

Auguste thought, however, of how often he had wanted to flee from the whole Balzac affair and what composure it took to hide this, especially from her. He tried to be calm, saying, "It only proves that Zola didn't trust French justice," and this time she was contemptuous. "Auguste, you can defend Zola after he stopped talking to you when you didn't sign the petition for Dreyfus?" She glared at him as if he were a fool. He wondered why she was so bitter and personal. It spoiled the vacation for him.

III

In Paris, Auguste believed things would improve. He felt rested; Camille looked better; now, he told himself, they were ready to work sixteen hours a day again—that should arouse her from her depression.

He had become so well known because of the Balzac affair that many people wanted to buy his pieces now—if only for the notoriety it gave them. There were offers for new commissions, mainly from private collectors, and it looked as if, with hard work and careful supervision of his expenses, he could recoup his losses from the "Balzac" and even pay back the money he owed the bankers. He knew he should be pleased, but he still felt torn apart, for "The Gates" and the Hugo monument remained incomplete, and the Société's charges made him more conscious than ever of his unfinished sculpture.

He decided that work was the only solution, the one thing that could restore their old happiness. He told Bourdelle and Desbois to sell his pieces for whatever they could get, to put off the offers for new commissions for a while, and started to work directly from marble. He began at the studio at the place d'Italie, thinking that if Camille wanted proof of his love he would give it to her in the way he knew best.

She was reluctant to embark on a new project, but she agreed when he declared that she would sculpt as his equal. But when the work became *his* work while she was the helper again, getting the materials, the tools, aiding but never initiating, her resentment returned.

After weeks of arduous labor a great hand rose from a large block of marble. It was as if the marble itself were the substance which had given birth to the hand and what the hand held. For out of the mighty palm and fingers emerged the interwoven forms of Adam and Eve, the man protective, the woman loving. And now it was as if the gigantic upthrust hand—as well as the marble—had given birth.

Auguste, pleased with this conception, named it "The Hand of God."

It seemed finished to Camille, but he was dissatisfied with the modeling. He felt the sculpting of the hand had been done hastily despite her approval. And he was not sure yet of the contours of the human flesh. He decided to pause for a week to refresh himself, and then return to "The Hand of God." Thus preoccupied with the piece, he assumed that she would not mind his absence, especially if she involved herself in her own work, as he suggested.

But she didn't believe him when he said he had to go to the country to study nature in the process of creation, stones rising from the earth, trees extending from their roots, the extraordinary structure of birds and insects.

When he didn't include her, she told herself that he was returning to Rose and Meudon, and that this was his way of doing it. And she became certain of this when Auguste's promised one week away became several. Then she knew she had to move unless he married her, and now she was almost sure he never would. She made arrangements for the concierge to move her and began to pack.

IV

He intended to return at the end of the week. He didn't go to Meudon or see Rose. He visited Versailles and Argenteuil, and Monet and Degas, but separately, since Degas was still not speaking to Monet because of Monet's support of Dreyfus. He enjoyed Monet, who continued to share his enthusiasm for nature. But Degas was more misanthropic than ever, complaining about the brightness of the sun they were sitting in, and unable to forgive Monet for supporting

Dreyfus, and burying most of his contemporaries, even Manet. This surprised Auguste: Degas had lauded Manet fervently when Manet had died.

What delayed Auguste the most was a letter from Henley. He was pleased that his English friend had prospective customers for several of his bronzes, but he was distressed that the usually ebullient Henley had become melancholy over the death of his five-year-old daughter, his only child, a short time ago.

He had to reply at once, though he disliked writing letters, often not answering them for months or at all. But it took him a week of pondering to find words that might console Henley. Then he wrote him an affectionate note, saying he understood Henley's suffering because he had suffered so much himself lately, and stressed his support of Henley as a friend and writer, congratulating him on the latter's recently published book, hoping this would ease Henley's grief. The business details—that the bronzes would be available for purchase—he left to the postscript.

He felt better, however, for having expressed his feelings to a friend he trusted. Thus he was unprepared for the news that Camille was leaving him, conveyed to him by the concierge.

V

Camille was not surprised to see Auguste standing wrathfully in the doorway while she completed her packing. She had used the concierge deliberately, so the concierge would tell Auguste and give him one last chance to halt her. But she said, "So Monsieur has returned from Meudon."

"I didn't go to Meudon. I visited Versailles and Argenteuil. I saw Degas and Monet. And I had to answer a letter of Henley's."

"That took two weeks?" She obviously didn't believe him.

He was shocked to see that she was dressed all in black, looking like a funeral bas-relief against the white "Hand of God." He heard the cry of the vegetable hawker outside, the whistle of the knife grinder. He didn't know what to say. Outside nothing had changed. He had seen the usual street cleaners in their blue denim, the gendarmes in their neat capes.

She said, "You've become one of the *grande bourgeoisie* with your home at Meudon. No wonder you don't want me there."

"Of course I want you there. But—"

"Rose is there."

"As I promised you." He moved toward her, but she evaded his embrace. "Let's take a ride in a cab, where we can talk things over in comfort."

"Will you marry me? Leave Rose for good?"

He found himself stuttering, and suddenly he halted. He didn't want to choose. He could not choose.

She knew it: she could see it in his tired, self-conscious, constrained expression. But she had to ask, "Why can't you leave her? You don't seem to love her."

"I don't love her. Not the way I love you."

"Yet you can't leave her?"

He shrugged, then said earnestly, "I haven't been to Meudon since we took our holiday. Believe me, Camille, I haven't!"

"I believe you." And she did, he looked so intense.

"So what are you upset about now?"

But this dismissal of what she had asked, had been forced to ask—marriage—struck her as an even worse effrontery. In a voice that made his blood run cold she said, "For the last time, Auguste, if you won't leave her and marry me, I'm leaving you!"

"That is blackmail." He grew rigid.

"Call it what you want. It's final."

"I can't abandon her, she's been my lifelong companion, my—"

"Your humble servant!" Camille interrupted explosively. "I know. I am only a servant, too! Oh yes, I am. I am supposed to wait patiently for you no matter where you go, what you do, just as long as it satisfies you. But I can't endure the intervals any more." She began to pack frantically, as if it took all her energy and courage, then to repack—for she had packed hours ago and had left a little only to keep her here until he arrived. But now she kept her eyes away from him, crying, "This is ridiculous, this life I'm living. It's intolerable and unnatural."

"Unnatural?" Auguste repeated. "That's nonsense."

"It is. How can you ask me to always wait for you?"

"I don't."

"Yes, you do. I don't mind being poor, but I do mind not living decently."

"I've been honest with you."

"And selfish."

"You're tired. Distraught."

"Because I've sacrificed my career to help yours!"

"You have been happy here."

Camille stared at Auguste. His eyes, under lids that were thicker than ordinary eyelids, seemed harsh. "But you won't commit yourself." She felt a hopeless grief when he didn't deny that. She coughed to get rid of the pain in her throat. He was caressing his figure of her in "The Hand of God," and she thought with a new bitterness, Never have I obsessed him as this statue does, as any of his statues have. His hand continued its slow, gentle caress of the unfinished marble. Sensual desire dominates him with a single-minded passion, her mind ran on, and because of this I've submitted. And now she felt an extraordinary humiliation in the sensual satisfaction with which he felt the naked "Eve." Never has he shown me such tenderness, such pure devotion, she said to herself, and I deserve this. I am being punished for loving him more than he loves me.

He said, "You must wait. I'll think of something."

"I can't. I can't go on any longer, Auguste. Not today, not tomorrow, not the day after. Either you marry me, or—" He became a blur. She couldn't stop the tears. She thought, I no longer exist, nothing exists for him but his work.

"You know I love you. More than anyone I've ever known."

"But I'm not your wife."

"Don't talk like that."

Even now, she thought bitterly, he was not really listening to her. An overwhelming wave of despair rose in her. She turned to the door and said, "Very well, I'm leaving."

He could not beg. Yet he blocked her way.

"Will you let me pass?"

She almost wished he wouldn't then, but he did, slowly, reluctantly.

She felt a hopeless grief—why must it end like this? But she could not endure any more. She forced herself to open the front door and said, "I'll send for my things. Tomorrow."

He had not moved after her.

She thought he looked as pale as death.

He wanted to weep; he felt broken with sorrow and dismay, at the end of his strength. But he could not be different. He could not make promises he could not keep. He hardened himself to say, "You will regret this, Camille."

"And you?"

He did not reply, but looked somber. His head slumped forward.

In this moment she realized that he was almost sixty, though no cracks showed—he still looked like a boulder. She cried, "You have to have it all your own way, like Louis the Fourteenth. You want Rose to wait for you at Meudon and me to wait for you in Paris, and sometimes I think you prefer Rose."

"She's had a difficult life."

"And I haven't?" Camille was surprised by the murderous rage she felt. "Then you won't marry me? Ever? And never intended to?"

He held out his hands in a gesture of helplessness.

She turned and rushed out of the studio.

He stood horrified. He made a vague gesture of reproach, but she had already vanished down the street with a panic-stricken haste. Trembling violently, he felt ill, but he could not follow her. He could not afford to. She was a fool. He made a silent prayer that she return.

The concierge came for her things the next day, and Auguste didn't stop him or ask where she was, too proud to inquire. His mind felt pitilessly clear. He had never promised to marry her—she hadn't been deceived. She had deceived herself—marrying him would have been an act of utter idiocy. To marry him when he was wed to his work would be a crime, a betrayal.

Yet when he heard footsteps in the street the next few days, he hurried to the door, hoping it was Camille, thinking how beautiful she was, how desirable. And when it wasn't Camille, he thought despairingly, What have I done to be so unhappy? I tried to do the right thing with her. But he could not give in, that would be an unforgivable weakness. Yet never had he felt worse.

After a week of waiting—when she did not return—he closed the studio.

VI

Auguste saw Rose in the garden when he returned to Meudon. She could tell that he had come to stay, though it had been three months since she had seen him. He walked awkwardly, looking older than she had ever seen him.

He asked, "How is the garden?"

"Fertile. It's good soil, country soil." She took his limp hand; it was as cold as stone. A shrewd gleam came into her eyes. She said, "She's left."

He hesitated, said, "I'm putting my studio here. My main one."

Rose tried to think of something else to say, but then realizing he preferred silence, did not speak. She went with him, however, as he walked back to the house, and he seemed glad to have her company.

Then suddenly he asked, "Is there anything to eat?"

"Fish, boiled meat, cabbage. What you have always liked."

In this moment he felt that Camille was a dream slipping away from him, and nothing remained but a sense of separation and anguish. He said, however, almost curtly, "That's what I like about you, Rose, it may not be elegant, but the workingman eats little else. And you, *ma chatte*, are a good cook. My poor Rose, what you've had to put up with."

Rose fled to hide her tears while he muttered, "I like obedient women, I would be a fool to give away such wealth." From now on he would trust only his sculpture, he decided. Sculpture could still take him anywhere. Yet he still felt icy, wondering if he would ever feel ecstasy again. He hurried over to the "Balzac" before missing Camille became unbearable. It stood stark and solitary. He had been right to amputate the hands. Whatever else he had spoiled, he thought, he had not spoiled this. The sunlight fell on the head. He wished "Balzac" could speak. He wondered if he would ever match this work. And now it was over. She had run away. It was still hard to believe.

Rose had returned, wanting him to eat. "Think," she said. "He will be here all your life."

"That's what makes me sad."

"But he will be in Paris someday, too."

"How can you be sure?" He disliked sentimentality, and what did she know?

"I remember when no one would give two sous for your work. How much did Carrière raise for this?"

He felt a rush of affection for her. She would not interfere with his work. Love and sculpture did not mix. He put his arm around her and said, "*Ma chatte*, you believe in me even when you don't understand me."

"I understand that you've come home," she said, smiling for the first time in many months.

He did not answer, but he went back to the house with her.

PART
SIX
THE
THINKER

CHAPTER 42

Auguste was excited when he heard that Paris was going to celebrate the coming of the twentieth century with its greatest exposition of all: the Exposition Universelle of 1900. He was told it would attract the civilized world to Paris. He decided to answer his enemies with an exhibit of his collected work for everyone to see. He was surprised by his own audacity. Only the exposition authorities refused to give him space to show his sculpture, saying it did not fit the exhibition's theme of progress. Then the Paris Municipal Council refused his request to erect a pavilion at his own expense, declaring it would not be attractive enough.

But finally, after much disputing and with the aid of influential supporters and the financing of the bankers who had helped him buy Meudon, he was able to get permission from the city of Paris to build his own pavilion. However, it had to be off the fairgrounds. As a compromise he was allowed to construct his pavilion of sculpture at the place de l'Alma.

He was pleased with the location. It was near the Seine and in the heart of Paris, close to the place de l' Étoile and the place de la Concorde and within walking distance of the exposition. He built a simple white structure with austere Greek columns and placed in it his collected works, 171 pieces. He was amazed by the amount of work he had done.

Yet the day before the opening he stood outside his pavilion and wondered whether anyone would come to see his pieces. His Temple

of Sculpture—the Société was calling it the Temple of Oblivion—
had a modesty which was in marked contrast to the spectacular pavil-
ions of Science and Industry. He stared at the nearby Palace of Elec-
tricity, the feature of the fairgrounds, which glowed with dazzling
lights that proclaimed a century of progress was assuredly ahead, and
doubted the wisdom of his own pavilion.

Everyone would prefer this tower of light, he told himself. But he
could not turn back. Eighty thousand francs had gone into his pavilion, sixty thousand lent by the bankers. He was committed. His future depended on how many visitors the Rodin pavilion of sculpture
would attract at one franc a person. The fee was cheap enough, but
his doubts increased. He was apart from the Exposition Universelle
itself, he had a sinking sensation that no one would come—that the
hostility of the Beaux Arts, the Institute, the Academy, which had
been behind the Société's savagery, would prevail. He was still shaken
by Camille's absence, though it was almost two years since he had
seen her. His pessimism grew as he remembered the sudden deaths
of Mallarmé and Chavannes, two of his best and most loyal friends.
When he had heard about their deaths, the news had devastated
him. Even today, thinking of them and of Camille, he missed them
very much and was very lonely.

II

Hardly anyone did come to his pavilion until the Minister of Education appeared in official recognition of its opening and expressed his
approval, stating that Monsieur Rodin's work, particularly "The
Gates of Hell"—which was in the place of honor—was the work of a
patriotic Frenchman. It was the greatest praise the Minister could be-
stow.

Patriotism was in favor again. Reconciliation was replacing civil
disunity.

Thanks to Zola, Dreyfus had been brought back to France, and
though he had been found guilty in a new trial a pardon had been
granted because of what the court called "extenuating circumstances."
This was considered the ideal French solution: it implied that Dreyfus was innocent, yet the honor of the Army had been saved. And
Zola's indictment had been dropped and Zola had returned to

France, a hero. After years of bitterness the Dreyfus affair had sim-
mered down. Though there was still hatred beneath the surface, the
affair had faded from the press. Now there was a need to praise
rather than to blame.

Gradually the Rodin pavilion became the place to visit, as if Auguste, because he had been persecuted also, had to be more appreciated, too.

In the next few months thousands of visitors came to see the unfinished "Gates of Hell" and to decide whether they were as horrifying
as people said they were. Many came also to view the "Balzac" because of its notoriety. But the greatest interest was in his nude pairings, especially "The Kiss." So much attention was paid "The Kiss,"
Auguste was revolted.

There was also much interest in his heads of Camille, Hugo, Baudelaire, Falguière, and Dalou. Everyone seemed to know that Auguste
and Dalou, once close friends, were bitter enemies now, and people
were curious to see how the rival sculptor's portrait had fared in Auguste's hands. There was even more interest in Falguière's head, for
Falguière, a good friend of Auguste's, had been given the final commission for the "Balzac" by the Société.

Yet they had remained friends. And Auguste—as a gesture of
friendship—had done a head of Falguière while the latter had been
completing his "Balzac."

Now Falguière's "Balzac," a large, stout man placed on a park
bench with the Dominican robe held around him, looked like a prosperous, commonplace bourgeois; and everyone was ignoring it to view
Auguste's vivid, powerful head of Falguière, showing Falguière as he
was, a little bull.

Viewers were surprised to see a "Baudelaire" with an expression of
profound melancholy, as if expecting his own imminent death and
dissolution. The heads of Hugo evoked admiration. But it was the
heads of Camille that drew the most attention. His relationship with
her had become one of the worst-kept secrets in a Paris that doted on
such affairs.

And though there were still those who declared that his work dis-
honored France and spoke of him with an abusive malice, to the
world outside of France he was becoming one of the glories of the
Third Republic. Czar Nicholas II of Russia, in Paris to open the

Pont Alexandre III, named after his father, visited the Rodin pavilion. The Prince of Wales, still curious to see how "The Gates" were progressing, spent an entire afternoon there. And finally, Loubet, the new President of the republic, not to be outdone by his foreign guests, came to the exhibit as an expression of national approval.

Faure, his predecessor, had died unexpectedly—because of an excess of copulation, it was rumored—and Loubet was not a hypocrite. The President thought the many coupled figures charming and regarded them good-naturedly, as republican love affairs, to be viewed with amusement.

Auguste thought Paris unpredictable indeed. What it punished one year it praised the next. Everywhere in Paris the word was spreading: "Rodin is the man to see, he is becoming the new Hugo." It took effort for Auguste to accept this. He liked the praise; he felt he deserved it; that in fact, it was overdue, but he wondered if he could survive such adulation. And he didn't see the connection with Hugo. But now even his nudes were regarded as fit for the *bourgeoisie*. His work became a matter of national pride when museums from everywhere but France competed for his statues.

Copenhagen bought eighty thousand francs' worth and created an entire room in their museum for his pieces, called the Rodin Room. The Philadelphia Museum purchased "Thought," for which Camille had modeled; the Chicago Museum bought "The Kiss," and then had to drape it when a shocked outcry arose. Museums in Budapest, Dresden, Prague, and London acquired more of his work.

Private collectors increased in number and avidity. He was offered more commissions than he could do. He didn't know what to charge, certain that if he raised his prices he would lose these orders, only to discover that when he did raise them—to discourage commissions he wished to refuse—his statues became more coveted by the wealthy. They wanted to pay. They clamored to pay. The more he charged, he learned, the more prestige the collectors got. A Rodin had become fashionable to acquire.

By the time the exhibit was over and he had moved his work from the place de l'Alma to Meudon, he had sold over two hundred thousand francs' worth of sculpture. After all the expenses had been deducted, he had sixty thousand francs. There was no more anxiety about money. He could sell anything he pleased. He could work without giving a damn. But he did not discuss this with anyone.

Carrière, his best friend, asked him if the exhibit had been a success, had he met his expenses, and he replied, "Just about, *mon ami.*" He knew he should not be suspicious of Carrière of all people, but there could still be disasters. "Do you need any help, Eugène?" The painter was still poor.

"No, no, no!" Carrière cried. Then seeing Auguste looking uneasy, he threw his arms around Auguste's shoulders and added, "It is just that I was hoping you would have enough success to bring you peace of mind."

III

Now it was not peace of mind that Auguste wanted, but time and energy to do the work he preferred. He had just reached sixty, and it reminded him that old age was no longer far away, that time and energy were more precious than ever. Yet when he heard that Camille was living in Paris, he asked Carrière to visit her in the hope of creating a reconciliation. The painter was the gentlest person he knew—an ideal peacemaker.

But Camille greeted Carrière coldly. She resented that the painter was a Dreyfusard, though the affair was no longer a subject of open discussion. And she didn't care for his work; she thought it misty, inconclusive. Yet she couldn't shut the door in his face, though she didn't invite him in.

The painter stood in the doorway of her studio-living room, trying not to appear as uncomfortable as he felt, noticing that she was living alone. He saw clay figures, plaster casts, several bronzes, but the only furnishings were a bed and a chair, as if she had to show she was even more austere and dedicated to sculpture than Auguste. And there was a pale, drawn asceticism on her face. She has aged, he thought sadly. There was gray in her hair, her features were sallow, there was only a little left of her beauty.

She ignored Carrière's hand and said with a weary bitterness, "Well, monsieur, you've found me. Maybe I deserve it." He groped for words, but she cut him short. "I don't want any help, monsieur. I didn't act from a spirit of revenge, but from principle." She refused to discuss Auguste.

Carrière found himself being ushered out of her room, which actually he had never entered, while she muttered, "Bourdelle preferred, always Bourdelle. His watercolors are unique, but his sculpture—I am far more realistic."

Auguste, however, learning that she was having difficulty managing, that her work, which he respected, was bringing low prices, arranged for the Minister of Fine Arts to buy several of her pieces for provincial museums—the Minister refused to consider them for the Louvre or the Luxembourg, though Auguste suggested this. And when he was given one-man exhibits in Brussels and Prague, he put her bust of him in the place of honor, but she disowned it, declaring harshly, "It is just a student's work. He could have gotten my work in the Luxembourg if he had really tried."

Unable to accept that, Auguste sent Carrière back to her with an offer of assistance, and she rejected it angrily. She stated that these offers of help were not an act of protective affection but a determination to persecute her. She was so hostile in a sudden burst of hysteria that Carrière was alarmed for her sanity. Camille was half sobbing and half laughing, "It's murder, my career was murdered, I must break free, be my own master. And no one will stop me, no one. No matter how I am attacked and repudiated. Monsieur, I am not a corpse, I am much better than Bourdelle, but exhibitions exhaust me."

He thought she was going to break down or attack him, and he excused himself, but she wasn't listening, agitated with a strange, feverish frenzy.

Auguste was very sad when he heard about this scene. And he was heartbroken a few weeks later when he was told that Camille had had a nervous breakdown and had been put in a *maison de santé*. The thought of her in an insane asylum, however they glossed over that with a fancy name, made his blood run cold. Yet he was not responsible, he told himself, she had been emotionally unstable for a long time. Poor Camille!

He went to see her and she regarded him as a stranger, as if she had never known this bearded, tired-looking man. She was in black, and so thin it was shocking. Only her musical voice remained of the beautiful girl he had fallen in love with, and suddenly she went off in a torrent of emotion, not talking to him, to anyone actually, yet having to blurt out, "These Dreyfusards they send me, they're dirty little beasts. My head "Grand'mère," won third prize, they kept the first from me, and now they want to put me in the women's prison of St. Lazare, the one they use for prostitutes, sick prostitutes."

Auguste turned gray. He tried to explain, "Chérie, marriage is a ghastly endurance contest, we would end by hating each other. Marriage may be your instinct, but it is unsound. Eventually we would never forgive each other, and develop an implacable hatred for the rest of our lives. Believe me, I may sound harsh, but it is true."

She looked at him as if he were crazy. She motioned to the attendant: Who was this man? Why was he here? She had work to do.

Only Auguste's prominence had gotten him into the maison de santé. Now as she grew worse with his visit, the doctor was called. The doctor informed Auguste that he must go and that he could not see Camille again.

She was mumbling, "Dreyfusards, sculptors," then suddenly screamed as Auguste walked away, "I hate them . . . hate them . . . hate them . . . !"

He was desolate. He could not sleep for weeks.

Yet a month later when he heard that Camille had been released from the maison de santé with the diagnosis that she had had a nervous disorder—not a mental one—and had returned to her studio-living room and was sculpting with a savage concentration, as though clay, plaster, and marble must be shaped to express her desperate, haunted dreams, he was sure she had used this illness as a way of attacking him. Then he was not sure when he learned that she was accusing him of having her followed, of wanting her put in the women's prison of St. Lazare, and that she was keeping her door locked.

IV

Rose had thought that with the departure of Camille she would have all of Auguste emotionally, and she was gratified that he had opened the studio at Meudon, for many people came to visit him there and he was home some nights each week. Only she still had very little of him. At Meudon he was usually in deep meditation, or ignoring her for his work—yet when she scolded him for this he looked sorrowful, as if afflicted like Job. And she was shocked to find him as preoccupied with his Paris studios as before.

He refused to discuss *petit* Auguste, who was living off occasional handouts from Rose. Ever since his son's absence during the crises of the Balzac affair, he had dismissed him from his mind.

He was attentive to other women, which upset her the most. She heard this from employees in his studios whom she paid to keep her informed. Often she thought she would burst with the knowledge, but what kept her from a final explosion was the awareness that he would return to her after each affair—he always had.

For Auguste each affair was a new effort to forget Camille. Gradually, though he continued to regard her behavior as a calamity, when he was pursued ardently by many predatory females he felt less lonely, and less vulnerable to the onrush of old age. World-famous now, he was sought out by the great, the near great, and those wishing to be close to the great.

Models were his for the asking: young women, beautiful women, society women, erotic women. Since it was believed that flesh was his passion, most of them felt his passion would be different from any other's. Moreover, now that Maître Rodin, as much as any artist, showed that women were the subtlest trap for the artist, he must succumb to them and so prove them irresistible.

Auguste allowed himself to succumb, as long as none of these liaisons were dangerous. No matter with whom he made love, a part of him was detached. He was accused of being a connoisseur of sex, a lecher, of using his studios as a harem, and he didn't care. He thought that love was so slyly arranged that no lover was ever truly happy. He told himself that it was enough that these affairs gave him pleasure, lessened his loneliness, and sometimes even gave him the illusion that he was still a young man.

However, he was furious when he came upon Bourdelle modeling a figure of Pan in the likeness of himself. Bourdelle, embarrassed, apologized for the two distinct horns he had set upon Pan's head, and Auguste shouted that this was "unfair, inaccurate!" He denounced Bourdelle as an ingrate, just a clever stonecutter, and in a rage ordered him out of his studios.

Then he was not sure he should have lost his temper. The large head Bourdelle had modeled was out of proportion to the satyrlike body, and the horns were too long, but the face was a dramatic likeness, even if it did resemble an old goat. He had to smile. A few days later he ordered Bourdelle to return, as emphatically as he had thrown him out.

But Bourdelle, though he agreed to return for two days a week to teach in the Académie Rodin the *maître* was starting, could not work with him any more in the studios or remain in discreet and devoted self-effacement. The pupil did not wish to compete with the teacher, but Bourdelle had become deeply involved in his heads of Beethoven and had to concentrate on them. Bourdelle had learned from Auguste the value of a single-minded focus.

Auguste could not argue with this justification; it was his own. But it made him melancholy. There had been times when he had thought of Bourdelle as a potential son, a need he had had of late with the coming of age and his disappointment with *petit* Auguste. Now he realized that was impossible. They had become competitors, whether they liked it or not.

V

Soon afterward he had an unexpected encounter which reminded him that he was aging faster than he liked. He had returned to the Hugo monument, hoping to find a final conception that would please him, and had ordered everyone out so he could work in privacy, when a young, very attractive woman stood in the doorway. This did not surprise him, many pretty women came to his studios these days, but what did was her manner.

She announced, "I'm Isadora Duncan, the dancer."

He looked blank. What dancer? He had never heard of her. But she was unusually pretty and quite young, actually just a girl, probably in her early twenties, to judge from her high color and freshness of skin. And now she was saying that she was madly in love with his work, which she had seen at the place de l'Alma, and she moved beautifully. As she approached him, he found himself sketching her movements without further thought.

She said, "My dancing is my own. I am my own choreographer. I am an American dancer, but I prefer the Greeks." She stepped out of her dress.

He was startled—her scanty dancing tunic was not what he had expected. He was glad she was not wearing that bastion of virtue: the corset. But she assumed he would be enchanted by her dancing. Was she a vagrant? he wondered.

When Isadora Duncan saw Auguste smile skeptically, her fear and hesitation faded before her flood of anger and she began to dance with a sensuous excitement. She was still overwrought, but there was an individuality about her movements that fascinated him.

Finished, she said, "I take my art from nature, too."

Auguste's eyes shone as he approached her.

She thought he was *exalté*. She was grateful that Carrière, whom she had met recently, had given her the great sculptor's address. Yet as she realized that in a few seconds her tunic would be off, she felt paralyzed with fright—he was so much older than she had expected. His statues were so youthful, vital, beautiful, but the sculptor himself was a gruff old man, with a thick graying beard down to his chest, shorter and heavier than she had expected, with a patriarchal face. Even as she assured herself he was a genius and she adored genius, and so he should be forgiven everything, her fear grew. She whispered, "I am not stone. I am a virgin."

It must not be too quick, she prayed. Didn't he hear what she said?

"I am a virgin," she repeated. Be gentle, she prayed.

He was amused—her virginity was so obvious—but he gave no sign. He had all the professional models he needed, with the best bodies in France, but he thought, What breasts this girl has! They were round and firm even when she danced. And her body was as lovely as her movements, and splendid for marble. He came close, intending to feel her flesh so that he could translate it to the working clay, to get its warmth into his fingers and work it into the clay. But as he caressed her arms, shoulders, and breasts, she grabbed his hand and held it against her cheek. Auguste, deciding he could model her later, started to embrace her, and she pulled away from him.

He did not pursue her. Since Camille, he could not pursue any woman.

Isadora took a deep breath, thinking there had to be a heroism about love, he had to accept her offering as precious or it was nothing

—and it could not be nothing. But he was sculpting again, while she felt clumsy and unhappy. She still felt his intensity, but he was so much older than she had expected. She mumbled, "I'm sorry." Her eyes filled with tears.

"Do not feel sorry. You are young and beautiful. Can you say I am young and beautiful? And I lost my patience a long time ago."

"I am sorry for myself, not for you."

"A man with patience will come along, my beautiful one."

She stared at him a moment more, then dressed, swiftly now.

He said, "What did you say your name was?"

"Isadora Duncan." She wanted to hate him for failing to remember, but she could not, he looked so impressive in his absorption with his sculpture.

"I like your dancing. I hope you will model for me sometime." Then he shrugged and returned to his work with a finality that was an *au revoir*.

Yet after she was gone, though he had sought to be the man of the world, he felt very old. This girl had made him feel like her father. But she had been honestly moved by his work. And that made him feel better. He began to draw his memory of her dancing, thinking that it would make several lovely sketches.

CHAPTER 43

When two years passed without any personal sculpture, the sketches did not satisfy him and neither did the busts or the pairings he was doing for private commissions. Yet never had he been so affluent. He remained in great demand; he was growing rich; he was courted by the celebrated and the mighty; attractive women pursued him in larger numbers than ever; and he was discontented. Whatever benefits fame and success brought him, he realized they did not alter his essential self. His most genuine satisfaction was still the work he did to express himself. Yet he was spending more time and energy in avoiding the interruptions than on work itself. But he could not avoid all of them, and there were some he did not want to avoid. He was proud of the dinner arranged in London in his honor, to celebrate the presentation of a bronze "St. John the Baptist" to the Victoria and Albert Museum by a group of voluntary subscribers.

The banquet was given on a mild evening in May. He was pleased by the weather and that the world was at peace this year of 1902. He sat in the place of honor, and everyone was congratulating him that this Rodin banquet was a huge success, many tributes were being paid him, and suddenly he felt out of place. Henley was on one side and Sargent on the other, friends he liked and trusted, and he felt isolated. He thought the dinner was good, considering it was English—out of consideration for him it had been cooked by a French chef—but he was not really aware of what he was eating. The conversation was disjointed, an odd mixture of French and English, and he kept saying to Henley in French, for he knew no English, "The work I've done is all that actually matters."

He did enjoy the speech by the French Ambassador, for he could understand every word of it. However, when the chairman of the Rodin dinner, the witty and handsome George Wyndham, Chief Secretary for Ireland, lauded him in English he felt uncomfortable. He liked praise as well as anybody, but this was confusing. He could tell there was much praise, for the audience applauded each time Wyndham said "Rodin," and there was frequent applause.

As a Frenchman he could not allow an Englishman to outdo him in civility. Each time he heard "Rodin," he bowed in acknowledgment. But this added to his discomfort. He sat thinking of the vanity of vanity. By the time he had to read his own speech of thanks, his notebook papers, which he had pinned together, kept coming apart and he kept losing his place. He found himself mumbling—he was sure that many in the audience didn't understand a word of his French—yet the applause was loud and continuous. He felt embarrassed.

Yet afterward he was told that he had made a splendid speech.

He was more comfortable when as he left the dinner with Sargent and Henley, English art students from the Slade and South Kensington schools unhitched the horses from his carriage and drew it through the streets themselves.

Then while Auguste was still enjoying this gesture—no matter how gruff he tried to be, he got his greatest pleasure from the appreciation of the students— a new representative from the Ministry of Fine Arts informed him there could be no more delays with "The Gates of Hell." Twenty-two years after the work had been commissioned, Rolf Balle said, "We have inaugurated a new policy at the Ministry, maître. Work must be delivered as promised."

Auguste said, "But the Museum of Decorative Arts hasn't been started yet. How can I complete an entrance for a museum that is not there?"

The positive young man replied vehemently, "That's not the point. You agreed to deliver 'The Gates' many years ago. We cannot wait any longer."

"It's almost finished. I've done one hundred and seventy-six figures."

"Yes, we know. But over thirty thousand francs have been paid you."

"Twenty-five thousand seven hundred. And I've spent every one of them."

"That's not the point. There have been many complaints in the Chamber of Deputies, particularly from the provinces, about a department that allows money to be spent without having anything to show in return."

Auguste could not admit that he was tired, even bored with "The Gates," that he had tried to do a Tower of Labor as diversion, yet he felt as far away as ever from completion. He said, "Two more years. That's all I need."

"Nineteen four?" The inspector looked suspicious.

"Yes." He had no feeling he would finish by then, but he would try.

Balle nodded, suddenly smiling as if he had won a victory.

Auguste asked abruptly, "How old are you, monsieur?"

"Twenty-six, maître."

"Then you were four when I started them."

"I've heard about them all my life. Do you really think you will finish this time? They will demand the money back if you don't. You will lose a lot of money, maître."

Auguste thought of his many lucrative sales since the Exposition Universelle and said curtly, "That will be France's loss, not mine."

II

It was also a matter of pride. He returned to "The Gates," determined to finish them. He went to work on them in his main studio, on the rue de l'Université, and ordered his concierge to keep everyone out. But weeks went by without any change. One gray day he was staring at "The Gates," thinking of the Inferno for the tenth time in as many days, when an intense young man stood in front of him.

He went to dismiss him, saying, "How did you get past the concierge? What did you pay him? Fifty francs?" This was the method most intruders used.

"I told him the truth. I am writing a book about you, maître."

"A book?" This was the last thing Auguste expected.

"To be published in Germany. I am the poet Rainer Maria Rilke."

The name meant nothing to Auguste. There seemed to be nothing out of the ordinary about this youthful foreigner—this was evident from his heavily accented French—except his admiration, and that was not unusual either these days. Yet Rilke was attractive: slim, small, dark, with intense blue eyes and a thin black mustache. Auguste paused in his scolding, not certain whether to dismiss this emotional young man who looked so eloquent.

Rilke declared, "Maître, 'The Gates' are so lyrical. All your work is." Before Auguste could halt him, the poet went on to say that his wife, Frau Clara Westhoff, was studying with the maître, and Auguste remembered her, an earnest, strong-willed, pretty young woman of some ability. Rilke spoke of the maître's sculpture with such thoroughness and understanding Auguste was impressed, though the veneration was so intense it was embarrassing.

He said suddenly, "I am not a monument historique."

"You will be," said Rilke. " 'The Gates' are a monumental work."

He still had no intention of succumbing to the poet's adulation, but he was pleased that Rilke, cultivated and sensitive, saw so much in his sculpture. And he liked the paternal feeling the young man aroused in him.

He found himself inviting Rilke to Meudon and allowing him the run of his studios. He was surprised by the way the poet's avid attention and comments prodded him to talk. He considered himself a reticent man, but with Rilke he was talking as a master to a disciple, and they were both reveling in it. And he was touched when Rilke created several verses in French and dedicated them to him.

One afternoon they were discussing "The Gates" when Rilke said, "Maître, why don't you make an individual figure out of the naked man sitting on top of 'The Gates'? He could be powerful and dramatic."

"The poet? Dante?" Auguste was dubious.

"He's no poet." Rilke was sure of this. "He's more the brute, with his heavy features and muscular body."

Auguste said, not sure he enjoyed this criticism, though Rilke could be right, "He's contemplating. That would be characteristic of Dante."

"Not if you made him life size. Then no one would see him as a poet."

Auguste hesitated and sat down, trying to decide. Unconsciously, from force of habit, he rested his chin on his hand and his elbow on his knee. However his mind turned, Rilke seemed right. And he could no longer fool himself into believing he could finish "The Gates," but if he could salvage this figure "The Gates" would not be a total loss.

"*Maître*, you look just like him!" Rilke exclaimed. "Especially when you are thinking. Thinking so hard. Thinking out your ideas. Thinking that—"

Auguste motioned for silence. Thinking—that was it. It was such a struggle. And this man was trying to do just that, with all his strength.

From that moment the poet became the thinker, while Auguste modeled him life size. But he still felt unsure, and there were more interruptions.

Zola died, asphyxiated in a room with tightly shut windows and a blocked chimney. There were rumors that he had been murdered because of the Dreyfus affair, and some gloated over his death, but others were saddened, like Auguste. Though Auguste hated funerals, he joined the long line following Zola's hearse, walking with Carrière and Monet. It was the least he could do, he thought, for though Zola had never spoken to him again after he had failed to sign the petition for Dreyfus, Zola had defended him at one time. Auguste sought to remain anonymous in the crush behind the casket, but he was seen by Clemenceau. Suddenly they were speaking to each other, though Clemenceau had stopped speaking to him also at the time of the petition. As they parted they shook hands, almost cordially.

III

The next day he visited Fantin, though he had not seen him for years, but they had been good friends and now he was driven with a need to recapture that. Fantin didn't seem surprised to see him. Fantin quietly accepted his outstretched hand, drew him inside, and said, "You look well, Auguste."

"I feel well as long as I am able to work."

"Yes, work, it is useful. I've been in this studio since 1868, over thirty years. It opens on a little court, like Delacroix's. Remember the day we watched him paint and we were amazed because he made his models move? I hear you are famous for that now."

"If anyone deserves credit for what I do, it is Lecoq."

"For me it was the Louvre."

"Still the Louvre?"

"Yes. I still admire the sculpture of Houdon, Rude, and Carpeaux."

"I like Carpeaux. But how have you been, Fantin?"

"Fantin does only flowers and fruit now. Not like *le grand Rodin*, whose patron is the State."

Auguste was unhappy with this sudden note of bitterness. As a young man Fantin had been one of the sweetest of artists. He said, trying to avoid any trace of hostility, "The State is a very unsatisfactory patron."

"Because of 'The Gates'? How much time have they given you now?"

"Until 1904. But it is not worth discussing. What about yourself? I see that you are working as much as ever." Wherever Auguste looked there were canvases. Fantin, however much he had withdrawn from the world, had not withdrawn from painting. "But no more portraits?"

"Occasionally." Fantin grew nostalgic, trying to recall how he had seen Baudelaire. "When I met him the first time I noticed his exquisitely tended hands, his closely cropped hair, and that his throat was carefully covered with an old violet silk scarf. But do you think anyone cares for exactitude any more? I used to make copies of the masterpieces in the Louvre to earn a living, of the painters I admired, Rubens, Rembrandt, Delacroix, and they said I was not too experienced but had a lovely line. And the gallery of the Louvre is still filled with copyists, only now some of them are copying me. Then I would have given anything to be hung in the Louvre, but now that I am, oh, I am pleased, but it is too late."

Auguste noticed that Fantin's light red beard had grown gray and yellow, his bushy hair was straggly, his strong nose was wider. Fantin, in his baggy trousers and green eyeshade and growing corpulence, was an old man. He wondered if he made the same picture. But he said, "I heard about your admission to the Louvre. Degas told me, said that he was partially responsible."

"I met Degas and Manet when I was copying at the Louvre, around 1855; I'm not sure of the year any more. And now I paint Baudelaire with a receding chin, and gray hair, and unhappy features."

Auguste shrugged, wondering if this impulsive visit had been a mistake.

"I hear that you are becoming a patron yourself."

"I own a few paintings. Renoir, Van Gogh, Monet. I like having them."

"Don't apologize."

But he was. Yet he had tried not to humiliate Fantin with his triumphs.

An elderly man walked in, poking his head in first, to make sure no one else was here, then was unable to retreat when Auguste saw him, though the newcomer wanted to. For a moment Auguste didn't recognize him, then he saw that it was Barnouvin, wearing a velvet coat and a broad-brimmed felt hat that was shabby from use. And still sitting on the terraces of cafés on the quais, thought Auguste, watching a world Barnouvin was no longer in.

Fantin said, "You know each other?"

Barnouvin flushed, but Auguste said hurriedly, "Of course," and went on to make Barnouvin feel more at ease. "No more *femmes parfaites?*"

"No," Barnouvin burst out with a sudden need to justify himself. "I make my living copying *le sujet religieux* and *le sujet patriotique* and when I meet a sentimentalist *le sujet de famille.* For that I have a great flair. I can shut my eyes and do it without a single blemish."

There was a heavy pause, and then Auguste said, "It has been a long time."

"Forty years?" asked Barnouvin.

"Just about," said Auguste, "but sometimes it seems like yesterday." Suddenly he saw Marie standing in front of him, and Papa and Mama. "Did you know, Barnouvin, that I went into the Church for a while, almost a year?"

"Oh yes," said Barnouvin. "I think I met you once after that."

There was a pause, as if no one knew what to say next. Auguste sensed that Barnouvin had come for a special reason, there was so much urgency in him.

Barnouvin said, "I hear you got caught in the affair over Dreyfus."

Auguste said, "Yes. I got damned for not taking sides."

Fantin asked, "Are you happy, Auguste?"

"I've had a few good things happen."

"A son?"

"He is not one of my favorite subjects."

"I remember," cut in Barnouvin, "you liked girls in white dresses."

"I still do."

Barnouvin said, "And now you are invited to the presidential palace."

Auguste said, "It doesn't make me a better sculptor."

Fantin smiled, but Auguste saw that the painter had grown weary. Auguste excused himself and they shook hands, but Auguste had a feeling they would not see each other again—there was no real point to it.

Barnouvin joined him as he left, saying, "I'm going in the same direction," though he had not said in what direction he was going. Barnouvin, breathless and agitated, swiftly destroyed the growing recognition of Monet, Renoir, and Degas, stating they were lucky, and added swiftly, "But you, *mon cher ami*, you worked hard."

And now Auguste's only anxiety was to end this as quickly as possible. He asked, "Would fifty francs help?" Barnouvin replied, "It's only a loan." Auguste said, "Of course," thinking it was better to give it to him than think of it as a loan, then neither of them would have to suffer under a sense of obligation. Auguste made it a hundred francs, and Barnouvin said, "I will always be grateful, *mon ami*," and they said *au revoir*, both of them relieved that neither of them had suggested another meeting.

IV

A year later Auguste was given his third award of the Legion of Honor, that of Commander. And though it did not help him finish "The Thinker," he was gratified by this new recognition, especially when his friends used it as a reason for giving him a picnic to celebrate. Bourdelle and Carrière made the arrangements, and after lunch in the forest of Vélizy, close to Versailles, Isadora Duncan danced. This was a pleasant surprise to Auguste. They had become friends and she had posed for him, but there had not been any romantic involvement. He thought her dancing lovely and Grecian.

Rose, sitting by Auguste's side, was happy. It was the first time he had invited her to a party with his friends; she felt this was recognition at last. To those who were new—she knew some of his friends from before—he introduced her as Madame Rose and said nothing more. She was surprised at how famous he was becoming. She thought Isadora a very pretty young woman, but she didn't care for her dancing, and was relieved that Auguste regarded the dancer paternally. She had heard about Camille's breakdowns, and she felt almost secure. She prayed there would be no more of the awful loneliness.

V

Soon afterward Henley died, then Fantin and Aunt Thérèse. Her passing and Fantin's were a shock to Auguste, but had the remoteness of the past. It was Henley's death that was the terrible blow. Henley had become one of the few artistic friends he could trust. It made him feel that his generation was being wiped out, that now with each passing year he was closer to death.

As always, when made desolate by the death of a friend, he turned to his work. He focused on "The Thinker" with a new resolution, as if this would stave off the onrush of death. He vowed that until he finished this figure he would not permit any interruptions. But he was facing a new, harsh difficulty: many days now he lacked the energy he needed. Often just when his conception seemed about to fulfill itself, he was afflicted with an immense weariness and he had to stop. "The Thinker" was becoming a race against time. He could still do busts, hands, and small work easily, but large works made serious drains on his precious energy.

Yet he labored on. If "The Thinker" was going to be his last epic figure, as he feared, he wanted it to be unforgettable. In life size, however, he thought it interesting, but not unique. And he had no desire to portray nobility, grace, or beauty, but man. The Greeks and Michelangelo had created bodies of great beauty and perfection of form, but he had to do something else, something more. When man had come to thinking, Auguste reflected, he had come to it only after the most laborious effort—even now it was as painful as it was difficult. To think was to suffer. To ask, Who am I? Where have I come from? Where am I going? Why?

Auguste redid his rough model larger than life size, and now he was sure that man was not a beautiful creature struggling against a corrupt world, but a brute struggling to rise out of the animal state, and not always succeeding. He felt this especially in himself. And he came to believe that the effort to climb out of the beast and into the thinker was such a burden he modeled the final figure twice life size, to show the magnitude of the struggle. He did this from memory, as Lecoq had taught him.

He remembered the many moments of struggle with his own efforts to think. He wondered about the position of the arm on the opposite leg, for it was not natural, and then he realized the strain of the position conveyed the effort to evolve from brute to thinker. The body became massive, the shoulders powerful, the feet and hands enormous.

At the end of many days of work he longed to make love, to get release from this burden, and was unable to, and this threw him into a deep melancholy, as if this were another way of approaching death. But he could not halt. Lately he had done too much work in which he had no vital interest, but this focused his feelings about life. He plunged on, though exhausted, seeing "The Thinker" as an expression of man's elemental tragedy even as the figure throbbed with energy and dominated the space about it. He stressed the brooding, stubborn strength, believing it characteristic of a life that was tragically arranged. But he put the greatest stress on the huge head and the magnificently robust hand that bore this immense weight. And as "The Thinker" came alive, Auguste became more depleted. When he finished, he was drained. Never had he felt so exhausted.

He asked Carrière to view the completed plaster—the first person to see it, for Rilke, who had stimulated him so, was out of Paris. Carrière stared at "The Thinker" so long in silence that he was certain he had failed. He started to say, "I was too tired, working on it," and Carrière hushed him.

There was another period of silence, while Auguste squirmed uneasily; then Carrière said suddenly, "For me he is the first man who could think, and in this effort he is being brought to the realization of the tragic destiny ahead for his species." Auguste was surprised: it was rare for Carrière to be pessimistic. Carrière added, "Such an effort to think, to be rational, such a terrible struggle, the flesh more powerful than the mind, yet the mind seeking to emerge from the slime, as the body has."

"Then you like it, Eugène?"

"Like it? No. How can you like such a vivid portrayal of our own struggles? He is me, my journeys, my efforts, my sufferings. This is very personal. 'The Thinker' could be any of us."

Auguste sighed. "I thought so, but I'm so tired I've lost all sense of perspective. I'm afraid nobody will care for it, I'm not sure I do myself."

CHAPTER 44

"The Thinker" was shown in the Salon of 1904, and again Auguste was severely criticized. Supporters of the Beaux Arts, the Institute, and the Academy called it "a monster, an ape man." Critics wrote, "Look at those horrible hands, they are not the hands of a moral man, they are a disgusting travesty of a man." There was an editorial in one of the leading Parisian papers declaring, "Monsieur Rodin has intentionally made this man ugly and clumsy, intentionally ignoble and degrading, intentionally bloated and gross, and unfortunately he lacks tradition and is too old to change." However, this time Auguste's friends were prepared. They replied by raising fifteen thousand francs by public subscription to buy the statue, then presented it to Paris.

Auguste was sure that the Municipal Council, still critical of him because of the "Balzac" and the Hugo monument, would not allow "The Thinker" to be placed in Paris, especially when the Panthéon was recommended as a site. But Rolf Balle, speaking for the Ministry of Fine Arts, suggested that if he returned the money advanced for "The Gates" a compromise could be worked out. When Auguste agreed to give back the 27,500 francs, plus interest, the Ministry persuaded the Municipal Council to accept "The Thinker," and Auguste promised to have the bronze finished for 1906. He was proud that a work of his would stand in front of the Panthéon, his first work to be in a Paris public square, and it eased the pain of "The Gates." It was more solace when the Ministry of Fine Arts bought a copy of the original plaster cast of "The Thinker" and presented it to the Metropolitan Museum of New York and the people of America as a gift from the people of France. He thought this was hardly a Statue of Liberty, France's other sculptural gift to the United States, but some Americans might feel it, though he was not sure they would understand it.

But Auguste's great pleasure came when he was asked to preside at a banquet to honor Carrière, and the twenty-fifth anniversary of Carrière's first exhibition. The guest list was distinguished: it included Clemenceau, Briand, Monet, Renoir, Monsieur and Madame Curie, Pierre Loti, Claude Debussy, and Anatole France. Auguste was particularly pleased that Renoir came, for his old friend's rheumatism had become so painful and crippling that it required a heroic effort for Renoir to go anywhere. Auguste was disturbed, however, when Carrière, usually punctual, was late. Then when Carrière did arrive, he looked haggard and gloomy. And Auguste noticed that the painter had to force a smile as guests congratulated him. He wondered why his friend was so somber and preoccupied in spite of the honors being paid him. He ordered a carriage to take Carrière home, knowing that the painter, still poor, would never incur such an expense. They rode silently up to Montmartre, where Carrière had lived many years with his wife and five children—the painter had not brought his wife because she had to stay with the children.

At the door Carrière said, "I don't know what to do, Auguste."

"Do? What's there to do? You will paint. The banquet will encourage you to paint more than ever. You will surely sell now, *mon ami*."

"Of course, of course. I will sell like Renoir now. It was nice of him to come. I wonder how he endures his poor health."

"How do we endure anything? With work, naturally."

"Yes, if you can work. Auguste, I have cancer."

Auguste was overwhelmed. He didn't know what to say.

"I felt so ill this week I didn't think I could go to the banquet. So I went to the doctor today, and since I wanted to know the truth he told me."

Auguste, though shaken to his roots, sought to be the consolation Carrière had been always and said, "The doctor could be wrong."

"He is not wrong." Carrière looked as if he had been given a sentence of death.

"What about an operation?"

"He may try, but he doesn't sound hopeful. For the time being, however, he wants me to continue painting, if I can."

"You will, you will!"

"Let's not lie to each other."

Auguste frantically longed to do something, but what?

Carrière sensed his emotion and said, "*Merci, mon ami,* it helps to know you are near. And perhaps you are right. Perhaps it is not that serious."

The next few months it seemed as if Auguste's hopefulness might be right. Carrière was able to work, though the pain continued, and as Auguste treated him with tenderness it helped Carrière to go on with dignity and resignation.

II

Auguste was pleased when he received an admiring letter from Rilke in September. It expressed the poet's continuing regard for the *maître's* work and inspiration and asked whether he might have the good fortune to see the *maître* when he returned to Paris shortly.

Immediately and with warmth Auguste replied that not only would he be at home to Rilke, he would like the young man to be his guest at Meudon.

When Rilke hesitated, writing that it could be an imposition, Auguste had his present secretary—his third in the last year—wire Rilke that the young man must come, it would be his pleasure. The more he thought of the idea, the better he liked it. Rilke's book on him had appeared the year after they had met, but he had not seen it, and he couldn't read it in any case, since it was in German. After Rilke had left for Italy and Germany, wandering from city to city and castle to castle, searching for roots Rilke seemed unable to find, Auguste had felt deserted, though he had not admitted this, even to himself. But Rilke made him feel differently than he had felt to any other young man: paternal, yet as master to disciple, hero to worshiper.

Rilke's first few days at Meudon were happy ones for both of them. They shared the beauty of the autumnal countryside, the variety and excitement of the sculpture—Auguste had a copy of everything he had done at Meudon. Auguste, even more than at their earlier meetings, was delighted with the poet's perceptive understanding of his work. He found himself mellowing under the heat of Rilke's praise and worship. Occasionally it made him feel like Louis XIV, but most of the time Rilke's regard put him in the role of the sculptor-philosopher-thinker. Yet it was a role impossible to sustain when the world intruded. There were constant requests for portrait commissions, most of which he turned down; people clamoring to see him; antique dealers he had sent for—he bought sculpture antiques whenever he could afford them; and letters from all over the world. He could not cope with this, especially the details; no one he hired understood his needs.

Thus when he was left without a secretary—the third time he had fired one within a year—and looked dejected at the thought of interviewing anyone else, Rilke suggested, "*Maître*, perhaps I could help you."

He beamed, then frowned. "*Merci*, but no, you are a poet, not a secretary."

"You need a poet. Someone who understands you."

Auguste hesitated.

"Oh, not full time, *maître*, but whenever you need me."

"Several hours a day?"

"Yes. And then I won't feel I am abusing your hospitality."

"Good." He liked the idea of Rilke's remaining. "And you will have time to do your own work. You will need to aid me just a little. Several hours each day."

At first Rilke helped Auguste two hours each day, chiefly with letters, though Auguste knew no language but French and Rilke, while he understood French, distrusted his ability to use it properly, particularly for such an important correspondence. But gradually, though the poet was still able to work on his *The Book of Images*, rewriting many of the verses, and he continued to feel this relationship with the great sculptor was instructive, the two hours lengthened to four, then six, and then often to all day. Rilke tried not to mind, and struggled manfully to remain enthusiastic and devoted, for as he wrote his friends, he felt the "great old man" needed him more than ever.

Carrière was operated on for cancer in November, and it was a failure. Afterward the painter was unable to leave his bed, and Auguste, in his concern for his failing friend, grew ill tempered.

Rilke blamed that on the burdens of fame and the *maître's* aging and tried to ignore the increasing inconveniences. But he was hurt when the *maître* suddenly and curtly warned him not to become involved with the models or he would be fired, though the *maître* still involved himself.

A short time later Auguste scolded him like a father to a son for preferring older women, saying, "It isn't natural. Even I prefer younger women. But remember, none of my models. I've lost too many models that way."

Auguste grew impatient with everything as Carrière grew worse. His correspondence was huge and becoming heavier, and he was always behind. He felt that Rilke, though a writer, didn't understand his French very well, often asking him to repeat his dictation, and this was another irritation. It was becoming difficult to feel relaxed with the young man, with anyone, as he saw life ebbing from Carrière.

Rilke was distressed most that the *maître* was coming to treat him only as an employee. Rarely now did he confide in him or discuss his theories of art. Most of the time he was curt and complaining, as if Rilke had come to represent the annoyances of the world. And Rilke had no time for his own work any more, unable to write, study, or even meditate.

Rilke became friendly with Madame Rose, as everyone called her. At first it was because of his desperate need to have someone to relate to, but finally because he was touched by her desire to mother him. Rose liked this gentle young man—he was even younger than *petit* Auguste, who was still young in her mind, though almost forty —and she enjoyed feeding Rilke her favorite dishes. She was not sure he enjoyed eating them, especially the cabbage soup, but she knew he needed milk, cheese, and eggs, he was so frail and sickly-looking.

Gradually a kind of understanding developed between them. They discovered that they shared the same complaint: often the *maître* would leave Meudon for Paris without telling either of them. Rose's carefully prepared lunch would grow cold, and an appointment made by Rilke on the *maître's* orders would be left waiting without a word as to when the culprit would be back.

One day Rilke came upon Rose talking secretly to a shabbily dressed man. Rose grew pale, hastily handed the man some francs, and motioned for him to go. Rilke didn't ask any questions, though he was curious—this man's features resembled Rodin's—and a few minutes later Rose blurted out, "Rainer, you won't tell Monsieur, will you? He doesn't like him. It's his son."

"His son?" Rilke was surprised. He had heard rumors that there was a son, and that the *maître* was not fond of him, but he hadn't expected to see him here.

"They've never gotten along. He wanted *petit* Auguste to follow him in the studio, but the boy is not like you, you understand art and Monsieur."

"Doesn't he have any talent? With such a heritage?"

"Oh yes. He engraves very well. But you know what sculpture is like, so difficult, and he can't work that hard. He's not very strong, and his father has always been so strict." She hurried to add, "Even with me."

Yet a few days later Rilke noticed that though there were days when the *maître* was so busy and preoccupied he acted as if Madame Rose were not about, when she hurt her ankle trying to protect her menagerie of dogs, ducks, and chickens from a marauding hawk the *maître* displayed sudden tenderness. He picked her up as he would a child, and despite his age—he was going on sixty-six—carried her gently to their old brass bed. There were appointments waiting for him, but he insisted on staying by her side until a doctor came and assured him the injury was nothing to worry about.

III

The next few months Auguste needed all the tenderness he could muster. He had been working on the plaster of "The Thinker" that was to be set temporarily in front of the Panthéon, so he could make the final bronze cast in proportion to its placing, but this became very difficult when Carrière died.

He was by Carrière's side every possible moment the last few weeks, much as he hated and avoided all aspects of death. Carrière kept mumbling, "One must go on," and Auguste felt a bitter inadequacy as his friend slipped away from him. At the grave he spoke of Carrière's gentleness and genius even as he thought there were times it hurt too much to care, it was too much of a demand on a man's strength and courage. Yet after paying for the funeral and giving the widow enough to live on temporarily, he had to go on, as Carrière had said. A prominent art dealer who had said it was impossible to sell Carrière's work gave the widow seven thousand francs for a canvas, saying that now that the painter was dead, his work was worth something after all. Auguste, suspicious about the dealer's sudden generosity, walked in on him abruptly and said, "We want all of the purchase price. I am Carrière's executor."

The dealer was surprised. He stated, "I gave her seven thousand francs."

"And probably got seventy," declared Auguste. *Mon dieu!* He had learned about the tricks of dealers since his work had become worth something.

The dealer blushed strangely and looked stunned.

Auguste said furiously, "I thought so. You were trying to cheat him. If you don't give the Carrières the balance, I will make a public scandal."

The dealer mumbled, "How did you know I sold it for seventy, Rodin?"

Auguste didn't. It had been a wild guess. He took the money without another word, wrote out a receipt for it, and gave it to Madame Carrière.

Soon afterward the temporary plaster of "The Thinker" was placed before the Panthéon. He approved of the placing, thinking it would look even better in bronze, not beautiful but appropriate. The next night "The Thinker" was shattered into a hundred pieces by students from the Beaux Arts, his ancient enemies. The vandals had been identified; some of them had been arrested by the gendarmes. There was only one consolation: there was still the original cast; the destruction had not been total.

CHAPTER 45

Auguste was in no mood to accept any new commissions when Rilke came to him with a letter from a Mrs. Charlotte Shaw, asking him to do a bust of her husband, Bernard Shaw, the writer. He refused at once, emphatically. He had never heard of the man, and he had had too much trouble as it was with the heads of writers. He told Rilke to write his refusal, grumbling that it was bad enough he did millionaires but at least they paid very well.

Rilke was astonished. He thought this was too much. He had heard of this writer's work; he was sure Shaw was a coming man, and he wanted to meet him. Rilke wrote Mrs. Shaw that the *maître* charged eight hundred pounds for a bronze and a thousand for a marble, and that if she deposited money in a Paris bank in the *maître's* name and persisted the refusal might be overcome.

A few days later Auguste received a letter from Charlotte Shaw that made him hesitate. She wrote that she had put a thousand pounds in a Paris bank in his name, to do a marble or a bronze, whichever he thought was appropriate.

Auguste was impressed. He liked such promptness.

She went on to write that her husband was a renowned writer, who adored sculpture. And that he would not allow anyone to do his head but Auguste Rodin, stating that he would be remembered as an idiot if living in the same time as Auguste Rodin, he failed to have his head done by this man, the greatest sculptor in the world.

Auguste turned to Rilke, who had translated this letter, and asked, "Is this Shaw really such a good writer?"

"Yes," said Rilke, thinking Shaw must be since he had obviously composed this persuasive note under the guise of Mrs. Shaw. "He has a most unusual face."

"Really?" He saw Rilke suddenly look very sad. "What's wrong?"

"My father. He died several weeks ago."

"Why didn't you tell me?"

"I tried, but Carrière was dying, and you were preoccupied."

"Did you like your father?"

Rilke was surprised by the directness of the maître's question. He wavered, then tried to tell the truth. "Not actually. He never understood me, as you do, but he was my father, it was a root."

Auguste said curtly, "We lose many roots before we die." Mon dieu! Why did this young man think he had the answers?

Auguste had started to walk away when Rilke asked, "What about Shaw?"

"Tell him to come to Paris and I will see."

Auguste expected this would be the end of the matter, but several weeks later Shaw came to Paris with Mrs. Shaw and made an appointment to see him. He was not sure he liked Shaw, but he was fascinated by his face. He felt there was a Christlike essence in the writer's features, and he approved of Mrs. Shaw at once. He was pleased with the way she hovered over her husband, always protecting him. He suggested, "It will be more comfortable if we work at Meudon, outside of Paris."

Shaw asked, "How long will it take?"

"At least a month." He expected this would discourage them, though now he rather looked forward to modeling this interesting face.

"You are thorough," Shaw said approvingly. "What time do you want us?"

Auguste paused. Ordinarily he didn't allow anyone but the sitter in his studio while he modeled, but Charlotte Shaw could be useful as a translator and he liked her. He said, "Ten in the morning."

Shaw said, "We will be there."

They were prompt, and work began at once. Rilke was disappointed that he was not included. He had expected to be present as the intermediary between the writer and the *maître*, but when he had met the Shaws the *maître* had not even introduced them, merely saying to the Shaws, "Monsieur Rilke, my secretary." He sensed they didn't even know he was a poet, widely read and praised in Germany. Yet Shaw was proud of his knowledge of Richard Wagner. Perhaps Shaw had no ear for poetry despite his love of music.

This was no consolation as the situation grew worse. Rilke wanted very much to become friendly with Shaw. One of the reasons he had taken this post was to meet important writers and artists, and being a secretary was removing him completely from the scene. With the *maître* modeling Shaw every day, all day, there was so much for him to do outside the studio. The *maître* told his secretary he could not handle any correspondence or see anyone until this bust was finished, and ordered Rilke to handle all these details. So Rilke's work accumulated to an average of sixteen hours a day while he tried to answer the mail himself, to keep the many visitors away from the *maître*, and to make appointments for the next month. And his unhappiness grew.

Rose was curious about this dignified couple who came every day, and she looked into the studio while Auguste was working, something she rarely did any more, and he ordered her out. He didn't introduce her to the Shaws. He saw an inquiring look on Mrs. Shaw's face and muttered, "She's not educated."

Charlotte looked embarrassed, but Shaw chuckled and said, "That's the way to treat women. They are always pursuing men."

"Yes," said Auguste. At least Shaw was not a barbarian. And he had such noble features. As he told Charlotte, "*une vraie tête de Christ.*" He wondered why she smiled strangely, but he went on working until there was another interruption.

A stout peasant Frenchwoman stood in the doorway with her young, pretty, slim daughter, declaring, "*Maître*, I've been told you need models. I can assure you, monsieur, my daughter has a good moral character."

Auguste retorted curtly, "I'm not interested in her moral character —are her breasts firm?" And when the mother looked shocked, he didn't even say *bonjour*, returning to his bust of Shaw with an abrupt swiftness.

Shaw asked, "*Maître*, you don't like women?"

Auguste snapped, "I love them. In their place."

That night Rilke was informed that if there were any more interruptions his usefulness as a secretary would terminate. Then Auguste strode away.

Rilke was confused. A painter-sculptor, Henri Matisse, was waiting to see Rodin, insisting that Rodin had said he would examine his work. Matisse had refused to budge and was still waiting, though hours had passed. So Rilke, though it could mean his dismissal, told the maître about the waiting artist.

Auguste didn't get irate, as Rilke expected. Instead he strolled over to where Matisse was waiting, said, "Where are the drawings?" and when Matisse brought them out nervously, he glanced at them swiftly and stated, "Too quick, too careless. Work on them more. When you have done them over ten times, return and we will look at them again." He walked off, leaving a bewildered, upset Matisse wondering if the great man's approval was worth it.

The next morning Auguste began his tenth version of the bust. Shaw was amazed. Shaw had come to scoff, but he was startled by the way the maître wiped out an entire head when Rodin was dissatisfied, though most of the clay heads struck Shaw as reasonable likenesses.

Shaw asked, growing restless, "Maître, is it true that you do a dozen heads before one satisfies you?"

"More, most of the time. My early heads are generally sketches. A bust is not a mere portrait, it is a blending of sculpture and character. But if you are tired, monsieur, we can rest today."

"Oh no!" cried Shaw as he squirmed to ease the strain of sitting. "I just wondered when you expected to finish."

Auguste said curtly, "That's my concern, not yours. Do you listen to anyone telling you when to finish your work?"

Shaw smiled, enjoying himself now, and said, "Of course not. But if you take this long on everything, you will never make any money."

"There are always millionaires."

"Do you charge more than a thousand pounds?"

"Do you, monsieur?"

"I am such a good model I should be paid for sitting."

"You will be. As you said, you will have a head by Auguste Rodin."

"My wife said that."

"With your mouth, monsieur."

But now they understood each other, and their mutual respect grew. Auguste liked this bust very much, and Shaw was absorbed by the way he was working. He measured Shaw's features to the fraction of an inch with his calipers. Then he made Shaw lie face down, and with his eyes and hands examined the back of the head and the neck where it met the head and the ears. Now he had Shaw lie face up while he studied Shaw's frontal contours with his eyes and his probing hands. Next he sat Shaw at eye level while he repeated his examination and measurements. Feeling on the right track at last, he did a dozen clay heads, all to the precise dimensions he had obtained. Shaw was quiet for once, fascinated by this exactitude, while Auguste pondered a moment, saying, "We have the physical features, now we have to pursue the expression. But you have so many."

Shaw asked, "You mean no head is better than the subject?"

Auguste said, "Yes. The sitter creates the quality or lack of it in his head. If he wants to be flattered, as most people prefer, the head becomes false. But if he allows the sculptor to be true to what the sculptor sees, to model without any preconceived notions but simply with his observation and skill, he may not be pleased with the portrait but it should be true."

Auguste ran his fingers over Shaw's skin, then over the clay to be sure the contours would be exact and have the subject's warmth, while Shaw sat silently and thoughtfully—as thoughtfully as Charlotte had ever seen him.

Then Auguste worked feverishly, as if finally he had caught the precious expression he had been seeking. There was no more talk that day as the shadows lengthened. Shaw sat intent on what the maître was doing while night fell, and Auguste worked on by candlelight. When Auguste said, "Merci, monsieur, bonsoir," Shaw was certain the head was finished.

But the next day Auguste resumed modeling the other heads, while he left the one he had modeled the night before untouched. To Shaw he was doing these heads in the style of a Canova, a Bernini, a Donatello, a Phidias, and Shaw said, "I prefer the head you did yesterday. It is Rodinesque."

Auguste halted, said, "I thought so also. But I couldn't be certain until I tried it in several other styles."

"Have we finished?"

Auguste looked at him, shocked, as if to say how could he be so obtuse?

Shaw reflected that for Auguste Rodin a head was never finished while the subject was alive and said, "I mean for me to take it home."

"It would mean a great deal to me, *maître*," said Charlotte.

"You like it, madame?" asked Auguste. He was surprised himself at this question; these days he never asked anyone else for such an opinion.

"Yes. You have captured a new, different expression. I didn't believe you when you said my husband had a Christlike essence, but now that you have given him this quality I realize he can be that way, whatever he pretends."

Shaw was silent. He felt humble, as if the sculptor had caught a side of him people seldom saw, one that he hid to keep from being vulnerable.

Charlotte asked, "*Maître*, may we have it?"

"Do you want it in bronze or marble?"

"What do you think?"

"I will make it in both," Auguste said impulsively. "Oh, *mon dieu*, there will be no extra charge. It will be my pleasure."

Shaw said, unable to endure the seriousness that had fallen on all of them, "The greatest writer in the world done by the greatest sculptor."

Auguste shrugged and said, "Time, occasionally just, will decide that."

II

The next day Auguste asked Rilke if anyone important had wanted to see him recently. Rilke said, "No, I told everybody that you had to finish a vital commission. Only one man was insistent, a rather nervous, elderly chap, André Cholet. He seemed hurt when I said you couldn't see him now."

"What do you mean, couldn't see him!" Auguste exploded. "Cholet defended me during the Balzac affair at great risk to himself."

"How should I know?" Rilke was bewildered; he had never heard of Cholet.

Auguste glared at him and said, "You should have known, that is why I am employing you. Cholet is a good friend and a fine writer. You should have known him by reputation. When did he say he would return?"

"He didn't say, *maître*."

"Of all the idiots!" Auguste stalked away, very angry.

Rilke felt dreadful. He had not been permitted to talk to Shaw, except as a secretary; Shaw had remained ignorant of his identity as a poet, which had been a great disappointment. And he couldn't maintain this pace much longer. Days were becoming more confusing and harder than ever. Meudon was chaos, with people waiting everywhere to see the *maître*, who had given orders he was not seeing anyone; the mail was heavier than ever; yet Rodin acted as if he were the culprit. The *maître* must be ill, Rilke decided.

Several days later when Auguste found a letter that his secretary had failed to give him, he was outraged. He refused to listen to Rilke's explanation that the secretary thought the letter of small importance and that it had only come yesterday. He had also found a letter to Rilke from Rothenstein, a young English painter with whom Auguste had become friendly. This struck him as treachery, the secretary was stealing his friends. He cried, "This is thievery!"

Rilke said, "*Maître*, the last thing I want to do is hurt you."

"But you have."

"Secretarial work is not my trade."

"You've made that evident."

"What do you mean?" Rilke's face went very white, and he looked ill.

Auguste paused, not sure he ought to plunge on, then he had to, telling himself he was the *maître* in the eyes of the world and this must be enforced or he would be regarded as a coward. "I mean that you have betrayed me."

"How?" Rilke felt more confused than ever.

"Stealing my friends, losing my correspondence, failing me in many ways."

Failing because I haven't been sufficiently subservient, thought Rilke, and recalled a favorite phrase of the sculptor's: "*Travail et patience."* He braced himself for what was coming, but felt crushed, unable to speak.

"I want you to leave at once. As soon as you pack your things." Auguste walked away, still very angry, but feeling triumphant and vindicated.

Two days later there was a letter from Rilke. Auguste was surprised that the carefully written note was not bursting with recriminations. Instead Rilke said eloquently that the sculptor would always remain his inspiration and *maître* no matter what happened. Only at the end of the letter did Rilke say a wrong had been inflicted on him. The portion Auguste liked best was where Rilke wrote that the *maître*, as a great and true artist, had to push aside anything that threatened his work, as eventually Rilke had.

That was true, thought Auguste. Rilke's adulation had become too much, even offensive, endangering his own view of himself. And the father-son relationship hadn't worked, couldn't have worked, he realized now.

He held on to Rilke's letter, but he knew he couldn't answer it, not now, his casters were asking him to examine the bronze cast of "The Thinker."

Soon afterward there was a warm note from Shaw, saying he would appreciate it if the *maître* could tell him where the idea of the statue of Pygmalion had come from—he was thinking of doing a play on the subject. And as an expression of gratitude he sent Auguste a precious Kelmscott Chaucer and wrote:

I have seen two masters at work, Morris who made this book,
The other Rodin the Great, who fashioned my head in clay:
I give the book to Rodin, scrawling my name in a nook
Of the shrine their works shall hallow when mine are dust by the way.

Auguste's answer was to send the Shaws two pencil-and-wash sketches of Charlotte, which he had done while modeling her husband, and on which he wrote, *"Hommage à sympathique Madame Charlotte E. Shaw."*

Then the finished bronze of "The Thinker" was placed in front of the Panthéon. There were speeches, reading of the poetry of Victor Hugo, whose monument by Auguste was still homeless, and many gendarmes to make sure no one damaged the statue. He was assured that the police would remain until there was nothing to fear.

But he felt lost. He had been living with "The Thinker" in one way or another since he had begun "The Gates of Hell," twenty-six years ago. And now he was through with it. He wished Carrière were here. He took a last look at "The Thinker," hunched before the Panthéon. He must say *au revoir*. He must turn to other things—if he had the strength. But the bronze was right. He had told the truth. "The Thinker" showed more than ever the terrible struggle of elemental man to reach thought from brute feeling.

He was startled to hear a familiar voice he had not heard for a long time. It was his old friend Boucher, still the *grand seigneur*, and looking very well. Boucher said, "Your 'Thinker' has the look of a man who, now that he has arrived at thinking, doesn't like what he sees."

"Yes," said Auguste, "I may have been more right than I thought. The longer I live, the more it looks as if man has come to thinking too soon, before he is ready."

CHAPTER 46

On July 12, 1906, Alfred Dreyfus was exonerated completely. All previous verdicts were canceled and he was declared innocent officially.

Auguste heard the news as if it were an echo from another time. He found it difficult to believe that the anguish of the affair had afflicted all of France just a few years ago and hurt him severely. Now it seemed centuries ago. His portrait busts were in such demand that even when he increased his fees to thirty and forty thousand francs, to avoid doing them, and more than he had charged for the entire "Gates of Hell," the fees were met willingly. His high prices made these subjects more avid than ever to have their features done in marble or bronze by the *maître*, as if only Rodin's hands could assure the esteem of posterity. But he was gratified by the total vindication of Dreyfus. Long ago he had become convinced of the officer's innocence. Then it made him sad, for it reminded him that many of the people involved in the affair and the "Balzac" were gone.

The recollection sent him in search of Cholet, to explain the secretary's mistake. Cholet, whom he found in a shabby room in a small hotel on the rue Jacob, looked aged and tired, but Cholet was glad to see Auguste. When Auguste apologized for Rilke's mistake, saying, "He was fired," Cholet said, "Oh, I'm sorry, the secretary meant well, but I was upset, I was in need of money." Cholet sounded unusually humble.

"How much, André?"

"I don't need any now."

"Are you sure?"

"I've written a new play that has been promised a production. I had a reputation once, you know. I don't think it will be suitable for Bernhardt, it's realistic, but I've been given some money in advance."

"If you need any help, let me know." Then suddenly Auguste thrust his hand into his pocket and gave Cholet all the francs he found there, not even bothering to count them.

Cholet, seeing that there were several hundred francs in this pile of notes, was amazed and touched. "You must be in great demand these days."

"Too much," grumbled Auguste. "The King of Sweden wants to see me, and the King of England. You can't refuse them, can you?"

"Michelangelo is supposed to have refused a Pope or two."

He muttered, "Between kings and millionaires, I'm becoming a society sculptor."

Cholet didn't believe him and said so.

"It's true. I do virtually nothing else. I hope this won't keep you away."

Cholet took his hand and squeezed it gratefully. "Take advantage of it, *mon ami*, take advantage. Poverty is a bad business, believe me."

Several weeks later the King of Greece visited Meudon to buy several Rodins for Greece, to present the sculptor with a torso from the Parthenon, and to invite the sculptor to Athens. Auguste was pleased with the gift—he loved Greek sculpture—but he didn't lower his prices, though he promised to visit Athens if he could get away from his work. He invited the King to stay for lunch and was happy when the King accepted. They were sitting at the table when Rose entered in her kitchen apron to serve the King—she had cooked the meal and she feared there would be no other way to see His Majesty. Auguste flushed angrily—they had servants—but when the King seemed to know who she was he realized he could not resort to subterfuge. He introduced her awkwardly, mumbling, "Madame Rose," but the King said, "How charming," and gallantly went to take her hand, and Rose backed away in distress, whispering, "I'm only a simple housewife," and fled.

"*Mon dieu!*" he shouted at her afterward. "Don't you have any taste?"

Rose trembled before Auguste's anger, but she didn't reply, still remembering the gracious way the King of Greece had treated her.

Rose saw no reason to be anything but herself when Auguste was visited by the Japanese Ambassador, who came to view Auguste's fine Japanese prints. Some people felt these prints were obscene, their anatomical designs too explicit, but the Ambassador agreed with the *maître* that they were lovely and must not be misunderstood. He insisted on thanking the mistress of the house for the hospitality, saying that he wouldn't think of leaving Meudon until he had. So Auguste reluctantly had Rose called. She came hastily, as she always did when Auguste called, wearing another apron and her arms smeared with soap suds from the clothes she had been rinsing. She was proud of her apron, it matched her eyes.

Edward VII of England visited Meudon soon after, and she did not understand why Auguste wouldn't allow her to meet him. She was hurt when Auguste forced her to stay in her room and view the King from behind curtains. It was very unpleasant that a servant was present to keep her there.

The former Prince of Wales, even stouter than before, still was curious about "The Gates." "*Fini!*" declared Auguste. "Oh, I still work on the figures, your Majesty, but they are for me, alone. The public, no more."

"Too bad," said Edward VII, observing them a few minutes later. But when the King of England desired to climb the ladder against "The Gates," to see the original of "The Thinker" on top, Auguste wouldn't let him. There was a bird's nest on top of the portal that he could not allow to be disturbed.

Edward VII was even more startled when he asked the sculptor to do a bust of a very good lady friend and the *maître* hesitated. The King made an impatient gesture, indicating money was no object. The fee the King suggested was generous, and Auguste couldn't say no. But when it came time to do the lady, who was a great beauty, he refused to allow the King in the studio while he modeled, though for an angry moment it looked as if the King were going to withdraw the commission. Auguste remained adamant. It was Edward VII who was diplomatic and generous; he gave in. Afterward His Majesty was glad. He thought the finished marble exquisite.

Three American millionaires followed, and Auguste liked the first two commissions. Joseph Pulitzer was a challenge, for he was blind, and Thomas Ryan also bought a number of pieces for the Metropolitan Museum, in New York.

But he wondered if he should have done the head of E. H. Harriman, for it had to be done from photographs; he felt they had no character. He kept reshaping this head, working in a skullcap and an untidy houppelande, but when Rose complained bitterly about his failure to introduce her to the King of England he said, "You wouldn't have dressed right. You're not educated."

She cried, "Then why didn't you educate me?"

"If I had, I would have lost you." He sighed, "I never should have done a head from photographs. All I accomplished was another photograph."

She stared at the head of Harriman and said, "It's not bad."

"Not good. The photographs must have been flattering. These rich men will never know what their money cost me."

"Then why do you model them?"

"We were poor a long time. We didn't get out of debt until I was sixty."

"Is that all?" He looked at her as if she were crazy, but she was thinking that she had been happier when they had less. Before she could say anything else, he asked her to prepare lunch. She hurried off, delighted to serve him. An hour later she went to call him and he had left for Paris.

It did not ease Rose's feeling of being abused when she returned to the kitchen and found *petit* Auguste eating the carefully cooked lunch. His indifference caused her to explode in a tirade against his father, and he shrugged, said, "What do you expect?" and continued eating. And when he finished, gulping down all the meat and wine, he asked for money.

Wasn't he ever going to grow up? She said, "I just gave you some."

"Two weeks ago. I need clothes."

"But I gave you some of his."

"They were old."

"*Petit* Auguste, don't you ever think of working?"

"You sound like him now." *Petit* Auguste stood up. "If you don't want me to come any more, I won't." He wrapped the pudding in a bag and put the soggy package into his pocket. "Poor old Rose, she's got pity only for herself."

"It's not pity," she denied angrily. "I've got friends in his Paris studios who tell me who he sees there. He doesn't fool me."

"Then you know he's making a lot of money. He must give you some."

"Just for the house."

"You've got thousands of francs stored away. Where are they, Rose?"

She stared at his gray hair, his alcoholic face, his black fingernails —Auguste was fastidious about his own hands—and she thought that Auguste's features were handsome in repose but that the boy had only the worst of his father. He was a poor, wandering dog, drifting from woman to woman, claiming to be an artist because his father was, though the only way he made money was by bartering Auguste's old clothes. Yet when he looked sad and weary, as he did suddenly now, her heart cried, How can I refuse him! He had been a good baby, a quiet baby. She gave him fifty francs and was hurt when he said, "Is that all you can spare?" She had a feeling he was calling her all the rotten names in the world, though he was returning to some drunken harridan. But she couldn't say a word, not even of reproach. He walked off, ignoring the entreaty in her eyes. The door slammed behind him. She felt forsaken. She should have given him more money. But she might need it herself someday, she thought apprehensively.

It was a week later that Auguste returned from Paris. And when he didn't explain his absence or apologize for leaving so suddenly, she declared, "It must have been another woman," and he replied, "Well, at least it wasn't Camille." Rose didn't take this hint to desist, and he added, "She was beautiful." He thought Rose would explode in her jealousy and rage, and now he was sorry for her and said, "But you were the one I cared for the most, we're still together."

"Because I was born to serve," she said bitterly.

"Oh, very well . . ." He turned to go, disgusted and tired.

Her throat ached with the desire to cry, "Let's have an end to all this!" How tired she was of duties and despair, of inhuman patience for one triumph! She could not speak. She felt in hell. Tears trickled down her cheeks.

Caught by her pain, he paused in his departure and said, "You know, *ma chatte*, I want you to be happy here at Meudon," and she said, "You don't have to feel responsible for me, I'll manage somehow," and he took her hands, which long ago had lost their soft, delicate quality, and brought them gently to his silver-gray beard and held them to his lips as if they held the beauty of the world while her cheeks were aflame and she trembled. "Camille was very beautiful, Rose, and I was reckless then. Now I need the peace of evening."

She wasn't sure she believed him; he was still a virile man. She murmured, "But suppose you get restless. You always have."

"I'm not made of stone. And emotion is sometimes a tyrant. But I know who my friends are. Could I have some lunch, *ma chatte*?"

"No, no, no," she wanted to cry. She said, "Meat and wine, Auguste?"

"Whatever you prepare, Rose."

CHAPTER 47

The following year Auguste was awarded an honorary degree by Oxford University. He sat next to Mark Twain, Camille Saint-Saëns, and General Booth of the Salvation Army, who were also receiving honorary degrees, and he wondered what he was doing here. He remembered how poorly he had done in school—arithmetic and spelling still baffled him—he had never gotten into the Beaux Arts, and Papa and Mama hadn't been able even to read or write. But now they were clothing him in a fine red silk gown and black mortarboard hat and bestowing upon him the degree of doctor *honoris causa* and describing him as a scholar of sculpture.

He was back in Paris just an hour, having stopped off at his main studio, on the rue de l'Université, to rectify the improvements his casters had made on the "Victor Hugo," when he was handed a letter from Rilke. He returned the monument to the way he had left it, then started to read the letter slowly and suspiciously, expecting this to be a request for a favor. He was surprised to find that Rilke had written him a friendly note of congratulations on the Oxford ritual, declaring, "*Maître*, no one deserved this honor more."

Rilke added that if he could see the *maître* again it would mean a great deal to him. A pleased Auguste replied that it was good to hear from the poet and that he would be glad to see Rilke within a few days.

A week later they met in the Luxembourg Gardens, where the trees were full of chestnuts and some of Auguste's work stood.

It remained one of Auguste's favorite parks, and he was in a good humor as they strolled along the walks in the clear autumn sunlight. The trees were thick and green, but starting to change. The flowers were a profusion of color and more varied than ever.

Auguste had learned that Rilke had gained a small income from his poetry, and had been living in the castles of patrons, mostly older women. But they didn't discuss that. They made a point of not talking about what had happened, but about what *was* happening.

The dark, slender Rilke with his intense blue eyes and slim mustache was still the enthusiast, full of praise for the Maillols he had just seen.

Auguste agreed, "His torsos are beautiful. There are things I could have learned from Maillol if I were younger."

Rilke was surprised by Auguste's generosity. "But you were his teacher?"

"More his guide. No one really teaches a man like Maillol. They used to say I surrounded myself with submissive disciples, Maillol, Desbois, Camille Claudel, Bourdelle, when four more different personalities and sculptors didn't exist in France. All they had in common was that they had come to study with me so that they could learn to be free, themselves."

"Did you like Manet? There is much talk about him now."

"Yes. Always. I'm delighted he is in the Louvre now."

"And Van Gogh? Cézanne?"

"I have several Van Goghs. I met him a few times, casually. He was very quiet, he always seemed to be deep inside of himself, a little like Cézanne."

"You knew Cézanne well?" Since Cézanne died, he had become a discovery of Rilke's and one of his great passions.

"Not really. I don't think anybody did." Auguste grew sad, thinking of Monet, no longer handsome or eager, but bitter about a success he said had come too late; Degas, whose lightning had struck even the mighty to earth, now turned into an impotent old man, humiliated by age and illness, wandering aimlessly about Paris, half blind, not even able to paint; Renoir, despite much success, able to work only from a wheel chair these days. Time had brought a tragic and autumnal corruption upon his closest contemporaries.

Auguste felt better when they walked over to the Hotel Biron, where Rilke was residing in the studio of his wife, who was out of Paris and whom he seldom saw. Auguste fell in love at first sight with this eighteenth-century château which had been converted into a series of nineteenth-century apartments. He thought the location ideal. It was on the quiet rue de Varenne, where the dignified street met the spacious boulevard des Invalides, and just around the corner from the Invalides itself, Napoleon's tomb. He was enchanted with the Hotel Biron's large grounds and fine gardens. It would make a fine refuge, he thought—it was Meudon in Paris. When Rilke showed him the rooms, he knew he had to have a studio here. The rooms were large, with lofty ceilings and lovely French windows overlooking the courtyard in front and the gardens in back. To do without this was unbearable. Everywhere he looked there was a grace of line that was rhythmic and harmonious.

He whispered to Rilke, "It is a château in the heart of Paris."

"*Maître*, it has been called the most superb house in Paris. Many unusual people have lived here: Peyrenc, a barber-adventurer, like Beaumarchais; then the Duc de Biron, one of the great *grand seigneurs* of French nobility; then the Papal Nuncio; the Ambassador of the Emperor of Russia; and finally, for many years, the nuns of the Sacred Heart."

"Who lives here now?"

"Isadora Duncan, De Max, Matisse. They have studios. And my wife."

Auguste liked Isadora. She had changed enormously since their first meeting, having become womanly and reckless and rumored to have had as many men as he had been reputed to have had women. He sensed she still desired him, as much for his reputation as for himself, and had regrets over the failure of their first encounter. But he was too old now, he told himself. After Camille there must be no more women half his age.

Rilke said, "The ground floor is available, but very expensive."

"I will rent it. Rilke, find out when I can move in."

For an instant Rilke was hurt. He wanted to shout, "I'm no longer your secretary, your slave." But the *maître* looked so imperious he said instead, "It will be wonderful, you living here, within sight of Napoleon's tomb. Napoleon and Rodin," Rilke added, absorbed with this comparison now. "Napoleon insisted on trying to shatter the world and remake it with his powerful hands, while you, out of soft clay, created an entire universe of real people. And for me, *maître*, yours are the more powerful hands."

"*Merci*, Rainer; you are gallant, but Napoleon's name will last longer."

"I doubt it. We can't see his hands any more, but yours will be on view for a long time to come."

Auguste smiled cynically and said, "At the moment I'll be satisfied if I can live in the Hôtel Biron. Then I'll be able to work as I used to."

II

Yet it was 1908 before he was able to move into the Hotel Biron. And though he resolved to remain here the rest of his life, his fellow tenant, Isadora Duncan, was pessimistic about his hopes. They stood in the rotunda which looked out on the garden—his favorite view on the entire floor, which he had rented for fifty-nine hundred francs a year—and he was surprised by her doubts.

Isadora said, "Ever since the republic took over this property from the Convent of the Sacred Heart, when the government legalized the separation of Church and State, there has been public agitation demanding that the republic sell Biron. I hear it all the time because of the parties I give. They say these parties are committing sacrilege."

"I want to work. I'm too old to give parties." And Isadora did give wild, bohemian parties which sometimes became loud and violent.

"Of course, Auguste, and we won't disturb you."

He thought, Not likely. Isadora was always on the move: Germany, Greece, Russia, America, England—God knows where she would be going next!

He settled down to work, and soon felt completely at home. Isadora and De Max dropped in occasionally, but gave him privacy when he was working, while Matisse stayed away—having organized his own Académie Matisse in the Hotel Biron. Auguste placed his favorite Carrière, Van Gogh, Monet, and Renoir in this new studio; he transferred the torso from the Parthenon and many of his marbles here; it became his chief domicile in Paris.

Rose was distressed by this move. He proudly showed her around the Hotel Biron, and she thought, He is returning to the days of Camille, but who is the new *amour*? There was no trace of one here. Yet she felt such anxiety she said suddenly, "You are only going to work here, Auguste? Yes?"

He frowned. She should know better than to expect any explanations.

"*Petit* Auguste worries me. He's becoming no more than a rag-picker."

"That's his affair."

"If you asked him to live with us at Meudon, he could still change."

"He will never change." But Auguste, though he disregarded her plea, felt sorry for her. He escorted her back to Meudon in a two-wheeled cab, though it was expensive and she was horrified by the cost.

III

A few evenings later Auguste was being received at the Élysée Palace by President Fallières—the invitation read "to honor Monsieur Rodin's contributions to the art of France"—and the President of the republic was telling him about the letters addressed to "Auguste Rodin, France," when a middle-aged woman insisted on meeting him. She interrupted the President to introduce herself as the Duchess of Choiseul, whom Auguste recognized as an American wed to a Frenchman with an old historic title.

He stood under the brilliantly illuminated chandeliers while the Duchess chatted animatedly with him about his "distinguished sculpture," and he thought here were all the accessories of an official salon under the ancient regime. There were many bemedaled chests, many jewel-laden women, more titles than republicans, and so much formality it made even intelligent people seem pompous and vain. But he could not withdraw. He was surrounded by her attention. And she appeared genuinely interested in his work.

She exclaimed, "*Maître*, this is the greatest night of my life! I've been wanting to meet you for so long. It's why I came to this function."

He looked incredulous, but as she kept insisting Auguste Rodin was the only reason she was here he almost believed her. He did like her awareness of his work. The Duchess of Choiseul discussed his pieces eloquently, as if she carried a catalogue of his work in her mind. Yet as he observed her, he was apprehensive. She was heavily painted, rouged, and powdered; her hair was dyed; she was a slim, sharp-featured, middle-aged woman with a thin red slash of a mouth and a pointed nose. The Duchess resembled a dozen other titled women who had flattered him the last few years.

Yet she insisted on enveloping him with her enormous interest, and she was vivacious, she never stopped talking about his work. She stayed by his side the rest of the evening, gradually coming to act as if she belonged there.

When it was time to go home, she offered to give him a lift to the Hotel Biron, saying, "*Maître*, surely you're not thinking of returning to Meudon this late, it's after midnight." He wasn't certain any more what he was thinking this hectic night, it had passed in such a whirlwind of conversation, mostly by the Duchess, but he found himself accepting her invitation, though generally he disliked automobiles and avoided them.

However, when they reached Biron, it wasn't too late for her to come in.

He realized that he hadn't actually invited her in, and that she hadn't insisted, and yet she had made it seem natural and inevitable.

She curled up in his favorite chair, looking coy, even as her pulses hammered and she wondered if she was acting insanely. Ever since she had seen his pairings, she had thought how wonderful to be his *grande amoureuse*—such a liaison would bring her honor, he must still be very virile. And her husband would be amused, and relieved, feeling even freer than before, if that was possible.

But when he stood in the center of the room, looking flustered, she decided she could solve his dilemma only by doing the courting. She cried coyly, "Auguste, we must be honest with each other. I've never met an artist whose work moves me more. You have great vitality." She wrapped her thin arms around him and snuggled close.

Before he knew what was happening, he found himself making love to her. Or rather, he realized suddenly, she was making love to him. He was startled by this actuality, her crude, vibrant energy. He hadn't expected her slight body to have such intensity. She became so skillful sexually she made him forget everything else.

As they lay next to each other afterward and she whispered, "Satisfied?" he could not disagree. He was surprised that an American-born woman could be so skillful. Her aggressiveness was a trespass, yet she made him feel so virile he could almost forgive her this.

The next few months an ambivalent attitude developed in Auguste. There were moments when he couldn't endure her obvious flattery, her heavy make-up, her extreme vivacity, but he came to depend upon their love-making with a kind of desperation, as if that would keep away old age. When friends wondered aloud how he could put up with her, he shrugged. He could not tell them that he needed these sexual encounters; it was not something to discuss with others.

Rilke implied that the Duchess was a leech, and Auguste was so irate he didn't speak to the poet for days. Then abruptly he invited Rilke to the studio and demanded to know why Rilke didn't like her.

Rilke said in his soft voice, "Maître, she's so forward."

"You are always involved with women who are aggressive toward you."

That was true, Rilke realized, but he was different. He needed such women, but Rodin didn't, the maître was a law unto himself.

Auguste pointed out, "You are quite friendly with the Princess Marie Hohenlohe, who is at least twenty years older than you."

"That's different," Rilke said unhappily. The maître was being unfair.

Auguste, feeling that Rilke was in a situation far more embarrassing than his own—the Princess was older than the Duchess—was amused and forgiving.

He pretended not to hear the casters in his studios mocking her statements that she was his inspiration by calling her "the muse." But he was furious when he caught Bourdelle referring to her as "Duchess Influenza." This was a betrayal; he ordered Bourdelle out of his studio. "For good!" he shouted, to show he was very angry, though he hoped Bourdelle would be intelligent and not take him literally. To suppress his feeling of guilt, he assured himself that she

was improving his social life, she was the ideal person to take care of
the many demands being made upon him, she understood his work,
and their intimate life was sensible—there was no nonsense about
young romantic love.

IV

She persuaded him to allow the Victor Hugo monument to be placed
in the spacious gardens of the Palais Royal, though he was still dissatisfied with the statue and the location. The erect, clothed figure
was not the Hugo he had visualized, but a compromise. And he
thought the site was too regal. But perhaps she had been right
when she had said the monument would die in the studio.

At the dedication he was surrounded by many important municipal and state officials, admiring his perseverance, that he had never
given up on this task, and she exclaimed, "How inspiring, it com-
pares with a Beethoven symphony!" and he thought, How foolish
can she be! It was far from his best work. He squirmed uneasily in the
clothes she had insisted he must wear, a Prince of Wales top hat and
a morning suit. He felt as overdressed as Hugo.

V

The Duchess was still arguing that she had been right about the
"Hugo," it had been his sacred duty to France to have this monument placed in the Palais Royal, when he decided to do a bust of her.
At first it was to avoid taking her to the races at Longchamps and to
one society dinner after another, but gradually as her features came
to life in his hands nothing else mattered. It was as if he had never
been ill, distracted, weary. Modeling again, he was being cleansed,
and nothing could divert him.

She grew restless, and he hushed her harshly. She complained that
he made her features too sharp, and he retorted, "That's the way they
are."

"But I'm prettier." He was grinding her face to a harsh edge.

He didn't waste time arguing. He worked silently now.

"Auguste, you're not listening. You're making me look like a
shrew."

She wanted him to pause for an amorous interlude, and he refused. He forced her to lie on the floor with her head between his knees while he felt her features, then transferred their warmth and contour to the clay. When he had finished, he thought it was good. She was upset that he didn't ask her if she was pleased. He asked Bourdelle to view it.

The younger sculptor knew he should not respond, Rodin was not even mentioning what had happened a few weeks ago, but he never could refuse the *maître*. He said, "I'm glad to see you didn't let her talking fool you."

Auguste was shocked. "Did you think I'd lie in clay?"

Bourdelle smiled and said, "It's accurate, and true."

VI

But when this work stopped, Auguste resumed the life the Duchess of Choiseul preferred. At Meudon, Rose felt alone in a new and worse way. Auguste was staying away weeks at a time. And she had learned about the Duchess, but she felt powerless. She had complained so often and so long that it had become an echo. The last time she had seen him and begged him to stay at Meudon he had regarded it as interference and said, "You can see Paris from Meudon, the Seine is nearby, and please don't try to improve my character," and he had returned to Biron without even remaining overnight. Rose was certain she was losing him for good, and she wandered around the grounds of Meudon like a lost soul, saving every franc for the day she would need it, hoarding, worrying, refusing even *petit* Auguste.

VII

Auguste was worried himself. After having found a studio where he wanted to live the rest of his life, he was informed he would have to move. The State had decided to sell the Hotel Biron to business interests. The sale was to occur in a few weeks, and everyone was supposed to move immediately afterward. To add to his dismay, it was happening just when he had agreed to illustrate a new edition of *Les Fleurs du Mal* and was doing fresh hands, searching for starker forms of sculpture. Shaken by the news, he went to see Clemenceau, who had been Premier since 1906, and asked him to prevent the sale, declaring, "Monsieur, it would be a disaster if this happened."

"Disaster for whom? For what?" Clemenceau said in his quick staccato.

"Monsieur, I'm not as young as I used to be. To make me move at my age is cruel. Can't you force the State to keep Biron?"

"*Mon ami,* you are naïve. Request another monument to Bonaparte and I can raise a fortune, but for art I will be ridiculed. Why did you come to me?"

"You've always been a friend of art. As Premier you are responsible for Manet's 'Olympia' being admitted to the Louvre. The art students adore you."

"And will probably support Briand or Poincaré."

"Should I go to them? I will not move. You will have to evict me." Auguste said with sudden satisfaction, "It will create a scandal."

Clemenceau wanted to laugh, but Rodin looked adamant, and one never knew how much of a stir such a commotion might make. The citizenry, unpredictable, might enjoy supporting such a fracas. He assured Auguste that he would do what he could, not sure he could do anything, not sure he wanted to.

But when Monet, a close friend, spoke to him on behalf of Auguste; when influential people went to see Briand, who was succeeding him as Premier; and then Poincaré, leader of the third vital political party and a potential Premier, was approached, as if now the retention of Biron was a nonpartisan negotiation for the glory of France; it became a question of which of the three parties could express their patriotism best. Four days before Biron was to be sold the Senate voted to defer the transaction and ordered the government to consider the wisdom of buying the property permanently.

This deliberation dragged on for two years, but when the State bought Biron for six million francs Auguste was sure he had won his battle. In the interval he had completed the illustrations for *Les Fleurs du Mal* and had modeled a number of stark hands and a few busts. The Duchess appeared to have become a permanent part of his life, and he was seldom at Meudon, for whenever he saw Rose there were tears, expostulations, and recriminations.

Thus it was a shock when, soon after the State bought Biron, Auguste was ordered to abandon the premises in three months. Terribly upset, he went to see Clemenceau, who said, "What do you want of me? I'm no longer Premier."

"Why did this happen?"

"The *bourgeoisie* are clamoring that everyone must be evicted, complaining about the wild parties taking place. They say that for this to happen in the Hotel Biron, which was once a convent school, is sacrilege."

"But this is absurd!" exploded Auguste. "I don't give such parties."

"De Max and Isadora Duncan do. But the State is being considerate of you. You have three months to get out, while they have to leave at once."

Auguste saw Clemenceau's cynical smile and thought it was useless to protest, he must think of something practical. Yet the idea of embarking on another battle made him weary. He would be seventy-one in a few weeks; he had hardly enough strength for his own work; even the Duchess was becoming exhausting. And this dispute might drag on for a few more years. He wouldn't be alive when it was resolved. But to move would be too upsetting. He had to make the republic feel like a comrade in arms. Yet as he thought of a plan that might accomplish this, it struck him as too simple and open to be trusted. Only there was no choice. He suggested, "Monsieur Clemenceau, suppose I turn over all my work to France? In exchange do you think I could live there the rest of my life?"

"And afterward form a museum?" Clemenceau grew thoughtful. The idea had merit, but no, it was too difficult.

"A Rodin Museum, if it wouldn't be too vain."

"And the six million francs? That's a high price to pay for art."

"I will sign over everything I've done to France. At the rate my work is selling, you will not lose any money."

"Just to live there?" Clemenceau was surprised by such a generous offer.

"Yes. And so there will be a Rodin Museum when I am gone."

"Is it that important, *mon ami?*" Clemenceau asked more kindly.

"I would like my work in one place, as much as it is possible."

"It's an interesting idea."

"Do you think it will work?"

"I don't know." However, Clemenceau was stimulated into action. "But it is worth trying, *maître*. Have a petition prepared on the terms we just discussed, oh, not by you, you can't afford to be directly involved, but by your most influential friends to make this appear philanthropic. Then approach me, Briand, and Poincaré. One of us should be Premier at that time, and under those circumstances something might be arranged."

Auguste had this done, and he found himself on the front pages of the French press again. His offer became a national issue. His supporters pointed out that his work should be worth more than six million francs in a few years at the rate its value was increasing, that it could become a great national asset.

The State negotiated with Auguste as to possible terms, but no decision was reached. But at the end of the three months given him, when he showed no sign of moving, though he was alone in Biron now, the State gave him an eighteen-month stay, with a possibility of renewal.

Auguste, grateful to Clemenceau, did a bust of him, though the latter seemed out of power permanently, while still an important voice in France.

He felt it was one of his better heads, showing Clemenceau in his vigor and resolution, yet with his dominant cynicism, and the politician would not take it, saying, "You've made me look as cunning as an Oriental potentate."

"Aren't you half Tamerlane and half Genghis Khan?" said Auguste.

Clemenceau still refused the bust, and when Auguste asked whether any decision had been reached about his offer Clemenceau snapped, "Your friends have become so militant it seems as if the government has nothing else to discuss. I spoke to Poincaré the other day, and the Premier said, 'What do you think is the main subject these days, Clemenceau? Not Germany, Russia, Turkey, or our Entente Cordiale, but Monsieur Rodin.'"

"Does that mean my terms are acceptable?"

"It means that Poincaré is annoyed. I doubt that your lease will be renewed any more. When does it expire, Rodin?"

"The beginning of 1913, I believe. Is there so much red tape?"

"Opposition. There are many things that Poincaré, Briand, and I do not agree on, but one thing we do—Biron is a damned nuisance."

"You are all against me."

Clemenceau sighed, "*Maître*, you don't understand. France is divided. If we accept your terms, half of France will be offended. If we don't, the other half will be insulted. In that Briand, Poincaré, and myself share a common anxiety, and we have to move slowly in whichever direction we go."

But Auguste understood. In politics the only person who was indispensable was a voter.

The Duchess was waiting for the results of this meeting, and when Auguste said tersely, "It looks hopeful," unable to admit anything else, she was distraught—acceptance of his offer could upset everything. A few hours later Rilke came upon the Duchess drinking heavily. She blurted out, "Is he married to this Rose woman? Is he really obligated to her?" Rodin had seen Rose very little since the Duchess had entered his life, Rilke reflected, but he could not imagine Rodin leaving her. The Duchess asked, "Does this *petit* Auguste have any chance to get the old man's money?" As Rilke looked horrified, she caught hold of herself and explained, "I want to know for the *maître's* sake, to expedite the museum. Rainer, I don't want anything to prevent that."

She wandered into the garden, and a few minutes later, when Auguste seemed receptive, Rilke tried to warn him about her and he wouldn't listen. Auguste kept saying, "Rainer, we must make sure nothing goes wrong." The more he thought about the idea of a Rodin Museum, the more vital it became.

The Duchess entered the studio, her face flushed but sober again, and as Rilke retired, she insisted, "You are happy now, aren't you, Auguste?"

He said curtly, "I'm as happy as a thinking man can be." He changed the subject abruptly and ordered her to get tickets for the Ballet Russe, which was coming to Paris for a return engagement. "I want a box as close to the stage as you can get." Isadora had posed for him, and Pavlova, and Loie Fuller and Hanako, and now he would observe Nijinsky from a vantage point.

"Are you going to model Nijinsky?"

"I haven't been asked. Now get the tickets, the best they have."

She resented his peremptory tone, and started to protest, but he wasn't listening. Angry, she interrupted his work to mention that there were stories that the Ballet Russe was doing a new ballet, *L'Après-midi d'un Faune*, which was lewd and shocking, and he regarded her severely and said, "I'm sure these rumors are lies. Nijinsky is a superb artist."

CHAPTER 48

Auguste arrived at the theater for the first performance of the new ballet with the Duchess, pleased with the tickets she had obtained—the box was next to the stage—and as he entered the box he was greeted with an ovation by the audience. He was surprised and pleased. He bowed slightly and mumbled to the Duchess, "I never thought I would feel so virtuous."

He was engrossed by the feature of the program, *L'Après-midi d'un Faune*, taken from a poem by Mallarmé. He thought how startled Mallarmé would have been at this use of his poem. He was not hopeful about the music, he rarely liked Debussy's music, though they were friends, but he was eager to see Nijinsky's dancing and choreography. Then he saw Clemenceau in an adjoining box and had to ask, "Have you heard anything about the museum?"

"Not a word. Not a word."

"It will never be resolved."

"Patience, *maître*. We are here to see a dancer."

The lights went down and there was an expectant hush. Auguste saw Nijinsky, the Faun, as half human, half animal, and was reminded of a world he had modeled many times. He was fascinated by the sensuousness and urgency of the dancer's performance, and watched intently and silently.

Nijinsky finished in utter quiet. Then as the curtain came down, the audience split in two: half applauded wildly and half booed and hissed. It was more than Auguste could endure, and he jumped to his feet and cheered.

After *L'Aprés-midi d'un Faune* was repeated as an encore, Auguste hurried backstage, embraced Nijinsky fervently, and cried, "We are comrades, *mon ami*, comrades. Your dancing is sculpture in motion." And when he sank into sleep later, ignoring the Duchess' desire to make love—she wondered if he was slipping away, he had been indifferent to her all evening—he kept seeing the Faun dancing on and on, like the pulse of marble beating.

Thus he was shocked the next day to read a vicious attack on the *Faun* in *Figaro* by its owner-editor, Calmette. He read with growing disgust:

Those who speak of art and poetry apropos of this spectacle make fun of us. It is neither a gracious eclogue nor a profound production. We have a faun, incontinent, with vile movements of erotic bestiality and gestures of heavy shamelessness. That is all. And merited boos were accorded the too-expressive pantomime of the body of an ill-made beast, hideous from the front, even more hideous in profile.

Auguste could not contain himself. It was as if it were an attack on himself. He was aroused further when reports circulated about Paris that the *Faun* was to be halted by the police because *Figaro* had convinced them that it was obscene. With the aid of friends he wrote a passionate answer to *Figaro*, which was also an ardent defense of the *Faun*. He was proud that it appeared the next day at the head of the editorial page of *Matin*, *Figaro*'s chief competitor. He felt self-expressed with the part of his article that said:

. . . today we see Nijinsky, who possesses at the same time talent and training. The intelligence of his art is so rich and so varied that it approaches genius . . . the harmony between his mimicry and his plasticity is perfect. His whole body expresses what his mind dictates. He possesses the beauty of the antique frescoes and statues; he is the ideal model for whom every painter and sculptor has longed. You would think Nijinsky were a statue when he lies full length on the rock, with one leg bent, and with the flute at his lips, as the curtain rises, and nothing could be more soul-stirring than his movement when, at the close of the act, he throws himself down and passionately kisses the discarded veil. I wish that every artist who truly loves his art might see this perfect personification of the ideals of the beauty of the old Greeks.

Nijinsky visited Auguste that afternoon to express his gratitude for this ardent defense, and the sculptor was startled by the dancer's appearance. He could not believe this short, slight, insignificant man in street dress was the faun who had enchanted him. However, Nijinsky wanted to model for him and he agreed, thinking if he got the dancer to pose excitingly enough a fine statue could still be achieved. He felt better then, and he was stunned the next day when he became the target for the vicious attacks. Calmette, taking his defense of Nijinsky as a personal affront, wrote in his newspaper:

I admire Rodin deeply as one of our most illustrious and able sculptors, but I must decline to accept his judgment on the question of theatrical morality. I have only to recall that in defiance of common propriety, he exhibits in the former chapel of the Sacré Coeur and in the deserted apartment of the excellent nuns at the Hotel Biron a series of objectionable drawings and cynical sketches which depict with great brutality and in further detail the shameless attitudes of the *Faun*, who was justly hissed at the Châtelet. And now that I am speaking my mind, I may say the morbid mimicry represented by the dancer on the stage the other evening moves me to less indignation than the spectacle offered every day by Rodin in the ancient convent of the Sacré Coeur to regiments of hysterical women admirers and self-satisfied snobs. It is inconceivable that the State —in other words the French taxpayer—should have purchased the Hotel Biron for 6,000,000 francs simply to allow the richest of our sculptors to live there. Here is a real scandal, and it is the business of the government to put a stop to it.

This was a terrible blow. Auguste felt as if Biron had been knocked out of his hands with this savage assault. He was sure he would be evicted, that the museum was doomed unless he could persuade *Figaro* to change its tune.

The next few days Paris burst with piety. Now many people, including public officials, regarded him as a lustful old satyr. His work was mocked and caricatured in other papers, there was agitation to get him out of the Hotel Biron at once. The Duchess said there was only one thing he could do.

"Auguste, you must apologize and disavow what you said in *Matin*."

When he didn't argue, too weary, ill, and old to fight any more, she composed a letter to *Matin*, disavowing his defense of Nijinsky, and signed his name.

Rilke, coming upon this, was appalled. "*Maître*, you can't send this!"

Auguste sat as if paralyzed by the misery of mankind and said not a word.

The Duchess looked triumphantly at Rilke and sent the letter.

Matin, already committed in this controversy, did not publish the disavowal. Auguste, realizing what a close call he had had, got the letter back and destroyed it. But when Rilke blamed the Duchess, Auguste cut him short. "I wrote it, Rainer, I let her put my name on it. Have you heard anything further about the museum? Do you think they will force me out?"

"I don't think so. You still have strong, influential supporters. Most of them don't even know about the Duchess' letter."

"My letter. I let her send it." He thought sadly he had made two mistakes he would always regret, this and the failure to support Dreyfus.

"Just the same," Rilke said encouragingly, "many people are for a Rodin Museum. Important people like Clemenceau, Poincaré, Briand . . ."

Auguste smiled bitterly and said, "Rainer, I learned a long time ago never to depend on politicians." The second letter, though unpublished, was still a reproach. He composed a statement which appeared in the press the next day.

I have no time to waste on answering Monsieur Calmette's attack on me. I admire Nijinsky's work and consider him a marvel of harmony. He is a dancer of genius. I wish so noble an effort as *Faun* would be understood in its entirety, and that all artists could come for instruction and communion in this spectacle of beauty.

The Duchess said this was insane, that he was betraying her, and he ignored her. Rilke congratulated him, and he nodded and asked to be excused. There was only work left at his age, he thought. He shut his studio to everyone while he prepared to model Nijinsky afternoons. He was not evicted from Biron, as he expected, but he was sure that when his extension ran out it would not be renewed. He closed the studio door to the Duchess, too, saying he had to work in privacy, but he didn't break with her, though this was his impulse.

Diaghilev escorted Nijinsky on the first session and was amused by the sculptor's distress over the controversy. The impresario laughed and said, "Pro-Faunists, pro-Rodinists, anti-Faunists, anti-Rodinists, let them scream, *maître*, it is making us an enormous success."

Diaghilev didn't stay, but Nijinsky agreed to come three afternoons a week until the statue was finished. Nijinsky, though he had been warned about Rodin's slowness, was so grateful for his support he was willing to do anything.

However, Nijinsky was taken aback when the sculptor told him to pose nude. He asked self-consciously, "*Maître*, is this your usual custom?"

"Of course." Everyone knew this.

Nijinsky's body was still insignificant when he stood naked before Auguste, but when he moved and then posed full length on rocks, as he had at the start of *L'Après-midi d'un Faune*, he came alive with vivid animation.

By the end of the first week they were good friends. Auguste noticed that Nijinsky was very shy when he spoke, hesitant with words, but vibrant when he posed or moved. The fog lifted from Auguste's brain and he began to feel like his working self. He struck out boldly, seeing this statue of the faun as the epitome of his plastic skill, just as Nijinsky was the epitome of movement.

Now there was only the sculpting, and a silence that had serenity. They came to understand each other without words. In the studio there was summer, the luxuriant sun, and a faun lying tenderly upon the rocks. Life became a trinity of work, nature, and respect. They were so involved they increased the sessions to five a week.

Nijinsky's absorption in the modeling upset Diaghilev. He didn't want to appear *bourgeois*, but the *maître* had a reputation as a fabulous sensualist in spite of his age. Diaghilev, telling himself he must not become jealous, grew very jealous as Nijinsky's interest in the sessions spread. He got into the habit of stopping at the studio to escort his protégé back to the hotel.

One hot day Nijinsky grew tired and drowsy from the constant posing and the heat. Auguste suggested a nap would help, and Nijinsky, liking the *maître's* paternal interest, lay down on the sofa Auguste kept for his own naps. Soon the dancer was sound asleep. Nijinsky looked like such a little boy in repose, reflected Auguste. He threw one of his smocks over the sleeping dancer, returned to his half-finished figure, and found himself yawning. He sat down on the sofa, there was no other place to rest—he kept this studio Spartan, as had been his lifelong custom—and gradually, tired, too, he fell into slumber, reclining alongside the dancer.

Diaghilev walked into the studio and was shocked. The smock had slipped off Nijinsky; the dancer lay next to the *maître* in total nakedness. How unfair, how frightening! thought Diaghilev, and saw them as faun and satyr. Frantic, he backed out of the studio without making a sound.

That evening Diaghilev didn't say a word to Nijinsky about what he feared, but informed his protégé that they had to leave for London at once, to arrange for their coming season before it fell through.

Auguste was deeply disappointed when Nijinsky didn't appear the next day and there was a message from Diaghilev, expressing his regrets, saying he was sure, however, that the *maître* would understand, Monsieur Nijinsky had more pressing commitments that had to be honored and the posing had to end.

"How ridiculous!" cried the Duchess when Auguste told her about this. "Nijinsky should have honored his obligation to you first. You are supposed to be the greatest sculptor in the world." Her voice became as sharp as the blade of a guillotine. She was outraged because he hadn't made love to her once during the time he had been modeling Nijinsky. She was glad to inform him, "You know that some of the greatest luminaries of the Ballet Russe are famous for their odd ways. There is much gossip about Diaghilev and Nijinsky's relationship. It is no wonder people are talking about you and Nijinsky. Now, don't get jumpy." Auguste had turned on her with such fury she was frightened. "What do you expect, associating with such people."

"Say what you mean." He was so shaken he could hardly talk.

"Now you are angry. But this gossip is all over Paris. Like this." She handed him a cartoon she had been keeping for this moment. It depicted a male model naked in a sculptor's studio and saying, "*Maître*, where should I place my clothes?" and underneath the caption "His Faun!"

He felt nauseated. In his life he had been accused of being obstinate, harsh, imperious, vulgar, obscene, and worse. "But to be called a homosexual!" he exploded. "How stupid, how absurd!" He, who still got excited when he saw a pretty girl, though the satisfaction was only occasional these days. "It's incredible!" For so many years he had loved women, too much sometimes.

"I still love you, *chéri*." She went to caress him, and he pulled away.

Then he remembered she was the proof he was not a homosexual. When it came to sex, she could be trusted. It was the one time she was genuine. But did it matter, he thought somberly, would anybody care? And all he had desired was to sculpt Nijinsky in marble. He felt so weary, he ached all over. He said, "I don't feel well. I need a vacation."

CHAPTER 49

"A very good idea," said the Duchess. "You were working too hard on that dancer, seeing too much of that young man. It was becoming unpleasant."

He didn't reply. He reached for a chair to hold on to. His nausea had grown worse. He thought he was going to faint, stricken with chills and dizziness. Never had he felt so weak. He sat down with a gasp of relief.

The Duchess wasn't alarmed. She had warned him this would happen, working so hard and neglecting her. She was gratified. Now she could take care of him the way she was capable. She said hopefully, "I'll call the doctor."

Auguste wanted to object, but he couldn't. In the last few years he had had severe aches in his bones, there had been days when the pain in his hands had been so harsh it had been a terrible struggle to work, but never had he felt so shaky. He could not stand. It was so foolish.

The doctor said the *maître* had bronchitis and that rest was the cure.

Auguste disagreed. As he lay in bed while the doctor examined him, the chills and aches and nausea vanished, but now it was as if a heavy weight pressed down on him, however he turned. It was such an effort to lift an arm or a leg. He thought what he really had was a severe case of fatigue.

The doctor insisted he must stay in bed for a few days, perhaps even several weeks, and the Duchess nodded in enthusiastic agreement. Using this as an excuse, she moved into Biron as his nurse and "devoted companion, on the doctor's orders," as she informed everyone. She forbade him to see anyone, particularly Rose, who, she declared, would only aggravate his condition.

He wanted to differ with her pontifical sway, but he didn't have the energy or strength. The more she spoke about his poor health, the more he thought about it, and when he did the pains in his arms increased. This was most terrifying of all; he wondered if he would ever be able to sculpt again.

The Duchess wasn't worried. She sat by his bed while the servant she had hired fed him, and assured him, "You've done enough work to support you, even if you live to be eighty-nine, like Michelangelo."

He winced. The way she made him feel sometimes, he was not sure he wanted to. But he felt so tired now, he needed someone energetic, like her. He asked, "What about Biron? Is there anything new? My extension expires soon."

"Don't worry, Auguste. My influential friends will take care of that. My husband, the Duke, is a personal friend of most of the crowned heads of Europe, and related to several. They wouldn't dispossess such a sick man."

"I'm not that sick." He was angry at her wish to mother him.

"Sick enough, monsieur," she said blithely, confidently.

"What about Nijinsky and Calmette?"

"Oh, that quarrel stopped long ago. As soon as Nijinsky went to London. Though Nijinsky didn't go right away, as Diaghilev said."

"Then the situation over Biron has been relieved?"

"Not completely. Calmette still questions strongly whether you should stay here, and says a museum is absurd, but I'll take care of everything."

Yet when a month had passed and the Duchess still insisted he remain in bed, though some strength had returned and he could walk without dizziness or nausea, he felt she was strangling him, even if it was out of concern. And he was worried about Rose. He said to the Duchess, "How will Rose live?"

She said with easy condescension, "As she always has. Like a peasant."

"No, no," said Auguste. "Rose is a good housekeeper. But she has to have money to live on. Who is paying for her household expenses?"

"She is, with the money she has hoarded throughout the years."

"Madame, she doesn't have fifty francs that didn't come from me."

"Because she has shamed you into it. But everyone knows that this woman has thousands of francs stored away."

"Everyone." He regarded her intently. "The Duchess of Choiseul, you mean?"

She shook her head at this childish ignorance of finance and said, "It's common knowledge that since your exhibit at the place de l'Alma you've been making at least two hundred thousand francs a year from the sale of your sculpture."

He was silent. To be accurate, he was not certain how much he had been earning in fees. Whenever he made a large sale, he put the money into a different bank so that he would not be obligated to any institution. But if he didn't know what he earned, how did she?

When she saw him looking grim, she hurried to say, "I hope you are not insulted, Auguste. I'm deeply concerned about your sales, so that you will get what you deserve and never have to want. You are careless about money."

"Your appraisal of my sales is very flattering."

"Didn't you tell Clemenceau yourself, when it was pointed out that Biron cost six million francs, that your sculpture was worth even more?"

He was upset. None of the other women he had known had shown interest in his earnings. Indeed, Rose hadn't dared and Camille had been too proud. Even now Camille was still struggling desperately to support herself as a sculptress, when, if she had accepted his aid, she could have been rich. And he couldn't get Rose out of his mind. He asked, "Why hasn't she come to see me?"

"She doesn't want to. She knows she isn't wanted."

"When I am sick? I don't believe you."

"Has she come?" the Duchess said triumphantly. "Has she, Auguste?"

"No."

"Do you think I would have stayed away if I had heard you were ill? No!"

He sank back on his bed, terribly weak suddenly. He couldn't tell where the physical pain ended and the emotional began.

The Duchess was delighted, he looked so acquiescent, manageable.

Several days later she decided to strike. She felt consummately attractive in her hobble skirt to the ankles, her long fur and feather piece. And he was in a better humor—the sun was shining through the French windows and on his body with a soothing warmth—and he could lift his arms without pain. She bestowed her brightest smile upon him, said he could sit up in bed, and served him some of his favorite burgundy. As this seemed to work as she had planned, he was affectionate, caressing her hands and saying, "You understand my needs," she answered, "Yes, I could work wonders, if you'd let me."

"What do you mean?" He was suspicious suddenly. He let go of her hands.

"Well, like the bust you made of me." She put her hands back in his.

"I thought you didn't like it."

"I love it. I'll always cherish it. But if I sold it, after you had it reproduced, you could make another ten or twenty thousand francs at least."

"If I sold it. But I didn't give it to you. You didn't like it."

She looked at him innocently. "Auguste, how could you think that? You said it was mine, whenever I wanted it, and now I want it."

He didn't answer, but he didn't indicate displeasure, as she had feared.

"Did you give the State the rights to reproductions of your work?"

"No. Not yet."

"Good."

"Why?"

She hesitated, but he still didn't look angry, just interested, and so she went on. "You know these reproduction rights are immensely valuable. With the amount of work you've done, and the easy way most of your work can be reproduced—without any effort on your part you could make a fortune."

"How?" His voice remained soft, but his face reddened a little.

The idea is exciting him, she thought jubilantly. I am being clever, he can become even richer without having to struggle with a single new piece. He was too old for that anyway. "You need someone to manage your affairs."

"You?"

"Someone must do it. I can't see you throwing away opportunity after opportunity. I've made up a document that will make sure you get the best price for your reproductions. There have been many orders for your old work since you've been ill, and I could have filled them if you had signed this. I prepared this document to save you any difficulties."

"Like the letter to *Matin?*" He started to read the legal document.

"Don't you trust me, Auguste?"

"As much as you trust me." He read the contract, which stated that Auguste Rodin was assigning all dealer rights for his reproductions to the Duchess of Choiseul, at a fee of one third of all she sold. He reflected a minute, then said quietly, "Very well. Where do you want me to sign?"

She had to struggle to hide her joy, and her voice trembled as she indicated the place at the end of the agreement.

He took the pen she handed him, tested it briefly on the white silk robe she had brought him—she could hardly believe her eyes—then handed it back to her, saying, "It's not even good for drawing."

"I didn't give it to you to draw with!" Must he torture her now?

"Where are my clothes?"

"Aren't you going to sign it? You promised!"

He put on his trousers and was surprised at how strong he felt. He said in a voice growing cold and harsh, "I've done no work for months."

She cried, quite injured, following him as he dressed, "You belittle everything I do. I give you all my time and have nothing to show for it."

"Not even money."

"Auguste, the rights of reproduction are very valuable. You certainly don't intend to give them to the State. Why, everything you touch is worth thousands of francs. You are going to live a long time yet."

He muttered, "You must think I'm an idiot, and maybe I was."

"What did you say, chéri?"

"That you said I was sick."

"You were. You still are." When she saw him all dressed and at the door, she shouted, panic-stricken, "Where are you going?"

"I had hesitated about giving my rights of repoduction to the State, but now you've convinced me. Who's Premier now? Poincaré? I'll speak to him at once about the reproduction rights. They can't turn down the museum then."

"Don't be sure. You have many enemies, not just Calmette."

He looked at her carefully. Her face, sharply outlined by the bright sun and taut with rage, was gaunt. It was fantastic, he thought, that he had found these pointed bones, this painted skin, attractive. Yet he had. He must have been ill indeed.

"When will you be back?" she asked, recovering some of her self-control.

"When you are gone, madame. For good."

II

Arranging to see Poincaré later, Auguste asked Bourdelle, "Would you do me a great favor and go to Meudon and tell Madame Rose that I'll be there tonight, after I see the Premier?" He was annoyed and surprised by the curious look Bourdelle gave him, but grateful that the younger sculptor didn't ask any questions, saying simply, "Yes, maître." Then it was Bourdelle's turn to be surprised as Auguste embraced him fervently.

Poincaré was glad to see Rodin; the Premier had heard that the maître was ill. He thought the sculptor's offer to give the rights of reproduction to the people of France generous, but there was the difficulty with the religious folk—just as they had become quiescent, Calmette had stirred them up.

However, when Auguste pointed out he had been in a religious order himself, telling Poincaré of the months he had spent as Brother Augustin, the Premier said, "That should reduce some of their objections. Now, if you could only sculpt the Pope, that would solve all your problems."

III

Rose had been working feverishly each day, cleaning, sewing, cooking with a dogged perseverance, as if this were the only way to keep her wits. Auguste had never stayed away this long before, not even with Camille. She was in her room, dusting the clay statuette of mother and child Auguste had given her after *petit* Auguste had been born, thinking if he stayed away much longer he would never come home and wondering if it would have been different if he had not become famous, when Bourdelle gave her the message from Auguste.

She almost dropped the statuette in her shock. Then she felt guilty. It was a long journey from Paris, it was late, and Antoine looked hungry. She said, "Antoine, you must have a bite to eat," and he said, "*Merci*, Rose, but I think it would be more appropriate if you got ready for the *maître*." And as she hurried to do that, he asked, "Did you know he was sick?"

"Sick?" She went white. "No. I couldn't reach him. What was wrong?"

"The doctor said bronchitis, but I think it was too much Duchess Influenza."

Rose was waiting for Auguste at the entrance to Meudon when he came into sight several hours later. She didn't say a word, but stepped forward to take his hand. He looked so old and tired, she thought, but not ill, thank God!

He said, "*Bon jour, ma chatte*."

She said, "*Bonjour, chéri*."

He turned to the studio, taking her with him, and as she cried, "Auguste, I didn't know you were ill, I didn't, I would have come at once," he said, "I know, I know." He walked through the studio to make sure all his pieces were still there, insisting that she accompany him. He said, "I must do a Christ," and she said, "I'm sure it will be unique, a Rodin."

IV

The next few months Auguste worked at both Meudon and Biron, but always spent his nights with Rose. After his interview with Poincaré things had quieted down about his occupancy of Biron, but as 1913 and the end of his extension approached he grew anxious again. It added to his apprehensions when the Ministry of Fine Arts ordered him to submit an inventory of all his work.

It took weeks to have this inventory done. He was astonished to learn that his sculpture was worth six million francs. He was a millionaire, though he still had very little money. He submitted the inventory to the Ministry, sure that they wouldn't believe these figures —he didn't believe them himself. Then he waited. Months passed and there was no word about Biron or the museum. Nineteen thirteen came, the extension of the lease expired, and nothing happened. There was no threat of eviction, but no promise of renewal or of a museum either.

One windy, wet March day while he was wondering whether he could endure this waiting much longer, he was visited by Boucher. He was annoyed by this interruption. As he had become better known Boucher had grown less friendly, as if his fame had become too much for the younger sculptor to bear. And he was still struggling with the conception of his Christ. But for once the *grand seigneur* was not jaunty. Boucher was pale and drawn as he asked somberly, "Have you heard about Camille?"

"No."

"You knew she had several breakdowns, didn't you?"

"Yes."

"And you did nothing?" Boucher said accusingly.

"*Mon dieu!*" Auguste shouted. "What do they expect of me! I tried to help her, but she wouldn't let me. Finally I kept away."

"But she was sick, mentally sick. Didn't you feel responsible at all?"

Auguste asked despairingly, "What could I have done?"

"Shown her sculpture."

"I did. And when she heard, she had it withdrawn."

"And you couldn't do anything else?"

"What happened, Alfred?"

"Yesterday . . ." Boucher broke down and for a moment couldn't go on. Then in a torrent of emotion he cried out, "It was dreadful. She hadn't been out of her studio for weeks, she hadn't eaten for days, her shutters had been closed for months. The only light was a candle, and she was kneeling and praying before a small plaster statue of the Virgin, which she had evidently done herself, and every so often she fondled it and mumbled, "*La petite amie.*" She didn't know anybody, not even her brother, Paul. She was like a child making a first penance for her sins. When her brother tried to open a window and let in some fresh air, she cringed in a corner, then grew hysterical. When he took her out of the studio, she was terrified and fought like a wild animal."

"He took her to another *maison de santé?*" Auguste asked in a low voice.

"It's called a nursing home, which means she'll get the best care, but it won't help. It's too late." Boucher was weeping as he said, "Auguste, the disintegration is horrible. She's insane. Incurably. I never thought she would be your *petite amie* when I brought her to you."

Auguste's eyes filled with tears. There was so much to say, and all he could say was, "France has lost a fine sculptor."

CHAPTER 50

Afterward Auguste kept telling himself that he had acted toward Camille only as any sane, sensible man could have acted. He sought to ease his grief by working harder, but it was exhausting these days. Whatever he pretended, her collapse had aged him. Weariness became common, and he had new, frequent spells of nausea and dizziness. He had trained himself to accept the painful stiffness of his joints which made it a strain to sculpt, but he could not be philosophical about the piercing pains in the head that came with terrifying frequency, the moments of numbness that left him limp and weak. Always before so robust and energetic, he was unprepared for ill-health. He didn't know where his feelings of guilt and sorrow ended and his sickness began. He wondered if he had caught some of Camille's nervous disease. He told no one, not even Rose, determined not to lose control of himself.

The waiting for a decision about Biron and the museum went on, and he craved peace, but there was no peace. War erupted during the summer of 1914. Within a few weeks the Germans were at the Marne and close to Meudon, and the government ordered him to leave before he became a prisoner. They informed him that they could not allow this, he was a national asset. He was amused to find himself a possession of France.

It was the only levity he could feel. Though he was passionately in love with France, with a nostalgia that increased with age, he could not regard the war as glorious. Most people, even his friends, were boasting about the bravery of the *poilu* and were swollen with *la gloire*, as if the days of Napoleon had returned, and he thought somberly of all the men who would be killed. Yet when he heard children singing the "Marseillaise," he felt pride in a France standing valiantly against the invading Germans.

As he prepared to leave Meudon with Rose, he took a last look at the "Balzac" in the garden—it was too huge to move on short notice—and he prayed that the Germans would not all be barbarians and damage or destroy it. His studio was crowded with other pieces, but he couldn't put a red cross on the building, and from what he had heard, that wouldn't help anyway.

Rose was calling, "Hurry, hurry, Auguste. You can hear the guns if you listen carefully. They say the Germans will break through at any moment."

He couldn't move. He couldn't desert what he had put his whole life into.

She had him by the arm. She reminded him, "The Germans are very angry with you because you refused to do the Kaiser last year."

"I made the proper apologies. I said I felt *malade un peu.*"

"They knew that was only an excuse, that you were expressing your feelings as a Frenchman about the way they were threatening us. And since the Kaiser himself asked you to do a portrait bust, they felt it was a national insult."

He shrugged. He couldn't worry about the Kaiser's displeasure, but he had been unhappy when Rilke was offended because he had refused to sit for Rilke's wife, Clara, for the same reason and with the same excuse. Rilke hadn't lived with his wife for years; Rilke allowed nothing to stop his work; but now the poet was back in Berlin, very much the patriotic German, not speaking to him, and they were supposed to hate each other.

Rose cried, "Do you have enough money?" She handed him a heavy bag of ten-franc coins, so heavy he could hardly carry it.

"No, no," he said, suddenly back in the present. *Mon dieu!* He couldn't leave all the money they had hoarded for the Germans. He said, "We need notes. Bring everything you've saved, Rose. Everything!"

A few minutes later Rose handed him a large package of notes, most of them dirty from much counting. He meticulously counted what she had saved and hidden. He didn't look surprised when it came to over ten thousand francs. As he pulled out the francs he had hoarded, which also totaled more than ten thousand francs, he chuckled, "You don't trust banks either, do you?"

She said defensively, "I've some in a bank. But you were away so much."

"Maybe we can't get away from our peasant backgrounds," he said. "Banks." He laughed. "I've tried them all, but it's good to have money in your hand when you need it." He grabbed the large pile of francs they had both hidden, and ignoring the large wallet she offered him, stuffed the notes in a bulging, untidy lump into the outside pocket of his greatcoat, saying, "I like to be able to reach it when I need it."

II

Paris was no refuge. Rumors that the Germans were breaking through at the Marne and would strip the city to the bone were everywhere. Auguste found this possibility unbearable, and he didn't want to retreat any farther, but he was advised by the government to go to England for his safety. He was afraid to argue, afraid it would hurt the museum. But when he tried to find out about Biron and the museum, no one knew anything.

He walked about Paris as if this could be his last view of it and bumped into Degas standing outside the Louvre, under the Arc du Carrousel. He thought Degas didn't see him. Degas was supposed to be almost blind.

Suddenly Degas said, "You've gotten old, Auguste, your beard is all white."

"I thought you couldn't see."

"I can't. I was sketching the other day and I almost got hit by one of those damned automobiles."

Auguste paused, wondering whether Degas really wanted to talk to him.

Degas grumbled, "Old age is a martyrdom. How is your museum coming?"

"No one seems to know. They want me to go to London."

"I won't go. Not that there is anyplace to stay here. You heard how they tore down my place on the Victor Massé. And after I had lived there twenty-seven years. But they called it progress. It was outrageous."

Auguste nodded. He had heard also how Degas wandered all over Paris like a homeless waif, though he was eighty and had become a pitiful, shrunken ball of a man in spite of his efforts to remain ferocious.

Degas mumbled, "You are avaricious, selling all your work."

"I never had an independent income, like yours."

"That was exaggerated."

"So were my sales. Besides, I'm willing to leave my work to France. Whom are you leaving your work to?" Auguste knew that Degas had no plans for his work, that it was a scandal the way the painter destroyed all his work he could get his hands on with a bitter, macabre cannibalism.

Degas muttered, "Why should I leave it to anyone? I painted for my pleasure, not for an idiot public and rancorous friends."

"Oh yes," said Auguste, "God save me from my friends."

Degas agreed, then said, "Were you going into the Louvre, Auguste?"

"For a few minutes. Do you think the Germans will harm it?"

"Who knows? Did you hear I'm in the Louvre now, without asking?"

"Of course. Congratulations."

"Why? People get ten times for my work what they paid me. And when Caillebotte left his collection to the State, it created as much commotion as your 'Balzac.' Everyone in the government was embarrassed. And now my work is stuck in a small room, in a corner, right off the lavatory."

"But you want me to see your paintings?"

"I can't. The room is too dark." Degas' voice took on an unusual tone as he pleaded, "You know, I never cared what people thought of my work, but your eyes are good, you can describe my palette to me."

III

Auguste left for London with Rose after his visit to the Louvre. He looked forward to viewing "The Burghers," which had been placed by the Houses of Parliament by the British Government; it lessened the pain of leaving France at this time. Rose, by his side constantly, all in black except for white lace at her throat, was content—as long as she was close to him.

But though he was gratified with the way "The Burghers" were silhouetted against the Houses of Parliament, one of his favorite buildings, he was homesick in London. He stayed at the Hotel Rembrandt because of its name, but he continued to worry that his work was being damaged by the Germans. And when the Germans were checked at the Marne, he worried that his casters would neglect his pieces. Then the news that the Germans had damaged Rheims Cathedral aroused him in a way nothing else had. For the first time they became the hated enemy, barbarians threatening to erase beauty and civilization. He was upset also by a London where all his old friends were dead and the young men were too young, reminding him painfully of his own mortality.

He was thankful when he was asked to do a portrait bust of the Pope. It would take him out of London; he would be following Michelangelo; and most important, it would be an opportunity to influence Benedict XV, so far distressingly neutral, to see the justice of France's cause.

He arrived in Rome in February 1915, determined to make Benedict XV one of his best portraits. He was surprised to find the Pope such a small man, but the head was good, with wide cheeks, a thin, decisive mouth, and a strong jaw. He set up his equipment, and the Pope said, "You will be brief?"

"I cannot rush, your Holiness."

"I can sit only a few times. I am very busy. The war, you know."

"Yes, and that's another thing, the war—"

"No!" The Pope cut him short. "It is not to be discussed. Hurry."

"But this must be a portrait, not a photograph."

The Pope wasn't listening. He insisted on sitting upon a high stand, built like a throne by his aides.

Auguste felt frustrated, the Pope was rigid, artificial, and far away. He knew he couldn't touch the Pope's face to capture the contours as he did with everybody else, but at least he could get close. He asked the Pope to walk about, and the latter was indignant.

Benedict XV said curtly, "The Pope below, the sculptor above, it is not allowed. Now hurry. I have only a few minutes."

At the second sitting Auguste made several heads, and in his disgust with the quick, superficial way he was having to model wanted to smash them. But when he went to alter the best of the heads, the Pope said, "No, it is a good likeness." Auguste started to argue, then remembered that a finished head of the Pope could remove the objections of the religious people to the conversion of Biron into a Rodin Museum.

He said, "Of course, your Holiness. Do you care for this?" even as he disliked himself for asking a subject's opinion. The Pope shrugged, as if to say it mattered little so long as it was a likeness, but smiled when the sculptor followed his judgment. Encouraged, Auguste stopped work to talk about the war, saying that surely a wise, understanding man like His Holiness knew that the Germans were beasts, and that France was one of the cradles of civilization. A word from the Pope to this effect would carry great weight. He paid no attention to the Pope's efforts to hush him. He talked the time away without doing any more sculpting, but for once it didn't trouble him. He could tell by the solemn, almost shocked way the Pope left him that he had impressed His Holiness.

At the third sitting Auguste started by asking, "Your Holiness, you will speak out against the brutal attack of the Germans on Belgium?" and the Pope replied curtly, "You had better finish. I will not be able to sit again."

Auguste was appalled. He cried, "I have just begun!"

The Pope stared critically at the head he had accepted the previous day. The sculptor must be insane; what had been recognizable had been changed back into a mass of clay. He asked, "What's this?"

"The truth. Your Holiness, you will tell the truth, too, about the war?"

The Pope regarded him scornfully, then said coldly, "Monsieur Rodin, you are naïve. If you can't finish today, copy a photograph."

When he saw the sculptor's look of horror, he said, "If that's too difficult, why not copy the portrait bust Count Lipai did of me?"

There was no sense in going on. Auguste stopped, but the Pope,
instead of being offended, was grateful. The Pope said, "You will
be paid for your materials, monsieur," and left without another
word. Auguste decided to finish the bust from memory, at Meudon,
if he could.

IV

The bust was difficult to finish. Everything was becoming difficult.
He worked on the head of the Pope, a head of Camille as she had
been when he had met her, and the Christ, but after many months
they remained unfinished. When people asked him about the Pope,
he snapped, "He should have remained a parish priest." But that was
not the worst disappointment. Often he was forced to lie down to
retrieve his ebbing energy and to bar the door to the fatigue that
threatened to engulf him. He sought to recall Camille's magnificent
gray-blue eyes, her fine brow, her delicate mouth, but it was as if
even the past was impenetrable and sculpture was alienated. Then he
could not rest. His body hurt no matter how he lay.

He didn't tell Rose, whose only interest was his health. He didn't
want to worry her, for she was ailing also. And when she suggested
they take in *petit* Auguste and the latter's woman, Nina, a blowsy,
fat slattern, who, however, was devoted to the boy, he agreed. He
thought that the couple, impossible though they were in many ways,
would take some of the burdens off Rose. The war had settled down
to a stalemate and servants were hard to get, and as Rose said, whom
else could they depend upon but their own?

Petit Auguste was willing when Rose told him that the maître
might marry her and then it was possible that he could be legitimatized.

Auguste promised *petit* Auguste room and board and two hundred
francs a month as payment for helping Rose, but avoided him whenever possible.

Yet he felt a little better with the arrival of his son, relieved that
Rose would have company and less work to do. He returned to his
studio and his sculpture, concentrating on his bust of Camille. It

didn't go much better than before, but he knew he had to keep busy. He found a huge medieval oak cross in Paris and bought it for a few hundred francs. Rose was bewildered, he had never been that religious, and besides, where would it go?

"In the bedroom," he answered.

"But it is bigger than the bedroom," she protested.

"I know. It's eighteen feet high and the bedroom is twelve feet high. But I'll manage. You'll see."

There was very little manpower about—most of the able-bodied men were away in the Army—but he rounded up all he could find and found himself supervising a group of elderly casters, workmen, neighbors, and *petit* Auguste. Rose warned him not to do any of the physical work himself, but he pushed and pulled with the rest in his enthusiasm to get the great oak cross set up. It took enormous effort to get this massive medieval wood carving to Meudon, but that was minor compared to the effort needed to move it upstairs and into his bedroom. Though everyone told Auguste it couldn't be done, he had the huge oak cross dragged upstairs and into his bedroom after many hours of backbreaking effort. He refused to allow the ends to be cut off. He lost his temper. He shouted that it would ruin the proportions. He felt like a young man pushing and tugging at this magnificent piece of medieval craftsmanship. He was proud that his hands and arms were still strong. In the moving many holes were made in the walls of the house, but he didn't care. He ordered other holes cut in the floor and ceiling of his bedroom. And while his helpers regarded him as crazy, he had the cross placed against the wall across from his bed, the top going into the attic, the bottom into the dining room, while the superb Christ faced him at eye level.

Rose asked when they were alone, "Are you becoming religious, Auguste?"

He shrugged as if to say one should try everything, smiling like a little boy in his gratification, and said, "I like the art, the design, it is fine sculpture." He went to adjust the crucified Christ and felt a stab of pain in his head, so fierce that he had to clutch the cross to keep from falling.

Rose noticed he had become very pale and asked anxiously, "What's wrong?"

"Nothing. I feel fine. Just a little tired." He sat down.

"Are you sure?"

He nodded, finding it hard to talk. But a minute later the pain was gone and so was the dizziness, and he said, "Have the dirt cleaned up."

"It will take a month to fix everything."

"We're not moving. I'm not going anywhere these days, *ma chatte*."

"You do feel better?" She didn't want to worry him with her concern, but more than ever he was all she had.

"Of course." He forced a smile to reassure her. "When I look at Jesus and see what He suffered, I can bear my own pain, I'm almost peaceful."

He returned to the bust of Camille, but a few days later while he was driving to finish the head before his strength ran out a wave of darkness swept over him. When he knew where he was again, the chisel was at his feet. He went to pick it up and couldn't. Had his hand gone to sleep? There was such a numbness in his hand. He called Rose, asked her to give him the chisel.

She did, looking stricken, exclaiming, "You are sick, Auguste!"

"No, it's just my hand. I hurt it, I think." But as he went to use the chisel again, he couldn't hold it and it fell to the floor once more. Yet when she wanted to call a doctor, he said it wasn't necessary, he was just tired.

Strength did not return to his hand, and he was unable to sculpt at all. His hand had become permanently numb, he realized sadly, but he could not tell anyone, as if that were a disgrace. Rose was growing so frail she was content to just sit and stare at the scenery, as long as he was by her side, but he couldn't give in, he couldn't accept inactivity. He spent his days in his studio, observing his work. He thought, viewing "The Age of Bronze," if he had the Belgian now he would do him better, more austere, he was still learning anatomy. He pressed his arm against his sculpture so that he could feel its warmth, grateful for this small favor. Everybody said he looked well, but he felt so tired.

He sought to become friendly with *petit* Auguste, but it was not easy, the boy was a washed-out copy of a man, an insult to his own life. Then *petit* Auguste drank so much. He mentioned this, seeking to help him, and *petit* Auguste turned hard, knowing the old man needed him now, and said, "What else should I do? You don't want me here. Not really."

Auguste wondered was he actually to blame for *petit* Auguste? All *petit* Auguste seemed to care about was the fortune the boy hoped to get, but how could he leave it to a shiftless alcoholic? But the harshest pain came from his inability to work. Without sculpture he was lost. He could not live this way, he told himself. He spent many days trying to drive life into his numb hand. But whatever he did, it hung limp. Finally in his desperation he held his limp hand in his alive one and pushed it against the clay—he would force life into it as he had forced life into so many pieces. He felt himself straining desperately, his head throbbing viciously, but he would make this hand supple again. He would massage it against the clay, that would bring life back to it. He pushed harder, harder. The pain increased in his head but he sought to disregard it, as he had disregarded so much pain, and suddenly there was a blinding flash. As he felt himself falling, he cried to himself, I mustn't damage the piece I'm touching, it's not finished yet . . .

When he knew what was happening again, he was in bed, staring at the Christ hanging on the cross opposite him and hearing a doctor say to a stranger, "He's had a stroke, from cerebral congestion which became a cerebral hemorrhage. We will have to declare him legally incompetent."

He was not legally incompetent, he thought indignantly. He couldn't walk and it was hard to talk and he couldn't move very well, but he could see Rose and Camille and Balzac and Victor Hugo. Hugo had worked until the poet was eighty, and he was only seventy-five—or was it seventy-six? He wasn't quite sure. They were telling him that he had been ill for weeks, but he didn't remember, it seemed like yesterday, but they hadn't moved Balzac, he could see him through his bedroom window.

And now they were introducing him to the stranger, Jean Grite, an official from the Ministry of Fine Arts, who wanted to discuss the museum.

"It's finished?" Auguste asked, alarmed.

"Oh no," said Jean Grite. "We want to draw up a provisional agreement."

"Provisional? What do you mean by that?" He sat up in bed when the doctor nodded that it was all right. He could no longer see Hugo or Balzac, but a man like so many others he had met in official circles, polite yet officious, knowing yet suspicious, and he thought, I've known so many of you and you are all the same, I can't believe a word you say.

"It will be a temporary contract, until we can decide on final terms."

"But I thought there were so many objections." His head had cleared, and he could see the official quite well. Jean Grite was middle-aged, stout.

"The religious people have been appeased. You did the Pope."

"I didn't finish."

"It was enough."

"That's not the only reason," Auguste said suspiciously.

"Well, you've been sick, *maître*."

"I know."

"And while you were, much of your work was being stolen. We want to put a guard on it, but we can't unless there is some sort of an agreement that it belongs to us—or will someday."

"Oh!" Suddenly Auguste realized the reason for the rush. "And I've had a serious illness and you don't expect me to live much longer."

Jean Grite looked embarrassed and didn't answer.

"You don't have to flatter me. I'm not afraid to die. There are worse things that could happen."

"Well, we are all mortal, *maître*, and we shouldn't wait too long."

"Especially since I'm mentally incompetent."

"We didn't say that."

"Legally, mentally, they mean the same thing. And you want my approval and signature while I know what I am doing." Suddenly it was hard to breathe as he realized they must be regarding him as they regarded Camille. With a great effort of his will he got out of bed and was surprised to find that he could. There was still life in his legs, and only one arm was numb. He put on his clothes by himself, refusing all help, and said, "What about Madame Rose? Will she be protected? I can't leave her penniless."

"*Maître*, you will outlive all of us."

"Is that why you've rushed here? What about a will?"

"One is being drawn up."

"Without my approval? I'm not dead yet, or crazy!"

"Of course not. The contract we want you to sign is provisional. The Ministry has to suggest its terms, then you suggest yours. We do not intend to leave you improvident after your most generous gift."

"Do I owe Clemenceau thanks for this?"

"No. He is out of power, though he may be Premier again if the Germans keep winning. He is devoted to killing Germans."

"And Poincaré?"

"He's President. He is deeply occupied with the war, too, maître."

"Oh yes, now I remember."

"His friendship will be useful when the Senate votes on the museum."

"Friendship? He's an acquaintance, a politician. I hope you have stronger support. Monsieur, could I read the agreement?"

Auguste was signing the agreement when Rose entered. Seeing him smiling, she cried in her happiness and took his hands in hers while Jean Grite bowed out with many thanks. He told her, "I'm giving the State all my work."

"I know, chéri. How do you feel? Your hands are so cold."

"I've been very sick." He stood up, holding on to the bed for support.

"But you are better now, I can tell. We will walk a little."

"First we must talk about a will."

"Not now, Auguste!"

"We can't put it off any longer."

"It's too soon."

"What about petit Auguste?"

She flushed. She was concerned about him, and Auguste knew it. She said, "You will leave something to the boy."

"Haven't you, Rose?"

"It won't be enough, Auguste."

"I'll leave him three thousand francs a year," he said with a flash of his old vitality. "He would squander any more." When he saw her hurt look, he added, "And the rest of the estate to you, Meudon, all my property."

She cried, "What will I do with it—without you?"

He shrugged and didn't answer. He walked slowly to his studio, to gaze at his pieces while he knew them.

V

Negotiations went on for months between officials of the Ministry of Fine Arts and representatives of Auguste, for though his mind wandered only occasionally, he grew more feeble daily and barely had strength to get about. But finally, on September 13, 1916, he signed over all of his art to France in return for establishment of a Rodin Museum at the Hotel Biron.

He was surprised at how much his work totaled. He was told that it came to fifty-six marbles, fifty-six bronzes, one hundred and ninety-three plaster casts, a hundred terra cottas, over two thousand drawings and sketches, and hundreds of valuable antiques: Greek and Roman sculpture, and ancient Egyptian art. He hoped France would be equally generous. Rose had been left Meudon and had been guaranteed a sizable income as long as she lived, but the agreement still had to be passed by the Chamber of Deputies and the Senate, and there was talk of considerable opposition.

The day after Auguste's bequest, despite the growing desperation with a war which was going worse and worse, the Chamber of Deputies passed the bill accepting the gift and establishing the Rodin Museum by a vote of 391 to 52.

Auguste heard the news silently, too tired to celebrate. Then there was the Senate, the Senate was always more conservative.

Several weeks later he was lying in bed, quite ill with a recurrence of bronchitis, when he was told that Poincaré, as President of France, had raised objections in the Senate. Poincaré was upset that the agreement guaranteed an annuity for life to a Mademoiselle Rose Beuret, when Monsieur Rodin was registered as unmarried. The President declared that this was immoral.

A distressed Jean Grite, who had become deeply committed to the success of the transaction for it would give him great prestige, informed the sick sculptor there was only one solution, the *maître* must wed Mademoiselle Rose.

Auguste nodded weakly, too exhausted to battle—it took all of his flagging energy to stay alive.

"You give your word?" an excited Jean Grite prodded.

"Yes. Yes." Papa would be amused; he had kept his word after all.

This was told to Poincaré, and the President withdrew his opposition, and the Senate approved the agreement by a vote of 212 to 27, making it final.

The wedding had to be deferred until Auguste recovered from his new attack of bronchitis; he refused to get married in bed and Rose insisted on a regular ceremony—she felt it was the least she deserved. But finally, on January 29, 1917, just over fifty years after *petit* Auguste had been born, reflected Auguste, it was happening. They had run out of coal, the water pipes had broken the night before, the weather was freezing, the Germans were attacking again, and the local Mayor was about to marry them.

Auguste heard the Mayor ask, "Will you love, honor, and cherish?" and he smiled slowly and said sardonically but quietly, "Naturally, your Honor."

Rose, not waiting to be asked, said fervently, "Yes, with all my heart."

Petit Auguste, standing behind them as one of the witnesses, was not happy as he had expected to be: Rodin still had refused to legitimatize him.

The day after her marriage Rose decided to have a honeymoon like a proper wife, though *petit* Auguste was whispering bitterly that they should be having their golden wedding anniversary instead. But Auguste was coughing violently and it was so cold, because of the complete shortage of coal, they had to stay in bed to keep warm.

Auguste, sensing that Rose was even feebler than he was, tried to get her to use his blankets, but she refused, saying he needed them more, though her body was so cold it felt like an icicle. He begged Jean Grite to bring some coal and fix the water pipes before they froze to death. The official promised to do what he could, but pointed out that the soldiers were freezing, too, every bit of coal was needed at the front, at Verdun.

Two weeks after Rose's wish for a honeymoon she was dead from the cold.

Auguste heard the news as if he were stone. He had no tears left. It took energy to cry and he had given it all to his work. He lost his apparent calm, however, when Jean Grite, who had become one of the executors of his estate, asked where Rose should be buried. As if there were any doubt! "Here!" he declared with a burst of his old vigor. "At Meudon, beside me!"

"What do you want on the stone, *maître?*"

"Our names and dates. It will be enough."

"No epitaphs?"

"They will come to their own opinion of me, whatever I say. But I would like one thing. I would like "The Thinker" to be placed over our graves."

"It will be done."

"*Merci.* For I shall be there for years—millions of years."

The night before Rose's burial Auguste sat beside the coffin without moving, his hands on hers. And when it came time to close the coffin, he kissed her gently on the lips and whispered, "What beautiful sculpture!"

Entering the bedroom a few minutes after the funeral, he came upon *petit* Auguste emptying the stockings, vases, and other hiding places where Rose had hoarded her savings. The boy looked up guiltily, still afraid of the *maître*, sure the old man would be wrathful and take the money away. Auguste said quietly, "It's your money now. She wanted you to have it."

"Twenty thousand silver and gold francs!" *Petit* Auguste exclaimed.

"There is more in the bank. You will have enough to live on."

Petit Auguste started to apologize for his haste, but he had wanted to make sure he would not be cheated again, and halted suddenly—his father wasn't listening. Auguste was staring at her things and thinking never had he felt so lonely.

VI

The weather improved with the coming of spring and so did Auguste. The next few months he spent every moment he could in his studio. He could not work, not even sketch, but he wanted to—he saw so many imperfections now.

If he had only ten more years, he thought, or five—he would even settle for one full working year—he could do so much now, so much he hadn't been aware of. Just as a man was learning, he reflected sadly, a man lost his strength and was taken away. He tried to be concerned about the war and was unhappy that it was still going badly, though he had heard that America had come in and should turn the tide, but it was very difficult to live in the present these days. He rarely had visitors. Almost everyone he knew was involved elsewhere or dead.

Then on November 12, his seventy-seventh birthday, he caught bronchitis again and had to go to bed. He looked at the Christ across the room, and as he lapsed into unconsciousness he wondered if they would ever meet again.

The next few days as his fever rose and his lungs grew congested he drifted on a vast sea without a beginning or an end. There were many faces in front of him, Marie, Papa, Mama, Father Eymard, Bibi, Peppino, Lecoq, but where were Camille and Rose? No matter how he searched he could not find them. Had they deserted him after all? Then he thought he heard Rose whispering, "What will he do without me?" as she had done just before she died, but everything was gray about him and he couldn't find her. He saw himself arguing with Papa about going to the Petite École—what a battle that had been—and the first nude he had seen, and how he had longed to be as gallant as Barnouvin and knew he never would be, and Marie's defense of both of them in spite of Barnouvin's lecherous ways, and Rose coming down the street the first time he had seen her, so erect and pretty, and Camille's excitement when they had stayed at Tours. One life, it was not enough, he found himself thinking.

Once again he could see "Balzac" and "Hugo" and "The Burghers" and "The Gates"—were they opening for him now? He had tried to work honestly, not to invent, but to observe, to follow nature: a woman, a stone, a head, were all formed by the same principles. So many moments to treasure if you had looked.

And then he saw the Christ looking at him and many people standing about his bed. He couldn't recognize any of them, they were too far away, but he thought he heard someone crying. "Don't cry," he tried to say, "no tears, no tears." He knew it must be Rose. Who else would cry that way?

He felt himself drifting away helplessly without being able to speak. Then he saw hands reaching out to help him, Carrière, Mallarmé, Lecoq, Papa, Balzac, even Hugo. He smiled at that. And now he saw sculpture as far as he could look: "Sorrow," "The Temptation of St. Anthony," "The Squatting Woman," "Psyche," "The Minotaur," "Gustav Mahler," "Mozart," "The Cathedral," "Misery," the "Last Vision," so many pieces he had forgotten he had done. He lay there marveling at the world he had created, and suddenly he cried out proudly, "And people say that sculpture is not a fine art!"

The crying stopped, and he was glad. They must have understood what he was feeling. Nothing terrible was happening. He was only going back into the earth, from which he had come.

He closed his eyes and fell into a dreamless sleep, looking like his own sculpture.

AFTERMATH

The next day Germany, though it was at war with France, declared, "Though Auguste Rodin is the greatest sculptor France has produced, like Shakespeare and Michelangelo, he belongs to Germany also."

Six days after his death, his ancient enemies, the French Academy, elected him to be one of their immortals.

Petit Auguste died nineteen years later, a shiftless alcoholic, without heir.

Camille lived until 1943 without ever returning to sanity.

In 1962, Father Pierre Julien Eymard, who so many years before had wisely returned Auguste to sculpture when he had become Brother Augustin, was approved for sainthood in a consistory led by Pope John XXIII.

And in 1963, "The Thinker" was the best-known and most widely viewed statue in the world. And perhaps that would have brought one of Auguste's rare smiles.